THE SNOW TREE

THE SNOW TREE

Elizabeth Walker

HEADLINE

First published in 1995
by HEADLINE BOOK PUBLISHING

10 9 8 7 6 5 4 3 2 1

British Library Cataloguing in Publication Data

Walker, Elizabeth
Snow Tree
I.   Title
823.914 [F]

ISBN 0-7472-1134-5

Typeset by Keyboard Services, Luton, Beds

Printed and bound in Great Britain by
Mackays of Chatham PLC, Chatham, Kent

HEADLINE BOOK PUBLISHING
A division of Hodder Headline PLC
338 Euston Road
London NW1 3BH

THE SNOW TREE

Chapter One

Mary sat in the apple tree, legs swinging, hair tangled and entwined with leaves and unripe fruit. She felt full of the smell of the orchard; dampness, greenness, with a dash of honey drifting from the hives by the far wall. She was dizzy with it. She flung back her head and almost imagined that she might fall, delighting in a nervous shudder. But she couldn't fall now. Nothing bad could happen today. She was home at last, at Gunthwaite, with all the summer to come.

Someone was calling her. The voice came reedily through the branches, 'Mary! Maaareeee!' Deborah always called like that, her voice full of wistful reproach, as if she was always left behind. So she should be, thought Mary, and moved her long legs higher in the tree. Deb had been a nuisance since the day she was born, and this year she'd been an absolute pain in the neck.

'Maaaareeeee!' She was coming into the orchard. She probably knew Mary was there all the time, but now everyone, Mummy, Dad, even Tom on the tractor, would know that Mary had left Deb out again. Out of what? An hour in the apple tree? The trouble with sisters was they never let you do anything at all by yourself and when you were followed and you yelled they went and told everyone you were being mean.

She nestled her chin uncomfortably against her knee. Dimly, through the leaves, she could see Deb's bright chestnut hair, shining like a conker just out of its shell. Although she could see no more, she let herself imagine the rest; creamy skin, a small neat nose, and those strange eyes, so much like glass, inherited like a talisman from her mother. I could at least have had the eyes, thought Mary, feeling resentment grow and burn. I wouldn't need to be clever or beautiful if I had those remarkable eyes!

When she looked down again, Deborah was looking straight up. Her eyes were so clear that the leaves of the apple tree were reflected back as if in a mirror. She looked like a forest creature, come from fairyland.

'Get lost' snapped Mary.

Deborah said, 'No. I'm bored. I've got nothing to do.'

'That's no reason to come and annoy me. Why don't you read something? Or ride Samson, he could do with the work.'

1

'You know I hate riding. Isn't it awful, stuck at Gunthwaite? I almost wish we were back at school.'

In one long, smooth slide Mary was out of the tree and walking away, crossing the springy turf like a young deer. Deborah, inches shorter, trotted behind. 'Now where are you going? Can we do something now? Please, Mary, it's so horrible here. I'm so bored.'

'Go away!' snarled Mary. 'When will you realise I don't want you around, you nasty little grub! You're bored because you're boring and all you can do is cry like a spoiled brat.'

Deb stopped. Her pretty face crumpled. 'I think you're absolutely beastly. Miss Stenson said you were the sourest girl in the Upper Fifth and I said you weren't, but you are. You're sour and nasty and I shall tell Mum.'

'Tell her what you like! I don't care what you do. Just leave me alone!'

Without any conscious thought propelling it, Mary's hand snaked out and slapped her sister's cheek. Deb was too shocked even to gasp. The imprint of her sister's palm showed like a brand on her skin. Mary stood looking down at her, wanting to cry, wanting to take back the blow, at the same time delighting in the act. Deb deserved it! Anyone who knew her must see!

Deb turned on her heel and fled through the orchard, across the lawn, into the courtyard and on to the house. 'Telltale!' shrieked Mary. 'Telltale tit!' But the words were hollow and she knew it. When Deb ran in with that mark on her face, there would be no pleasure left anywhere in this day.

She ran to the orchard wall, hitching her stupid skirt, tearing it in the scramble. It wasn't her fault. If they let her wear trousers she wouldn't tear them. Some of the girls in her year wore denim jeans, and all she was allowed was jodhpurs if she was riding and a skirt if she was not, and this year, because she was older, even the skirt had to be long. But they'd say it was her. Everyone always did.

She made for Long Meadow, and the horses. Deb's pony, a fat grey, blinked and increased its munching, in case someone wanted to take it out. Diablo, Mary's tall black darling, tossed his head and called to her, while Bonny, the old shire brood mare, turned her vast rump and ambled away.

Mary's heart untwisted a little in her breast. The very air seemed to soothe and caress her. The chestnut tree was a green so true and fresh, and the marsh marigold shone like gold itself. Why wasn't she happy, as she used to be, in this lovely, lovely place?

She returned to the house only when it was getting dark. Dusk came late at this time of year, it was just after ten, and she was sick with hunger and fright. The light in the kitchen shone out across the cobbles like a beacon. The beacon on Roundup Moor hadn't been lit since the end of the war, she thought abstractedly. Its first lighting had been for the Spanish Armada, when Gunthwaite was said to have been built half of wood, surrounded by a wooden stockade. Miss Stenson, *bloody* Miss Stenson, had said she was showing off when she said that. She wouldn't have said that to Deb.

Fired by the thought, she stormed through the kitchen door, letting it clatter shut behind her. But where was her father, where the accusing Deb? Only her mother was there, quietly ironing.

'Your supper's in the oven,' said Laura peaceably. 'I expect it's a bit dried out though.'

Mary said nothing. Suddenly tears were thick in her throat, nothing could pass them. Silent herself, her mother took up her oven gloves and drew Mary's supper from the side oven on the range, still in use even though they had an electric cooker nowadays.

She put a cool hand on her daughter's shoulder. 'Come on, darling. Sit down and eat. You'll feel better.'

But she was the one who was sour and mean! Why should anyone care to make her feel better? She sat at the table, dripping tears between mouthfuls, while her mother damped sheets with lavender water.

Suddenly she could bear it no more. 'I'm sorry!' she burst out. 'I didn't mean to!'

'Didn't you?' Her mother glanced at her.

'It's just – she's such a pest. And she hates Gunthwaite, and she doesn't ride Samson, and – and—'

'And she's pretty, and clever, and everyone at school thinks she's nice,' finished Laura. 'It's my fault really. We shouldn't have sent her to Silverton with you. I didn't think.'

'It's not your fault she's pretty and clever and nice!' wailed Mary, giving up on her supper and letting the tears run. 'It's mine because I'm not!'

Laura put down her iron and went to embrace her daughter, her dear, irreplaceable firstborn. Some part of her longed for the days when it was in her power to make things better. Contentment used to be a plaster on a cut knee, or a yard of her own garden, or a hen to call by name with each chick separately loved. What could she do now when some bitter, misguided teacher wrote that Mary was 'rebellious and lazy, lacking in intellectual and social skills alike' while Deb's report was a glowing paean of praise?

She rocked her and held her, whispering small French endearments left over from years ago. That terrible school! They were even grudging in their admission that Mary was good at French, putting it down to 'the undeniable advantage of a native parent', as if Laura herself came endowed with feathers in her hair and a grass skirt, as well as a foreign language.

3

Mary began to calm. Laura said, 'Deb can't help being what she is. Do you think you can help hating it?'

Her daughter swallowed noisily. 'I don't know. I couldn't today. Why is she everything I'm not? It's so unfair!'

'It would be if she was,' said Laura reasonably. 'But you imagine a lot of it, you know. She isn't really cleverer than you. She's too young to be annoyed with the school yet, so she does what they want. You don't. You don't make it easy for yourself.'

'They hate me. All of them. They want to see me fail.'

Laura's hand stroked her daughter's thick, dark hair. 'And you oblige them, don't you? Oh, Mary, it isn't right!'

They sat in silence. There wasn't a lot to say. With the exception of French, Mary had failed every exam other than English, a subject she loved.

Mary let out a long, heartfelt sigh. 'Is her face badly marked?' she asked miserably. 'I hit her really hard.'

'It's only a bruise. She's being good about it.'

'I wish she'd hate me for it! I really do!' She flung away from the table and her mother to stand in the middle of the kitchen, a girl too tall and too shapeless, with nothing to commend her but a mane of thick black hair. Suddenly she gathered up that hair, pulling it back from her face, going to stare at her reflection in the darkened window pane.

'Mary, don't. You're being silly.'

'No I'm not.' Her face was outlined against the night, a pale oval lit by dark blue eyes. But in the centre of her forehead, made livid by crying, was a V of discoloured skin. And beneath one eye, almost a devil's thumbprint, was a mark like a rotting strawberry.

'You're upset,' said Laura desperately. 'That always makes it worse.'

'Like when I'm cold, or when I'm hot, or when I laugh? I must remember not to laugh or cry, or get cold or hot, and then I'll be all right, won't I? Won't I?' She stared out at herself, hating what she saw. Not for nothing were the mirrors in this house confined to small, utilitarian squares in bathroom or bedroom. This was a study which never seemed to pall.

Laura went to the window and drew the curtains. 'It isn't that bad,' she said determinedly. 'You know you make too much of it. You've said so yourself.'

'It's bad enough, though! No one likes me. Everyone likes Deb.'

'They don't know you,' soothed her mother. 'And who doesn't like you? Girls at school?'

Mary flushed. Laura watched as the marks on her face darkened to purple, praying that she didn't know that happened, that she had never seen, that no one had ever told her. 'Not girls,' she said stiffly.

4

'Darling, you're not quite sixteen!'

'It isn't going to get better though, is it? Tom's still going to ignore me, and comb his hair for Deb and buy her sweets!'

'Tom? That stupid man? He's only good for tractor driving. And besides, he's courting that dumpling of a girl, the one from the fish shop in Bainfield.'

'Mummy, you know what I mean!'

Laura turned aside. Of course she knew. But somehow, when Mary was born, her life saved by the forceps that had marked her, she had felt that they were both so lucky, and so blessed. She had never expected to have children, and there was her wonderful child. Neither then, nor in all the years since, had she found it in her to think that Mary would not be loved as she deserved. She didn't think it now. But if the girl persisted in this terrible, pointless self-loathing, Laura didn't know what might be the result.

There was a step on the cobbles outside. Mary pulled her hair over her face and turned her back, but it was only her father, Michael. Big, dark, moving as if his daughter were a nervous calf, he took off his boots and went to wash his hands at the sink.

'You were ages,' said Laura. 'She's been back half an hour.'

'I went down to the horses. I thought she might be there.'

Something caught at Mary's heart. It was the thought of her father caring enough to look for her at night, when they all knew he could see hardly at all in the dark. She thought of him stumbling through the fields, in search of his wayward child.

'You shouldn't have bothered, Daddy,' she burst out. 'I'm not worth the trouble!'

Michael dried his hands carefully on the towel. 'If you're not, I don't know who is,' he said calmly. 'You've worked yourself up over nothing. Children argue, that's all there is to it. Deb's got a bruised cheek and deserves an apology, but after that we'll forget about it. You're home. It's a time of happiness, for us all.'

'Oh, Dad.' Mary got up and went to him, pressing her face against his burly shoulder. He patted her once or twice, but no more. The girl needed calming, she needed natural, firm handling. He wouldn't make more of this.

Laura took her up to bed with a glass of milk. The ancient stairs creaked and groaned, but thankfully Deb didn't stir. Returning from her unruly daughter's room, she looked in to see her younger child sleeping peacefully, her hair spread across the pillow like a glorious tumble of embroidery silk. Even the bruise, darkening now, seemed like a beauty spot, matching the two curving crescents of lashes resting against pale skin. Laura's heart ached with love. Deborah was such a golden child. She would have her troubles no doubt, just as Mary did, but she would never have cause to despise her face.

5

She closed the door and hurried down to the kitchen. Michael was at the sink again, bathing his eyes with some mixture the doctor had prescribed. Although the damage was not in the eyes themselves but in the optic nerve, straining to see, especially at night, always caused him discomfort. How like him to say nothing to Mary.

'I'll make you some tea, shall I?'

'No thanks, love. I'll get to bed.'

'Have you a headache? I'm sure you have. I'll get aspirin.'

'I don't need aspirin. What I need is a good night's sleep.'

But she hovered still, wanting to undertake some service that would please him. How else could she show how much she needed him, loved him, relied on his calm constancy? He was her unfailing support.

He turned, wincing slightly as the light came on to his face. A headache, then. They came about once a week nowadays, although directly after the injury, a shrapnel wound in the desert, they had been as frequent as every day. In another ten years they could be gone altogether, she thought. But they seemed fierce lately.

She felt the cold stirring of fear. Perhaps something in his brain had moved and he was in danger. Forcing herself to be rational she admitted the more likely explanation; farming was so pressured nowadays, so full of change. New grants, new seeds, new fertilisers, something different every week, and so much of it against Michael's instincts. He hated to ask Gunthwaite to yield by the ton, when bushels had provided enough and to spare in the past. She knew what they said about him in town; that he was slow, and old-fashioned, and hopelessly sentimental. Who but Michael would keep four or five shires, simply for the pleasure of their company? Who but he would refuse to widen gates for new machines, or grub up hedges to make harvesting simple? He loved Gunthwaite, and kept it as his sacred trust.

She put a hand on his shoulder, wishing she could draw the pain from him, sure that if it was hers she wouldn't care. He said, 'You let those girls worry you too much, love. They'll be all right.'

'Will they? Mary hates herself. And every time she looks at Deb she hates herself more.'

'Deb's blooming early, that's all. She won't look so pretty the rest of her life as she does now.'

Laura snorted. 'I don't want Deborah to fade just to make Mary happy! She's a beautiful young girl, she should be able to enjoy it, not walk around in a sack in case Mary's jealous. And it isn't only her looks. You know Deb, she's so easy and friendly, she can't help but make friends. And Mary—'

'Our wild young mare,' supplied Michael. 'Nothing but gangling legs and nerves.'

6

'If she were a horse you'd sell her,' said Laura miserably.

'I might not. I might keep her and be prouder of her than any when she came good.'

Briefly, thankfully, she rested her forehead against his arm. Then she moved away, clearing the room for the morning, banking the fire. There wasn't so much to do nowadays, with Sophie and Marie in one of the cottages and old Mrs Cooper dead more than two years since. Paula, one of the land girls they had had in the war, settled in the village with twin boys, came out to see them now and then and always remarked on the change. 'It used to be you couldn't get moved in this kitchen. You wouldn't think a few years could change things so. It's the same everywhere. Everyone's gone.'

The thought depressed her, although why she should want a houseful of waifs and strays again was a mystery. She ran some water into the sink and added some bleach, immersing the dishcloths and mentally running through what must be done the next day. A cow to prepare for market, they milked commercially now they had electric and did quite a trade in quality cattle; Mary to take into Bainfield to buy some new shoes; Deborah to be enrolled in Gunthwaite Village Guides, to give her something to do. All to be mixed in with the everyday round of cooking, washing, and livestock care.

Michael was going up to bed. Laura felt heavy suddenly, almost too heavy to follow him. Mary should have friends at her age, go to parties, visit the cinema. Out here, at Gunthwaite, it wasn't enough just to exist. Friends had to be cultivated, be they children from the village or hunting people. But Mary had no knack for easy acquaintance; she would rather turn into a recluse than subject herself to tongue-tied embarrassment at a tennis party, or a dance. It wasn't right – not for a girl of sixteen.

Laura turned out the light and stood a moment, letting her eyes grow accustomed to the dark. All at once a memory flashed vividly into her head – herself at that age. A skilled whore, lying on her high-priced bed while some fat stranger threw off his clothes. She put out a hand and clutched the frame of the door. That was so long ago. It had nothing to do with who she was now, and nothing to do with Mary.

Her fingers were hurting. It took an effort of will to prise them from the wood. She went slowly and stiffly up to bed.

7

Chapter Two

The market was bustling. Cattle trailers mixed with cars and trucks in Bainfield's narrow main street, made narrower by stalls and carts. Michael drew in his breath angrily; if he had been alone Mary knew he would have sworn. They should have come earlier, but all the upset of yesterday had made everyone slow. Her mother had still been washing the cow as they led her into the wagon.

Deb said, 'Is it busier than usual? Look, the bus is stuck.'

Sure enough, the bus that served the outlying villages, bringing housewives and old men for their weekly shop, stood athwart the bridge hooting uselessly at a broken down car.

'It certainly does seem crowded,' said Laura. 'If we don't get to the pens soon Tulip will be so far down the list there won't be any point in selling her at all.'

'It's the fault of that car,' said Michael. 'Why doesn't somebody push it?'

Mary leaned out of the side window. 'They're trying. But someone won't let them. Man in a dark suit with a horrible squashy hat. Looks like a gangster or something.'

Laura chuckled. 'Perhaps the car's full of guns.'

'Do you think so?' Deb was wide-eyed. She would believe anything, provided it added sparkle to ordinary days.

'No, of course I don't. Michael, do you think we should walk the cow?'

He considered. 'We'll not get her there otherwise. But she might not lead in all this upheaval. We can always put her back, though. I daresay it's worth a try.'

They pulled the wagon into the side of the road and got out. When the farmer behind saw what they were about he got out of his van and stood watching, saying, 'You'll never get her through this lot. Give it up, Cooper. Give it up, I say.'

'We'll give it up when we've tried,' said Michael. 'Laura, you take the rope, and you girls go either side of her head. I'll chase her up from behind.'

'Wouldn't be in your shoes, Missis,' said the farmer to Laura.

'I showed her last year,' said Laura. 'She knows me.'

Tulip came cautiously out of the wagon, her large eyes liquid with

8

uncertainty. She was a shorthorn, dark red and creamy white, her back flat as a table, her udder tidy. 'Bit narrow,' said the farmer.

'She's young yet,' said Michael. 'And yielding well. I wouldn't be selling her but we've some good cows this year. Can't keep every good cow Gunthwaite breeds.'

A small crowd was gathering. A few years ago no one would have looked twice at cows being led through the town, but times had changed. The war had caused Bainfield to grow and prosper, losing some of its agricultural roots. The result was today's market, with produce stalls cheek by jowl with people selling cloth or car parts or plastic plates.

Laura patted the cow and said, 'Come on, Tulip,' in an encouraging voice.

'Right pretty bunch of tulips,' said a voice from the crowd.

'I know which one I'd buy,' said another, and a laugh went up.

Mary's face turned a slow, dull red. She shook her hair over her face, hunching her shoulders and slouching. Deb merely looked around her, seeing nothing frightening or disturbing in the crowd. She too put her hand on the cow's neck. 'Come on, Tulip, there's a good cow.' And then, 'If you'd all be quiet she'd lead better. We've got to get her to the sale or she'll have come all this way for nothing.'

The chatter diminished. Placed between her two girls, Laura could sense Mary's humiliation, Deb's unconcern. The cow paced down the cobbled street, picking her way delicately between stalls and cars, stopping only once to sniff at a discarded cabbage. Deb picked it up. 'You can have this when you get there,' she promised the cow. 'For being good.'

And from the crowd there came audible whispers. 'Little smasher, isn't she? Pretty as a picture, and good as gold with the beast.'

At last they reached the cattle pens. By now, Tulip's progress had made her famous, and a positive flurry of interest arose. Michael was quietly pleased. 'Well done, girls,' he said. 'No one can doubt she's a good, quiet cow. She'll follow you anywhere, Laura.'

'Weren't people nice?' said Deb. 'Everyone got out of the way when I asked.'

'What else did you expect?' demanded Mary. 'A red carpet, perhaps?'

'Mary,' said Laura in a warning voice. Mary gave her a beseeching look and turned her back.

Laura left Deb with her father and took Mary off to buy shoes. As soon as they were out of earshot Mary said accusingly, 'You heard what they said! You see?'

'They could have been talking about any one of us.'

9

'It was Deb. You know it was Deb. Look at me for once, just look at me! No one's ever going to say I'm pretty in my whole life!'

Laura struggled for calm. 'I don't believe that for a moment, darling. But even if it were true – and it isn't – would it matter? It doesn't matter what people look like, what matters is being good and kind and – and making the most of your talents. No one's exactly the way they want to be! Look at me, wrinkles, no proper waist and hips – like one of your father's older cows.'

Mary stopped and surveyed her mother. She was a woman of medium height, dressed today in a tweed skirt and sensible shoes. She could be any farmer's wife, except that she wore a simple cotton jacket, caught almost casually at the shoulder; and her hair, the occasional strand of grey standing out like silver, was caught up too with a matching scarf. There were no wrinkles that Mary could see, just a gentle fanning at the corners of her mother's eyes that might almost be feathers from an artist's brush. 'You're beautiful,' said Mary heavily. 'You know you are.'

'I know I'm not! Darling, everyone has faults. We just learn to make the best of them, that's all.'

Mary turned away. There was no making the best of hers.

Laura felt tears rising in her throat. She was too vulnerable where Mary was concerned. If there was anything to be done to make Mary happy then she would do it, she thought. No matter what it cost, no matter that everyone said the girl was spoiled and undisciplined and didn't deserve her parents' tolerance, nor yet an expensive horse. The horse had served for a time; what now?

They had reached the shoe shop. The window was full of boringly sensible brogues and sandals. Laura felt sudden irritation with such practicality. What wouldn't she give for a window crammed with Parisian style and expense and sheer, unnecessary frivolity? She recalled a pair of elegant little button boots, heels like pins, as wicked a pair of shoes as could be bought, that had made her own teenage self happy for a week. Was she really to buy her daughter square-toed, brown, buckled sandals?

She turned to Mary. 'What would you like? I mean – really like?'

Mary blinked. 'I don't know. Clothes, you mean? Aren't we going to buy the sandals?'

'No. To hell with sandals. What about a pretty dress? A blouse and skirt, even. Something you'll love, something summery, something just to make you smile.'

Mary grinned ruefully. 'Mum! What would Dad say? You can't make people happy with things.'

'You can cheer them up a bit, though. It just seems to me that people like – well, people like Deb don't need any help looking wonderful. It's people like you and me that do. And I haven't helped you. I've just gone along with the way everyone else does things. There's no reason why girls your age have to dress in horrible clothes. It's time you acquired some style.'

Mary almost grimaced. 'Style won't make my face better!'

'It could. If you had enough style those marks could be an asset. Something different. You can't want to look like everyone else.'

'Can't I?' Mary was wistful. All she wanted was smooth, white skin. Well, not all perhaps. What about small hands and feet, shoulders that were less square, legs that were less long, and – embarrassingly – something less of a washboard for a chest? She wanted to stand in a roomful of unremarkable pretty girls and go unnoticed.

Laura sighed. Nothing with Mary was ever easy. She turned without a word and began making her way towards Relham's Department Store, and their 'junior' floor. Mary strode unhappily behind.

Relham's was not in the forefront of design. The 'junior' clothes were modelled in the main on extremely dated fashion. Young girls were supposed in summer to wear endearing little blouses with flowered skirts, with perhaps, for parties, a slip-on shoe. If they were really to dress up then it was in a parody of the clothes their mothers might have worn; stiff cocktail frocks, boned bodices and unforgiving box jackets. Here and there could be seen women with strained faces, waiting for their lumpish daughters to emerge from fitting rooms in yet another hopeless creation. Laura felt well-worn despair. English fashion!

An assistant was bearing down on them. Mary watched in fascination as her mother underwent the change that always overcame her in shops; a slight lifting of the chin, a narrowing of the nose, a stiffening of the back. Those who knew nice Mrs Cooper in so many other spheres wouldn't recognise this Mrs Cooper – haughty and difficult to please.

Laura ignored the assistant for some moments. A chubby young customer was standing disconsolate before a mirror, her frilly collar as tight round her neck as her gathered skirt around her waist. Her mother was twittering, 'Possibly, darling – if we moved the button?'

Laura sighed audibly. 'Don't you have anything that isn't – pretty?' She imbued the word with absolute contempt.

'Not pretty?' The assistant blinked.

'You must have something distinctive. A good jacket, perhaps. A well-cut skirt. God knows that child over there could do with one.'

'Yes.' The assistant smiled glacially. 'Some of our customers do still have such a struggle with puppy fat.'

'Then stock clothes to accommodate it!' snarled Laura.

She spun on her heel – a sensible flat heel, but to the onlookers it could well have been a stiletto – and demanded that the assistant consider Mary. The girl wilted beneath their combined, assessing stares.

'She is quite tall,' said the assistant, nervously.

'Indeed. Tall and slender. And so striking.'

'Indeed—' echoed the assistant doubtfully. 'Perhaps you'd like to see our Miss Bainfield range?' She waved a hand at a rail of white-cuffed dresses.

'No,' said Laura. 'We don't want sweetness. We want style!'

'Madam, we don't have style for young girls!'

Laura blinked. 'Whyever not?'

'Most of our customers want their daughters to remain – remain—'

'Dowdy,' supplied Laura.

She approached the rails of clothes, sweeping aside the woman as if she wasn't there. 'Would Madam like – is there something I can select—' In Relham's it was an unpardonable sin for the customers to touch the rails. But Laura's quick fingers were extracting dress after dress. 'Try this, Mary. It looks nothing but could be wonderful. And this red – oh, yes, and this!' She held aloft a tube of grey knitting.

'That isn't in the junior range,' the assistant managed. 'It's on its way to Models.'

'If we find nothing here we may perhaps accompany it,' said Laura drily. 'Come on, Mary. Try them on.'

Mary was scarlet with embarrassment, the marks on her face livid and stark. Laura thought of the mirrors in the fitting rooms and shuddered inwardly. 'Come on, Mary,' she snapped, and led the way herself.

Gradually, in the privacy of the room, Mary's blush subsided. 'You were horrible to that woman,' she whispered, struggling out of her clothes.

'I wasn't! At any rate, she should be better at her job. Imagine allowing that fat little girl to go out in that skirt.'

Mary, in her underwear, surveyed her own long, pale limbs. 'I hate clothes,' she said viciously. 'I'll look just as bad in these!'

'Try the blue,' said Laura, and smothered her difficult girl in folds of cotton.

It was a dress with a deep scooped neck. The colour was wonderful, lighting up Mary's dark, rather sombre eyes. But the dress needed breasts, and Mary had none. She plucked miserably at the empty folds.

'This would suit Deb,' she said, with truth.

'Deb is getting a guide uniform,' retorted Laura. 'We could take this in, I suppose. But at this price! As if a young girl is going to have a bosom like Mae West!'

Mary said, 'I ought to have something by now. I'm the flattest in my year.'

'I had nothing until I was seventeen,' lied Laura.

She stood back and tried to be dispassionate. She remembered Madame and Marie, dressing her for her first customer. If this expedition had been planned she would have brought Marie, there was never anyone with a better eye. But the girls hated to take her shopping, because she always made a scene. As for Sophie ... she giggled.

'What's so funny?'

'I was thinking we could have brought Sophie.'

'Mum! She can be rude as anything!'

'She'd say you needed a French brassiere. And she'd be right.'

Mary took the dress off with an air of finality. No French brassiere was going to supply what nature could not. She stepped into the red shirtwaister, very plain, in all but colour very dull. 'Oh,' she said. Reflected back from the glass was a tall, slender girl with long, shapely, marble white arms and legs. Her hair was a cloud of darkness, the marks on her face no more than echoes of the vivid colour of the dress.

'It works,' said Laura with relief. 'Severity. That's the secret.'

'It makes my face look red.'

'It's so red you don't notice your face. We'll have it, darling. You can wear it to Graham Beacham's tennis dance.'

'You know I won't go to that!'

'Well. We'll see.'

Laura expertly removed the dress. Even Michael had once remarked that she could remove clothes more quickly and gracefully than he would have believed possible, even on someone else. Laura called it her French knack, which it was. Her French prostitute's knack.

She tossed the grey sheath over her daughter. 'My God, look at the price! But we'll just see.'

'It's horrible,' complained Mary. 'It's just nothing.' She forced her arms through the clinging knitted sleeves. 'See?' Laura pulled the neck straight and eased the long skirt over her daughter's snakelike hips. They had never seemed snakelike before – only narrow and unformed. But in the clinging dress a young and shapeless body was transformed into an erotic statement. Each tiny breast was outlined, topped with its own pert nipple. The long back swept down to a neat rear, with the dress snuggled beneath it like an old man's knee. Even Mary's angular collarbone, rising like a cliff above the fabric, suddenly seemed to have point; it marked those wide, square shoulders, and exaggerated the narrowness beneath.

The assistant swept aside the curtain. 'Has Madam – oh!'

'What do you think?' asked Laura ingenuously.

The assistant swallowed. 'I think – I think – I think I should take that dress straight up to Models,' she blurted.

Laura grinned. 'I believe you may be right. Take it off, darling. If you went to a tennis dance looking like that you'd be eloped with. We'll have the shirtwaist.'

'But Mum – Mum! Couldn't we keep it till I was older?'

Silently, Laura turned the ticket on the sleeve. Mary's eyes grew enormous. 'Really?' she mouthed. Her mother nodded. After a last, lingering look in the mirror Mary took the dress off.

They were silent as they walked back through the shop. Laura stopped once or twice, in fabrics, to check the price of lining, and again in menswear to buy some collars for Michael's shirts. As they waited for the change to descend along the tube from the fastness in which the money was kept, Mary said, 'It was a very indecent dress, wasn't it?'

'Shockingly indecent,' said Laura, running her finger along the wide expanse of polished mahogany counter. 'You must have a dress exactly like it one day.'

'Mummy!'

Laura widened her eyes. 'You don't always have to look respectable, darling. One day there'll be a young man who makes you want to be quite unrespectable. Is that a word? Unrespectable? You know what I mean.'

'I wouldn't ever dare wear it! I'd – I'd just like to know that I could. To have it – and know.'

'And you do know. You can look wonderful, darling. Even I didn't know how wonderful.' She idly turned a packet of collar studs and wondered if she should buy some. But this was taking too long as it was. She glanced at her watch. 'Will you look at the time! Where is this change? Your father will be worried to death.'

At that moment there was a whoosh and a thud and an object like a cartridge case came visibly to rest in the glass end of the tube at their counter. The assistant came bustling over, extracting the change and dispensing it as if he were doing them both a favour. Laura snapped her purse shut.

Walking back through town, Mary couldn't believe she could feel so different. Beneath these schoolgirl clothes, behind this ordinary exterior, there lurked a cool, sophisticated woman, one who could walk into Graham Beacham's tennis dance and cast a world-weary glance over this little country amusement. Not for her orange juice and biscuits, she would probably be offered cocktails. Or something. Perhaps gin? She wrestled with the problem. Since she didn't know anything about anything except wine, would it be better to ask for water? Or would that look as if she was being judgmental? They

14

might think she was religious. Against pleasure. Not if she wore the grey dress, of course. She let her mind drift off into delicious, tempting imaginings. 'Is that the Cooper girl? There really is something about her. I know her sister's pretty enough but Mary Cooper has a certain – quality – don't you think?'

The wagon was in view, parked on the broken tarmac beside the market. Laura and Mary picked their way across the rough ground, avoiding potholes and discarded chip papers. The door of the wagon suddenly flung open. 'Laura! Where in God's name have you been?'

They both stopped, disconcerted. Even Mary was shocked out of her daydream. This wasn't like Michael. He strode towards them, face set in an unnatural glare. 'Two hours we've been waiting. Two bloody hours!'

'Michael!' Laura put a hand on his arm. 'Michael, please.'

Something seemed to ebb from him. 'You've been so long,' he said in a softer voice. 'I've been waiting.'

'Has something happened? Is it Deb?'

'No. No.' He passed a hand across his eyes. He had a headache, thought Laura, it was the headache, that's all. Everyone was looking at them, wondering what had got into old Cooper all of a sudden. You never knew with these remote farms. They all went bonkers in the end.

'We'll go home,' said Laura shakily. 'Shall I drive?'

Michael looked at her. 'You don't understand.' He seemed unutterably weary. 'Gabriel's back.'

All at once Mary saw her mother waver like a leaf in the wind. Every part of her, body, legs, hands, was wracked by a long shudder. She watched her father put out his hands and hold her, watched the shudder pass from her to him and back again. She felt afraid suddenly. Her parents had never been other than controlled, in control, of themselves and of events. Like a baby taken from familiar hands, she knew herself lost.

Chapter Three

It was noisy in the wagon, and Mary could only just hear what her parents were saying to one another. Usually they sat on either side of the cab with the girls between them, but today Michael sat at the wheel with Laura next to him, then Deb, then Mary at the far side. They were excluding her, she thought. Whatever this might be it was something they didn't want her to hear.

'It was his car . . . stuck on the bridge . . . automatic transmission or something, impossible to push.'

'Trust Gabriel . . . flash so and so. What about Dora? Piers? Is it a holiday? . . . you should have . . . we're entitled to know.'

Mary shifted uncomfortably. What was the matter with them? All that had happened was that Uncle Gabriel, her father's brother, had returned from America for the first time since the war. He had married Dora Fitzalan-Howard, from Fairlands, further down the valley, so of course they were staying there. Weren't they pleased? Excited? She couldn't believe her father hated him. Dad didn't hate anyone, with the possible exception of that man who hit his horses in the mouth out hunting.

She thought of Piers, her cousin, and felt a frisson of pleasure. The very last time they met had been how long ago? Three years? Four? He had been left at Fairlands with his grandparents for years while his parents settled in Canada. Except that they hadn't settled, and had moved to Chicago and then to New York, while Piers and Mary formed a childhood alliance built on mutual isolation. For years he had been Mary's closest friend. When he left, reclaimed at last, the hole in her life had seemed vast, a wasteland impossible to fill. But filled it had been. What would it be like to see him again? Would he know her? What would he see?

She tuned again to her parents' conversation. 'Could have written . . . you don't think . . . perhaps Gunthwaite?'

She felt herself go cold. Were they here to claim Gunthwaite? She had known for years it wasn't hers. Gunthwaite wasn't owned in the ordinary way, it was held in a trust set up by her father's grandfather, who thought women didn't count. Because of it the house and land passed always through the male line, and her father had no male heir. Once, when she was quite small, she had found her mother crying in

16

her room because, she said, she'd thought they were to have a new baby but it seemed that now they weren't. Aren't we enough? demanded Mary. Me and Deb? Her mother had said that certainly they were. But if there wasn't a boy then Gunthwaite would go to Piers and, nice as he was, he wasn't their family. Was he?

Mary had thought about it and decided her mother was right. Piers was her friend, right enough. He was even a Cooper. But he wasn't a Gunthwaite Cooper, and Gunthwaite was theirs.

They were nearing Gunthwaite village. Her mother, pulling herself together, said:'Stop here Michael, please. I've to see about Deb's guides in the Post Office. Old Mrs Tims keeps the list.'

'I don't want to go camping,' said Deb warningly. 'If they make me go camping I'll leave.'

'Of course you can't go camping,' said Michael absently.

Mary said, 'And why not? The scouts do. There's no earthly reason why Deb shouldn't rough it for a change.'

Michael said nothing, simply manoeuvring the large vehicle into the side of the road. Laura chivvied the girls on to the pavement and climbed out after them, hurrying at once into the Post Office. The girls leaned on the side of the cab. The engine's warmth was pleasant, the smell of oil mingling with roses from the churchyard wall.

Deb said, 'They're in a state, aren't they? Do you know why?'

Mary shrugged. 'Haven't a clue. Dad can't like his brother much. I don't know when he last came to England, even. When Piers was at Fairlands he used to spend holidays with them, but they never came here.'

'Why didn't Piers live with them all the time?'

Again the shrug. 'The schools here were better or something. But I bet that was just a story. Couldn't be bothered with him more like.'

Deb leaned her shoulders on the cab and walked her feet up the wall opposite. Mary said, 'Don't! People are watching.'

'What if they are? Mum isn't here. And I don't mind if people see my knees.'

'Well, you should!'

Mary walked away. Deb was such an exhibitionist. Even now, a couple of farm lads, calling at the blacksmith for a welding job, were sauntering with studied aimlessness towards the wagon. It only happened when Deb was there, thought Mary. It always happened when Deb was there.

Laura came out of the shop. 'Pull your skirt down at once, Deborah!' she rapped. 'Mary, stop gawping and get in the cab. You can make some bread when we get home. In all the rush I forgot to buy any.'

She climbed up into the wagon, her irritation palpable. Deb said, 'Can't I join the guides then?'

17

'Of course you can. Seven o'clock tomorrow, church hall.' Then, in a low voice to Michael, hoping to be covered by the engine, 'They've been in the village already. Gabriel, Dora and Piers. They're using the Fairlands car.'

Michael took a short breath. 'They won't call.'

'Won't they? I can't bear it if they do.'

The girls exchanged a glance. Here was a mystery. Mary found herself instinctively thinking the worst. She would lose her home, her pony; Uncle Gabriel would come back and take it all. She thought of Piers, as she had last seen him; a stocky, blond boy, shy with strangers. He had never been shy with her. But in her imagination the image changed; friendship had become challenge, generosity was now greed. Piers Cooper was his father's son, come riding out of the west to steal her home.

When they arrived back at Gunthwaite everything was a scramble. The range was almost out, and because they had been short of time this morning the dairy still had to be scrubbed. Michael was sharp with Tom, it seemed he'd spent the day doing nothing very much. Bill Mayes, the foreman, a cantankerous old bloke, caused trouble by remarking that scrubbing milk pans was women's work. If Laura had heard him there'd have been a row, but fortunately she was busy in the house. So it was left to Mary to point out that since she could drive a tractor, why shouldn't tractor drivers scrub pans?

Mayes glared at her. He had a face like an earthed up turnip, thought Mary, covered in unappetising lumps. 'Here, Master,' he rumbled. 'That girl's getting above herself. Not too old for a hiding, she ain't.'

'I don't beat my daughters,' said Michael. 'And if I did it wouldn't be for telling the truth. But you're impertinent, Mary. Go in the house and help your mother with the bread.'

Mary went bad-temperedly off. She had been hoping to talk to her father about Uncle Gabriel. Her mother never said anything she wasn't quite sure she wished you to know.

She went into the kitchen, cleared a space on the long pine table and weighed out flour. 'Have you washed your hands?' snapped Laura.

Mary sighed and went to the sink. 'I shouldn't be doing this now, anyway,' she said. 'The oven's too cold.'

'It'll be hot in an hour. It takes you more than that to make bread.'

Mary watched her mother from the corner of her eye. Under Laura's hands the kitchen seemed to settle down and become once more a place of good things. With order restored, Laura's mood visibly improved. She went to the dresser and got out a table cloth embroidered with daisies and edged with lace. It was her favourite.

Whenever there was a crisis she soothed herself by laying a perfect tea table, best cloth, new bread and fairy cakes. Mary knew she would bake while the oven came up to bread heat, and then finish some pies as it died. The thought of it made her unexpectedly sad. She knew her mother so completely, down to her littlest routines.

Mary rubbed lard into the flour perfunctorily. 'Why didn't Dad ask Uncle Gabriel to tea?' she asked.

Laura barely turned her head. 'Even you must have grasped that he and Dad don't get on.'

'What do you mean, even me? Are you saying I'm stupid?'

'Of course not. Don't start, Mary.'

They subsided into silence. After a while Laura switched on the radio. It was dance music, and Mary kneaded in time to the beat, wondering why her mother hadn't sent her upstairs to try on the new dress. Everyone had forgotten about it. Even her.

The kitchen door opened. They both looked up, and Mary saw her mother put her hands to her face and gasp: 'Oh!' But it was only Sophie and Marie.

'*Mes anges*! We had to come! Such news. Have you heard? He's back. And the wife . . . Mon Dieu, would you believe, more a harlot than most! And her so very well bred, wouldn't you know. Cake, for us? We must eat together. Wonderful Lori, always right.'

Laura's face relaxed into a little smile. 'Come if you want, darlings. Sophie, sit down. Mary, put the kettle on, please.'

She watched as she obeyed. All three of them lapsed at once into French, talking nineteen to the dozen. The old ladies waved gnarled, ring-encrusted hands, Marie's still long and expressive, Sophie's emerging plump from the sleeves of a lace blouse much in need of a wash. Their hair was dyed, their lipstick thick, their inhibitions non-existent. As she talked Sophie hitched her blouse and scratched her armpit while Marie lounged back and propped one still shapely leg against the range, pulling her skirt up the better to warm her bottom. They talked so fast partly to exclude her, she knew. But her French was almost good enough. She strained her ears to catch the words.

'My dear, she's a dog's dinner. Dog's vomit, more like. As for him, you remember the man who shot himself? Yes, you do, Zelma's bloke. Nothing but drink and sex, and didn't he look it? Same as him – Gabriel. You know how thin they get, and their eyes take on that look. Well, you know what look. No, I don't mean he's going to shoot himself, someone else more like. That sort did well in the war, and no wonder. Killer's eyes.'

'He never enjoyed killing,' said Laura, a little ruffled. 'That wasn't him. He was a pilot, you know he was.'

'Killed people, didn't they? You can always tell. Now, the boy. We haven't seen the boy, he wasn't there. They saw us now, oh yes they

19

did, for all they looked over the rooftops. Poor kid, they never wanted him, either of them. She only took him in the end to spite his grandma if you ask me.'

'I was sorry when he went,' interjected Mary.

It was a mistake. They all stopped talking and looked at her. Laura got up and said in English, 'Mary has a beautiful new dress. Go and put it on, darling, and let us all see.'

So she went slowly upstairs, listening all the while to the buzz of talk. And when she came down they admired her, although of course Marie sniffed and said she needed decent underwear and a haircut and some jewels. But Marie always said things like that. She thought everyone should always look as if they were going to a ball.

The bread rose quite well, considering the atmosphere in which it was made. Laura's cakes were good as usual, and Sophie and Marie were funny and made even Michael laugh. Deb made Sophie sing some French song she had taught them as babies, complete with actions. When she got rather carried away, rolling her eyes and adding bits in colloquial French, Michael said smoothly, 'Deborah, go and fetch Aunt Sophie's coat. She ought to be home before long,' and they all knew the party was over.

Michael and Deb walked them home. Deb still loved to hear them talk about Paris in the old days, but for Mary it was a story heard too often. She began desultorily to clear the table, while her mother sat over a cup of tea, gazing into space. The beautiful tea table, so richly set with cakes and hot bread, china and glass and lace, had disintegrated into crumbs and mess. Suddenly Laura said, 'Nothing ever lasts. That's the pity of everything.'

Mary turned at the sink. 'Are we going to lose Gunthwaite then? Is that what it's all about?'

And her mother's surprised, bewildered face looked back at her.

Just then there was a knock at the door. A voice, a woman's voice, called: 'Laura! Laura darling, it's me. Dora.' But before they could move the door was open and she was there. Aunt Dora.

Her hair was sculpted gold curls, set firmly against her head. She wore a long coat in dark wool, edged with a fur collar, and her shoes were fashionably high-heeled. But it was her make-up that fascinated Mary, a pale enamel covering her skin, eradicating every line, every colour change, every sag. She could have been six or sixty, somehow achieving a remarkably timeless beauty. Next to her Laura looked nothing, she thought. Aunt Dora was like a cinema star, and her mother was just ordinary.

Dora put out her hands. More slowly, her mother extended her own. 'You haven't changed a bit,' said Dora.

'Neither have you,' said Laura, although that had to be a lie. No one living around here ever looked like that, thought Mary.

20

Laura said 'Is Gabriel—'

'No. He thought he'd better not. Sent me ahead to test the water. But it's been so long, darling, and everything's such ancient history. Every one of us has changed.'

'Yes.' Laura looked wistfully back at the tea table. Perhaps to her that symbolised the changes. Order to chaos, whatever you did to thwart it.

Mary stepped forward. 'Hello,' she said bravely. 'I'm Mary.'

She could feel her aunt's eyes assessing her, taking in the height, the thinness, and most of all, the marks. She turned her head as she always did, so they could see everything, all at once. Sometimes, if people only saw her from the good side, they flinched when she turned round. She couldn't bear that.

'What a wonderfully tall young lady,' said Dora.

Mary felt her teeth clench. Don't patronise me, she thought fiercely. Don't pity me. 'Have you brought Piers with you?' she demanded, sounding even to her own ears gauche and aggressive. 'I thought you might. He and I used to be good friends.'

'When you were children,' said Dora. Mary knew she was being put down.

The visitor turned her shoulder and said to Laura 'Why don't we go and sit somewhere and talk? I've got so much to tell you. We've had an exciting time, you wouldn't believe how exciting. Done pretty well for ourselves. And we'll be staying at Fairlands for the next few months, so it's foolish to go on avoiding one another, isn't it? Time to forget old wounds.'

'I don't think Michael's ready to forget anything,' said Laura thinly.

'If the men are stupid, we don't have to be,' said Dora, spreading her hands.

'My father isn't stupid,' said Mary.

Dora fixed her with a firm eye. 'If you don't mind, my dear, I was talking to your mother.'

'Either I'm a child or I'm not,' said Mary rudely. 'You can't have it both ways.'

'Mary, don't,' said Laura, almost pleading with her daughter. She led Dora off into the little used morning room, full of cold and dust.

Mary cleared the table and washed up, leaving the dishes to drain because it wasn't fair that she had to do everything. The evening was grey and overcast, threatening a warm rain. She felt restless, unable to settle to anything. For a minute she entertained the notion of going upstairs and trying to listen. Her mother would open the morning room window to air it a little, and if she leaned out from above she might hear something. She was so tired of knowing nothing at all.

She was suddenly seized by an almost painful longing to try! But

21

someone would see her and she'd be in trouble. To avoid the possibility she threw off her apron and flung out of the house.

Her steps led her down to the horses. She hadn't ridden today so tomorrow Diablo would be a handful and a half. Her stomach tightened, half in fear, half in excitement. There was nothing so good as mastering a horse that frightened you, and nothing so dreadful as failing to master it, because then you had taught the horse a bad lesson. It sometimes seemed to Mary that horses remembered only the things that went wrong; a lifetime of good experience could be ruined by an hour of bad.

The grass was still short in the fields. It had none of the deep, uniform greenness that so typified fields fed with nitrogen from a bag. Her father relied on muck and good management, to the scorn of his neighbours, all of whom had their dairy herds knee deep in luscious sward. But Gunthwaite cows bloomed late and milked forever. That was why Tulip had sold so well today.

She leaned on the fence of the pasture. The horses were down by the stream, grazing the sweet turf. Mary whistled to them, which she never dared do when her father was around, or any of the men for that matter. '"A whistling woman and a crowing hen, Brings the devil out of his den",' she quoted, and laughed as her own pet devil, the black, Diablo, cantered towards her.

She had brought sugar from the house, a pocketful of granulated that made a mess of her skirt and had to be licked by horsey tongues from her fingers. Diablo was bullying the others away, quelling Deb's Samson with a threatening hoof, the shires with a lift of the eyebrow. Giants though they were, the shires were gentle souls. Mary reached out a hand to them, holding Diablo tight by the forelock with the other. He fixed her with his mad, clever eye. 'I'll teach you to be better than you ought to be,' said Mary, and suddenly wild, she climbed another rail of the fence and slipped on to his back.

It was an idiot thing to do. She had nothing to control him, not even a headcollar. Diablo stood rigid with surprise as he felt the girl's bare legs beneath her skirt. Feeling the tension within him, Mary longed to get off, but dared not. He would know then he'd won.

She squeezed his flat sides with her calves. 'Walk on. Walk on, I say.'

The pony lurched sideways in a half plunge and she clutched at the mane. 'Walk on!' she said again, and at that he leaped into a gallop. Past the trees, through the dell, hurtling towards the stream. Let him not buck, she thought desperately. But he did, twisting his haunches, and only Mary's bare legs, glued with his sweat and hers, kept her in place. The stream was upon them. The gelding gathered himself and flew, forced to check on the far side by the abrupt rise of the land. 'Steady,' gasped Mary. 'Steady, Diablo.'

22

The first rush of energy was abating. He slowed as he topped the incline, dropping into a trot. Using her weight Mary turned him and put him back down the slope, knowing he couldn't rush or he'd fall. They hopped the stream again, the pony meek with surprise. He'd tried to lose her and she was still aboard. Gently, cautiously, she steered him in loops and long curves back to the fence. Now she could dismount with honour.

'Great! Mary, wait a minute!'

She swung round, her face as always flaming. Someone had seen her riding in her skirt. They would have seen her knickers! A young man was jogging towards her from the shelter of the willows. He was large and blond, broad-shouldered yet still with the gangling bones of youth. As he ran his hands were loosely clenched into giant fists.

'Piers?' said Mary doubtfully. 'Piers, that isn't you?'

'Of course it's me. I'm not that different.'

'You used to be eleven and smaller than me.'

'You used to be just like you are. I recognised your riding. Hi. It's good to see you, Mary.'

He stood before her, his hair falling loosely over his face. He looked foreign, thought Mary. His clothes, his way of standing. That stiff, unforthcoming smile. She had been right about him. Everything had changed.

'Great horse,' he said awkwardly, looping his thumbs in his belt.

'His name's Diablo. He cost a fortune and everyone thinks I'm spoiled because of it.'

'Are you?'

'No!' But then she looked at him under her lashes. 'Well, yes, a bit. Indulged, shall we say. I've got two of the nicest parents.'

'I wish I could say the same.'

There was an uncomfortable silence. Years ago, when they were both properly children, they used to talk about Piers' mother and father. They had decided, between them, that Gabriel was engaged in dangerous work with Dora as his loyal companion. Although they loved their son, they had selflessly left him in safety. Now, Mary said, 'Your mother's at our house. She's awfully glamorous.'

'She ought to be. Takes her half the day to get ready. She broke her nail today. Boy! You should have heard her.'

'Because she broke her nail?'

'She said it was the nail. Really it was everything. We brought over a car and it's too big for these roads, and Gran baked a special 'Welcome Home' cake that Mother thinks is tacky, and Dad opened a bottle of bourbon at lunch and glazed over. So it wasn't really the nail.'

'Oh.' Mary was impressed. Although not quite a year younger than she, Piers had always been the junior partner. Now he seemed

23

worldly wise, witness to real drama. She took a breath. There was no longer the easy friendship between them, she didn't know if he'd come with her if she walked off. So she said, 'I'm going to look at the swans' nests. Do you want to come?'

'Sure.'

They wandered together down towards the pond. The swans were recent arrivals, driven to these heights by drainage and disturbance lower down. They nested bad-temperedly next to moorhens and ducks, like royalty forced to live cheek by jowl with commoners. Bill Mayes was always warning people to stay away from them. 'Break your leg soon as look at you, they will. One blow from one of them wings and it's curtains.' But it sounded like rubbish to Mary. In fact, she thought Bill rubbish through and through.

There was much hissing and flapping as they approached. Only one of the birds was sitting, and she rose and stood anxiously by the nest while her spouse threatened and honked. The others patrolled in stately menace up and down the too small pond. Piers laughed. 'They look real stupid.'

'They probably feel it,' said Mary. 'I think they came from the lake at Bainfield, but it's full of boats now. Dad says he might make them something bigger somewhere, it's ridiculous having everything trying to nest here.'

'He'd do that? Just for some birds?'

Mary was nonplussed. 'If the birds need it – of course he would.' Then she flushed. 'I suppose you won't do anything for the birds when you have Gunthwaite?'

'What?'

'When you own this. After all, you will. Is that why your father's come back after all this time? To see about Gunthwaite?'

The boy ran a hand through his hair. It seemed too adult a gesture. 'I don't think he's thinking anything like that. When he talks about it – well, it's like something primitive. Worse than old-fashioned. Almost – well, almost a disaster.'

'Gunthwaite?' Mary was affronted and amazed. After a moment she said, 'Then why is he here? My parents are in such a state about it.'

'They want to live here again. In Yorkshire. Dad made a lot of money in Canada and the States and he says he wants to enjoy life in England. Says he wants to come home. Mother's none too pleased about it, but he's promised she can go back and visit. And I was kicked out of a school and Dad thought it might be best if I came back here for an education.'

'Were you expelled?'

'Sure. So what?'

'Nothing.'

She looked at him again. Was he the same Piers? The one she used to know would never have been expelled. He had been such an open-faced, open-hearted boy. Looking at him now, she could guess nothing of his thoughts.

She turned to go back. It was getting dark and people would be wondering where she was. In the old way, with the old complicity, Piers silently accompanied her. Their feet were soft on the rain-soaked earth, and again rain was falling. Small birds in the trees all around trilled and twittered as they settled for the night. Mary thought what a strange day it had been. She would go home and tell her mother there was nothing to fear for Gunthwaite and they could be happy. She was happy. She had to be. A friend was restored to her.

They took the short cut over the orchard wall. Piers remembered it, springing over easily, and Mary cursed her skirts and wished she could do the same. 'You should wear jeans,' he said. 'Tell your mother. All the girls do.'

'Not in this family,' said Mary primly. 'My father doesn't like it.'

'What's it got to do with him? You wear what you like, don't you?'

Mary was embarrassed. Of course not.

The feeling of awkwardness was growing. This didn't seem like Piers at all, but some young man she really didn't know. She felt conscious of herself in a way she found disturbing. She always felt like this when there were boys about. She knew so few. The blush that always threatened at such moments was starting to engulf her. She started to run, skirt or no skirt, like the child she used to be. But he kept pace, shortening his stride to hers, when years ago she was always the faster and always left him behind.

They came racing through the orchard gate and slithered into the yard. The car his mother had arrived in was no longer there. 'The bitch wouldn't wait, of course,' he said sourly. Mary gulped at the words. She didn't know anyone who would talk of their mother like that. He was watching her from the corner of his eye. She thought how provincial she must seem and tossed her hair and laughed, to be sophisticated.

'See you tomorrow?' said Piers. 'I'd better go. It's miles to walk.'

'You can come tomorrow. If you like.' She lifted her hand to wave. But at that moment Deb came running across the yard, calling, 'Piers! Piers? It is you. I thought so. You've grown so big!'

He stood looking at her in the fading evening light. Auburn hair, creamy skin, a figure bountiful with promise. Above all those clear, reflecting eyes, returning admiration with interest. She seemed to look at you through pools of clear water, fringed with the thick banks of her lashes. A study in beauty.

'Deb?' he said cautiously. 'It can't be little Deb!'

'I don't know who else it could be. Trust Mary, keeping you all to herself.'

'She wasn't. We went to the pond. Oh, Deb.'

Mary turned away and began to walk back to the house. She didn't want to stay longer. She had seen that look of dazzlement on so many faces, boys to stringy old men. She felt a huge bubble of sadness where her happiness had been. It wasn't that she begrudged Deb her looks. What she begrudged was this; the immediate diminution of herself. Like a candle placed next to a searchlight, she was doomed to stand beside Deb and count for nothing.

Chapter Four

Laura put on her boots and coat and dragged a hat over her hair. The rain was falling steadily now, darkening the evening to night. Michael must still be out on the hill with the sheep.

Her breath came hard as she trudged up the steep path. Once she would almost have run up here, she thought ruefully. Was it age or merely that nowadays she spent too much time in the house? During the war she had run this place efficiently and with ease, but afterwards the reins had slipped back into Michael's hands. Stopping to catch her breath she felt irritated suddenly. Her life was full of little things. There was nothing big.

She found Michael up at the stone circle by the moor. It was an old lambing pen, erected by some long-dead farmer but still well placed and useful. A ewe was lying within it, panting with the effort of birth. As Laura watched, Michael felt within her, gently withdrawing a motionless lamb.

'Let me,' she said, moving to take it. 'There'll be more.'

'Dare say.'

He handed her the slimy bundle. She quickly bent down and cleared its nose and mouth, then lifted it by the back legs to swing it vigorously. The creature coughed and gasped. She laid it on the wet grass, but she had nothing with which to rub it. She took off her hat, turned it inside out and used that. When the ewe's struggles were over she would do the rest. It was a good, big lamb.

'She's very late' said Laura. 'Did you know she was due?'

'Thought she was barren. I was going to draft her at the end of the month.'

'How many more?'

'Two, I think.'

The third lamb was very poor. It had barely the strength to lift its head. 'Best let it go,' said Michael, cradling the limp form in his big farmer's hands. 'She won't rear more than two anyway.'

'Let me have it,' said Laura. 'It might come through.'

'I'll milk her out a bit then.'

She wrapped the lamb in her hat and sheltered it within her coat. Its little body felt frail and vulnerable. She felt a pulse deep within her, almost a contraction of her womb, and was suffused with longing.

27

Giving birth, however painful, was such a joy. What wouldn't she give to experience that again!

Michael was cursing softly as the recovering ewe made a bid to escape. He had less than an inch of yellow liquid in an old milk bottle, but he wouldn't get much more. 'I'll try with that,' said Laura. 'Let's get back.'

He straightened up. She could see he was bone weary and in this light would barely be able to make out the path on the way down. Unbidden, unwanted, a memory flashed into her head: Gabriel, here. Head bent towards her, framed against the windblown sky. It was as real as a physical blow. She let out a gasp, turning to hide her face, although Michael would see nothing. Let her not think of him now. Ever.

Michael said, 'What is it?'

She licked her lips. 'Dora came to the house. Everything's stirred up again.'

'That girl always was brass-faced. Did she say anything?'

'Lots. They've moved back to Yorkshire for good. They're staying at Fairlands while they sort themselves out, although Dora's already fallen out with her mother. Something about Piers.'

'They shouldn't have left him as they did, and they shouldn't have taken him as they did,' said Michael. He picked up his shepherd's bag, threw it over his shoulder and cast a last assessing glance at the ewe. She was standing against the far wall of the pen, sheltering her twin babies. They'd be all right.

'She said something about Gabriel,' said Laura abruptly. 'I don't know whether it's true. She says – she thinks he's had lots of affairs.' Michael said nothing. After a moment Laura burst out, 'I hate myself for being such a fool!'

'You thought I was dead,' said Michael softly.

'I should have known you weren't! And I should have known – Gabriel's that sort. He always was.'

Michael reached out and held her. They stood, in the rain, the lamb weakly alive between them. 'I wish we could have a boy,' whispered Laura. 'Why can't we?'

'Perhaps we wanted it too much. It won't happen now.'

'I asked Sophie and Marie once, if they knew of anything I could do. But it was disgusting and I didn't bother. I wish I had. I'd do anything to keep Gabriel out. He doesn't deserve this place.'

'He won't get it. Not till I'm gone.'

'But he shouldn't have it then!'

It was very dark now. The rain was falling in earnest and the lamb at her breast was fading. Why did they struggle so to preserve this farm? she wondered. It wasn't for them or their children. It was for Gabriel.

Slithering down the track, one hand on the lamb, the other on Michael's arm, she stopped to catch her breath. Michael stopped also, and they stood looking at the sky. It was pale still, the clouds like ragged shawls blown across it. The rain came steadily down, soaking Laura's bare head.

'Dora thinks we should all meet,' said Laura abruptly. 'A civilised tea, or some such.'

'The woman's mad.'

'She thinks it's all forgotten. Perhaps it is for them.'

'Did Gabriel suggest it then?'

'I don't know.'

Suddenly Michael burst out, 'If I could leave this place I would! There's no peace with them here. Always thinking you'll see them. Knowing they're there.'

'I won't talk to him,' said Laura. 'You do know that?'

Michael's half-blind eyes turned towards her. 'I know what I shall think. That you're seeing him.'

'You know that won't be true!'

'But I know I shall think it. I can't help myself.'

She said nothing. Against her breast the lamb stirred momentarily. Would it die? she wondered. It seemed an omen. Yet they were safe in their marriage, secure behind walls built of years of trust and love. Old quarrels and mistakes couldn't harm them. Memories could, she thought fearfully. Grubs, eating at them from within. Gabriel must hate her to do this. Or perhaps he simply discounted her. She had become merely one of his many adulteries.

When they returned to the house Mary was in the dining room, playing the same piece badly over and over again on the piano. Deb was in the kitchen, copying a picture of a Devon village from a book. She was a good artist, and they had several of her water colours displayed on the walls. As her parents came in she said, 'Mum, I met Piers. He's coming to tea tomorrow. Is that all right?'

Laura felt a shock. She looked at Michael and he sighed. 'We always used to have him here,' said Laura feebly. 'It seems silly now—'

'He can come,' said Michael. 'But not his parents. Make that clear to him, Deb. He's not a foot in the door. I don't want any misunderstandings.'

Deb said 'I thought we weren't supposed to bear grudges?'

'Deborah!' Laura glared at her younger daughter. 'Behave yourself. This isn't something your father and I want to discuss. Get a box and help me with this lamb.'

Distracted, Deb peered down at the wet little bundle. 'It's nearly dead,' she said with distaste. 'You should have left it to die.'

29

'It deserves a chance,' said Laura. 'Go and get a feeding bottle, will you?'

'I'll get Mary to do it. She likes lambs.'

'Deborah, I asked you.'

But in the end it was Mary who sat up until ten, spooning tiny drops of nourishment into the lamb. She would have sat up all night if necessary. 'I'll come down,' promised Laura. 'You can do the early morning. Though it might be dead.'

'It won't be.'

Such confidence, thought Laura, thinking how attractive Mary became when she lost herself in something that absorbed her. Pretending unconcern, she said, 'Did you know Deb had invited Piers to tea?'

'Did she?' Mary's colour at once came up. 'Trust her. I met him by the horses. He came back with me and saw Deb.'

'Oh.'

'I thought Deb was going to guides tomorrow.'

'Good heavens, yes, so she is. Oh, well.' Laura busied herself with the lamb. 'He'll just have to have tea with us instead.'

She could feel Mary's uncertain gaze. The currents of emotion flowing through the house must seem like rivers to someone of Mary's sensitivity, she thought. She knew exactly how little was being said. All at once, as she let her eyes rest on the loved face, it seemed to Laura that her daughter's features seemed subtly to change. She looked as she always did, and yet – she looked like somebody else. Laura gasped and fastened her gaze again on the lamb, feeling her heart pound and her stomach turn over. 'Mum?' said Mary anxiously.

'I felt sick for a moment,' said Laura, not turning round.

'It's the smell of the first milk. Really sickly.'

Laura breathed carefully in shallow, cautious breaths. After a moment she permitted herself another glance at her daughter. Everything seemed normal. Like a room in which someone says they have seen a ghost. Her nerves were getting the better of her, that was all. Mary looked nothing like Gabriel, and never had. But in that moment Laura could have sworn that her daughter looked at her with Gabriel's eyes. Within Mary, for those who cared to see, was Gabriel's face.

In Michael's absence, Laura sat at the head of the table. Piers was on her right, with Mary next to him, while Sophie and Marie occupied the rest of the table. As if to emphasise that this was no ordinary, casual tea, Laura had put on an afternoon frock and brought out the good china. She saw that it made Piers uncomfortable and she was glad. He would think twice about coming again.

'Offer Piers some more bread and butter, Mary,' said Laura.

30

Obediently Mary picked up the plate. 'Would you like some more bread and butter?'

'No thanks. I mean – no thank you.'

He looked nervous, thought Laura. And disappointed. He'd hoped to be seeing Deb.

Marie bared her teeth at the young guest. 'Did you have a girlfriend in Canada? Someone you liked?'

'I knew some girls,' said Piers, almost defensively.

Marie snorted. 'Your father's son. I knew it. He too liked women from an early age.'

'Marie,' said Laura warningly.

Marie shrugged 'Why should I not say? His father was always a man who loved women. This boy will be the same. It's in the genes.'

Piers' cheeks flamed, as did Mary's. Laura choked on a giggle. They thought Marie meant denim jeans.

She pressed her advantage. 'What time are you expected home?' she asked, as if he might already have stayed too long.

'No special time. Dad said I was to call when I was through. He'll come in the car.'

'That won't be necessary. One of the men will run you home. Please tell your father, Piers, that we'd rather he didn't come to the farm. Michael doesn't wish it.'

An uncomfortable silence fell. Laura wrestled with herself, refusing to give in and be nice to this boy. Until he left he had lived almost as one of the family, but things had changed. He had grown up. So had Mary and Deb. And while it had once been commonplace for Cooper cousins to marry each other, keeping the land and money in the family, she was determined that those days were firmly past. Not that there had ever been any trouble with peculiar offspring; the Coopers were relentlessly healthy stock. Nonetheless she had no wish at all to encourage Piers, and even less to hear herself larding her conversation with questions designed to make him tell her things about his father.

There was the sound of a car in the yard. Laura half rose, suddenly dreading that it might be Gabriel. But the back door clattered open. It was Deb.

'What on earth are you doing home?' demanded her mother. 'It doesn't finish until eight.'

'They're going camping,' said Deb, throwing the beret her mother considered suitable headgear for a would-be guide on to the settle by the fire. 'I knew Dad wouldn't let me go so I told them there was no point in my joining. The vicar gave me a lift.'

'They do other things as well as camping!'

'But that's what they're doing now! I won't bother with guides, Mum. There isn't any point.'

31

She advanced on the tea table, giving Piers a brilliant smile. 'Hello. I'm glad you're still here. I'm starving, I had hardly anything before I went out. Move up Mary, and let me squeeze another chair in. There! Have a salmon paste sandwich, Piers.'

Laura felt her heart sink. It was as she feared, Deb was a natural coquette. Every apparently unconscious movement was all for his benefit. She tossed her hair, she stretched her neck, she smiled and talked, always as if he was the audience and she the star. And the boy was accordingly dazzled.

Sophie said in French to Marie, 'We should take him in hand, my dear. Wear him out. He's already thinking with his cock.'

Marie chuckled. 'We'd be out of luck. He's after our little red hen and no other.'

Mary felt herself colour. The old women were so crude at times, she didn't understand why her mother allowed it. They must have been talking like this for years of course, and it was only now that her French was good enough to understand. What did they mean, wanting to take Piers in hand?

Laura said, 'I gather you were expelled from school, Piers. For what, exactly?'

He mouthed at her like a landed fish. She felt cruel, deliberately destroying his memory of her as kind and encouraging. But then he was a child and now, half boy, half man, he was something else; his very presence was a threat.

He said, 'I – I played a trick on a teacher.'

'What sort of trick?'

'I set his room on fire.'

'You didn't!' cried Mary.

'Oh! How brave,' added Deb.

Laura almost ground her teeth in fury. She had hoped to discredit him and had allowed him to seem a hero.

'Did the master survive?' she asked thinly.

'He wasn't in the room at the time.'

'How fortunate. Do tell me if you feel the urge to incinerate anything here, won't you?' She got up and left the room. Marie and Sophie, delighted at such evidence of the spirit which had seemed so sadly lacking in Laura these last years, got up and left too.

Behind them, Piers said, 'She doesn't like me much any more.'

'No.' Mary looked down at her plate. 'But I think it's your father she doesn't like really.'

'She doesn't like any boys that like us,' said Deb. 'She's going to be a terrible mother-in-law.'

'You're so sure you're going to get married,' sneered Mary.

Deb said, 'We shall both have to marry. After all, Piers is going to get Gunthwaite, not us.'

'Maybe that's why your mother hates me,' said Piers.

Deb leaned across him for a piece of cake. Her breast brushed his arm. When she leaned back to munch her prize she rested her knee against the table, letting her skirt fall back to reveal a smooth, pale thigh. 'We don't hate you,' she said between mouthfuls. 'Do we, Mary?'

Again, Mary's colour flamed. 'Of course not,' she said stiffly. 'Deb, sit properly will you? You're like some tart.'

'Sophie and Marie do this all the time,' said Deb. 'They only smarten up when Dad's around.'

'You don't honestly want to be like Sophie or Marie!'

Deb laughed and sat up. 'No. You won't believe what someone said at guides. They asked if I was the girl who lived at Gunthwaite with a couple of French prostitutes.'

Neither of the others said a word. At last Mary said, 'Is that why you left?'

Deb shook her head. 'I just didn't want to go camping. And I don't mind what they say. They could have been, after all.'

'I think it's horrible to say things about old women.'

Piers was gathering the wits that Deb seemed so easily to scatter. 'Aren't they your mother's relatives, though? I mean, they could never have – it isn't possible—'

'I don't think they're blood relations,' said Mary. 'Sophie brought her up. They lived in a big house. I think Sophie must have been a maid.'

'A maid? Sophie?' Deb looked at her in amazement. And it was unlikely. Sophie was the least tidy, least organised, least dependable person in existence. If it wasn't for Laura and Marie she'd have drowned in a sea of disorder years ago.

Mary felt the familiar, corrosive irritation. There Deb went again, contradicting her, showing her up, being pretty, being right. 'I'm going for a walk,' she said, waiting for Piers to say he would come too.

'Then Piers and I will stay home and do a puzzle,' said Deb.

Mary realised she had put herself out on a limb. Why hadn't she suggested they all go for a walk? 'You're such a lazy cow,' she said to Deb, and saw from Piers' expression that she had surprised him. He might swear but he didn't think girls should. Now he thought her foul-mouthed and mean as well as plain, she thought dismally. She took herself off for her solitary walk.

When Laura came back half an hour later she found Piers and Deb nose to nose across a jigsaw puzzle in which barely a piece was laid. Deb was flushed and talkative, the boy bright-eyed and absorbed. Laura felt her stomach tighten. Deb had him wound into a tangle of sexual excitement. Practising her art for the first time, she was delighting in her new-found power. She needed a talking to, decided Laura. She said abruptly, 'It's time for Piers to go home.'

But it was early. No one was around to drive. 'I can telephone my father,' offered Piers, and Laura knew that for a barb.

'It's not necessary,' she said tightly. 'I shall drive.'

'I'll come too,' said Deb, but Laura turned on her. 'No you won't. You'll go in the kitchen and feed that lamb. It's time you did something to help around here.'

'Yuck! It's dying and it smells.'

'Don't be so pathetic, Deborah! Do as you're told.'

The girl pulled a face at Piers. He grinned encouragingly back. They made a striking pair, thought Laura, each gloriously smooth-skinned and shining-haired. But this was Gabriel's son. He was not to be encouraged.

He took the front seat in the big old car. She would much prefer that he had sat in the back. As it was, she felt constrained by the silence, forced to make some effort to talk. She decided to push forward the cause of his disenchantment with her family. She said, 'You must realise, Piers, that I do expect you to behave yourself at Gunthwaite.'

He glanced at her. 'I'm sorry, Aunt Laura. Did I do something wrong?'

She wished he wouldn't call her 'Aunt'! In the old days she'd helped him with his buttons and played hide and seek. But that was when his parents were safely elsewhere. She took a deep breath. 'It's just – Piers, the girls are older now. Deb's very pretty. And I can see you like her. I'd rather you weren't on your own with her.'

'Why not, Aunt?'

'Don't be silly, Piers!' In desperation she retreated into a mealy-mouthed lie. 'Her father doesn't consider it proper. He can be very old-fashioned.'

'My father says he needs to be hauled into the twentieth century.'

'Your father always did have a very patronising manner,' said Laura waspishly.

They were silent. The road snaked to the bottom of the hill before branching left towards Fairlands, nestling comfortably within a sheltered valley. The very position of the two steadings spoke volumes. Gunthwaite on its windy promontory, stark and undefended amidst its difficult land, and Fairlands, with its river and its woods, feeding generations of its children so well. No rich son of Fairlands deserved more, thought Laura grimly. Least of all should he have proud Gunthwaite.

The late rhododendrons were still in flower, great gaudy banks of pink and red. They wouldn't grow at Gunthwaite, and besides, they wouldn't want them. The plant was poisonous to stock, and many a

Fairlands ewe had died of it. But then, Fairlands could afford a few losses. Laura changed gear unnecessarily. This drive might be beautiful now, but in winter it was dank and unpleasant. She would take Gunthwaite's windswept acres any day.

'You don't mind if I'm alone with Mary, then?'

Laura caught her breath. She hadn't thought of that. But she could hardly say no, she didn't mind, and if he sneaked a kiss from her elder girl then so much the better! But that was what she meant. It was Deb who was likely to find herself out of her depth.

'Mary's older!' she prevaricated. 'More sensible. Deb's very young.'

'So it's OK for me to see Mary but not Deb?'

'You can see them both! But I won't have you sneaking off for tête-à-têtes with Deb. I hope you can be sensible about this, Piers. I don't want to have to speak to your family.'

'You don't want to speak to them anyway, it seems to me.'

They had reached the long, gravelled drive up to the house. Laura stopped the car. 'I think you can walk from here,' she said, continuing to look straight ahead.

'Sure. Thanks.'

His voice sounded a little thick. She glanced at him. He was flushed, suspiciously bright-eyed. She'd been unkind, he was barely more than a child. She'd invaded his private thoughts, mocked his family, exhibited not an ounce of trust. Instinctively she put a hand on his arm. 'I'm sorry, Piers. None of this is your fault. You've got to realise – it's difficult for me.'

'Because Deb's so pretty and Mary's not.'

She closed her eyes for a second. But why pretend? She fooled no one but herself. She looked at the boy again. She said, 'It's hard for us all. And it's hard to accept that this quarrel with your parents won't be made up. But it never can be. Explain that to your father, will you? He has to understand.'

The boy got out of the car and began walking up the drive. His long legs seemed ill at ease with the pace, as if he knew she was watching and wanted to run. She felt desperate suddenly. What was happening to her? She had spent years telling her children not to be vindictive, to forgive and forget, not to judge. Now everything was conspiring to make her do what she despised in others. But then, she more than anyone should know that if the need arose, anyone would do anything.

The car turned awkwardly in the narrow lane. The rhododendrons brushed the windows. She found herself wondering how anyone could bear to be so closed in. The long bonnet of the car edged round, she let in the clutch, accelerating away – and screamed. There was a man in the road. Her foot stamped on the brake, the wheels locked, the big car slid across the tarmac. It slithered to a halt an inch from the standing figure. He didn't move, and neither could she, simply sitting there, hands clenched on the wheel. I should have run him over, she thought. Why didn't I? It was Gabriel.

Chapter Five

She had stalled the engine of the car. She pressed the button again and again, but it wouldn't catch. He flung open the passenger door, she jabbed the button with her thumb and the engine fired. At last! But he reached out and turned the key. The motor coughed into silence. There was to be no escape.

'Hello, Laura.'

Did he sound different? A little, perhaps. The deeper note of maturity. They'd been so young before, having to face things for which no one was ever old enough. But they were braver, then. You lost your nerve with age.

She turned her head to look at him, bending across the seat towards her. Fair hair, controlled these days instead of falling into his eyes – Mary's eyes. At once she crushed the thought. They were just blue eyes, ordinary blue eyes, in a thin mobile face. He'd been good-looking when he was younger. He looked drawn, she thought. Not quite handsome any more.

'I – I don't want to talk to you,' she said stiffly. 'I promised Michael.'

'He doesn't need to know.'

'I've done with lying, Gabriel.'

'You? Don't make me laugh.'

He wasn't in the least amused. He sounded bitter and angry. She said, 'Dora told me you wanted to make up. I didn't think it seemed very likely.'

'It isn't. But we should be civil at least. The children are bound to see something of each other.'

'I don't see why,' she said abruptly.

'For goodness' sake, Laura! We can't carry this even unto the third generation.'

She turned and stared at him. 'I imagine we could do that very easily. After all, my daughters will be disinherited by your son. Quite enough for a feud, I should have thought.'

'How is Mary?' said Gabriel, very quietly.

Laura's cheeks flamed. She felt her heart stutter, she was finding it hard to breathe. If only she could get away from here, away from him!

37

But she knew there was no escape. You couldn't run from what you knew. You couldn't undo anything.

'I want to see her,' said Gabriel. 'No more than that.'

'You can't,' said Laura. 'She isn't yours and never has been. Michael's her father.'

'You know she's mine! We both know it. That gives me the right.'

'You don't have any rights! If you care anything for her, and if you ever cared anything for me, then leave us alone!'

He didn't say anything for a long moment. She sensed a movement beside her, and when she looked, he was sitting in the seat with his head bowed. He smelled of whisky, she thought. He'd had to bolster himself to confront her.

The thought caught at her emotions. That was the trouble with Gabriel, it was never easy to dislike him, he was too vulnerable. At least, she thought wryly, he was strong enough not to worry about showing his vulnerability. He had always shown it to her.

He turned to face her. Close to, she saw that his face was a mass of fine lines, as if he had been exposed to too much heat and cold. The little scar was there still, from shrapnel. She'd remembered that over years. 'Where's the point in hating me?' he asked simply.

The answer rose at once to her lips. She closed her teeth on it. If it wasn't obvious to him then it wasn't something he should know. She had to hate! He had to be kept out, kept away. Like this, he was just too dangerous.

'You've had lots of women, Dora said,' she remarked. 'I wasn't even the first, was I? But I was Michael's. Having me meant getting the better of him. That was all it was.'

'Don't try and belittle it,' said Gabriel. 'Don't be stupid.'

She lifted her chin. 'I don't suppose I'm very clever, actually. That's why it was always so easy for you to make me do what you wanted.'

'God damn it, Laura, it was what you wanted! Why won't you remember? You wanted the sex, you wanted the love! You wanted Michael too, I don't deny that, but not for what I could give you. What we could give each other.'

She gripped the wheel again, her knuckles white. 'It was filthy,' she whispered. 'I'd lived a filthy life.'

'Honest passion,' murmured Gabriel. 'I've not done anything so honest since. And I'll bet that neither have you.'

She turned on him in a fury. 'Get out of here! Get out, get out! You want to start it again, don't you? You've never had enough. Weaselling your way into my life, trying to take things that aren't yours, trying to make me do wrong! I don't want you any more! I've forgotten why I ever did!'

Her arms flailed at him and he caught them. 'You? Forget?' She wrestled with him, trying to break free. His fingers bit into her wrists, and she hissed, 'Damn you, don't mark me! Michael will know!'

He let her go, then.

After a moment he said, 'I never wanted to hurt you. Not from the first. I don't know how it all happened.'

She was calmer now. She rubbed her wrists. 'I know you didn't mean it. I wish you had. I wish – oh, Gabriel, I've worried about you so often these last years. There wasn't any need, was there?'

He sighed. Such a long, tired, painful sigh. 'I don't know. I'm not who I thought I was going to be, I know that.'

'You can't say that's my fault!'

'I haven't said it was anyone's. For God's sake, Laura, can't you stop trying to fight?'

Tears were lodged in her throat. She couldn't swallow them down. The years had blurred things, let her believe he was less than he was. But then, that was what she had wanted to believe. The real Gabriel, fitting her like the other half of a broken cup, was something she had refused to remember.

In a low voice she said, 'It's cruel of you to disrupt my life like this. You must have known how it would be.'

'I just wanted to come home. I'd been away so long. You can't imagine what it's like, living in a country that isn't really yours. Dora loved it, knew everyone, went everywhere. Swimming pools, parties, game fishing in the sea. It should have been paradise.'

Laura said, 'You know there's no such place. People aren't meant for paradise.'

'They're not meant to lose their roots, either. When Piers came out he was homesick for a long while. He used to talk about it all the time. Drove Dora mad. And I remembered things. Little things. The smell of a rainy evening, the sound of sheep out on the hill. You know how noisy they can be. I began to wonder if I could bear not to be here again. And then I had an offer for the business and Piers was expelled and everything seemed to fall into place.'

'But you're not just visiting! I could have understood that.'

'I don't know what we'll do.'

Some small ray of hope seemed to strike through the gloom. They might not stay. This might not go on forever. She thought of going home, back to Gunthwaite, to its safety and its warmth, and never again being made to feel like this.

She said, 'I must go. Everyone's waiting.'

'Yes.' But he stayed in the seat, as if the effort of moving was too much for him.

'You're not ill, are you?' she asked.

He shook his head. 'I find it all very tiring, that's all. Dora and her mother; Piers; you. I keep thinking how good it would be to come over to Gunthwaite one evening and talk to Mike. I miss him.'

'I'm sure he misses you.'

'So you see?' He turned to her. 'We could settle it! Really.'

'No, Gabriel. Michael won't.'

He nodded, as if it was only what he had been expecting. He climbed slowly from the car. Light rain was falling, but he didn't put on his hat, simply walking away up the gloomy drive, not looking back. Laura watched him in her mirror until he turned the corner and was gone.

Mary swung the saddle easily on to Diablo's back. Just as easily the horse sidestepped, dropped a shoulder and discarded it. 'Pig,' said Mary automatically. She tied him up a little tighter, put her body weight against him and pushed him into the stable wall. This time the saddle stayed put.

'Needs mastering, that horse,' said Bill Mayes, who always seemed to be around when you least wanted him, and never when you did.

'He's all right,' said Mary. Inwardly she cursed. Everyone round here seemed to think the horse was too much for her and needed a man. What she saw as naughtiness they classed as devilment. But if you crushed it out of him you crushed out the life, she had told her father, more than once. Fortunately, he agreed.

She led Diablo out into the yard, hopping on before he had time to realise. Nonetheless he plunged and tossed his head, and she caught him up before he could get any ideas. At that very moment Deb appeared. She was running up from the field, towing Samson behind her on a worn piece of string. 'Wait for me! I'm coming.'

'But I'm ready to go,' complained Mary, who could normally never persuade Deb to ride. 'You know this horse won't wait.'

'I'll be quick, I promise.'

Diablo danced while Deb flung a saddle and bridle on the patient Samson, who blinked sleepily in the warm air. They had woken this morning to an unexpectedly beautiful day, as if the long, wet spring had finally given way to summer. Swallows whirled above the steep barn roof and the orchard was alive with bees. Mary felt happiness welling up from deep down in her soul.

'Right. Ready.' Deb was kicking the mud off her shoes and scrambling into the saddle. She wore Mary's old jodhpurs, turned up at the bottom, a white shirt of her father's and a red scarf in her auburn hair. She should have looked a wreck, but as always served only to make every woman who saw her wonder why they couldn't look as good in a shirt five sizes too big. But today Mary didn't care. She merely said, 'I know Sam's kind but you really should wear a hat.'

'I'll be OK,' said Deb, and rattled her heels on the old horse's ribs to urge him into a trot.

Mary planned to hack down the edge of the fields and up into the woods, galloping down the firebreak before taking a breather in a wide circle down into the valley. Diablo was keen and insisted on trying to take off, despite all her cajoling. Finally, as he sprang on to the headland bordering standing corn, she let him go.

'Mary!' shrieked Deb in horror. 'Mary, don't!' Even staid Samson couldn't resist. He kicked up his feathery heels and charged behind. Mary, glancing back, yelled, 'Sit down to him, Deb! Take hold!' But they had stopped at the gate before Deb was back in control.

'That was horrible,' she said with feeling.

'Sorry. I had to let Diablo have a run, he was going to explode.'

'I hate it when you can't stop.'

'You could have. You won't sit into him, that's all.'

They slipped through the gate and on to the moor. The woods rose up above them, out of land that had once been cultivated, or at least used for sheep. But Michael's grandfather had planted oak and ash, and Michael himself had added elm and rowan and chestnut. Badgers lived there, and foxes and rabbits in abundance. Mary lived in dread of Diablo putting his foot down a rabbit hole and breaking a leg. She had developed the habit of cantering down the rides muttering the Lord's Prayer under her breath.

To her surprise, Deb pushed past and went in the lead. Diablo at once began yawing at his bit. Mary pulled him up, he couldn't always do as he wished. She followed Deborah's joggling back at a controlled hack canter, Diablo's pent-up energy turning every stride into an inflated balloon. All at once Deb veered off the main ride and down the track back into the fields. Without thinking, Mary followed her, although it wasn't what she had planned. But this ride was as good as any other. The woods were as familiar to them as the palms of their own hands.

This track led down into the long spur of planting stretching up like a finger from the valley below. It reached out from the Fairlands estate into Gunthwaite meadows, put there deliberately as cover for game birds and foxes. Mary wished they hadn't come this way. It meant riding in the shade instead of out in the sunshine and air. Now and then, on either side of the ride, there were pheasant feeders, still with a bit of corn, to attract the birds back into the woods at night. Mary kept her wits about her; at any moment a pheasant might clatter up from the trees, startling her horse. Painful experience had taught her that it never paid to take anything for granted with Diablo. One lapse of concentration and she would probably walk home.

Deborah was trotting now, and Samson was blowing. As she drew in her horse two yellowhammers flashed through the trees. 'Did you see that?' Mary called, but Deb didn't look round. Both horses pricked their ears, and Diablo whinnied. Sure enough, there was an answering call. Someone was riding towards them.

Mary pushed up beside her sister. 'You arranged this! Is it Piers?'

Deb shot her a look of wary complicity. 'I had to. You saw how stupid Mum was being. And you like him, don't you? I know you do.'

'He's all right. I don't see the need to sneak, that's all.'

She felt in a fluster. Her shirt was torn and her hair was tied up anyhow under her hat. Then she sighed. There was no point worrying. He would notice only Deb.

He was riding his grandfather's big bay, a roman-nosed hunter with a back like a table. He didn't look comfortable, Mary thought, and neither did the horse.

'Hello!' called Deb eagerly.

'Hi.' He slithered to a halt beside them. 'Deb. Mary.'

'Don't jab him in the mouth like that,' said Mary critically. 'You look really rusty.'

'Do I? I haven't ridden since I left.'

'Then you shouldn't be riding the Bombardier. He can get some steam up when he wants.'

'Thanks.'

She flushed. Deb shot her a furious look. 'You look fine to me,' she declared. 'Let's go down by the village, we can get some sweets at the shop.'

'I didn't bring any money,' said Mary. 'And we'd have to go past the pig farm. You know what Diablo's like.'

'Oh.' Deb turned those clear guileless eyes on her sister. 'I'd forgotten the pigs. Why don't you ride round through the park and meet us on the other side?'

Mary waited for Piers to reject the plan, but he said nothing. So it was up to her. 'You know Mum said we weren't to go off with people on our own,' she muttered. A fiery blush was turning her scarlet, darkening the scars on her face to deepest purple. She could feel Piers watching her, as people did, as if she was some kind of experiment.

'You don't do everything your mother says, do you?'

'Of course not,' said Mary uncomfortably.

'I bet you do! And I used to think you were real daring.'

Deb let Samson's reins dangle and lay back over the cantle of the saddle, her head on his round grey rump. 'Mary is quite daring,' she remarked. 'She rides like anything, she's never scared.' She put her hands beneath her neck and flicked her hair provocatively.

Mary was caught in a maelstrom of conflicting emotions. Who could help but be jealous of Deb? Who could help but be mollified by her? Who could help but be enchanted by the picture she made, as beautiful as the woods, as careless as a child, as seductive as any creature in her confident youth? She looked at Piers, his face intent. She couldn't blame him.

'All right,' she said stiffly. 'I'll go round. Don't be long.'

'What shall we get you at the shop? Rhubarb and custard?'

'I haven't had those for years,' said Piers delightedly.

Deb sat up. 'They're Mary's favourite. What did you used to have?'

'Sour apples,' supplied Mary. 'I bet you won't like them now. People change.'

'Yeah. Sometimes they do.'

He turned the Bombardier awkwardly on the track. Deb was sitting properly now, a better position than she ever bothered to achieve with no one but Mary to see her. For her part, Mary reined Diablo back, executed a perfect pirouette and set off at a good collected trot, a faultless performance quite wasted. There came the sudden, machine-gun rattle of wings. Two cock pheasants had seized their moment to cannon into view.

'Oh!'

Mary rode Diablo's plunge, and turned to see why Deb had shrieked. She was off, lying still in the bracken. Next to her, his feet hammering the ground, the Bombardier bucked on the spot.

'Get him away from her!' shrieked Mary. She flung off Diablo and ran to grab the Bombardier's rein.

'The brute won't turn!' Piers was sawing on his mouth.

'I've got him. Let him be.' She was dimly aware of Diablo seizing his opportunity and thundering off home. Oh, well. One less horse to worry about. He'd done it before.

With the Bombardier calming, Piers jumped to the ground and knelt beside Deb. Mary, hanging on to the ponies, couldn't see. 'Is she all right? Deb? Deb, say something!'

'She's out,' said Piers.

'Oh God! Is she dead? She isn't dead? Damn you, take these horses and let me see!'

When he didn't come, she couldn't bear it. She tangled the reins anyhow into a tree and fell sobbing at Deb's side. Let her not be dead. Not Deb, who a moment before had been so lovely.

There was blood in her auburn hair, as red as the scarf that she had liked so much she had refused to wear her hat. Her eyes weren't quite closed, and she muttered a little. 'Mum? What you doing? Mum?'

'We've got to get Mum,' said Mary hysterically. 'I'll put her on the horse and lead her home.'

'We shouldn't move her,' said Piers. He was very white but seemed calm. Mary was aware that he was behaving better than she, snivelling and shaking like a fool.

'I'll ride home,' she gasped.

43

'Fairlands is closer.'

'Then you ride!'

'No. You'll be quicker. Take the Bombardier.'

It made sense. Why couldn't she see that for herself? She scrambled up and ran for the horse, leaping easily into the saddle. Deb was starting to thrash about and Piers was holding her still. 'Don't let her die!' yelled Mary, gathering up the reins. 'If you do I'll make you pay!'

'Just go and get help, damn you!'

As she galloped away, stirrups flying, she felt amazed at the passion in his frightened young face.

The Bombardier was a big, long-striding horse, bigger than anything Mary had ridden, except the shires. But this was a quality horse, a man's horse, courageous and hard to hold. Halfway down the track she wished very much she'd bothered to adjust the stirrups, but she couldn't stop. Instead she lay across his neck, hands halfway to his mouth, ready to do what she could if another bird flew up and he shied. He was galloping steadily now, the raking stride that kept him hunting all day. As they turned the corner out of the wood and saw the gate across the path no more than twenty yards away, Mary felt her heart lurch. It was Piers' fault. That gate was always left open!

She took a pull, at once aware that she couldn't stop. Without stirrups it was a waste of time. But the horse was clever and experienced, he knew what he was about. She put her faith where her courage should be, and put her legs to him. The horse flew.

They even galloped up the Fairlands drive, sliding at first on rhododendron juice, putting him on the lawn turf in preference to the gravel when the drive opened up. She felt sure Mr Fitzalan-Howard would prefer to have his lawn ruined rather than his horse's legs. It was only sense. He appeared on the terrace as she thundered to a halt.

'What the devil – Mary Cooper, what are you about?'

'Deb's had an accident. Piers is with her, she's dying, in the Long Plantation.'

'Dying? What on earth do you mean?'

Mary was sobbing, tears and runny nose together. 'She hit her head and the Bombardier almost trod on her and she doesn't know what's going on!'

'Right.' He went back into the house, calling: 'Judith! Gabriel! Deborah Cooper's had a fall, I'll get the shooting brake and bring her here. Call the doctor, will you?'

People were everywhere suddenly. Someone came and took the Bombardier, and Mary heard herself babbling, 'I saved his legs as much as I could. He jumped the gate. I wouldn't have let him without bandages, but he wouldn't stop.'

44

'It's all right, Mary. Calm down. Gabriel, get her a brandy, would you?'

A tall man with a lined face brought her the disgusting drink. She'd only had it once in her life before, when she was very sick, and it only made her sicker. It stung her lips and made her eyes water.

'Drink it down, Mary. We should introduce ourselves. I'm your Uncle Gabriel.'

'Hello. I mean – how do you do?'

'Rather better than you just at the moment. Piers is with her, you say?'

Mary nodded. 'He knew what to do. I went to pieces. I must be really stupid.'

'So she isn't dying, then?'

Mary's eyes flooded. 'I don't know! She was talking rubbish. She wanted Mum.'

He put his hand on her shoulder. 'All right, my dear. All right. Come in the brake and show us where she is.'

The brandy had gone to her head. It was as if the world was at a distance, with her own life happening quite separately. The sensation was horrible, she would rather feel as she had, as if her brain was disintegrating under the pressure of its thoughts. In the brake, sitting on the slatted wooden seat, Gabriel held her hand. Even then, feeling as she did, it seemed odd.

Mr Fitzalan-Howard had brought one of the gardeners, who leaped out at the gate and opened it. 'The Bombardier flew it,' said Mary, because it looked bigger from the ground and she thought his owner should know.

'So I gather,' said Mr Fitzalan-Howard, driving carefully through. 'We'll have to think about you riding him in the point to point.'

'My mother wouldn't let me,' said Mary.

'And neither should she,' said Gabriel. 'Neither would I.'

Piers waved as they drove into view. Deb was half sitting up against a tree, crying a little. Mary scrambled out and ran to her. Piers stood up and said nervously to his father, 'I tried to keep her still, Dad. She's delirious, she wouldn't. I think her back's OK.'

'I should hope it is,' snapped Gabriel. 'If I take the trouble to send you on a first-aid course, I hope the least you can do is put it into action.'

'But he did,' interposed Mary, taken aback at this sudden transformation. He'd been so kind to her. And now this.

Deb said, 'Mary? My head hurts. I want Mum, I want to go home.'

'We're going to Fairlands, it's closer. Someone's bound to ring Mum. Come on, Deb, can you get up?'

45

'She shouldn't stand,' said Piers. 'She might have cracked an ankle or something.'

'You should already have checked,' said his father. 'I'll carry her. She looks feather light.'

'She might look it, but she's not,' said Mary wryly. 'Deb weighs a ton.'

She was certainly a solid little parcel. Gabriel struggled to fit her into the brake without banging her head, and his son remarked, 'Now who's making a hash of it?'

'Do shut up, Piers!'

'I think the boy's done remarkably well,' said Mr Fitzalan-Howard. 'Both he and Mary. And I don't think Deb's too much damaged. A concussion, I should say. You'll have to spend a few days in bed, my dear.'

'I want Mum,' repeated Deb, and began to sob again.

They drove slowly back down the track. By the time they arrived at Fairlands a gaggle of people had assembled, the doctor, Dora, an ambulance and its crew, and standing embarrassed and anxious on the periphery of the group, Laura and Michael.

Mary fell from the car and ran up to them. 'I couldn't do anything! It was a pheasant, you know how they clatter, and she never will sit down to him. I let Diablo go ... did he get home? I hope you didn't worry. Well, you know what he's like. I had to ride the Bombardier, he nearly trod on her, and Piers was the only one who knew what to do.'

Michael put his hands on her shoulders. 'Slowly, Mary. It's all right. You've done very well.'

Her legs didn't seem strong enough to carry her. She sank on to the terrace balustrade, watching her parents go to Deb. She felt very tired all of a sudden. If the sun had been only a little warmer she would have lain on the stone and gone to sleep.

Piers came over. He sat nervously at her side. 'They want to take her to hospital. She must be hurt bad.'

'She looks all right now Mum's here. She's such an idiot. I told her to wear a hat.'

'It was my fault. I wanted to see her.'

Mary grinned wryly. 'I shouldn't worry about it. That's just the way things are with Deb. The boys in the village are always trying to get her to go off with them.'

Piers said, 'And does she?'

'No!'

She yawned capaciously. Piers was biting his nails. Mary felt easier suddenly. They could be comfortable together. He was the Piers she remembered after all, a companion and a friend. She said, 'I'm glad you're back. I thought I wasn't, but I am.'

He glanced at her. In the last few days he had grown cautious, less certain of his ground. He said, 'I'm not sure it was such a good idea. No one really wants us around.'

She looked across at her parents, close together, close to Deb. Uncle Gabriel and Aunt Dora were there too, wanting to talk to them, using Deb as an excuse. Mary had never seen her father look so hard.

They were putting Deb into the ambulance. Laura came running across. 'Mary darling, your father and I have to go to the hospital with Deborah. Will you be all right? He'll be back for milking, but I might not be back until tomorrow, the doctor says.'

'She can stay here' said Piers.

Laura said, 'Oh. I don't think—'

But then Mrs Fitzalan-Howard came across and said, 'Laura dear, of course Mary must stay. Someone can run her across to check on the horses and collect her things. So you'll have nothing at all to worry you.'

Laura seemed to pull herself together. 'That's very kind,' she said, and pinned on a tremulous smile.

Chapter Six

Mary brought with her not only her night-things and toothbrush, but her new red dress and a sick lamb. Dora, recovering from the upheaval with a drink and a cigarette in the conservatory, watched her arrival with one eyebrow sardonically raised. 'That girl gives a whole new meaning to the word gauche,' she remarked. 'I didn't think they made them so plain, shy and neurotic any more.'

Gabriel poured himself a whisky from the trolley. 'You can't have been all that sophisticated at her age.'

'I was never that bad! You might have noticed, if you hadn't been more interested in your mother's sexually active friends.'

Gabriel snorted with laughter. 'I didn't know I'd told you about that.'

'Told me? Everyone knew. At least, I couldn't know, because I didn't know anything then, but I suspected. You know how it is when you're young.' She took a mouthful of gin and sighed. 'That poor girl. Her face is just terrible. And Deborah can't make it easier.'

'Piers is very smitten,' said Gabriel in leaden tones.

Dora gurgled with laughter. 'Who wouldn't be? She's gorgeous. A sexy little moppet, you mark my words. We shall have to watch Master Piers.'

'Good God, Dora! If he lays a finger on that child I'll personally slaughter him!'

'A bit late to develop morals, isn't it?' She held out her glass for another drink. 'As long as he doesn't get her pregnant, I really don't care.'

Gabriel poured the drink in silence. Sometimes he hated Dora's worldliness. She seemed shallow and hard, and he didn't know any more if it was all there was of her. Youthful innocence – or ignorance as she chose to call it – had turned itself into cynical sophistication. In Dora's world, love was nothing more than sexual or pecuniary desire.

He wondered which she felt for him. Perhaps neither. She liked sex and she liked men, she'd have wanted him in bed whoever he was. He felt his body stir. He looked across at his wife and raised

48

an eyebrow. She got up, catlike and sinuous, and came across to him.

'Like that, is it? What does Laura have, may I ask? One sniff of her faded cotton skirt and you're some kind of stud.'

Her fingers brushed his groin, but her words repelled him. He gave her the drink and turned away, but she wrapped an arm around his neck and undulated against his hip. 'Sorry. That was mean. We ought to laugh. Laura and Michael are too ridiculous. Two country bumpkins clinging together as if you were Lucifer himself! Michael hasn't got a clue what makes that woman tick. I bet he still doesn't give it to her more than once a week. No wonder she looked so miserable.'

'Her daughter was half conscious, you may remember.'

'No one cared about her! We all wanted to know if you and she still wanted it. And you do, don't you? You can't think of anything you'd like more.

She was whispering in his ear, nibbling at his lobe. He'd seen her like this before. She had only to sense that he had someone new and she'd be all over him, talking about her, guessing what they'd done. Dora was a third in any bed. Her own affairs never seemed to excite her as much as his.

'Let's go behind the palm and do it,' she whispered.

'Here? Piers. Mary—'

'Who cares?'

'I do. Let's go upstairs.'

She went sulkily up to their room. She took off her skirt and briefs, brisk, businesslike, and stood in stockings and suspenders. 'How do you want it?' she asked. 'How did she used to be?'

Gabriel took off his jacket. 'Stop it, Dora. It was years ago.'

'She was remembering. You could tell. Did she lie there and wait? She's that sort, I'll bet.'

'She wasn't, actually.' He was entering the game, teasing her, exciting her.

Her mouth was wet. 'She was desperate, then. Would be. Years Michael was gone. Couldn't wait to have it.'

'Had to have it,' said Gabriel. 'Just like you now.'

He opened his trousers and came to her. She opened her legs, falling back across the bed, but she wasn't getting him that easily. He gripped her arms and turned her face down, a position he knew she hated.

'Bastard. Pig.' He went into her and she let out a long groan. Then she said, 'Oh, look. We can see ourselves in the mirror. That makes up for a lot.'

He looked away. He didn't want to see her. In some part of his mind, conscious, unconscious, he wanted to imagine that the body

49

beneath him was indeed Laura's, compliant, eager, that only he could satisfy. And it was as if Dora knew, mimicking the French intonation of Laura's voice as he moved in her. 'Oh, Gabriel! Don't – don't stop. Please, more, more, more!' dissolving at last into Dora's own orgasm.

He felt his own seed flood out. He was drained and yet dissatisfied. Lying on her on the bed, he heard her chuckle. Dora at least was happy.

Outside, on the stair, Mary stood as she had for minutes past, frozen in fascinated horror. She had never heard such sounds before. Groans and gasps and the rhythmic, unexplained thumping of bodies on a bed. Brought up on a farm, used from her earliest years to the bull and the ram 'getting on with the job' as the men called it, she knew what was happening. But she couldn't believe it. Not of people. Not her aunt and uncle, Piers' parents, not even doing it at night! She felt the shame they neglected to feel, the embarrassment that ought to have prevented them behaving in such a disgusting way. How glad she was that her own parents never did any such thing.

Dora's voice carried clearly from the room. 'Don't get dressed, Gabriel! Come here, you know you want to. I bet Laura never let you get away with a quick one.'

Mary gasped. What did she mean? What could she mean? She stood rigid, even when a moment later the door opened and Gabriel came out. They stood staring at each other.

'What on earth are you doing here?'

'Nothing. I mean – I was going downstairs.'

'Didn't your mother ever tell you not to stand outside doors? Listening were you?'

'No! I – I heard someone cry out. I thought—'

'I see.' Some of the anger seemed to drain from him. His blue eyes no longer looked like steel. 'Your aunt – she cut her finger. Can't bear the sight of blood. Is your room up here? I'd have thought you'd be at the other end.'

'Mrs Fitzalan-Howard said she thought I'd like to be near Piers.'

'And where is Piers? Has he been listening too?'

'He's in the stables. I was going to find him. And I wasn't listening. Truly.' She put up her chin, as she always did for a lie.

But he'd lost interest in her. Dora called, 'Gabriel? Who are you talking to?'

He sighed and didn't reply, turning instead and going slowly down the stairs. Mary followed, padding silently in his wake, not daring to go past him, hating to stay where Aunt Dora might find

50

her. He went straight into the conservatory. A half full whisky glass stood on a tray, he took it up and drained it down in one. 'Oh God,' he whispered. 'Oh bloody God.'

Mary couldn't bear it. He was mad and depraved, and at the same time miserable. She backed away, her shoes silent on the tiles, out of the conservatory, down the hall and clattering through the outside door. A bird was singing in the creeper on the wall. The world ceased its crazy tilting and became still.

In the stable, Piers was grooming the Bombardier. Mary leaned on the door and watched him for a while. 'You've not done his belly. If you don't do that the girth rubs.'

'But he's ticklish. He'll kick me.'

'You've got to be firm. Here, I'll do it.'

She slipped into the box and took up the brush, stooping with total confidence beneath the horse's giant belly. As she swept the brush firmly across him, the horse lifted a hind leg in threat. 'Stop that!' growled Mary, and he put it down again.

'You're very good with him,' said Piers.

'I like horses. They're easy. The easiest thing.'

'No they're not! I should have thought Deb in hospital would show you that.'

'It was her own fault. She should have worn a hat. Mum will be furious when she gets over being upset.'

She finished the brushing. She was keeping half an eye on Piers. He didn't look much like his father, apart from the hair, although in Gabriel that was faded. 'Your father's younger than mine, but he doesn't look it,' she ventured.

'It's because he's a bastard.'

Mary blinked. Piers said, 'Don't look so shocked. I mean he's a creep. And he hates me worse than I hate him.'

'What do you hate him for?'

He looked at her with what she now saw was his father's cold eye. 'Chasing women, mostly. He's always doing it. If you ask me that's what the quarrel's about. He had a go at your mother.'

Mary felt a blush beginning at her toes and rushing upwards. She hid her face against the Bombardier, hating herself, hating Piers, but most of all hating Gabriel. Of course that was it. Her mother – and Uncle Gabriel. It made everything fit.

Piers said, 'I wouldn't get too upset. It must have been years ago. During the war, probably, when your dad was away.'

'My mother wouldn't!'

'I know. It's hard to believe anyone could. With him.'

Her heart was pounding in her throat. She thought it might choke her. She struggled to say something, anything. 'Poor Dad.'

'It's him. He spoils things for everyone in the end.'

51

The stable clock chimed the hour, a restrained, elegant bell. Mary wiped her face with the Bombardier's stringy mane. 'I've got to feed the lamb. Does your gran like people to change for supper?'

'She makes me put on a suit.'

'Oh.'

So it would have to be the red dress. Walking back to the house, in whose kitchen the lamb seemed so out of place, she wished with all her heart for Gunthwaite. Despite its leisured style, so different from Gunthwaite's workaday face, Fairlands was tainted. It was odd that she'd never before been aware of it. But then, in these last weeks and months, it was as if she was seeing everything anew. No one was as she had thought them, not even her mother! She pushed the thought away. It was nonsense, when she got home she would see it for just that. She tried to conjure an image of the family round the table, Mum and Dad, she and Deb, Sophie and Marie. Then she discarded Sophie and Marie. They were embarrassing too nowadays. So many things were.

The lamb was sucking quite strongly now, so it seemed likely to live. But the Fitzalan-Howard cook didn't approve of lambs in the house. 'That creature should be in the stable, if it's anywhere,' she said again.

'It needs to be warm,' said Mary, for the umpteenth time. 'If you had a heat lamp it could go in the stable. But I'd have to go out each time it needed to be fed.'

'You don't keep horses in the house!'

'I'll take it out in the morning. I promise.'

Horrible woman. Mary wondered if she'd smother the little creature. Anything seemed possible in this house. She went upstairs, along carpeted, polished corridors in which large flower arrangements stood as a matter of course. Aunt Dora's laugh came ringing from downstairs. She sounded drunk.

In her room, neat, carpeted, looking out across lawns, she changed into her new red dress. But her hair was wrong, bushy and uncontrolled. In this house everything had to be held down, she thought, and dragged her brush through the wiry strands. Deb could do her hair better than anyone; on her own she could only just manage to fasten it. After much struggle she achieved a pony tail. It left her face more exposed than she was used to, and made her feel shy. She unfastened it again, and instead tied her hair loosely back with a black ribbon.

The bell went for supper. She went shyly downstairs; when she used to visit Fairlands before she had been too young for anything but nursery tea. Mrs Fitzalan-Howard came out of the drawing room and said, 'There you are, Mary! We won't eat just yet. The bell's to get everyone gathered for a drink. Come in and have some sherry.'

Piers was standing by the fireplace. His parents, very hard and glittering, sat at either end of a large sofa while Mr Fitzalan-Howard stood at the drinks tray. Despite her welcome, Mary was aware that all was not well. Dora and Gabriel were drunk.

'Sherry, my dear.' Mr Fitzalan-Howard handed her a glass of brown liquid. Used only to Gunthwaite's frugal supply of wine, Mary sipped and was revolted. The drink was cloyingly sweet.

'You look lovely, dear,' said Mrs Fitzalan-Howard. 'I'm so glad you could stay. We've seen nothing of you since Piers left.'

'It was a mistake,' he said abruptly. 'I was happy here. I should never have gone.'

'You loved it!' said Dora. 'Really, Mother, he took to the life like a duck to water. He's only complaining now because he fell foul of that school. And to make up with you.'

'Don't screech, Dora,' said her father. 'How much gin have you had?'

'Bottles and bottles, darling,' she said, flapping her hands. 'Don't you think you should really ask how much whisky Gabriel's had? He starts before breakfast these days. Did you know?'

'Shut up, Dora,' said Gabriel wearily. 'You're embarrassing our guest.'

'I thought you liked to embarrass people,' said Piers.

His father looked at him with distaste. 'Be quiet, boy.'

Mary felt desperately uncomfortable. She hunched her shoulders, wishing she could shrink away into invisibility. Gabriel ran a judgmental eye over her. 'Do stand up, girl. Your mother never taught you to slouch, I'll be bound.'

'Slouch? Laura? Too short and dumpy,' declared Dora.

Mrs Fitzalan-Howard almost writhed. 'Dora! Please. Give Mary some more sherry, dear. And Piers – Piers, tell us what you plan to do this summer. You and Mary used to go fishing, I remember.'

They looked glumly at each other. 'We'll probably go,' said Piers. 'Deb might like to come. I don't suppose they'll let her ride again for a bit.'

'She'll be back on a horse before the week's out,' said Gabriel. 'I know Michael and horses. No child of his can be permitted to give them up.'

Mary felt her hackles rise. 'He's never made either of us do anything we didn't want,' she said stiffly. 'Deb doesn't often ride actually. And nobody makes her. *My* father isn't a bully.'

Dora laughed. 'That's telling you, Gabriel. She's as stiff-necked as you are.'

Gabriel coughed. It was the briefest hiccup, an inhalation caught halfway through. Mary felt the hairs on her neck prickle with alarm, watching like a hawk as Gabriel went unnecessarily to the drinks tray and topped up his almost full glass. No one else seemed to notice anything. She took a gulp of her sherry, sure that she must be going mad. These thoughts were nothing more than wild imagination. There was nothing to see, nothing to know. Her mother and this drunken, cruel man? Of course not.

It was time to eat. Mr Fitzalan-Howard took Dora's arm, and his wife should have gone through with Gabriel. But he came quickly across the room and put his hand under Mary's elbow. As he touched her she flinched. He looked into her face and said, 'Are you afraid of me?' She shook her head. 'I frighten Piers,' he went on. 'Why is that?'

'Perhaps you're mean to him,' she said.

He guided her through the wide double doors into the dining room, placing her firmly at his side for the meal. 'And how am I mean? I don't beat him.'

'You treat him like a fool,' said Mary simply. 'My father would never do that.'

A flicker of anger passed across his face. She knew she ought to be careful. He was very drunk. 'Michael always was too soft for his own good,' he snapped.

'He isn't soft and you know it,' retorted Mary. 'He's strong and kind, that's all. There isn't anyone more respected around here.'

She sat herself down in the chair he held for her. Her face felt as red as her dress, she felt red all the way through, on fire with indignation. Gabriel sat down beside her. She shot him a glance, and saw that he looked almost anguished. Was it possible that his eyes were bright with tears?

He poured himself some water with a trembling hand. 'Is he proud of you?' he asked jerkily.

Mary, too young to prevaricate, struggled to find something to say. There was only the truth. 'There isn't anything to be proud of,' she said simply. 'I'm not like Deb. I'm not pretty or clever. Dad loves me, though. I do know that.'

'He loved me too, once,' said Gabriel. 'And believe me, there was a lot less to be proud of there.'

He seemed to stare without seeing. She sat very still, hoping that he would forget that she was there. Piers, across the table, made a face at her. Mrs Fitzalan-Howard said, 'Gabriel? Gabriel, dear?' But he didn't seem to hear. He got up from the table and walked blindly out of the room.

Mary lay for a long time without sleeping that night. Eventually, unable to lie any longer waiting for the stable clock to chime, she

54

got out of bed. She would go and see the lamb in the kitchen, and somehow fill the hours that lay between her and Gunthwaite. Thoughts kept clicking round in her head, like cogs on a machine; images that she couldn't begin to realise. Her mother and Uncle Gabriel. Uncle Gabriel and Aunt Dora. Herself and some nameless, faceless man who might even be – horrors – Tom who drove the tractor. She shuddered even to be thinking such things.

She had brought her dressing gown but forgotten her slippers. Her bare feet padded down the stairs. The house was silent. She hesitated outside Gabriel's room, but all was still. Thank goodness. She dreaded seeing anything more of him, ever again.

The kitchen flags stung her feet. She scurried across them to the lamb, blinking in the glare of the light. Cook had pushed the little creature as far from the stove as she dared, and already it was cold to the touch. Glad to have something ordinary to feel angry about, Mary noisily filled the kettle and set it to boil. A feed and a hot bottle would soon perk it up. She knelt on the kitchen bench, keeping her feet well off the floor, letting her mind wander.

'Mary?'

She spun round, colouring to her hair. It was Mrs Fitzalan-Howard. Her mother would find out she'd been the worst sort of guest, upsetting everyone at dinner and waking up the household at night.

'I'm sorry,' she gabbled. 'It was the lamb. I couldn't sleep and he was cold and I didn't think anyone would mind—'

'It's all right, my dear. You didn't wake me. I couldn't sleep either and came down for a cup of tea.'

'Oh. I put the kettle on. A bottle for the lamb.'

'I daresay there's enough for some tea. I'll make you a cup, shall I?'

Mary nodded.

Mrs Fitzalan-Howard was an older, paler, altogether less glamorous version of Dora, thought Mary. Her hair was pinned up in a net for the night and she wore a sensible dressing-gown. Mary knew her only as an acquaintance – not quite a friend – of her mother's, and as hostess of the local fête, held annually on the Fairlands lawn. Now she seemed reassuringly ordinary. She sat at the table, watching as Mary fed her lamb. It was rather peaceful.

'Are you worried about Deborah? It's only natural to be.'

'Oh.' Mary flashed her a smile. 'I'm not really worried. I mean, it was just concussion. It was a bit silly of me to make such a fuss, but at the time—'

'It wasn't a fuss. She could have been very badly hurt.'

'But I ruined the lawn.'

Mrs Fitzalan-Howard sighed. She was very fond of her garden. 'I was reminded of the war, actually. The lawn was a mess then. The village school was billeted here and if it wasn't football it was air raid drill, and everyone churning everything into mud. But I daresay if we repaired it once we can do it again.'

Mary bent her head over the lamb. She shouldn't have reminded her about the lawn. Suddenly Mrs Fitzalan-Howard said, 'Did he say anything to you? At dinner? I thought perhaps—'

'Say – anything? Uncle Gabriel, you mean?'

Mrs Fitzalan-Howard swallowed visibly. 'Yes. He'd been drinking, you see, and people don't always watch their words. I wouldn't want – you must understand that the war was a very difficult time. Your father was posted as missing, believed killed, for months.'

Mary licked her lips. 'I didn't know.'

'It's not the sort of thing people want to remember. I've tried to explain to Piers, everything was breaking up. It wasn't as if anything was settled. It wasn't that no one wanted him. It's hard to explain now, how confused everything was.'

'Confused?'

'Yes. No one knew if they would live or die. Even your mother was sent to France. I never knew the details and in those days one didn't ask.'

'Mother? My mother?'

'Well, yes. As an agent. She was a French national, she was terribly well suited.'

'Oh.'

Mary looked back at the lamb. Her thoughts were whirling in her head. No one had told her anything, she didn't know anything at all! Only one piece of information seemed solid and unchallenged; whatever had happened between her mother and Gabriel had been during the war. She had been a baby then. She couldn't be Gabriel's daughter.

The kettle was boiling. Mrs Fitzalan-Howard got up to make tea, and Mary chatted a little, lulling her fears. 'I should have guessed, I suppose. Sophie and Marie talk about the war, but Mum never says a word. She hardly ever talks about the past. I don't even know how she and Dad met.'

'Good heavens.' Mrs Fitzalan-Howard put out two pretty china cups. 'I believe Gabriel brought her to Gunthwaite,' she remarked, selecting silver spoons for this dead of night tea party. 'Your grandparents were alive then and I believe there was some sort of fuss. But Gabriel's always been the same. He never took any notice. He brought Laura for a holiday and she never went away.'

Blood pounded in Mary's ears. She forced herself to get up and put the lamb in its box, refilling the hot water bottle from the kettle's dregs. Mrs Fitzalan-Howard prattled on and on. Mary stood before the darkened window, trying to see herself in the glass. If only, like Deb, she had her mother's eyes! At the table tonight, when Gabriel stared, it had been like – like looking at herself.

Chapter Seven

Deborah sat between her parents, pale but self-important. It was not often that she was given chocolates and hours of undivided care. The tedium of three days' bed rest still to come could be offset by the glamour of her situation. She imagined Piers coming to visit. She drooped in practice.

'Are you feeling dizzy again, darling?' Her mother put an arm around her shoulders.

'It's only when we go over a bump.'

'Best you lie down on the back seat then,' said her father.

'I'm not that dizzy!' declared Deb, and sat up again.

Across her head, her parents exchanged grins. They knew their Deb. Laura said, 'I hope Mary's been all right.'

Deb said, 'She'll have been silly and shy. People don't notice her face nearly as much as she thinks they do.'

'It's easy when it's not you,' said her father.

'I know.'

They left the main road and began the tortuous drive up into the hills. Deb was feeling less robust with each yard, a headache pounding above her eye. If she could only get to bed, she thought. She wouldn't see anyone, not even Piers.

As they topped the rise before Gunthwaite she put her hands over her mouth, giving a strangled gurgle. Michael pulled into the side of the road. Deb fell over her mother and out on to the grass verge, casting up her breakfast in its entirety. 'Now will you lie down on the back seat?' said her mother.

Deb nodded and crawled into the car.

As they drove into the yard Sophie and Marie came chattering out to meet them. '*Mon Dieu*, but she's pale. It's these horses, so dangerous. You remember that one you rode in Paris, Laura? Owned by the daughter of Monsieur le Comte, I know you recall! The one who shot himself in bed with his whore. Zelma, you must remember! How I worried about that horse . . . every day I thought you'd come back dead.'

As always, Deborah noted, her mother said nothing. Whatever tales Sophie and Marie recounted, her mother neither confirmed nor denied. Did she know how much her daughters understood?

Michael spoke little French, but now that school had improved their grammar both Deborah and Mary were almost fluent.

'We'll get you upstairs, young lady,' said Michael, steering his daughter with a firm hand towards the house.

'I ought to go for Mary,' said Laura doubtfully. 'You've got the sheep to see to.'

'The sheep can wait for once. I'll fetch her now.'

Laura smiled at him. Despite her headache Deborah suddenly felt quite happy, as if she and the whole of Gunthwaite were enveloped in the warmth of her parents' love.

Michael drove quickly to Fairlands. He wanted this task over and done with, as soon as he could. On the lawn by the side of the drive a man with a wheelbarrow was trying to repair the damage caused by the Bombardier's galloping hooves. It wasn't going to be easy.

Mary was sitting on the front steps. As her father approached she got up and ran to him, flinging her arms around his chest. 'Daddy! Oh, Daddy.'

'What's all this then? Deborah's fine, a bit of a headache, she has to stay at home in bed.'

'I hated it here. I wanted to come home.'

'And that's just why I'm here. Go get your things now, will you?'

Mary ran off into the house. Ill at ease, Michael leaned on the car, reflecting that it had come to something when a man couldn't feel comfortable passing the time of day with a neighbour. Someone came walking round the side of the house, and for a moment Michael thought it was Mr Fitzalan-Howard and was pleased. But it was Gabriel.

'Hello, Mike. I thought I'd heard a car.'

'I've come to collect Mary. I don't want to talk.'

'Mary. Ah, yes. A difficult sort of girl.'

'I'll thank you not to criticise my daughter.'

'Went to pieces at the accident, I gather.'

'She's young yet. She'll do.'

Gabriel said nothing. He had been hoping for a chink in Michael's armour, some hint that Mary wasn't all that he dreamed. But his brother was so damned loyal! 'You shouldn't put your daughters up on keen horses.'

'The horse is fine. Deb should have worn her hat, that's all.'

His tone was flatly discouraging. But Gabriel persisted. 'I'm trying to remember if you ever had a bad horse,' he remarked. 'I can't think of one.'

'Timberman,' said Michael laconically.

'What? Oh, yes. Reared all the time and tried to wipe you off under trees.' He laughed, although nothing funny had been said, and kept the laugh going uncomfortably. At last he was forced to stop.

'I wish – I wish I could come across and see the old place,' he said wistfully.

'Laura wouldn't like that.'

'Damn Laura! I mean – you were my brother before she was anything to either of us. We're brothers, Mike. We can't break that bond even if we wanted to. We've been apart for too long.'

'To my mind, not long enough.'

The muscles in Michael's cheeks were clenched to knots. Mary was coming down the steps of the house, encumbered by the lamb and her suitcase. Before Michael could move Gabriel was there, taking her bag. 'You must come and see us again,' he said abruptly. 'Here, at Fairlands. We've started to be friends, haven't we?'

She recoiled a little, startled by his intensity, his unlooked for approach.

'Mary has a great deal to do at home,' said Michael heavily. 'She can't go running about to people's houses.' He came and took the lamb, bearing it carefully to the car. He slotted the box on the floor behind the front seat and the little creature put its head up and went: 'Maaaa!'

'She can find time to come and see us,' said Gabriel, insisting beyond the point of politeness.

'Gabriel.' Michael came across to him. He put his big, farmer's hand on his brother's shoulder. 'Leave Mary alone. Leave us all alone. We can't give you what you want.'

'You don't know what I want,' said Gabriel bitterly. 'I didn't know until it was too late!'

'You're gaining nothing by wishing for what you can't have and drinking yourself to death. You're turning into a man that nothing and nowhere will ever suit. Whatever you have is never what you want, and if you had what you wanted it wouldn't be enough. Get a grip on yourself, Gabe. Your son will have Gunthwaite one day. Make him man enough to deserve it.'

He nodded to Mary, who scuttled into the car. As they drove away, she looked back and saw Gabriel, slumped on the steps of the house.

'What's the matter with him, Dad?' she demanded. 'What does he want?'

'To do as he likes and have no one mind,' said Michael grimly. 'Look at the state he's reached. Drunk more often than he's sober, if you ask me. Getting into these wild states, making everything out to be ten times worse than it is.'

'Like me,' said Mary. Her voice was a thready whisper.

'If you like. But you're young, and learning about the world. Pray God you never make his mistakes.'

Soon the familiar dark roofs of Gunthwaite drew into view. Mary knew she should be relieved, and she was. But the dark mood of Fairlands could not easily be brushed away. If only she could live at Gunthwaite forever, she thought, and never set foot beyond its meadows and fields and streams, she would live always in happiness and peace.

Laura came out of the house to meet her. 'Are you all right? Was it awful?'

'Dreadful,' said Mary. 'But my new dress was right. Uncle Gabriel got so drunk before dinner that he stormed off before we'd even had the soup.'

'Oh no. Poor Gabriel.'

'You can't feel sorry for him, Mum! He's just a drunk. A horrible, slobbering drunk!'

'He wasn't always like that.'

'He is now, though. And he's cruel to Piers. They hate each other.'

Laura turned away. Mary felt wretched suddenly, as if she knew everything and it was all far worse than she hoped. If only she could ask someone what had really happened. All these half truths and dark suspicions could be so very wrong. If only she could go back to a week ago, when she had nothing more to concern her than the inevitable, boring, marks on her face.

Upstairs she ran in to see Deb, who was grumpy and complained about a headache. Mary took her some books and a puzzle, but then Laura came in and insisted that the curtains be drawn and Deb left to doze. So Mary went and changed into her riding clothes, feeling at once freer, more alive. She dashed out to the field to fetch Diablo. Today would be a schooling day, careful circles and small jumps over poles. The horse had a small cut above his knee, legacy of his wild dash home. Mary powdered it to keep off the flies, and inevitably Bill Mayes came by and said, 'That horse knows too much. He'll do for you one of these days, just to get home.'

'I let him go,' said Mary grimly. 'When Deb had the accident he was one horse too many.'

'He'll do for you. Mark my words,' intoned Bill, and Mary shivered. She hated that man!

But Diablo behaved well that day. He was happy in himself and eager to learn. Mary kept him working longer than she had planned, delighting in his airy stride and quick response. When she had finished she stood him in the stable for half an hour, and wandered about, waiting until he was cool enough to take back to the field.

'You should wear trousers often,' said a voice. 'They suit you.'

She turned. Marie was sitting on the sunwarmed stable bench, doing some of the exquisite embroidery with which she passed the time. In the bright light her dyed hair seemed garish, her face a made-up mask. But she had been like this all Mary's life. It seemed wrong to notice and criticise, even if she only did it mentally. When Marie patted the bench beside her, encouraging Mary to sit down, she felt it would be churlish not to oblige.

'You're coming on,' said Marie, stitching a complicated knot at the heart of a flower. 'Deb's a beauty, of course, but you will have elegance. Like me.'

Mary said nothing. Marie's style of dress seemed to her most peculiar, too long and narrow, her brightly coloured head emerging from collars cut high enough to seem like a frill on a dish ready for the table. She had seen a boar's head displayed like that once, upended on a plate, the severed neck neatly disguised. But as immaculate as Marie, for all that.

'You must have been very glamorous when you were young,' said Mary, hearing her own words ring false. But Marie didn't seem to notice.

'I was renowned for it,' she said easily. 'At the place where I worked, they used to make me sit in the window. To impress people, you know.'

'Where did you work?'

Marie looked vague. 'At a house. A big house.'

'But what did you do?'

'What women do. What women always do. We entertained people. Men. Don't be curious, child.'

It was infuriating. Nobody told her anything, nobody told her enough! She moved her ground a little. 'How did my mother come to know Uncle Gabriel?' she asked. 'He brought her to Gunthwaite, didn't he?'

'She worked for him,' said Marie.

'But what as? I didn't know my mother had ever worked. She never says a thing.'

'He managed a nightclub. He did it badly. Your mother saw how it was and took the place in hand. There was bad food, dirt, stealing. She was well trained, it wasn't hard to put right.'

'I didn't know she'd been trained.'

'But of course. By Madame Bonacieux, who ran the best house in Paris.'

The sun was high now, and the bench was becoming uncomfortably hot. Mary wanted to move, but Marie seemed settled. She was old and thin, she loved it when the sun baked her bones, unlike fat Sophie, who sweated like an elderly sow looking for a wallow. 'So my mother was good friends with Uncle Gabriel? Before she knew my father?'

'My dear.' Marie put down her sewing. 'Why all these questions?'

'I was just – curious.'

'Don't be. The past has nothing to do with you. The future is yours, to do with as you wish. Leave others their history. Leave them in peace.'

Mary was beginning to feel sick. It was the heat and last night's lack of sleep. But it was also the realisation that there were secrets being kept. She wasn't imagining the silence, the deliberate omissions. There was something that nobody thought she should know.

She felt the bile rise up in her throat and swallowed it down. 'Was my mother in love with Uncle Gabriel?' she asked. 'Is that what the quarrel's about?'

Marie stabbed her needle hard into her work. 'Your mother has always loved your father.'

'But – when he was away.'

'My dear.' Marie put down her work and took hold of Mary's soft young hands. She looked into her face with compassion and not a little exasperation. 'What do you want me to tell you? That your mother isn't a saint? Of course she isn't. No mother can be all that her children would wish. We grow up and we understand that. And it is very English to concern yourself with this or that man in a woman's life. She can sleep with men and it can mean nothing or everything. Most of them are nothing at all.'

Mary felt the shock running through her like electricity. No one had ever spoken to her frankly, not in all her life. 'You mean – it doesn't matter if my mother loved Uncle Gabriel?'

'She didn't love him! How could she? She loved your father.'

'My father.' Mary forced herself to look full at the old woman. To find the words. 'He is my father, then?'

A flicker passed across Marie's face. She covered it with an immediate smile. 'But of course, *chérie*. The things you imagine!'

Mary was subdued at lunch. Laura was up and down stairs seeing to Deb, but Michael noticed. 'Here's something to cheer you up,' he said. 'Your cousins are coming at the weekend.'

'With Aunt Rosalind and Uncle Howard?'

'Certainly. Howard's taking a holiday from the Foreign Office and my sister fancies a bit of rural peace. Actually I think they

63

have the decorators in. You know Rosalind. Won't put up with a bit of paint. But we could do with some visitors to take our minds off Fairlands and all that silliness.'

'Are they quarrelling with Gabriel too?'

Michael grunted. 'As it happens, they are not. Go and pour another cup of tea, Mary, will you?'

'So it's just us?'

'Go and pour the tea, Mary please.'

She did as she was told, quietly fulminating. They all thought she was still a child, to be fobbed off with easy distractions. They behaved as if it was none of her business, when it was nothing but that. She found herself staring at her father. What did he think? What did he know? He must be her father, he had to be. He was the bedrock of her life.

'What are you staring at, miss?'

'Nothing. You.'

'Shaken you up all this, I see. Silly girl.' He got up from the table and came round to envelop Mary in a brief, fierce hug.

'Oh, Daddy!' She buried her face against him, letting the tears flow.

'Silly girl,' he said again. 'Take life as it comes, my sweet. You fight it every inch of the way.'

'I don't! It's just all so difficult.'

'Be a good girl and help your mother. Everything will work out.'

She felt a flicker of unusual irritation. He wanted her to be easy and domestic and childlike. She wasn't like that! She couldn't be like that! She was a fighter and didn't know what else to be.

When her mother came back downstairs she was rattling the dishes in the sink. 'What's the matter with you?'

'Daddy.'

'Oh?'

'He thinks I'm a baby. He thinks I'm a girl.'

'Well, you are a girl.' Laura laughed.

'You know what I mean. Not important. Not – not useful. If I was a boy he wouldn't tell me to be good and mind the house.'

'Did he say that?'

'More or less.'

'More or less. I see.'

She was being gently mocked. Mary turned on her, suds flying from her fingers. 'It's all very well for you to laugh. I suppose they taught you that in your Paris house. I suppose you were trained for everything!'

'Mary? What on earth do you mean?'

'I mean – I mean it's horrible to know about you and Uncle Gabriel.'

64

Laura said nothing. As Mary watched, the colour drained from her face, leaving it deathly pale. Her lips seemed blue, and in contrast her eyes shone like the clearest glass, suspended over a dark well. She began to shake so badly that her teeth chattered.

'Mum?' Mary couldn't believe that her words had resulted in such a change. 'Mum, are you all right? I only meant – you worked with him in a nightclub.'

'What? And what if I did?'

'You never said. You kept it secret. You don't tell me anything at all.'

Her mother turned away, hands pressed to her diaphragm, trying to restore her breath. 'You should tell me the truth,' said Mary miserably.

'I don't have to tell you anything.'

'Mum? Mum, please! What's the matter with you?'

'Mary, will you just mind your own damned business!'

Mary abandoned the dishes and fled from the house. Her heart was beating high in her chest. What was happening to her? She hadn't felt normal, calm, in days. Everything she did seemed to upset someone. One wrong word and her mother fell to bits.

Someone was calling her. She stopped, and saw that Piers was leaning a bicycle against the barn. He was carrying a bunch of Fairlands hothouse flowers, brilliantly red. 'Mary? I came to see Deb.'

'You can't. She's asleep.'

'But I brought flowers.'

Mary ignored him. She went into the barn, up into the hayloft, and Piers put down his flowers and followed. It was like the old days, she the autocratic leader, he following loyally behind. She flung herself down in a heap of last year's crop, still sweet and fragrant. People were talking about silage as a better feed for cows, but Michael prided himself on the quality of his hay. He never believed anything anyone told him, thought Mary. Whatever anyone said, he kept on in his own stubborn way.

'You were right,' she said as Piers climbed up beside her. 'My mum and your dad. I think I'm your sister.'

Piers stopped in the very act of piling up a pillow. 'That's just foolish. Honest Mary, you don't change. Still making things up.'

'Suppose it was true, though. She knew Gabriel before she met Dad. And I look like your father. A bit.'

'He's your uncle. There's a family resemblance.'

She rolled on her stomach and looked across at him. 'Do you really think that's it?'

He nodded. Mary let her face fall softly against the hay.

65

They lay there for an hour or more, talking desultorily. They discussed Alan and David, Rosalind's children, departed into adulthood and lost to them. The parents didn't realise the gulf, of course. But Alan was nineteen now, and David twenty-one, they would have nothing in common with Mary, Deb and Piers. Alan was at Oxford, while David was something in the City. 'What does he do, then?' asked Piers.

Mary shrugged. 'Search me.'

'It's the Beachams' dance soon. We could all go.'

Mary wriggled uncomfortably. 'I don't fancy it.'

'Don't you? I think it sounds like fun.'

The tide of her misery, ebbing and flowing, crept a little further up the beach. Her loyal household was only loyal to a point, it seemed. Where Deb might be going, Piers would surely follow. Was she to go to the dance and spend the evening cringing in a corner, or stay home and be lonely? It was a dismal choice.

'You can go and see Deb,' she said suddenly. 'Mum said if you came it would be all right.'

'Did she? You're sure she doesn't mind?'

'No. She said she didn't.'

She climbed down from the hayloft, and waited in the yard while Piers brushed himself down and collected his flowers. She took him into the hall, saying, 'Deb's room is the first on the left. I'll come up later, I've got some things to do.'

'OK. You're sure your Mum won't mind?'

'I told you. She said it was all right.'

She went back into the yard. He might get away with it, after all. If he didn't, none of them would be going to the dance.

She fetched Diablo's sweat rug, hung it on a gate and began scrubbing. Half an hour passed, forty minutes, almost an hour. The rug had never been so clean. All at once Piers erupted from the house, followed by Laura. 'How dare you flout my wishes? I won't put up with this behaviour, Piers. You're just like your father, I should have known.'

'But, Mrs Cooper, Mary said—'

'Don't drag Mary into this! I found you in my daughter's bedroom, only days after telling you that you were not to see her alone. I never thought to tell you her bedroom was out of bounds. In my foolishness I thought that might be understood!'

'I only took her some flowers!'

'You were lying next to her in the bed!'

Mary crept through the barn and out of the side door, making her way unseen into the house. She went up to Deborah's room. Her sister was lying white-faced against the pillows. 'Were you in bed together?' asked Mary with interest.

Deb made a face. 'Of course not. I was in, he was on. She's going mad.'

'She thinks we're like her,' said Mary. 'You know. Her and Gabriel.'

Deb blinked. 'What do you mean?'

'They were lovers in the war. Surely you realised that, Deb? It's obvious.'

Deborah said nothing. Her pretty face, already white and drawn, seemed to diminish, leaving nothing but eyes. Mary felt ashamed suddenly. But unless she repeated the words, turning them this way and that, holding them up for her own and others' inspection, she didn't know what to do.

'I didn't mean it,' she said abruptly. 'I made it up.'

Deb said, 'Mum never used to hate Piers.'

'But that's because of you. She thinks he's a bad influence, because his father is too.'

There came the sound of Laura's angry feet on the stairs. She burst through the door, flushed and avenging. 'That's the last of him. I won't have him here. You should never have let him in, Deborah, surely I've taught you better than that?' She put her hands on her hips and glared at her younger daughter. What a state to be seen in!

Deborah's white cotton nightgown belled seductively over her breasts, the sheer, flower-printed fabric failing to conceal the dark aureoles. Her hair, disordered and in need of washing, seemed like a net of glowing threads. The child looked glorious, even now!

'I don't know what to make of you girls. You're getting quite out of hand.'

'I suppose you'd know,' said Mary rudely.

'What?'

Laura felt the shaking begin again. Now they were both staring at her, two accusing faces looking into her soul. She felt naked before them, defenceless in the glare of their lack of understanding. Did they know anything? What did they know? The fat men, the ugly men, the ones who made her lick them? If they despised her for Gabriel, what would they think about the rest?

She turned and ran out of the room. The girls looked at each other, appalled. They were used to their mother's calm, her self-control. This was someone they simply didn't know.

They could hear her dialling on the telephone. 'Hello? Hello?' Her voice was high, thin, hysterical. 'This is Laura Cooper. Hello, Mrs Fitzalan-Howard. Piers has been here, being disgusting. I won't have it and he's not to come again. What? He – he was on the bed with Deborah. Yes. Surprised? I don't see why. Not with the father he has. I don't want any of that family to set foot here.

67

None of them. And if I find that boy has so much as spoken to Mary or Deb, I shall send Michael to see him with his gun!'

The receiver slammed down. 'She's gone mad,' whispered Deb.

'Didn't I tell you?'

They sat and waited. Sure enough, Laura came slowly back into the room. She sat on the bed, endlessly pleating the fabric of her skirt. At last she said, 'You do understand, don't you?'

Both girls shook their heads. 'How can we?' asked Mary. 'You never explain.'

Laura bent her head and said nothing at all.

Chapter Eight

Howard, Rosalind and the boys arrived late on Wednesday night. Howard still employed a chauffeur and the family waited in the long, black car until he emerged from the driving seat and opened the doors. Rosalind came out first, wonderfully smart in a houndstooth-checked suit, immediately making Laura feel dowdy. Like Dora, she too wore perfect make-up. Laura felt her own skin to be fast becoming a joke.

'Rosalind! You look wonderful.'

'Thank you, darling. You look tired. You should make Michael take you on holiday, staying here all the time just isn't fair. Boys, come and give Laura a kiss.'

David and Alan came grinning across. They were both tall, grey-eyed with mousy hair, but where David had his father's large and ugly nose, his brother was blessed with Rosalind's aquiline proboscis. It made a startling difference; Alan was handsome, while David looked nervous and overbred. Seeing them so rarely, Laura found it hard to relate them to the bouncy small boys who had spent years with her during the war. With her they had learned French and farming, but not much else. Rosalind had spirited them back to London at the first opportunity.

'You both look so prosperous,' she managed.

'True in David's case, but not in mine,' said Alan. 'Pa keeps me on far too short a rein. I keep telling him, I barely have enough money to eat.'

His father, a serious-minded man – far too serious in Laura's opinion – failed to catch the light tone. 'This isn't the time to talk money, Alan,' he said, obviously shocked. 'I should have thought that was obvious.'

'It's all right, darling,' soothed Rosalind, although it was unclear which darling she meant.

'Good heavens,' David was saying. 'You've grown enormous, Mary. And I can't believe this is little Deb.'

Mary sighed. She couldn't believe that her cousins had so soon forgotten the 'how you've grown' routine. She steeled herself. Inevitably, people made comparisons. Sure enough one after another everyone acknowledged her height and Deb's beauty. 'Goodness me!

69

If it wasn't for the lovely hair, Deborah, I wouldn't have known you.' And afterwards, in a whisper to Laura, 'She'll break a few hearts!' Mary knew only too well which 'she' they meant.

She went heavily into the house. Her father and Howard were exchanging pleasantries about the weather. They lived in worlds so far apart that they had nothing of which they could talk, but they liked to signal goodwill. 'Getting your subsidies, are you?' remarked Howard. 'I was talking to the minister the other day.' Such comments could not be responded to.

The girls were soon sent to bed. Downstairs the buzz of conversation sounded like bees round a hive. Deb, padding along to Mary's room, said, 'Why don't we take David and Alan to the Beachams' dance?'

'We won't be allowed to go,' said Mary, hunching her knees up in the bed. 'Not after the fuss about Piers.'

'You are silly. Mum won't want Rosalind to know there was a fuss so we'll go all right.'

Mary hadn't thought of that. 'Well, I shan't,' she said crossly.

'Mum's sure to make you. And if we take the cousins you'll at least have someone to talk to. You know you ought, Mary. You can't be a recluse all your life.'

Mary ignored her, pointedly opening a book. Deb, who still had a dull headache when she stayed up late, hung around for a while. But Mary was always difficult nowadays. She was forgetting if there had ever been a time when she was anything else. She flounced noisily back to bed.

Laura had opened the drawing room for the visitors. A fire was lit, because it was late and also because the room smelled damp sometimes. She had left the curtains undrawn across the arches of the windows, and outside the soft summer night beckoned with moths and owls. Rosalind got up and went to look through the glass. 'I forget how bright the stars are in the country. How quiet it all is.'

'Wait until we take the ewes from the lambs.'

'Don't be prosaic, Laura!'

It wasn't a rebuke. Laura knew Rosalind well enough to know that. But the comment stung, as so many did nowadays. Like sunburned skin, she was unable to endure the slightest touch. Her nerve-ends twitched with every passing breeze. And after all, she had spent years at Gunthwaite, becoming more prosaic, more provincial, with every day.

Rosalind said, 'So. Have you seen Gabriel?'

Laura flinched. 'Yes. Unfortunately.'

'Oh, Laura! It's all years ago. Surely you're both old enough to let it pass?'

'I don't think Michael or I will ever be old enough.'

Rosalind sighed. 'It wasn't all Gabriel, you know. Remember, I was there.'

'Do you think I don't know that?'

Laura glared and tried to move away. Rosalind caught her arm. 'Don't, my dear. Don't be angry. I'm sure Gabriel would never do anything to cause you pain.'

'Then why did he come back?'

The force of Laura's passion caused Rosalind to pause. After a moment she said, 'You realise we want to see them, don't you? It was partly why we came. That and the decorators.'

'They can't come here.'

'But Laura! He is my brother. And Dora, and Piers. None of it had anything to do with them.'

'Piers is just like his father,' snapped Laura. 'He's chasing after Deb like an animal. I've banned him from seeing her.' Her eyes suddenly filled with tears and she put up her hand to hide them.

'Laura! This isn't like you! Surely the children—' She looked away, towards her husband, but he was still earnestly trying to talk to Michael, and the boys were sorting through the record collection, laughing at what they found. And Laura looked ravaged. Quite uncontrolled. In a low voice Rosalind said, 'What is it, my dear? What is it really?'

Laura drew in her breath, struggling to compose herself. 'The girls know,' she whispered. 'About me and Gabriel. I don't know what else. Perhaps even about – my past.'

Rosalind grimaced. 'Well. If you will keep those two old tarts about the place. I never thought it wise.'

'You know I could never throw them out. I never thought – I never realised how much I wanted my daughters to think well of me. And now they can't.'

Her sister-in-law said nothing. She knew a little of Laura's past. More than Michael, less than Gabriel, and she was sure no one knew the whole. She wondered how much she dared say. How much she dared ask. Mary's premature birth had always been a matter of conjecture, and her blue eyes one of speculation, if not more. But Michael had always seemed to accept Mary as entirely his own.

'Would you like me to talk to the girls?' she asked. 'Perhaps I could tell them a little of what you did in the war. Redress the balance.'

Laura tried to laugh. 'You know why I did that. It was all Gabriel. All of it.'

'But no less praiseworthy because of that.'

Laura took a long breath. Thank goodness for Rosalind. If she had kept it all bottled up much longer she might have gone mad. But Rosalind could do something. 'Talk to Mary,' she suggested. 'It's Mary that you always have to convince.'

71

'It's Deborah you'll have to watch,' said Rosalind darkly. 'Really, Laura! What a beautiful child.'

Laura nodded. 'She's lovely. Inside and out.'

She looked out at the night sky once again. Her face was wistful, as if she saw a place where she longed to be. Rosalind felt anxious, suddenly. Laura had spared no effort in giving her children what she had never had herself. It had left her pale and weary, diminished by the years. What had happened to her spirit? she wondered. Perhaps it was like liquid in a bottle, to be poured and poured until there was nothing left. It might be like that. But she hoped it was a flame, one that fed on hope and dreams fulfilled, that might one day burn brightly again. She had known Laura strong and powerful and happy. She wasn't that now.

Howard turned from his long, opaque conversation with Michael. The boys were playing 'Teddy Bears' Picnic' quietly on the gramophone, and talking about Oxford. Remembering her manners, Laura said, 'Can I get anyone anything? We don't have to stand on ceremony, do we? Come into the kitchen and have something to eat.'

David came across and took Laura's hands. 'I love this house, Aunt Laura,' he said enthusiastically. 'It fits you like a glove.'

'Rubbish,' said Rosalind, with more force than she intended. 'You'd be surprised at the gloves that fit Laura. She's worth more than you think.' She could feel Michael looking at her. Not for the first time, she wondered how much he knew of what was going on.

They drove over to Fairlands on Friday afternoon. Laura worked in the garden, pretending she didn't know. When Rosalind invited the girls to accompany her, they both refused politely. They well knew what storm would have broken if they had said yes. Mary took her horse out and rode along the crest of moorland high above the farm. The wind froze her to the marrow, icing her feelings, her thoughts. When she came back, tired and peaceful, she found Deb sitting on the stairs, kicking her heels against the wormeaten wood.

'What's the matter?'

'Mum. She's in a foul temper. I went out to talk to her about my dress for tomorrow night. She wants to make me wear a pinafore.'

'What?' Mary was dumbfounded. No one could go to the Beachams' dance in a pinafore. Not even Deb should suffer so.

'She says I'm trying to grow up too quickly.'

'She doesn't mean that. It's Piers.'

'Honestly, Mary! He was only sitting on the bed!'

Mary sighed. Her mean-spirited actions always seemed to cause more trouble than she expected. She felt guilty and rather ashamed, because it wasn't Deb's fault she was so gorgeous. When she herself wasn't involved, Mary could actually feel some pride. No one else's family could boast such a beauty. No one she knew, at any rate.

The kitchen door opened. Laura was back to prepare the evening meal. Once they would have moved easily from hall to kitchen, ready for a comfortable chat, but not now. They waited in silence, wondering what sort of mood she might be in.

The kettle filled, and the radio was switched on. The Light Programme. They exchanged glances. 'I'll talk to her,' said Mary, and crept up the stairs so that she could descend again with appropriate commotion. She breezed into the kitchen. 'Hello, Mum. I've been riding. Diablo was super.'

'I hope you wore your hat.'

'You know I did. I don't want to lie out on Roundup Moor for hours. The foxes and crows might get me.'

'Mary, don't! That's a horrible thought.' They saw lambs enough with their eyes pecked out.

Laura was chopping herbs from the garden. She grew them fanatically, spending hours in their care, covering them with cloches, surrounding them with orange peel which she thought kept away the slugs. Now she was tossing them into a pot with three farmyard chickens barely old enough to cluck. 'Yum,' said Mary, who had been brought up to be quite unsentimental about food. 'Shall I go and steal some wine? It always tastes wonderful when you slosh in half a bottle.'

It was blatant, but Laura smiled thinly. 'All right. Not your father's best, though. And not the stuff Howard brought. We'll have to drink that at dinner, and don't you dare say a word.'

'I won't.'

Howard Dalton was mean about wine. He laboured under the misapprehension that Laura, being French, would drink anything. His gifts were always a disappointment. 'I bet his London cellar's stuffed with good claret,' mused Mary.

'Probably. Darling, pass the pepper, would you?'

Mary obliged and gauged that this was the moment. Her mother liked to cook. It soothed and satisfied her. 'You don't really mean Deb to wear a pinafore to the Beachams', do you?'

Her mother stiffened. 'It's a very pretty pinafore.'

'But she isn't six.'

'She's still too young to go all done up.'

Mary rocked her chair back on its legs. 'It won't do any good, Mum,' she remarked. 'She'd be the centre of attention whatever she wore. So you might as well not embarrass her.'

Laura looked at her unpredictable daughter. 'You're being very kind for once.'

'It doesn't matter to me. I'm not going.'

73

'What? After I bought you that red dress? Let me tell you my girl, you most certainly are!'

Deb sat on the stairs and listened to the battle. She grinned. The pinafore was out of it, there would be no more discussion. Everything would now be directed to winkling Mary out of her shell. The time-honoured pattern of threats and cajolery and more threats and more cajolery achieved its usual result. Mary still wouldn't go.

A car was drawing into the yard. The Daltons were back, full of a Fairlands tea which would spoil them for a Gunthwaite dinner. Deb wandered out to meet them, expecting to be more or less ignored by her lordly cousins. But the years had changed even that. To her surprise Alan beamed at her. 'Hello, Deb. You don't know how I've suffered, trapped all afternoon by Aunt Dora. Come for a walk, I'll tell you the tale.'

His brother shot him a frowning look, but Alan merely smiled. Rosalind, laden with Fairlands flowers and early peaches, rushed into the kitchen, into the midst of the row.

She stopped in the doorway, at once grasping the gist of the conflict. 'Goodness me, Mary,' she declared. 'Of course you must go. Everyone will be there, including David and Alan. Dora telephoned and arranged it.'

'There you are then,' said Laura, in a strained voice.

She warily eyed the flowers and fruit that were about to be pressed upon her. Olive branches came in many forms these days, it seemed. She wanted none of it, but could see no civil way to refuse. She turned her back, and Rosalind put everything carefully on to the table.

'Don't be petty, Laura,' she murmured.

'But they are so flagrant!'

'They want to make up. That's all.'

Mary watched in silence, hoping that no one would remember she was there. But Rosalind turned quite suddenly and bestowed a brilliant smile on her niece. 'Mary,' she murmured. 'Come up to my room. We really must have a little chat.'

'About the dance?' she asked cautiously.

'I suppose it could be. Amongst other things. Come along, my dear.'

She felt nervous as she followed her aunt up the stairs. There was something menacing about Rosalind's smile. Her aunt was a powerful and perceptive woman, and it was as well to remember it.

As soon as the bedroom door was closed, Rosalind sat on the bed and said, 'Well, Mary. You certainly excelled yourself. Piers is not very pleased with you.'

Mary coloured to her hair. But she still put up a weak defence. 'What have I done? I didn't do anything.'

'I imagine Roman emperors said as much when the Christians were thrown to the lions. They didn't actually throw them after all. They merely caused the throwing to take place. If you understand me?'

Mary abandoned subterfuge as hopeless. 'I didn't know Mum would find him.'

'You just hoped she would. Well, that's as may be. You've succeeded in having Piers banned from ever speaking to either of you again. Was that what you hoped for?'

'No.' Mary went to the dressing table and fiddled with her aunt's silver brushes. 'I just wanted us not to go to the dance. I thought she'd say we couldn't, that's all.'

'I see.' Rosalind hid a smile. 'I think it's best then if you go to the dance without complaining. Any more fuss and I shall tell your mother what happened, and let her deal with you.'

Mary lifted eyes dark with anger. 'That's mean!'

'Almost, but not quite, as mean as you.'

Rosalind swung her legs on to the bed. Age had thickened her ankles a little, she thought, and her knees weren't what they were. Looking at Mary's long, slender figure, encased in jodhpurs, she felt a pang of envy. How fortunate it was to have sons. With daughters you were confronted every day by your own ebbing beauty.

'Can I go now?' asked Mary rudely.

'No, you may not. I don't like the way you've been treating your mother lately.'

'Me?' Mary was aghast. 'I haven't done anything. She's the one who's gone bonkers, ever since Uncle Gabriel came back.'

'What a dreadful expression!'

'What would you call it then? She used to be sensible. Now we don't know what she might do next.'

Rosalind took a long breath. 'Your mother – your mother's a very unusual woman,' she began carefully. 'Very brave. Very daring.'

'But she and Uncle Gabriel were lovers.'

Rosalind was taken aback. She took refuge in uncharacteristic shock. 'Really, Mary! What a thing to say. I don't know what you girls are being taught nowadays, but to say such a thing. About your own mother!'

'But they were. Whether I say it or not, they were.'

The girl's eyes were a piercing, unwavering blue. Rosalind blustered, 'I've really no idea what you're talking about. Your mother was a heroine in the war. Quite wonderful. And after all, your father was thought to be dead.'

'There you are! That's another thing. Why wasn't I told that? I should have been told!'

'I really don't know why you weren't. Weren't you? Perhaps you forgot.'

'Aunt Rosalind, I'm not an imbecile!'

That sadly appeared to be true. Rosalind was beginning to wish she'd never started this. 'Why don't you sit down?' she murmured soothingly. 'I can tell you everything right from the start.'

'The start of what?'

'I don't know. From the start of the war, I suppose. You were just a baby and your father decided to go off and fight. He shouldn't have gone, he hadn't any need, and he was posted missing. Your mother – Laura was very upset.' She waited for Mary's interjection. None came. The girl just stared at her. Waiting.

'Your Uncle Gabriel hadn't been married long,' went on Rosalind. 'I don't think he was very happy. No one was, in the war. Everything rushed, no time to think. Perhaps he'd got married in a hurry. I think – I think he might have wished he'd married your mother instead of Michael. He – and your mother – became very fond of each other. And then of course, thankfully, your father was found to be still alive and everything could go back to normal.'

'Except she was in love with Uncle Gabriel.'

'No! She loved your father.'

'So why did what happened – happen?'

Rosalind closed her eyes for a moment. 'Be that as it may,' she said firmly, 'your mother behaved very bravely. I was responsible for recruiting people – special people. She became an agent for us and was sent to France.'

Mary said nothing. The girl was dumbfounded, thought Rosalind delightedly. She had at last managed to expand her view of her mother. Mary could see something of the real, complex, admirable woman her mother really was.

'This is outrageous!' Mary exploded.

'What?'

'My mother could be anything! Anybody! She's never said a word about her life before, not one little word! And she's let us go on believing rubbish, pretending she's one sort of person and all the time being someone else. Why? She can't tell us anything, can she? She's terrified we'll find out the truth!'

'There's nothing to find out,' said Rosalind, feeling her temper start to go at this impossible, wayward girl. 'The war was a difficult time for us all.'

'She knew Uncle Gabriel before the war, didn't she?' demanded Mary. 'Before she even met Dad. Who am I, Aunt Rosalind? Is my father really my father at all?'

Rosalind blinked. She knew she should laugh, mock the idea, make Mary seem very young and silly. But all she could say was, 'Who put that idea into your head?'

'It came, all by itself,' said Mary nastily. 'Even girls can think, Aunt Rosalind. You're not the only one that ever managed it.'

'Don't be rude Mary, please!'

'Then don't treat me like a fool. I need to know.'

Of course she did. Mary was someone who would never avoid truth. Like Gabriel, thought Rosalind, feeling her heart lurch. Oh God, how was she in this mess? 'Your mother's a very brave – loyal – resourceful—'

'Aunt Rosalind!'

'For God's sake, Mary! I really don't know. And your mother is the only person who might.'

Mary said nothing. Her eyes at last dropped and looked away. 'When people keep secrets,' she said softly, 'you end up wondering about everything.'

'Children can't be told everything. Some things are too difficult to understand.'

'But she doesn't tell us anything. She never has.'

'But she loves you, Deb and your father more than anything in the world. Mary, I'm sure you're being silly. The war was a terrible time, everything was upside down, people were desperate for comfort. Afterwards, when your father came home blind—'

'What?'

'He got better! It all got better!'

'Except no one thought any of it was something I should know. I'm sorry I'm not more stupid, Aunt Rosalind. If I was you could all be very happy.'

Rosalind pulled herself together. 'None of it was important, Mary! It isn't important now. We won't talk of this again, you know. And I don't want you bothering your mother. Or anyone else for that matter. And you're not to think any more about this. You won't, will you?'

Mary turned and gave her a look of complete scorn.

Chapter Nine

The Beachams' dance was an elaborate affair to which everyone always went. Even Michael and Laura usually attended, although this year they had refused. They knew Gabriel and Dora would be there.

Laura was emphatic with her girls. 'You are not to speak to Piers under any circumstances. Either of you. Especially not Deb.'

'So I can speak to him a bit then, Mum?' asked Mary in mock innocence.

'Don't annoy me, Mary! That boy and his family are absolutely out of bounds. And I shall ask Rosalind what went on, mark my words.'

The girls went sulkily upstairs to change. 'Mark my words,' mocked Mary. 'Don't worry, Deb. Aunt Rosalind can't watch us all the time. You'll get to talk to him.'

'I don't care if I don't,' said Deb, unconvincingly. 'Will Mum notice if I wear lipstick?'

'You bet. Put it on when you get there.'

But lipstick or no, Deb looked wonderful. She wore a plain blue dress that Laura had made to Marie's design, seamed on either side of a central panel. It fitted to perfection, the sweetheart neckline dipping down to the merest suggestion of Deb's bosom. But nothing could disguise the new voluptuousness of her shape. Her chestnut hair, her father's gift, hung brushed and shining to her shoulders and her eyes drew colour from the light. Almost a woman, no longer a child, she was enchanting.

She watched Mary wrestling with her unruly hair. 'Let me,' she advised.

Mary dropped her arms. 'It's no good. If I pin it back it shows my marks and if I don't it looks a mess.'

'Forget the marks,' advised Deb. 'It doesn't suit you all in a heap over your forehead. I'll put it in a pony tail.'

'That's too little girl!'

'But a French pleat's too severe. How about – how about tying up the front and letting the rest hang loose?'

'Like Sophie when she's in one of her *jeune fille* moods?' They both giggled. 'All right.'

It was a moderate success. Mary's agitation brought the marks on her skin into prominence, and the neatness of her hair only seemed to exaggerate the length and angularity of her face. Perhaps it might have been better if Deb's anxious and unblemished countenance wasn't so visible behind her in the mirror. But there it was.

Mary said bravely, 'At least one of us will hold up the family honour.'

'The dress is great,' said Deb. 'Mum does know her stuff.'

'I'm all right from the neck down,' said Mary. 'Oh, well. Let's see what Aunt Rosalind considers appropriate for a country party.'

In fact, Rosalind had taken dressing down to extremes. She was wearing a simple cotton frock, and no jewellery. She might have been going for an afternoon's shopping in Bainfield. Laura said doubtfully, 'I suppose you don't want to overdo things in the country.'

'My own feelings exactly, dear. No, Howard, not my stole. I'll take my suit jacket.'

Laura raised an eyebrow at her daughters. They wrinkled their noses back. It was entirely possible that there would be ladies there tonight in floor-length satin and heirloom emeralds. It was only the young set who did not dress up. 'I think the stole – don't you, girls?' ventured Laura. 'And why not your diamonds?'

'Really, Laura! You'll make me look a dog's breakfast. I'm not going to come the sophisticate in the country.'

'But I'm sure it's black tie!'

'I can think of nothing more crass than to come on a late invitation dressed to the nines in Paris couture. I'm sure you'd all find it very amusing, but I should not. Come along, everyone.'

Laura conceded defeat and stood at the window watching as they left. Michael said, 'She's certainly in a temper.'

'She took it upon herself to make Mary agree to go. But then I think she tried to give her some advice.'

Michael chuckled. 'Not used to defeat is Rosalind. You don't mind staying home, do you, love? You don't wish we'd gone?'

'I couldn't bear to have Gabriel and Dora trying to get on our right side all night. They don't realise. There isn't a right side as far as they're concerned and there never will be.'

She went to Michael and put her arms around his neck. He held her waist, saying, 'That's right, then? That is still what you feel?'

Laura buried her face in his chest. 'Yes! Yes! It always was.' But the vehemence was out of place. She didn't know if it was Michael or herself that she was trying to convince.

They drew up at the Beachams' house behind a line of cars disgorging gorgeously dressed people. The lady immediately in front of them was wearing a black lace sheath that looked much like Chanel. 'Oh my God!' said Rosalind in strangled tones. 'Laura was right!'

'My goodness,' agreed Howard. 'It does seem very grand.'

'Never mind, Mother,' said Alan. 'You can always pretend you're the char.'

'I'll thank you not to be offensive,' snapped his mother. 'I can't come like this. I shall have to go back and change.'

They couldn't dissuade her. The girls barely tried. They too were overcome by what appeared to be a sudden rise in the style quotient of the Beacham dance. Deb thought of the threatened pinafore and shuddered.

It was decided that the chauffeur would spirit Rosalind back home while the rest went in. It meant that she wouldn't join them much before ten, or later if she took her time in changing. If the girls were to leave at twelve, as planned, there would be little time for the party. But needs must. Mary and Deborah were in essence to spend the evening chaperoned by their vague uncle and two youthful and high-spirited cousins.

But Mary's nerve was going. She felt hot and flustered, the palms of her hands clammy with sweat. She knew she was blushing, knew that her face must look like a side of bacon. She tugged at her hair and Deb said, 'Don't, Mary! You'll pull it all out.'

'I don't care if I do. Oh, look. There's Graham Beacham. I do so hate parties!'

She pinned on a stilted smile as Mrs Beacham welcomed her, responding in monosyllables to enquiries about her parents. As usual it was left to Deb to say that Laura and Michael sent their regards and would be in touch about the hunt towards the end of August. And it was Deb that Graham Beacham beamed upon when the girls, as 'young people', were despatched to his care.

'Hello, you two. You've got to dance with me, Deb, I've told everyone you will. You have to, I'm the host.'

'Can't I say no then?'

'No, it's rude. You won't, will you?'

'No, of course not. I don't dance very well, though.'

'I don't care.'

Mary stood glumly by. She might as well not have existed. But then Graham, remembering his duties, said awkwardly, 'I'll dance with you too, Mary, if you like?'

'If you dance as well as you ride I won't bother, thanks,' she retorted waspishly. Graham muttered something and retreated.

'Mary!' Deb glared at her. 'You didn't have to be horrid.'

'He doesn't want to dance with me.'

'He won't now, that's certain. If you're going to be like that every time someone asks you to dance, you'll spend the whole evening sitting by yourself.'

'That's what I always seem to do anyway at these things. I told Mum but she wouldn't listen.'

'But it's your own fault!'

Deb sighed in exasperation. But then she spied Helena Carter, who went to the same school although she lived twenty miles from Gunthwaite, and rushed across to talk. Mary, who hated Helena for being Miss Stenson's pet, was left bereft. She went to stand next to a pillar – the Beachams had a house of giant proportions – and longed for the evening to be done.

People were arriving all the time. All at once she saw Aunt Dora, gorgeous in cream satin, the collar a wide bow enveloping her shoulders and dipping down between her breasts. In fact it dipped so far that Mary could feel herself blushing. You could see almost everything. Almost – the ends.

Dora's searching gaze passed her, returned, and fixed itself on Mary's shrinking form. She swept across the room, her painted mouth beaming.

'My dear Mary. You look very uncomfortable, standing there alone. Piers is here, you must dance with him, he can just about waltz.'

Mary felt her blush rising. If Aunt Rosalind had been here she might have explained perhaps. As it was, she struggled for words. 'My mother said – she thought – she doesn't want me and Deb—'

'Don't be silly, dear,' said Dora in clipped tones. 'You have no quarrel with Piers. Actually there's no real quarrel with us either. It's just your parents bearing silly grudges over things that happened a hundred years ago. It's all so silly.'

Mary summoned her courage. 'I don't think my parents would like me to disobey them.'

'Wouldn't they, miss? Well, I think you should do as I say. Come and talk to Piers. I insist.'

There was nothing to be done. With her aunt's hand firmly beneath her elbow Mary was transported willy-nilly to the dance floor. There, next to his father and uncomfortable in a bow tie, stood Piers.

'See what I brought you,' said Dora, as if she was presenting lions with a kill.

'I do see,' said Gabriel. 'Hello, Mary.'

He looked drunk, she thought. He always looked drunk. She ignored him, and instead greeted his son. 'Deb's been snaffled by Graham Beacham. He says she has to dance with him because he's the host.'

'Oh.' Piers avoided her eye and instead looked at his feet.

Mary said gruffly, 'I'm sorry I got you into trouble. I wanted Mum to stop us coming tonight. I hate parties.'

'I can't dance anyway,' said Piers, relenting enough to look at her.

'I could teach you! I mean – if you wanted or anything.'

Piers' face made it clear that it was the last thing he wished.

Gabriel said, 'He could have learned if he hadn't been so damned stubborn. But I told him he should, and of course that was it. You never do a thing I want, do you, Piers?'

'I hope not,' said Piers rudely. 'I do my very best.'

'Do stop squabbling,' said Dora in a bored voice. 'I don't know anybody here, Gabriel! Only that man Hodgkins and his peculiar wife. What's happened to all the people we used to know?'

'Perhaps it's so long ago they're all dead?' said Mary brightly. Dora fixed her with a stare of intense dislike.

But Gabriel chuckled. 'You must dance with me before Piers, my dear,' he said, and took Mary's arm in a firm clasp. Like it or not, she was propelled on to the floor. The band was beginning a quickstep. Gabriel's arm slipped neatly around her waist and she was swept away into the dance.

'You're good,' he remarked, as they completed a smooth circuit of the room.

'I think it's you,' said Mary. 'I've only ever danced properly with Dad. And the dancing teacher, of course, but she's a woman.'

'Michael was never any good at parties.'

'Wasn't he?' Mary beamed. 'Then I must take after him, mustn't I?'

Gabriel looked down at her with sudden intensity. 'Actually, I doubt that you do.'

They were silent. Mary ducked her head, letting her feet follow instinctively. Gabriel said, 'What are you thinking?'

She lifted her eyes. 'Nothing I want to tell you about.'

'I'm surprised Laura permits you such appalling manners.'

'Why? My mother isn't what she seems, in case you hadn't noticed.'

He grinned at her, his mood suddenly lightening. 'Oh, I had, actually, Mary. There's more to your mother than dolts like Michael will ever see. I doubt if anyone knows everything about her.'

'But you know a lot.'

'Yes. Actually I do.'

He swept her down the length of the room, twirling her in double time. Mary clung to her wits, wondering fleetingly if people were staring, not having time to care. She gasped, 'I wish you'd tell me. It's only fair.'

He paused for the corner, pushing her into a reverse then twirling her away again. 'Tell you what?'

'Who she is. Where she came from. How you met.'

He chuckled once more. 'Haven't you asked Sophie and Marie?'

'Marie. She wouldn't tell me.'

The music was ending. He stood apart from her, still holding her hand. She was breathless, she knew she was flushed. What must she look like? But he lifted her fingers briefly to his lips. 'Thank you, my dear. You're going to be a very good dancer.'

He let her go, but she hesitated, still wanting to know! She couldn't quite believe he wouldn't tell her. 'Is it very bad?' she asked in a rush.

'What? About your mother?' He swayed a little. She hoped he was too drunk to watch his words. 'She thinks it's as bad as it can be. It's not. She's had a terribly rough time, that's all. Talk to Sophie.'

'But she's so old! And so – silly.'

'Sophie always did have her moments. The old hag.' He spoke with something like affection. Then he looked again at Mary. 'Your mother's a sweet soul. You're like me, and you have to know, but – don't hurt her. Be kind.'

A waltz was beginning. Gabriel seemed unaware that they were in the way. Mary took his arm and pulled him to the side, looking in vain for Dora and Piers. They were nowhere to be seen. Gabriel muttered, 'Where in God's name can I get a decent drink?' and wandered off into the throng. She was alone.

She suddenly realised that no one was really looking at her. She could do what she liked. Unlike Deb, who could never go unobserved, when people saw Mary's face they always looked away. She strolled to the long table where they were serving punch, picked up a cup and drained it. There. No one cared what she was doing. She could turn cartwheels in the middle of the room if she wanted.

'Oh, Mary! You're not drinking, are you?' It was Alan. She was trapped again.

'It's only punch. Anyway, I think you're drunk.' His hair was disordered and his bow tie crooked. But in the unfair way of things, it only added to his good looks.

'Not drunk, just annoyed. I can't get a single dance with your sister. If it's not Graham Beacham, it's that pipsqueak Piers. I'd watch him if I were you. Deb's entranced.'

'And you're jealous,' said Mary sourly. 'You ought to dance with me. I'm the eldest.'

'Elder, my dear Mary. Let's not forget our grammar, shall we?'

She administered a cousinly kick on the leg.

Alan began hopping about, gasping and groaning. David appeared, and took no notice. 'There you are, Mary. Father's been giving me strict instructions to keep you away from Uncle Gabriel for some reason.'

'I'm nowhere near him,' said Mary ingenuously.

'So I see. You haven't been drinking punch, I hope? Come and dance, Alan appears to be having some kind of fit.'

They took to the floor for a foxtrot. Mary was almost defeated,

David wasn't nearly so good as Gabriel and in the long sweeps down the room she felt rudderless and at risk. But enthusiasm stood David in good stead. He launched himself on moves he was barely competent to perform, and muddled through somehow. Mary was confirmed in her earlier view; dancing was fun.

'You're good,' said David condescendingly, when the music finished. 'Have you tried jiving yet?'

Mary shook her head. 'A few girls at school do it. I don't.'

'They're going to do some out on the lawn later. We'll have to give it a go. Look, Mary, do you mind if I buzz off for a bit? There's a chap here I used to go to school with at Fairlands during the war, and I simply must have a talk. He and I dug a tunnel in the shrubbery and the gardener fell in.'

'Oh. Good. Go on, I don't mind.'

He disappeared into the party. Mary wandered out on to the terrace, trying to decide if she really didn't mind being viewed as an obligation. Perhaps not. To be alone all evening might be more than she could bear. She began vaguely looking for Deb or Piers, suspecting that to find one would mean finding the other. She strolled into the gardens, lit tonight by strings of fairy lights, although the sky still glowed with the sunset. Half-past nine. Aunt Rosalind would soon return.

The Beacham gardens were small in relation to the house. There was a formal area, giving way within fifty yards to controlled wilderness, beyond which stretched the fields. People in evening dress stood about on the lawns, laughing and talking. Mary went down a path into the wild garden, and almost immediately the sounds of the party were lost in the bushes and trees. A field mouse ran across the mossy flags on which she walked, making her start. There was a muffled groaning in the bushes.

It sounded like a woman. Fearfully Mary crept forward. Perhaps someone was ill, or upset. Leaning against a tree was her Aunt Dora, lovely dress pulled down to expose her breasts. Her head was thrown back, her eyes were closed, and a man – Mr Hodgkins, of all people, from the estate! – was touching and kissing and licking her. Licking them. And all the time Aunt Dora was groaning. Mary could see a small trickle of saliva oozing from the corner of her mouth.

She turned and ran back the way she had come, not caring that they would hear her and know they had been seen. She hated Aunt Dora. No wonder Uncle Gabriel got drunk. Reaching the terrace she leaned against the balustrade, catching her breath. Heat coursed up from within her, shameful, embarrassing warmth. Her own breasts, so small, stuck on to her rib cage like stunted apples, tingled and throbbed.

She couldn't go back into the party yet. Her face was scarlet, her marks like beacons, she'd be stared at by everyone. Taking long, calming breaths she walked round the side of the house to the stables. As she heard the horses stamping in their boxes, she felt the beginnings of peace.

The Beachams had a good string of hunters, strong and well ribbed up. Mary stopped to talk to a big grey, his neck still soft from summer grass, impatient with confinement on a warm summer's night. They were starting early, she thought. Perhaps they were getting him fit for the September point to point. She imagined riding him, imagined winning! With her arms around his neck and her head against his, she could almost imagine it was true. How much more pleasant than this awful party.

Footsteps were approaching. She shrank back into the shadows, wondering what she might say. It might be Aunt Dora. Then what? But into the yard came Deborah and Piers.

He had his arm around her waist, holding her close to his side. He was smiling down at her, and she was smiling back, her body leaning pliantly towards him as if she knew him, trusted him. Mary felt a shock run through her. Didn't Deb realise, couldn't she see? This was dangerous. He was dangerous. Deb's precious, vulnerable girlhood could be lost.

'Take your hands off my sister!'

They both jumped. When they saw who it was Piers drew Deb protectively to his side.

'Let go of her! Deb, you know what Mum said.'

'And you said we didn't have to bother. We're not doing anything.'

'Yes you are. He's only making up to you because – because there isn't anyone else. I shall tell Mum. I will!'

'Beast.'

Piers was looking fraught. He said, 'Look Mary, you don't have to tell anyone. I won't hurt Deb. I – I'm very fond of her.'

'Huh!' retorted Mary.

'Do you want your mother to know that you and my father danced together?'

Mary gulped. 'I really don't mind,' she managed.

'Oh yes you do,' said Deb. 'Anyway. It doesn't matter. I'll go on seeing Piers whatever anyone says and no one can stop me.'

'Deb!' said Mary in shocked tones. 'Deb!'

It was so out of character. Deb was the biddable one, the easy one. It seemed that overnight she had changed. 'I don't know what's got into you,' said Mary in bewilderment. 'You hardly know Piers! He was my friend, not yours.'

'But you're not very friendly any more, are you?' said Piers. 'You can pretend all you like, don't expect me to believe you.'

'Believe what you like,' snapped Mary.

She began to storm away, but then stopped. She couldn't leave Deb with him. Look what his mother did, how his father had behaved! Their son was a worthy successor. 'If you don't come, Deb,' she said shakily, 'I'll go and find Uncle Howard and tell him to fetch you.' It was clear that she meant it. After a moment, sulkily, Deb came.

They argued all the way back to the party. 'We weren't doing anything!' Deb insisted.

'You would have done,' said Mary darkly. 'I hate Piers. I wish he'd never come back.'

'You're just jealous.'

'No. Really I'm not. It's – Deb, you don't know what you could be getting into. He doesn't love you. He can't. You don't want to end up like Susan Stanley, do you?'

'The girl who had a baby in the village?'

Mary nodded and said nothing. Neither did Deb. Susan Stanley had been forced to leave the village and find lodgings in Bainfield, and they only knew because Laura had insisted on going to see her and they had heard her talking to Michael about it. The baby had been born sickly, because the girl couldn't afford to eat, according to Laura, and no one would take a sick child for adoption. It had gone to the orphanage, and eventually a home had been found. For some reason they didn't understand, their mother had been miserable about it for days.

'That won't happen to me,' said Deb at last.

Mary took a deep breath. 'That's how it starts. Going with boys in the dark. Deb, you know all about that! You know you do.'

But even as she spoke she felt the futility of it. How could words have reality? What was real to Deb was the touch of skin on skin, the feel of another's hand, another's face, the quickening of the senses, the heating of the blood, the delicious, whirling delight. Mary felt ashamed. She was denying Deb what she herself could yearn for.

They went together from the terrace into the lighted room. One or two people nudged each other and said, 'That's Deborah Cooper. Gorgeous, isn't she? Her sister's nothing like.'

Alan came up at once and said 'There you are, Deb. My dance, I think,' and snatched her away before Graham Beacham could battle his way across. Mary waited to see if he would ask her to dance, but he veered off and left her. It was her own fault of course. But all the same.

Someone was banging a gong. Alan was too late, the dancing was finished until after supper. Now Mary felt really miserable. She was alone with no one to take her in. She would have to join the jostling queue by herself, amongst all the men fetching plates for ladies. She'd rather starve.

This time she slipped into the hall. The library door was open and she peeped inside. No one there, which wasn't surprising. It was a room full of light-sensitive mildewed leather volumes that might one day prove of value, so the blinds were never lifted and the whole place smelled musty. She pulled out a book at random and sat on a hard chair to read. *The Collected Works of Alfred, Lord Tennyson, Vol 1*. Oh well. It would have to do.

No sooner had she settled to read than the door was flung open. It was Aunt Rosalind, dramatic in black silk and diamonds. 'So there you are, Mary! I've been looking everywhere, I was beginning to think you were dead. Out of this room at once. I've told David how shocked I am at his behaviour. He knows better than to leave a young lady unattended. And you won't have had any supper.'

Mary was propelled into the supper room, scarlet with embarrassment, the focus of dozens of eyes. She wanted to perish, then and there, explode in a fiery plume that consumed her down to the very last atom. Everyone was murmuring, she could feel their pity like claws against her skin. A plate of ham was thrust under her nose. She felt her stomach begin to heave and clenched her teeth and swallowed. Never again would she suffer this, she vowed. Never again would she subject herself to this – this torment! They could plead and order as much as they liked, but this was, without doubt, the last party of her life.

Mary slept late the next day. When she eventually surfaced and came downstairs her mother was at the kitchen table, doing the farm accounts. She put down her pen and said expectantly, 'Well? How was it?'

Mary shrugged, and Laura said, 'It was all right then? You're glad you went?'

Mary fetched herself a glass of milk. 'I'm never going to another party as long as I live,' she announced.

She watched her mother's spirits visibly decline and all she could feel was annoyance. What had she hoped for? That Mary had suddenly become the belle of the ball?

'You must have met some nice people.'

'No, actually. I saw Aunt Dora in the garden with Mr Hodgkins from the estate. He was kissing her.'

'Dora? Really?'

Mary nodded. 'You were right about them. They're a disgusting family. You must make sure Deb doesn't see Piers. I'm sure she means to.'

Laura took a few moments to absorb this avalanche of information. She said feebly, 'Poor Gabriel. I mean – Mary, you're not making this up?'

She shook her head. Why on earth did her mother have to take that man's side? They each did, she thought, her stomach lurching with nerves. She took another gulp of the milk. They might wish to hate each other. The trouble was, they didn't.

She went out soon after. She was wearing her jodhpurs, so everyone would think she'd gone to see Diablo. In fact, she slipped out of the yard by the field gate, and walked up the track towards the cottages. There were three in all, one right out in the fields, the other two snuggled up next to each other like very good friends. Mary's grandmother had lived in the right hand side until her death, and since then it had been empty. No farm worker appeared to relish life with Sophie and Marie as neighbours.

She knocked on the left hand door, calling 'Sophie? Are you in?' She had timed her visit carefully. Marie usually begged a ride with the milk wagon down to the village in the morning. She had the French habit of daily shopping, and liked to prowl around the post office and the general store, prodding disappointing vegetables and factory-wrapped bread. Every now and then she was returned by the vicar in his car, who then went in to have a long and secret talk with Laura. When he'd gone she invariably went over to the cottage and relayed whatever had been said. The confusing thing was the gales of laughter that always erupted on these occasions. Laura always emerged from the cottage chuckling.

Mary knocked and called again: 'Sophie? It's me!'

An upstairs window was thrown open and Sophie called in French, 'Mary? Come on up, sweetheart, I'm still in bed.'

Mary pushed open the door, picked her way across the over-crowded living room thick with papers and sewing and books and dust, and ran up the stairs. She found Sophie sitting up in her high bed, half smothered in blankets, a breakfast tray at her side and a fashion magazine covered in crumbs and drips on her knees. The room smelled of perfume and too little washing.

'My darling, how good to see you. Look at this dress, could I wear it, do you think? Not too young?' Sophie gestured with her good hand. She had a weak side from a stroke, and her mouth was pulled down. Mary leaned across to look at the illustration of the dress. It was high fashion, with a nipped in waist and lacy hem. Mary said diplomatically, 'I like the lace.'

Sophie cackled. 'You think I'm too fat! You're right, my sweet. I'm fat and old and silly.'

Mary's heart went out to her. 'No, you're not,' she lied, and watched Sophie's face look hopeful.

'You don't think so? Perhaps with the waist not so tight?'

'Perhaps we'd better ask Marie.'

The magazine was cast aside. They both knew what Marie would say. Sophie looked depressed and mournful, a little bored. Mary hunched her knees to her chest. 'I wish you'd tell me what my mother was like when she was young.'

Sophie was distracted. 'What was she like? A good girl. Sweet. Liked clothes.'

Mary tried again. 'But what was she really like? I mean, you knew her better than anyone. And she's so fond of you. More than Marie.'

Sophie bridled. 'I should think so! She didn't take her in. Wash her. Kill the fleas. Persuade Madame to give her a bed, when no other girl could keep a child, I tell you, not one other!'

'I knew you'd been kind to her. Marie told me all about it. Was she really the one who did most?'

Sophie's eyes flashed. She leaned forward, luxuriating in Mary's attention. No one much listened to her any more. 'That's what that woman would say! What else was it? That the men liked her more than me? Rubbish! I was the one they all wanted, she was too cold! Madame wouldn't have taken a dog in for Marie. But for me she took little Lori.'

'Where was she from?'

'Marie? Some place in Bordeaux, I believe.'

'Not her. My mother. Lori.'

Sophie waved a hand. 'Some godawful farm. A savage when I found her. And why not with that old woman and her perverted son? But he might have done her a favour. A girl can't make good in the life unless she's had something to take the innocence away.'

Mary said slowly, 'What do you mean?'

'*Chérie*, you're so young still! You've got to know what men are, that's the thing. Then you don't get confused. Not all men, you understand. If you knew this young man I had, he loved me, he really did . . .' She waved her hands, as if dancing, closed her eyes so the old veined lids were all that Mary could see. She felt confused. A little frightened. She thought she would get up and go, before Sophie said one word more. But before she could move Sophie opened her eyes and said 'The best house in Paris! But Madame was hard. The old goats she used to give me, enough to start a herd. I should know, I got served by most of them.'

Mary swallowed. 'My mother – my mother too?'

Sophie looked vague. 'No. Not those. She had her own, you see, politicians, you know. High class. Always had something, she did. Bit about her. Even as a child.'

Mary stood up. The blood was pounding in her head. Sophie would say anything. She hadn't before because she hadn't been asked. 'I've got to go,' she said abruptly. 'Did you want anything?'

'Some bonbons,' said Sophie at once. 'I gave your mother bonbons when first we met. The first in all her life.'

The front door was opening. Mary ran down the stairs and saw that it was Marie. They stood, facing each other. Mary felt herself colour. Marie said, 'You have been talking to Sophie.'

'No I haven't,' said Mary, caught in a stupid and obvious lie.

'Go home,' snapped the Frenchwoman. 'You should know better than to disturb an old sick woman. Her mind wanders. She – she doesn't know what she says.'

'I asked her questions. That's all.'

Marie took off her old-fashioned hat, placing the pin carefully within the folds of ribbon on the crown. 'You shouldn't ask questions when you cannot understand the answers. I've told you. Go home.'

But Mary stood where she was. Marie pushed past her and went to put the kettle on the stove, moving with unaccustomed fluster. The words she wanted to say seemed stuck in Mary's throat. She couldn't speak, not even to pass the time of day. Images flashed through her mind; Aunt Dora, groaning, dribbling; Uncle Gabriel, looking reckless and wild. Her mother's closed and secret face. If it was only Uncle Gabriel! If it was only that!

But she didn't know. She could only guess. Sophie, Marie – the children in the village whispered about them all the time. But her mother? She almost laughed. It wasn't possible. She must be going mad. She turned to Marie, because if she voiced this foolishness it would be ended once and for all. 'Marie,' she said conversationally. 'It isn't any use pretending. Were you and Sophie prostitutes? And was my mother?'

Marie stood with her back rigid. Mary could see the muscles in her jaw bulging. Waiting and waiting, sure that she must speak, Mary at last realised that she would not. Why not? But of course she knew.

She was finding it difficult to breathe. She forced her lungs to open and suck in the air. 'Was she starving?' she asked plaintively.

Marie slowly shook her head. 'But there was nothing else. For any of us. Why should a woman live poorly, meanly, because she comes from nothing? We were in a good house. The best. But Sophie got thrown out, and after that your mother had to earn her keep. Younger than you, she was. And how would you live if you had to?'

Mary said nothing. She turned to go, but the other woman crossed the floor in a rush and grabbed her. 'I didn't tell you! Don't ever tell your mother that I did.'

'You're just frightened she'll throw you out.'

Marie looked down her nose at her. 'I can't be frightened, child. Not any more. It's her I care about.'

Mary shook her off and made for the door. She dashed through it and out into the little garden, falling over an overflowing tub of flowers. Her jodhpurs ripped and she had barked her shin She ran on, back to the farm, feeling warm blood running down her leg.

Her mother was in the courtyard, hanging washing. When she saw her daughter she said, 'Mary, your leg! Come in and let me see to it.'

Mary stopped, speechless and panting. She wanted to fall on her mother and sob. Every day here was horrible now, discovering something vile. Once home had been her sanctuary, but not any more. Even her mother was a stranger.

But Laura bathed and dressed her leg with absolute gentleness. Mary looked down on the dark head, so like her own, and wanted to sob and scream. She wouldn't of course. She was older now. She felt ancient. She thought suddenly, If I don't say anything now I'll have to live in silence forever. It wasn't possible. Something had to be said.

'Mum,' she managed. 'About Sophie and Marie?'

'Yes, darling? What about them?' Her mother's face, clear and untroubled, lifted towards her.

'They were prostitutes, weren't they? In France. And so were you.'

The colour rose and fell under her mother's skin. She got up and staggered back. 'Why do you say these things to me? What have I done?'

'Is it true, Mum?'

'Gabriel told you. Damn him! I didn't think he hated me so.'

She was taking off her apron, getting her coat. Mary hopped after her, bare-legged. 'Where are you going? Mum?'

Laura said nothing. She rushed from the kitchen, leaving Mary struggling to get dressed. A moment later the car swept out of the drive.

Chapter Ten

Mary struggled back into her jodhpurs. The cut on her leg was stinging badly. She wished her father would come, anyone. But Michael was out with the sheep and Deb had gone shopping with Aunt Rosalind and the boys. Only Uncle Howard remained, working on some papers in the study, and she didn't want him.

She ran out to the barn, intending to get her bicycle. But to her surprise Diablo's fine black head looked out at her from a loose box. One of the men had brought him up for shoeing, and he was waiting restlessly for the blacksmith to call. It was an omen. She would take Diablo.

It was the work of a moment to tack him up. It took longer to find her hat, but she didn't dare ride him without. Besides, if her mother was heading for Fairlands, as she thought, there was nothing for it but to gallop through the fields, jumping walls and hedges. She dragged the horse out into the yard and scrambled up. Sensing her distress, he sidled and jogged, but instead of calming him she put her legs to his sides and urged him on. For the first time in his life Diablo and his rider were in complete accord; they were to go just as fast as they could.

The first fields were easy, flat grassland bounded by low hedges. Further on the standing crops sighed and shuddered in the summer breeze. Mary pushed Diablo on to the headlands, wide in Gunthwaite fields, narrow and trappy once they trod on land owned by other, more mercenary men. The walls too were high and forbidding. She thought about Diablo's legs and winced. She thought about her own frail bones and shuddered. But there was nothing for it. She put him at wall after wall and each time his proud heart found joy in pleasing her.

They came to a crop of roots and slowed to a trot. She stood in the stirrups to see further. Sure enough, the Gunthwaite car was racing along the twisting lanes. She was behind it by no more than five minutes.

The kale smelled green to the point of rottenness. But then, everything about today was rotten and bad. Everything about this year, perhaps. Mary had never felt so sad and uncertain in all her life. Nothing was as she had believed. Her life was a fiction, her own mother was a lie! Why had she lived all these years and not seen it?

A wide dyke was before them. Diablo snorted and shied and Mary turned him away, but only to give him enough room. She put him into a fast canter, her legs urging him to lengthen his stride. Let him not stop, she prayed. They would both slide in and drown. Did she care? Not much.

At the last moment she dug her heels into his flanks. Stung, the horse leaped out and away, his stride rolling out like plaited ribbons on the other side. Mary knew she couldn't stop him and didn't try. She thundered down the hill, into the lane, and up the Fairlands drive. Once more the soft grass verge gave way beneath a horse's feet. Today, she didn't even feel guilty.

The house seemed very quiet. The black Gunthwaite car stood empty and waiting before the steps. Mary flung her horse's reins over one of the stone lions, and then thinking of chills, took the travelling blanket from the back seat of the car and put it over her mount's back. Then she ran up the steps and into the house.

At once she could hear her mother. Laura's voice was rising and falling, hysterical, without pause. 'And she knows, Gabriel, she actually knows and it was you! How could you? I would have died rather than have her know, and you knew that, I know you did, and you said that you loved me!'

Mary followed the voice along the passage and into the small sitting room, hidden behind the stairs. In contrast to the rest of the house it was rather shabby, a family place not much seen by visitors. Her mother's words faltered into sobs. As Mary reached out and pushed at the door she saw her huddled on an old, faded sofa, crying into a cushion. Gabriel had his arm around her.

'Hello,' said Mary. She sounded high-pitched and very young.

'Oh God.' Laura turned her face away.

Gabriel said, 'Close the door, Mary, and come in.'

'I don't want her here,' whispered Laura.

Gabriel said, 'She wanted to know and you must tell her. Believe me, you must.'

All at once Laura looked up. Mary found herself staring into those clear glass eyes, so like Deb's and yet so different. Here there was no tranquillity, and there never had been. She hadn't seen it before, but locked behind these pale windows was nothing but pain.

'I don't want you to know!' wailed Laura.

Mary licked her lips. 'But I do know. You can't rub that out.'

Folding her arms across her breast, like someone in desperate pain, Laura moaned, 'I wish I could be rubbed out. I don't want this, I don't want any of it. Gabriel, I've tried so hard, why won't it come right?'

93

Her glass was spilling on to her skirt. He took it away and knelt at her side, holding her, soothing her. Mary saw him kiss the back of her mother's neck, where the hair had parted to show soft white skin.

'No!' she shouted, and her voice was raw with rage. 'Don't touch her! I'll tell my father!'

Laura looked up. 'He is your father,' she said dully. 'I used not to be sure, but I am now. You're so like him. You don't know how to accept.'

Mary felt as if all the breath in her body had been suddenly squeezed out. Her head began to throb. Spots floated across her eyes. But her lungs reacted, and gave a convulsive heave. She began to pant, as if she had been running for a very long time.

Laura got up and began to pace the room. 'What else do you want to know? That I was a whore? A good one too, one of the best, men would pay anything to have me. But I gave it up, Mary! When I met Michael I hadn't done it for a very long time!'

'Except with him,' said Mary contemptuously. 'Or didn't he count?'

Laura looked away. Gabriel said, 'Didn't I tell you to be kind? We made mistakes. Both of us.'

Laura swung on her heel. 'I didn't know! I didn't understand! I thought – I thought what I did with my body only mattered if somebody else found out! But it hurts me. Always. Here.' And she pressed her hands beneath her breast. And the tears began to flow.

Watching her mother cry, seeing her weak and defenceless, Mary was suddenly angry. This wasn't how she should be! Only a little time ago, days, perhaps even hours, she had been strong and sure. Why was she crumbling? Why was she taking away all the little certainties of her daughter's life?

'You don't care, do you?' she burst out. 'About me, or Dad, or anyone. You've cheated us. Just so you could go on pretending you weren't all that bad. And you are. I know it and so do you.'

She watched her mother flinch, and then recover. That was her, she thought. It wasn't possible to hurt her as other people could be hurt. The anger began to diminish. In its place there was a cold, hard stone. Her mother didn't love as others loved. How could she? She was too well defended. Nothing reached her soul.

Mary turned and went to the door. Gabriel came and stopped her, putting his hand on hers to prevent her turning the knob. 'Don't touch me,' she said dully. 'I don't want anything to do with you.'

'You mustn't tell Michael,' said Gabriel quietly. 'Please.'

'You wouldn't care if I did!'

'You don't know that. Mary, can't you see that if you tell what you know it won't make anyone happy? Not Michael, not Deb, no one.

I'm sorry you're angry. We'll talk again when you've had a chance to calm down.'

The door closed behind her. She stood for a moment listening, and sure enough, her mother began to cry. Gabriel must have gone to her, because the sobs became quieter, and finally ceased. She heard Gabriel – her father – let out a long, anguished groan.

His hands were on her buttocks, holding her hips against him. He moved her against him, creating an inevitable excitement. 'It's been so long,' he whispered.

'Yes.' But she moved like a woman who did this every day. She lifted her skirt around her waist, letting him feel the naked flesh of her upper thigh above her stockings, letting him slide his hands into her underclothes. He touched between her legs and she shuddered and almost fell. He couldn't help himself. He said, 'I thought you didn't want this any more.'

'I need it. To stop the hurt. It's never good with Michael.'

'Christ! All you ever do is use me. I could be anyone.'

'No. It has to be you.'

He was iron hard, but if he entered her now it would be done, and could only be remembered. Part of him wanted to wait forever, to be always in this state of anticipated bliss. But the other, greater part had to be in her, to have it achieved, to know that she was still what she had always been. His.

He opened his trousers and she held him in both her hands, trying to make him come into her, like a street girl with no time to lose. Her knee kept sliding to and fro across his hip. With a groan, he pushed her clothes aside and penetrated her. She let out a long, guttural sigh.

Mary ran from the house, desperate to get away. She wanted to run and keep on running, leaving her knowledge behind like the droppings of a rabid dog. Obscurely, childishly, she felt that if she went fast enough she might return once more to innocence.

Racing down the steps she saw her horse, and he put his head up and whinnied. He loved her. He cared. Her eyes flooded with tears and she fell on him, hugging his neck and sobbing. But the crying stopped almost at once. Emotions chased through her, one after another, unrecognised, unacknowledged. She pulled the blanket from Diablo's back, letting him trample it as he wished. She kicked her hat into the hedge – she didn't care today if she died – and leaped into the saddle.

Cantering back down the drive, earth flying in great clods, she saw the Fairlands car. Mr Fitzalan-Howard sat in the front with Dora, and Mrs Fitzalan-Howard was in the back. Diablo swerved unnervingly, but today Mary was without fear. She pulled him back, letting his high-stepping feet pound the turf, watching the Fitzalan-Howards rush towards her.

'Mary? What's the matter, child? The grass—' Mrs Fitzalan-Howard flapped her hands and Diablo half reared.

'Get off the horse, girl!' roared her husband. 'It's obvious you can't hold the brute. See what he's done to my driveway, and no excuse this time. I'll make your father pay, I promise you.'

Mary felt laughter bubbling up. Her father! If they only knew. She wanted to tell them, just to see their faces. But then the bubbles seemed to pop to nothing. Her throat was full of tears.

She turned the horse and sent him on his way again, holding him in and letting his stride balloon beneath her. Mr Fitzalan-Howard began roaring and cursing in her wake. When it was clear that Mary was not going to stop, he turned to his wife and said, 'The girl's gone mad. But I take it back, you know. She can certainly ride.'

Dora, teetering on the ruined turf in high heels, said, 'She's a mess. Ugly and wild. Now if Hitler had put down people like that I don't suppose anyone would have minded.'

'Really, Dora!' Her father looked shocked.

But his wife said, 'Did you see her expression? Poor child. I hope she doesn't do something silly.'

'You don't count this as silly?' Mr Fitzalan-Howard gestured to the scars in his beloved land. She didn't deign to reply.

Mary was heading for Roundup Moor. Diablo began to tire on the long, uphill climb. She was riding him off summer grass and not much more. She let him slow to a walk, picking his way between rabbit holes. She had planned to gallop here, to let fate take a hand to kill her if it wished. But she would probably just have killed Diablo. Not even in her misery could she bear to think of her beautiful horse with his leg smashed.

Below her the valley stretched wide and lovely. Gunthwaite's dark stone walls seemed natural, an inevitable outcropping in the lee of the hill. Further down, the manicured elegance of Fairlands seemed to her false and loathsome. She thought of Michael's discomfort there and knew that he alone in all this was good and true. Yet he wasn't hers! Her mother had taken him from her. She had snatched away Mary's father and put an impostor in his place.

She was crying again. It was odd, she didn't intend to cry, but the tears welled up and fell. She wanted to go home. She turned her horse and tried to look through her tears, to pick out Long Meadow from the patchwork of fields. She saw the horses first, the shires, standing patiently in the shafts of a wagon. Then she saw Michael – although at such a distance it was hard to be sure. But she knew it was him. Who else would climb up behind a pair in just that steady, deliberate way? He had taught her everything she knew about horses. He had shown her, by example, how to persuade them to give you their trust. There was a pain in her chest now, an agony of feeling. She loved him, as her father, and now he was taken away!

A cold breeze was blowing. As the sweat cooled Diablo was starting to shiver. She rode on down the hill, feeling lost, as if she no longer had a home to which she could return. The intensity of it surprised her. She had suspected, after all. But all along she had thought it would come right. That was the child in her, sure that in the end her mother would banish the nightmare, smooth her forehead, offer her restful sleep. Now, in daylight, with her adult mind, she knew that it wasn't to be.

This was real and could not be denied. But how was she to go on? For a moment or two she entertained the thought of going back home and pretending all was well. Her mother would come home, pale, subdued; her father – Michael, that is – would come in from the fields and talk of the horses. He would see how it was and would cover the rawness with easy, everyday talk. He never lanced boils, thought Mary distractedly. He poulticed them, drawing out the poison over weeks. If the poultice wasn't strong enough though, the wound simply healed right over, and festered in the dark, quite unseen. As her mother festered. And had always done.

A great weariness was coming over her, a longing to sleep and forget all this. But there was always the awakening. She thought of the days and months and years facing her mother across the breakfast table, both knowing, neither saying a word. It wasn't to be born! It was impossible.

Suppose she told Michael? She thought of his face, and closed her eyes, trying to blot out the image. She knew she wouldn't tell. Not for her mother, who had so completely betrayed him, but for herself. She couldn't bear that Michael should look on her differently. She knew he was not hers any more. That he should know it too was terrible.

The horse was picking his way carefully down a rough track. She couldn't remember bringing him here, the way was too steep for his delicate legs. Nonetheless it brought her straight down to Gunthwaite, slithering and sliding on the shale. Bill Mayes was in the yard, puffing out his chest ready to berate her. 'What do you think you're playing at, young miss? Give you a good horse and you treat it like a knacker, and that's what he'll be if you take him down Stony Slide. Your father shall hear of this, I warn ye!'

'Shut up, Bill,' said Mary. He stood open-mouthed, silenced as much by her cheek as by the instinctive, unchallengeable authority in her tone.

'The little madam!' he whispered underneath his breath. But he thought better of following her as she tied up her horse and ran quickly into the house. After a moment she came out again and took

Diablo into the barn. For once, Bill decided against continuing the lecture.

Mary rugged her horse up, sponged his mouth, ears and eyes and gave him a feed. He was as comfortable as she could make him. There was nothing more she could do. All the same, she stood at the door for quite a minute, absorbing the smell of good hay and honest sweat. It would be a long time before she smelled such scents again.

Laura was still not back. But time was pressing, Mary knew she must hurry. She went into the house and ran up to her room, passing Deb on the stair. 'I wish you'd waited,' said Deb. 'I wanted to ride today.'

Mary stopped and gave her sister a jaundiced stare. 'I suppose you wanted to see Piers again. Well, it's none of my business. But his family stinks and if you've got any sense you'll keep well away.'

In the hall below the door to the morning room opened. It was Uncle Howard, looking deliberately vague. He thought it suited his persona. 'Mary? I thought I heard you. Where is your mother, dear? Rosalind was asking.'

'She went over to Fairlands,' said Mary flatly. 'Don't ask me why. Excuse me.'

She ran the rest of the way upstairs, followed in high excitement by Deb. 'You do know why she went! Was it about me and Piers?'

'No' said Mary shortly. 'Buzz off, will you? I'm busy.'

'Doing what? Don't be mysterious.'

Mary turned on her. 'If you must know, I'm packing,' she declared. 'I'm leaving. Satisfied?'

Deb fell back a step. Her face lost some of its sparkle. 'Why?' she managed at last. 'Have you and Mum had a row?'

'Not really,' replied her sister. 'I just don't think there's any point in staying any longer. I don't want to go back to school. That's all.'

'That can't be the reason.'

'Well, it is. It's all the reason you're getting, anyhow.'

But Deb persisted. As Mary stuffed blouses and skirts into a suitcase she bombarded her with questions. 'Is it Piers? It is, isn't it? Or the dance. But no one noticed you. At least, not in the way you think! And you could try, you know. It doesn't help when you're rude.'

'It isn't the dance,' said Mary.

'So it is Piers! You don't even like him! Or do you? I bet you do.'

Mary rounded on her. 'Shut up about Piers! You may think he's wonderful but I don't. Look at his father, and his mother's a tart. Did you know she let Mr Hodgkins kiss her last night? I saw her. She was utterly disgusting.'

Deb briefly fell silent. Then she said, 'I won't tell Piers. It can't be nice to know something like that about your mother.'

98

'No.'

Mary pushed past her to the wardrobe and pulled out her red dress. There was a stain on it, she realised. Some time last night someone had put a seal on the occasion by dropping pickle down her frock.

'Oh dear,' said Deb. 'Well, it might wash.'

'I haven't time,' said Mary, and stuffed it willy-nilly into the case. There was no room for more. She banged the lid shut and forced the catches home.

'Now what?' said Deb cheerfully. 'You'll never get that to the station. Not before Dad catches you, anyway.'

'I'll manage,' said Mary. She went to the window and picked up her china pig. She spared a regretful glance for his faded blue eyes before she rapped him firmly against the brass knob of her bed. He shattered into a dozen pieces, showering the rug with coins. Mary picked them up carefully. In the midst of the pennies and shillings there were two carefully folded five pound notes. Howard and Rosalind's Christmas and birthday presents.

'That isn't anything!' said Deb. She was beginning to take her sister seriously. This wasn't just Mary in one of her moods. 'Where will you go? That won't keep you going for even a week.'

'I'll get a job,' said Mary. 'I don't know where I'll be.'

'I'll tell Aunt Rosalind. Look, she's in the orchard, I'll run down and tell her now.'

'Don't you dare!' Mary rounded on her and Deb quailed. When her sister glared like that it took a stronger heart than hers to withstand her.

'I will,' said Deb, but very feebly.

'Tell her when I've gone,' retorted Mary.

There was the sound of an engine. She looked out, dreading to see her mother. But it wasn't. The taxi had come, as requested on the telephone, to take her away.

The hall was deserted as she dragged her case downstairs. From the safety of the stairs Deb called: 'Uncle Howard! Uncle Howard!' but he did not appear. Mary crossed the yard with stiff, uneven strides, expecting at any moment some familiar voice to call, 'Mary? Where on earth do you think you're going?' But no one called. She had to go.

The driver took her case and put it in the front well. Mary got stiffly into the back. Movement was no longer natural and easy, it had suddenly become a conscious effort. 'All right then, love?' said the driver. 'Bainfield station?'

She nodded. It was too simple. Why didn't someone come and make everything right again? But that was a childish thought, and she rejected it. There was nothing to do but go on.

The taxi began to draw away. She kept her eyes fixed on the back of the driver's head, not daring to turn round. Behind her she left

99

everything that she loved. Before her was nothing that she knew. But even as the thought formed in her head, a car came quickly down the lane, passing them in a swish of rubber. Gabriel was driving and her mother sat beside him. Her parents, thought Mary, and almost gasped aloud. She used to think she loved her mother more than herself. But now she knew she had loved her mother's care, and no more. How could you love someone you didn't know? She had been tricked in her affections, loving what she now knew to be – a monster!

Not the tears again. Not now. In time she would learn to think of her mother without this agony. Suddenly she could bear it no more. She turned and stared, trying to catch a glimpse of her home. But she was too late. The house and all it held was hidden by a bend in the road.

Chapter Eleven

The train pulled in to King's Cross just after nine in the evening. Mary stayed where she was, not sure what to do, and a gentleman opposite said, 'King's Cross, my dear. Can I help you with your bag?'

'Oh. No. Thank you.'

She scrambled up, blushing, and tried to wrestle her suitcase down from the rack. The gentleman did it for her, whether she liked it or not, and tipped his hat at the door. Mary was glad to see the back of him. Interest was dangerous, however kindly meant.

The station was draughty and everything seemed covered with a thin layer of soot. Her feet adhered to the platform at each step, as if it were smeared with weak glue. She had only been to London once before, a daytrip when staying with Rosalind, and they hadn't travelled by train. She didn't know where she was but knew she must look as if she did. Taking up her case she marched purposefully down the platform, only to stop at the barrier and fumble for her ticket. It had been checked and punched so often it almost fell apart, and the man said, 'You've come a long way. Country girl, eh? Being met?'

'Yes,' said Mary. Why did everyone insist on noticing her? She longed for anonymity.

She hurried out of the concourse and into the street, stopping in bewilderment as taxis rushed by. It was almost dark and lights were everywhere, and a warm, dusty wind. All at once her fear seemed to drop from her, to be left like baggage in the road. This was exciting, even a little dangerous. This was life!

A taxi swerved to a halt beside her. 'Where to, luv?'

'Er—' Mary stared at him. 'I don't know if I can afford you,' she admitted.

'First time in the smoke, is it? Want lodgings? Take you to a place I know, cheap but clean.'

She gulped. He might be wicked. She couldn't tell. But he had a round, no-nonsense face and a tattoo on his hand saying 'Mother'. Mary felt threatened by tears again. What was the matter with her? She see-sawed from one thing to another in the blinking of an eye. Wordless, she got into the cab.

The driver whistled as he drove, a long, tuneless twittering. Mary found it grated on her nerves and at last she said, 'Where is this place?'

He glanced at her in the mirror. 'Backside of Chelsea. Takes a lot of kids like you, she does. Runaways, like.'

'I haven't run away!' Mary was indignant. 'It's just – I need a job. I live in the country. There isn't any work.'

He appeared to accept this. 'What you looking for?'

'I don't know. Anything really.'

An ambulance screamed past, ringing its bell, and the taxi drew up on the pavement. A bus was forced up in front of them, and couldn't get back when the ambulance had passed. In the lull, while they waited for things to sort themselves, the taxi driver turned round and stared at his passenger. As usual, Mary blushed.

'Always had those marks, have you?' he asked with interest. She nodded. 'London's the best place then,' he went on. 'You can make something here. A career, like. No point sitting at home wishing you was pretty.'

She gulped. 'That's what I thought.'

'Right, then. Get anything to start off, waitress, cinema. But keep out of the clubs. Only one sort of girl works there, know what I mean?'

'Yes.'

'Get yourself to night school. Learn typing and that. In a few years' time you could be in a nice little office.'

The bus wheezed its way back into the road. The taxi driver followed, making rude gestures to the hooting motorists behind. But he continued his homespun advice. 'Keep clear of shop work. Ruins your legs. And hotels. Slave labour that is, let the foreigners do it, it's all they're fit for.'

Mary tried not to giggle. 'But waitressing's all right?'

'What? Oh, yeah. But not at Lyons, you don't get no tips. Go somewhere smart. Right. We're here. Three and six that is, but let's say three bob, since you're strapped.'

'Thank you very much.'

She paid and got out, waiting in vain for the driver to carry her suitcase. When he made no move she hauled it out herself. It was very hard to know when to be a lady and when not, she thought distractedly. She looked up at the building before her, large, gloomy, with peeling paint. 'Wait!' She rapped on the driver's window. He opened it. 'What shall I say?'

'You want a room. Say you've been recommended. Her name's Mrs Harris.'

'Harris. Thank you. Thank you very much.'

When he had gone she stood on the pavement and watched the traffic stirring the litter. Further down the street, two women in silk dresses were walking with their escorts, all four of them laughing wildly. They were going somewhere for the evening, thought Mary enviously. They only had to think about fun.

She turned and looked again at the house. The front door was rotting in one corner, but the bell push was polished brass. Now it was almost dark. She should have asked the taxi to wait. Suppose this Mrs Harris said no?

She pressed the bell. After a moment an upstairs window was flung up and someone yelled, 'Doreen? Is that you?'

Mary stepped back. 'I wanted Mrs Harris.'

'Oh.' The window closed. Mary pressed the bell once more, and then again. Just as she was beginning to give up hope, the door was flung open and a large woman stood there, hair dyed an improbable black. 'Do you think we're all deaf?' she demanded.

Mary could feel herself blushing. Why, oh why did that tormenting crimson tide always rise? 'I'm sorry,' she stammered. 'I didn't think you'd heard. I've been recommended. I want a room.'

The woman stared at her for long minutes. Mary could feel the assessing eyes moving inexorably from her sensible school shoes to her Sunday coat to her mop of unruly hair. 'Does your mother know where you are?' demanded the woman.

But Mary was ready for this. 'She's dead,' she said promptly. 'That's why I'm in London. My dad's gone to pieces and there's nothing at home.'

She imagined the pitiful scene. It almost moved her. She drooped perceptibly and Mrs Harris, convinced, held wide the door. 'Third floor front,' she declared. 'Pound a week, that doesn't include linen, that's an extra shilling and a shilling a wash. No cooking in your room, if you want to eat in you ask me and I see if I can spare the kitchen. Gas is charged by the five minutes. There's a meter. Sixpences. Don't ask me for change.'

'No. I won't.' Mary followed her across the hall drugget and up the stairs. The place smelled of bleach and floor polish.

'No young men, obviously, and don't think of asking me to make an exception. I don't believe in brothers, miss, and that's a fact. Bathroom's here—' She flung wide a door on to a damp and chilly room '—and I don't provide towels. No more than twenty minutes a bath please. Hot water's from the Ascot. There's a meter.'

Mary was panting now, the heavy case bumping her legs as they mounted the third flight of stairs. Mrs Harris pushed open the final door. A room, a bed, a cupboard. There was a small rug on the floor and one small window. 'Cold in winter, hot in summer,' said Mrs Harris matter-of-factly. 'Because it's under the roof. If you stay long enough I'll consider moving you.'

'It's very nice,' said Mary in a rush. 'Very clean. Thank you.'

Mrs Harris smiled. 'Nice to have someone who appreciates it,' she said smugly. 'Rent in advance, please.'

As the door closed behind her Mary sank thankfully on to the bed. She was unbearably tired, and for once felt nothing but relief. She was safe here, for a little while at least. She could rest. Outside and far below the buses roared past in the busy street, while on the roof and clearly audible city sparrows and starlings stamped and squabbled. She was very hungry, and thirsty too. Perhaps she should go out to find somewhere to eat. But she couldn't face the world again tonight.

There was a peremptory knock on the door. She froze, suddenly wary. Mrs Harris? 'Who is it?' she called nervously.

The door opened at once. Two girls stood there, one small and blonde, the other tall with a dark, stylish bob. 'I'm Angie,' said the small one.

'And I'm Jane,' said the other. 'We heard you arrive. I know her speech off by heart, but the only bit you need bother with is the one about food. She's frantic about dirt, you know, so if she finds a crumb you're out. Hungry, are you?'

Mary thought of lying. But there wasn't any point. 'Yes,' she admitted.

Angie said, 'Knew it. Come to my room, we've got cocoa and biscuits. We'll show you how it works.'

Mary scrambled off the bed. For a second the room swam about her and the girls' faces seemed bizarre and threatening. She blinked and steadied herself against the door. 'You are in a bad way,' said Jane. 'How long since you ate anything?'

'Breakfast,' admitted Mary. 'There was a buffet on the train, but I wasn't sure about leaving my bag.'

'Well, come on,' said Angie encouragingly, sliding what Mary hoped was a friendly hand beneath her arm. 'Let's see what we can find.'

She was whisked down the stairs into a room much like her own, except that it was large enough for two beds and two cupboards. Angie spread a newspaper on one of the beds while Jane rummaged behind a cupboard. She emerged with two biscuit tins and proceeded to remove a primus stove from one and cocoa, sugar and tinned milk from the other. While Angie spread meat paste on to crackers, the newspaper catching every morsel, Jane rigged up the primus in the biscuit tin and proceeded to boil up a glutinous mixture of water and tinned milk. Mary began to feel sick.

'Have you been here long?' she asked awkwardly.

'Six months,' said Jane. 'It's OK really. As long as you're clean, clean, CLEAN she's nice to you. Some places are much worse. Rats and stuff.'

Angie spread another sheet of paper across Mary's knees and

handed her a cracker. Mary nibbled cautiously, but her stomach subsided and she was hungry again. Starving, in fact. She was four crackers down when she realised neither girl had eaten anything.

'I can't have it all,' she said, suddenly guilty.

'You look as if you need it,' said Jane. 'Why did you run away?'

'I didn't!' But the blush was starting again. She ducked her head. 'It's not – I can't tell you.'

No one said anything. Jane made three mugs of oversweet cocoa and they all sat sipping. 'I'm going to need a job,' said Mary shyly.

'Can you type?'

She shook her head. Angie lounged against the pillows of her bed. 'Then it's waitress, shop or hotel. What's it to be?'

'She'll only get hotel,' said Jane. 'No experience.'

'The taxi driver said hotels were only for foreigners.'

'Well, they do get a lot. Dolores downstairs works for one. You get meals sometimes. She doesn't think it's so bad.'

Mary said nothing. She had barely thought what she would do, except for a vague idea of tripping down the street in a smart suit and high heels. Angie reached out and squeezed her arm. 'Don't worry,' she said. 'It's not as bad as all that. You can always go home.'

'I can't. Really, I can't. My – my mother's dead.'

The girls exchanged a look. A moment later Jane began to pack up the primus stove and Angie to fold the newspaper. Mary stood up. The girls had administered their casual kindness and now it was time for her to go.

The house woke early. At six Mrs Harris began cleaning the stairs, starting at Mary's door, and by six-thirty the first of the girls was leaving for work. Mary watched her from the window as the front door slammed and she walked off down the road, pigeon toed in black shoes, black skirt and white blouse. Was this Dolores? She looked like the vicar's cleaning lady.

She crawled back into bed, so much more familiar than it had seemed last night, but still strange. Before she could stop herself her mind had leaped from the vicar and his cleaner to Gunthwaite. What would her room be like now? She thought of the sunlight dappling the ceiling and the cockerels crowing. She buried her face in the pillow.

By half-past eight, everyone was up and about. Mary waited and waited, peeping out now and then to see if the bathroom was free. Whenever it was and she returned for her spongebag, by the time she came out the bathroom door was closed again. Eventually, desperate to use the lavatory, she went and sat on the stairs right outside.

The occupant was Angie. When she saw Mary she grinned. 'You look better today. Look, I'm off at quarter past. If you're ready by then I'll take you to the end of the road. Show you where to get a coffee.'

But Mary wasn't a natural intimate. She said, 'It's all right, thanks. I'm sure I'll manage. I'll buy some crackers and stuff. To make up.' Then she dived into the bathroom.

She left the house just before ten, dressed in a plain blue skirt and cream school blouse. Peering at herself in the bathroom mirror, she wondered if she looked very young. Suppose everyone knew she had run away? So far no one had been fooled, with the exception of Mrs Harris, and Mary doubted that she cared. People seemed to take one look at her and assume. She decided it was best to offer a story before they had time to imagine anything.

She slipped cautiously out of the house. To her surprise the air felt warm, and smelled of city dust. The cold, grim cleanliness of the boarding house had insulated her against the world outside to the extent almost of making her forget it. She hurried down the road, trying to look purposeful in case someone was looking. But no one was. In this great city, she was lucky to have found anyone to care.

There was a little shop on the corner where an Italian man sold coffee and hot doughnuts. The cups were tiny, but there didn't seem to be anything else to buy. She went to sit on a stool, taking an incautious sip, discovering that this coffee was hot as hell and strong as vinegar. It was nothing like the sort she drank at home! Her stomach knotted and she took a bite of the doughnut. Then she discovered that if she took alternate bites of the doughnut and sips of the coffee things weren't too bad at all.

When she finished and returned her cup to the counter, as she had seen others do, the man said, 'Too strong for you, eh? How you going to be a big girl if you don't drink good coffee?' And Mary blushed to the roots of her hair.

But she felt strangely exhilarated afterwards. She had only left home yesterday and she had a bed and some acquaintances, and had drunk strong coffee. She walked and walked, looking at everything, excited and impressed. So many tall buildings, so much traffic, and people of all kinds. In one street the shop windows held nothing but single items, an elegant bag, a diamond necklace, a glove, while in another the windows teemed with lengths of fabric or carpet or cups tumbled anyhow on a rug. Elegant mannequins appeared to loiter realistically behind glass, when in Bainfield they always looked risibly artificial. She gazed for long minutes at one in a blue afternoon frock. Laura would say it was too old for her, she thought gloomily. But then she remembered. Who cared what her mother thought?

Yet again Gunthwaite intruded. They would be worried. Her mother deserved to be but not Michael. At the end of the street a kiosk was selling postcards and she bought one of the Tower of London, and then went back and changed it for a view from Box Hill. She would write just a line, telling them she was safe. That would be all.

After a while, and feeling that she was walking in circles, Mary asked the way to Selfridges. A vague memory lingered from years ago, when Aunt Rosalind had thought to show her nieces the sights. 'If a girl must work in a shop it might as well be Selfridges,' she had said. 'If a girl has to serve, let her learn to serve well.'

But now, wandering down the aisles, up the brass-banistered staircases, through the softly carpeted fashion departments and book rooms, she was overwhelmed.

Her feet were aching. In the furniture department she sat on a sofa for as long as she dared, but the assistants started staring. She moved to the powder room, and sat in a cubicle for ten minutes, thinking how nice it was to be out of sight. When she emerged and saw herself in the huge mirrors above the basins, she felt the usual dimming of her spirits. She looked like a schoolgirl; her face was grimy; her hair was a mass of unruly curls.

The cloakroom attendant was polishing taps. 'Excuse me,' ventured Mary, 'do you think I could get a job in the store?'

The woman glanced at her. 'You can try, love' she said disinterestedly. 'Personnel, top floor.'

'Thank you.'

She checked her fingernails and pulled at her hair. But she never looked better with primping. She went out to the lifts and stood nervously waiting for the one that went up to the floor above. Two staff members joined her, a black-suited gentleman and a girl in a grey suit. Beside them she knew she looked foolish.

When at last the lift came no one spoke. All three stood in silence, until, as the doors opened, Mary blurted, 'I was looking for Personnel.'

'I take it you want a job?' The man stopped and looked down his nose at her.

'Yes.'

'You know you're wasting your time? But if you must. The door at the end.'

He walked off. The woman in the grey suit, who had stopped to listen, said, 'He's right you know. We don't take anyone without references. And I don't think—'

'I see.' The blush was starting again. The longer she stood there the more people stared. No one looked in the least friendly. She looked down the hall towards the end door. It looked forbidding, like the wall of a fort. As the woman in the grey suit walked away, Mary stepped back into the lift and escaped.

Her retreat was a mistake. In a place like this to drop your defences just once meant that doubt and uncertainty rushed in. Suddenly everywhere looked unwelcoming. She went to a tea shop and failed to attract a waitress's attention, so she came out again and bought a chocolate bar from a kiosk instead. She stood for ten minutes outside a big hotel, trying to summon the courage to go in, and the doorman crossed the road and said, 'It's time you hopped it, my girl. You should have better things to do than hang around street corners. Take yourself off, now.'

So she went to the park. Pigeons eyed her speculatively, but she had nothing to eat. She sat on a bench but a tramp came and sat on the other end so she got up and walked on. When next she sat down there were two women nearby, talking while their children played on the grass. Mary took out her postcard and wrote, 'I have a job and somewhere to stay. Please don't worry. Mary.' But she didn't have a stamp, and spent the next hour following misdirections to a Post Office.

It was four in the afternoon. She was terribly hungry again. She made her way tentatively back to the cafe of this morning, and the friendly Italian, but he only served cakes. She ate two and drank two more coffees. They were so strong they made spots float before her eyes.

The Italian was busy polishing cups and reading the racing form. She wished he would talk to her – or at least that someone would. Not having anyone know you was by turns terrifying and liberating. She supposed this was freedom. If she floated like a balloon or fell like a stone, it was all the same to the unknown, passing faces.

When she left the cafe she walked slowly back to the boarding house. The key was on a string inside the letter box, and as she fumbled for it the door opened from within. A dark girl stood there, the girl she had seen this morning. 'Excuse,' she said shyly, dropping her eyes. 'You are new. Welcome.'

'Thank you.' Mary tried to smile. It was difficult, her face felt stiff. She had not smiled in hours. 'Are you Dolores?' she asked.

'*Sí*. I work at hotel. But I am finished.'

'Did you do something wrong?'

Dolores smiled and shook her head. 'No. For today I am finished, only.'

'Oh. I see.'

Dolores smiled again and moved towards her room under the stairs. Mary wanted nothing so much as to scuttle up to her own bare sanctuary. But she said abruptly, 'Dolores—'

'*Sí?*' The wide, foreign smile.

108

'Could I work at the hotel? Angie said they give you meals and if there was something I could do—'

Dolores put her hand to her face. 'But it is not good job. Hard. No money.'

'I'm sure they must pay you something! Could I, Dolores?'

The woman sighed. 'Come and see,' she said. 'Tomorrow at half past six. They no like if late.'

Mary nodded. 'All right. Thanks.'

She retreated back upstairs to her bedroom and lay on the bed, feeling her heart pound erratically and her stomach lurch. Miserable tears trickled from the corners of her eyes into the pillow. If only she could go home. If only everything could be like before. But there was no going back.

When she felt better she sat up and counted her money. So much had gone, already. And yet she had done nothing, eaten hardly at all.

When Angie and Jane rapped on the door and asked if she wanted to come out for pie and chips, although her stomach groaned in protest she said, 'No thanks. I had something before.' Then she went to the door as they ran downstairs and heard Angie say, 'Really, that girl! She thinks we're going to white slave her.'

Jane said, 'With her face? They'd have to be desperate.' And they both laughed.

Mary slept badly that night. It was partly hunger, partly nerves in case she didn't wake in time to go out with Dolores. She got out of bed at half-past five and went down for a bath, but her sixpence only gave her a few inches of tepid water and she couldn't afford more. She stood at the mirror brushing her hair into a neat bun at the base of her neck. It was a style she hated usually, since it showed her marks in stark clarity. But vanity took second place today.

She only had one suitable shirt, a white riding blouse that was fraying at the collar. Teamed with her blue skirt she looked plain and poor – like Dolores, in fact. What would happen if she didn't get a job? What would become of her? She stood in her bedroom, listening to Mrs Harris clumping on the stairs, and knew that if this came to nothing she simply did not know what she would do.

She was at the door waiting when Dolores came out of her room. The other girl looked surprised. 'I did not think you would come,' she confessed. 'You're sure?'

'Yes,' said Mary. Together they went out into the early-morning street.

The hotel was The Meridian, an unglamorous place much used by businessmen. Dolores took Mary through a back door, past overflowing rubbish bins and two of the young chefs, smoking. 'Christ Almighty!' said one to the other. 'These girls get worse.'

'Right pair of dogs,' replied his friend.

Mary stopped, her hackles rising, but Dolores grabbed her arm and hurried her past. 'They are always rude,' she muttered. 'It is best not to notice.'

The kitchen itself smelled of hot fat and too little ventilation. Badly washed pans stood around on perfunctorily wiped surfaces, but Mary would have given anything for some bacon, or even some of the burned toast she could see lying discarded on the side. She was so hungry! If she didn't eat soon she thought she might collapse and die. They said you could survive for weeks without food, but she felt sick and shaky and her head seemed full of stones.

Beyond the kitchen was the housekeeper's domain. 'This is the household,' explained Dolores. Mary looked critically about. Clean and dirty linen was piled up everywhere, and a harassed black woman was sorting items for the laundry. 'Isn't it ready yet, Rita?' yelled a woman's voice. 'They're coming at half-past seven!'

Rita rolled her eyes at the two girls. 'She knew that last night,' she confided. 'She just don't say. She like me to be in trouble, that's all.'

Dolores nodded and whispered to Mary, 'It's Mrs Sweet. The housekeeper.'

Mrs Sweet appeared out of the inner recesses of a linen cupboard. She was tall, well-corseted, and imperious. Catching sight of Dolores and Mary she stopped. 'What's this?' she demanded.

Dolores cast her eyes down. 'My friend, Mrs Sweet. Mary. She want a job.'

'Does she now?'

The housekeeper advanced upon Mary. She had to crush an urge to extend a hand socially and exclaim, 'How do you do?' Imagining the horror, she folded her lips on a giggle and stared at the floor. Mrs Sweet tweaked the fraying collar of her shirt. 'Can't you even turn a collar, girl?'

Mary wrestled with possible replies. She could indeed turn a collar, although she doubted anyone would want to wear any that she had. Besides, if she'd been in less of a rush she could have packed very much better. But instead she settled for a whispered, 'My mother's dead.'

'What a pity she didn't teach you anything useful before she passed away,' rapped Mrs Sweet. 'What have you done before?'

Mary was struck dumb. Dolores kindly said, 'She very young, Mrs Sweet. She make bed good. And clean. Good chambermaid.'

The woman stood back and considered. She did, after all, need chambermaids. This one was tall and thin and very plain, which was all to the good. But she was young. She thought with jaundiced memory of all the endless failings of young chambermaids. She sighed.

110

'A month's trial,' she said heavily. 'Spend the morning with Dolores. She can show you how we go on.'

The two girls stood with bowed heads until their mistress had once more retreated into the sanctity of the linen store.

Mary lifted eyes luminous with joy. 'I've got a job! I've got a job!'

Dolores smiled. 'You got a job.'

'Do you get food? Can I have breakfast?'

'We get the leftovers. We have to wait.'

'Oh.'

Mary felt some of her pleasure disappear into the void that was her stomach. They collected a trolley piled high with sheets, towels, pillowcases, soap, toilet paper, buckets and disinfectant. It was very heavy. Mary could barely push it by herself. She pushed disconsolately beside Dolores up into the hotel, trailing along the worn carpets, past rooms full of flushing, gargling, radio-playing guests. Dolores was on the fifth floor. Together they hauled their unworthy burden to the end of the corridor where Dolores knocked and called: 'Clean room, sir? Sir?' There was no reply. Dolores unlocked the door and went in.

Mary had never seen such a mess. Plates, cups and glasses lay tangled in a shambles of bedding. Something red had been smeared on the dressing-table mirror, and an upturned bottle of beer dripped steadily on to the floor. The occupants of the room, an older man and a young woman, lay sprawled across the bed. The man didn't wake, but the girl, stark naked, sat up and said, 'Christ! What a night. Hello, Dolores.'

'Hello. Meet Mary. She new.'

'Hi. I'm Sandra.'

Mary muttered a greeting. She couldn't look at the girl, her long breasts swinging, her thighs covered in blue marks. What's more her companion's naked buttocks were highly visible beside her.

Dolores began collecting crockery. 'Good night?'

'Not bad. He paid, that's the main thing. I'll give you ten bob Dolores, OK?'

'Sure.' Dolores stood and waited. Sandra got up, causing Mary to blush scarlet and stare at the floor. Sandra's pubic hair was cut into the shape of a heart. A ten bob note changed hands.

'Right,' said Sandra. 'I'll be on my way. Keep me in mind, won't you, dear?'

Dolores sniffed. 'I see. I get into trouble.'

'Why? I won't split on you. But if Stevie comes round, say you haven't seen me.'

Dolores made a face. 'You think I stupid?'

Sandra patted her cheek. 'Just remember whose side you're on, that's all.'

111

Mary and Dolores retreated back into the corridor. Without a word of explanation Dolores rapped on the next room, called and went in. To Mary's relief there was just a man in his shirt sleeves, fastening his cuffs. 'Can't you wait to do this?' he asked irritably.

Dolores smiled. 'I no speaka da English,' she murmured.

The man muttered xenophobically. Dolores began to bustle about, singing, moving the man's coat, pretending to throw away his newspaper. Mary wanted to stop her. Why was she doing this? Surely they weren't supposed to make the guests uncomfortable?

The man swore beneath his breath. 'Will you please come back later?' he said very slowly and loudly.

'Pliss?' Dolores grinned foolishly and began to put some of the man's papers in her rubbish sack.

'For God's sake!' He seized his jacket, rummaged in the pocket and thrust money at her. 'Go, woman! Just will you go!'

Dolores retreated, still grinning, the unearned tip joining the ten bob note in her pocket.

Out in the corridor once more, Dolores chuckled. 'You can tell the ones to try,' she confided. 'Always very tidy.'

'Do you do this sort of thing often?'

Dolores shrugged. 'Not the girls, no. Dirty work. That Sandra, she always want me to find men, and Mrs Sweet, she sack me if she know. But the other – why not?' She beamed happily and rapped on the next closed door.

Mary's head was spinning. Sandra was a prostitute, then. As her mother had been. But there was no way in which she could visualise Laura sprawled naked on a stranger's bed. Sophie, possibly, Marie with a struggle, but her mother? The world tilted crazily as she tried to bring knowledge and experience into line. It wasn't possible. Something was wrong. Whatever her mother said, she had never done that!

Tired and bewildered, she followed Dolores like a lamb. But there was to be no more escape from the tedium of scrubbing baths and making beds, confronting other people's filled ashtrays and unpleasant habits more closely than anyone would ever wish. The hotel had once been glamorous but the years had taken their toll. Large rooms had been divided into smaller ones, and bathrooms crammed uncomfortably into corners. The lifts were slow and erratic, so staff were commanded to use the back stairs. The porters took no notice and travelled up and down side by side with guests, but woe betide a chambermaid who tried to save her legs. They were the worker bees, condemned to toil in long, unseen corridors and up endless flights of stairs.

At ten, Dolores declared a break. 'We eat now,' she told Mary. But it seemed too much to hope for. She followed her mentor listlessly down the dark staircase, passing a chambermaid and a porter smoking and whispering, his hand on the firm swell of her buttocks in her drab chambermaid skirt.

'That girl a fool,' muttered Dolores as they passed. 'He always go for the new ones. You watch out.'

'Me?' Mary almost snorted. 'I don't think he'll bother with me.' There was no point in deceiving herself, after all. Not even a greasy-skinned porter was going to find her worth his interest.

The staff ate at a long table in the kitchen. At this hour great trays of bacon, eggs, toast and fried bread were lined up around the walls, and everyone took a plate, helped themselves and sat down to eat. Mary darted forward eagerly, but Dolores held her back. 'We must wait,' she confided. 'Not our turn.'

So they waited. Doormen, waiters, porters and kitchen staff all came before chambermaids. When Mary finally confronted the food there was little left but cold eggs, congealed bacon and iron-hard fried bread. She would have turned up her nose if anything so awful had ever been put before her at Gunthwaite, but this morning she was grateful just to eat. She sat down beside Dolores and didn't speak or look around until she had cleaned her plate.

The relief was wonderful. She could feel vitality begin once more to course through her veins. No longer was she vaguely cold, vaguely ill, vaguely miserable. She looked around the kitchen, at the fat and angry head chef, the bucolic head waiter, the tremulous early shift doorman. And she considered her fellow chambermaids, their shoes broken down, their manners humble. She wondered how many of them were as skilled as Dolores in adding to their wage.

A thought came to her. She turned to Dolores and said, 'Are you going to stay here always?'

The woman made a dismissive gesture. 'Here? Never. I work to send money to my family. I have a little boy.' She reached into her pocket. Mary found herself studying a worn photograph of a serious toddler. She looked up into his mother's dark eyes. 'I have no husband,' she said, as if that explained all.

Mary returned the picture. The head chef began to berate one of his white-aproned henchmen, the point of a knife resting threaten-ingly against his chest. No one but Mary seemed concerned. The shouting increased, and the pair became surrounded by the entire kitchen staff. Mary wondered if she was about to be witness to a murder. But Dolores sighed and stood up. 'We should have five more minutes. But they are going to fight again. Come.'

As they left to trail back up the stairs to the fifth floor there was the sound of breaking china.

Chapter Twelve

Laura stood at the window of her kitchen, a cloth twisting endlessly in her hands. From time to time she would move away, begin some task, but sooner or later she would be back at the window, watching, waiting. One day – perhaps today, perhaps this very hour – Mary would come home.

The postcard lay on the windowsill. Although it had arrived only three weeks before, it was as faded and creased as if it were years old. Try as she might she picked it up twenty times a day, trying to find some hidden message in the picture, the writing – even the positioning of the stamp.

Michael came in. She turned guiltily. He said, 'You know you shouldn't.'

'But I can't help it. To go like this – she must hate me so. Why don't you hate me too?'

'She wants you to be perfect. But to me you are.'

He crossed the room and put his hands on her waist. She couldn't look at him. He would hate to see that she was crying again. She bent her head and said thickly, 'I'm not the woman you think. I never have been. And this is all my fault.'

'She found out something she'd have been better not knowing, that's all. She'll come to terms. It's all over, all in the past.'

Laura whispered 'She thinks it isn't. I know she does.'

'You don't know anything of the kind. Now, it's half-past one. What am I to eat?'

She hadn't realised the time! She began to rush about the kitchen, flushed, anxious. Hadn't she promised herself, years ago, that Michael would never want for anything it was in her power to give? She had cared for him devotedly all these years, knowing – hating – that she could not offer her fidelity.

In a panic she buttered home-made bread and heated onion soup, sliced a roast ham and opened a jar of her own special pickle, made a salad with tarragon and chives, sliced the remains of a rabbit pie with the juices turned to golden jelly. Always trying to make up, she thought miserably. He deserved more, far more than this. In the end, by her own weakness, she had driven away the daughter he loved as his own.

The tears were coming. She blinked furiously. She had never imagined that her life would come to this again, this turmoil, this inner pain. Before Gabriel came back she had known peace. She had lived in shallow waters, never venturing out into the mysteries of the cold dark lake. She had lived a lie, she thought to herself. But she had loved that lie, treasured it, given it her trust. She wanted her lie back again, safe in her heart.

She set three places at the table, remembering only when she went to call her that Deb wasn't home. She had gone to stay with the schoolfriend she had met at the Beacham party, driven out by the atmosphere at home. Laura and Michael sat opposite each other, she with her back to the window, and every few minutes she made an excuse to get up and see if Mary was coming home.

Michael ate on, munching with determination. But willpower alone could not restore things to normal. Suddenly he couldn't face the rabbit pie. He pushed it aside and said, 'If only she wasn't so headstrong! We could have talked. Explained things. What happened with you and Gabriel has nothing to do with her.'

'No.' She felt again the utter misery of this. Why did Mary have to be as she was, prying, questioning? Because she was Gabriel's, she thought. If she came home and told Michael everything, even that, especially that, what then?

She let out a small, unhappy moan. Michael said, 'She'll be all right, love. She's a survivor.'

'She doesn't know anything! She says she's got a job, but I don't believe her. What could she do?'

'Work in a shop?' he suggested.

'With her face? You know what people are like about things like that. They think – they think it puts people off.'

She got up again and went to the window. One of the men was leading Mary's horse through the yard. She said, 'They've taken his shoes off. Poor Diablo. Will we have to sell him, do you think?'

Michael got to his feet, outraged. 'Sell Mary's horse? What in God's name do you mean, Laura? I'd never forgive myself if she came home and found him gone. Now, listen to me. She's coming back. I know she is. Our good girl's going to come home.'

Laura looked at him, words pinned back behind her face. Mary couldn't come home. If she was honest with herself, if she peeled away the longings and the hopes, the deceptions of years, everything was clear. Mary was Mary, incapable of dissimulation. Her daughter couldn't live with Michael, knowing what she did. Loving him, needing him, she had gone to spare him pain. But somehow, inevitably, Laura turned back to the window. She was waiting for her daughter to come home.

Deborah sat on Helena's bed. 'I don't know if I should,' she said ingenuously.

'Oh, go on, Deb! He's dying to see you. I'm sure he's in love.'

'Did he say so? What did he say?'

'He said – well, he just said tell Deb to come tomorrow, but it was the way he said it. He's awfully good-looking, isn't he? I mean, so American.'

'That's only his hair. He's ordinary really.'

'I suppose he must be. His mother's horrible.'

Deb lay back to think. But Mary intruded, as she always did, just when she was letting her mind stroll down pleasant pathways. Mary didn't think Piers was ordinary. She thought he was dangerous. But then, Mary always saw things differently from other people. Deb felt empty suddenly, as if she hadn't eaten in hours. If only Mary hadn't gone! She imagined how wonderful it would be if she went home and Mary was there, but the reality, knowing that she wasn't, was too horrible. If only she could talk to someone. Not Helena. It was too important. Too family. She wanted to talk to Piers.

'I'll go,' she said abruptly.

'Really? Can I come? I won't say anything.'

'But you can't come anyway. He might – he might want to kiss me or something.'

Helena's brown eyes widened. 'Will you let him?'

Deb sank her chin into her hands. She and Piers kissed whenever they were alone together, there was no letting or forbidding about it. But it was best to pretend maidenly modesty. 'I don't know.'

'I'll come and stay in the field, then.'

'For God's sake, Helena, no!'

It was uncharacteristic. Deb wasn't usually the least snappy. She was starting to realise that she didn't actually like Helena, who seemed young and silly and flippant about things that mattered. About Mary. Suddenly she felt a great longing for Mary's acid tongue. What a thing to miss!

'I'm going for a walk,' said Helena huffily.

Deb pulled herself together. You couldn't fall out with your hostess. 'I'm sorry,' she said stiffly. 'I'm a bit on edge. Why don't we go to the shop and buy some sweets? Then you can walk home and I'll go on and see Piers.'

'I might tell my mother,' said Helena, still in a dangerous mood. 'She knows you're not allowed to see Piers Cooper. Your mother said.'

Deb sighed. 'All right then! You can come. But wait in the field.'

She got up, tossing back her heavy mane of hair. She was tired of

Helena already, and there was another week to go. She thought of Piers with longing. Someone to talk to, at last.

That same afternoon Laura went walking. She took the steep track up to Roundup Moor, partly to exhaust herself, partly because at every pause she could turn and scan the valley to see if Mary was coming home. She knew it was foolish. If she kept on like this, turning at every second stride, she would go mad. Perhaps she was mad. The same thoughts whirled round and round in her head, never changing, on a never-ending loop.

She tried to force herself to walk for five minutes without turning. But five minutes was too long. She decided on fifty steps, but turned after ten. Why walk at all? she thought frantically. Why not simply stand here, watching, until it grew dark? She could stay then too, and listen in the quiet of the night. She would know if Mary was coming.

Her eyes closed. She listened intently, hearing none of the birdsong, hating the rustle of the wind. Her heart was thudding in her ears, she tried to still it, will it to silence. She held her breath, held it until her lungs turned to flame, holding it still. She would hear! She must!

'Laura? Laura, my dear!'

He was holding her. Strong hands gripping her upper arms, shaking her awake, not letting her go. He smelled of whisky and expensive men's cologne. She dragged air into her starving lungs and opened her eyes, panting with the effort, seeing only starbursts of colour against a red-tinged sky. He didn't let go. She breathed on, more easily now, until at last he said, 'What were you doing?'

'Trying to listen. When it's dark I can't see if she's there.'

He put his arms around her and held her close. She began to cry, her face against his chest, the sobs growing and growing until she was howling like a dog. Then she began to hit him, pummelling with sharp and painful fists. 'It's your fault. We were all right. I hate you for this, you didn't have to come home!'

He grunted as she caught him painfully on the ribs. But he made no move to defend himself. He simply stood there, taking what she chose to give. After a while the blows diminished. She reached out, took hold of a handful of his hair and pulled. Some came away in her fingers. She was done.

'I'm sorry,' he said quietly. 'I didn't think it would all go so wrong.'

Laura shrugged wearily. 'You might have guessed. I don't know why I'm waiting for her really. She can't come back. She'd have to face Michael, and she's no sort of a liar. Transparent honesty is Mary's besetting sin. The truth will out, however painful.'

'She's very black and white, isn't she?'

Again the shrug. 'Perhaps. She takes things hard.'

He laughed. 'So did I, at her age.'

Laura stood back and looked at him. His face was puffy from drink, his eyes red-rimmed. 'Are you ever completely sober?' she asked.

'Not if I can help it, no. You should try it. Blurs the edges wonderfully. Stops you walking the hills trying to suffocate yourself, at any rate.'

'I wasn't doing that! It's just – Gabriel, sometimes I really do think I'm going mad.'

He sat down on a rock and gazed down the valley. Smoke from Gunthwaite's chimney drifted lazily on the breeze. Somewhere far away a cow was lowing. 'What do you want to be, Laura?' he asked. 'Nothing? Nobody? You're always trying to rub out the parts that are you, trying to make yourself bland and ordinary. You're a sexy, worldly, vibrant woman. You've lived your life, made your mistakes, learned from them. Why try and pretend that isn't you?'

She sat down beside him. When she talked to Gabriel she always felt calmer, she thought. 'I owe it to Michael and Michael's children to be – good,' she said simply. 'A good woman.'

'You were never bad! Even in the brothel you weren't. You're living a lie, without good reason. Who do you know who's as perfect as you want to be?'

'Mrs Fitzalan-Howard,' said Laura promptly.

Gabriel guffawed. 'Judith! Good God. A nice woman, I grant you that, but pretty bloody dull.'

Laura chuckled. It felt unfamiliar and she realised she hadn't laughed in days. She took a long breath of summer air and felt some of the threads that seemed to have tied her mind in knots begin to unravel themselves. 'I like talking to you,' she murmured. 'Why is that?'

'We go back a very long way.'

'All the same.' She got up and brushed at her skirt. There was a stain on it some days old. Clearly she had been letting herself go lately. 'I'll get back. Michael worries. And I must telephone to see what Deb's doing. She's staying with some schoolfriend near Bainfield.'

'Really? That explains things.'

She blinked at him. He grinned, and for a moment he looked like the boy she had known so many years ago. 'All of a sudden Piers has taken to cycling,' he explained. 'To Bainfield.'

Laura felt a sudden, overpowering rage. 'You pig! You bastard! If that boy lays one finger on my Deb I'll kill you both. As if we haven't got enough to worry about. Why can't your family ever leave us alone?'

He was laughing at her. Gabriel was a snake, sliding beneath her defences, inveigling his way back into her life. She didn't want him!

All he ever did was upset her and cause trouble. 'I wish you'd die,' she screamed at him. 'If you were dead then I'd know it was the end of you and I'd never have to worry again!'

The words flicked him from amusement to anger. He grabbed at her, pulling her close. Her breasts were against him, full and soft, loose within her petticoat. 'You really are a mess,' he murmured. He slid his hand into her blouse and took hold of her. 'Is this what you're worried about? If I was dead you'd never have this again.'

'I don't want it. Let me go.'

'You wanted it enough the other day. And what about me? Don't I deserve something?'

He was hard against her, like a customer, like anyone. The illusion of sobriety was suddenly gone. He was drunk and aroused, the sort of man you dealt with as quickly as you could. But it wasn't her job any more. She didn't have to do this. She brought up her knee in a quick, practised jerk, left him crumpled on the ground and walked down.

Deb said, 'Do your parents know you're here?'

Piers shook his head. 'I just go for rides on my bike. Do you really like that Helena girl? What's the matter with her?'

'She thinks you're in love with me. She's very romantic.'

'Oh.'

The wood was full of small blue flowers, nestling deep in the grass. Helena lurked on the outskirts, acting as look-out, although no one knew for what. Laura was hardly likely to come thundering out of the summer afternoon. And they weren't doing anything. Just sitting in the wood, holding hands.

'I wish Mary would come home,' said Deb. 'Mum's beside herself. And she won't say what it's all about. I can guess though. It was all stupid, wasn't it? Mary said something once. About my mum – and your dad. It was all stupid, wasn't it?'

'I – I don't think so.' He put his hand on her knee. Preoccupied as she was, she didn't seem to notice.

'So you think it's true?'

'Yes. I suppose they broke it off when she met your father. But in the war it started up again.'

'What about now? Is it all over?'

'I don't know. I should think so. I mean – yes.'

Deb sat very still. Piers gathered his courage and stroked her cheek, his hand moving with apparent unconcern across the front of her jumper. 'That's horrible,' said Deb, and he whipped his hand away.

'It probably isn't true,' said Piers, patting her shoulder manfully. But she didn't seem to notice anything he did.

'But if Mary thinks it is! Poor Mary.'

His hand descended once again. God! She felt so firm to his touch. So smooth and heavy. He imagined touching her without the clothes in between and had to suppress a groan. He was in danger of embarrassing himself.

'Don't do that,' said Deb absently.

'Why not? Don't you like it?'

She looked at him. He was flushed and a little breathless. 'I do love you, Deb,' he blurted. 'Your friend's right.'

'But you shouldn't touch me there.'

'You touch me then.'

Her face flamed. 'I couldn't!'

'But no one's ever going to know. It hurts me like this. Please, Deb.'

'Hurts you? Why?' She looked utterly bewildered, her lovely face still rosy from her blush.

'You're so beautiful,' he whispered.

'But why are you hurting?'

Suddenly he couldn't bear it. She had to look at him, had to see. Even as he unfastened his belt he thought, This isn't happening. This can't be. I never thought this was something I could do! What would happen if she turned and ran away, told her mother, told his father, told her friend? But he could not stop.

He pulled himself free of his clothes. Her eyes were fixed on him, a little curious, a little afraid. She said, 'It's like the bull, isn't it?'

'Yes.'

It looked raw, and obviously painful. She put out a finger and touched the tip and he gasped. 'Just hold it,' he whispered. 'Just for a second.'

'Wouldn't it hurt?'

'I wouldn't care. I want you to.'

She thought how horrible it must be to have a thing like that attached to you. It seemed the most terrible affliction. She felt drawn on, repelled and yet fascinated, ashamed and excited at one and the same time. She closed her hand around the swollen pink shaft. At the touch of warm skin Piers jerked, gasped and ejaculated.

Deborah wiped her hand on the grass. 'I see,' she said thoughtfully.

Piers was fastening his jeans. 'You hate me, don't you? I'm sorry. I didn't mean – you should have said no.'

She turned her eyes away. 'Will you tell?'

'Hell, no! Will you?'

She shook her head.

He realised she wouldn't look at him. And he felt better now, suffused with a deep calm. He took her by the shoulders, turned her to him and kissed her gently on the lips. 'I love you,' he said honestly. 'It's only because I love you so much. Say you love me back.'

She looked away. 'I don't know. Everything's different, isn't it? Mum, Mary, you.'

He felt annoyed with her. She should have said she loved him, if only to be polite. He'd made a mistake, of course, he'd known that even as he was making it. But she was so warm and lovely, those pale eyes full of innocence and youth. He felt ancient, as if he knew all about the world and she knew nothing. But shaming as this was, it wasn't wrong!

They walked to the edge of the wood. Deb was silent still, and he was terrified that this might be the end. She wouldn't ever want to see him again. He had revolted her entirely. They could see Helena sitting in the grass. He said urgently, 'Will you come tomorrow? I'll be here. You must.'

'I don't know.' She turned those pale eyes towards him. What was she thinking? 'I might not.'

'I'll be here anyway. I won't – we could just talk.'

She nodded. But still he didn't know if she would come. Helena, seeing them, jumped up and came over. Something about Deb's face silenced her usual babble. 'We're late,' she said feebly. 'We ought to be getting home.'

Deb walked away without once looking back.

Sophie and Marie were sitting in the sun. Marie was embroidering a delicate pattern on to a napkin, peering through spectacles perched on the end of her nose. She put down her work and said, 'I wonder if she will come home?'

'Never,' said Sophie. 'And a good thing. If she came back Lori couldn't go on.'

'She can always go on! She always has.'

Sophie made a face. 'But not the same. Everything changed.'

'Sometimes things ought to change.'

'But not here! Not this. We've been happy here for so long.'

'Yes.' Marie took up her sewing. 'I sometimes think too long. Peace isn't good for us.'

Sophie struggled to her feet and limped into the house. She fetched a bottle and two glasses, and hobbled out again. 'You're not young any more. Have some wine and stop fretting. If the sun shines and there's no one trying to screw us or shoot us, what more do we want?'

'More than a little wine,' said Marie with a sigh. 'We weren't put on this earth to rest peacefully. Don't you worry about that girl? You know what happens to girls on their own.'

'Pretty ones, yes,' said Sophie. She settled comfortably back in her chair. 'There's no need to worry about Mary. Too plain. And too clever to get seduced.'

Marie gave a crack of laughter. 'You certainly never had brains.'

Sophie lifted her glass. 'So what? Who wants to be clever? It's not doing you any good.'

Marie sighed. Whatever Sophie said she couldn't stop worrying. It was like a bad tooth, a constant niggling pain. There was nothing to do but lift her glass, drink wine, and forget it.

Chapter Thirteen

Beds had a mind of their own, thought Mary. Although much depended on age. A new bed was difficult and pert, throwing sheets off its shiny mattress with all the wilfulness of a young horse. An old bed was stubborn and lumpy, like an elderly resident of Gunthwaite village refusing to extend her arms for her coat to be put on, although she was cold and would have liked it. In between there was a legion of stained mattresses and wobbly legs, each one just sufficiently off centre to ensure that she caught the bedside lamp with the first flap of the sheet.

But if beds were difficult, bathrooms were downright unpleasant. Mary had never before realised how repellent people could be. Every day she left basins shining and towels in folded rows, only to confront less than twenty-four hours later a cess pool of wet, hairy, smelly and unmentionable remains. People didn't care about hotel rooms, she realised. It was the chambermaid's job to put it right, and they didn't care about her either.

She began to understand Dolores and her schemes. You couldn't like hotel guests. They weren't people to a chambermaid, any more than she was to them. A little exploitation was simply a way of redressing the balance of power. Anything was possible, short of robbery, and that only because it was a quick way to lose the job.

But chambermaiding had its good side. Work finished at three in the afternoon, and Mary would emerge from The Meridian's dull corridors into a warm and sunny day. She took to walking in the park, watching the ducks squabbling on the pond, trying not to think of Gunthwaite. What would she be doing now if she were there? Lying in the orchard, on the damp, cool grass. The sky was bluer there, the trees more green. There was none of the dust and noise that pervaded even this oasis.

Sometimes memories made the park unbearable. It was then that she wandered the streets, trudging to Buckingham Palace, spending some of her meagre wage on a bus ride to the Tower. She looked at the churches, St Paul's, Westminster Abbey, the prettier, lesser places. She loved the peace and the emptiness. She loved the beauty. Sometimes she felt that she had left beauty behind and would never encounter it again.

123

Weeks passed, three, five. Summer was ending, the afternoons sultry and dull. After the first flurry of interest the girls at Mrs Harris's forgot about her. She hadn't after all seemed to want to make friends. Dolores was older, and a week after Mary started she took a second job, evenings in a bar. Her life wasn't in England, she was passing the time, saving money, waiting to go home.

But Mary was lonely. Some days, some nights, she thought she would die of the world's indifference. All around her groups of people met, talked, laughed, loved, while she moved in the spaces between. She might have been invisible. Round and round she went, in her little daily routine, like a paper cup bobbing in the water and never reaching land. She began to wonder if she were truly invisible, although once, in Harrods, when she touched a vase, a girl strode across and said icily, 'If you don't mind! This is worth three thousand pounds.' But then, Mary looked like a chambermaid in her down at heel shoes.

She calculated that in another month she could afford some new shoes, and a month after that a shirt. Such little steps, and so pointless. She hadn't brought a winter coat, she realised. What would she do when it snowed, if indeed it did snow in London? But it didn't do to think ahead. As the days grew colder she took to sitting in the library reading in the warm. In less than three weeks she finished *War and Peace*.

One morning, as she arrived on the fifth floor, pushing her own trolley now, she saw Sandra emerging from a room. She was yawning and in an obvious hurry, still tucking her blouse into her skintight skirt. When she saw Mary she teetered across in her three-inch heels.

'Hello, love! Haven't seen you for ages. Listen, I had a hell of a time last night, he was a right sod. Didn't pay the full whack, though he gave it me, right enough. You won't say you saw me, will you? Tell Dolores I got the wrong room and didn't find him. You will, won't you, love?'

Mary bit her lip. She had no wish to offend either Sandra or Dolores. But Dolores had been kind. She said, 'I think I'll have to tell her. It's not fair to cheat.'

'It's not cheating, love! I didn't get paid, honest!'

She fiddled with her belt, obviously trying to decide on her tack. 'Look,' she began confidingly. 'It's Stevie. My pimp. He's threatening me, see, he knows I work here some nights and he wants his cut. I can't pay him and Dolores, now can I? I'm the one that gets some bloody big cock stuck up me, not them.'

The blush that Mary had tried so hard to suppress suddenly flamed. Sandra saw and chuckled. 'Aren't you the innocent! Sorry, love.

124

Didn't mean to shock. Here, take five bob and go and get your hair cut. Look nice you would, with it short. I'll make it up to Dolores next time. Promise.'

'You do promise?' Mary stammered, automatically closing her hand on the coins.

''Course. And you know where to find me, don't you? If anyone asks.'

'Why should they ask?'

Sandra sighed patiently. 'If they want a girl for the night, of course. Tube station, Leicester Square, I'm usually there about eight. But make sure it's all night, I don't come all the way up here for a quickie. I'll see you right, love. OK?' She waggled her fingers and was gone.

The coins were sticky in her fingers. She slipped them into her pocket, wondering if she ought to tell Dolores, what would happen if she did. But she didn't see Dolores until almost lunchtime, and the other girl said nothing about Sandra. So the five shillings was hers.

After lunch Mrs Sweet, the housekeeper, told her to do out one of the suites, ready for the morning. It was almost an honour, Mrs Sweet never usually let new girls do suites. And this one wasn't even dirty, it had been empty for a week and just needed dusting and the beds made up. Alone in the sitting room, Mary drew back the long net curtains and polished the windows, looking out on to a dull view of streets. But this was London, and a Rolls-Royce was driving by, and a nanny in uniform was leading two small children by the hand. So much money! People who had Rolls-Royces and nannies would never be thrilled by a sticky five bob.

She left the windows and went through to the bedroom. The wardrobe was a small room, one side of which was all mirror. Mary stood in front of it, looking at herself. She looked thinner than she had ever been, and her skirt bagged in front and behind, just like a char's. Her hair was drawn severely back from her face, but when she was calm, as now, her marks were no more than faint stains. Would short hair suit her? It suited Sandra. She might be a slut but her curls lent her a certain pert charm.

Mary undid her hair and bunched it up against her cheeks. She couldn't see it somehow. It was such thick hair, and so unruly, that if it was cut it might rise up round her head like a vigorous pruned shrub. Ought she? She might look foolish. But after all, who cared?

She finished her work and reported to the household. Mrs Sweet took her keys and said, 'Thank you, Mary. I think you should know I'm very pleased. You're a good worker.'

'Thank you, Mrs Sweet.' It was the first nice thing anyone had said to her in weeks. It emboldened her. She plucked up her courage and said, 'Mrs Sweet – someone said I should have my hair cut. I don't know where to go.'

The housekeeper paused in her endless sheet sorting. She looked critically at the girl. That hair certainly did nothing to help her, nothing at all, she was long and thin enough already. And those terrible marks. She felt a sympathy that was never aroused for all the silly, giggly, pretty girls who passed through her hands. Mary was shy and different. 'Tell you what,' she said, 'we have Monsieur Raymond comes to do the guests. He's French and all, but he's good. You could go round to his salon, it's only in the next street.'

'Wouldn't he be awfully expensive? I've only got five bob.'

'Five shillings, my dear. Tell him Mrs Sweet sent you for a five-shilling cut, and will he be free on Friday? I'll get him a guest or two to make up.'

Mary's cheeks flamed with pleasure. Those marks. Such a pity, thought Mrs Sweet. 'Thank you. Thank you very much.' And Mary rushed off, quite overcome.

To Mary's disappointment Monsieur Raymond's salon was only a dusty little shop. True, the pictures in the window were stylish and gave her hope, but the drab pink curtains and baby blue paint depressed her. Still, she had asked for Mrs Sweet's recommendation and had to take it. She pushed the door and went in.

A bored girl looked up from a doodle. 'Yes?'

'I have to see Monsieur Raymond,' said Mary. 'Mrs Sweet sent me. From The Meridian.'

The girl turned her head. 'Raymond! Someone to see you.'

A short, balding man stuck his head through a curtain. '*Oui*?'

Mary moved automatically into French. 'Good day, Monsieur Raymond,' she said. 'Mrs Sweet of The Meridian sent me for a five-shilling cut. She promises to recommend you to some guests this Friday.'

He came out from behind his curtain, hands extended. 'But you are French! This is truly wonderful! I have lived amongst savages for months!'

'My mother's French,' said Mary. 'I – I haven't been to France.'

'No? I'm amazed. You sound Parisian. Come through, come through, we must talk.'

In the end he talked and Mary listened. It was a torrent of French, a river of homesickness. He missed the food, the people, even the traffic of his native land. 'I shall be killed!' he announced, raking a comb absently through Mary's mane of hair. 'Each time I step from the shop I am nearly run down. Why must the English be different, even in driving? What does driving matter? They want to kill us. That's what it is.'

He paused and looked at Mary's face in the mirror. 'What are these marks?' he demanded, spreading his fingers across her brow and cheek. 'Has someone struck you?'

126

'They're from when I was born,' said Mary. 'Forceps marks. I think I nearly died.'

'Oh.' He used the comb to block off her forehead, the side of his hand to shield her cheek. He altered the angle of the comb a little. 'A full fringe is bad. Your parting must be this side, and the fringe that. The hair curls, but not enough. Longer than the chin, I think. With the curl it will be right.'

The bell in the shop rang. Another customer had arrived, this time with an appointment. But Raymond was absorbed. Ignoring his affluent client, who came here because, as she told her friends, 'He's a genius, just waiting to be discovered. He'll be in Bond Street in a year, believe me,' he began work on the head of a badly dressed chambermaid.

It took until six. After an hour, driven at last to deal with his official client, he left Mary with half her hair at chin length and the rest of it untouched. She gazed miserably at herself in the mirror. She looked a fright, she knew she did. She thought of running out of the shop, but she couldn't leave in this state. What was more, Raymond kept up two conversations, one in French, telling her how terrible England was, and one in English, telling his customer that English women were the most beautiful and charming in the world. He twirled his customer's hair into vicious rollers, stuffed her under a drier and returned to Mary. 'This hair has dried too soon,' he said contemptuously, and made her put her head in a bowl of freezing water.

She grew tired and very hungry. She had been up at six, and had worked hard all day. Her head ached from the unaccustomed parting, her neck from Raymond's endless tugging. But again she had to wait while his real customer was unrolled, brushed out, and finally thrust into the street. 'Now,' said Raymond, and poured half a pint of icy setting lotion over Mary's head. He took up a handful of giant rollers, wound them tight as drums, and turned on the drier.

When at last he set her free she was past caring. Her Italian café would be shut, there would be no coffee and cake. She would have to walk down to Lyons and get some tea there, served by waitresses more downtrodden and miserable even than a chambermaid. She said acerbically to Raymond, 'Isn't it finished yet?'

'You have a lot to learn,' he said, running his fingers through the tight curls. 'Did your mother not teach you? Does she not have style?'

'She has wonderful style,' said Mary, remembering too late that she hated her mother. 'It isn't – I don't – I don't want to look a fool.'

Raymond began combing, giving each separate strand of hair a long stroke. Gradually Mary's hair reasserted itself. But instead of the unruly mop there was now a softly angular bob, the fringe arched over one eye, disguising but not obscuring the red V. And the length was right to a centimetre. No longer did her face look long and narrow. She was elegant. She looked good.

'*Mon Dieu*,' she said.

Raymond chuckled. 'Is that worth five shillings?'

'I'll pay you more. When I have it.'

'Pouf! Mrs Sweet can give me clients. I shall be famous soon, I shall leave this shop. And you are French. You must learn make-up, get rid of those marks. I cut you again in one month. Not so hard the next time. I'll take the five shillings.'

She handed over her cash. She would have to get another five shillings by the end of the month, and she didn't know how. Her head felt light and buoyant, like a balloon that might at any moment float off into space. She often felt like a balloon, she thought. Rootless. Unattached. She lifted her chin and shook her new curls and Raymond said, 'Wonderful! You walk like a Frenchwoman and not some English cow. To the next time, *chérie*!'

When she woke the next morning she went cautiously to the mirror and peered at herself. Although rumpled, the hair was just the same; short, soft, flattering. It drew attention to her dark blue eyes and the hair itself seemed darker and more shiny. She turned her head this way and that, looking at her profile. Her nose was still too long, but the hair helped.

She dressed in the skirt and blouse with more than usually bad grace. She should be wearing her red dress. If her hair had been like this for Graham Beacham's party then in all likelihood he would have danced with her after all.

The moment she saw her Dolores said, 'The hair! So different. Good. Very good.' And when they walked past the young chefs who always made a point of tormenting the girls in the mornings they clowned about and pretended to faint, saying, 'Blimey, what's happened? Who's the new girl?'

Mary merely tossed her head and strode contemptuously past.

'I shall congratulate Monsieur Raymond,' said Mrs Sweet, handing Mary her mountain of sheets.

'He's very good,' said Mary. 'It was very kind of you to send me.'

'Here.' Mrs Sweet added something to the stack of linen in Mary's arms. 'A girl left these some time ago. You can probably make use of them.'

'Oh. Thank you.' Mary was bemused. When at last she could put everything down on her trolley she found that Mrs Sweet had given her two almost new cotton blouses and a heavy serge skirt. She was so overcome that she went into a bedroom, sat down and started to cry.

A man came out of the bathroom. Mary saw the feet on the carpet in front of her, looked up and said, 'Oh.'

'What on earth are you doing crying in my bedroom?'

128

'I'm the chambermaid, sir. I thought you'd gone.'

'As you can see, I haven't. What's the matter?'

'Nothing. I'm sorry, sir. I'll go.'

She got up and began to sidle towards the door. He moved to block her way, a tall man, about thirty, stocky and thickset. He had a grim, thin mouth that gave no hint of smiling. 'Tell me what you were crying about.'

'Nothing! Someone gave me a present. I was pleased.'

'Oh. I see.' But he leaned back and set his shoulders against the door.

She was surprised, but not yet nervous. She knew this room better than he did, she knew this hotel. In half an hour she'd go down for some breakfast and Rita would show them all photographs of her daughter's baby. She didn't have to worry about a guest, for goodness' sake. Guests didn't count.

He said, 'Look. I don't have to go for an hour or so. I'll give you five quid.'

'What?' Mary was confused.

'Five pounds. Take a long time to earn that making beds.'

'But – what do you want me to do?'

He grinned. He had large sharp teeth. 'Just the usual.'

He reached out and began to unfasten the buttons of her blouse. Mary was so taken aback that for a moment she did nothing, and simply stood there. 'Yes,' he said, looking at her thin frame, tiny breasts covered by her white schoolgirl brassiere. 'That is really rather nice.' He put his hand on her naked skin.

Mary shot backwards like a startled gazelle. 'No!'

The man's face darkened. 'Now look here, my girl, you don't come unasked into a room and get this far and then say no!'

She gathered her wits. 'I mean – I haven't the time right now. If I don't go down in ten minutes they'll come looking.'

'Three quid for ten minutes, then. Quick, get on the bed.'

'No. I'd rather not.' She took a deep breath and attempted a smile. 'How about if I come back tonight? I've got you down until tomorrow. We could – take some time.'

Thankfully, fatefully, Dolores' trolley squeaked past the door and some guests walked by, chattering. The room seemed less private now. Mary fastened her blouse again, her fingers shaking.

'All right. Make it nine this evening. We can have a few drinks. Enjoy ourselves.'

'Yes. I'd like that.'

The trolley was squeaking by again and Mary called out, 'It's all right, Dolores! I'm just coming.' She gave the unknown guest a shy smile. 'Until nine.'

In the corridor she felt almost too weak to stand. She almost staggered to where Dolores stood and gasped. 'He wanted to sleep with me! He thought I was a prostitute.'

'Did he hit you or something?' When Mary shook her head Dolores seemed bemused. 'Then why the fuss? It happen all the time. Everyone. If you want to do it, make sure Mrs Sweet don't catch you.'

Dolores walked to the stairs, ready to go down to breakfast. Mary longed to use the lift, but instead walked down beside Dolores, her head in a whirl. Sitting over her breakfast she looked surreptitiously up and down the tables. Most of the chambermaids looked tired and plain, but here and there a girl opened her blouse a little low, or wore her skirt a shade too tight. They had a different air about them, too. An expectant self-awareness. Was that how they survived on a chambermaid's wage?

Unbidden, her mind clicked back to her mother. She had never looked vulgar in her life. If Laura had ever been a prostitute, which Mary was finding harder and harder to believe, she had never been one like this. Of course, now that she understood more, she knew there were different grades of girl, as in everything. It was perhaps possible to envisage her mother in a flat or somewhere, being charming to an important man. But all that rumpled, messy, Sandra sort of thing? Never.

Anxiety nagged at her still. She was her mother's daughter. Was she tainted in some odd, invisible way, so that men – that sort of man – knew? Probably she was being silly. Men like that were opportunists, always on the look-out. But all the same.

Mary was cautious all the day, knocking very hard before entering a room. She kept thinking about nine o'clock that night, when the guest in number 531 would wait in vain. He couldn't complain, could he? She was starting to see that this hotel was only superficially respectable. It was quite likely that the hotel would prefer its chambermaids to sleep with the guests if it kept them happy. If she was complained about she might lose her job.

She considered confiding in Mrs Sweet. But she discarded the idea. It would look too much like taking advantage of her kindness. The best thing would be for someone – anyone – to go to Room 531 tonight. It would have to be Sandra.

When she finished at three she walked down to Leicester Square and stood outside the tube station, looking around. Sandra was nowhere to be seen, and she resolved to go to the library, buy something to eat and wander around until the evening. It was cold and blowy, but it seemed too far to Mrs Harris's and back. She went into a department store and looked longingly at the coats. 'Would you like to try one, dear?' asked an assistant.

Mary was surprised. She put down her parcels and slipped her arms into a double breasted coat in navy blue wool.

'Well!' said the assistant, and stood back. Mary looked at herself in the mirror. The coat was almost military, the skirt sweeping down almost to her ankles. It suited her perfectly, setting off the squareness of her shoulders and the long, long length of her leg.

'Some people always look best in tailoring,' mused the assistant.

'So my mother always says,' said Mary. 'How much is it?'

'Fifteen guineas.'

Mary set her teeth. She turned sideways to look at herself again, as if she was considering. 'I'll think about it,' she said at last. 'It's rather a lot.'

'Worth paying for what suits you, I always say,' maintained the assistant. Mary picked up her parcels and departed, trying not to run.

When she left the store it was even colder. It was growing dark and a thin rain was beginning to fall. This time of night always made her think longingly of home, and suddenly she was blinking back tears. If Deb wasn't at school she'd be sitting by the fire, reading or talking to Mum. Dad would be out with the stock, but soon he would come inside to sit with the paper while Mum made the tea. It was all rubbish of course. She knew that. The whole damned thing was no more real than the set of a play, shored up by plywood and pretence. Mum wasn't good and kind, home wasn't safe. But it had seemed so. It comforted as if it was.

She went to the station and waited. Sandra wasn't there. But other girls were, five or six of them, talking, smoking, eyeing her with obvious hostility. Finally one came across. 'You working?'

'I'm waiting for someone. Sandra.'

'Got a message for her, have you? You can tell me.'

'No. It's just – I know someone who'd like her to visit.'

The girl drew on her cigarette. She had lines around her mouth beneath the make-up, though she wasn't old. There was a burn mark on her arm. 'Sandra's busy. I'll do it. Give you your cut.'

'I'd rather wait for Sandra.'

'As you like.'

A man came up, ordinary-looking, not very old. He talked to a girl for a moment and they went off. 'Was he a customer?' Mary asked.

The others sighed. 'They weren't talking about cricket, darling. You can have the next one, if you like. Go on, you could do with some experience. Like the hair. Where d'you get it done?'

'A friend,' lied Mary. She didn't imagine Monsieur Raymond would appreciate three prostitutes as customers. But in this crazy world the rules were not as she supposed. Anyone might do anything.

At that moment Sandra came sidling into the station. Her long skirt was slit almost to the tops of her thighs. She was yawning and

131

scratching her hair. 'Some filthy bastard's given me fleas,' she confided.

Mary said, 'Hello, Sandra.'

Sandra turned. 'Hello, love. Christ, I like the hair. What you doing here?'

'One of the guests wants you. Well, he wanted me really but I wouldn't. I thought you might like to go.'

'A whore can go where good girls fear to tread,' said Sandra, striking a pose to make the other girls laugh. 'What's he like?'

'A bit dangerous, I thought.'

'And aren't you the connoisseur! OK, love. I'll give you five bob, like before.'

'I thought – a pound. Now.'

Sandra opened her eyes. 'Come off it, love. Dolores only gets half a nicker. If it's that easy you do it.'

'If you don't want it someone else might,' said Mary, fixing her thoughts on the coat.

'Christ! You aren't as soft as you look, are you? All right, here's a quid. Which room?'

Mary gave her the number and pocketed her pound. How many beds would she have to make for a pound? Fifty, a hundred? She couldn't calculate, she was lousy at maths. She went to the station kiosk and bought herself a Kit-Kat, and ate it on the bus going home.

She found herself visiting Sandra several times over the next few weeks. It was the season for business conferences and businessmen away from home seemed to like to have a girl. Mary began to learn which rooms she should linger in, striking up some sort of a conversation. Sometimes the men got the wrong idea, but she was ready for them now. She offered her 'friend' with ever increasing ease. After just a month of this she went back to the shop and paid fifteen guineas in crumpled notes and jangling coin for a navy blue double breasted coat.

The only problem seemed to be Mrs Sweet, of all people. Although Mary continued to work hard and well, there was a perceptible cooling on the part of the housekeeper. On the day that she appeared for work in the coat, Mrs Sweet drew in her breath and said, 'Some people are going up in the world, I see. One just wonders which ladder they're using.'

Mary's face flamed. Did Mrs Sweet know? If so, why did she mind? As Mary now knew, almost everyone was running some kind of racket here, be it escorts, tourist guides, cars. It was whispered that one of the porters could even provide young boys. For a consideration. Did Mrs Sweet think she was doing something like that?

The housekeeper's real thoughts came to light when the chambermaids were having lunch. Mary made to sit down next to Dolores, and Mrs Sweet rapped, 'I'm sure you'd be happier at the end please, Mary.' She looked down the table. Two of the other girls sat there, tight-skirted, made up. One of them said, 'Yeah, come over here, Mary. We like a girl with a bit about her.'

'I – I think I'll sit here.' Mary sat herself down on Dolores' other side, and kept her eyes on her plate.

It was horrible being despised. Perhaps it might not have been so bad if she had friends, but really she had no one. She had come to like the housekeeper's approval. Having nothing else, she valued it far more than it was worth. After the meal, sick and shaking, she went to see her.

The older woman was sitting in her room, checking her accounts. She looked up from the book, her face cold. She did not ask Mary to sit down. 'Yes?'

'Mrs Sweet – I wanted to tell you something.'

'Indeed? Are you sure it's something I want to know?'

'I'm not sure. I know you think – today, when you said – I'm not like those other girls, Mrs Sweet. I don't – you know.'

'I'm afraid I don't, Mary.'

'I don't sleep with them!' she burst out. 'I know some of the girls do, but not me. And I don't want you to think badly of me because of something I don't do.'

Mrs Sweet closed her accounts book. 'Then perhaps you will tell me how you have managed to acquire such an expensive coat?' she said quietly. 'I wasn't born yesterday, Mary. I've been in hotels for a very long time.'

'But it isn't anything!' she insisted. 'At least, not anything much. It's just that if one of the guests asks me to – you know.'

'Sleep with them,' supplied Mrs Sweet. 'Go on, Mary.'

'If he asks me – I say I won't, but I've got a friend. There's this girl. She does it all the time. I give her a room number and she gives me a pound.'

Mrs Sweet looked into Mary's young, innocent face, so confidently awaiting forgiveness, if not outright approval. She sighed. 'Why do you think that is all right, my dear? Don't you think it might be more honourable to sell your body yourself rather than to sell someone else's by proxy?'

'But it's Sandra's living,' said Mary. 'If I didn't give her the numbers she'd have to spend all her time on the street.'

'So you see it as doing Sandra a favour. Making her life as a sexual object a little easier. Why then do you take money?'

'Because I talk to the men,' said Mary, in bewilderment.

'I see. You actively procure clients for this girl. Mary, Mary! What would your mother say?'

Mary was silent. She had no idea of her mother's views on this or

133

many other subjects. Over the last months she had suddenly come to realise that outside the narrow confines of life on the farm she barely knew her mother at all. Had she really sold her body? One part of her believed it, while at times the rest stood and laughed. Her mother, the same as Sandra? Two people could not be more different.

But every day here she learned that things weren't always as straightforward as they seemed. She didn't know what she herself might do from day to day. Her mother might have done anything at all.

'She might think it was all right,' she said falteringly. 'After all, Sandra needs the men and I need the money.'

'But don't you see, child?' Mrs Sweet got up and came round the desk. She put a firm hand on Mary's shoulder. 'It's dirty. It isn't something you should do. This friend of yours, this Sandra, is being paid to have her body treated with contempt. And the men – married most of them – they wouldn't seek out a prostitute. But you provide one. You make it easy. Can't you see, Mary, that taking money for this is almost worse than being a prostitute yourself?'

Mary blinked. 'No.'

'It's also illegal. You are living off immoral earnings. It's exactly the same as all the vicious and lazy men who prey on these girls, sending them out when they're sick, beating them when they won't do as they're told.'

'I only give room numbers,' wailed Mary. 'Everybody does it.'

'That in itself should be enough to tell you that it probably isn't right.'

Mary turned to go, but Mrs Sweet restrained her. She was much taller than the housekeeper, but felt half her size. 'You will stop,' said Mrs Sweet quietly. 'There'll be no more of this. You're an intelligent girl and can make your way honestly in the world.'

'You could starve on a chambermaid's wage,' whispered Mary.

'I can assure you that a housekeeper's salary is hardly the lap of luxury. But it's a question of honesty, child. Women don't have to stoop to the gutter to survive. We're not that weak.'

Mary flew through the rest of her work that day. She barely noticed the beds and the wet towels, the fluff in the corners and the unmentionable bathroom slime. She was trying to make sense of Mrs Sweet. Was it so bad? Truly?

She had a number for Sandra that night. But she didn't go. Instead of facing the by now well-known crowd at the station she went back to Mrs Harris's, and ate bread and jam crouched over a newspaper, huddled for warmth in the bed. This was the honest way, she thought. Forget that in the streets outside there were men driving cars for which they had not struggled, women wearing jewels for which they had not had to make a single bed. If everyone began poor she wouldn't begrudge anyone their wealth, she thought. But it wasn't like that. In London, the poor stayed poor. And the rich simply didn't give a damn.

Chapter Fourteen

For a week or two, Mary was the model chambermaid. She cleaned and polished and made beds so unobtrusively that most of the guests barely noticed her, let alone felt drawn to conversation. Not that she was in the least sure about what Mrs Sweet had said, but she was convinced that it wasn't sensible to upset her. By no coincidence the hotel was suddenly in the grip of a subtle crusade to exclude call girls and everything to do with them. No longer could tickets for a Soho show be obtained from the porter, and even girlie magazines were frowned upon in the hotel shop.

But gradually, as the days passed, things began to return to normal. One evening, as Mary was wandering back to Mrs Harris's, her bag stuffed with kitchen leftovers that she planned to eat in bed, Sandra stepped out in front of her. 'Hello, stranger! Long time no see.'

Mary was delighted. She had so few friends in London that even Sandra was someone she welcomed. Especially Sandra, perhaps. She had that open, uninhibited worldliness that reminded her of Sophie and Marie.

'You can come in if you like,' she said, gesturing to Mrs Harris's unappealing door. 'She hates men but she doesn't mind girls.'

'All right then, love. I'd like a chat. Could do with a sit down too, the streets are killing my legs.'

She took off her high heels when she saw the stairs, and hitched her tight skirt. When they had puffed up to the third floor, Sandra said, 'You live right up here? Ought to get yourself somewhere a bit better, love. Place is freezing. About as bloody comfortable as a convent, if you ask me.'

'It's all I can afford,' said Mary. She unpacked some rather squashed vol au vents from her bag, left over from a function the previous night. Sandra took one and munched, letting crumbs fall anywhere. Mary wondered how she'd get rid of them. She'd have to take a nail file to the cracks in the floor.

'They still kicking the girls out at The Meridian then?' asked Sandra.

Mary shook her head. 'Not so much. Mrs Sweet got in a state, but the management don't really mind. Dolores said they always clamp down now and then, in case things get out of hand.'

'They're out of hand in my neck of the woods, that's for sure,' said Sandra.

'What?'

Sandra made a face. 'Stevie. My pimp. He's giving me a terrible hard time. I need the hotel work, love, and I don't get it.'

Mary was confused. 'But Dolores used to get you jobs too. And you said you didn't give Stevie money from the hotel.'

'I never did more than a couple for Dolores. It didn't help, her being Catholic. And she didn't trust me. Always barging in, in case I didn't give her a cut. You never did that, Mary love. We trusted each other. You don't know where you are with foreigners, do you?'

'Don't you?'

'Take my word for it.'

Sandra leaned back and lit up a cigarette. Mary thought of Mrs Harris but didn't dare open the window. It was cold enough already.

Sandra said, 'So how about some business?'

Mary sighed. She would have to be honest. 'I'm not sure I should. It's immoral, isn't it? Me getting money for you doing it. I mean – you're selling your body as a sexual object, aren't you?'

'What?' Sandra looked bemused. 'I'm making a living ducks, that's all. I need the work and you need the money, what's wrong with that?'

'I don't know,' said Mary miserably. 'I thought it was all right but now I'm not so sure.'

'It's a bloody sight more moral than me standing on a street corner half the night and then getting worked over by Stevie.' She leaned forward to whisper, 'He's always round the streets. I can't sneak nothing by him. In the hotel it's different. He don't know what I get. I can make a bit. Put something by. He don't know how much things cost in hotels. There's a bloke on the desk puts it in the safe for me, and I come back in the morning and put it in the bank. My retirement fund. For when I get so's nobody wants to screw me.'

Mary kicked her heels against the bed. 'If Mrs Sweet finds out I'll lose my job.'

'But she needn't find out! I won't say nothing. And you lay off the new clothes. It were that coat, weren't it? Daft, you. Still, you're only young once so they say.' Sandra was given to the homespun cliché, always attributable to 'they', as if she wasn't going to open herself to criticism by taking the opinion as her own. But her life must make her defensive, what with Stevie and the

137

men. Mary allowed herself a rare feeling of superiority. Sandra's way of life was Sandra's choice, but how much better was her own. After all, she wasn't just getting money out of it; she was helping Sandra.

The next day she hung around in the room of a German businessman, a large, florid gentleman made exuberant by freedom from his even larger wife. She chatted and dusted at the same time, asking what he meant to do in London, had he seen the Tower? 'I have never seen the sights,' he declared. 'Three times here and never. I have no one to go with you see. No friend. You should be my friend.'

Mary side-stepped his bear-like embrace. 'If you really do want a friend,' she said breathlessly, 'I do know someone.'

'What? A young girl?'

'She's – she's very nice.'

'And she will take me to see the Tower of London?'

She blushed, and then realised he was teasing her. She shook her head at him and her curls bobbed. 'She's just a friend. For the evening. Or the night.'

He sighed heavily. 'Even the chambermaids – and so young. My daughter is almost as old as you.'

Out in the corridor once again, Mary felt shaky. Someone else was trying to make her ashamed. But the true shame wasn't in what she was doing, but that she had to do it! You couldn't live on a chambermaid's wage. You could barely eat. What else was she to do?

She went straight after work to the station and left a message with one of Sandra's friends. The girl swung on her heel and said, 'Pay you well, does she? Sandra?'

'We've got an arrangement,' said Mary cagily. She didn't like talking about it to the others. She knew they thought it was unfair. Their hotel contacts were mostly with Chinese girls, or Filipinos, who didn't have Mary's natural native advantage when it came to chatting up the guests. They were lucky to get a booking a week, while Mary could manage one a day, if she set her mind to it.

She went off as quickly as she could. The afternoon was cold and blowy, with no hint of spring. She walked past the huge department stores, looking at the drab sale goods in the window displays. At Christmas there had been animated gnomes and woodland creatures, nodding or hammering jerkily. When she and Deb were small their parents sometimes took them into Leeds to look at the windows and visit Father Christmas's grotto. They had chestnuts from a man selling them in the street, and burned their fingers even through their gloves. This year she had stayed at the hotel and eaten dried-up turkey with people who cared nothing for her.

An ache began in her heart, swelling until she thought she would burst with anguish. If only she could go back, not just to her home but to her childhood! The world had been laid out for her then, an enchanting vista, before knowledge and experience put dirty fingers on the glass.

It was almost dark. She thought about the long, dull evening at Mrs Harris's. She had been there forever! Perhaps in the summer she would have enough to move to somewhere better. Or if not quite that, perhaps she could ask Mrs Harris for a different room. Such a little, miserable ambition.

As she walked on someone hailed her. 'Mary! Mary, love.' It was Sandra, trim and ebullient, with a tall, thickset man. 'This is Stevie.'

Mary eyed him cautiously, to find him eyeing her. She could tell by his face that he wasn't impressed. She stood up straight and tossed her hair. Let him think what he liked! She wasn't going to wilt when some pimp stared her down. He grinned and said, 'Fancy a drink?'

She didn't have anything else to do. It was either that or a cold evening reading in bed. Stevie took hold of her arm and propelled them both down some steps into a small, dark drinking club.

'What you having?' Stevie grinned again, as if he was sure she was too young to choose.

'Gin and tonic,' she said easily. It was what her mother sometimes drank, and her mother's friends.

'Same for me, Steve,' said Sandra, and leaned back in her chair. 'You look worn out.'

'It's just the cold. I'm sick of winter. I was missing my home.'

'Didn't know you had one. Most down here don't. Going back, are you?' Mary shook her head.

The drinks arrived. Stevie was drinking whisky, looking around him all the time to see who was there. Every now and then he'd give Mary that smile again. It made her uncomfortable, and she drank too fast. Her head began to swim.

'Tell you what,' said Stevie suddenly, 'Sandra's got to work, but you and me could go get a feed.'

'I'm sorry?'

'You're posh, I can see that. Classy. We could go somewhere a bit smooth.'

Sandra put down her glass. 'No, Stevie. She's just a kid.'

'Needs friends, she does. On her own in London.'

'Not friends like you.'

Without warning, without a word, he lashed out a fist, catching Sandra a blow on the side of the head. She let out a gasp, but nothing more. Everyone in the bar fell silent.

'I've told you before,' said Stevie in a low, calm voice, 'I won't have none of your cheek. Mary knows how to behave. She don't give me lip.'

'I – I can't come out with you,' said Mary stiffly. 'I'm expected home.'

'Don't believe you, sweetheart. I'll take you to the Dog and Duck. I won't have no complaints from you about that.'

As if she would dare complain! Sandra was trembling quietly, trying to light a cigarette. Stevie simply put a hand beneath Mary's arm and pushed her before him, up and into the street.

Walking beside him, his arm through hers, she felt sick with nerves. He had a tattoo on his neck, only half an inch of which showed above his collar, a rolling eye and a dripping fang. It was there to frighten people, she decided. People like her. Had she happened to see Sandra or had they been looking? Stevie hailed a cab, pushing her before him, and she didn't hear where they were to go. Stevie kept tight hold of her hand, as if they were lovers, as if she needed support. They twisted and turned through the streets, and she knew she was absolutely lost.

'Here we are,' he said at last. It had seemed like a lifetime. It was a pub by the river, quiet and badly lit. She thought of running, but discarded the idea. He was big and might catch her, and then what? He might want nothing after all. She would do nothing until she was sure.

He steered her to a table in a corner of the saloon bar. The proprietor seemed to know him, and sent over free drinks. Stevie waved expansively, showing off, and Mary wondered why. Did he really think she was worth impressing?

He leaned back in his seat, taking a long gulp of his whisky. 'Sandra's a slag,' he said reflectively.

Mary said nothing. He went on, 'Quiet, aren't you? Nothing to say. Not scared of me by any chance?'

'No,' she lied quickly. 'It's just – you shouldn't talk about Sandra like that. I thought you liked her.'

'Sandra? You must be kidding. She's business, that's all. Bloke like me can do better than a mucking tom, know what I mean?' He reached out and touched the ends of her curls. He had short, wide hands with bitten nails and swollen knuckles. Mary suppressed a shudder.

'You need someone to take care of you,' said Stevie. 'Look at you! Skin and bone. Tits no bigger than a sparrow's arse. I could make something of you. Feed you up. Get that face sorted out. A decent paint job and you'd be a looker, legs like yours.'

'What? What could you do with my face?'

'Get you some make-up, darling! Decent stuff. Bloke from the

140

theatre could turn you out a star. Wouldn't have to live off Sandra's shagging then, would you? High class you'd be. Real tasty little piece. Worth a packet.'

Mary swallowed bile. She should have realised he'd found out about her and Sandra! So far he was teasing her, no more than that. He was biding his time. She said boldly 'I'm hungry. I thought we were going to have something to eat.'

'So we were. So we were.' He lifted a hand and the barman came running, a whisky and a gin already on his tray. 'Drink up,' urged Stevie, pushing her glass towards her face. 'Get it down you, love.'

'No thanks.' She caught his wrist and held it. If he wanted he could crush the glass against her teeth. But after a moment, he shrugged and put it down again.

He ordered a mixed grill for two. It was the last thing Mary wanted; she imagined it settling in oily unease on top of the gin. 'I'd prefer something else,' she said, assuming arrogance.

'Tough.' He grinned at her. He was like a man with a pet dog, playing now but at any moment likely to kick it into the canal. She was starting to shiver and exerted all her willpower in bodily control. Fear demeaned her and excited him. She had to stand firm against it.

The food arrived. Chops, bacon, mushrooms and glutinous baked beans. Mary looked at it in revulsion, but she had eaten nothing in hours. She picked up her knife and fork and tried a mushroom. After a while, nibbling, she managed the chop. The food helped, sobering her and giving her strength. She began to wonder what Stevie was really up to.

When he had finished he pushed his plate away and said, 'You don't eat much.'

'I told you. I didn't want mixed grill.'

'Not posh enough for you, I dare say.'

'Well, you said this was a posh place. Pity you lied.'

He choked on his whisky. 'Don't call me a liar!'

'Why not? I bet you lie all the time.'

For a moment he stared at her with real venom. Then he laughed. 'You're a right one. Show Sandra a thing or two, you could.'

'Sandra's been good to me,' said Mary, sipping again at her gin. 'I don't see any reason to be mean about her.'

'You would if you was me. Cheating, she is. You and her. Cheating me.'

Mary said nothing. She stared across the bar towards the door, wondering how long it would take to get there, and what then? Stevie was drunk, but not drunk enough. She thought of Mrs

141

Harris's, and wondered how she came to be here at all. She should be there, in her cold hard bed, not in a badly lit pub with a violent man. She turned and looked at Stevie. 'I've never met anyone like you before.'

'No? Why's that?' The curiosity of a conceited man. She massaged it a little.

'You know what you want. You don't mess about. Sandra said you were tough, it's what she likes about you. She's nice, is Sandra.'

'She's a cheating bitch. And so are you.' But he softened the words by bringing his face close to hers and pursing his lips in a silent kiss.

Mary chuckled. 'Go on. You're kidding.'

'Christ, but you're a fucking little tease.'

Her heart was pounding again. He was either going to rape her, murder her, or simply beat her up. She tried to imagine any of them, but could only run her tongue across her teeth and imagine them broken and smashed. It wouldn't take him much, just look at those knuckles! He knew how to fight. He'd take less than a minute to wreck her.

He said, 'You're scared, ain't you?'

'Of you? Not likely.'

''Course you are. There ain't no one to care if you was never seen again. That's the trouble with girls. Ten a penny. Everywhere. But I'll say this for you, you're different.'

She said, 'If my family don't hear from me each week they'll call the police.'

He burst out laughing. 'And you're a bloody liar! Girls with families don't make money out of toms. You think I was born yesterday?'

'I think you don't know anything about people like me.'

He was quite drunk now, she thought. She got up, pushing the table aside and evading his grasping hand. 'I'm going to the powder room,' she said determinedly. 'Where is it, please?'

'To powder your fucking nose?' he said, waggling his head from side to side. 'Keep it in your knickers, do you?' At that moment Mary hated him, truly hated him. He was so coarse and brutal, a male animal of some unknown species. He was so unlike Michael that she couldn't imagine they had anything in common. Kind, gentle, tolerant Dad and this – this smelly, drunken, dangerous thing! It should be kept in a zoo, she thought dispassionately, making her way to the end of the bar. People could poke sticks at it through the wire.

She found herself in a small, cold, concrete-floored room with a lavatory at one end. She relieved herself, teeth chattering from strain as much as the chill. The window was high in the wall, a rusted metal frame set in stone. She closed the lavatory lid and climbed on to it, pushing at the window handle. It gave quite easily, but the opening was small and very high. She gritted her teeth. Not for nothing had she spent her childhood vaulting on and off ponies. If this was Deb, now – she felt a frisson of dread. If Deb ever found herself in this position she wouldn't have a hope. As it was – Mary gripped the stonework and heaved. Her feet scrabbled against the lavatory lid, and then against space. Shoulders through – her head was in darkness and light rain – suppose she got stuck? Or broke her neck in the fall? But her fingers caught hold of the overflow pipe and she hung on, twisting herself out through the window, hanging for a second with her feet on the sill, her fingers aching to let go. But then her feet were free. She dropped on to concrete smeared with leaf mould.

She could hear voices in the pub. The lavatory door was locked with a bolt, they'd have a job to break it down. She crept away into the darkness, keeping back from the car park and the road, sneaking off down the river bank. Water lapped and gurgled, once she nearly fell in. Damn the water! She didn't know if they were following. But Stevie was drunk, she'd hear if he was.

When she came to clear ground she began to run, keeping on until her breath burned in her lungs. But she could hear a car on the road nearby, and voices. It was Stevie come after her. It had to be. The moon was peeping from behind a cloud, illuminating rough, uncultivated ground in its pearly light. There were no houses nearby. Just the pub and the river and the road. Close at hand, too close, Stevie laughed. Mary backed, slowly but without hesitation, into the cold, dark river.

Chapter Fifteen

Deborah sat on her bed, watching the other girls larking around pretending to be the high mistress. They were taking it in turns, dressing-gowns draped like capes around their shoulders, hands extended from the wrist. It should have been funny. She should have joined in. But, as everyone said, Deborah Cooper was no fun at all these days.

She flopped back and stared at the ceiling. If only, if only, she found herself thinking. But there were too many things to wish for, too many things that were wrong. She didn't like school without Mary. She didn't like home with her mother in a state. She didn't like anything much any more.

Then she thought of Piers. Her mind settled on him, like a bee on a flower. Piers. She imagined his pale, determined head, bending down to her, lips soft and warm like – like nothing else. When he touched her – when she touched him – she experienced pure pleasure. It had taken her by surprise, a sensation she hadn't yet imagined. But for him, she thought, she would never have known. Now, she found her thoughts returning again and again to how it was. Like a pattern of molten silver on her skin, exquisite, painful, yet searingly beautiful. I love him, she thought, and her heart thudded against her ribs. I love him so much I can't ever have enough.

One of the girls came up to her. 'You're not asleep, are you, Deb? Honestly, you're a dead bore. Wouldn't kill you to join in, would it?'

'I don't want to. Sorry.'

'No you're not. I thought your sister was bad, but you're just the same. What is it about your family? Too used to the rustic pleasures of Yorkshire to benefit from a bit of civilisation?'

Deb turned on her side, quite unmoved. The girl gave up, there was no point in tormenting someone who refused to be tormented. Mary Cooper had been different of course, that blush for a start, making her look like a lobster with spots, and her terrible, lanky legs. But Deb was different. Too lovely ever to be teased about her looks, too self-possessed ever to be discomfited. She had become serious, though, this term. She hadn't come back with everyone else but had arrived two weeks late, minus the unmissable Mary, just saying she'd been ill. Perhaps someone was ill. Perhaps her mother had died. The girl went back to her friends, resolving to pay her no more attention.

Deb reached into her locker. She would read her father's letter once again.

My dear Deborah,
Just a note to let you know that all is fairly well here. Your mother remains downcast, as I fear she will until Mary comes home. You will be sad to learn that there is scab in the sheep we bought at market, so we have been dipping again, and I have had little time.

Your mother is too much alone. I have decided to send her to Rosalind for a week or two, in the hope that the change will restore her. Don't be alarmed if you telephone during the day and find no one in the house.

I hope that you are keeping up with your studies despite everything. Although our thoughts are much with Mary you too are our dear daughter and your welfare, although not as pressing at this time, is always our first concern.

These are difficult days for us all, but if we have strength and faith they will surely pass away.

Your loving,
Father

The tears were threatening again. Michael loved so honestly, so unconditionally. He didn't ask for high standards or creditable thoughts, he loved despite the failures. Nothing she or Mary could ever do would make him stop caring for them.

Helena Carter came and sat on the bed. Deb folded her letter hurriedly. 'Is it from Piers?'

'No. From home. My mother's having a holiday.'

'Oh.' It was commonly supposed that Deb Cooper's mother had gone barmy. When she came to school at the start of term, pale, nervous, one of the girls had asked after Mary and she'd burst into tears. 'Do you think she's really going into hospital?'

Deb stared at her. 'Of course not! How dare you say such a thing?'

'I just thought – well, it's the sort of thing they say, isn't it? Going on a visit. When they don't want to tell you.'

Deb sank back against the pillows once again. People did always try to spare you. Or at least to cover things up. Why? For you or for them? It was so much easier to pretend that all was well. At first. But then you built and built on the falsehood, and everything seemed fine, until suddenly, without warning, it all fell down.

She looked at Helena. 'You can't believe anything anyone says really,' she said thoughtfully. 'It's all to do with trust, I suppose. Someone has to trust you to tell the truth, and you have to trust them enough to believe it.'

'Like you do with Piers,' said Helena, always and unswervingly romantic.

Deb considered. She didn't really think of Piers in the same way as other people. He was private, occupying some central space in her mind around which thoughts and feelings revolved. What would happen if he wasn't there? She couldn't imagine it. Everything would be different. There would be no firm constant anywhere.

She hunched her knees to her chin, feeling restless and unhappy. School was no place to be when you felt threatened, although she didn't know what it was that she feared. But tonight she felt as if she sat in a tiny pool of light, and all around was dark. The pool was getting smaller, she thought. The darkness threatened. Quite suddenly she thought of Mary and felt terribly afraid.

Laura sat rigid in Rosalind's beautiful drawing room. The fire was crackling, there was a brandy at her side and one of Rosalind's little toy dogs lay curled attractively on a cushion. All the same, she couldn't relax. Howard, who would clearly prefer to be working in his study, tapped uncomfortably at the pipe he was not permitted to smoke in here. Rosalind said, 'Put on a record, would you, dear? Something light.'

He got up and obliged, happening upon one of David's jazz records, full of screeching trumpets and unlooked for excitement.

Rosalind stared at her sister-in-law's tense face. She sighed. 'Drink the brandy, Laura. You can't go on like this.'

Laura attempted a smile. 'I know. But it's so hard. I keep thinking about her. What's happening, if she's happy. Tonight I feel as if she isn't, somehow.'

'Don't get all fey, darling. Tonight's no different from any other night, except you're here and not at Gunthwaite. You should get away more often. Stuck up there you're turning in on yourself. There's more to life than husbands and children, you know.'

Laura felt a stabbing irritation. Of course there was more, she wasn't a fool! But life was soured by one's children's unhappiness. With two sons leading distant and unknown lives Rosalind could be confident now, but what if disaster struck? She would know then what it was like to wake up each morning with one's happiness dependent on something over which there was absolutely no control.

Howard said, 'It seems to me that Laura needs some diversion. Learning a new language, perhaps. Shall I fetch you my books on Japanese?'

She took a breath. 'Thank you.' She had been about to continue, saying that she wasn't up to much Japanese at the moment, but Howard was gone. Japanese? She couldn't concentrate on a shopping list just now.

She felt so sick. Why? It could be the brandy. But it was probably the terrible, griping fear that churned her guts to water a dozen times a day. It was worse tonight. Perhaps it was the garden here, lit by unearthly moonlight, the unfamiliar trees and bushes crowded upon a formal and intimidating lawn. She tried to settle herself, thinking of Michael at home, of Deb safe at school, of Mary's courage. Courage? She had it all right, the sort of foolish bravado that led her to take on the world. But what of her shyness, and her embarrassment, and her generous, untried heart? Suddenly Laura couldn't pretend any more. She sank her face into her hands. The child she had cherished was tonight beyond any sort of help.

The water was very cold. Something brushed against Mary's legs and she choked back a shriek. It was only weed, surely. Or an eel. Out here in the river the moonlight glistened like sunlight on steel. She sank deeper, feeling the chill rush up into her hair. Her face must be so white against the blackness. If she swam the ripples would gleam too. She held her breath, sinking her face into the water, letting the current take her away. Oh, but she was cold. You could die of cold. When she was little a shepherd died one winter, lost in the far high hills. She had listened when they whispered. His hands had been frozen into the fleece of a long-dead sheep.

There was a rushing in her ears. She was in an eddy at the bank, and her lungs were bursting. She broke surface, gasped, and heard a voice yell, 'She's there! In the river!'

Help! She kicked and pushed away, out into the stream. She heard feet splashing, flailed a stroke. What now, what next? Roaring water, a rock, another. She clung for a second, her fingers slipping on algae, and the men were in the shallows, watching her.

'You bitch!' yelled Stevie. 'You mucking bitch!'

She knew then that if he caught her she was done. He didn't let girls annoy him. To him they were flies, to be tormented and then left in a bloody mash. She let go her precarious hold, and the river

147

took her, and she longed quite desperately for her mother to come and make this right. There was a gurgling in her ears, and the water was tumbling. She looked ahead, but before she could realise, she was gone.

Stevie waded to the rocks and stood looking out at the moonlit weir. The water slid smoothly over and away, to emerge like tumbled bedclothes after the drop. He saw something dark, twisting and turning like a ragdoll in the stream. He laughed. That was her, then. Ugly cow. Finished.

David Dalton came out of his club into the quiet peace of St James's. He felt restless. He had eaten a good dinner and drunk some good wine, but the company had been old and unexciting. He could feel old age creeping up on him. Fresh from Oxford frivolity and saved from National Service by short sight and string pulling, he had been thrust too early into the life his father lived.

He looked about him with a jaundiced eye. Everything was ordinary, nothing out of place. Sometimes, on an evening like this, with tomorrow destined to be much like today, and yesterday, and the day before that, he had a longing for the war. Child as he was, at least then there had been the excitement of the unexpected. People coming, people going, battles, bombs, like a particularly absorbing game in which you were occasionally permitted to be involved. But it had all gone. Nowadays young men of good birth and good education were condemned to live out their lives in drab offices, with drab people at their sides.

What could he do to cheer himself up? He thought of telephoning Daphne. But she didn't seem to like him a great deal more than he liked her. She probably liked Alan better, but then he was good with girls. David was cursed with the sort of looks and manners that meant that the pretty girls went to others, and he was left with the rest. And Daphne wasn't even very pretty. In Alan's book, she was a 'take to dinner if you have to' girl, and nothing more. Daphne could never aspire to the dizzy heights of Alan's ultimate accolade: 'She'd give Deb Cooper a run for her money.' But there weren't many of those about, and none of them ever looked twice at David. No, he was left with the Daphnes of this world, too good to be exciting, too ordinary to be good.

He reached into his pocket for his cigarette case. It wasn't there. Damn! He'd left it on the table in the club. He turned in irritation, striding back up the street, wondering if he'd be nobbled by old Winterton again, and if he honestly minded. What was the world coming to when a man could think of nothing more thrilling than being talked at by the club bore? He was in a rut, deep and inescapable, and every move seemed to ensnare him more.

The club steps stretched into the street like an old-fashioned spreading skirt. Someone was sitting on the very bottom step, hunched up in the shadows, out of the light. A tramp, thought David, preparing to hurry past. If the doorman saw they'd be moved on pretty sharpish. As he approached, deliberately brisk, the tramp stood up. David sprang up the bottom steps, two at a time. It was coming to something when a man couldn't get into his club without drunks getting hold of him.

'David?'

He stopped dead in his tracks. 'What the devil?'

'David, it's me. Mary.'

It wasn't a tramp at all. It was a thin, miserable, exhausted-looking girl, and, yes – it was Mary. 'What the dickens are you doing here?'

'Waiting for you. I don't know where you live, but I knew your club. I just hoped you might be here.'

'My good girl, do you realise how worried your family's been? They're in a total, complete panic!'

'Yes. I sent them a card. I'm sorry to bother you David, but I can't go home. I do need help though. Sorry.'

She was wearing a rather nice blue coat, pulled on over what looked suspiciously like pyjamas. She had a bag with her too, stuffed so full that the zip wouldn't close. And she was shivering, trembling so violently that she was clenching her teeth to stop them chattering.

'What in God's name has happened?' he demanded. 'You're freezing to death!'

'Yes. Can we go somewhere warm, please, David?'

The door of the club was opening. He looked up and saw that it was Winterton himself, the club gossip as much as its bore. This would be all round the City by the morning. He abandoned all thoughts of his cigarette case, he'd have to pick it up tomorrow which was a hellish nuisance, and slipped a hand beneath Mary's slender arm. God, the girl was stick thin. He picked up the bag with his free hand and turned her smartly towards the park. With any luck they'd pick up a cruising taxi and he could get her home!

David lived in a service flat that belonged to his parents. They had kept it on all through the war and afterwards Howard used it when he stayed over in London. But it was large, with three bedrooms, and rather too much for one man, so David had taken it on when he came down from Oxford. He let one of the bedrooms to an Irishman, recommended by someone his father knew, and the third was reserved for Howard should he wish to use it.

By the time Mary arrived at the door she was more dead than

149

alive. The lift was old and erratic, stopping at every floor and needing constant slamming of the inner iron gate. She began to sag, sliding down the wall, her hair leaving a slick of moisture. 'Were you caught in the rain?' asked David curiously.

Mary dumbly shook her head.

Nothing much had been done to the flat since they bought the Surrey house. There were large brown armchairs, an old turkey carpet and a gas fire that popped into roaring, flaming life. David put a match to it, saying, 'There you are then! That should warm you up.' But Mary just leaned against a chair. David wondered if she might be drunk. Or taking drugs. You never knew with girls nowadays.

The lift clanged again in the hall outside, and a second later the door opened. 'Hello, Con,' said David awkwardly. Trust him to choose this one night to come home uncharacteristically early. A girl here, in her pyjamas – he'd be bound to make assumptions. 'This is my cousin Mary,' he tried in explanation.

'Hi,' said Con.

Mary said nothing. She leaned against the chair still, her face and its marks half turned away. But there was almost nothing to see. Tonight the marks had paled to a faint blue stain.

'Christ,' said Con suddenly.

'What?' David knew about the Irish and religion, but it seemed unlikely that Con was having a vision.

'What have you done to her? The girl's half-dead.'

'I haven't done anything! She was waiting outside the club. She's run away, you see, it's been months, not a word, and suddenly—'

'Stop wittering and run a bath, for God's sake. She'll be a corpse if you don't move. Feel her hands, she's cold as death already!'

David stood, bewildered. Con was pulling Mary out of her coat, and the pyjamas were sticking to damp skin, damp flesh. He could see the long, slender back, each rib clearly outlined, and when she turned her breasts were as visible as if she were naked. A flush of embarrassment suffused him. 'Get the bloody bath!' yelled Con. And David went.

He came back with a bathrobe, holding it in front of him like a shield. 'Twat!' said Con explicitly, and bundled it around Mary's shoulders. He began half dragging her to the bathroom, and her head rolled on her shoulders, as if she were asleep. David followed at a discreet distance. Steam was billowing into the hall. He was dimly aware of Con immersing his cousin, pyjamas and all, into the steaming foam. Mary cried out, once, and was silent. 'My God,' said David. 'Is she dead?'

'Not yet,' said Con. 'And no thanks to you. Poor kid.'

Half an hour later Mary was wrapped in the bathrobe in front of the fire, sipping a mug of cocoa laced with rum. Her head still felt cold, the scalp shivering beneath its feathery fronds of hair, but her fingers and toes burned with returning life. Only now did she regret looking for David. He was sitting opposite her, his face the picture of accusation. She wondered if it might have been better to die.

'I hope you've got something to say for yourself,' he said importantly.

Con flung himself down on the rug. 'Give her a break, why don't you? She's done in.'

'And so she should be. Have you any idea, Mary, of the fuss when you left? Your mother was in rags, not knowing which way to turn. Your father too, beside himself, and Deb in tears and everyone blaming her, because they thought she should have stopped you, and—'

'What happened tonight, Mary?' broke in Con.

She looked at him. Hair as black as her own, but without the curl, falling in a shock over his face. Brown eyes, warm as hazelnuts, looking at her now with interest and concern. She felt herself colour and thought of her marks. This good-looking man had seen her naked. He'd undressed her, easing her out of the sopping pyjamas into this fleecy robe. And now he'd notice her face.

'I – I got into some trouble,' she said abruptly. 'A girl I know – her boyfriend got hold of me. He's horrible. Dangerous. I ran away, he was after me, I had to get in the river. He knew I was there, he was waiting. There was this weir – and afterwards, ages after, I got out. A man in a lorry gave me a lift to town, I said I'd been fishing, I know he didn't believe me. When I went to my lodgings – someone had been there. I don't know what they said but the landlady said I had to go, then and there. But they'd taken my money, and lots of my stuff. I grabbed everything that was left, I was scared he'd come back and find me, so I ran. I'm sorry to land on you, David, I didn't know where else to go.'

'You're making this up,' he said scornfully. 'What sort of girl is likely to have that sort of boyfriend?'

Mary swallowed. 'She's a prostitute. He's her pimp.'

'Good God!'

Con said, 'Do you want anything to eat, Mary?'

She shook her head. But after a moment he got up and went to the kitchen, returning with a plate of bread and cheese. He cut her some and she nibbled at it. His kindness was too much. Tears began to fall.

'A fine time to start crying,' said David righteously.

'Oh, shut up, will you?' snapped Con. 'The girl's past it. She's had a rough time down here, anyone can see that. London's no place for such as her.'

'She's a thoughtless, silly child,' said David unforgivingly.

'And perhaps you don't know the first thing about it!'

Mary looked at Con gratefully. He didn't know her but was prepared to take her part. She said, 'I know it must seem terrible to run away, David, but really I didn't have a choice. I can't explain. It's just the way it is.'

Con said, 'Was it a boy? Was that it?'

Mary coughed on a laugh, a sob, something. 'I don't have trouble with boys. My face, you see. Stevie was only interested because I was young and he wanted his own back. It was just – well. My parents. Trouble. In the family.'

'You've broken your mother's heart,' said David, and Mary flared, 'And how would you know? My mother's not what you think she is, not at all! If her heart's broken then she deserves it to be. She broke mine first.'

David gave a dismissive nod but Con said, 'How?'

Mary put her hand to her eyes. She couldn't tell him. She didn't want anyone to know.

They put her to sleep in Howard's room, an austere, under-decorated place with a hard bed and a thin rug on the plank floor. Lying in the dark Mary found herself wondering if Howard had arranged it like this, or if it was the work of Aunt Rosalind. Perhaps she wanted to make him uncomfortable and keep him at home. Or perhaps she didn't like him very much and this was her way of showing it. As so often near sleep, her thoughts drifted to Gunthwaite. She'd have to go early in the morning or they'd phone. There was no point in thinking that David would do anything else. Alan might have been persuaded perhaps, but not David.

She wondered if he'd always been so unimaginative. She could vaguely remember that as a child he'd been daring, and fun. Now he was boring old David, just like his father, predictable and dull.

She turned to go to sleep, snuggling into the smooth, clean pillow. But suddenly the weir was there, suddenly she was falling, drowning, unable to breathe! She tried to scream but the water was in her mouth, the weed was in her hair, she was clinging to rocks, to a wire, she held on but she still couldn't find air!

Someone was holding her, shaking her. That man. Con. And David, by the door. 'Wake up, Mary. It's only a dream.'

'I was drowning,' she said feebly.

'You're not now. Shall I leave the light for you?'

She nodded and they left. So silly. They'd think she was a child.

She lay down again, and tried to remember. She'd lost consciousness, perhaps for only a second, perhaps longer. The rocks had battered her legs. And then breaking water again, finding the air, looking up into the star-filled sky and knowing she was alive! She'd simply lain there, on her back, taking in great draughts of life, knowing that the current was taking her away, saving her and killing her at one and the same time.

She'd thought that like the shepherd she was really going to die. And then, coming up against a little rowing boat, feeling her way along its painter towards the shore. No one there. Her feet without feeling, until she'd walked for five minutes or so, her hands too stiff to move. It was more a dream than many a dream she'd known. Where was she? Dead or alive? Place and time, people and ghosts, they were all come to nothing. She fell, finally, into sleep.

Chapter Sixteen

Mary woke as she always did, just before six. She lay in the unfamiliar bed, trying to decide where she was. Gradually she became aware of a sense of disquiet. Of course. She was going to have to leave.

As she got out of bed her legs felt stiff and barely part of her, and when she stood they trembled disconcertingly. Was she ill then? She took a deep breath, but felt no pain, and yet when she walked it was as if she had to instruct each muscle individually. She felt very odd, at least.

But she had to go. David would telephone home just as soon as he could. They had put her bag in the room and she rummaged for something to wear. Her chambermaid's skirt came to hand and she paused. She couldn't go back to her job, Stevie would find her. And all her money was gone. She'd have to see Sandra and hope she could lend her something, but if she told Stevie – Mary felt herself quail. He had caused her to be more afraid than she had ever thought possible. Everything seemed to be conspiring to make her think less of herself, day by day. She used to think she had courage, of a kind. Now she knew that it had only never been tested.

She pulled on a jumper and the worn black skirt, wondering where they had hung her coat. If she wore that to an interview she might get a live-in job somewhere. Would Mrs Sweet give her a reference? Dared she ask? She zipped up her bag and staggered with it out into the hall. The front door was closed with a complicated lock, and she fiddled with it. Aunt Rosalind must think they were likely to be attacked by storm troopers to put up with such a thing. Just as she swung the brass hasp free and began to investigate the catch a door opened behind her. Connor said, 'Actually, the lock's misleading. You can't get out without a key.'

She turned, blushing fierily. He was wearing thick blue and white striped pyjamas, the sort her father wore. But on Con they looked exciting. She said, 'I was only – didn't mean – you see, I have to get on.'

'I wasn't born yesterday, you know. David hasn't told anyone yet. And you should get back to bed.'

'He'll telephone as soon as he wakes up! It isn't fair. He doesn't have the right.'

He moved from the doorway and took hold of her bag. 'You need to eat. I've never seen a girl so thin. You've got an hour or so, he never wakes before eight.'

'I'm not hungry. Please. I've got to go.'

'But I've not got to let you.'

She remained by the door, looking speculatively at the lock, then eyeing the telephone. He chuckled. 'You don't give up, I see. Look, I don't care whether you go home or not, but you'll not get to the street as you are. Admit it, you feel bad.'

'I feel odd,' she admitted. 'If I had some coffee—'

'I make brilliant coffee. Coffee and toast, and then see?'

She nodded.

He made bacon and eggs as well as coffee and toast. Mary sat on a hard kitchen chair, but after a while, feeling disorientated, she slid to the floor and leaned against the wall. Con fetched a blanket and wrapped it around her, dispassionate, practical. He handed her cups and plates, and she ate and drank from her blanket nest, curled by the wall. Her eyelids felt heavy. She couldn't eat the toast. She allowed herself to doze, thinking that in a moment she would get up and go.

Con said, 'So, then. It's all the fault of your mother.'

'I didn't say that. But it is.'

'Does she make you come home early? Does she make you work?'

Mary cast him a contemptuous glance beneath her lashes. 'I'm not a child. It wasn't trivial.'

'Forgive my lack of imagination, but I can't think of anything so serious that a girl of your age should have to run away.'

'A year ago, I would have said the same,' she murmured. 'Odd, isn't it? I used to think my face was my biggest problem.'

'What's a bit of pink, here and there?'

She giggled. 'It's the difference between people liking you and not.'

'You mean boys?'

'I mean everybody. People see the marks. They don't see me.'

She slipped a little deeper into her nest. Her eyes were closing. Con leaned on the cooker, studying her. She couldn't know how pretty she looked, that elegant, thin face with its unexpectedly tender lips, framed by a mass of wispy hair. She was right about the marks, though. They spoiled her. It was hard to look without thinking how different she might have been.

He could hear David getting up, clattering noisily in the bathroom. But she wasn't going anywhere. Like an exhausted animal, she was drugged with sleep.

Rosalind came slowly into the breakfast room. 'You're not going to believe this, Laura.'

'What?' The hope, the expectation. It was almost pitiable.

'She's been found. She's at David's. I don't know how.'

'Mary? Mary? Oh, thank God!' She fell into a paroxysm of weeping.

Howard, looking ruefully at his boiled egg, thought that the woman was really getting worse as she grew older. She'd always been unpredictable of course, although with her background it was only to be expected, but nowadays she seemed to have lost that underlying calmness he'd always rather admired. Laura had always seemed to him to be the sort of woman you wouldn't mind finding next to you on a life raft. Domestic, but still intelligent, self-possessed but never strident, sexual without overt display. But this hysteria was a sad development. It really would do her the world of good to concentrate on some purely cerebral task.

'I've looked out those books for you,' he said encouragingly. 'You might find it interesting to scan *The Fundamentals of Japanese* as an initial study.'

'Do shut up, Howard,' snapped Rosalind. 'She'll be going to London, of course. I'll come with you dear, we'll take the ten-thirty train. David says Mary's perfectly well, rather thin and tired but no more than that. So you needn't worry any more, Laura. Do you want to telephone Michael?'

'Yes. Yes, I must.'

But it was too late in the day. The telephone rang and rang, but Michael would be out in the byre or up on the hill with the sheep. Laura felt the hollow within her growing as she listened to the unanswered phone. She longed for Michael's voice, Michael's calm. She was going to see Mary and she didn't know what she could say!

They had to hurry if they were to catch the train. She dressed in a pale blue suit, some years old, with a jaunty hat adorned at the front with a cockade. Although she had given her outfit no real thought Rosalind said, 'Good heavens, dear, you always amaze me. Your clothes always look so bang up to date.'

Laura glanced at her sister-in-law's own smart two-piece, immaculate grey wool. Rosalind was being disingenuous, she thought. Her suit must be obviously past it. When all this was over, when Mary was once again safely within the fold, she would buy some new clothes.

It was the first ordinary thought she had had in weeks, she realised. All her time, all her energy had been devoted to Mary. And it was worth it! The reward had come! When she reached London and the flat she would have her child once again.

But on the train, in a crowded carriage, Rosalind said quietly, 'What are you going to say to her, my dear? I don't suppose she really wants to come home.'

156

'Doesn't she?' Laura looked suddenly vulnerable again. 'But she went to David! I thought—'

'She was down on her luck. She didn't want him to telephone, you know.'

'That's just Mary being defiant. She doesn't like to give in. I know she really wants to come back, she must know how much we all worry. Mary isn't a bad girl, Rosalind. You mustn't think that. She doesn't mean to cause us all trouble.'

Rosalind, remembering that difficult interview, pursed her lips. Whatever Laura might think Mary was no sugar-coated plum. She was honest, tough-minded, and in some respects quite admirable. But she was also stubborn and judgmental. Whatever judgment she had passed on her mother might not have been revoked.

Laura was picking at the stitching on her glove. Rosalind began to wish she hadn't spoken, at the same time wondering why Laura deceived herself so. She had never been like this before. But it was all about truth, thought Rosalind dismally. All the deceptions of Laura's life had conspired to come together in Mary and ask for an explanation.

They arrived at the flat shortly after twelve. Laura fell from the taxi and buzzed insistently for the lift, holding it impatiently while Rosalind followed. They ascended in silence, Laura gritting her teeth as the ancient mechanism stuttered and stammered. 'One of these days someone will plunge to their doom,' muttered Rosalind, slamming the inner gate once more, and Laura thought, Not yet, not yet. Yesterday she wouldn't have cared, but today – today she would see Mary. Her heart was as erratic as the lift, she hadn't felt this nervous since – since Gabriel. The first time. When she was younger than Mary now.

They were there. She hammered on the door, but no one came. She looked wildly at Rosalind, and knocked again, but then there was the sound of many bolts being drawn and a key turning in the lock. At last. As the door opened David looked cautiously out. 'Thank goodness,' he said, and stood aside. 'She's been trying to leave for over an hour.'

For a moment Laura couldn't see her. She looked up and down the hall, and then moved instinctively towards the sitting room. She was at the farthest corner, near the window, almost hiding behind an armchair and a curtain. 'Mary?' Laura's voice cracked. 'Mary, is it really you?'

She put out her arms, thinking for one terrible moment that her daughter would turn away. But she didn't. Letting out a strangled sob, Mary pushed the chair aside and ran to her.

No one could say who was crying most. Just the feel of her daughter's skin, the smell of her hair, seemed to Laura miraculous.

157

And for a moment Mary luxuriated in the comfort of her mother's embrace. Since babyhood she had known nothing more secure, she longed for the safety and the warmth. But she wasn't a baby any more. Gradually she disentangled herself.

'You shouldn't have come,' she said finally.

Laura pushed at her own wet hair. 'Of course I should. I was only at Rosalind's. Darling, you're so thin! But your hair's wonderful. You look much older, you know. Almost grown up.'

'I am grown up. I grew up the day I left.'

Laura said nothing. She could think of nothing to say. Rosalind came in, bearing a tray of tea, closely followed by David and a reluctant Con. 'The trouble you've caused, Mary, both these boys should be at work you know. But I hear you've been difficult. Imagine, needing two strong men to take care of you!'

'I only wanted to leave,' said Mary quietly. 'They wouldn't let me. That's all.'

'But you're glad you didn't?' asked Laura in a trembling voice. 'You didn't really want not to see me?'

Mary said nothing.

Con, who was there at Rosalind's insistence, said, 'Look, everyone, I think I'll be on my way—'

But Rosalind interrupted, saying with a steely look, 'Thank you, Connor, but I'd be obliged if you could spare us a moment of your time. Family things can get so intense, you know. An outsider can often – restrain things.'

'I suppose you imagine I'll say something embarrassing if he isn't here?' said Mary. 'Don't worry. I don't want to say anything at all.'

'Except that you'll come home?' pleaded Laura. 'Please, Mary. You can't imagine how worried your father and I have been.'

Mary flinched and looked away. 'Do you have to say that?'

'What? Of course we were worried.'

'About my father!'

Rosalind said smoothly, 'David dear, how about making some sandwiches for lunch? No Connor, not you.'

'I'm really much better at sandwiches than David,' said Connor. But it was a perfunctory protest. He looked interestedly from Mary to her mother and back again. The girl had a case, it seemed. This was more than adolescent trauma.

David shot his mother a look of venom, but withdrew nonetheless.

Rosalind said, 'Mary dear, I know you've some silly idea about your mother and your uncle but I thought I'd explained. Can't you please accept that you've been making things up?'

'No,' said Mary flatly.

'Honestly, Mary—' Rosalind began crossly, but Laura lifted her head.

'Please, Rosalind. Mary knows the truth. Gabriel is her father, and Michael doesn't know.'

Rosalind let out her breath in an astonished gasp. Now the cat was out of the bag. How could she say such a thing, so baldly, in front of the child? But Mary wasn't the least surprised. It was what she had known. Why she had gone.

Laura said, 'The thing is, I can't bear it to make a difference. Why should it, after all? She and Michael love each other as a father and daughter should, and that's what matters, isn't it? That's what counts?'

'No,' said Mary. 'How can it? I can't be a daughter to him any more. You took that away. You ruined it. If you had to tell a lie, you should at least have made sure that I never found it out!'

No one said a word. Finally Connor said, 'How did you find out, as a matter of interest?'

'My real father came back,' said Mary. 'Although it's no business of yours.'

'Then it wasn't your mother's fault you found out. You can't blame her for that.'

'If you'd seen how she behaved! She went to pieces!'

'I'm sorry. I'm sorry,' whispered Laura.

'Don't apologise, Laura,' snapped Rosalind. 'Of course you went to pieces! Who wouldn't?'

Mary got up and walked to the window. She stood playing with the window cord, looking out into the street. 'But you see why I can't come home. I'd have to face Dad. And not tell him. I'd have to live a lie.'

'I managed it,' said Laura, her voice lilting with hope. 'It's only the start that's hard.'

'It comes out in the end,' said Mary flatly. 'And then it's worse. He'd know I'd lied to him for years, and that you had too. Honestly, Mum, can't you see? If the family's going to keep anything of what it used to be, I can't come home. We were happy, once. We've had that happiness, we can't go back to it. If we're not to destroy even that, then I can't go home.'

Her mother put her hands to her face and groaned. Mary said, 'Really, Mum. You must see. It just isn't possible.'

'It is! It has to be! Don't you care that Michael's unhappy? Don't you care that I am, and Deb? You're thinking only of you, and not us at all.'

'And who did you think of? Then?'

Her mother's eyes, Deb's eyes, the same and yet so different, looked like white fields of snow. They were horrible, thought Mary. Why hadn't she ever seen that? She'd wanted those eyes, envied Deb, yet they were windows on an unquiet soul.

159

She turned and made for the door. Rosalind said, 'No, Mary. At the very least we have to sort something out. You look terrible, you can't have been managing. Perhaps you won't go home. That doesn't mean we can let you simply run off again. Have you any money?'

Mary said nothing. Connor, clearing his throat, said, 'You can eat David's sandwiches, perhaps. You don't have to rush off. No one's going to drag you anywhere.'

That much was clear. Mary stood undecided, all the energy she had husbanded for the fight vanished into the air. She was so tired. And even with things as they stood it was comforting to be known by her companions, to be honest, to be understood.

They ate in the kitchen, the atmosphere soured more by David's angry glances at his mother than anything else. Rosalind began to discuss what Mary might do. 'If you're determined on living away from home. A secretarial course, perhaps? I know the principal of a college. Or I could get you a job at Selfridges, quite a few girls fill in there.'

'Fill in what?' asked Mary.

'Their lives, dear. Between school and whatever. The season, marriage, that sort of thing.'

'But I wouldn't be filling in. It's my life.'

David said 'I hope you're not suggesting she stay here, Mother? Con and I can't be expected to babysit just on some whim.'

'I've been managing pretty well up to now, thank you,' flashed Mary. 'No one provided me with a flat and an allowance and I got by.'

'Until last night,' said David, meanly. 'Falling out with a prostitute and her pimp.'

'What?' Laura's head came up. 'Mary, you didn't—'

'No.' Mary challenged the question in her mother's eyes. 'No, I didn't. Even at my lowest, I didn't stoop to that.'

To fill the silence, Rosalind began to chatter about hostels and introductions, perhaps Mary could stay with a friend of hers and go to some parties at least. 'Mary hates parties,' whispered Laura.

'She'll have to get over that, I'm afraid,' retorted Rosalind. 'She has to meet some decent people. You may wish to disown your family, Mary, but you can't abandon your class.'

Connor snorted into his waterglass. Mary giggled too. Rosalind was such an impossible snob! David said, 'Honestly, Mother, you're like something out of the ark. As if nothing mattered but getting Mary back with the right sort.'

'Nothing else does matter,' said his mother firmly. 'I have no doubt that Mary will have several changes of heart in the coming months. It's our job to make sure she hasn't given up on anything she may regret. And abandoning the sort of life she's always led is not something she can be permitted to do.'

Laura looked up wearily. 'Mary, she's right. When I first came to England I didn't know anyone. I lived on the outside of everything. I couldn't break in. I was never part of anything in England until I married your father – I mean – married Michael. Why not go back to school? You needn't come home in the holidays, if you don't want.'

Mary sighed. 'I'm too old! And you know I hated school.'

'Yes. I know you did. But at least – at least it gave you time. If you're too old for school you're still too young to be out in the world. Believe me darling, I know more than anyone how hard it is on your own. And I think, so do you.'

They were all looking at her, forgetting for once that she of all people hated to be the focus of everyone's eyes. She got up abruptly, pushing at the table. 'If you don't mind, I think I'll lie down.' As she left, she heard Rosalind say, 'My God, Laura. If anything proves she's unfit to live at home, it's this.'

And David said, 'What are you on about, Mother? I should at least be told what this is all about, I'm not an infant any more!' only for Rosalind to snap 'Please don't you start, David. You can't all misbehave at once, I simply won't stand for it,' whereupon David stormed out and slammed the door.

Laura left Rosalind and Connor in the kitchen and wandered back to the hissing warmth of the gas fire. She felt drained, as if all emotion had been used up. If only she could talk to Michael. She went to the telephone and asked the operator to try her home number, but again there was no reply. She tried to imagine where he might be; at market, up on the hill? If only she could speak to him!

It was like the war again, she thought. No Michael to anchor her, left to herself like a drifting barge, rudderless, powerless, without purpose. Mary was right to despise her. She had never doubted that. But all these years she had striven to conceal from her children that she was just that. Despicable. She was a woman who gave herself as easily as others shook hands. Once it had been everyone, or at least anyone who could pay. Then it had been Gabriel, because he wanted it, because she wanted it, because there had seemed no good reason not to. And it wasn't as if she didn't know it was wrong! But what use was knowledge, when the fires flared into life, scorching her from within? Sometimes – sometimes it was worth anything. Any risk, any disgrace. She could live for months, perhaps years, bobbing along like anyone, being ordinary, doing ordinary things. Until the fog began. Smothering her, smothering everything, a curtain between her and the joy, the reality of life.

It was then that she needed it. Another's body, another's touch, so raw and intimate that everything was clear. You couldn't hide forever, she thought simply. She had hidden herself from everyone for years. She had hidden even from her own thoughts. And now all that effort, all these years had come to nothing. Mary knew her for what she was. How long before Deb knew too, and finally, terribly, Michael?

A shaft of pure agony stabbed at her heart. She bent over, muffling a cry. It always hurt, she thought desperately, there was always the pain, the same now as the day her mother died. You could think yourself secure, you could think yourself safe, but it was never true. All she had achieved in her life were interludes of stillness; until, back it came.

She was so tired of it. She was so very, very tired. She thought, If I was dead Mary would go home. Michael would never know she wasn't his child, she wouldn't add to his grief. They would gather together, the three of them, Michael, Mary and Deb. With her gone, they would be free to be a family again.

She got up and went to the door. There was an old faded velvet draught excluder by the wall, to be rolled against the bottom of the door on cold evenings, and Laura pushed it into place with her foot. It was very heavy, filled with sand perhaps. Nothing would get beyond it. She quietly turned the key in the lock.

She went to the windows and drew the curtains, bunching the hems up on the sills. How long would it take? She had absolutely no idea, perhaps minutes, perhaps an hour. She would have to be quick. She moved to the gas fire and switched it off, waiting a moment before turning the gas on once more. It hissed out obediently, and for a second she thought the residual heat would relight it. She might blow up. She'd rather not. It had terrified her in the war.

She lay down in front of the fire, but her head was too low, so she sat up again to fetch a cushion. There. Like the Jews in the gas chambers, how long did they take to die? Why didn't she mind? They had. But then, she was finished with it all. In her heart of hearts she'd always known it might come to this. She'd be discovered, be unmasked, and there'd be no way out.

She thought of Michael and the tears stung. She would miss him so. He wouldn't understand, but then no one except Gabriel ever had. They were completely known to one another, they had complete understanding, just as if two whales of the same species swam towards one another in the vastness of the sea and at last saw another of their kind. She and Gabriel had always swum amidst alien lifeforms. The trouble was, she didn't want to be Gabriel's sort.

Her head was beginning to swim. Her limbs felt leaden and unusable. Let Mary and Deb be happy, she thought. Let my love go with them throughout all their lives. I'm worth nothing except for that. The gas fire hissed, the curtains swayed a little in the unaccustomed breeze, and Laura slipped silently away.

Chapter Seventeen

Deborah was summoned to the high mistress's study. 'Now what?' said the girls. 'Has your grandmother died? It's usually that.'

'That was years ago,' said Deb. 'It could be Mary, I suppose.'

'What about Mary?'

Deb coloured. 'Nothing.'

She went to the study and rapped. Seeing the high mistress was never easy: if you knocked too hard she told you off about it, and too soft an approach left you standing there for hours. She was impatient today and erred on the side of vigour. But the high mistress simply called, 'Come in.'

She was a small, grey woman who was popularly supposed to hate all girls. And it was true that years of them had disillusioned her. Nonetheless she retained some spark of sympathy for pretty Deb Cooper, so much nicer than that sister of hers, all gracelessness and bad temper. 'Deborah,' she began, 'your mother's ill. You are to return home.'

'Ill? What's the matter with her?'

'I cannot say.'

'Do you mean you know but won't tell me?'

'I was not informed, Deborah. I know merely that she is ill and your presence is required at home.'

Deborah was silent, taking time to absorb the implications. 'Could I telephone?' she asked. 'Speak to my father?'

'If you wish.' She gestured to the telephone on her desk.

Deb sat beneath the intimidating eye and waited to be connected. The ringing went on and on, but no one answered. Finally she replaced the receiver. 'Was it my father who rang?'

'I prefer to use the word telephoned, Deborah. Less colloquial. It was in fact your uncle who telephoned the school.'

'Uncle Gabriel? Oh.'

She felt sick. She knew something was terribly wrong. The high mistress was handing her a rail ticket. If she hurried she could telephone Fairlands from the station. At least Piers might tell her the truth. Then she remembered; he was at school too. She couldn't speak to Gabriel or Dora, or even the Fitzalan-Howards! Not about this. She would have to sit on the train, enduring each and every stop, not knowing. 'Slaithwaite – Marsden – Denby Dale.' The ever familiar litany. Taking her home – to what?

She arrived at Huddersfield at around four. A fine drizzle was damping the pavements and washing away the dirty remains of winter snow. She looked around to see if anyone was there to meet her, wondering what she would do if there was not. But then she saw Aunt Dora, muffled in fur, elegantly smoking a cigarette.

'At last, Deborah.' She threw her cigarette, barely started, to the ground. An elderly gentleman hissed disapprovingly, but Dora swept out of the building, leaving Deborah to struggle behind with her bags. She thought with distaste of the drive to come. Aunt Dora was incapable of respecting anyone's privacy, she would ask what should never be asked and no doubt expect a reply.

'How's my mother?' asked Deb, the moment they were safely in the car. Dora glanced at her, before sending the car fizzing backwards out of the parking space. Damn the child! All big eyes and glorious hair, enough to make anyone feel old.

'I believe she was taken to hospital in London. As far as I can gather she tried to kill herself. I've no idea why your father thought you should come home, no idea at all. For one thing he's gone to London, so you're to stay with us. Quite pointless.'

Deb felt the air in her lungs freeze solid. She forced lumps of ice up and out. 'Why – does anyone know why?'

'Something to do with Mary, no doubt. That tiresome girl turned up at David's, your mother rushed to see her and then this. Ridiculous, all of it.'

Deb sat absolutely still. She wanted to cry, but would die rather than do so in front of Aunt Dora. The Huddersfield traffic was thick as glue. It seemed an age before the long nose of the car could point to an open road and Dora accelerate away. Relaxing, pulling open her coat as the car warmed, she looked across at her youthful passenger.

'Tell me,' she said cosily, 'are you in love with Piers?'

Deb coloured to her hair and Dora laughed. 'Don't be embarrassed, my dear. He's besotted with you. But then boys of that age do fall very easily and you are a lovely girl. I think you could have more or less anyone you wanted, you know. Are you really going to throw yourself away on my son?'

Amazed, Deborah said, 'Why would I be throwing myself away? Don't you like Piers?'

'But of course. It's simply that a girl like you could make a wonderful marriage. With a little effort, moving in the right circles, you could have money, a title. Whatever.'

'Is that why you got married? For what you could get?'

Dora chuckled. 'I wasn't so clever, then. No, dear, I married for

164

love. And look where that got me. A dull life in a dull corner of dull little England.'

Deborah was glad the woman was so unpleasant. Thinking of that, fielding her horrible questions, she need not worry about Mum. But why would she try and kill herself because Mary was in a mess? What sort of mess? How bad?

Dora said, 'Are you and my son sleeping together?'

'What?' Deborah turned astonished eyes on her. 'You can't possibly ask me something like that!'

'Why not? I won't be shocked if you are. Too many girls marry for sex, you know. There's no need. Not if you're sensible.'

Deborah was silent. If it had been possible to jump from the car she wouldn't have hesitated. The things she and Piers did together were private. Special. It wasn't something common, something animal, to be discussed matter-of-factly by a woman with a coarse mind.

Dora lit another cigarette. Deborah ostentatiously opened the window. 'It's such a pity,' remarked Dora. 'You really are your mother's daughter. Totally bourgeois.'

It was dark by the time they came to Fairlands. Mrs Fitzalan-Howard greeted Deborah on the steps, saying, 'There's no news, I'm afraid. Michael promised to telephone from the hospital, we'll let you know as soon as we can.' She ushered Deb through to the sitting room, but as they passed the library the door opened and Gabriel lurched out. Even Deb could see that he was terribly drunk.

'What's she doing here?' he demanded, squinting at the new arrival.

'You know very well!' said Mrs Fitzalan-Howard, a little stiffly. 'There's no one at Gunthwaite just now. I'll have your dinner sent up to your room, Gabriel.'

Deb doubted that he could get to his room. He seemed to be supporting himself on the door as it was. 'I'd rather join you,' he said, adding disarmingly, 'if I won't be too much of a trial. I'm not drunk, you know. I mean – I've drunk a hell of a lot, but I can't get away from myself somehow. It was the same when Philip died.'

Deb gasped. Was her mother dead? Was that what they were trying to say? Mrs Fitzalan-Howard, realising, said, 'We don't know that anyone's dead, Gabriel. This isn't like the war. Come to the table if you must, but please, don't upset Deborah.'

But she was already upset. In the sitting room, before a crackling log fire, they gave her brandy. 'It's only medicinal, dear. I know that when one sees Gabriel in that state one can't but wonder – but at times like these alcohol can be quite a blessing. We only know your mother's ill, you see.'

'What did she do? Did she fall? Did she cut herself?'

'I'm afraid we just don't know.'

Deborah felt so sick. She wondered what they would say if she threw up then and there, on the immaculate pale blue rug. Mrs Fitzalan-Howard, being such a lady, would be charming. Dora, who wasn't a lady at all, would be foul. As for Gabriel, he was probably doing much the same thing in the library. She had the sudden desire to talk to him. He was drunk for the same reason that she was sick: Laura.

He arrived at the dinner table halfway through the soup, and took a few hurried mouthfuls, stopping all at once and saying, 'Sorry. Sorry. God, what a terrible day.'

Dora said, 'Damn you, Gabriel, you might at least try to put a face on things! Or don't you care at all about me?'

He looked blank. 'What about you? It's my fault she's tried to kill herself.'

But Deborah suddenly wanted that not to be true. This was a private affair, and these people didn't understand privacy. 'I think it was to do with Mary, actually,' she declared in a high, strained voice. 'I'm sure you think you know Mum well, Uncle Gabriel, but I am her daughter. I'm sure it was something to do with Mary.'

He said, 'You think I'm trying to be important to her. More important than you. The thing is, people aren't clear to their children, you know. They can't be.'

Mr Fitzalan-Howard said, 'I think that's very true. Any more than children are clear to their parents. There's a sort of barrier, don't you think? A necessary one, perhaps. I suppose it might come down with age.'

'I still think we know Mum better than any of you,' declared Deborah. 'I know you don't realise, but she pretends an awful lot. And no one can pretend all the time. She doesn't with us.'

Gabriel leaned forward, trailing his tie in the soup. 'What you see of her is real, of course. But as children, you can't see everything. In a way, all parents lie to their children. They pretend to be more grown-up than they are.'

Deborah could feel the tears building. 'You think we're stupid, that's all,' she burst out. 'You think we don't know about Sophie and Marie. You think everything has to be told and understood, you don't realise people can feel things, know things just by feeling. You think you're the only one who can. But we know Mum, and you don't, you don't, you just don't!'

She was beautiful, thought Gabriel. More beautiful now than Laura had ever been, all heaving bosom and tear stains. Mrs Fitzalan-Howard made as if to get up, but Gabriel put out a hand and stopped her. 'I'm sorry, Deb,' he said gently. 'I'm not very good with children. Less good with people who aren't children any more. Stay and have your dinner. Let's talk about something else.'

166

She had never liked him before. He had always seemed to be one of those people best avoided, someone you would dread to think you might ever in any way resemble. But tonight he had permitted her to glimpse his charm. She saw that he kept it sheathed and out of sight, a weapon he didn't want and would not use. Perhaps Aunt Dora had once loved him after all. Oddly, unexpectedly, she found herself pitying him.

Connor pulled the coat a little more firmly around Mary's thin, shaking shoulders. 'Will you keep warm, at least? No point in everyone dying.'

She winced. But he had used the word deliberately. He could see no way in which the girl's mother might live.

He could still taste the gas on his tongue. But more than that, he tasted the shock, the realisation, the amazement that you could talk with someone, find them sensible, when minutes later they would decide that they wanted to die. A pretty, subdued, young for her age woman had eaten a sandwich, risen from the table and gone off to kill herself. It was all completely ghastly.

David came along the corridor. 'Mother says you should take Mary home, Con. Stay by the phone.'

'But my father's coming. I should be here.'

'Mother thinks – you're upset. She thinks not.'

Mary struggled with things. Rosalind thought that in her distress she would blurt everything. Well. She might. It was all so utterly terrible. Without complaint she permitted Con to lead her out into the street, push her into a taxi and take her back to the gassy flat.

All the windows were open and it was very cold. Connor closed up the kitchen, putting on the kettle, although he winced when he struck the match. Mary said, 'She could have blown everyone up. That's not like Mum.'

'I don't suppose people are much like themselves when they decide to die.'

'It was me, wasn't it? My fault. I wish you'd say.'

He shrugged. 'I don't know if it was. How can I know? Perhaps it wasn't you, it was simply your knowing. Everyone's knowing. Your mother's sins have found her out and she can't live with that.'

'But how am I to live with it? She was going to die and leave me. Let me struggle with it all alone.'

'I thought that was what you wanted?'

'I did! Until I thought she'd let me. Oh God. I need my mother. Like a snivelling little baby. I need her so much.'

She bent her head and sobbed. After a moment Connor moved awkwardly to pat her shoulder, saying, 'There, there,' ineffectually.

When Mary surfaced, instinctively covering her face with her hand, she said, 'I'm not a dog, you know.'

'I wish you were. I'm good with dogs.'

'Are you? I'm better with horses.'

'I'm good with those too. You have to be, at home. And now it's my job.'

She looked at him with renewed interest. 'What do you do, in London?'

'I'm a runner for a man who buys racehorses. I go through the papers and check on the breeding and form. One day I might get to look at a real horse, now I only get photographs. And the pay's bad. I should have stayed at home.'

'And why didn't you?'

He turned his back to make the tea. 'I wanted a sniff of the big wide world. And so did you, I guess.'

Mary sighed. 'No. I didn't want that at all. I wanted to stay at Gunthwaite for ever and ever and never leave it more.'

They drank their tea in silence. Mary wondered if they were both seeing the same thing; Laura's face, eerily white, hair and lashes still dark and lustrous, still alive against that dead-looking face. Was she dead? It seemed so. But no one would say until Michael arrived. Until then, they were all in limbo.

Con broke the silence. 'If David hadn't come in – I mean, he'd have asked me where his coat was, except he didn't want to see his mother. He only went in because of that. And it was temper made him force the door. We could have just sat there, while she died.'

'She looked dead. She wasn't breathing.'

'Yes she was. In the ambulance, they got her to.'

'But that was an age. Oh, I wish Dad was here! And Deb. I can't bear this by myself. Is it my fault? If it is I don't know what I shall do.'

She got up and stood in the centre of the floor, poised for some action, any action, that would take her away from this. Looking at her, so young, so thin, so marked and defenceless, he felt an unexpected lurch in his stomach. He turned back to his tea. My God, it was coming to something when he desired such as this. He must be desperate for it.

Mary, sensing something, felt herself blush. In her heightened state, every nerve at full stretch, she could almost smell the change in atmosphere. She folded her arms around herself and sank back into the chair. She looked at him, fearfully. He kept his eyes resolutely on his tea.

'I'll go back to the hospital,' she said at last.

'No. You can't do any good.'

'Suppose she comes round and wants to see me? Last words. You know.'

'So you want forgiveness?'

She nodded. He got up and put their cups in the sink. 'You denied it to her though.'

'Yes.'

She was so touchingly honest. So hard on herself. He wondered what would happen if he turned round and told her that he wanted her. That at this most inappropriate time he wanted to take her to the bedroom and make love. He chuckled to himself, and she said, 'I'm glad I amuse you. Actually, I don't think anyone takes me seriously.'

'It would be pretty hard to take you as seriously as you do.'

She blushed again, and the marks lit up like beacons. He felt his heart contract.

A bell sounded. Mary looked bewildered, but Con said, 'It's only the door.' He went out into the hall, letting in great gouts of cold air, as well as that smell again. Would it ever go? It clung to everything, causing them to cough. Mary hovered, wondering if it was the caretaker again, furious and bewildered, wanting them to stop the ambulance and the smell and the public removal of a body, as if they had wanted any of it, intended anything at all! But it was not. It was Michael.

'Dad! Dad!' He looked so different here, so out of place. Big, brown, his hair too long and ruffled by the wind, his old tweed jacket redolent of sheep sales and cattle markets. She ran to his arms.

'Dad, Dad. I'm so sorry.'

'I know. My God, despite all of this you're still my good girl. My wild one. My darling.'

It wasn't like him. Whatever wild and raw emotion she displayed he always responded with calm and ordinariness. But he was different, and that alone proved how terrible all this was. She buried her face in his jacket, smelling of everything that was home, and wished she could die there.

Michael said, 'She's better. I wanted you to be the first to know.'

'Better? I thought you'd come to tell me she was dead.'

'No. Thank God, no. What got into her, Mary? Why?'

Mary thought of what she might say. But there was no hope of explanation. Instead, she put her face against him once again and murmured, 'It was because I wouldn't come home. I'm sorry, Dad. Truly I am.'

He was silent for a moment, patting her shoulder. 'How could you, Mary?' he managed at last. 'Knowing she was fretting?'

'I didn't do it to hurt her. Not really.'

'But you knew she was hurt. Oh, Mary. Mary, Mary.'

Never in her life had he looked at her with disappointment. He did now. She felt her heart break, felt it disintegrate into a thousand useless pieces. But better that, better by far that. Her heart instead of his. She must never let him know this pain.

Connor appeared in the kitchen door. He had been discreetly listening, thought Mary. She could feel him looking at her and deliberately avoided his eye. 'I made you some tea, sir,' he said. 'And perhaps you'd like something to eat?'

Michael nodded, not asking who this might be, not interested. Mary thought that she had never seen him at a loss before. At home, at Gunthwaite, he seemed invincible. Here, he was a big, lost, vulnerable man. She knew she would do anything to put him back where he belonged, to restore his confidence, his strength.

Connor was watching her again. She twisted her head, letting him see the marks, not caring. It was the way things were today, for him and her. They knew everything, saw everything. They were the two from whom nothing was concealed. Everything had to be clearly seen.

That evening, they went to the hospital. Rosalind was there, sitting beside Laura's bed. Mary couldn't help thinking how much her mother would hate that. Being watched. But Rosalind thought she was being kind.

She went off for some tea while Michael and Mary were there. Michael said, 'Well now. Feeling better?'

Laura's eyes opened a slit. 'I don't want – I can't – I'm sorry. It was because—'

Mary said, 'And I'm sorry, Mum. I know it was because I wouldn't come home. I will now, I promise.'

Her mother's pale, parchment-like face contracted into a frown. 'You won't tell?' she asked.

'What?' Michael rubbed her hand.

'All the things I said?' supplied Mary, taking her other hand and squeezing it invigoratingly. 'I'm so sorry, Mum. I know it was my fault. But I will come home. I promise.'

Laura's head moved restlessly on the pillow. She looked confused and still upset. But that didn't matter, thought Mary, she'd get better, she'd get well. At home, at Gunthwaite, they would all pretend to be as they used to be. That had to be the way it was.

In the flat that night, everyone was everywhere. Rosalind was sharing Howard's room with Mary, while Michael had Con's room, and he moved in with David. Mary was perhaps the most uncomfortable. She and Rosalind were forced into either side of a double bed, a proximity neither of them relished. When Rosalind made as if to go to bed, and Michael was persuaded to do the same, Mary took herself off to the sitting room, still with its windows wide.

170

She went round closing them, automatically pulling the curtains straight. As she shook the folds the smell of gas was released again, and she wondered if she would ever smell it and not remember this day. It was very cold. She perched on the sofa and looked at the gas fire, wondering if she should light it. Before she could decide the door opened and Connor came in.

'Light it,' he said at once. 'No point in freezing.'

'We ought to go to bed,' said Mary. 'It's very late.'

'But I imagine that you don't relish sharing a bed with Rosalind any more than me with David. Much as I like the chap, his public school did him no favours. He's looking as if I might rape him.' He bent down and put a match to the fire, and at once the room began to warm.

Mary laughed, disguising shock. She had never heard anyone speak openly about that sort of thing. Sandra, perhaps. She hated queers, as she called them. Said they blighted her trade.

'And would you?' asked Mary, greatly daring.

'Would I what?'

'You know. What you said.'

'Rape him? Good God, no. I'm more inclined to rape you.'

She blushed fierily. But he didn't look. He sat in the armchair across from her, staring at the fire, gnawing on the side of his thumb. She thought, He doesn't mean it. Does he? Since coming to London she had realised that prettiness wasn't everything. Sandra wasn't pretty, but that didn't mean men didn't want her. For the night, at least. Men might want a beauty to take about, but in bed they looked for other things.

She said shrilly, 'I don't know what I'm going to do. I've said I'll go home, but then what? I've finished with school, and I can't spend all my life hanging about at home. Especially not now.'

He glanced at her. 'You should leave it to Rosalind. She'll set you up, you can see she's just dying to.'

'She doesn't like me, you know.'

'I don't suppose she likes anyone she can't push around.'

She giggled and moved to kneel in front of the fire, holding out her hands to the popping flames. She had long, thin fingers, held together by a fragile lacing of bones and sinews. He said, 'I don't know what I'm going to do either. This job's a washout.'

'What would you like to do? If you could.'

'Horses, I suppose. Dealing. Breaking and schooling. There's a market for jumping horses these days, I've sold no end of bad racehorses to people who want them to jump. But they need the work, you know, it's not done in a day. I'd like to do that.'

Mary hugged her knees. 'Me too. You know where you are with horses.'

171

'And where's that?' He was laughing at her and she made a face. 'On top.'

They were both laughing when Rosalind came in. She looked from one to the other and said briskly, 'Time for you to go to bed, Mary. I can't possibly go to sleep knowing you're going to start clattering about at any moment.'

Mary got to her feet. 'Con and I want to go into business, Aunt Rosalind,' she said easily. 'A horse business.'

'At which you would undoubtedly fail,' snapped Rosalind.

'Oh, I doubt that,' said Con, leaning forward to turn off the fire.

Rosalind paused. 'You're not serious?'

Mary and Con looked at each other. 'We'd have to talk to Dad,' said Mary. 'But it would be something, wouldn't it? Something for me to do. For us both.'

Rosalind eyed Connor. He sank his hands into his pockets to stop them trembling, and she thought, Yes. You mean it too. And he was good for Mary. Good for them all. He'd been a Godsend today, and at Gunthwaite he might be again. She said, 'I'll talk to Michael, then. In the morning.'

'It's only an idea,' said Connor deprecatingly. 'We'd have to look at the money side, buildings, everything. I don't want you to think we'd go off half-cocked.'

'I can assure you, Connor, I'll see you don't do that. To bed with you both, please.'

In separate beds, uncomfortable and ill at ease, both Connor and Mary lay wakeful. They thought of each other, and of the horses, and of the day; of David's shout of horror, of Laura's almost dead face, the horrible, heart-stopping fear. Towards dawn they heard Michael get up and make a cup of tea. Mary longed to go to him, and instead lay still. She was going to have to learn what her mother had learned: to keep her secrets in silence.

Chapter Eighteen

Deborah stood on the platform, jiggling a little. It was partly cold, partly tension but mostly the desire to go to the lavatory. She had tried earlier, but there was a very long queue and she thought she might miss the train. Now she jiggled uncomfortably.

Gabriel said, 'They're late. These bloody trains!'

Deborah glanced at him. He was sober for once, and a little bleary. They had risen at six to be ready and he wasn't used to it. What's more, she had asked him several times not to come.

'Here it is now.'

The train was moving smoothly into the station. Deb jiggled again, wondering which carriage, if she would see them and they her. Perhaps she should have waited at the barrier. But they were at a door only twenty-five yards away. She saw Mary and Dad. She rushed forward waving, and Gabriel called out: 'Mike! Hey, Mike!' just as if they were friends.

But where was Laura? People poured from the train, and only when everyone had gone did Michael help Laura gingerly down. Deb said, 'Mum? Mum?' in a voice shrill with tears, and her mother put out her arms and said, 'Darling, darling Deb.'

Deb thought she looked terrible. Chalk white and nervous, her hair in a mess. Michael stood on one side, and on the other an unknown young man. In a voice like glass Mary said, 'Deb, this is Connor. A friend of David's.'

She said hello, and took no more notice, being far more interested in her mother and Uncle Gabriel. They, and Michael, were talking, which was a miracle, surely. Only Mary, nerves at hair trigger, saw Connor take in the wide eyes, the perfect cheek, the swell of breast and thigh. She felt the old, familiar canker begin again and closed her mind to it. What man could not admire Deb? Why should she care? Connor was a friend and prospective business partner, no more than that.

The car was impossibly squashed. Michael insisted that Connor and the girls take a taxi and pushed money into Mary's pocket, but before they left Laura leaned out and said, 'Take Deborah to the Ladies, Mary, do. She can't stand still.'

As the car swept away, both girls laughed. It was such a

welcome reminder that Mum was still Mum. 'Do you really need me to go with you?' asked Mary.

Deb shook her head. 'I'd have gone before, but there was a queue and I thought I'd miss you. Hang on here, will you?' She dashed away, an elf of a girl, shining head bobbing through the crowd, and Mary stood looking after her. 'Stunning, isn't she?' she said.

'Yes. Do you mind?'

'Terribly. At least, I did. I hope I don't any more. I've got used to it. Deb's pretty, I'm not, that's all.'

Connor took a breath. At not quite twenty-two, he wasn't all that used to women. In London he'd visited a girl occasionally, someone he knew who had a job but did favours for friends, and he'd known girls in Ireland of course, but nothing much. He'd never thought himself to be properly in love. Somehow he wasn't prepared for Deborah. She was the most lovely girl he had ever seen. Which left Mary – where? He was filled with a boiling confusion.

'You're very attractive,' he managed.

Mary coloured, as always. 'You don't have to pander to me, you know.'

'You're different from your sister. Interesting.'

'Oh, please! Don't go on, Connor. You're embarrassing us both.'

'All the same. You are, you know.'

She couldn't resist. 'Am what?'

He looked away across the taxi rank, to the statues of nymphs arrayed in the square. Why not tell her the truth? 'Desirable,' he said. 'Sexually.'

She was struck dumb. She said nothing until Deborah began walking back towards them. Then she said quickly, 'Where I worked, before. Men tried – you know. But you won't? I mean, we've got to work together, haven't we? I don't want you to think – I mean, this is business.'

He looked at her. Christ, you fool, he was shouting inwardly, couldn't you wait, you bloody fool? He sidestepped away, saying smoothly, 'Of course it's business. I only said it to cheer you up.'

'Did you? Thanks. There was no need, you know. But it was kind.'

They didn't talk much on the trip home. Connor was looking at the scenery, an unnatural interest to avoid looking at her, Mary thought. Or at Deb. Deb herself was constrained by his presence, and could only hint at things. 'I don't mind Uncle Gabriel as much as I did. He was so worried about Mum, you know. And he can be very kind.'

174

'Can he?' Mary was frosty. She didn't want to talk about Gabriel, or to think about him. Ever.

'Aunt Dora was a cow, of course.'

Absently, Mary said, 'You wonder how it happens, don't you? The Fitzalan-Howards, I mean. Two nice people producing something like that.'

'It's the same with horses,' remarked Connor. 'Good stallion, good mare, and you still get a rogue. It's the way it's meant to be. Makes life exciting.'

Did he mean her? Mary glanced at him and looked as quickly away. He was looking back. Deb, who had caught the exchange, was bemused. She opened her eyes wide at her sister, but Mary didn't explain. Why was this man here? Who was he?

It was Connor who took it upon himself to enlighten her. 'I'm not just a hanger on,' he said abruptly. 'Mary and I are going to do something with horses together. It was just an idea, but your Aunt Rosalind took it up.'

'Dad was all for it,' contributed Mary desultorily. Now that she was almost home again, it didn't seem much of an idea at all. She didn't want Con around, she realised. With him there she couldn't slump back into surly, rebellious girlhood. And that, she realised suddenly, was exactly what Rosalind had intended. Damn the woman!

'You know Dad and horses,' said Deb, and gave Connor the benefit of an encouraging smile, dazzling him in the process. 'Mary's a whiz. Rides anything. Dad's the same, but he hasn't the time. You'll have to watch him, given half a chance he'd turn the whole farm over to horses.'

'Like us at home,' said Connor. 'It's all we do.'

'Then why come here?'

He shrugged and grinned at her lopsidedly. 'Oh, you know. Reasons.'

Gunthwaite was coming into view. Mary craned at the window, wishing she was alone, wishing she could express what was in her heart. Winter was ending, and the last of the snowdrops dotted the hedgebottoms, mingling with crocus and aconite. Small birds flitted across the lane, absorbed with the coming of spring. The cycle went on, year in, year out, never changing, never tired. Knowing this was here, knowing that the fields and hills, walls and houses were just as they had always been, Mary felt herself relax. Everything passed but this. It would be the same forever.

Deborah said, 'Look at you, Mary! Anyone would think you'd been away a hundred years.'

'It feels like it,' said Mary. She gestured to Connor. 'That's Gunthwaite, on the hill. Can you see?'

175

'Yes. It looks like a stronghold.'

'It was. It is. Oh, damn it to hell, the oak's gone!'

'Blew down in a storm,' said Deb. 'Dad was pleased, it was getting dangerous. He's planted new.'

Mary grunted. 'Trust Dad. Can you see, Connor? The big barn? Half of it's stables, right out of the wind.'

He looked and politely admired. Deborah privately wondered if he thought the place utterly bleak. Gunthwaite wasn't to everyone's taste, after all, it wasn't soft. In the yard there was straw blowing and unfed bullocks bellowing from the barn. Home before them and hurriedly changed, Michael was storming from the house. 'I'll swing for that Bill Mayes,' he said shortly. 'Gets more idle by the day.' Without a word, Connor handed his jacket to Mary. 'I think I'll be giving your father a hand.'

She winced. He of all people shouldn't call Michael her father. But she would have to reconcile herself. That was why she was here. 'There's an overall in the barn you can have. I'll make some tea.'

She went into the kitchen. It was cold, the range was out. Her mother was sitting slumped at the table, Gabriel standing away from her, face set. They had been arguing, thought Mary. One minute alone and it all began again.

'I'll light the range,' she said tersely. 'If you could move yourself, please?' She pushed rudely in front of Gabriel.

'Don't, Mary,' said Laura in an exhausted voice. 'I've had enough for one day.'

Gabriel snapped, 'Had enough of what? Lying? Can't you see, Laura, can't you understand? It's time to come clean about everything. You must let me talk to Mike.'

She lifted her head. 'One word to him and I'll shoot you first and me second.'

Gabriel turned away. Neither he nor Mary could doubt that she meant it. Everything about her spoke of despair. The next time she tried to take her life she wouldn't get it wrong.

Mary rattled paper and kindling efficiently. One thing that could be said for chambermaiding was that it made you efficient at least. She set a match to the fire and dropped coal neatly down, hearing it begin to crackle. It wasn't everyone could light this range. She turned and dusted her hands. 'I think we'll all just keep quiet,' she said firmly. 'I know you don't want to, Uncle Gabriel, but we can't bother about you. You'll have to be content with being friends with Dad again. We might let you be that.'

He said, 'God, but you're a vindictive little minx.'

Her eyes blazed at him. 'Someone should be. If people had

known what you were like years ago, there wouldn't be any of this mess.'

Laura lifted her head and said wearily, 'It wasn't all him, Mary. You won't get anywhere hating him.'

Mary said nothing. She filled the kettle and banged it heavily on the cold stove, and began rummaging in drawers for a table cloth. She felt tearful suddenly. She had thought so often of coming home to Gunthwaite, but never to a cold house, a sick mother, and lies. She supposed it was the price you paid for growing up. You weren't a passenger any more.

By the time Michael and Connor appeared for tea, order had been restored. Gabriel was still there unfortunately, making it plain that this was a new era and he wouldn't be chased out. Michael eyed him with obvious speculation.

'Come off it, Mike,' said Gabriel evenly. 'Isn't it better this way?'

'It was better with you abroad,' said Michael. He finished washing his hands and passed the towel to Connor, resting a hand on Laura's shoulder in passing. She had done nothing towards this meal. It was all Mary and Deb.

With nothing in the house and no hot oven they had prepared a sort of breakfast of bacon and eggs and sausage, cooked on the soulless electric hob. There was tea, and Deb had discovered the remains of the Christmas cake, only nibbled at this year. She sliced it into small pieces and arranged it prettily on a plate, but all the same Mary could but wonder what Con thought about it all. The meal offended her sense of propriety; there should have been scones and homemade bread and cake, with jam and cream and new butter, and perhaps a winter salad of shredded carrot and cabbage, the way Laura had taught them. But everyone ate heartily, just the same.

When it was finished and they were sitting over their cups of tea, Michael said, 'Well then. We'll have to talk about what you and Connor mean to do, Mary.'

Connor said, 'If we mean to do anything. Nothing's settled. It's capital we need, sir. To buy a few horses and see what we can do.'

'And what makes you think you can do anything at all?' demanded Gabriel, with what seemed unnecessary force.

But Michael said, 'I think they can try. There's a market for good horses, and if good people can make them there's money in it. But you won't make it buying cheap.'

Connor flushed. 'No sir. But if that's all we can afford. We could make a start.'

'You should never put hope where money should be,' said

Gabriel portentously. 'Should they, Mike?' He grinned at their blank faces, and Mary felt a shaft of dislike. He managed to look so unbearably smug.

Michael said, 'Don't torment them, Gabriel. Connor, Mary – my brother has offered to finance this new enterprise. He's being – very generous.'

Mary was astonished. She stared from Michael to Gabriel and back again. 'No! she burst out. 'We don't need his money!'

Gabriel laughed. 'You need it Mary, you just don't want it. Or is that difference too subtle for you?'

'Don't talk to me about subtlety,' she blazed. 'You can't wait to get your foot in the door again, can you?'

'I am opening the door, Mary,' said Michael.

His tone silenced her. It was the old Michael again, calm, ordered, in control. He didn't need her to defend him from his brother. At Gunthwaite Michael was king.

All at once, and unexpectedly, Michael was businesslike. 'Connor and I have talked a little. He agrees that the way forward is adding value to horses. Point to pointers, jumpers, that sort of thing. I won't say I'll get rid of my shires, but they don't need all the space I give them. Now, if I provide the stabling and Gabriel puts up the money, you two can busy yourselves finding the stock.'

Mary looked down at the table. It was the only way she could avoid looking at Connor, who she knew was looking at her. Everyone wanted this except her. They were all intent on making her agree. Making her join forces with Gabriel, the man she liked least in the whole world. Then she thought of Stevie, and changed her mind. One of her least liked people. There were certainly some that were worse.

'It sounds good to me,' said Connor.

'You would think so,' said Mary waspishly, and quite without foundation. She didn't know Connor well enough to know what he might or might not think. 'We don't need much money. What about the Bombardier? Mr Fitzalan-Howard's bound to pay us for training him. If we take a few like that we'll soon be able to buy our own stock.'

'In about a hundred years,' said Gabriel lazily. 'Face it, Mary, you're going to have to take what's offered with something approaching good grace.'

'No need for grace of any sort,' said Connor. 'It's business, after all. We'll pay you a return on your investment. If we fall behind you'll be entitled to take and sell the stock.'

Gabriel looked at Mary's face. 'Don't encourage me. I might just do that. Very well. We'll draw up an agreement and begin.'

178

* * *

That night, Mary couldn't sleep. Thoughts were buzzing in her head, she felt unsettled. Her abiding sense was that she shouldn't have come home. In London she had at least been responsible only for herself. Here, she felt the combined weight of Michael, Laura, Deb, even of Con. What's more, she didn't believe in this business idea. Connor might not see, but it was an amusement, a diversion, the sort of thing indulgent parents provided for demanding little girls. It wasn't anything serious.

Suddenly she couldn't stay there a moment longer. She went to the cupboard and found her jodhpurs, hastily pulling them on. All this talk about horses and she hadn't ridden one in months. She could have lost her nerve, her touch, anything. She grabbed her hat from the top of the wardrobe and crept stealthily out.

Diablo was in his loose box, rugged against the night. Mary went to him, whispering, watching him throw up his lovely head and blow worriedly. 'It's me, have you forgotten? Mary. Oh, but you're so beautiful. What have they been doing? I believe you're getting fat.' Where once there had been hard muscle, his shoulder was soft now, and round. She slipped the rugs from his quarters and fetched saddle and bridle, while Diablo blinked at her out of wide, puzzled eyes, and wondered what she was doing. He wasn't used to night time disturbance. This was new.

The moment she swung into the saddle she knew it was a mistake. Fat he might be, but Diablo had spent months idling his time away, doing as he wished. Restriction and coercion seemed to him things of a long-forgotten past, while there rose in him a much older instinct – the longing to be free!

Mary held to his head, knowing that if she so much as breathed on him he would explode. He felt like a gun on a hair trigger, and she knew that if she had any sense at all she would get off. But she couldn't. She had never yet retreated from a confrontation with a horse, however ill-advised. Bad lessons were taught so much more easily than good ones, it seemed to her. Above all else, the horse must not know she was afraid.

She turned his head to the drive. She didn't particularly want to take him down the road, where any fall would be on to stone, but at least she wouldn't be troubled by gates. Gently, gingerly, she put her legs to his sides. Diablo threw up his head, plunged and bucked. Out of practice, Mary simply hung on, until he gathered himself and began to gallop. She had lost a stirrup, her hat was coming off, she couldn't stop! By the time she had sorted herself out he was well into his stride, bolting hard. 'Now then,' she said breathlessly, 'do I just wait till you run out of steam?'

179

But she knew she couldn't. Diablo wouldn't forget. He'd try this again and again, a good horse spoiled and dangerous. She sat down in the saddle, folded her legs like a vice and pulled.

'Whoa! Whoa, damn you!'

The horse set his teeth, as she'd known he would, bending his head to relieve the pressure and still charging on. She shifted her grip, pulling and snatching, feeling him alter his stride. He threw up his head but she was ready for him, taking inches from the reins. His nose was rammed into his chest, she forced her legs to increase the pressure, squeezing him up from fore and aft. Something had to give. Amazed and not a little impressed, he slithered to a halt.

'You stupid horse,' panted Mary. 'You couldn't see a thing, we could have been killed.'

Her legs were shaking and her arms felt like over-stretched elastic. But she'd done it! He'd tried it on and she'd mastered him.

Wonderful! Tired as she was, she couldn't go home yet. She took him on down the lane, his unshod feet silent on the verges, eerily padding on the road. A fox slipped by, giving her a knowing look from his triangular eye. An owl in the treetops startled her. Deep inside she felt the beginnings of something she had almost forgotten; not quite happiness, not yet contentment – simple pleasure.

She rode back just before three. The horse was very tired, he'd be a duck tomorrow. She thought what a pity it was that Connor wouldn't see him at his worst. He'd think she rode a donkey and thought it was a star.

But to her surprise, Connor was in the yard. He was sitting on the mounting block, collar turned up against the cool night air. 'Well then,' he said as she rode up. 'You came back a deal more quietly than you went.'

'Did you see?' He'd nearly had her. She'd been a mess.

'He's got one hell of a buck in him. I thought he'd beaten you, to tell the truth.'

'That's what he thought, too.' She slid down to the ground, and loosened the girth. 'But he always thinks he can have a go. I shouldn't have tried him when he could win, it was stupid.'

'All right if it works. I should say you should have cut his corn ration and started him on the lunge before you saddled him.'

'I know that! Do you think I don't?' She glared at him, leading the steaming horse into his box.

'You can't take chances on things any more. Not when it's serious.'

180

'He's my horse and I'll do what I like.'

He said nothing while she sponged Diablo's eyes and mouth, letting him stand in a sweat rug before rubbing him down. At last, he said, 'You are good. It's a relief.'

'Sorry to have caused you so much anxiety,' said Mary sarcastically. 'As for you, I think you could be all talk. Neat and tidy on a horse no doubt, but no guts.'

'You think so?'

She glanced at him. No, she did not. But she said, 'I suppose we shall just have to see.'

She had succeeded in annoying him. The muscles in his cheek twitched gratifyingly. She set about rubbing down Diablo with a sense of a job well done.

He said, 'This one's knackered, he won't give me a run. What else is about I can try?'

Mary blinked. 'Nothing here. It's all right, you don't have to prove anything.'

'But I do. You think I'm a no-talent sponger. You think I'm all talk.'

'I didn't say that.'

He pointed a finger at her. 'Let's get this straight. We're equals here. You are not in charge of this outfit.'

'And neither are you! You think you're the only one with ideas and I've just got the connections.'

'And the courage, and the skills. Let me tell you, girl, I'll see you dead before you ride better than me!'

They glared at each other. Mary said sulkily, 'There's only the Bombardier, and he's not bad. He's at the Fitzalan-Howards. And I rode him once without stirrups over a five barred gate, so you can't prove anything there.'

'Lead me to him,' said Connor uncompromisingly.

'I can't. It's the middle of the night.'

'So it is. Then it had better be first thing. Six o'clock, I don't like a late start.'

'It's half-past three now!'

'So, you can't take the pace?'

Mary sighed in exasperation. 'Six o'clock then. Damn you.'

She couldn't sleep for the scant time left to her. She lay in bed, thinking about Con, Diablo, everything. What a pity men weren't like horses, she thought feverishly. Clear rules, clear commands, nothing hidden. If a horse was thinking something it didn't matter, most of the time. But with men, their thoughts mattered more than anything they did. She didn't understand Connor or any other man. They were different. They wanted different things. They weren't like her.

At six o'clock she was back in her jodhpurs, waiting in the yard. Con appeared seconds later, and went without a word to the car. 'I suppose you asked permission?' she said unkindly.

'Not at this hour, no. We'd better get ourselves a car, actually. There'll be a lot of travelling.'

'Why?'

'Buying horses, of course. They're not like fallen leaves. Get on with you, before someone wakes up.'

The motion of the car made her sleepy. She yawned and gave poor directions, so twice they had to reverse. But when they came to Fairlands, that Palladian house with its wide lawns and clear windows, she fully expected him to be impressed. But Con said nothing. Mary was puzzled, he'd been kind about Gunthwaite so why not this?

'Don't you think it's nice?' she asked at last.

He grunted. 'Bit Home Counties for Yorkshire I should have said. Ireland's thick with such as this. And we've got a darn' sight more horses.'

'Then I really can't think why you didn't stay,' said Mary airily, and marched off to the stables.

The Bombardier was looking out over his door with a mild, enquiring eye. Connor twittered to him, the horseman's greeting, and Mary felt the first stirrings of anxiety. Suppose he was miles better than her? He was older and he was a man. She'd have nothing to equal him.

She fetched the tack, quiet now, wishing they hadn't come. Connor swept the Bombardier's rugs to the ground in a neat, practised gesture. Mary picked them up and folded them, watching his fingers deft on the buckles. The horse was beginning to blow and stamp, he was always excitable. Connor pulled him from the box and mounted.

He was a horseman all right. He sank deep into the saddle, his legs long on the gelding's barrel sides. He sat straight and square, his shoulders relaxed and flat. Mary felt herself staring. There was something delicious and illicit about it. He was busy with the horse, and besides, she was allowed to watch him ride. The indulgence made her dizzy. His shoulders were so very wide, she thought, and before she could stop herself imagined standing behind him and running her hands over his naked back.

The colour flooded into her face. Why would she think something like that? At once she turned her mind to respectable things; his hands on the reins. Such firm, brown, responsive fingers. She closed her eyes and tried to think of nothing, nothing, nothing! But when she opened them again there was Connor, dark-headed, absorbed, and she could stare and stare and it didn't matter. Surely it wouldn't hurt.

A minute or two later, deciding that the horse was warm enough, he began to shorten rein. Mary pursed her lips. No one ever got very far with the Bombardier's schooling. He was a cross-country horse, pure and simple, stop, go, and nothing in between. But somehow, under Connor's hand, he was changing. His big, heavy head began to drop, his back end bunch and strive, powering him forward. The horse that Mary had never seen perform anything more than a workmanlike pace was accepting his bit and collecting himself like a continental dressage star.

Connor circled and tried the shoulder in, sending the horse diagonally across the arena. It was tough on the big horse, and tiring. Halfway across, muscles struggling with the unaccustomed strain, he ducked his head, half-reared and dived towards the gate. But Connor never moved. It was as if he and the horse were glued together. In a moment, without alarm, the horse was back on the track, performing well. When they reached the corner, as a reward, Connor let him relax in a canter, taking him up after a stride or two into the classic ballooning gait.

He glanced across at Mary. 'He'll win nothing till he learns to use his hocks. He jumps flat, I can tell.'

'He does a bit. It's always hairy, but he often gets round.'

'Teach him to use his hocks and he'll always get round, with fewer crashes to strain his nerves. He's a nice horse. Have you seen enough, or do you want me to ride him Indian style?'

Without a word of warning he slipped from the saddle and hung beneath the horse's belly. He aimed a mock gun at Mary. 'Pow, Pow!'

'What are you doing? You'll frighten the horse to death!'

'This chap don't frighten easy. You'd have a good day's hunting on him and be pleased with the chance. Don't girls play Cowboys and Indians, then? We did it all summer at home.'

Mary shook her head, watching him slip easily to the ground. She felt shy. He rode so well, and all her boasting, or at least her family's boasting, must have seemed so silly. He must have ridden hundreds of horses. He could do things she had only read about in books.

'Who taught you?' she asked, as he led the horse back to his box.

'My father. He's the best, taught all us boys. Four of us,' he supplied, answering the unspoken question. 'And not enough room at home for all. No, I've to make my way in the world with what few skills I possess.'

Mary picked up a scraper and began sweeping the sweat from

the Bombardier's broad flanks. 'You're brilliant. You know you are. You didn't have to prove it, I'd have seen the moment you got on a horse.'

'But think of the sneers you'd have suppressed before then. I don't like being despised, Mary Cooper.'

'And I don't like being taken for a fool.'

He stood back, considering. 'Your foolishness is all for lack of caution. Don't worry about it. It's a good way to be.'

Mary glared at him, unable to think of a crushing reply. In her agitation she caught the horse on the point of his elbow, and he grumbled. Connor made a face. 'If you please, Mary. Mind on the job.'

'Get knotted,' she said rudely.

By breakfast time the Bombardier was immaculate. As a gift they had plaited his mane and tail, and he looked like a show prospect, handsome and neat.

'We make a great team,' said Connor. 'Will they feed us here, do you think?'

'You don't want to meet Aunt Dora, surely!'

'The appalling Aunt Dora? No one more.'

There was a certain measure of surprise when they turned up at the house with their garbled story. But Mr Fitzalan-Howard had said often enough, without meaning it, that Mary could ride the Bombardier in a point to point, so he could hardly object to 'our assessment' as Con blandly put it. 'A good horse, sir, and once he's schooled he'll win for you. Can we send you a note of our terms?'

'Your terms?' Mr Fitzalan-Howard blinked.

'Discounted, of course,' said Mary. 'Connor thinks the horse doesn't use his hocks enough and jumps too flat. And he does. Keep it quiet and cure him, and we could make a killing on the day.'

Mr Fitzalan-Howard laughed uncomfortably. 'You amaze me, young lady. Now, will you have bacon and eggs? Gabriel's not down yet, but I think Dora's about. Oh, and Piers.' He looked uncomfortable and Mary vaguely wondered why.

Dora was already at the breakfast table, smoking and stirring her coffee. She looked singularly fed up. 'Good God, where did you two spring from?' she asked, tossing a newspaper off a chair. 'A new man, at last. Sit down, won't you? Mary, introduce me.'

'This is Connor,' said Mary feebly. 'Connor—'

'O'Malley,' he supplied. 'And you must be Dora? The elegant aunt. It can't be anyone else.'

Dora laughed. 'Irish charm, I see. We don't have enough

184

interesting men around here. I should say any interesting men. Sit next to me and be entertaining.'

By the time the bacon and eggs arrived Mary found her appetite had gone. Connor was a ladies' man, she realised, watching him sparkle and flirt with Dora. She blossomed in the glow of his attention, her cheeks flushing, her gestures intimate and slow. When she lit a fresh cigarette she leaned on her elbow and puffed smoke into his face and he grinned.

'You're a very attractive man,' she murmured, under cover of a clatter of silverware.

'Thank God,' he replied. And they both laughed.

Chapter Nineteen

Deborah replaced the telephone and chewed on her thumb. The back of her mother's head was in full view, drooping unmistakably. She sat like that for hours nowadays, saying nothing, doing nothing. If anyone took her to task about it, she would look at them, apologise, and her eyes would well with tears.

'That was Graham Beacham,' said Deb, picking up some knitting and putting it handily at Laura's elbow.

'Oh.'

'He wants me to go into Bainfield to the pictures.'

'That's nice.'

'I said no.'

Laura stirred herself a little. 'Wasn't there anything you wanted to see?'

'There is, actually. But I thought I'd go with Piers.'

Laura said nothing, and Deb felt a great rage beginning. Apart from the odd, almost reflex comment, her mother had ceased to care. What was she thinking? It was impossible to say. She dressed each day in whatever came to hand, dragged herself downstairs and did nothing at all.

She went on determinedly, 'So I thought I'd ring Piers and ask him if he wants to go. And we'll go back to Fairlands and play records and things. In his room.'

Still her mother said nothing. Giving up on her, Deb stormed into the hall and dialled the Fairlands number. 'Hello, Mrs Fitzalan-Howard. Is Piers there? It's Deborah Cooper.'

She waited for him to come to the phone. Suddenly she was aware of her mother, standing in the doorway. 'I wish you wouldn't,' she said abstractedly. 'But you won't stop because I tell you, I see that now. There isn't any point in telling people things. It's all a waste of time. But you will be careful, won't you, Deb?'

She hunched a shoulder. 'I don't know what you mean.'

'He's such an odd boy. He always seems to be angry with me.'

'He would be. You're so mean to him.'

'Am I? It's just so hard. I thought I was doing right. But in the end I just don't know.' She rubbed her head and looked vague. After a moment she wandered aimlessly away.

Later, Deb went to find Mary in the barn. She was rubbing down a hot, restless, energised Bombardier, his flanks dark with sweat. Three weeks into his training programme, he was starting to buzz.

'She talks as if she's at the end of everything,' said Deb worriedly. 'As if there isn't going to be anything else to come. Does she mean really to kill herself do you think?'

Mary stopped her work and leaned against the horse's twitching shoulder. 'I don't know. It's on her mind, you can tell. And she used to be so strong, she and Dad were the strongest people you could ever meet!'

'That's the trouble, isn't it?' said Deb. 'Dad. They're not like they used to be. It's as if she's keeping her distance.'

'And he won't push her. He never has.'

The sisters looked at each other glumly. 'Your hair needs cutting,' advised Deborah.

Mary made a face. 'Why bother? In London I went to a brilliant bloke, but they won't be able to do it in Bainfield.'

'Better that than a mop,' said Deb. 'Are you or Con going into Bainfield this afternoon? I need a lift.'

Mary didn't ask why. It would be some boy, of course, Deb was never short of dates. 'We could drop you off. But you'll have to get back under your own steam, we're going to see a horse.'

Mary drove as far as the outskirts of town. She was a very new motorist, and hadn't yet passed her test in the little Morris the horse concern had acquired, so Con took over once they were in traffic. Deborah said, 'I can't wait until I can drive. Will you let me use this when I can, Con?'

He glanced back at her, grinning. 'Who could ever refuse you, Deborah?'

'Me,' snapped Mary. 'Easily. This is a car for the business, not pleasure trips.'

Piers was waiting outside the Odeon. When Mary saw him she drew in her breath. 'I told Mum,' said Deborah defensively. 'She didn't mind.'

'She wouldn't care if you were going to see Jack the Ripper,' said Mary miserably. She wound down her window and said, 'Hello, Piers.'

'Hi.'

He was wearing blue jeans and a leather jacket. As Deb got out of the car he took her hand possessively, and glared at Mary in case she said anything. But she was silent. As she and Con drove away she looked back and saw that Piers had his arm around Deborah's waist, and stood watching them.

187

'Damn,' she said flatly.

'He's in love,' remarked Connor. 'I can see why, too. But what about Deb? She's too young for that much devotion.'

'She likes him,' said Mary. 'He's almost family, I think it makes her feel safe. You're just jealous.' She said the words lightly, but her heart lurched in case it might be true. He glanced at her and laughed.

They were going to see a gelding they had been offered. That in itself was strange, it wasn't usual to be urged to see something someone had to sell. Would-be sellers normally let it be discreetly known that circumstances prevented them from bringing out the horse's full potential, and that a suitable price might persuade them to part, wrench though it would be. To state baldly that 'the bugger's got to go' was odd indeed.

It was a farm on a windy and treeless plain. The farmer, known slightly to Mary from trips to market, was a small, wizened, battered-looking man with two strapping sons. As soon as they went into the stable it was clear to Mary that although the old man was a horseman neither of his sons could lay claim to any skill. A rawboned chestnut stood at the back of a box, rolling his eye. As soon as anyone made to go in with him he swung his back end round menacingly.

'Does he mean business?' asked Con.

'Aye,' said the old man. 'I left the boys to see to him and this is the result. Only advice I've had is to shoot him.'

'But he's broken to ride?' asked Mary.

'Just about.'

Mary looked gloomily over the door. The horse was miserable, she thought. But although there were many miserable horses, it was rare for one to take it out on humankind. The animal lashed out an experimental leg, connecting only with air, sending a draught past her face. She felt a shiver run down her spine. 'Does he bite?'

'That he does. Right devil, this 'un.'

It was clear why they'd been called. The farmer could do nothing with the brute, not even load him for slaughter. If she and Con paid killing price, and took him away, the farmer would count himself well suited.

'We'll take him,' said Connor suddenly.

Mary turned to him, her eyes big with horror. He returned her gaze blandly, giving nothing away. She was furious suddenly, and turned back to the horse. They should at least have discussed it!

The farmer blew down his nose with satisfaction, trying not to show he was pleased. 'You can pay when you come for him,' he said. 'I'll not deceive you, he's a devil to handle. But he's yours for the price and then it's up to you.'

'We won't have much trouble,' said Connor, watching the back of Mary's rigid and disdainful head. Quick and deliberate, she moved to the box door, swinging back as the horse's long, snakelike head whipped out savagely. Thwarted, he squealed and kicked at the door.

'I told you he's a one,' said the farmer in strangled tones. Mary contented herself with snort of withering scorn.

On the way home, Connor began to cajole her. 'At worst we take him straight to the knacker. Mary, we can't lose.'

'He could break up the wagon. He could kill us!'

'He won't do that. He's a horse, we're too clever for him. Not that he's stupid. There's something about a horse that fights back. Makes you think he's worth a bit, perhaps. A bit of respect, at least.'

There was indeed something admirable about the horse's futile, determined stand. 'Did you see the scars on his face?' said Mary. 'They took a whip to his head, the fools.'

'I'd rather be dead than in the care of foolish men,' said Connor, and looked sideways at her. 'But that horse deserves a life. A chance at something a bit kinder.'

She felt resentful. He shouldn't appeal to her soft heart. The horse had touched her the moment she had seen him with his brave, angry, bashed about face. But this was business, and she should be businesslike. She knew instinctively that Connor would use her sympathy against her as quickly as now he added it to his cause.

He said, 'So why don't we stop for a drink? We should make a plan for him. Make sure we load him without getting hurt.'

'We can plan at home,' said Mary distantly.

'And don't you think a drink would help? You've been ignoring me for weeks, Mary. Why is that?'

She stopped the car in a gateway. The headlights, small and weak against the gloom, seemed like twin paths wavering towards a pointless destination. She turned to look at Connor. He had shifted in his seat. She was aware of his excitement, because of the horse, because they were together in the night. He knew nothing at all of what she was thinking.

'Tell me,' she said silkily, 'how are you and Aunt Dora getting on?'

His face changed, although at once he tried to hide it. But she had seen enough. She rammed the car into gear and screeched back on to the road, not once looking to see if anything was coming.

'You'll have us killed!' said Connor, for something to say.

'Aunt Dora would be upset,' retorted Mary, refusing to be diverted.

'What about her? What has she to do with me?'

'Damn you, Connor, don't lie!'

He fell silent, forcing himself not to grip the dash of the car. She was driving with no care at all, braking hard on greasy corners, not once looking behind. He hadn't realised before that she was so stark, so clear-cut, he thought. He should have done so. Mary's need for truth and clarity had brought them together in the first place. He should have known there was no room for shilly-shallying with her.

'It's the sort of thing she does all the time!' he said at last.

'And you? Do you do it all the time?'

He turned towards her. 'What? What is it you think I do?'

If he hoped to embarrass her he was denied that pleasure. 'I think you sleep with her,' said Mary baldly. 'Is that what you'd like to call it? Or do you perhaps – make love?'

He was the one to be embarrassed. There was no brazening this out. They screeched around a corner and he said distractedly, 'Pull over, will you? I'd better drive.'

To his surprise she did as she was told. Her hands were shaking, she sat for a moment not getting out. He said, 'Are you jealous? Is that it?'

'Of you?' She imbued the words with absolute contempt. 'But did you have to, Connor? Did you have to paddle in that dirty pond?'

'You don't understand—'

'No! But you're not what I thought you. Not at all.'

She flung out of the car and round to his side. He could have moved across, but instead he got out and faced her. Tall as she was, he was taller. He felt a surge of masculinity, caused by the talk as much as anything, that and the somehow touching stains on her pale and angry face. She seemed so bruised and open. Where Dora was all aggression, Mary was all need.

He bent his head to kiss her. 'Don't you dare!' she hissed at him, her breath hot on his lips. 'Touch me and I'll bite your damned head off!'

He recoiled, wishing in an instant that he hadn't. She'd have given in. She'd have had to. But Mary pushed past him and into her seat.

They didn't speak until they were back at Gunthwaite. In the kitchen, Michael said, 'No good then?'

'Godawful,' said Mary. 'But we're having him. It's a brute.'

'Needs handling,' supplied Connor. 'A bit of feminine guile.'

190

'What he'll most likely get is a bullet,' snarled Mary, and even Laura looked up and said, 'Mary!' in a reproachful tone. So. Everyone thought she was the difficult one. Her heart ached with the pain of it all.

Deborah came in just before midnight. Mary heard her and got up, padding along to her sister's bedroom, staying to watch her undress.

'I couldn't get a lift any earlier,' said Deb quickly, countering the expected criticism.

'You could have got a taxi. Dad would have paid.'

'No point in wasting money.'

She pulled off her blouse, turning away. All the same, Mary saw the blood red marks on her breasts. 'What's he been doing to you?'

'Who? What?'

'Deb, you shouldn't! They're all the same, that family. You know they are.'

Soft colour was flooding Deborah's cheeks. 'We don't do anything we shouldn't. You don't know, Mary. He's – he's lovely to me. I can talk to Piers. He's the only one who understands.'

'If Mum sees you there'll be hell to pay.'

Deb turned and met her eyes. 'Do you really think so? I don't. Mum doesn't care about anything any more.'

Mary turned and went back to her bed. There was a weight in her chest made up of misery and confusion. It was her fault that her mother was so changed. It was because of that change that Connor was here, that Deb was taking chances, that everything was different and out of control. If only she could put things right. But there was no going back, no unravelling it all. The sins of her father had been visited on her, and with a vengeance. How she hated Gabriel!

That night she tossed in her sleep, dreaming of wild horses and horrible ends. But in the morning, heavy-eyed, she knew there was nothing to be done but to go on.

They went to fetch the horse the next Friday, going in the evening when the wagon was free. Michael was interested and wanted to come, but Mary insisted that they could manage. 'We could do with an extra hand, Mary,' said Connor, and she knew that but for Dora he'd have insisted on having his own way. But he wasn't on solid ground.

'We can't rely on other people all the time,' she said ingenuously. 'You'll see, Connor, that I'm very well able to do my bit.'

'Your bit of what?' he muttered, following her out to the yard. 'Putting in your three pennorth of mischief, I'll be bound.'

She turned and smiled brilliantly as she climbed into the cab.

When they arrived they found the farmer hovering in the yard, jiggling from foot to foot with anxiety. 'Thought you weren't coming,' he said. 'He's bad, that horse. Near had my lad today.'

Mary went to the box and stood at a safe distance looking at the horse. He had a weal down his face, the mark of a businesslike whip. 'What a pity he didn't,' she said thinly, and the farmer shot her a sharp look.

'We've got to get on, Mary,' said Connor warningly, and she went to the wagon and brought out their own secret weapon.

It was a long length of cane. A rope was tied to one end, extended on a wire in a loop to coil back into the hand. It was a primitive lasso, all they could think of to let them get a collar on the horse.

'I thought you'd drive him,' said the farmer.

'We guessed you'd tried that already,' said Mary. The man pretended he hadn't heard.

Connor reached out to take the stick. 'Let me.'

'He's worse with men. I'd better.'

'Oh, for Christ's sake, Mary!'

'Get the headcollar, then! Connor, I can manage!'

They glared at each other. She was conscious of something delicious in the conflict, something intensely pleasurable. She loved to oppose Connor! All her anger against Gabriel, her mother, placid, accepting Michael, even against Deb, could be gathered up and flung at the handsome and deserving Irishman. Even her fear of the horse could be used against him, instead of building up within her to make her hand shake and her voice quiver. She turned to the box. 'Hello, sweetheart,' she said happily. 'Come along, then. Come along.'

She inserted the stick over the door. The horse squealed and spun round, but she was expecting it and was prepared. The rope looped out, caught, and the horse was held by the neck.

'By! That were quick!' exclaimed the farmer. The horse was throwing himself at the door, snatching with his teeth. Mary was hard put to keep out of reach. 'Bring him sideways on,' urged Connor. 'I'll put the collar and blindfold on.'

'You can't reach!'

'I'll stand on the door.'

'Damn it, you'll fall in!'

But he sprang up and stood balanced on the narrow edge of the door. The horse was plunging, enraged by terror, his head thrashing against the unlooked for rope. Connor leaned into space. She thought for a moment he would sit on the wide back and be thrown and killed. She wanted to reach out and clutch to his belt, to save him. But in a plunge of the horse the collar was on, and in another it was buckled. A hood was pulled down over the animal's wild, terrified eyes.

'Put a twitch on him,' advised the farmer.

'If you do he won't forget,' said Mary.

Connor slipped down from the door and said, 'I can hold him now. Go and get the bullstick from the wagon, Mary.'

She wanted to say that he could go and fetch it, but her arms were shaking from holding the horse. She did as she was told.

As they were leading the blindfold horse into the wagon, screaming out whinnies, swinging his vicious kicks this way and that, the farmer was loud in his congratulations. 'Never seen anything like it! By, but you're professional, I'll give you that. When I saw the girl I had doubts, I warn you, but she's game. That she is. Well done, lad.'

'Thank you very much,' said Connor, trying to seem nonchalant. 'She's a hard worker, is Mary.'

He jumped quickly off the ramp, knowing that a second more and she'd slam it up and lock him in with a mad horse, as his just desserts.

On the drive back Connor was exultant. After a while he began to notice that Mary had said hardly anything at all. 'What's the matter with you, girl?' he demanded. 'You're like a wet weekend. Don't you realise? We did it! We must know what we're doing after all. Jesus, I thought the brute was going to kill us straight.'

'That would have been a pity,' said Mary icily.

He sighed and drummed his fingers against the wheel. 'You can't go on hating me. We have to work together, you know.'

'Do we? Everyone assumes I'm just the hired help.'

'They do not! You're too sensitive. And the fault's half yours, if you slink about with your head down and your hair over your face.'

'So it's my fault now, is it? I don't look right! Would you like it better if I looked like Dora? Or Deb?'

He clenched his teeth, feeling trapped and harried. Mercifully there was the sound of loud kicking from the back. Con pulled over near a wall, and they stood on it to look in through the side window. The horse, still blindfold, was smashing the back of his stall. Even as they watched splinters of wood flew high into the air.

'It's going to cost more than we make to mend the box,' said Mary.

'It's only a panel.'

They climbed down and started off again. Gradually the kicking diminished, presumably as the panel was smashed to nothing.

193

Connor said, 'Look. About Dora. It doesn't mean a thing, it's just something we both enjoy. I can't say I even like her all that much.'

'Don't you think you ought to like people you sleep with?'

He looked at her. 'Not always, no. Not if you're a man.'

'Are women different then?'

'I suppose so. I suppose they should be.'

'Unless they're Aunt Dora. That's different again.'

He changed gear unnecessarily on a hill. The wagon coughed and the horse in the back let out a raw, screaming whinny. The rain of these steep, Yorkshire valleys began to lash at them again as they sat in silence, gazing out at the mist, thinking their own secret thoughts.

They left the horse to settle the next day. He stood huddled in his new box, specially painted in his honour, refusing to look out at anything. He wore a headcollar now, from which a length of rope dangled, to make catching him possible again. Both Con and Mary came separately to look at him. He wasn't a pretty sight.

Later, Con took the Morris. Mary heard him go, and went to the barn again to look at the new horse and think. 'What shall we call you?' she mused, tempting him with a bucket in which lurked a handful of molassed feed. 'How about Sweet?' Because he wasn't, she thought. Not at all.

The horse's nostrils quivered as he was tempted. He took a tentative half step towards her. 'Good lad,' said Mary, tilting the bucket to let him see what was promised. 'No need to fight, Sweetness. See what's for you!'

He stretched his neck, teetering on his toes rather than take another step. She thought, men are the same. Offer them something and they all reach for it, even when they know it's wrong. Piers and Deb, Con and Dora, Gabriel and – her mother. She pushed the thought away.

'Come on, horse,' she urged, and his lips quivered at the bucket rim while his eyes rolled and his ears lay flat against his head. She held her breath, coaxing him, tempting him. Was Dora even now doing this to Con? she wondered. Perhaps he didn't need tempting. Perhaps, if you were Dora or Deb, you simply allowed yourself to be approached. But Mary, her arm breaking with the weight of the bucket, felt as if she would always be hanging over a metaphorical stable door, failing to attract a reluctant friend. Just then the horse stepped forward, snatched some feed, and jumped back. They looked at each other, the horse wary, the girl exuberant. 'There are some things I can do, at any rate,' she told the horse. 'Come along, Sweet. Have some more.' She rattled the bucket again enticingly.

At Fairlands, Con was in the summer house. The weather wasn't suitable, the cushions were mildewed and damp while a cold wind whipped beneath the ill-fitting door. He stood at the window, awaiting Dora's pleasure, feeling today as if he would give anything not to see her approach.

He hadn't known it could be like this. Nothing in his sexual experience had fitted him for the maelstrom of feeling that Dora unleashed within him. At first he thought he loved her, but that soon changed. Sometimes, when she sat astride him and laughed cruelly into his face, he knew hate. For the rest, he vacillated from wild excitement to depression and lethargy, longing to see her, longing to have her, hating it when he did. Sex left a bad taste, he thought gloomily. He never left Dora's arms refreshed and replenished, ready for what was to come.

She was tripping lightly up the path towards him. She was wearing a long tube of a dress in pale cream wool, no doubt with nothing underneath. She never pretended that they met for anything other than this, not for a minute did she indicate that she cared. As he'd tried to say to Mary, this was entirely physical. A dish he hated, but couldn't push away.

She came in, closing the door and pulling the scarf from her head. 'Really, you'd think Gabriel wanted to be difficult. He's been hanging around half the morning. Hello, darling. Thought I'd never get away.' She put her arms around his neck and kissed him, undulating her hips against his groin. He was as yet only semi-erect. She slid her hands inside his trousers, cradling his buttocks, digging her nails into his flesh. He said, 'You're keen.'

'And you're not! Look, I haven't much time, I can't be all day.'

'Sorry.'

He tried to will the blood to flow and the nerves to respond. All at once Dora knelt before him, pulling down his zip. His senses tingled, he couldn't believe – wouldn't believe! She said matter-of-factly, 'You'd be amazed how many men need this to get them going.' She took him in her mouth. He felt himself engorge, a great rush of feeling. He wanted her to go on and on, needed it, would give anything – she released him, stood up and stripped off her dress.

He'd never seen her completely naked before. Her breasts were as heavy as a boat's fenders, her nipples raspberry red. He took them in his hands, feeling the softness and the weight. Her hips were slim, still. She was a woman who had grown top heavy with age, all breasts. She was pushing herself on to him, trying to gain the upper hand, dictate what would be. Suddenly he wanted none of it. He wasn't her plaything, her toy! He was a man, he didn't need her encouragement in this. He pushed her backwards, feeling her trip over the rough boards, fall back against the glass of the window. She cried out, and he laughed. 'Let's do it my way.'

She brought her legs up on to the window sill, shameless, open. She was panting. He thought, She's more animal than woman. In her need for this, she was more like a man. He too was aching with need, and she was ready for him, crouched on the window sill, eyes closed and lips apart. He pushed forward, feeling her take him in, grinding against her for a second until she began to pulsate. She let out gasping cries, and he was brutal suddenly, pounding at her, feeling her fingers raking down his back. Suddenly, in a rush, he was done. She throbbed against him still. He could only hear their breathing.

'God,' said Dora, wrapping her legs around his pelvis. 'And I thought you might be getting bored.'

'I am,' he said weakly. 'I've had enough.'

'Have you?' She held him into her. It was exquisite anguish. He knew he'd be here again.

Outside, from the terrace, the window was no more than blur. But Piers put up the binoculars and saw his mother's naked shoulders, her head against a man's. He saw her uncurl her legs from him, and for a second stand easily on the sill, facing whoever it might be. It didn't matter to Piers who it was. He'd known for weeks that his mother had someone. She was always the same with a new man, prowling, restless, criticising Gabriel with venom. For the duration of the affair she would despise her husband, taking less and less trouble to hide what she was doing, challenging him to notice. Why didn't he kill her? thought Piers. She deserved it. He'd kill any woman that did that to him. But his father just drank and ignored her, while his mother, hating to be ignored, let strangers use her body in what was almost a public place. Piers shuddered, a long tremor that would not cease. He was like an overfilled bag, the seams so strained that at any moment they might burst. Again the long shaking, pressure building and building with no legitimate release. He felt afraid suddenly, and ran to the cloakroom to try and be sick. Nothing came. All he could hear were his own harsh sobs and he knew, without doubt, that one day he would explode in an orgy of loathing.

Returning to Gunthwaite, Connor felt weary and drained. Just when he thought he had the woman's measure she surprised him. He saw again the sight of her crouched against the window, and his sex reawakened. It was like a curse, he thought. He was condemned to make love to her whatever it cost. Love? There was no love. Theirs was an animal mating.

196

When he went to see the new horse, he found Mary in the barn. She was sitting on a stool the same height as the stable door, dangling her legs inside with the horse. She was feeding him titbits from her fingers, but when he saw Connor he leaped away and turned his back end, sending swinging kicks towards the door. Mary said, 'Silly Sweet,' in the voice she reserved for horses that were being foolish rather than wicked.

Con said, 'You'd better get out of there. You're taking chances.'

She looked at him. 'You're a fine one to talk. He's OK, he's coming round. I've called him Sweet.'

'You haven't? That means he won't be. Call him Killer and you might have a chance.'

'Is that some Irish superstition? He'll be what he's going to be, and that's that.' She brushed her fingers together, retracted her legs and slipped down. As she walked away she sniffed and said, 'I do think you should wash. Aunt Dora wears terribly strong perfume.'

He felt himself colour. She was the oddest girl! He wanted to feel angry at her, for putting him in the wrong, but he knew it was justified. If only he needn't go, hadn't been, and had instead spent the last hour looking at a horse or something. But that was what he felt now, after the encounter. He couldn't think like that before. He looked at Mary's stiff, slender back and felt hopeless suddenly. It wasn't his fault about Dora! Surely Mary ought to try to understand?

Chapter Twenty

On the day that they put Sweet on the lunge, Michael came and watched. He stood at the field gate as Connor held the line and Mary walked behind, chivvying the horse up. They used no whip – the horse had seen too much of that already. Only the suspicion of a blow and he became unmanageable.

'Now,' said Michael as they finished. 'Who will you ever sell him to?'

'He's not half done yet, sir,' said Connor.

'But you're right, Dad,' agreed Mary, putting her hand up to pat the horse and then thinking better of it. Even pats could be misconstrued. 'He's never going to be quite right in the head.'

Michael grinned at her. He and Mary so often thought alike. 'It's good to have you back,' he said suddenly, catching her unawares. She felt the tears rise, and swallowed hard.

'I wish Mum—' she said harshly.

Brightly, too brightly, Connor said, 'Ah, she seems much better to me. She went for a little walk yesterday, down by the stream.'

'She went to see Sophie and Marie,' said Mary. And sighed. 'She makes an effort for them. But it doesn't help, seeing them old. I think they make her feel that nothing's got any point.'

Michael said, 'Anyone can feel like that. Before I met your mother I thought that life was made up of that feeling, with little interludes that were better. But really, it's the other way round.'

'Is it?' Con had wiped his smile away. He looked grim. 'We all have a different mix, it seems to me. It's just how life goes.'

He began walking the horse back to the barn. As he passed the big, open-fronted shed, Bill Mayes came out and rattled a stick against his boot. 'Get up! Get up, there!' he intoned, and the horse erupted.

Connor hung on for grim death. The horse struck out in front, catching him a glancing blow on the cheek, and as he fell plunged earthwards himself, feet flailing. Bill Mayes rushed ponderously forward, yelling, but Mary was before him.

'Shut up, Bill!' she hissed in passing, and saw that Michael was

198

putting his large hand over the old man's mouth. Sweet stood inches from Connor's dazed head. 'Silly boy. Silly boy,' crooned Mary. The horse's mad expression was giving way to bewilderment. 'Sweet baby,' oozed Mary, and took hold of his rein. She led him quietly away.

When she came back, horse safely stabled, she found Connor with a swelling bruise on his cheek.

'Is it broken?' she asked cheerily.

He glowered. 'Much you'd care.'

'If you want sympathy, you'll have to go somewhere else.' She looked at him meaningfully, but he avoided her eye. It hadn't occurred to him before now that she might let people know. She wasn't that sort. Was she?

Michael said, 'It's nasty. Best take him to the hospital, love.'

They sat at the front in Casualty. Visitors stared at them as they passed, and Mary wondered if they thought she might be the patient. People quite often mistook her marks for burns. After an hour's wait Con was seen and sent for X-ray, and Mary sat alone, looking through out-dated magazines. Suddenly a voice said: 'Mary.' She looked up. It was Gabriel.

'What on earth are you doing here?' she asked in bewilderment. Then she saw Piers. He was passing on a stretcher, his skin blotched and ghastly. He seemed half-conscious. 'Oh my God!' exclaimed Mary, leaping up. 'What is it?'

'Alcohol poisoning,' said Gabriel simply. 'He's here to have his stomach pumped. The doctor insisted.'

The stretcher was carried past. Mary looked up at Gabriel. 'How?'

'Bottle of whisky. But I don't know why.'

She thought at once of Con and Dora. She said, abstractedly, 'He should have been at school.' With children safely at school parents could behave as they wished, she thought. Was that why children were sent away? So their parents could be children again?

Gabriel ran his fingers through his hair, looking distraught and overburdened. 'They've thrown him out. At least, there was an upset and they said he was welcome to leave. I won't find another for him. The boy's a complete waster!'

'Oh.' Mary fiddled with the draw-cord of her coat. 'Is that why, then?'

'God knows! I don't think so, it was weeks back. But he won't make any plans, won't even work on the estate. And now this. I don't know what he wants.'

Except Deb, thought Mary sourly. She looked away.

'And why are you here?' he asked, as if it had just struck him that it was odd to find her there. 'Nothing serious, I hope.'

199

'Con got kicked by a horse. He's being X-rayed.'

'I see.'

She wasn't comfortable next to him. She was on the point of making an excuse to get up and move when he said, 'I think you should spend more time with Piers, you know. You owe him that at least. Since we came back home you've been very distant.'

She almost gasped. How dare he expect her to be involved with him? But she could only mutter, 'I'm not distant! It's just – it's all too difficult.'

'But he is your brother.'

A flush lit up her face. Suddenly, and just to spite him, she got up and went towards the treatment rooms. There was the ghastly sound of retching and a nurse said, 'I'm sorry. Could you wait outside, please?'

'Piers Cooper is my brother,' said Mary in carrying tones. 'Our mutual father won't come in, but he ought to have someone with him, don't you think? Some blood relation.'

She looked round defiantly at Gabriel. Did he really want the whole thing made public? But he was sitting as if turned to stone. So, she thought bitterly. He really didn't care.

On the way home, sent away with nothing more dramatic than a plaster on a bruise, Connor said, 'The boy must have half killed himself with whisky. Does he take after his father or was he trying to prove a point? Did he say?'

Mary was for once carefully negotiating a bend. She put her foot down and screamed round instead. Connor gasped.

'He was still pretty drunk,' remarked Mary. 'He said he wanted to blot out his mother and all she stood for. He's been working up to it for days. He'd seen her in the summerhouse. I suppose it was with you.'

After a moment Connor said, 'Oh, God.'

Mary glanced at him. 'You needn't worry. He doesn't know it was you. It's only me who knows that.'

'All the same. Christ, I knew this was going to happen.'

'Did you? And you did it just the same? Actually I should think it's worked out pretty well. They're keeping him in tomorrow. So you could nip round and see Dora quite safely.'

'Stop it, will you?'

'No.'

But she didn't say any more.

They heard nothing about Piers for several days, and could only assume that he was home again. For Mary, the days were acquiring a certain routine; in the mornings she handled Sweet, and in the afternoons helped Con with the Bombardier, and rode Diablo. On about two evenings a week they went to look at horses, but they were always too expensive or too finished or too unpromising.

Small doubts were beginning to worry her. She seemed to be doing so much of the hard work of this horse business, leaving Con the riding and the fun. Day after day she wielded the muck fork while he rode out on the Bombardier, returning with the horse in a lather, saying: 'I'm bushed.' It was Mary who saw to the horse and cleaned the tack. And it was she who sat for hours in Sweet's box, a book in one hand and a bucket of feed in the other.

On Thursday, she was struggling with a loaded barrow when Gabriel drove into the yard. She stood, hair blowing, straw whisking from her load. He came slowly towards her.

'Why are you wasting your time with that?'

'And a very good morning to you. Someone has to muck out horses.'

'You can get someone to do it, can't you? Free you for more important work. In any business you've got to invest.'

So, even Gabriel thought he had a hold over her. He had put up money she didn't want for a business that wasn't hers to give her advice she didn't need. If she said they hadn't the money he'd simply offer them more. And she hated being beholden to him! 'I'll thank you to leave the organisation to us,' she said tartly, and began pushing her steaming load away.

'Is your mother in?' called Gabriel to her retreating back. She didn't deign to reply.

He knocked at the back door, but there was no answer. He went in, looking askance at the unwashed dishes in the sink and the litter of papers and unopened letters on the table. Laura never used to be untidy. Her kitchen used to be one of the most pleasant places he had ever dreamed he could be.

She came in from the hall, carrying a vase of dead flowers. 'Oh. Hello.' She went to the sink and poured the flower water away. It stank quite horribly. 'I should have thrown this outside,' she said vaguely, looking about her in weary despair. Gabriel felt his heart ache for her. How had the young, pretty, brave girl he used to know become this grey-streaked, helpless woman?

'I needed to talk to you,' he said awkwardly. The idea seemed foolish now. What could Laura do about his troubles, when she so clearly had enough of her own?

She sank into a chair and looked up at him. Her eyes were pale and empty. Like the ashes of a dead fire, he thought, and brushed dust and crumbs from a bench so that he too could sit down.

'Stop staring at me,' said Laura suddenly, pushing at her hair. 'I know I'm a mess. I wasn't expecting anyone.'

'You look fine,' he lied. 'Did Mary tell you about Piers?'

She nodded. 'I'm sorry. He's better, isn't he? Lots of boys get drunk, you know. And I suppose he sees you and Dora drinking and thinks he can too.'

He looked at her witheringly. 'Not an entire bottle, Laura!'

'A bottle? Of Scotch? Oh. I didn't realise.'

She got up and went to the sink to start the washing up. The smell of stagnant water still hung in the air and she ran the tap for a minute or two to dispel it. Then she said, 'He did it to spite you, then.'

'Not me. Dora. She's having an affair.'

'Really?' Laura turned in surprise. 'Who with?'

'God knows. It doesn't matter. She just is.'

Laura went back to her washing up. After a while she said, 'I thought I was a bad mother.'

'Oh no you didn't,' challenged Gabriel. 'You thought you were a bad person, but a good mother. You made a point of it. Too much of a point, if you ask me.'

'You can't be too good a mother!'

'You can lead your children to expect perfection! And then they discover you have feet of clay.'

'Or the morals of an alleycat,' said Laura tartly. 'To think I encouraged you to marry her. Well. Who'd have thought?'

Gabriel was feeling thoroughly annoyed. He had come here to have his own failing spirits raised, not to restore Laura's vision of herself in comparison to Dora. He found himself being pushed from the table while she gave the surface a thorough wiping, then moved to another seat while she dealt with the chairs.

'For God's sake!' he burst out then. 'Will you just listen! I don't know what to do with the boy. Not out of hospital a week and I find him drinking my whisky. And his school's kicked him out and when I suggested he might start work on the estate and do some farming he told me to go and – go and shoot myself.'

'Did he really say that?'

'You know what he said!'

'My, my.'

Laura leaned her back against the sink. She chuckled. 'Poor old Gabriel. A man can't even call his whisky his own any more.'

'Don't you think you could take this seriously?'

She considered. After a moment she said, 'I don't think you and Piers like each other very much. The poor boy hasn't anyone who really loves him.'

He looked away. Without realising, she followed his own earlier thinking, remembering how he used to look when they were young. Nothing had greatly changed in him, there was still the golden springing hair, the deep eyes, the even teeth. But he was puffy and florid from drink and too little exercise. His eyelids, always heavy, drooped in spurious menace, product only of dissipation.

'He – he enrages me,' said Gabriel suddenly. 'He's got everything in front of him and he just throws it away.'

'To spite his parents,' said Laura. 'Well, people do.'

'Not my son, Laura! Not my damned son! He's good-looking, he's intelligent, he's got courage and backbone and – and everything a boy could need, and all he wants to do is drool after your daughter or hang around Fairlands drinking himself unconscious!'

'That's all he wants to do this week,' corrected Laura. 'But then, he's had a shock. It isn't so often you find out the truth about your parents. Look what it did to Mary.'

Gabriel clenched his teeth. 'She's pure gold, that girl,' he muttered.

'Oh. So you see it now? There might be gold in Piers, too, if you looked.'

'You know there isn't, Laura! He's like Dora. Exactly like. Selfish and self-centred and lazy.'

'And you're not?'

His eyes met hers. 'I might not have been. I need not be now. Laura—'

She turned away from him. 'I think I should tell you,' she said quickly, 'Michael and I have decided to send Deborah away. To Rosalind. She needs something new. She can do a term or two at finishing school and meet all the right people.'

'People who aren't like my son,' said Gabriel thickly.

'If you want to see it that way.'

As if suddenly energised by the thought, she swept all the papers into a pile and began ruthlessly sorting them.

After a moment Gabriel said 'Damn you, Laura. Is that all you can say? If you look at it coldly he's not a bad catch, you know. He's going to be rich one day. He's going to have Fairlands, and Gunthwaite too. Are you sure you know what you're throwing away?'

She glanced at him. 'I think so. The days of looking no further than a cousin are well gone, I think. Deb could have anyone. She doesn't need Piers.'

He glared at her. She had rarely annoyed him so. He said, 'By God, you can be an ungrateful bitch. Turning your nose up at my son. My son! And your daughter may be pretty, but think whose daughter she is!'

It was an underhand stroke. Laura's mouth thinned to a narrow line. 'Am I more or less the whore than Dora?' she asked quietly. Gabriel visibly flinched. He turned on his heel and stalked out of the door.

When everyone came in for lunch they were pleasantly surprised. Instead of the usual messy table and cursory bread and cheese, there was a clean blue cloth and a cauldron of soup. Laura was flushed from the fire, her hair straggling around her face. She said, 'Mary, could you help me in the house this afternoon, please? Everything's got in such a mess lately. I really need to get on top of it.'

Mary was taken aback. 'We were going to ride Sweet this afternoon, Mum. We haven't before.'

'Oh, that doesn't matter,' said Con airily. 'I'll do it.'

And Michael added, 'You shouldn't on your own. Never mind, I'll come and keep an eye. I might even be able to help.'

Mary was cornered. How clear they all made it. She was a girl, responsible for home and hearth, not to mention her mother's health. They were men, the natural leaders. She had no doubt that she would go into the barn tomorrow and find today's tack still uncleaned. They wouldn't have thought of it, of course. That wasn't their job. It was for others to do.

She took a deep breath. 'I can't work in the house and look after the business. Con and I need to make the business work.'

'It's only one day, Mary!' said Con, revenging himself for her comments on Dora. 'You'll not begrudge one day.'

'When your mother's got so much to do,' reproved Michael.

'We could get Dinah from the village,' persevered Mary.

Laura said, 'She's visiting her sister. I already asked.'

So it was decided. Mary scrubbed and polished and brushed, looking out of the window now and then to see Con and Michael between them struggling with Sweet. He was being difficult, she could see, rearing again and again, not caring if he went over backwards. Con clung to the saddle, glued there, immovable. She hated him for staying there. She knew she could not.

She had thought to be done by four, but Laura was embarked on a major clean. She set Mary to waxing the stairs, laboriously applying polish and then buffing it to a deep shine. It was something she used to do, cosseting the old oak and soothing its creaks and groans. The stairs would be slippery for a day or two, but no one had yet come to grief.

In the kitchen, Laura was preparing a sumptuous meal. Mary knew she should be pleased. Her mother was better, soon she would be well. But she could see how it was all going to be. As she had suspected, the horse thing was nothing more than a ruse to keep her home. They had given her a hobby, while her real work, housework, waited to be done. It wasn't fair!

It was her face, of course. What was there for a girl who looked as she did? Her parents would deny it, but she was to be the spinster daughter, biding her time at home, her mother's companion in activity, her support in old age. Lots of farms had girls like that, the plain one, the shy one. Her life would be happy, in its way. But the thought made her want to weep.

Everyone was cheerful at dinner that night. Even Mary couldn't resist a shoulder of prime lamb, casseroled in wine with shallots and rosemary, and potatoes crisp with cheese. Michael said, 'What a pity Deb's not here. This feels like a celebration.'

'I think it is,' said Laura. 'I feel so much better. And you've all been so patient and kind.'

'We've done nothing,' said Connor gallantly, and Mary thought, No, damn you. You haven't.

'Did you clean the tack?' she asked ingenuously.

'What?'

'Sweet's tack. You did clean it?'

'I left it for the morning.'

'And you'll do it in the morning?'

Michael said, 'Mary, do we have to be so mundane? Don't you want to know how the horse went?'

'Badly,' she snapped. 'I saw from the window.'

'Not so bad,' said Con. 'I got him going a bit.'

'Up and down isn't going,' retorted Mary. 'For that, you need up and along.'

Laura chuckled and got up to remove the plates.

Later, when the moon was high, Mary went out to see Sweet. He was standing in his box, the old, sour expression on his face. When he saw Mary he laid back his ears. 'Not this again,' she said, and fetched her stool. She settled herself, feed bucket in hand, and waited for him.

After a while her mother came in. Mary jumped, she wasn't expecting visitors. 'They've upset him again,' she explained. 'I knew they would.'

'It should have been you riding him,' said Laura. 'He trusts you.'

'Yes.'

They were silent. Laura came to lean beside her daughter, looking up into her face. 'It was only one afternoon,' she said. 'I don't mean to make you stay in the house and forget about this.'

'Dad does,' said Mary shortly.

Laura considered. 'Maybe he does. But you and Connor have a

205

business together. If I'm better there's no need for you to do much.'

'Are you better?' asked Laura nervously. 'I mean, really?'

Her mother sighed. 'I don't know. It comes and goes. But I don't feel – I don't feel despairing.'

'It was my fault, wasn't it?'

'No, darling. Mine. For being so silly as to try and pretend to you.'

Mary swung round on her perch. 'Mum, don't you think you should talk to Dad? I mean, if it all came out—'

'No!' Laura shocked herself with her vehemence, and the horse leaped in fright. 'No,' she added more quietly. 'I shall never tell him. He won't ever know.'

A cloud dimmed the moonlight falling through the high arched door. A cat stalked by in the shadows, intent on hunting. In a lighter, quieter voice, Laura said, 'Does he really leave you to clean the tack?'

Mary nodded. 'And the horses. And do the mucking out. He humps bales and feed bags and things. And rides, of course. He thinks that's fair.'

'You don't.'

'No.'

Again Mary rattled the bucket. This time Sweet stretched his neck and nibbled. Mary risked touching him, light fingers on his cheek. He twitched, but did not pull back. He remembered something, then.

'You haven't bought many horses,' remarked her mother. 'Didn't Gabriel give you enough?'

Mary sighed. She didn't want to burden her mother with all these problems. She was grown-up now, she had lived on her own. The girlish habit of confidence was more or less gone. But she ought to explain.

'It's just that – just that Connor likes one sort of horse and I like another,' she burst out. 'Take yesterday. We went to see a mare. Small, a bit cobby, but good. She needed bringing on, so she was just right, but Con wouldn't look at her because of her size. But it's not as if men are riding everything. Girls need horses too. He won't look at anything under sixteen hands, and nothing a bit common over it. And you get a strong horse with a bit of common blood.'

'It's the Irish in him,' said Laura. 'They like blood and bone.'

'And he's got Dad on his side,' said Mary darkly. 'Imagine! After the shires, he won't look at a cross. Connor can make Dad think anything.'

They sighed, in unison, and laughed. Sweet, relaxing in the

atmosphere of feminine approval, sidled over to the door. Mary put her fingers in the base of his mane and scratched him. He groaned in ecstasy.

'You've got what it takes,' said Laura softly.

'Have I? Try and tell it to Con.'

All the feed in the bucket was gone. Mary quietly slipped into the horse's box and forked out some muck. He let her, much like hotel guests with a chambermaid, aware but uninterested. She let her mind dwell on what would happen if he took fright. She'd be killed, in all likelihood, smashed against the side of the box. But it didn't happen. Task completed, she left him for the night.

As they were walking back across the yard they heard something. 'My God,' said Laura. 'What was that?'

'Vixen?' suggested Mary.

'It was more of a groan. It sounded human.'

'Hare,' supplied Mary, who had more than once heard a hare scream. It was why she neither ate nor hunted them.

They walked on, only to hear the noise again. It was midway between a groan and a scream. 'Someone's there,' said Mary fearfully. 'There's really someone there!'

'Who is it?' called Laura. 'Run in, Mary, and fetch Michael and Connor. Tell them to bring a gun.'

For a second Mary hesitated. She didn't want to seem feeble and weak. She walked forward, into the moonlight, towards the darkest shadows by the wall. 'Mary! Mary, don't!' Her mother called out in horror and tried to grab her back. But Mary was bending. 'Oh,' she said in a quite different voice. 'No need for a gun, at any rate. It's Piers. He's being horribly sick.'

Michael and Connor moved him into the house between them. He looked terrible, almost as bad as the time in hospital. His face was like chalk, with lips to match, and the whites of his eyes were threaded with red blood vessels. When he vomited, as he did at three-minute intervals, the bowl was streaked with blood.

'There's no point in calling the doctor,' said Mary. 'He'll only send him to hospital, and he doesn't need a stomach pump. I think they only do it to frighten people off, anyway.'

'He needs something,' said Michael. 'The boy looks like death. Is there nothing we can do to calm him?'

Laura reached for her coat. 'There might be. I'll go and ask Marie. Or even Sophie, if she's up. They've dealt with a million drunks in their time.'

Somehow, no one doubted it. After twenty minutes or so, Laura returned with Marie. Dressed in a tattered but magnificent lace peignoir, she stood over Piers, wrinkling her nose expressively.

'He's got a skinful. Silly child. Make a tisane. I'll put some

207

laudanum in it, numb the stomach. When he stops throwing up we'll give him a purgative, clean out the system. He'll be ill for three days, and then some. Ruins the digestion. He'll be on milk for a month.'

'I shall write and tell Deborah,' said Laura with emphasis.

Michael said, 'Good idea. He really is a stupid young puppy! I'll talk to Gabriel. He should be ashamed.'

'I put the blame squarely on Dora,' said Laura with satisfaction. 'How can she let a child get into this state? That woman's no sort of a mother. She should be ashamed!'

Connor, in the background, flushed to the roots of his hair.

Chapter Twenty-one

Gabriel and Dora arrived quarrelling. Dora was highly coloured and furious, her lipstick smudged and her hair awry. She swept into the kitchen, saying to Laura, 'What on earth is he doing here? Honestly, I've had quite enough!'

'Really?' said Laura in a colourless tone. Connor, at pains to efface himself, winced.

But Dora wasn't interested in him now. She sank into a chair, lit a cigarette and said bitterly to Gabriel, 'I suppose you'll try and blame it all on me. You always do. When you're the family lush, for God's sake!'

Gabriel looked at her with distaste. 'Do shut up. This isn't the place.'

'And where is, may I ask? When will you ever take it upon yourself to listen to criticism?'

Michael came into the kitchen. 'Good evening,' he said pointedly, and went to the sink to wash his hands. 'You can be heard quite clearly upstairs. The boy's better. Marie's with him, and he's sleeping.'

'That raddled old ewe,' said Dora, puffing furiously at her cigarette. 'What good's she supposed to be? You've sent for a doctor, of course?'

'No,' said Michael. 'He doesn't need one.'

'Then why have we been dragged here in the middle of the night?'

There was a silence. Laura looked to Michael and met his eyes. It was a telling glance. Gabriel said, 'It isn't that we don't care, of course. But he's done these things before. He likes to have us running after him. It encourages him. Makes him worse.'

Mary laughed. Her mother looked shocked, but the girl was unapologetic. 'I'm sorry, everyone,' she said. 'But really! All you care about is your own inconvenience. Not about Piers at all.'

'Coming from a child who almost drove her mother mad, that's very good,' snapped Dora. 'I suppose you'd like me to crack up. Prove to my son that I care about him.'

'But you don't,' said Connor slowly.

She tossed her cigarette on to the flags and ground it with her toe, all the time fixing Connor with an unblinking stare. He coloured, holding her gaze. She chuckled knowingly. 'God, but you're two-faced.'

Gabriel said, 'Leave it, Dora. Let's go and see Piers.'

'Are you sure you can spare the time?' asked Mary, her voice like acid.

Laura moved quietly over to her, and put a restraining hand on her shoulder. Mary quivered beneath her touch. It brought the tears to her eyes, for no good reason. And she had thought that she and her mother would never be properly close ever again.

Dora and Gabriel went noisily up the stairs. Michael said, 'I don't understand him, Laura. He's my brother, but I simply don't. He doesn't care.'

'I think he does,' she said softly. 'He's angry, that's all.'

'The boy's a young fool, of course. But only that.'

Was it only that? Mary went to put the kettle on, aware of the oddest sensation. She almost understood what Piers had done. Understood it in some fundamental way. Was it the relationship? The blood tie? She and Piers shared their need for an ordered world, shared their outrage when it was all upset. But Mary had been cherished all her life. Piers had not. Her instinct might be to run away, protecting her own precious self, but not his. He had turned inward, burning himself with the force of his anger at a world gone wrong.

Laura said, 'I'm so glad Deborah's not here. He ought not to see her, Michael. He's so unstable.'

He nodded. 'I know. It's not that we dislike the boy, of course. But he is a bad influence.'

Mary looked at Connor. 'Do you think people can be bad influences?' she asked. 'Or do you think people do what they want to do, just the same?'

'I don't know what you mean,' he said stiffly.

'I think you do.'

There was a crash on the stairs. Laura rushed into the hall, to find Dora half sitting, half lying in the hall. She was holding her ankle, and it was swelling even as they watched. 'These stairs are lethal!' she burst out. 'I could have been killed.'

'Surely not,' said Mary optimistically, and Dora shot her a fierce glance.

'Much you would have cared! Why in God's name do you polish the stairs, Laura?'

'It was me,' said Mary smugly. 'If only I'd known you were coming. You'd think I'd have more sense.'

Dora tried to stand and winced. 'What you need is a good hiding, my girl! Look at this ankle. I'll swear it's broken. Connor, give me your arm.'

He came forward reluctantly. Gabriel, coming down the stairs, said gruffly to Michael: 'I suppose it's all of a piece. Mind if I leave him here, Mike? I'll have enough bother with Dora's ankle. She does this once a year, just when she wants a rest.'

'Are you saying it's deliberate?' demanded Dora from the doorway.

'Just that it's always convenient,' said Gabriel nastily. 'Now you won't have to nurse Piers, or even visit him.'

'And what excuse are you going to provide for not doing it either?' She giggled, clinging to Connor's arm. 'Come along, my dear,' she murmured. 'Be a good boy and take Dora to the car. I shall wait for my husband there.'

Mary stayed up after her parents had gone to bed. Marie was sitting with the patient, delighted to be of use, and Connor hadn't come back in since taking Dora to the car. She felt restless and on edge, and knew she wouldn't sleep. To soothe her nerves she took up the accounts book for the horse business and made notes. Then Connor came in.

'I thought you'd gone back with her,' said Mary shortly.

'I went for a walk.'

She watched him from under her lashes. His dark hair was on end, his face grim. He had been all smiles when first they met. Someone who didn't take life as seriously as she did. Dora was good at making people feel bad about themselves, she thought.

'I thought I'd ride Sweet tomorrow,' she said.

'I'd rather you didn't.'

All sympathy for him vanished. 'And why not? Do you think you're the only one who's any good? You're ruining him. Putting him back.'

'I'm staying on him. It's more than you can do. And once he gets you off he won't forget.'

'You're not the only one who can sit a horse!'

'I'll tell you this, I can sit one better than you.'

They glared at each other. Mary was the first to look away. She wasn't as good as he was. But he didn't have her sympathy, her gentle understanding of what it meant for a fine, brave horse to be afraid! She felt instinctively that men had soured him and women must turn him sweet again. But to say it would sound foolish. She said sullenly, 'I think you should at least let me try.'

He said nothing. She didn't know if he meant her to ride the horse or not. She didn't know him well enough to decide if he stood firm behind silence or moved position while his meaning was obscured. If she talked of it again would he think her a nag?

Without another word she closed the accounts book and went upstairs. Marie was dozing by the half-open door of the guest room.

211

Mary put her head in, and saw that Piers was awake. Laudanum had made his eyes very dark and soft. She went in and said, 'How are you feeling?'

His blond hair was standing up against the pillow. 'Don't know. Better.'

'You're to stay here for a few days. They can't manage you at home.'

'Don't want me, you mean. Wish Deb was here.'

'Why? She hates people being sick.'

'All the same.'

She glanced towards Marie. The old lady was fast asleep now, snoring a little, her chin quivering. On impulse, Mary knelt at the side of the bed, taking Piers' hand. 'We really are brother and sister, you know,' she said slowly. 'And we might be almost that, one day. With Deb. So we ought to stick by each other, oughtn't we?'

He blinked dopily. 'What do you mean?'

'We should be loyal. Help each other. I mean – what I wanted to say – I know it's hard with your parents. I can see that you might think – well, that Deb's the only person to care. But there's me too. Not the same, of course. A sister.'

He said nothing. Mary wondered if he had heard her, or if he was drifting off to sleep. She let go his hand and went quietly off to bed.

The presence of an invalid seemed to give Laura a new focus. She bustled about the house, turning out scones and cakes, soups and stews, purposeful and busy once more. As Marie had predicted, Piers took his time getting well. Two days later he was only just strong enough to come downstairs.

'You gave everyone a fright, young man,' said Michael seriously, holding out a chair.

'I'm sorry, sir,' said Piers, with his ingratiating smile. Laura found herself wondering how often he had looked like that in some headmaster's study, and knew she didn't trust this boy.

'We don't need an apology,' she said. 'But your parents were very upset.'

'Oh yeah?' Piers laughed scornfully and Laura raised her eyebrows at her husband. She hardly remembered the Piers from before when she saw him now. The likeable, friendly little boy was gone forever. He had been transformed into this hard-shelled, difficult young stranger.

Connor came in from the yard. He had been riding the Bombardier and was brisk and warm. 'Good to see you're better,' he said to Piers, going to the sink to wash his hands. He could feel Piers watching him and scrubbed a little too vigorously. God, how had he got into this mess? When he turned round the boy was still looking at him. Did he suspect? Probably suspected everyone. Connor began to hum with studied unconcern.

They all sat down to breakfast, although Piers could only eat a little bread. Laura had cooked bacon and egg, but only Michael seemed to have much appetite. Mary moved her food around the plate and then said, 'I thought I'd ride Sweet after breakfast.'

Connor pushed his chair back from the table. 'I thought we'd decided. I'm to ride him.'

'You decided. I didn't agree.'

Michael, swallowing a giant mouthful of bacon, said, 'He's a handful, Mary. Too strong for you. There'll be others more suited.'

She said, 'But I don't want to have to muck out and clean tack while Connor does the riding. It wasn't what we said when we started and it isn't fair.'

'A difficult horse needs a man on his back,' said Connor flatly.

'Oh yes?' flared Mary. 'Call yourself a man, do you? I can think of a few other names.'

'Mary!' Laura was shocked. 'Mary, you're being rude!'

But she didn't take it back. Instead, Connor got to his feet and stormed out to the yard.

When breakfast was over Mary endured a lecture from her mother. She listened without saying a word. At last Laura fell silent. Mary seized her moment and made for the door, only for her mother to turn and say, 'So what did you mean? Really?'

Mary flushed. She should have realised that given time to reflect her mother would see straight to the point. She said, 'It wasn't anything. I was just annoyed. He – he's just so bossy.'

'It isn't Dora, then?'

Mary's eyes grew big. She stared at her mother, who shrugged and said deprecatingly, 'A guess, that's all. And the way he didn't look at her the other night.'

'He's – he's horrible,' said Mary, her voice deep with revulsion.

'He's young,' said Laura. 'Young men will do these things. Take no notice.'

Mary stamped across to the barn. As if she could ignore it! Pretend she didn't know, when it made her feel – so discarded. She had thought, briefly, foolishly, that at least Connor would be her friend. It might be nothing more, but they could have come together over the horses and been good to one another. Nothing physical, nothing like that. So why was she offended?

She went to the boxes and saw that the Bombardier still stood in his sweat rug, Sweet still waited to be mucked out and Diablo was gone. He'd taken her horse. Connor, who deserved her contempt, had revenged himself by leaving her the work and taking her horse. Not only did he make her feel worthless and ugly and barely feminine, but he completed the picture by using her as a drudge. She wished she could murder him!

She slammed into the Bombardier, took off his rug and groomed him with manic energy. He was done in barely twenty minutes, and in another twenty the boxes were neat and clean. Yet still she fizzed with unexpressed rage! Soon no doubt Connor would return, looking a little too big for Diablo, but having him well in hand. How smug he would be.

She looked at Sweet. Connor intended to work him next. Well he wasn't the only one who could do as he wished!

She went to fetch saddle and bridle. Her heart was beating fiercely, and she felt light-headed and a little sick. The horse might kill her. Connor would gloat. She might be utterly wrong about the horse and it might take a man to ride him. But returning, and looking at the watchful, sceptical animal, she felt a flicker of confidence. She knew this horse. She knew what went on in his head.

She went in and racked him up short. Tied like that, he couldn't whip round and bite while she saddled him. All the same, he cow-kicked as she tightened the girth. Oddly enough, the bridle was less of a problem, although he'd been so difficult about his head early on. Was it a good sign? Did it mean he trusted her? Connor never tacked him up, it was impossible to say.

She led the horse into the yard, but she wouldn't mount there. The field was the place, away from the hedge, where the ground was soft and forgiving. But the horse was very tall. Ideally she would have liked a leg-up, but this was best done alone. So, there was nothing for it. Knowing she was likely to startle the horse into fits, she jumped across the saddle, wriggled furiously, and swung a leg aboard.

The horse fidgeted a little. Nothing more. 'Good boy!' said Mary, in surprise. She stroked his neck, the familiar gesture, reminding him of the nature of his passenger. She slipped her feet into the stirrups and took up the reins. She could feel the horse's tension, was almost expecting the half rear and plunge with which he greeted all Connor's attempts to move him. 'Come on, then,' she said, meaning to sound comforting. It came out half strangled. She touched her legs to his sides. Suddenly, without any ado, the horse relaxed and ambled away.

She took him up through the woods and on to the moor. It was foolish of course. If she came off anywhere she could lie there for days and not be found. But she had the sense that the horse needed an hour or so of gentle paces, taking in the pleasures of life. She and the horse both. The dull afternoon smelled of heather coming into flower on the moors, and a skylark twittered somewhere. The horse trotted easily along the path, Mary's riding becoming less and less tentative. And then, round a bend, came Connor and Diablo.

The horses let out screaming whinnies of recognition. Their riders were less pleased. 'What in God's name do you think you're doing?' demanded Connor.

'I could ask the same of you,' retorted Mary. 'That's my horse.'

'And doesn't it show! No collection. No discipline.'

'Oh, I am sorry! But it does seem the horses go well for me, doesn't it? This is Sweet, by the way.'

'I had noticed. You're foolhardy. You could be killed. I should have known.'

'Known what? That I can sort this horse and you can't?'

'That you can never do as you're told!'

He made to ride past her. She was aware of a surge of fiery anger, and without thinking pushed the horse to block his path. 'You don't give me orders, damn you!'

'You spoiled brat! The horse will have you off. Take care, won't you?'

'Don't tell me what to do!' She pushed the horse to shoulder him off the track, but Diablo pushed back, and they circled, round and round, neither giving way. On the smaller horse, his face was on a level with hers. They glared at each other, each holding their ground, alight with rage.

'Do you give Aunt Dora orders?' demanded Mary.

'So, is it all about that still?'

'That and your laziness. And bossiness. And general assumption that you're in charge.'

He grabbed at her rein. It was a mistake, Sweet felt the strange hand and plunged. 'Let go, damn you!' Mary swung her horse away. Diablo, thinking he was being left, dived sideways. Connor fell off.

Mary laughed enough to hurt. She rode down the track, caught the horse and came back. Connor was dusting himself off, white with rage and humiliation. She couldn't resist teasing him. 'Who's the master horseman now, then? Who never gets thrown?'

He got back into the saddle. He said, 'If you were so fed up, don't you think you might have said so?'

She was stopped in her tracks. 'I thought it was obvious.'

'All that was obvious to me was that you like to work all the hours in a day. If it wasn't the mucking out it was accounts, or tack, or grooming.'

'Someone has to do it!'

'And you always do. I thought that was the way you wanted things. You could have discussed it, Mary.'

She felt bewildered. She pushed her horse up beside him again. He

215

had a great smear of leaf-mould down his shirt, everyone would know he'd fallen off. 'But you did stop me riding. You know you did.'

'I thought I was the better horseman. But you have a knack with wild horses. And I always give credit where it's due.'

Somehow, he had seized the initiative. She had been praised, like a good employee, and in the same breath told it was all her fault. She felt helpless suddenly. Bewildered. Going straight for the throat, nothing in her way, she found herself blundering.

The Fairlands car was in the drive when they returned. Mary pointedly ignored it, and as pointedly rugged up her horse and left. There were straw beds to make and feeds to prepare, but she wasn't doing it. Looking back over her shoulder she saw Connor start to work, his movements neat, practised, fast. So what was she to do? She couldn't go into the house. She went back into the stable and began to help.

But the car was still in the yard when they went in for lunch. Gabriel and Dora sat in the kitchen, the air blue with cigarette smoke. Gabriel held a glass in his hand and was talking volubly to Michael.

'I tell you, Mike, it's the new thing. We're doing it at Fairlands, we've had more than enough of hay. I mean, a few acres for the horses and some for the sheep, but that's about it. Silage is the thing. Ideal.'

'Expensive though. Setting up.'

'Well, yes! But I'm paying for the Fairlands machinery. I might get a discount worth having if I order for you too. After all, it's coming to me in the end.'

Michael said nothing. Mary could tell merely from the set of his jaw that his brother had annoyed him. But Gabriel had been drinking and had forgotten his tact. They all knew that since Michael had no male heir Gabriel could look on Gunthwaite as his own. But no one ever said it straight out.

Laura made a face at her daughter and Mary went to help. It seemed that everyone was staying for lunch, and there was the table to lay and bread to slice. Mary opened a jar of bottled fruit and went to the dairy for cream. When she returned Con was talking to Dora, leaning over her chair, while she smiled up at him, all red lips and predatory teeth. She wondered what Piers would think if he saw them. She realised she didn't know where he was.

She asked her mother and Laura looked blank. 'He was supposed to be coming down. Is he still upstairs?'

Mary went to see. He wasn't there. She slipped out into the yard and into the barn, but there was no sign of him. Looking about her, squinting against sunshine that seemed to blow on a gusting wind, she saw him. He was at the top of Stony Slide.

She climbed up to him, slipping on the shale. He was sitting in the wind wearing only a thin shirt, tossing pebbles into a tussock of grass. He looked thoroughly miserable, she thought.

'Aren't you coming down?' she asked breathlessly. 'Lunch is about ready.'

'They didn't send you, did they? I bet they didn't notice I wasn't there.'

'But they will,' said Mary. 'And they'll be cross. It's not worth it, especially when Mum's taken trouble.'

'Don't know why she bothers. For them.'

'To be hospitable. She would for anyone. It's only right.'

He was shuddering with cold. He looked like a sick animal, skin too tight, eyes dull, hair without a gloss. She took off her jacket and gave it to him. 'You'll catch your death. I've got a jumper and you haven't.'

He took the jacket and slipped it round his shoulders. It was far too small. Sometimes Piers surprised her by being so big. In her mind's eye she saw him as younger, weaker, in need of her help.

She said, 'Why do you keep drinking, Piers?'

'It makes me feel good. And it makes them so mad.'

'It doesn't help, you know. And if you go on, you won't be allowed to see Deb.'

He grinned then, and looked young again. 'They can't stop us. I'd like to see them try.'

'Well, you will.'

He showed no sign of moving. Sighing, she got to her feet and prepared to slither back down the track. Piers said suddenly, 'Did they talk about me? Say what they want me to do?'

She turned back to him. 'No. At least, if they did I didn't hear. You're going to work on the estate, aren't you?'

'I don't know. I've heard them talking but they don't say anything to me.'

She felt unbearably sad all of a sudden. The sensation was strange. It occurred to her that for ages past she had felt nothing so strong for anyone except herself. Even her fears for her mother had been centred on her own horror of being left alone. But now she was conscious of a deep, impersonal sorrow for someone so much less loved than she. Perhaps this was what it meant to be growing up.

She said quietly, 'Do come down. I'll bring up the subject at lunch. Then everyone can join in and it won't be just them and you.'

'They never talk to me. They rant on, that's all.'

'They can't with everyone there. Please, Piers. Come down.'

Going in together, Gabriel exclaimed 'At long last! I'm sorry,

Laura, the boy's got no manners. Never where you want him, however much trouble's caused.'

'It's all right,' said Laura, and gave Piers an encouraging smile. But then she thought of Deb, and pulled her lips straight. It was cruel to deceive the boy.

Connor said something to Mary, but she pretended not to hear. Dora said silkily, 'Mary dear, I think Connor's trying to attract your attention.'

'But he has all yours, Aunt Dora,' murmured Mary, and Laura banged a dish on the table and glared. She mouthed the word 'Don't' at her daughter, and Mary looked wide-eyed back.

Assembled in haste, the meal was patchy and unremarkable. Dora lit a cigarette and smoked it intermittently, disregarding Michael's pained expression. Finally he said, 'I wonder, Dora, if you'd go outside if you want to smoke at lunch? Or wait until we've all finished eating.'

'Well, I for one have finished,' she declared and got to her feet. 'Are you coming to chat to me, Con, in my enforced exile? I'll come back for the coffee, Laura, I'll give the fruit a miss.'

She swept from the room, and Connor, painfully aware of Mary's sardonic eye upon him, followed. Piers said 'Bitch' quite audibly. Michael and Laura glanced at Gabriel, but he pretended not to hear. So it was Michael who said, 'Please don't talk about your mother in such terms, Piers.'

The boy flushed, scarlet patches against the strained white of his skin. 'I hate her,' he said bitterly.

Gabriel said in exasperation, 'What in God's name am I to do with the boy? Whatever I do with him, he's just so damned uncivilised!'

'I tell the truth, you mean,' said Piers. 'She is a bitch.'

'Sometimes there's more than one truth,' said Michael quietly. 'It all depends on how you look at things. Your mother has many good qualities, Piers, but at the moment you're blind to them. Believe me, in the future you'll feel differently.'

Gabriel laughed and drained his glass. Piers said, 'I can't believe that I shall ever feel different about either of my parents. And believe me, I should know.'

'I'm sure you do,' said Gabriel. 'And I feel sure that you'll take the greatest care never to make the mistake of impressing me.'

Mary hung her head over her plate, letting her hair shield her face. She wondered if her parents were waiting, breath bated, to be impressed by her. Was that what you wanted from your children? A creditable performance? Then you could bask in the knowledge that you had passed on your genes to a worthy vessel, and not to some waster like Piers.

She looked through the curtain of her hair. The fragile, flyaway cut was quite gone, she was a bird's nest again, a riot of tangled strands. Since coming back home she'd barely thought about how she looked. Even her face had seemed less important than horses and people and things to do. She wondered if she added to Gabriel's disappointments. Michael and Laura had Deb to be proud of, but Gabriel was faced with the double burden of her scars and Piers' temperament.

She looked up and said abruptly, surprising Gabriel who was sunk in thought, 'What do you mean Piers to do, please? I gather there's been talk of work on the estate.'

Gabriel stirred himself. He glanced across at Michael and then at Laura. There was an assumption of adult intimacy that flicked Mary on the raw. 'We've talked of a few things,' said Gabriel stiffly.

'Have you talked of them to Piers?' asked Mary. 'There might be something he wants to do. Some job.'

She looked hopefully at Piers but he looked sullenly down at his plate. Gabriel laughed and said, 'That's your answer, my dear. Nothing can motivate that young man. He's prepared to spend his days loafing around at Fairlands and sponging off me.'

Michael said, 'There's work here if he's a mind for it.'

Laura sat up. 'What? What work?'

Michael met her eye. 'Helping out. Bill Mayes is more or less past it, the cantankerous old goat. It would do no harm for Piers to learn a thing or two about Gunthwaite.'

Laura mouthed helplessly. 'Yes, but—' She looked at him in entreaty. What was he saying? She didn't want Piers here. What about Deb?

But Piers had brightened visibly. 'I'd love to work here,' he said, his voice imbued with sudden energy. 'After all, this is a real working farm, not just a glorified shooting gallery full of tame birds and a few fat sheep. And if it is mine one day—' He flushed and looked guiltily around at them all.

'It's as well to see what everything's about,' supplied Michael kindly. 'You could have the flat over the barn.'

Laura was gazing steadfastly at her plate. Christian charity behoved them to take Piers, but she didn't want him, not at any price. But Michael said, 'There are conditions, of course, Piers. We want no more trouble with drink. And when Deborah comes home we'll have no trouble there either.'

Piers took a breath. They waited on tenterhooks for the explosion. But all he said was, 'No, sir.'

Michael got up and poured his wife another glass of wine. The gesture held such tenderness, such understanding. Mary felt her eyes prick with tears. If only Michael could be hers again, really hers! His calm, brown bulk held quiet authority, the reassurance of a good and steadfast man. Next to him, the city veneer like a coating of plastic on

219

a cheap table, Gabriel fingered his glass again. He wasn't part of this place, as Michael was. He seemed not to be part of anything. Disgruntled, disappointed, he lurched through his life without any of Michael's certainty.

Chapter Twenty-two

Mary rode Sweet every day for three weeks. The horse improved visibly, sure that he had fallen amongst friends. When he and his rider disagreed, an event which Mary tried to make rarer than hens' teeth, she cajoled him around the problem, terrified of giving in, terrified of fighting. She wanted to ask Connor for advice, but of course could not. Only Piers understood.

He said, 'There's no point with Connor, really. He knows it all.' Mary sank her chin into her hands. 'He didn't seem like that at the start. When Mum was ill – he was nice. Kind. He didn't treat me like a child.'

Piers jumped up on the straw stack and effortlessly threw down a bale with either hand. He had the casual strength of young manhood.

'But this is horses. He doesn't like you being better.'

'I'm not better.'

'You are so! Anyone can ride. Only you can ride Sweet.'

Mary allowed it to be true. It wasn't vanity, she told herself. She'd always been good with horses. They were her only talent, and always had been.

But that evening, Connor and Michael talked by the fire. Mary fulminated, feeling left out. What was it that didn't concern her? Or was it her concern, on which they thought they knew best? It was confusing. All her life, in a household of daughters, she had never been in competition with boys. She had felt some of Michael's prejudice, but never its full weight. But, with Connor and Piers on the scene, she was no longer Michael's full partner, Michael's confidante. There were others to whom he gave more.

She spent the evening machining the braid on a horse rug, turning a standard hessian blanket into something smart. She wasn't good at sewing, but she at least was prepared to make the effort. Not even to herself did she admit that she was enjoying her martyrdom. She might just as easily have gone to talk by the fire.

At last, when it was bedtime, Michael said, 'Come over here, Mary. We've been talking about that horse of yours.'

'Sweet? He's not mine. He belongs to the business.'

'Whatever. You're the one who's turned him round.' Connor treated her to his devastating smile. She returned a sour stare. 'We

221

watched you with him today,' he added, and at once she was on her guard.

Because she didn't like to feel overlooked, she worked the horse most days in one of the meadows, out of sight of the house. They must have made quite an effort to see her. Had they stood on the haystack, and laughed when she struggled to get the horse turned, or to back him, or to persuade him to strike off on his inside leg? She tried to remember if she had done anything stupid that day. But it was just one of those difficult, struggling times that might or might not be going forward. You never knew with horses. Sometimes, after weeks like that, it all unravelled and came good.

'We weren't doing anything special,' she said defensively.

'No,' said Connor.

'What do you mean? What do you think I should have been doing?'

'You were riding him. It's hardly for me to say.'

'But you will say, won't you? You've been talking about it half the night.'

'We've merely been discussing what might become of the horse,' soothed Michael. 'He could have a jump in him.'

'I'm sure he has. He's not ready to try,' said Mary flatly.

Connor said, 'But we think he is.'

She looked from one to the other. She could see they thought her obstructive. They'd been talking for hours about how to bring her round. 'You want the ride, don't you?' she said bitterly to Connor. 'Now I've got him going you want to take over.'

'It's what I'm good at,' he said soothingly. How she hated being soothed! 'We'll buy some more horses for you. We could see if that cobby little mare's still for sale. Get her cheap after all this time.'

To keep me happy, thought Mary. To keep me quiet.

There was the sound of the back door. Laura had been doing the last minute checks round the stock. She came in flushed from the night, her arms full of eggs. 'The Rhode Island hen's been laying by the hedge,' she said. 'Look at all these! Shall I put her to sit or not bother?'

'She'll brood if you sit her or not,' said Mary in a brittle tone. 'She always does.'

'I suppose so. I'll let her bring them off, then.'

Laura looked from one face to another. It was at once obvious to her that Mary was feeling beleaguered. She took a deep breath and waded in. 'I hope you've not been trying to persuade Mary to give up that horse?' she said determinedly. 'It wouldn't be fair.'

'Perhaps not,' said Michael. 'But it would be businesslike and sensible.'

'But she brought him round! She did the work.'

'She started the work,' said Michael. 'She has to realise, Connor's the man to complete it.'

'But Mary's a brilliant rider!' insisted her mother.

'She certainly is,' said Connor. 'But you know, it takes experience to bring on a difficult horse. And to know when to hang on to something and when to let it go.'

'It takes a man's hand,' added Michael.

Mary felt all her certainties crumble into dust. These two were united in betraying her! It was all settled. She could say what she liked, but nothing would change. She licked her lips. 'I certainly know one thing,' she said slowly. 'It takes two men together to decide on something they would neither of them do on their own. All right, I give in. Have it your own damned way!'

Evading her father's restraining hand, she stormed out of the room.

She hadn't thought that Connor would move all that quickly, but the next morning, while she was still wondering if she was speaking to him or not, he took the horse. She stood by the house, watching him ride straight and collected out of the yard. Damn the horse, she thought furiously. How dare he give in like that?

Piers was washing out the dairy. She went across to him, instinctively seeking out an ally. 'Did you see? He's so tactless. But he doesn't care what I think.'

'He won't stay forever. He'll be back in Ireland soon, you wait.'

'A week's too long. I hate him!'

Piers sluiced the floor with a bucket of hot water, took up the long-handled brush and began to scrub. He was a conscientious worker, thought Mary. They were alike in that. Given a task it never occurred to either of them to find someone else to do it, unlike Deborah, or even Con. Perhaps it was only fools who did as they were told, thought Mary glumly. Perhaps the really successful people in life established what they wanted and then took it, no questions asked.

'I should have stood my ground,' she said miserably.

Piers was refilling his bucket. 'What about?'

'The horse, of course!' Not even Piers realised the enormity of last night. She had been put in her place, the girl's place, specially made for the stay-at-home daughter, and no one cared but her.

Unable to settle, unable to think, she finally went back in the house. Her mother was baking.

'I thought you had work to do,' said Laura, expertly cubing a block of lard.

'I have. I can't get on. Connor's taken Sweet without so much as a by your leave. I hope he gets killed.'

'Don't. If it happened you'd never forgive yourself.'

'Wouldn't I? Just watch me.'

223

She knelt on a chair, leaning her elbows on the table. Her mother automatically put a spoonful of dried fruit in front of her and she began to nibble.

'Is Deb really going to Rosalind's this holiday?'

Laura glanced up. 'I don't know. Don't you think it's a good idea?'

'I think it's the best one you've had. You know what Piers is like.'

'Yes. Young boys! What a good thing they grow up.' Like a conjuror, Laura folded pastry handkerchiefs, imprisoning a concoction of fruit and brown sugar.

'It's the same with Deb, though. She adores him.'

'Does she?' Laura looked unusually sardonic. 'Deb could have a brilliant time with Rosalind. Piers would be forgotten in a week.'

'Poor Piers.'

'Don't take his side all the time, Mary!'

'Why not? It's the least a sister can do.'

There was a long, unpleasant silence. At last, Laura unclenched her fists and said shakily, 'I wish you wouldn't.'

'And I wish you hadn't! Oh, Mum.'

'I know, I know, I know!' She turned blindly away, fighting tears, and Mary felt again the sick, cold sinking in her guts. How she wished her mother was really strong again. But in all likelihood she had never been as strong as she appeared. It had been an illusion, manufactured and sustained for the benefit of Mary and Deb. How could she despise someone who had tried so hard?

Mary said bracingly, 'Honestly, Mum, you do get in a state about nothing. Come and finish the pastries. You know, if Deb does come home for a week or two it might be all right. She's sensible. And she and Piers might go off each other, if nothing stands in their way.'

Laura took command of herself again, resolutely squaring her shoulders. 'Do you think so? That would be good.'

A movement in the yard caught their attention. It was Connor returning with Sweet. The horse was dark with sweat but moved easily and comfortably. Mary let out a squawk of pain and rage. 'How could he?' She sprang towards the door but her mother caught her arm. 'You can't yell at him for doing the horse good! Think, Mary. It's a business. He's done the right thing.'

Mary struggled with herself. But it was obvious. Connor was being sensible and she was not.

When she went out to the yard, leaving just sufficient time so that Connor would have to see to the horse, she found him cleaning tack in an unusually benign mood. 'He went well,' he said. 'You've done a grand job, Mary.'

'Don't patronise me, please.'

'And what am I to say to you? A word of praise shouldn't come amiss.'

'I don't need praise from you! Will you stop thinking you're the senior partner, damn it!'

'Since I'm a deal older than you it's only natural I should know a bit more though. Isn't it?'

She resisted the temptation to wipe the understanding sympathy from his face with a backhanded slap. 'We came into this as equal partners,' she said, her teeth almost gritted. 'Nobody talked about age then.'

'And you didn't talk about unfairness, until you found out about Dora.'

Mary fought with her temper and lost. She reached out a long arm, picked up four bridles and flung them into a heap on the floor. Then she upended an open tin of staples all over them. 'All right, I'm being childish!' she yelled at Connor's forbearing expression. 'How dare you assume I'm jealous! How dare you assume anything as far as I'm concerned! But you and Dora just proves that you're not the sort of person anyone should do business with. Lying, untrustworthy – and influenced by people of the very worst sort!'

'Unlike you,' retorted Connor. 'Consorting with a prostitute in London.'

'I did not consort! If it comes to consorting, you're doing a damn' sight more than that!'

'And how would you know? Or aren't you as innocent as you pretend?'

'Innocent?' She hesitated. She was sick of being treated as a child. Would it hurt to let him think – let him imagine – that she wasn't the virginal young girl he liked to assume? She turned her head slowly, sending him a sly glance, extending her long, graceful neck with the elegance and deliberation of a woman of the very highest class. A woman who knew – everything. 'Of course I'm not innocent,' she said, giving a slight laugh. 'Really, Connor. I thought, after my time in London, that it was obvious. You're too provincial sometimes.'

This time he was the one who stormed out. She was overwhelmed by a sense of victory, until it dawned on her that he had left her with a pile of dirty tack and a muddle of staples and leather on the floor.

Deborah returned home for a fortnight, before going on to Rosalind. In her last term at school, she had graduated to classes on deportment and dress, and seemed suddenly not a schoolgirl any more. Laura talked to her sister-in-law almost nightly on the telephone, arranging a programme of race meetings and dances, with the added lure of a trip to Biarritz if Howard finally agreed to tear himself away from office crises for a few weeks. Mary listened with a sense of exclusion that she knew was unjustified. She didn't want to go to parties and race meetings! She didn't want to suffer the horrors of the beach at

225

Biarritz! She had her heart's desire at Gunthwaite, her horses, her life. All the same, she couldn't escape the feeling that it was somehow unfair.

The feeling was partly due to her defeat over the horse. Under Connor's careful riding Sweet was turning into a respectable mount. Mary and Connor had also acquired two more prospects, the little mare they had squabbled over and a big, over-muscled chestnut that Connor liked and Mary didn't. The way the horse held together displeased her. She thought that under strong work he would probably break down and prove unsound. But, in the way that things tended to, and as she was coming to expect, Connor had his way.

They were dealing, too, in an undramatic style. A hunter bought cheap from a farmer who hadn't time, sold on looking smart for a turn of a few hundred pounds; children's ponies, held in the paddock, hairy and unassuming, until the required parent came sniffing around and could be steered in the direction of that which was most suitable for a bumptious, or retiring, or energetic child; the spirited mount that had unnerved its rider and only required someone better to realise a good price. They took them all, and prospered, moderately.

They had a celebration dinner when Deborah came home. Piers had been tactfully sent back to Fairlands for the night, but the inclusion of Connor was annoying, although how he could be excluded was difficult to say since he always ate with the family. Nonetheless, watching him be charming and talkative with Deb when he was so often silent and sullen with her put Mary in a mood far from festive.

But whoever was there, it would have been hard to be cheerful in the face of Deb's glowing good looks. Never had Mary felt quite so shapeless and lanky. In the last few months Deborah had acquired new poise, wearing her hair in a chic pleat, disguising the ugly waistband of her skirt with a French belt of her mother's. She could be cool, too, thought Mary, watching her depress Connor with a sideways look. The days of her girlhood were ending. She was learning to use her Godgiven powers to remarkable effect.

When the long meal was over Deborah went up to her room. Mary followed and flopped on the bed. 'I hate Connor,' she said with venom.

'He seemed OK,' said Deb, sinking with newly studied elegance into a chair. 'Bit fond of himself, perhaps.'

'Fond of you! He was falling into your sweater. He'd have got in it with you if he could.'

'But I thought that was your fault.' Deborah pulled the pins from her hair and let down a waterfall of chestnut silk. 'He was doing it to annoy.'

Mary blinked at her. 'You must be mad! You don't know Connor, he'll chase anything. And he's a brute to work with, wants everything his own way. Honestly, I almost wish I was the one going to Aunt Rosalind's.'

Deborah kicked off her shoes and took off the borrowed belt. She looked young again, thought Mary with relief. When Deb was tricked out like a mannequin it was hard to believe she was the younger sister. It made Mary feel all of ten. 'You ought to go to London,' said Deb. 'Your hair's a mess.'

'Is it?' Mary pushed ineffectually at the heavy black curls falling over her forehead. 'No one in Bainfield can do a thing with it.'

'You should go back to the place in London. Why don't you go away? If you're not happy here.'

Mary sighed. Deborah didn't understand. 'They've given me everything I wanted,' she explained patiently. 'The horses, everything. And Mum needs me. She isn't as strong as she looks, the slightest thing and she's upset. I can't go.'

'Not even for a visit? Mary, you could!'

'No.'

Deborah sighed. She went to her case, threw open the lid and began to unpack. There was a great wad of letters held by three elastic bands. She tossed them into a drawer. 'Piers?' asked Mary. Deborah nodded.

After a moment Mary said, 'Does he know you're going away?'

Deborah said nothing. Mary didn't know if she should persist. Whatever it was between her and Piers seemed so private that questions couldn't be asked. Did Deb love him? Was he special to her? But before she could frame even the mildest enquiry, Deb said, 'I don't know what I would have done. Without him. When Mum almost died.'

Remembering, Mary shuddered. 'You didn't see the worst of it.'

Deb turned on her. 'And that was dreadful! I didn't know what on earth was going on. Everyone thought I was a child, no one told me a thing! But then, Piers was there. I needed him so much.'

Mary wondered what she was being told. 'But you don't need him now,' she ventured.

'I don't know! Perhaps. It's been such ages. He writes such things—'

'What sort of things?'

'Oh, you know. That he loves me. That I'm all he cares about. That he's got nothing in the world except me.'

'Oh God!' said Mary gloomily. 'How's that for responsibility?'

'To be honest, it feels like blackmail. As if I've got to feel the same or I'll destroy him. You know what he's like, Mary!'

Her sister considered. Did she know? Sometimes she thought so.

227

She recognised in him the same intensity and passion that she had herself. And she simply did not know if in loving Deb he was loving reality or a myth. She wasn't only the heart-stopping contours of her face.

He came to work early the next day. Deborah ran out to meet him and they stood in the drive holding hands. Laura, at the window, said, 'That boy!' in exasperation. But they made the loveliest picture, their faces alight with pleasure, their young bodies leaning towards each other like sapling trees. Connor, coming in from the barn, said to Mary, 'Isn't that enough to soften even you? They're lucky, so they are.'

Laura said tartly, 'Deborah is going away. I wish Michael had never had him here, it makes everything impossible!'

When Deborah came in for breakfast she was flushed and happy. To Mary's surprise, her mother said brightly, 'Well then. What are you two girls going to do today? Go into Bainfield? You can have the car.'

'I've got to work,' said Mary feebly, but her mother brushed aside her protests. 'Deborah's only here for two weeks, darling! Surely you can spare the time?'

Clearly, the time must be spared. Mary resigned herself. Her mother expected it. She was to be the instrument that kept Deborah and Piers apart.

They shopped the first day, went to the cinema the next, and then, urged on by a burgeoning summer's day, they went swimming at the outdoor baths. But that wasn't such a good idea; the sight of Deborah in a swimsuit, all swelling breasts and pert bottom, did little for Mary's self-esteem. She knew only too well that beside her voluptuous sister she looked like a stick insect. Boys appeared from nowhere, splashing, rioting, smiling boys, vying for Deb's unconcerned attention. One actually came over to talk. 'Hello,' he said happily, and grinned. About to administer a stinging retort, in the nick of time Mary recognised Graham Beacham.

'Hello,' she replied sourly. 'Deb, it's Graham.'

'Is it? Oh, hello. I thought you were just one of the creeps.'

'I hope not.' He flushed, from shoulders to hair, Mary noticed. She was a connoisseur of the blush. He coughed awkwardly. 'I was just wondering – we're having a tennis do tomorrow. Do you want to come?'

'What? Just Deborah?'

He met Mary's direct blue stare. 'And you, if you want. It's open house really. For tennis.'

'Piers can come, then,' said Deborah. 'And why not Connor? He doesn't know anyone round here.'

'He knows more people than you think,' said Mary darkly.

She got up, pulling at the leg elastic of her costume, balanced on the swimming pool edge and dived. Her body described a beautiful long arc. 'Athletic, isn't she?' said Graham, wonderingly. 'You don't really expect it in a girl.'

'Don't you?' Deb lay back and closed her eyes. 'Mary's never what anyone expects, actually. You ought to get to know her, Graham. She's great fun.'

He looked at Mary's long arms cutting rhythmically through the water, and thought of her tongue cutting as easily through his fragile self-esteem. No, he thought. He'd concentrate on the gorgeous Deb and leave Mary Cooper very well alone.

Turning up at the Beacham house the next day, expecting an informal afternoon, it was to find a party in full swing with drinks laid out on the terrace and refreshments in the dining room, as well as a gramophone churning out dated dance music in the great hall. Tennis dress had been interpreted liberally, and Mary for one, in her short white skirt, felt herself to be all legs. Girls drifted past in ankle-length pleated white cotton. She looked at Deb, who wore a skirt as short as her own but which somehow looked right, and whispered, 'This is horrible! We can't stay.'

'Don't be silly, Mary. You look super in a tennis dress, you know you do.' She wandered off to talk to Graham Beacham.

Mary stood behind a large terracotta pot, hoping her legs couldn't be seen. In the mirror when she came out she had been moderately pleased with herself, knowing that she showed to advantage in boyish clothes. Even Marie, stomping by as they got in the car, had said, 'My, my. The sporting look. A good choice,' as if Mary had simply decided to take to tennis clothes as a fashion statement. She looked cautiously at the men, all glamorous in white trousers. And Deb was quite unconcerned.

Why did no one else ever feel as conspicuous as she did? wondered Mary miserably. She looked at them all, talking, laughing, their hair obedient, their skins unmarked except by the occasional spot, which at least would pass. She was the only awkward, ugly girl in the place, she thought. Saying the wrong thing, wearing the wrong thing – she imagined people laughing later on. 'That poor Mary Cooper. What with the blushing, and the hair, and the terrible short skirt – one can only feel sorry for her. But really!'

Connor was standing on the terrace, looking for somebody. Her, probably. She had a horrible vision of him catching sight of her, hiding behind her pot, obviously unhappy and out of place. He'd laugh at her. He'd know that her pretended sophistication had been nothing but lies. Galvanised into precipitate action, she marched out into the open, taking great strides, like a flamingo in a lake.

'There you are, Connor. Can you imagine, a tennis party and no visible tennis?'

'They're still putting the net up. But at least you can get a drink. It's flowing like water in there.'

'Is it?' Mary went to peer in at the door. Ranged beside the orange juice were bottles of whisky and gin. 'Where's Piers?' she asked, thinking she sounded casual. Connor laughed.

'He's following Deb. Don't worry about him, Mary, have something yourself. What's it like having everyone staring at your legs?'

She tried not to clench her teeth. 'It always happens,' she said with forced airiness. 'I have very good legs, I'm told.'

'You've been told right.'

He was drinking gin, and she joined him. She remembered the evening with Stevie in the pub, and thought how unexciting everything had been since. Did she want that sort of excitement? The gin was making her reckless, that was all. She wanted – she wanted something to happen!

She looked into Connor's dark eyes. They seemed very close to her own. Mrs Beacham's voice suddenly broke in on them, saying loudly, 'Come along, you two, no canoodling! Get off and play tennis, do.'

Walking down to the tennis court, the thin sunshine warm on her face, she said, 'I suppose you wish it was Dora here with you.'

Connor said, 'Why should I wish that?'

She turned to face him. She wasn't playing any of these silly games! 'So you could sneak off with her into the shrubbery and make love,' she said in ringing tones.

The colour surged into Connor's cheeks. Mary felt savagely triumphant, as if she'd injured her enemy with a dangerous wound. But Connor said, 'I'll have you know that I've finished with all that.'

'Since when?' She knew exactly how often Connor sneaked away to Fairlands. She could give times, dates, everything. She had radar as far as that was concerned, could piece together every minute of his day and know which hours were missing. And he'd gone there yesterday. He said, 'I'll tell her. Next time.'

'Oh. I'm sure you will.'

She stalked off to the tennis court. It was grass, with netting only at either end. Balls and racquets were heaped by the gate, and Mary seized on them and began sending practice serves fizzing across the net. Connor moved to the other side and returned every one. Mary knew herself once again to be outclassed.

She felt a rising tide of fury. Connor seemed able to do everything better than she. Gritting her teeth, she put everything into her shots, and at last managed to wrong-foot him. 'Right,' he called. 'That's enough of a warm-up. Let's play.'

She knew from the first game that she would be annihilated. Only her reach saved her, letting her grab a point or two here and there. Connor was accurate, competitive and skilled. He won every game.

At last Mary put down her racquet and said, 'Happy now that you've established your male superiority?'

He came to the net. 'I didn't think it needed establishing.'

She turned away and went to put the racquet in its press. 'You ought to play mixed doubles,' someone said to her. 'You two should do well, you're both strong.'

'Connor's no good in a team,' said Mary sweetly. 'He tries, but it just isn't in him. He likes to please himself.'

She was on her way back to the house when he caught up with her. He grabbed her arm. 'I'll thank you not to say things like that about me! Everyone knows we're in business together. Do you want them all to be party to our squabbles?'

'I've no need to keep them secret,' retorted Mary. 'What with your affair and your high-handedness, you must be the talk of the county.'

'And if I'm not, it's no thanks to you!'

'Blame me if you will,' said Mary self-righteously. 'It's as I said, though. You only ever please yourself.'

They were engulfed in a crowd of people going down to play tennis. Mary pushed on back to the house, thinking that she'd have another gin and to hell with it. But then she saw Deb.

To anyone else, she looked calm and composed, but to anyone who knew her she was in a panic. Her eyes were very wide, mirrors of grey glass in a face set in studied immobility. Mary went over at once. 'What on earth's the matter?'

'Piers. I was talking with Graham and he got in a state. He's dead drunk.'

'Oh God.'

Deborah's face was becoming whiter by the minute. Mary knew that at any moment she might cry. She took her wrist and said firmly, 'Don't worry, he's done it before. Where is he?'

'Upstairs. He wanted me to go in a bedroom with him, but he was so drunk I just pushed him in and ran. Anyone could find him. He could be sick or something.'

Connor was stamping by, on his bad-tempered way to the bar. Mary shot him a look and he stopped. 'What's the matter?'

'Piers. Upstairs. Drunk.'

'That bloody boy!'

It seemed a Gunthwaite emergency, something to be dealt with and concealed. Mary and Deb went upstairs first, trying to look as if they were going to powder their noses, and Connor followed on his own. As he crept along the upstairs corridor, confronted by twin ranks of closed bedroom doors, one opened. 'Quick!' hissed Mary.

231

Piers was lying sprawled on an immaculate blue quilt. His shoes had left a spreading muddy stain at one end and a half-finished bottle of whisky a puddle at the other. He was snoring and asleep.

'I hate him,' said Deborah, her voice thick with tears.

'That's what comes of flirting,' said Connor, and Mary snapped, 'Go on, tell her it's all her fault! Are you sure you can't blame me instead?'

'Aw, shut up, Mary, do. We've got to get him home.'

Between them they hauled him off the bed, legs trailing. Deborah began frantically trying to save the bedspread, but the whisky had soaked through to the mattress. 'If we get out without being seen they won't know it was us,' said Mary urgently.

'Aren't we the honest guest?' taunted Connor.

She blazed at him. 'Don't talk to me about honesty! Some of this can be laid at your door, you know.'

'If you'd just stop quarrelling,' said Deb, her hands pressed to her cheeks. 'Is he going to be sick, do you think?'

'Pray God, no,' said Connor.

But the thought galvanised them into action. Deb went ahead to discover the back stairs, and could be heard having an awkward conversation with a maid. When she returned, flushed and bright-eyed, she said, 'Hurry! Everyone's about to eat tea. Come on, will you!'

They descended in a rush. The outside door led into a shrubbery, and they left Piers there while Connor fetched the car. He brought it as near as he dared and they bundled Piers inside. 'We'll have to make our excuses,' said Mary. 'We can't just leave.'

'Suppose they find out about the bed?' said Deb in an agony of embarrassment. 'Should we own up?'

'Never,' said Mary, with a shudder. 'Let's just go. We'll get Mum to telephone later and say you were ill or something. Come on!'

They all got into the car. Deborah, squashed beside the inert form of Piers, began to cry.

Chapter Twenty-three

'This settles it,' said Laura to Michael that night. 'Either Piers leaves or I send Deborah to Rosalind right away.'

Michael said nothing. The unspoken accusation hung between them. Why had he brought Piers to Gunthwaite? The presence of someone so unstable was unsettling them all.

He went to sit by the fire. His head was aching, caused no doubt by the extra work in the dairy. He had become used to Piers being there, doing his not inconsiderable bit. 'The boy's a good worker,' he managed at last.

'And Deb's a good daughter. Why must she be driven out of her home? My poor girls. My poor, good girls.' Laura flung herself restlessly down.

Michael said, 'The boy deserves a chance.'

'He's had every chance. And sorry as I feel for him, I won't have him bringing this into our home. He's got to go, Michael.'

The door opened and Mary came into the room. She was wearing jodhpurs and a baggy jumper, and looked tall, thin and tired. 'Did you telephone?' she asked.

'Yes. They were very nice. But then, I don't suppose they've discovered the bedspread yet.'

'Should we have said, do you think?'

'Yes,' said Michael firmly. 'When Piers is better he can write and explain. It's his problem, not yours.'

Mary went to sit on the sofa. Her mother wondered if she dared ask about the party. Perhaps, in the time before Piers had disgraced himself, Mary had had a good time? She lived in hope that one day her daughter would be a social success. If only Mary would believe in herself a bit more! Despite the hair, with which she would do nothing, she had a waiflike, angular beauty that caught at the heart of those who chose to see. She wondered why Mary couldn't be the one to entrance Graham Beacham. But, visualising Mary in the glossy Beacham house, she rejected the daydream out of hand. No. Graham was right, in that smooth, expensive life he needed someone like Deb. And Deb did not need Piers!

'I've told Michael that Piers has to go,' said Laura firmly.

'What?' Mary blinked. 'Where will he go? Not back to Fairlands.'

'Yes. Why not?'

'There's nothing for him there. Oh, Mum, Deb's going anyway. And – and besides, I don't think she's as keen as she was. He frightened her today. She didn't realise what he can be like.'

'I've told her often enough,' flared Laura.

'That isn't at all the same.'

Laura felt a little humbled. Sometimes nowadays Mary could make her feel quite immature.

Michael said, 'I can't convince your mother that we should keep Piers on. I'd like to, I admit. He's a good boy underneath, a good worker. He'll have Gunthwaite one day. I like to feel that he's learning what life here's about. I want to teach him what's important about Gunthwaite. It should be passed on.'

Mary drew in her breath. He didn't realise what he was saying, she thought. How it slighted her. The invisible ropes of tradition that held Gunthwaite firm between past and future were as real to her as the sinews of her own hand. She had absorbed Gunthwaite lore with her mother's milk. And yet to Michael it was nothing. She was only a girl.

'It must be nice to have a boy about the place,' she said gruffly. 'He does work well.'

'To be honest, I don't know what I'd do without him,' confessed Michael. 'You don't realise you're getting older until someone young comes along. With Deborah in London he'll get over all this silliness and steady down. You see, Laura, even Mary agrees.'

Laura looked at her daughter's downcast head, sensing unease. Mary was the most difficult girl! She simply didn't know what it would take to make her happy. 'So you want Piers to stay, Mary?' she asked.

Her daughter raised dark, unfathomable eyes. 'Yes, Mum. All in all, I think that would be best.'

There was a scene the next morning. Gabriel arrived before eight, demanding to see Piers. In the meantime, while his son was assembled for inspection, he berated Michael. 'The boy was supposed to be working, damn it! And then I get a telephone call from the Beachams, telling me he's made a complete cake of himself with drink at a party and ruined a bedroom! Threw up on the bed, I gather, and worse. You know what he's like, Michael. I thought I could trust you. He's not fit to be let out in company.'

Deborah, very pale, said, 'He wasn't sick, Uncle Gabriel. Some whisky was spilled on a bed. We should have apologised but we thought it might be better for Mum to explain.'

'Oh, make Laura do your dirty work. I shouldn't have expected anything else!'

Laura said, 'Do stop shouting, Gabriel. There isn't any need. I shall telephone Mrs Beacham later today and try and smooth things over. And Deb will write a note and we'll send it over with some butter and eggs.'

'And Piers does nothing!'

Michael chuckled. 'He's in no state to do anything as yet, Gabe. But he'll be sent over to apologise as soon as he is.'

Gabriel felt the wind leaving his sails. He had stormed across, determined to confront Piers, imbued with a fury that he didn't himself understand. But somehow his son's failures seemed to have direct bearing on Gabriel himself. It was as if the boy were the tangible evidence of the man's life, and any lapse, whatever its nature, only served to prove that despite appearances, Gabriel wasn't a success. He sat down at the table and mutely accepted Laura's proffered cup of tea.

'You take these things too hard,' said Michael, helping himself to a little more bacon.

'But this is the third time,' said Laura. 'It's getting to be a habit. It's got to stop.'

Gabriel consoled himself with a slice of hot buttered toast. 'I blame his mother.'

'You would!' remarked Mary, picking up a bridle she had cleaned before the fire last night and sauntering out to the sunlit yard.

Connor was lunging the chestnut in the meadow. Mary stood and watched for a moment, trying to decide if the animal was really as top heavy as he seemed, or if it was simply that she was determined to prove Connor wrong. But those legs looked as if they belonged to a very much lesser horse! As Connor brought him in she said, 'We'll have to take his condition down. He's far too burly.'

'Be off with you! He's looking great. Coming riding? Take Diablo.'

It was her treat. Instead of the mare, all wilfulness and ignorance, she could hold high courage on gossamer threads. She grinned at Connor, and went to tack up. He, of course, was taking Sweet.

They rode up through the woods and on to the moor. The sky was flecked with feathered clouds, the skylarks almost invisible against the sun. Sweet was going happily, his neck rounded in obedience to Connor's careful hand. In contrast Diablo was sidling and yawing, a miniature thunderbolt straining against Mary's hold.

'You should boss that horse!' complained Connor at last, unable to bear Mary's light-hearted acceptance of her mount's wicked ways.

'He doesn't take bossing. He takes cajoling.' She put him at a stream and he flew over it. At once she made him turn on his hocks, neat, obedient, and jump back. 'He only works for treats,' she explained. 'We understand each other.'

'You do him too many favours. He could be ten times the horse!'

The familiar irritation began to swell in her. 'Even Michael thinks I handle Diablo well,' she said quietly.

'Pah! He says what he thinks you want to hear.'

Her anger ignited like petrol to a match. She hated him! Truly she did! 'You only know how to crush spirits,' she said shrilly. 'Everything has to be made to bow down to you! Horses, women, everything. You've got no real understanding, no real charm. You're just a bully.'

He pushed his horse up to hers. 'I understand you too well, Mary Cooper. The little girl of you. The spoiled brat.'

'You said yourself I know my horses!'

'You know yourself you'd never say it back!'

'Because it isn't true! You ride like a champion, that I'll admit, but you don't know horses and you don't know me.'

She turned to ride away, but he was beside her, his big striding mount matching hers with brilliant ease. She began to canter, and he was there, stride for stride, keeping in step whatever she did. She hated him! She reined in, hard, and he went a stride past before turning. Now they were face to face. 'Aunt Dora deserves you,' said Mary bitterly.

'That's over. I'm telling her today.'

'Are you so? What should I care?'

'Is it that Beacham boy, then?'

She stared in shock. 'Him? You mean that he and I—?'

'Are you in love with him? I know he's one of Deb's. But all the same . . .'

She was incensed. That he should think her nursing a hopeless passion! 'I'm in love with nobody,' she said with dignity. 'There was the man in London, of course. But you can't call that love. I mean, I was so young.'

'So there *was* someone in London?' His face was wary. He suspected the lie.

'He was much older than me,' she said, struggling for convincing sincerity. 'I was lonely. He taught me a lot. I'm still fond of him.'

'Do you write?'

She laughed. He really did believe her! 'Of course not! He's married. Young girls don't send letters to married men. Don't they teach you anything in Ireland?'

She sent her horse dancing away from him, hopping the dykes, sure-footed and nimble. He followed, suddenly leaden. She felt a grim delight. He would like her to be in love with him, no doubt. And once she was, he'd be gone.

Deborah was despatched to Rosalind the following day. Everything had been a scramble, but Laura was determined to have her gone before Piers was back in circulation again. She had sent him to Fairlands with his father, and he had yet to reappear. No one knew quite what to say when he did, least of all Deb.

Before the last breakfast, Deb and Mary walked in the orchard together. The day was full of promise, warm, scented, the unripe fruit not yet weighting the branches. In a good year, in the early-spring the blossom on the trees was like snow, but now, in summer, they walked in a green forest.

'I wish you were coming,' said Deborah.

'Me? I'm a misfit at parties. You know that.'

'But you don't have to be. Not any more. Aunt Rosalind would get your hair cut again, and you could learn how to dress and so on.'

'It isn't me, Deb!'

'Only if you don't want it to be.'

Mary reached up into the apple tree and climbed on to a low branch. This had been her place, years ago. Her sanctuary. 'Will you mind leaving Piers?' she asked, hidden by the leaves.

Her sister sighed. 'I don't know. Probably. He's such an idiot though. I used to love being with him. I wasn't happy unless I was. But now, he's always accusing me and things.'

'He's bound to be jealous.'

Deborah's pale eyes looked up at her through the leaves. 'I can't live with someone who's going to be jealous forever.'

They walked back to the house. Laura was brittly cheerful, trying to make Deb eat, eating nothing herself. She wasn't coming to the station. Connor said, 'Don't let David take you to his club. Terrible place, full of unburied corpses.'

'And don't let Alan take you to anything,' added Mary. 'It's bound to be disreputable.'

'And you'd know, would you Mary?' demanded Connor, and she met his gaze bravely.

'Of course.'

When Deb was gone, waved off with Michael in the car, the day seemed to hang in the air. Mary knew she should get on with something ordinary, but there had been so few ordinary days since Deb came home. She went into the barn and began the endless cleaning of tack. Connor came in and said sourly, 'Do you never stop? God, you're the most conscientious girl I ever knew.'

'Only in contrast to your lack of application,' she said sourly.

But he had put her off. She hung the bridles back on their pegs and wandered into the house. Laura was sitting at the table, surrounded by the aftermath of Deb's departure. Mary began automatically to tidy things up. 'What would I do without you?' said her mother shakily.

237

Mary turned to her. 'I don't know. What would you do? Mum, I don't think I can stay here forever.'

Laura looked up at her daughter. She felt the tears that she had held back for Deb suddenly pricking her eyes. 'You mean – you want to go? As well as Deb? When?'

'Soon.'

Mary sat at the table. She knew she must try and explain, honestly, carefully. She began to talk, knowing that her mother would hear only part of what she said, that she wasn't capable of understanding the whole. She didn't believe that Mary was stifled here. Hadn't she always loved Gunthwaite, never wanted to leave?

'It isn't because – because of Dad and everything?' Laura asked pathetically. 'I thought we'd got over all that.'

'I haven't,' said Mary. She sighed and tried again. 'But it isn't that. Honestly. Not this time. It's mostly Connor. And the business. Mum, there's no real place for me here!' She got up and began to pace the room.

Laura looked up at her, bemused. 'But if it's Connor that's the problem then *he* should go! I won't have my daughters chased from their home by these men. I simply won't.'

'It isn't really him.' She took a deep breath. 'Without Connor there isn't a horse business. He's got the real skills. I admit, we should be a great team, but we're not. It doesn't work. And Dad can do my part every bit as well as me. When I've gone they'll hire a girl to do the tack and the mucking out, and they'll have endless fun. As for me – this is such a backwater, Mum. I really can't stay. I've got to make something of my life!'

Laura was silent for a moment. In her heart, she knew Mary was right. She was stagnating at Gunthwaite, doing nothing, going nowhere. But imagining the days without her daughter in them, her firm and constant friend, she felt her heart quail. 'Where will you go?'

That was the rub. Where was she to go? Mary stood disconsolate before the range. 'Deb said I should go with her to Rosalind. Do you think I should, Mum? I mean, I'm no good at parties or anything but Rosalind can find people jobs. She knows everybody. All that sort of thing.'

'Yes. Yes, she does.' Laura folded her hands together, trying desperately to stop their quivering. What was happening to her? She didn't need this girl, she had existed very well before she was born. But the years had entwined them in some inescapable knot. Mary was her ally, in league with her against the truth. Together, they stood firm before Michael and the world, holding up the myth that was Laura. Without her daughter, she didn't know if she could hold it up alone.

The decision made, Mary had only to tell Connor. But he was nowhere to be seen. She waited all day, sure that he was with Dora, hating him and grateful at one and the same time. This proved how right she was to go. He was a liar and a cheat. He hadn't finished with Dora at all.

He didn't come back until late-evening, when Mary had taken herself up to bed. She saw the lights in the yard against her curtains and heard the car door slam. She turned over, wondering what she would say in the morning. But to her surprise, a moment or two later, there was a soft knock at her door.

She sat up. 'What do you want?'

The door opened quietly and Connor stood there.

'If my mother catches you there'll be trouble,' said Mary prosaically.

'All the same. Can we talk?'

She shrugged. 'I suppose so.'

He sat on the bed, pushing the door closed with his foot. Mary huddled beneath the bedclothes, warm and cosy in her den, taking in the smell of spirits, his tousled black hair, the cut on his lip.

'Did she do that?'

He put up his hand to touch. 'Yes. Like I told you, it's finished.'

Mary made a noise, half laugh half growl. 'You can believe it,' he said defensively. 'It's true.'

He put out his hand and touched her cheek. She lay very still, wondering what he saw. How red was the stain on her skin against the white of the sheet? She never wore white if she could help it. Her hair was such a mess. He thought she was like Dora, and that was her fault, leading him to believe—

He said, 'Your skin is like silk.'

'You don't come from her to me and say things like that.'

'It's because of you I left her.'

She flinched from his hand. 'Don't touch me. I'm not like her. You won't get a welcome here.'

His hand moved away. She realised suddenly that he was very tense and on edge, almost trembling with suppressed emotion. 'I wanted to talk to you!' he said desperately. 'I'm so sick of your cold, silent shoulder.'

'You don't want me to talk, just to agree. It's you who stays silent the moment I say anything you don't want to hear.'

'About horses?'

'About anything! I don't know why you came here really. With me.'

He said nothing, although he could have said much. He had come because of her. That strange, tense time in the flat had left him with

239

the sense that there was something here to be pursued. She had attracted and intrigued him, promised something – he didn't know what. All he now knew was that he seemed to be at her mercy.

He very much wanted to kiss her. The undischarged electricity of the meeting with Dora was fizzing through his body. Mary's shadowed eyes stared at him beneath her heavy hair, that whipcord and quicksilver girl! He lunged at her, taking her by surprise, finding lips that parted in shock. For a brief, heady moment he felt the warmth of her tongue, followed, almost immediately, by a stinging blow on the back of his head.

'Get off me! You think I want that, don't you? You want to get rid of Dora and start on me!'

'No! No. Mary, don't make such a noise.'

'I'll make all the noise I like. Well, that's decided it. I won't stay here to be walked over and made a fool of and – and mauled by you! Be happy, Connor. It's all yours. I'm leaving.'

She flung back the covers and got out of bed, as if she was about to pack and go that very minute. Instead she seized her dressing gown and stormed downstairs, putting on the kettle with grim determination.

Connor followed, waiting until the storm eased a little before saying, 'And where did you think you were going? This is your home.'

'I'm going to my Aunt Rosalind,' said Mary, not deigning to spare him a look. 'I shall keep Deb company. She'll need someone to keep track of her admirers. You and Dad can do as you like, with no useless girls to get in the way. All we're good for is keeping house, you know.'

'I can't stay without you!'

'You should have thought of that earlier.'

She shook the tea caddy aggressively and spooned the leaves into the pot. 'Anyway, Dad won't let you leave. You and he can run a very good horse business, no doubt. You won't keep the chestnut sound and the little mare's too small for you, but those are minor problems.'

She turned to stare at him with a blue and unforgiving gaze. 'I think you should sell Diablo. He's not your sort of horse. And I could do with the money.'

'I won't sell your horse, Mary. If you want him sold, you do it.'

'And there you go again! You're never anything but difficult.'

He leaned against the dresser, trying to look into her face, trying to reason with her. 'It isn't me, Mary! Don't you see how prickly you are? Everything I do upsets you.'

'Because you never consult me first! You just do what you want and expect me to agree. If I don't, I'm being difficult.'

'That's a distortion of the truth, girl!'

'Don't call me girl.'

'And why not? It's what you are.'

'But with you—' she spread her hands, trying to explain '—with you it's a term of abuse. You don't respect girls. You don't respect me.'

They stood facing each other, very still. There was no sound in the house but the low hum of the kettle and the shifting of coals in the range. They had the sense that they were quite alone in the house, perhaps even in the world. And yet, there was a force between them, drawing them inexorably together. As if he couldn't help himself, Connor suddenly reached out and took hold of her shoulders, finding her mouth, drawing her in. Mary's head fell back, she felt his tongue, his teeth, the pressure of his body against hers. A great spasm of feeling swept through her. Like flying, like dying, like – like heaven!

It was too much. She broke free, and stood away from him. She put her hand up to her mouth, touching where he had touched. He could see her short, broken, horseman's nails. 'I don't know – I don't know why—' he couldn't make sense of himself or her.

'That was – odd,' she muttered.

'Christ! Is that what you call it?'

He turned away and went to the window, looking out into the night, trying to cool his blood. If he looked at her a minute longer he would rape her or strangle her, he thought. Probably both.

After a while she said quietly, 'So you see, I really do have to go.'

Not looking, he said, 'Yes. I see it's for the best. I'm – I'm sorry. It should have worked, you know.'

'You and Dad will be good together. He's loving the horses. Farming's all about machines and chemicals nowadays. This is right up his street.'

Suddenly he said, 'I wish you cared for me as you do for him.'

Mary took in her breath. 'Only because then I wouldn't fight you. You're not used to having enemies, are you, Con?'

The kettle was boiling, but she was past thinking of tea. She took it from the stove and listened to the water bubbling and sighing within. Gradually it calmed. She thought of a dozen things she might say and decided against all of them. It was for him, surely, to explain what had happened here tonight. Was she Con's enemy? They always seemed to fight. They hadn't touched out of love. Suddenly he said, 'Oh God,' in a voice full of grit, and went quickly into the night.

241

Chapter Twenty-four

Mary looked gloomily about the room. She should have been delighted. Rosalind had decorated it with her nieces in mind, indulging the girly fantasies of a mother of sons. The wallpaper was floral, the curtains edged with lace, the beds covered with quilts of baby pink and white. Even the dressing table wore a demure skirt, and the wardrobe opened to reveal rows of beautifully padded hangers. It was Deb's sort of room, thought Mary. It did not suit her.

Deb sat on one of the beds and sparkled up at her. 'This is mine. Gorgeous, isn't it? Like something out of a film.'

'I think it's the sort of film I'd talk through.'

'What on earth do you mean? Anyway, you always talk through films, unless they're meaningful and boring. Oh, I'm so glad you've come. I was scared stiff of going to everything on my own, but now there's two of us we can have fun.'

'I'm supposed to be getting a job,' said Mary.

'And you will! But you have to acquire some of what Aunt Rosalind calls "town bronze" first. I do like her, you know. Even if she is out of the ark.'

Mary said nothing. She wasn't sure if she did like Rosalind, in actual fact. She was almost sure that Rosalind didn't like her. But in that she might be doing her aunt an injustice, she decided. It might simply be that she and Rosalind knew each other rather well. It was an instinctive and unsettling understanding. They neither of them made the mistake of thinking the other a fool.

Mary washed her face and hands in the little bathroom that was hers and Deb's alone, and went down to tea in the drawing room. Rosalind was presiding over a silver pot and cake stand, an arrangement that Mary at once suspected of being staged. Rosalind liked the image of herself as a beautiful and sophisticated aunt and was giving it her full attention.

'My dears.' She motioned them to sit down, and said, laughing, 'My goodness, Mary, you're almost invisible behind that hair. Whatever shall we do with you?'

'I have a London hairdresser,' said Mary airily. 'If we're going up to town tomorrow I thought I might make an appointment.'

242

'Oh.' Rosalind was nonplussed and Mary pressed home her advantage.

'Dad's given me quite a bit of cash, actually. I thought Deb and I could go shopping for clothes. Not Knightsbridge, it's so pricey. I thought Kensington.'

Rosalind laughed uncomfortably. 'What an expert you sound, Mary. I don't think I realised you knew London quite so well.'

'I don't think anyone can claim to know London well,' said Mary, with a world-weary smile. 'But Monsieur Raymond is definitely a remarkable hairdresser.'

Rosalind almost dropped her cup. 'Raymond? My God, Mary, you'll never get in. And if you could, you can't afford it. He's desperately fashionable.'

'Is he? Oh.' Mary dropped her pretence and grinned. 'I went to him when he only had a horrid little shop. You never know, though, he might remember me. We talked in French, he hates England really. Thinks English women are frumpy cows.'

'Lots of them are,' said Rosalind, without thinking. Then she collected herself. 'Really, Mary! You simply must stop saying such things!'

But it was Rosalind who found the number, and leaned on the sidetable to listen while Mary 'phoned. She spoke in French from the start, with the result that Raymond himself had to come to the 'phone.

'Oui? 'Allo?'

'Ah, Monsieur Raymond' said Mary, delighted, 'I had to speak to you! It's Mary Cooper – you may remember, I came to you when you were in your little shop. I've been in the country and my aunt says you're too fashionable to cut my hair now. But – but I wonder if you could? I – I have marks on my face. You cut my hair to hide them.'

'The little hotel girl! Very French. From Paris.'

"No – er – yes.'

'Come tomorrow. I see to you between clients. My salon is full of rich old women.'

'I can be there by ten, I think. Is that all right?'

'Yes. Tomorrow, Mary Cooper.'

The 'phone buzzed as he put it down. Rosalind said, 'You don't know what it's going to cost.'

'He's worth it, whatever it is. I wonder if he'd do Deb as well? I didn't dare ask.'

'My dear, anyone can do Deb! She only needs the ends trimming, and barely even that. Her hair's naturally magnificent.'

Mary heaved a long sigh. 'Deb's naturally magnificent, you mean. Oh, well. I'll feel better when I've had my hair cut.'

243

She stood looking at herself in the hall mirror. Rosalind felt a sudden warmth towards her unruly niece. She tried to be brave about her face, tried to stand firm against jealousy of Deb, who had the looks, and the parentage, that Mary craved. Rosalind put an arm briefly around her shoulders. 'We'll make something of you yet, my dear,' she said bracingly. 'Have some fun, and then we'll see about finding you something to do.'

The early train was crowded with London commuters. Mary felt shabby and out of place amongst them, a country bumpkin who should have stayed at home. Rosalind and Deborah sat opposite, the one elegant in a houndstooth suit, the other delectable in schoolgirl skirt and blouse. Mary wondered how she would appear in Monsieur Raymond's salon. She was wearing her churchgoing grey skirt, a wrapover which kept her legs free from draughts, and a jacket her mother had pressed upon her from her own wardrobe. Although too short in the arms for Mary, otherwise it fitted very well. She had folded back the sleeves to make it seem as if she meant to show her wrists.

As they got off the train Rosalind said, 'Do you know, Mary, you can look quite chic when you try.'

'The sleeves of this jacket are too short,' she said glumly.

'All the same! I don't think you need worry, dear. You look very well.'

'If only it's not full of really rich people,' said Mary, whose nerve was failing badly.

'Talk French, dear. No one expects anything of foreigners, you know.'

Rosalind and Deborah left her. Mary trudged glumly into the tube and sat amidst cigarette ends and peculiar people, feeling the old sense of unimportance begin again. In this huge city, amidst so many, she was less than a grain of sand. She had survived before, she told herself, when she had far less to rely on than now. This time she need not freeze in Mrs Harris's attic room, need not scrub and polish and connive to earn her bread. The grain of sand had enlarged to be almost a little pebble.

The hair salon was huge. Mary stood outside a window of expensive belled glass and saw a dozen girls in navy blue inscribed with 'Raymond' on the pocket in red. The reception area was heaped with flowers and soft chairs, and a girl with Dora's enamelled complexion sat at the desk. Mary pushed open the door to confront her bored and intimidating stare, launching at once into French. Sighing, the girl rang a little brass bell and a minion appeared. 'Take her through to Raymond, would you Mandy? She's French. Friend or something.'

'Thought he hated everyone,' said Mandy grimly. But she treated Mary to her stage smile and whisked her through.

She was shampooed without ceremony, and Raymond came out to her as she sat, wet and bedraggled, before a huge and unforgiving mirror. She was staring miserably at her undisguised face, taking in every inch of blotched skin. Sometimes, if she didn't stare at herself for a while, she could imagine the marks had shrunk, or faded, or were not in fact as bad as she had thought. But when she looked as she looked now she saw they were as they had always been, blurred red blemishes on the porcelain of her skin.

Raymond stood behind her, unsmiling. 'You will never be beautiful,' he said. 'But there can be charm. It is not the marks that will ruin you. It is how they make you feel. A woman of distinction would bear the scars as if they were nothing, and those around her would think them nothing also.'

'I do try,' said Mary forlornly. 'Sometimes it's very hard.'

He took up his comb and began raking the thick mat of her hair. 'The hair will help. *Mon Dieu*, it's like a nest of snakes.' He turned and lapsed into English. 'Mandy, tell Lady whoever she is I am detained. Give her some cake and make her fatter than she already is.'

Mary giggled. 'What shall we talk about?' asked Raymond, placing his comb against her face to measure proportions. 'You? Me? Love?'

'Talk about France,' said Mary ingenuously. He settled happily to snipping her hair while talking lyrically about the beauties of the land of his birth.

She emerged at two-thirty, starving and tired. Her hair was once again shining, feathered, setting off the angles of her face like a beautifully designed hat. He had charged her a pound.

She took a taxi to the teashop where she was to meet Rosalind and Deborah. They were sitting in the corner, a pile of packages on a chair, the remains of lunch in evidence. Mary hurried across. 'I'm so sorry, both of you! He took forever.'

'We thought you'd died,' said Deb. 'And perhaps you did. You're a new woman.'

'Do you like it?' She turned her head this way and that.

'It's – it's stunning,' said Rosalind. 'Quite stunning. My dear, you look like a girl who spends her life adorning the deck of a yacht in Cannes.'

'Perhaps I should buy a pair of white trousers and one of those striped tops?' said Mary, giggling like a carefree ten year old.

'It would suit you,' said Rosalind. 'We'll invest if you come to Biarritz.'

Mary insisted on eating, although the others had sat there long enough. She had a sandwich for speed, an unpleasant slab of ham between two stodgy squares of bread. London food wasn't good, she recalled dismally. Thank heavens for Rosalind's exceptional cook.

'Now,' said her aunt, gathering everything up, 'I think Simpsons, for a few things, and we could look in at Harrods, and do Kensington another day? You need something for Friday, Mary.'

She swallowed down a mouthful of stodge, like a ship taking on coal. 'What's on Friday?'

'The races, dear. Only Epsom, it isn't smart. But you'll meet lots of people, so you really do have to look your best.'

Mary looked down at her sandwich. Her appetite had quite deserted her all of a sudden. She thought of all the new people, people who knew nothing of her but what they saw. People who would see Deb and think one thing, and her and think quite another. People who would pity her and say: 'Such a shame about Mary Cooper. Her sister's so lovely.' She looked up and saw Rosalind watching her, knowing exactly what was going through her mind.

'The horses will be fun,' she said lamely. 'I've never been to a flat meeting before. What should I wear?'

'We'll find something,' said Rosalind, giving her hand a firm pat. 'Deborah's wearing palest lime green.'

Deb smiled at her, Rosalind smiled at her, together they willed her to be happy. So she smiled back. And tried to be.

The skirt of her new two-piece creased under the pressure of her clammy hands. Mary tried not to clutch at it, and instead confined herself to gripping the leather seat of the car. She wanted to go to the lavatory, quite badly, but they were still miles away from the course. Besides, she didn't really want to go. She knew her own nerves, sending false messages to confuse and confound her. If she did find a loo there wouldn't be any point.

Deb looked delicious of course. Like mint ice cream topped with glorious hazelnuts. Mary, in her oatmeal suit with a long swinging skirt, felt bland and colourless. Aunt Rosalind had insisted on a dark cerise lipstick, although Mary was convinced that all it did was clash with the marks on her face. She should have worn blue, she thought miserably. But Rosalind had said it was too unsophisticated and had insisted, and at home she'd thought she looked all right. It was now, in the car, about to confront strangers, that her confidence had fallen through the floor.

'Nearly there,' said Rosalind bracingly. Mary clutched at her skirt again. Her hands were starting to shake.

'Will you stop it?' said Deb urgently. 'What are you worried about?'

'I'm not worried! You know I'm not worried! Honestly!' She turned her head firmly to the window and stared out at a car park. In the distance flags waved above long rows of stands and the dim sound of loudspeakers filtered across the short, breezy grass.

They were to lunch in a box, at the invitation of some people Rosalind knew. Flowers were banked along the walkways and everything was very clean and brightly painted. Rosalind strolled along, waving now and then to a familiar face in the throng. A man almost collided with Deb, stopped and tipped his hat. 'Good afternoon, my dear.'

She gave a cool half smile and stepped around him.

'Very good, Deborah,' said Rosalind in an undertone. 'Men drink rather a lot at race meetings. You don't want them getting out of hand.'

'They're always out of hand where Deb's concerned, drunk or sober,' remarked Mary. The exercise was making her feel better. And there was a sense of excitement about the place, a rough glamour that stung the senses. Dimly seen and faintly heard, ordinary racegoers milled about by the track, amidst tic-tac men and touts, studiously ignored by those in this sleeker, neater enclosure. Everyone seemed busy, although racing hadn't started as yet. Every now and then, mingling with the scent of flowers, came the smell of frying onions.

'Come along, girls.' Rosalind bustled them into the stand, thinking longingly of a gin. She hadn't expected to get here without incident, Mary had looked positively green in the car. She trotted up to the box, and saw at once that it was a larger party than expected. Some fifty or so people overflowed into a function room, drinking and talking without pause.

Mary let out a strangled yelp. 'Shut up, Mary,' said Rosalind through gritted teeth. But she had frozen to the spot. Between them, her sister and her aunt put a hand under either elbow and propelled her forward.

'Roger!' Rosalind extended her hand to her host. 'Roger, this is just lovely! Let me introduce my nieces, Deborah and Mary.'

'Deborah! Good heavens.' A man of forty or so stood gazing into Deb's lovely face. 'Goodness me,' he said again, and she tried to retrieve her hand. 'How do you do?' she murmured. 'We're so happy to be here.'

'My dear, the pleasure is all mine.'

'And this is Mary,' said Rosalind firmly, moving Deb aside.

'Mary. Indeed.'

And so it went on. No one was intentionally rude, of course, it was simply that Deborah cast a light against which no other could shine. Mary looked well that day, but no one noticed anyone but Deb.

247

'An exceptional young girl,' said one woman to another. 'It isn't often you see one quite so lovely. The young men are bound to be silly over her.'

In a matter of minutes Deb was in conversation with the son of a racehorse trainer and his indigent friend. Mary, finding herself edged aside, went to seek out her aunt, only to find that she was enveloped in a group of cronies, drinking and gossiping hard. Mary was lost in a roomful of strangers. It was her worst nightmare come true. She looked longingly at the door, but dared not leave. Aunt Rosalind would wash her hands of her, and then what?

A small man with a bright, enquiring expression passed her carrying two drinks. 'You look a bit bereft, sweetie,' he said bluntly. 'Know anyone?'

Mary shook her head. 'I came with my aunt and I've lost her.'

'Probably just as well. Most people's aunts deserve to be lost without trace. Mine, without a doubt. Here, have a drink.'

He handed her a tall glass full of pale yellow liquid. Mary sipped and brightened. 'Lovely. What is it?'

'Champers, darling. The best, our Roger never skimps, such a treasure. I'm Clark Donaldson, the famous actor. What's your name?'

Mary laughed and told him. 'Are you very famous?'

'Can't be. You've obviously never heard of me. Toast of Broadway last year, my dear, an absolute star, but back here in boring old Blighty I'm lucky to get a part as the butler in a Whitehall farce. Can't imagine why I came back, to tell you the perfect truth. Except I can imagine. It was all for love.'

He struck a theatrical pose and fixed his gaze longingly on a tall, blond young man in a cream jacket. Mary felt the hairs on her neck rise up and took a gulp of champagne. Did he mean what she thought he meant? He was watching her, his birdlike eyes sharp and amused. Mary said breathlessly, 'Are you really in a Whitehall farce?'

'No. My agent suggested it, that's all. But as I said to him, what do you think I am? I've served my time, dear, I said. I'm due some respect! But you might just as well ask a monkey to play the banjo. What happened to your face?'

She was completely taken aback, shocked into matter-of-factness. 'Forceps marks. When I was born. It saved my life, so I'm supposed to be grateful.'

'Pity they didn't haul you out by your bum, if you ask me.' No taller than her chin, he came very close and peered up at her. She felt herself blushing, knew the rising tide was investing her skin with new and livid colour. He put out a twiggy finger and lifted her hair.

'My God, you do light up, don't you? Poor darling, you'll have to do something. And you've got such lovely skin.'

248

'There isn't anything to do,' said Mary grimly. 'I just have to live with it. And not mind.'

'The things people expect! Of course you sodding mind, love! Who wouldn't? Hang on a tic, I'll get Kristian to have a look at you, and while I'm about it I'll get us another drink. Don't you dare move!'

Mary stood bemused where he had left her, watching him flit over to his tall blond friend and on to the bar. They returned together, Clark with his hands cradling three more glasses of champagne. 'Get this down you, Mary my darling. Take a look at that face, Kris. What do you think?'

Mary felt her insides cringe and shrivel. The blond stranger bent his large, white-toothed face to hers and peered under her fragile fringe of hair. In an act of bravado, hating herself and hating him, she put up her hand and pulled her hair back, saying, 'Go on, have a really good look. You see? There's nothing you can do.'

Her tormentor straightened and put out his hand for some champagne. Clark at once supplied a glass, saying, 'Drink another couple, Mary. What do you think, Kris love? Do a paint job, could you? Lights up like a whore's bellpush when she blushes, you've no idea.'

'It is possible,' said Kristian. He had an odd, lilting accent that Mary thought might be Scandinavian. 'It would take perhaps an hour. Two, the first time. The skin's good, very smooth. Without that I wouldn't try.'

'Try what?' she asked in strangled tones.

'He's a make-up artiste, sweetie,' said Clark. 'Makes even me look beautiful sometimes. When he's in the mood. Moment I saw that face I thought: Kristian, here's one for you. Loves a challenge, does Kris. That's my trouble, I'm too easy these days. His old pair of slippers. His dull old mate.'

Kristian said nothing, simply staring at Mary's face and sipping his champagne. 'This is a good face,' he said, as if he had been making a considered assessment. 'There is character here. I can do something. Come to my studio in the morning.' He parted his lips in a brilliant and confusing smile, and walked away.

Mary looked in bewilderment at Clark. 'Well!' he said expressively. 'You are a hit – I'm almost jealous. Don't look so worried, sweetie, I'll give you his card. Don't get there before eleven, he's never there – well, with the life he leads, you don't expect it. He'll do you the make-up job of your life.'

Suddenly a hand fell on Mary's shoulder. 'Where have you been?' demanded Aunt Rosalind. 'You haven't been drinking?'

'I've been guzzling the most wonderful champagne,' said Mary. 'Clark, this is my aunt, Mrs Dalton.'

'Absolutely charmed,' said Clark, and took Rosalind's hand to kiss it.

'Delighted,' said Rosalind frostily, and propelled Mary towards the dining table with the force of a battle cruiser under full power. The moment they were out of earshot, she hissed, 'What do you mean, falling into the clutches of that terrible old queen?'

'He's lovely,' said Mary, bolstered by the bubbles in all that champagne. 'Give me an old queen any day.'

'Mary!'

But a lecture was out of the question. Mary was placed at table between a racehorse trainer who was too worried to eat and a boy who must have been starving, judging by his concentrated munching. Eating roast beef, Mary gradually sobered up. The trainer, who had said virtually nothing throughout the meal, suddenly turned to her.

'Do you know what's the worst thing about this whole business?'

'No?'

'It's the owners. Load of misfits who don't know a horse's arse from his ears. Half of them don't pay and the other half don't pay on time. It's not as if they have to face the bank manager, though. Not them.'

'Poor you,' said Mary feebly.

'Too bloody right. My horse won't win today. Vaselingus. Great horse, but that's nothing. Can't win today. It's too important. He's in good form all right, but he won't win. That way I'll have to go into that bloody bank without a leg to stand on. The wife will leave, of course. And take the kids. I'll probably have to shoot myself in the yard.'

She choked on a giggle. 'I'm sure it's not quite that bad.'

He gave her a panicky, end-of-the-world glance. 'If anything it's worse. Do you know how much stable lads want these days? And what do they do for it? Drink and womanise and take no notice when the horses go wrong. Dope them too, most of the time, and who carries the can for that, may I ask? Lads are the people I hate most in the world.'

'I thought that was owners,' said Mary unwisely.

'What?'

'Nothing.'

He subsided into silence, merely taking out his racecard and looking again and again at the runners.

The boy on her other side said, 'I say, do you mind if I have your bread roll?'

'Not at all.'

He grabbed and devoured it, saying not another word. She sat marooned between her two dismal companions, watching Deb across the table, laughing and hardly able to eat for the attention paid to her by those on either side. She was imposing rules on them, five minutes

250

each with no interruptions or timed forfeits must be paid. The trainer said lugubriously, 'That your sister talking to the Cummings boy? Don't know what he's got to laugh about. His father's almost bankrupt.'

'Perhaps he doesn't know,' said Mary.

'You're right there. Couldn't laugh like that if he did. No one knows what it's like. I tell my wife that all the time.'

'No wonder she's about to leave.'

'What?'

'Nothing.'

The meal was running late. Although pudding had not been served people suddenly began to get up and rush about. 'I'm going to be late,' said the trainer, in an agony of misery. 'I've got a runner in the first. They'll probably disqualify him.'

'Probably,' said Mary. She got up as he did, and followed him. He didn't appear to mind. He trotted down the stairs and she trotted after him, supplying the punctuation to his miserable monologue as and when needed.

They whisked past the flowers and the racecard sellers, the tote and the paddock, past miles of white railing and a glimpse of the green ribbon that was the course. Suddenly Mary found herself backstairs. The place was full of horses and stable lads, thick with the familiar smells of horse-sweat, leather and nerves. A small, wizened man wearing a trenchcoat two sizes too big was holding a wiry chestnut wearing a saddle many sizes too small.

'Who's she then, guvnor?'

'God knows. He's lame, then?'

'No. Sound as a bell.'

'Oh, God.'

The lad began to lead the horse towards the paddock. Mary and the trainer followed, he trying to light a cigarette, only to leave it crumbled on the ground.

'Has he got a chance?' asked Mary.

'Not a hope. Bound to break down. Probably have to be—'

'Shot?' supplied Mary.

In the paddock a jovial and loquacious owner laughed and chatted to them. The trainer said nothing, the jockey looked small and cold, so it was left to Mary to fill in the gaps.

'My, he looks well!' exclaimed the owner.

'Doesn't he?' she said.

'You've done well with him, George, I'll say that.'

'Hasn't he just?'

The horse was led to the gate, to be flung free like a pigeon released into the air. 'What an action!' said Mary spontaneously.

'I've always thought he moved well,' said the owner.

The trainer chewed on an unlit cigarette.

The horse won by four lengths. Somehow Mary found herself in a bar drinking champagne again, making meaningless conversation with the owner and his friends, finding herself in her element. A man said, 'Known George long, have you?'

And Mary thought of Deb and smiled enigmatically. It didn't do to play it too straight, after all.

George was at her elbow. 'Coming then?' he barked. 'We've a runner in the next.'

'Oh. Right.' She downed her drink and left with him. For some unfathomable reason they were a team for the day. Down in the stables, with the same lad but a different horse, all was made clear.

'You were great in the paddock,' he said gloomily. 'Good with people, I can see that. Not my style.'

Mary thought of the many, many times she had been considered too three-cornered for any company. She was only a social expert in comparison to George. She looked at the big, well-muscled horse.

'How's this one going to run?'

'Dunno. Might have a chance.'

She abandoned any thoughts of having a bet.

The horse came third, and George mumbled another two cigarettes, confiding to Mary that he fully expected the bank to foreclose. 'The worst thing is,' he added, 'they'll shoot the horses. The ones that don't race. They'll make good jumpers when I get the time, but I haven't the time, see? Bank won't like it. Shoot 'em. That's what they'll do.'

Mary felt a prickle of interest. 'You should sell them,' she advised airily. 'Or send them away to be trained.'

'They'll bust me first,' he said.

For the third time that day, she found herself in the paddock. She stood in an earnest group around the favourite, the doomed Vaselingus, engaging in conversation with his rich Italian owner.

'He break blood vessel last spring. I think it the end.'

'What a good thing it wasn't.'

'I long for this victory. I live my life hoping for it.'

'Let's hope for the best, then.'

George, who hoped for nothing but a quick end to his torment, let out a long, miserable moan. 'Be brave, George,' said Mary bracingly, and he looked at her with lugubrious eyes.

A familiar figure stood at the edge of the paddock. Rosalind. She was staring at Mary in amazement, lacking the magic escort or owner's badge, forced simply to mouth at her to come out. Mary excused herself for a moment and walked across to the railing. 'Sorry, Aunt Rosalind. Can't come now. Put five pounds on Vaselingus for me, will you? To win.'

'What? Mary!'

But Mary had returned to her horse. Rosalind stood for a moment, watching incredulously. At this distance Mary seemed tall and elegant in her oatmeal suit, the sort of woman who belonged in the paddock at race meetings. She might have been at least twenty-five.

The horses were going to the start. Rosalind tore her gaze from her chameleon niece and rushed to the Tote, to get her bet on before the off.

The drive home was made peaceful by exhaustion. Deborah had been invited to two parties and a weekend, of which Rosalind was more than doubtful. Mary had an open invitation to visit George at his stables, and to go racing with him whenever she wished.

'But he says the bank's going to foreclose,' she said sleepily to Rosalind.

She snorted. 'Foreclose on George Reynolds? He's this year's leading trainer. Nice of him to give you that tip though. Fifty pounds!'

Mary had the beginnings of a headache. She had never in her life imagined she would ever drink so much champagne. Trying to doze in the corner of the car, she turned uncomfortably. A square of cardboard in her pocket was digging into her hip. 'Oh,' she said, remembering. 'I've got to go up to town tomorrow, Aunt Rosalind.'

'You can't, dear. It's a Saturday. I'm giving a buffet lunch.'

'All the same. It's – it's about my face. Clark Donaldson's friend is going to make me up.'

'What? You've made an appointment with those two deviants? Mary, I think not!'

But, as Laura had discovered before her, when it came to stubbornness Mary had no equal. She was adamant: she was going to see Kristian at his studio. 'You said yourself they're deviant,' she said reasonably, getting out of the car and wandering through the house into Rosalind's delightful sitting room. 'They only like other men, so I'm perfectly safe.'

Too late, she realised that David was there. 'Good God, Mary,' he said, looking down his large nose. 'You haven't got mixed up with queers, have you? Mother, what have you let her do?'

'I'm not letting her do anything!' said Rosalind in despair. 'I shall telephone your mother, Mary. I warn you!'

Deborah, flinging herself down in a chair, said, 'Why not just let her go, Aunt Rosalind? You can't tell Mary anything, you know. I don't suppose she'll get in that much of a mess.'

'She certainly won't!' said David portentously. 'If you insist on going, Mary, I shall go too.'

She sank on to the sofa, feeling suddenly light-headed and silly.

She imagined David faced with Clark and Kristian and began to laugh.

David, taking his mother aside, said anxiously, 'Honestly, Mother, that girl! She really does need someone to take her in hand. She's impossible.'

Chapter Twenty-five

Mary awoke clear-headed and ready for the day. It was a mark of her iron constitution, and perhaps too the iron will that drove it. She put on her new pair of jeans – a purchase made locally, free from Laura's doubtful eye and out of sight of Rosalind's not necessarily more liberal one. Topped with a cream jumper and her lovely, floaty haircut, Mary knew she looked good.

She bounced downstairs, expecting to be the only one up. Buffet lunch or no, Rosalind wouldn't rise before ten. After all, she had a cook and a maid to see to that sort of thing and her duty was to be rested and on form. But the breakfast table was not in fact deserted. David sat there, neat in sports jacket and flannels, determinedly reading the paper.

'You're not really coming?' Mary paused in the doorway, affronted and dismayed.

'I most certainly am. We can't possibly let you go jauntering off to some theatrical flophouse—'

'What's a flophouse? Like a whorehouse, only worse?'

'For God's sake, Mary!'

'Oh, David, stop making faces! You're not my keeper. I won't go to pieces if you take your eye off me for a second.'

She went to the sideboard and discovered bacon and eggs. They weren't as good as Gunthwaite's, having invariably sat on hot trays for twenty minutes, but she was starving and they were edible. After some minutes David said, 'I can't believe anyone can eat so much and stay so thin.'

'Connor says I'll wake up one day and suddenly be fat,' she remarked. 'Do you keep in touch with Connor at all? He never says.'

David rustled his paper. 'We don't, actually. To be honest, I thought he was encroaching rather. Latching on to the family as he did.'

'We latched on to him a bit too, you know.' Mary poured herself some coffee. 'He's terribly good for Michael.'

David cleared his throat. 'Yes. About Michael – and your mother—'

But Mary did not want to be inveigled into chitchat about her family. She drained her coffee cup, pushed back her chair and got up.

255

David trailed after her, watching her gather bag, book, silk scarf, whisking from room to room in a whirlwind of energy. He was still trailing as she whisked out of the house to the station.

Kristian's studio turned out to be an upstairs flat in Drury Lane. The entrance was between a dubious café and a ticket agency, with last night's blown rubbish heaped against the door.

'What did I tell you?' said David self-righteously.

'Shut up, David,' said Mary. 'You don't have to come in.'

'And you don't have to go in! Come away, Mary. Mary!'

But she had pushed at the door and left him in the street. He followed her up the bare staircase, the very air suffused with an odd and he thought probably deviant smell of something oily. He wished that Mary would pay him some attention! He was supposed to be taking care of her and she treated him like a pursuing stray dog.

She rapped on the door at the top. By the time David arrived, panting, behind her, she was inside, talking to someone. He followed her in, stamping aggressively on the bare boards, and they both stopped and looked at him. A very tall, very blond man in a white boiler suit said, 'Who is this?'

'My cousin,' said Mary glumly. 'This is Kristian, David. He's a make-up artist. You can see he's OK, so you can go now.'

'What on earth do you want a make-up artist for?'

Mary gritted her teeth. 'I've no idea. But I do. Go away, David. Come back in an hour.'

'Come back in two hours,' said Kristian. 'Go away, silly man. We have work to do. She can leap from the window if need be.'

David looked around the room. A bench ran round three sides, beneath which stretched a curtain. Above it was a mirror again encircling the room, and above that again a shelf laden with wigs and moustaches, greasepaints, powders, a confusion of things. There was a large dentist's chair and nothing else. It was what it seemed – a make-up studio.

'I'll – I'll come back for you,' he said, trying to regain the initiative. 'I'll go to my club. Afterwards we can have lunch.'

'Connor says everyone in your club's an unburied corpse.'

'Well, Connor would.'

They stood regarding him. They were waiting for him to go. Routed, David turned and clattered back down the stairs.

The encounter had left the others feeling like allies. Kristian took Mary's hand and led her to the window, telling her to hold her hair back from her face. He stared at her in the cold north light, and then fetched a magnifying glass and stared again. His breath smelled of mint and something herbal. Mary wondered if she smelled of bacon and egg. Golden hairs curled up from the neck of his suit, tangling in a thin gold chain. 'Most interesting' he murmured. 'A thousand broken blood vessels covered by smooth skin. You have tried make-up before, of course?'

'Just foundation and powder,' said Mary. 'It looked worse than ever. The colour always shines through and the rest of me looked yellow.'

'Your skin colour is very delicate,' admitted Kristian. 'It will be very hard to match it.'

'Oh.' Mary allowed herself a flicker of disappointment, when she hadn't known she treasured hope. But she should have known how much she wanted her miracle. People could bear the unbearable, thinking that one day all would be well.

Kristian wrapped a band around her hair and sat her in the dentist's chair, reclining it. She let out her breath in a long exhale, trying not to mind, trying to think of nothing. She closed her eyes. Cold cream was rubbed into her face, the man's long fingers firm and decisive. A moment later dollops of something were arrayed on her forehead.

'What are you doing?'

'An experiment. Keep quiet.'

She subsided. More dollops. After a while he wiped it all off, irritably, and started again. Mary's spirits declined still further. It was too difficult, the colour too intractable, he hadn't known how hard it could be. Again everything was wiped off, again more was applied. She said, 'You don't have to keep on at it, you know. I don't expect it to work.'

He didn't pause in his careful application of this and that. 'It does work. I am choosing the exact shade. You have no patience. If it was easy you would not be like this now.'

Of course it was true. She thought of all those miserable afternoons in her room, trying this or that, expensive stuff, cheap stuff, powder. It made her look like a gargoyle. That's what she would look like now. And this man would charge her, and expect her to be pleased.

Again he wiped everything off. But this time he pushed the chair into an upright position and said, 'Go and make coffee. I have to mix.'

She got up and went to the kettle in the corner, looking at herself in the mirror. She looked just as she always did, greasy with cream, her eyes unnoticeable beneath the reddened V on her forehead, challenged and beaten by the thumbprint on her cheek. If only David hadn't come. Her stupidity should be kept private. She wondered if he would mock her at lunch.

Kristian was working with a small pestle and mortar, adding this by the spoonful, that by the drop. He ground away at it, thinning the mix again and again, letting it run into the bowl like thin cream. Mary thought of putting that on to her skin, and knew it wouldn't stick.

257

That was why he lived in this far from prosperous studio, of course. Kristian really didn't know a thing.

She perched on the chair and drank her coffee. Outside the buses ground along, their roofs a foot below the window. She wondered if her face mattered as much as she had thought. The races had been fun, after all. And if a face like this meant that men would never look at her as they looked at Deb, did it matter so very much? It only mattered if she cared. She must learn not to care.

'Now.' Kristian took her coffee cup from her grasp and pushed her back in the chair. 'Close the eyes.'

She lay back obediently. A soft brush coated with liquid began to slide across her face. She thought of watercolour painting, washing in the sky, a lovely ethereal blue. What a pity skins weren't blue, she mused. Or black. If she'd been black then none of this would matter.

A hair dryer was switched on nearby. Suddenly soft, cool air struck her face. 'Are you drying it off? Can I look?'

'No. It is only the beginning.'

She lay still. The dryer was switched off and the painting began again. Twice more. She wanted to yawn, to frown, to smile, but dared not. The surface of her skin would crack.

'Now.' He wound the chair upright again. 'Open your eyes and look.'

She peered anxiously into the mirror. At first she thought she was disorientated, there wasn't a mirror there. Instead there was a picture, a girl about her age, wearing a headband and a towel around her shoulders. A girl with an ordinary, morning, getting out of bed face. Unmarked.

She stood up. She leaned towards the mirror, put her face an inch away from it. All she could see was pale, undressed skin. Except – now she could detect something. Running into her eyebrow, under the hairs, was the trailing edge of the mark. The rest was gone.

She stretched her mouth, to see what would happen. Nothing. She smeared, very gingerly, with her finger, but nothing came off.

Kristian said, 'This is the base, of course, for your look. I suggest strong eyes and lips. Some colour under the cheekbones – you can take shadows.'

'It's a miracle,' she said quietly. 'How is it done?'

'I tell you later. Always take an hour. Less and something will show. The hour is needed for drying, each stage must be dry. Come. There's more to being beautiful than only not being ugly.'

She sat again in the chair. She felt distant, dreamlike. Kristian touched her eyelids with browns and blues, brushing her eyelashes and eyebrows with mascara as black as her hair. He gave her a lipstick fierce enough to please Aunt Rosalind, and dark, sultry shadows on her cheeks. Then he whisked off her headband and with a few deft ruffles of his fingers set her hair just so. Mary looked out at herself.

'Fabulous,' she breathed.

Kristian leaned on the chair and trailed his fingers down her cheek. 'I have created beauty,' he murmured.

'It's an illusion.'

'What isn't? You are the slender young gazelle, taken by the Sultan for his pleasure.' He lifted her fingers and breathed kisses on their tips.

Mary laughed, a little breathily. This big, blond man was looking at her with decided intent. 'At least you know what's really underneath,' she declared.

His ice blue eyes stared down at her. Without a moment's hesitation he slipped his hand under her jumper and enveloped her breast.

She gasped. The sensation of his hand on her was like red hot needles dancing on her nerves. She stared up at him, transfixed as a mouse swooped on by an owl. Marooned in the dentist's chair, he seemed to her suddenly huge. He swung his leg across her knees, straddling her. Baring those square, invincible teeth, he reached for her other breast.

'No!' squeaked Mary, trying to writhe away.

'Yes.' Her tiny breasts were no more than undulations under his hand, the nipples as hard suddenly as nails driven into her flesh. The sense of her body, the closeness of his, suffocated her. His thumb stroked her nipple and she was shocked into a groan.

He smiled and knelt on the chair, Mary half lying between his legs. 'I made you,' he said happily. He shifted position, releasing her to hold on to the chair. The fly of his boiler suit bulged an inch from her newly restored face. Her hands flapped like fish, helpless on a slab. Was she to hit him? What if she did not?

'I thought – you and Clark?' she said helplessly.

'You don't care about that. You are beautiful. I love beauty.'

His body seemed to elongate. His groin touched her and slid away, until he and she were lying in the chair, face to face. She stared into his cold blue eyes. He smiled at her. His body began thrusting at hers, she could feel it through their clothes. A gathering billow of feeling was growing in her. She wanted to part her legs and thrust back, hard, harder, two bodies that didn't know each other, two needs that had no need to care.

Footsteps clattered on the stairs. Kristian muttered some Scandinavian oath and got up. Mary, stunned, flustered, shot out of the chair and stood shaking and disorientated in the middle of the floor, looking helplessly at the door as David rapped and came in.

He looked from her to Kristian and back again. Mary shuddered, waiting for the accusation. Shaking girl, flushed and dishevelled man, pulling his clothing straight. Surely the scene was crystal clear? But David simply said, 'I can't believe it. Mary, I hardly recognise you.'

'My – my face?' She went to the mirror, wondering if the last few minutes had blurred any of its perfection. Not so. The girl who looked back at her, dark-eyed, elfin, was someone lovely, someone she didn't know. 'Do you think it's all right?'

'More than that. It's unbelievable. Mr – Mr Kristian, was it? I really must offer you my heartiest congratulations.'

He went to Kristian and shook him warmly by the hand. Kristian's limb participated not at all, and was simply pumped like a handle. 'I did not do it for you,' he said contemptuously.

'All the same! It's bound to make all the difference, isn't it? Have you paid him, Mary? How much did it cost?'

'We – we haven't talked money.'

She went to her bag but Kristian said irritably, 'It's ten pounds. I always charge ten pounds. I give you three bottles, three layers, take the hour to make it set. Afterwards put anything on – some stupid stuff you buy in Woolworth's. Pale blue eyes . . . look like everyone.'

'I'll do it like this,' said Mary shyly. 'If I can.'

He put down the three bottles, and tossed in a brush. 'When this is gone you must come back,' he said, looking down at her.

'Of course. Of course I will.' She smiled at him, a little questioning, a little on edge. Almost – encouraging. All at once the grim Scandinavian face split to a huge grin, and she grinned back.

'The next time,' he said, and took both her hands.

She said, 'We'll have to see, won't we?' And they both laughed.

Downstairs, walking in the street with the precious bottles in a bag, David said, 'I've just thought, you're wearing jeans. They might not let you into the club.'

'Even with my new face?' Mary was looking at herself in shop windows as they passed. She looked normal. Better than normal. Perhaps even glamorous.

'I could try and bribe the doorman. You could sit in a corner with your legs under the table and not move.'

'But I want to be noticed. For the first time in my life!'

'I wish you'd be sensible, Mary!'

She subsided reluctantly. They came to the club, and she ran up the steps almost expecting to see her old self cowering at the bottom. But no one was there. Instead the new, improved Mary treated the doorman to a dazzling smile and said, 'I'll keep my legs under the table. Promise.' The head waiter, harder to please, conducted them to a corner and flung an enormous napkin over her offensive knees. His expression made it clear that it was coming to something when even men of David's calibre could so lose their grip.

They avoided the soup and chose fish to start. It was tasteless and bony. Mary began to wonder what would have happened if David hadn't come up to town. She might have eaten a decent lunch for a start. Then she thought of Kristian's boiler suit. She was sure he wore it over nothing but bare, golden skin. She remembered the weight of him lying on her. What a good thing David had come!

Her blush mounted. She ducked her head instinctively and David said, 'What's the matter? Dropped your fork?'

'No – no.' She had forgotten. Her skin had no colour now except that which was applied. It was like wearing a mask, one that absolutely hid her personality. Behind it, she could be whoever she pleased.

Two old men across the room were looking at her. She realised she had assumed that they were looking at her marks. But it couldn't be that. Was it possible that she might be admired? Greatly daring, her fish gone, she said, 'Do you think I'm attractive, David? Now?'

He stared at her in amazement. 'What sort of question is that?'

'A fair one, I hope. After all, everyone says that Deb's wonderfully attractive. They mean sexy, of course. Men only have to glance at Deb to want to take her to bed. Do you think you could feel that way about me?'

He took a gulp of water, playing for time. But she continued to regard him across the table, long slender hands supporting a chin he had never before realised was delicate. She had such eyes, too – dark pools of blue in that pale, dewy face. What a difference! You could look all day into a face like that, when always before he had wanted to look away.

'Do you – want me to feel that way about you?' he asked breathily.

She sat up, laughed, and tossed a bit of bread at him. 'No, of course I don't. I was just saying. I've never been attractive before, you know.'

It was the oddest sensation. She didn't know when she had experienced such a peculiar day. They arrived home at four, to find some late lunch guests being treated to tea, in the hope that they'd take the hint and leave. Two young men were talking to Deb, and she looked bored and tired and restless. When Mary walked in Deb's face was a picture. 'Mary! My God. Mary!'

The boys stood up and straightened their ties. They put on welcoming expressions. She realised she had never before been introduced to someone who didn't, for the briefest second, show that they were repelled, or if not that, at least – aware. It was in the eyes, or the momentary set of the mouth. But these boys looked at her as if she might almost be someone like Deb.

David said aggressively, 'Mary's had a hard day, Deborah. She's very tired.'

'Am I?' Mary sank on to the sofa and accepted a cup of tea. 'You never used to worry if I was tired or not, David.'

'Don't be silly.' He perched next to her on the sofa arm, a little ridiculous with his seriousness and his spectacles. Deb looked at the men with something approaching exasperation. She wanted to be alone with Mary, and talk.

One of the boys said, 'How is it that both you girls are so terribly pretty?'

Mary and Deb looked at each other and giggled. 'It must be the Yorkshire air,' said Mary glibly.

The excitement of Mary's transformation inflamed the whole house. Rosalind and Deborah crouched with her before the mirror, searching for a flaw. 'I really must recommend this fellow to Howard's Covent Garden cronies,' said Rosalind. 'Some of those divas could do with a lot of extra help.'

'Really?' Mary found herself wondering if Kristian's taste ran to large ladies. It certainly seemed to encompass everything else.

'Do you think you can do it yourself?' asked Deb, taking the lid off a bottle and sniffing.

'No idea,' said Mary. 'But I'm keeping this on for as long as I possibly can.'

'You'll get spots,' said Rosalind dubiously.

'I absolutely don't care!'

But the make-up didn't survive the night. By morning it was streaked, and by lunchtime on a warm and humid day, the telltale red was shining once again. Mary looked dismally into the mirror, and reached for the cold cream. Deb said, 'Never mind. You can do it whenever you want.'

'I want it always,' said Mary gloomily.

When she had finished cleaning her face she stared at herself in the glass. Once again the marks dominated. All the delicate charm of her face was lost. She felt like crying and hated herself, because she had been given the means to escape, and it wasn't enough. She must be unbearably greedy, she thought. She must be one of those people who can never be satisfied, whatever the gift.

There was a call for her that evening. It was Connor. She sat in the hall, tensing herself against whatever he might say. But he was simply genial, telling her that all was well. 'Sweet's jumping four foot. Michael wants to put him up for sale, but I'm not sure. Mr Fitzalan-Howard took the Bombardier for a spin, and reckons he's twice the horse. He's going to let him race this time. Swears it.'

'He was always going to let me ride him.'

'Well, then. Perhaps he would. If you were home.'

There was a silence. They both started talking at once, and both fell

262

silent. Mary said, 'We're going to a party tomorrow. A London hotel.'

'Sounds very glamorous.'

'It probably is. Aunt Rosalind's making me wear the longest, thinnest dress you ever saw.'

'Would you rather be here, then?'

'Why do you ask?'

'I just wanted to know.'

She paused. She had barely begun in London. She wasn't ready to return. But the thought of Gunthwaite, lovely, tranquil Gunthwaite, fusing yesterday and tomorrow in the reality of today, remained like a jewel in her mind; something radiant, something valuable, her prize.

'I don't miss it as much as I did,' she said prosaically.

'You don't miss me.'

'Connor, that's a terrible thing to say!'

She heard him take in his breath. All at once she was angry with him, for what he had done and what he was doing now. 'You're making things up about us,' she flared. 'You used me as your drudge. We were never a pair, not in business, not in anything. You had Dora for that, after all.'

'Perhaps we should have been a pair.'

'Should we?' She was taken aback. 'Why do you say that now?'

'Because – because I miss you, Mary.'

He had taken the wind out of her sails. He had taken away her direction, tempting her with possibilities overlooked. She could hear him breathing, waiting for her response. She had none. She said, 'Could you put Piers on, do you think? I know Deb wants to talk.' Placing the receiver on the table, she went to fetch her sister.

Afterwards both girls sat glumly in the sitting room. Rosalind, flitting about discovering rings on polished surfaces from yesterday's party, said, 'I hope you two aren't getting homesick.'

'Horsesick,' said Mary. 'I miss my horses.'

'If that's all, I'll get you a ride tomorrow. Colonel Forbes is bound to let you borrow his hack.'

But the Forbes gelding proved to be dependable and dull. Mary took it on a trudge through the lanes, with a short canter down a bridle path in which she terrorised a mother and child. Coming back past a farm hemmed in by neat houses, she relieved her feelings by putting the horse at a large steel trough upturned on the verge, and flying it. The farmer came out and shouted at her, and by the time she rode back to the stable, word had spread. Colonel Forbes berated her for risking his horse's legs.

'It was the most fun he's had in years,' retorted Mary. 'Look at him! The poor old boy's bored stiff. Got a jump in him, though. I'll school him for you if you like. Fire him up a bit.'

But Colonel Forbes did not want his horse fired up. He liked to know that a ride would end in a whisky and soda by the fire, and not a hospital bed. He made a mental note to speak to Rosalind Dalton about her niece, and have her restrained.

Mary returned home still restless and on edge. The evening's party preyed on her mind. What if people could see that she was marked and had tried to hide it? There was something pathetic about attempts at concealment. They opened the door on her vulnerability. Let people know that she cared. She had almost decided to forget about the make-up, but Rosalind and Deborah were waiting after her bath.

'We're going to watch,' said Rosalind, trampling with her usual vigour on the frail shoots of Mary's confidence.

'We're going to help,' interjected Deborah. 'And encourage. Otherwise you'll rush and insist on wiping everything off.' Deborah knew her sister only too well.

There was nothing for it. Mary settled in front of the mirror, dribbling make-up into individual ramekins scrounged from the kitchen. It was very hard to paint her own face. 'Let me,' said Deborah, agonised by her ineptitude.

'No. I've got to learn.'

She struggled on, prevented by Rosalind's time-keeping from impatience. Gradually, as each coat dried, she acquired smooth, even colour. 'It's not as good as before,' she said doubtfully. Here and there she had lapsed into heavy handedness.

'You're bound to improve,' said Rosalind. 'Anyway, you can put powder on now, can't you? I always think powder makes a difference.'

The girls both thought of Rosalind's frequent appearances in imitation of an enthusiastically floured loaf. Instead, Mary confined herself to eye shadow.

'Do me,' said Deb enthusiastically, as she finished. 'It looks great, please do me.'

Mary experimented, turning her sister's lids brown. At once she seemed foreign and mysterious. 'I much prefer pale blue,' said Rosalind. 'Take it off, Deborah.'

'Yes,' said Deb in non-committal tones, and did nothing.

Mary was wearing a dark blue sheath. With so little flesh on her bones it clung to every protuberance, and Rosalind had insisted on a firm support bra, needed only to insulate her niece from the revelations of clinging jersey. Mary thought it ruined the dress; her bolstered outline seemed to her full of frumpy respectability.

As a complete contrast, Deborah was in frothy cream lace. Her auburn hair shone against it like an expensive metal, she seemed tiny and voluptuous and sweet. Looking at herself and Deb, standing together reflected in the hall mirror, Mary knew herself outclassed. With her face painted, she might pass as a pretty girl, but next to Deborah she paled to nothing. She took a long breath, waiting for the expected sick loathing, of herself, of her jealousy, even of Deb. It didn't come. She felt her eyes prick with unshed tears, and quickly turned away. She had spent years thinking herself wicked and cruel, imagining that she wanted to defeat Deborah, eclipse her, see her gone. But it was enough just to be almost pretty. She didn't need any more.

'Are we ready then?' said Rosalind, shrouding herself in a disgusting mink wrap, complete with claws.

'I wish you'd take off that bra,' hissed Deb, under her breath. 'Do it at the party and stuff it in your bag.'

'Everything will show!'

'Let it!'

Mary giggled. She felt ebullient suddenly, casting off the shadow that had hung over the day. Thoughts of Gunthwaite had no place here.

Chapter Twenty-six

A band was playing dance music in an enormous hall. Every pillar was decorated with pink and white ribbon, and buds of pink and white roses. Numbered tables stood around the dance floor, each with place names. Rosalind was gratified to see that she and her nieces were deemed worthy of a table near the floor.

She moved down the receiving line, kissing the air next to every cheek. 'My dear, it's so lovely to see you again. Such lovely girls. Whereabouts in Yorkshire did you say?'

But Rosalind was vague. She saw no need to let it be known that her nieces were heir to nothing very much. After all, she had spent many years fostering the impression that she was the product of a great Yorkshire estate, of which she was too modest to boast. But for her nieces . . . suddenly she found herself painting pictures of wealthy seclusion and rural bliss. She hinted at a grouse moor – Gunthwaite had moorland grazing rights, after all – and made much of Laura's foreign origins. It was all too easy to imply that she had emerged fully fledged from a grand Parisian dynasty, all gilded sofas and Louis Quinze desks.

Gradually people drifted into the ballroom. Aware of the buzz of interest that seemed to surround the girls, Rosalind felt a twinge of anxiety. But then, nobody could expect her to be entirely honest about everything. People weren't, in society. But she was aware all the same that she had permitted wishful thinking to run away with her. Retrieving her nieces, she said, 'I hope you girls have the sense to smell the fortune hunters. A number of people seem to think you're very rich.'

'And whose fault is that?' demanded Mary, with her usual irritating bluntness. 'Honestly, Aunt Rosalind, I've heard you! We live on a farm, nothing more!'

'You don't want to be snubbed, I take it?'

'If people snub us because we're respectable farming stock, then they're people we don't want to know.'

They were brave words. But Mary was feeling brave this evening. She wondered if she had the courage to take off the hated bra. Never having worn anything like it, she felt as if she was struggling to breathe. And the dress didn't deserve a bra like this! She excused herself and whisked into the cloakroom, taking it off in the privacy of a cubicle and handing it airily to an attendant. 'Look after this, will you? If I forget to collect it, you can use it as a truss.' She didn't know what a truss was but it sounded disgusting.

When she returned, unfettered and svelte, Rosalind glared at her across the table. But young men were present, and nothing could be said. Deb grinned, and Mary sat down with a flourish, feeling sophisticated, feeling happy. She let her mind wander, responding automatically to introductions, looking about her at the dresses and the lights. She was right to have come. There was more to life than Gunthwaite's peaceful acres.

A face across the dance floor seemed familiar. The band was playing a quickstep and one or two people were dancing, although it was too early for most to be in the mood. A man, grey-haired and portly, was urging his much younger partner to dance. She seemed obviously reluctant and he rather drunk. At one point he tried to drag her on to the floor. Mary felt a sudden shock of recognition. It was Sandra.

There could be no mistake. There was the stringy blonde hair, tonight dragged up into an approximation of a French twist, there the bony shoulders and stubby-fingered hands. Even from this distance Mary could see the reddened knuckles, the result of Sandra's habit of standing in stations waiting for business, rolling her fists against the wall. She got up, leaving her companion in mid-sentence, and walked across. Sandra was hissing in agitated tones, 'Honest, Giles! I can't. I can't dance!'

'Hello, Sandra,' said Mary. 'I didn't expect to see you here.'

Both Sandra and her escort froze. 'Who's this?' said Giles urgently. 'Another one?'

'No,' said Sandra flatly. 'What you doing here?'

'I'm invited. Are you?'

'Came with Giles, didn't I?'

The two girls looked at each other, Sandra chewing at her lip. 'You've come up in the world,' she said.

'No thanks to Stevie,' retorted Mary. 'Is he here?'

'Bloody hell, no! I won't tell him I seen you, love.'

'OK. As long as you don't. You still working the station?'

'Yeah. Pop round one evening. Have a chat.'

Mary nodded. Giles, gathering his wits, said, 'If you two girls have finished your little gossip? We're going to have a dance.'

'No, you ain't, love,' said Sandra. 'I never learned, see? When there's more of a crowd you can teach me.'

Giles began to argue that he had paid for an evening companion, and had specifically asked if she could dance. 'No one thought you

267

meant dance, love,' explained Sandra. 'Not that sort of dancing! Never you mind. I'll make it up to you. Promise.'

Mary returned to her table. Everyone stared at her. 'Who was that?' demanded Rosalind, raising her eyebrows to her hair. 'She doesn't look in the least respectable.'

'She isn't,' retorted Mary. 'But honestly, she's all right. I mean, she won't steal anything. I don't think.'

'Where on earth did you meet her?' enquired her neighbour, a very tall, very thin public schoolboy.

Mary considered. Rosalind was making faces, and Deborah was frozen into panicked immobility. 'It was when I worked as a chambermaid,' said Mary, dropping the words like icicles into a pond. 'I wasn't trained for anything and it was the only job I could get. And Sandra was doing the only job she could get. So you see.'

'I do indeed!'

Rosalind was looking as if she wanted to die, while Deb talked with totally false animation to her neighbour. But Mary's instinct had not failed her. In this privileged world it was easy to be bored and easier to be boring. There was barely a girl in the place who had done anything more exciting than ride to hounds and go to school. They were too young and too sheltered. But Mary, who might so easily have been exactly the same, had dipped her toe into the great ocean of life, and dwelt amidst the flotsam on the beach. In this select company she was glamorously exciting!

Mary's companion asked her to dance. She was delighted, she was fizzing with energy. How good it felt to dip and sway and accelerate up the floor, turning just before they crashed into the band. Her dress belled out behind her, outlining breast and belly as she turned.

'What a very unconventional girl,' said one woman to another. And they didn't entirely disapprove.

No sooner had she sat down than she was asked to dance again. Stranger after stranger came up to her. Soon she was hot and dishevelled, and retreated to the cloakroom to cool off. Rosalind was hot on her trail. 'Mary! What on earth are you doing?'

'Having fun, Aunt Rosalind.' She leaned towards the mirror, blotting the fragile make-up with a tissue soaked in cold water. Thank God. Nothing showed.

'You're being outrageous. There's no need to behave like some devil may care American. All these stories!'

'You're a fine one to talk! At least I haven't said anything that isn't true.'

'That's got nothing to do with it, Mary. People are talking about you. And that dress is indecent. I should have known.'

Goaded into anger, Mary turned to face her. 'Yes, Aunt. But then,

I'm my mother's daughter, aren't I? And you know who my father is. What else can you expect?'

Rosalind's face froze. She came very close and said, 'I won't have you thinking such things! You are yourself, Mary. Parentage has nothing to do with it. It's up to you to decide who you want to be, and I don't think you're going to be pleased to be seen as fast and wild.'

'I'd rather be that than a milksop,' said Mary heatedly. 'Oh, Rosalind, I've never been pretty before! No one's ever wanted to talk to me, let alone ask me to dance. I don't want to be timid, and shy, and – and ordinary.'

Rosalind sighed. In her heart, she sympathised with the girl. It wasn't hard to imagine the sensation of release that Mary was experiencing. She had spent her life in a straitjacket of ugliness, only to be suddenly set free. No wonder it was going to her head.

She made one last attempt to apply the brakes. 'Just remember, my dear. You might have to live with what people think of you tonight. Can you really go on being daring and unconventional? Don't you think it might be very tiring? As well as a little dangerous. I really don't know what happened when you were in London before, but I think you know what I mean.'

Mary turned away. Rosalind suspected that she was blushing. What an odd thing this make-up was, a sophisticated mask behind which the real Mary lurked unseen. 'You never say anything like this to Deb,' the girl muttered. 'And she's always in danger of getting in a mess.'

'To my mind, Deborah is far more capable of handling men than you, Mary,' said Rosalind tartly. 'But then, she's had far more practice.'

They marched back to the dance floor together, prickling with mutual irritation. Deborah was being leered at by a man with a paunch, but she extricated herself without difficulty and came across. Mary felt her spirits dip. In the end, parties were always the same. This evening was entirely an illusion: her face, the fun, everything and everybody. It was a performance, as far from reality as a pantomime. Everyone was pretending to be something they weren't.

Deb said, 'Those boys Aunt Rosalind knows have asked if we'd like to go on to a club. I said I'd ask.'

'What club? Who?' Rosalind was all ears.

'Peter and Tim. They're in the Guards.'

Rosalind looked thoughtful. Peter Murray-Gill would one day inherit a vast sporting estate, and his friend, although only a younger son, was said to be very well heeled.

'Please, Aunt Rosalind,' said Deb, looking beguiling.

269

Her aunt laughed. 'Do stop it, Deb. I'm not likely to be taken in, I can assure you. You may go, provided you're home no later than two. I expect your escorts to bring you right to the door, mind. No putting you in a taxi and hoping for the best.'

The girls grinned at each other. Mary's spirits, mercurial at the best of times, zoomed skywards once again. There was a world beyond here which she would explore. New worlds always existed, she could move on and on, endlessly. So nothing really mattered. Whatever she did could always be left behind.

The boys were charming to Aunt Rosalind. They assured her that everything was under control. As soon as the car door was closed and they were driving away, Peter leaned back from the wheel, lit a cigarette and said, 'That's the old bag done with. Right, girls. Who's for some hooch?'

He reached into the glove compartment and brought out a hip flask.

'What's in it?' asked Mary.

'Scotch. It's from our own distillery.'

'What a good thing you weren't too modest to mention it.' She took the top off and sniffed. 'No thanks. You could strip paint with that.'

'Can I taste?' Deb took it and sipped. Her eyes widened. 'It's what I think it would taste like if you set fire to an oak tree and then ate it.'

'With pepper,' supplied Tim, availing himself of the flask and downing a hearty slug. 'Peter gets gallons of it. Kept the whole house pickled at school.'

'And now he's pickling the army.' Mary leaned back against the car's sleek leather. 'Pickled privates; pickled corporals; pickled people on all sides. Do you pickle the horses while you're about it?'

'Only on Sundays,' said Peter. 'You know, you girls are very unusual.'

'Not me,' said Deb. 'I'm ordinary. In our family we leave it to Mary to be different. That's the way it has to be. I behave properly and Mary never does.'

She sat up and stared at her sister. 'I'm sure it isn't like that really, Deb.'

Her sister rolled her lovely head against Tim's arm. 'We're not supposed to think it's like that, you mean. And it's probably our fault. It's what we've led them to expect.'

Tim said, 'I know what you mean. Like in a play, everyone in a family has a role. We all know the parts and we have to play them. That way the play goes on. It's only when we stop playing that things go wrong.'

'Just consider, Mary,' went on Deb, 'if I'd run away instead of you. What then?'

'I don't know,' said Mary, bemused.

'Chaos, that's what,' said Deb. 'At least you were expected to be difficult. Not even Dad could have coped if it was me.'

Tim leaned across and nibbled at her ear. 'You're a very clever little girl,' he murmured. 'Who would have thought it?'

'And what do your family expect of you?' she enquired.

He made a face and reached for the flask again. 'Don't know, really. Actually, yes, I do. To be irresponsible. My brother's getting the title, so I don't count. I just have to be amusing and a bit of a rake, getting into scrapes. Keeping up the family tradition for wildness. That sort of thing.'

'Then don't look at me,' said Deborah sweetly. 'I'm too good for a black sheep. You and Mary should get together, while Peter and I behave well.'

'But in my family . . .' said Peter, taking the flask and drinking. He closed his eyes for a second and grimaced. 'In my family the heir is supposed to be wild. We only sober up when we marry for the succession. Which we never do before the age of forty.'

Mary chuckled. 'And to think Aunt Rosalind doesn't know! How wild do you mean to be?'

He pulled the car into the kerb and stopped. Then he leaned towards her, his mouth still wet with whisky. 'Positively manic,' he breathed, and pushed his tongue between her teeth.

For ten minutes or so they stayed there. It was very dark. In the back seat Tim was kissing Deborah, his hand periodically fumbling between her thighs. She wished she knew him better. She wanted him to reach up and touch her naked skin. She felt heavy and aching with the need to be touched, barely cared that this was a stranger. It was because of Piers, she thought, feeling the inept hand press down on her dress once again. Piers had touched her and awakened her to touch. She had leaned against a tree, staring at him, while his hand moved between her legs. At the beginning it had frightened her, she had thought she might explode. And then she did. And she understood what Piers felt when she held him.

Deb moved a little, letting the taffeta folds of her skirt ride up. Tim's hand was on her stockinged thigh. She parted her knees, wondering if he would tell people, and what they would believe. Nothing, probably. Nobody would believe that gorgeous Deborah Cooper, the pure young beauty, let herself be seriously groped in a car. He had reached the bare flesh at the top of her stocking. His hands were clammy with sweat, quite repulsive really. Deborah's breath caught in her throat. What was she doing? She didn't even know this man! A moan broke from her, desire turned to protest. She sat up, breathing hard.

'Stop it, Tim! How could you?'

271

Mary was keeping Peter more or less at bay in the front seat. She pushed him away and said, 'What on earth's he doing?'

'Trying to get into my knickers. Honestly!'

Tim said, 'Oh, Christ. I'm sorry. I got a bit carried away.'

'I should think you did.' Deborah pulled her skirt down and ran her fingers through her hair. 'Anyway, I thought we were going to this club?'

Mary and Peter straightened up. He started the car once again. They were all a little subdued.

In the club, drinking champagne at a table too small for four, Mary felt tired suddenly. She wasn't sure that she liked Peter very much. He was too sure of himself, too convinced of his own inestimable worth. At every opportunity he made some reference to his inheritance, as if that alone rendered him important and of value. She tried talking to Tim instead, but he was enslaved by Deborah. Another one, thought Mary ruefully. But then, with Deborah glowing in the soft lights, who could blame him?

The music was dreadful. Records of American ballads belted out at full throttle, the sound level of their generation but the material of the last. Peter said, 'We've got a horse running at Ascot next week. Why don't you come?'

Mary's interest was reawakened. 'Oh, yes, please,' she replied. 'I love racing. As a matter of fact, I know George Reynolds quite well.'

'He's our trainer. Actually.'

'That's a turn-up for the books.'

She was using Sandra's expressions because they wrong-footed him so. They made him look at her in total confusion. Deborah, getting up to dance, said, 'Don't worry, Peter. You won't understand her so it's better not to try.'

'What is there to understand about you?' he asked, looking at Mary bemusedly. 'Are you a tease? Is that what she means?'

'I'm not what I seem,' said Mary, thinking of her face. He sat, gazing down at her, drunk and getting drunker. If he saw her as she really was he wouldn't look, she thought. It was odd that she could feel so detached from her appearance. When the marks were showing she felt as if her nerves were stripped bare, lying twitching on the surface of her skin. Now, with them hidden, suddenly she barely cared how she looked. She was concealed. This could be anyone.

She got up to dance, putting out her hand to Peter. He took it and staggered after her on to the floor, clutching her round the waist more for support than anything. 'Can Tim drive?' she asked, her arms around his neck, her mouth against his ear.

'Sure.'

'He'd better, then. You can't.'

'Right. I can't. God, but you're lovely.'

She chuckled. It was as if the compliment belonged to someone else. Kristian perhaps. Would he like Peter? He seemed to like her. Did it matter who liked who, was she silly and provincial to care? She bent and swayed to the music, discovering some attraction in maudlin ballads. Her mother used to work in a place like this. Looking about her, over Peter's shoulder, she could see women in long dresses drifting between the tables. They looked beautiful and in command. As Laura used to be.

She pushed the thought away. Her mother was better, much better. One day she would regain her self-possession. But an image of her persisted, a woman grey, nervous, grateful to everyone for not treating her as she thought she deserved. Suddenly Mary was blinking away tears, trying to substitute the old Laura, the clear-eyed mother who had stood steadfast throughout her daughter's childhood. But the image would not come.

She tapped Peter on the shoulder. He was almost asleep. 'Let's go back to the table.'

He obliged, blearily, taking obvious mouthfuls from his flask now and then. One of the club hostesses saw him and moved to say something to a man in evening dress. Mary wondered with detachment if they might be thrown out. She didn't really mind.

Deb and Tim were sitting down too. Tim was gazing at Deborah with sheeplike devotion, while she looked around the room, rather bored.

'Ought we to be going?' asked Mary, who didn't have a watch.

Deb yawned. 'Perhaps we should.'

'Let's drink another bottle first,' said Peter, and almost fell off his chair.

'Oh God,' said Tim. 'He swore he wouldn't get pissed.' He hiccuped, not much better himself.

The girls exchanged glances. 'You'll have to lend us the money for a taxi,' said Deb firmly. 'You can't drive us and we've got to get home.'

'No taxi,' said Peter. 'You'll have to come home with us. Stay the night.'

'Thanks awfully, but not just now,' said Mary. 'Look, you promised you'd get us home. I warn you, Aunt Rosalind's dangerous when she's annoyed.'

'Better get them a taxi,' said Tim, still holding on to something resembling sense.

They got up to leave the club. When Tim asked the neanderthal doorman for a taxi he looked at them as if they were grubs. 'I tell you – my father – great man—' ventured Peter, but Mary shoved him into

273

the road before he got himself thumped. Deb approached the doorman with a tentative smile. 'Could you tell us where to get a taxi, please?'

'Down the road, love. Watch it. He's going to throw up on your pretty little dress.'

At once Peter turned and ddid that very thing.

Back in the cloakroom of the club, Deb did what she could to clean up the mess. 'God, but I hate drunk men!'

'Except Piers,' said Mary.

'Especially Piers! And Gabriel. And Peter can go and drown in one of his bloody lochs!'

Wet, the dress clung unpleasantly against Deb's legs. She looked at her watch and saw that it was almost a quarter to two. They were certain to be late home.

They rushed out of the cloakroom. Surely by now Tim would have found them a taxi? But there was no sign of anyone except the doorman, blinking at them stonily. 'Do you know where they've gone?' demanded Mary. 'Are they getting a taxi?'

'Went staggering off somewhere. Doubt no taxi driver would want to know. State they was in.'

'Oh, God.' Deb started searching in her bag. 'I've only got ten bob.'

'And I haven't got that. Could we telephone, do you think?'

'And wake Uncle Howard? We'd have to be desperate.'

'We could go to David's.'

'We'd still need a taxi. And then we might as well go home. She leaves the money for the fishman in the kitchen, we could pay the driver off with that.'

As if in answer to a prayer a taxi came cruising up the street. Mary waved at it frantically and it drew up to the kerb. She hurried across, giving Aunt Rosalind's address. The man looked dubious. 'Money up front if I'm going out there. And I won't get a fare back, double.'

Mary blinked. 'We'll pay when we get there,' she declared.

'Pay now or it's no go, love.'

They were stuck. Mary and Deb looked helplessly at each other, and then at the disinterested doorman. 'This'll teach you to go off with a couple of drunken sots, won't it?' he said conversationally.

'Yes,' agreed Mary. 'Can you lend us the money, though? We'll send you a cheque tomorrow.'

'Don't know as I trust you,' said the doorman. 'Have to ask the owner. He prides himself on knowing an honest face. Lucky he's in tonight.'

He disappeared into the fastnesses of the club. Mary, Deb and the taxi driver exchanged measuring looks. 'She'll have us back in

Yorkshire before the night's out,' muttered Deborah. 'Those useless boys! We should have known.'

The cold night air was stinging her wet skirt against her legs. She thought of the warm car they had come in. How dare those boys desert them like this?

The door opened and a tall, blond man in beautiful evening dress came out, followed by the doorman. 'Like I said, sir,' he muttered respectfully, 'it's two pretty young ladies. Stranded, like. Thought you'd want to know.'

'Indeed. I most certainly do want to know.'

He cast a cursory eye over Mary and a lingering one over Deb. He reached out and matter-of-factly touched her hair. Deb flinched.

'Don't be afraid of me, child. Your colouring is very unusual. And I have only seen eyes of that hue once before. In – in Yorkshire, I do believe.'

'We come from Yorkshire,' said Mary.

The man spun on his heel and stared at her. When he spoke Mary had thought him foreign, and now he looked at her she was sure of it. He had a long, narrow head that was somehow quite un-British, and his opulent neatness was the same. She felt his eyes boring into her and dropped her own. 'You two are sisters?' he demanded. 'You are, I am sure.'

'Yes,' said Mary, surprised.

'I knew it! That hair. Those eyes. Put them together and who do we have? Laura Cooper.'

'You know our mother?' Deborah let out a little crow of delight. 'Laura Cooper of Gunthwaite Hall?'

His face was inscrutable, a mask they could not read. 'But yes,' he said, with a certain reserve. 'In the war, I knew her well. Also Dora. Dear Dora. I heard she had gone abroad?'

'She's back,' said Mary at once. 'She and her husband. They're staying at Fairlands, they mean to settle.'

'Indeed?' The man shot his cuffs and adjusted the links. 'That is interesting. And your mother? She is well?'

'Yes. Perfectly,' said Deb. 'We'll write and tell her we met you. Who shall we say?'

'Just an old friend.' He was reaching into his pocket for his wallet. It was of calf's leather, embossed in gold. Another distinctly foreign touch. He took out a ten-pound note and gave it to Mary. 'I am so glad I could be of assistance. It is time I repaid your mother for all she did to me.'

'We'll pay you back,' said Mary urgently. 'We'll write, tomorrow first thing.'

'The money is nothing,' said the man. 'But I insist you let me know you are safe.'

275

The taxi driver revved his engine impatiently. The girls retreated towards it, murmuring, 'You're terribly kind', 'We'll write tomorrow', 'Thanks once again.' When they looked back from the taxi as they drove away they saw that he still stood in the doorway. He raised his hand in some foreign kind of salute.

Chapter Twenty-seven

The repercussions of the late night rumbled on for days. Rosalind was furious, first with Mary and Deb, and later, when the story had unfolded, with Peter and Tim. Nothing could dissuade her from making a blistering telephone call to their commanding officer, with the result that two bunches of flowers and two letters of apology were received the following day. They were followed by telephone calls from the miscreants: one from Peter, insisting that he'd been taken desperately ill and repeating his invitation to the races, the other from Tim, saying that Peter had insisted that he drive him home, which he had done, and the girls should be grateful not to have been included in the party, since Peter was sick everywhere and Tim was so drunk.

'You could have got us a taxi. And paid for it!' declared Mary in a fury.

'Couldn't you put Deborah on? Is she cross too?'

'Livid,' said Mary, and handed over the receiver. But Deborah was much more forgiving.

'The only person to come out of this with any credit is the owner of the club,' said Rosalind decisively. 'Who was he, do you think? Didn't he give you any sort of a clue?'

'None.' Mary took a bite of a cheese and pickle sandwich, reflecting that London cheese was a poor reflection of Gunthwaite's own. They really should send some to Rosalind from time to time, to remind her that real food existed. 'We owe him ten pounds, though,' she went on. 'I thought we'd write. And he might write back and then we'd know.'

'Incredible that he recognised you, whoever he was. But then, Deborah's eyes are very distinctive. It must be someone Laura met when she was in London. Or on that course, perhaps. You said he was foreign. I can't get over the luck.'

So Rosalind wrote a letter of effusive thanks, in which she did not enclose the ten pounds. Instead, she said, he was invited to lunch a week on Sunday, when they would repay him properly.

'Suppose he doesn't come?' said Mary.

'We'll have to take our chances. Was he good-looking, did you say?'

'Yes, quite. Old, of course. I mean, not young. And too smart. But, yes, he was handsome. All cold blue eyes and long nose.'

He was forgotten until the Sunday. Instead they wrestled with the dilemma of the race meeting. Should Mary be so insulted that she would not go? On the other hand, there were few young ladies who would turn down an invitation from a gentleman so very eligible. Even Mary's assurance that Peter wasn't about to marry until he reached forty did nothing to dampen Rosalind's enthusiasm. 'He won't be the first to discover he's more inclined than he thought he was,' she declared. 'Just think, Mary! You could end up running a castle. Rather better than serving in Selfridge's. Or playing around at Gunthwaite for that matter.'

Mary went up to her room. She hated sharing with Deb. There was no real privacy, no sense that here was a sanctuary into which no one could intrude. If she was married, she thought, she would have to have a separate room. Like the queen. How else could you gather your thoughts around you, letting the world go by until you could once again confront it? But here, in this frilly place, she felt out of touch with reality. If only she could go back to Gunthwaite, just for an afternoon. It was odd. The moment she had decided that Gunthwaite wasn't needed any more, she found herself longing for it. The big cool barns, the ancient house, the orchard. Perhaps a ride, with Connor, on to the moor. An afternoon only. An hour perhaps. But she must make do with a memory.

True to form, a moment later Deborah came wandering in, leaving the door wide open and flopping down with a groan. 'We've both got to go racing. Honestly, Mary, she's almost got you married off. But you could do worse, I suppose.'

'Actually, he's a bit of a bore.'

'He was drunk! He might be nice. Anyway, you'd be rich as anything, which must be good. Just think. Racehorses. The Scottish acres.'

'I hate shooting. He'd divorce me for sabotaging the drives.'

'You wouldn't get divorced, you'd be hanged.' Deb yawned and rolled on to her back. 'Boring, isn't it?' she said.

Mary stared at her. She at least was expecting to be bored. After all, she was the also-ran at parties, the inveterate no-hoper. But Deb had always been the acknowledged belle of every ball. 'Are you cross because Peter's keen on me?'

Deb shook her head. ''Course not. But I am bored with being nice to people we don't really know. I've met dozens and dozens of men, and they're all the same, don't you think? Same background. Same jokes, half the time. There's no one really amusing, is there? No one prepared to take a risk.'

'What sort of risk?'

'I don't know.'

Deb put her arms above her head and stared at the ceiling. She was dissatisfied and didn't know why. It was partly her bodily restlessness, the needs of a healthy young woman constrained to deny her own desires. Perhaps it wasn't normal, she thought dismally. Perhaps she was a slut. But she found herself thinking more and more of men. A man. Any man, if need be. Deborah was finding in herself an acute need for physical satisfaction, with no way of being satisfied.

She got up and began to sort through her wardrobe for something to wear the following day. 'I'm wearing blue,' said Mary. 'I don't care if it is unsophisticated.'

'Rosalind won't mind now,' said Deb, absently. 'She used to think it made your marks look like bruises. As if we'd been beating the hell out of you.' She held up her own choice, a dress in pure virginal white. Advertising to all the world her unhappy state. She threw the dress on the bed and went dismally to the window, looking out at the pretty summer scene. David was coming into the garden, still in his business suit. Then she saw Alan, following at a distance, and her heart lifted. 'Alan's come home,' she said happily. 'It must be end of term.' She ran down the stairs.

That night, after dinner, Alan took his lovely cousin for a moonlit walk. She seemed to him very small and very lovely, a pocket princess made out of porcelain. Her hair might have been painted from pure copper, her eyes made from clear glass. For all his Oxford sophistication, Alan knew himself entranced.

'Do you have very many people in love with you?' he asked.

'Dozens,' said Deb, sending him a mocking glance.

'I suppose they all kiss you too?'

'Only when I let them.' She turned towards him. 'Do you want to kiss me? You can if you want.'

Alan thought of what his mother would say. But David was dancing attendance on Mary, and never a murmur was spoken. He put his hands on Deborah's waist and drew her to him. She lifted up her face and parted her lips, taking his tongue into her mouth almost fiercely. Was he kissing or being kissed? He felt her small, voluptuous body against his, felt her press her heavy breasts into him. Then she broke free.

'There,' she said defiantly. 'Did it make you feel better?'

'No. You know it didn't. You wanted to make me feel worse.'

'Of course I did. I'm sick of all this – this messing around.'

He didn't know what she meant. She stared at him balefully, wondering if she knew herself. She wanted something special, something exciting, that much was clear. But what? Everyone had told her that the London season was wonderful, that she'd be a great success. And it was, and she was, and it wasn't enough. Where was the use of being complimented on one's looks? She hadn't made herself. Beauty wasn't to her credit. Where was the use of being loved by people who didn't know you? She was beginning to think she was impossible to know. Men never looked beyond her lovely face.

'Sometimes I wish I was Mary,' she said venomously. 'At least people know who she is.'

'She's nowhere near as sweet as you,' said Alan.

Deborah turned on him. 'And how do you know? I could be sour as hell. But I mustn't be. I'm Deb, sweet of face and sweet of nature. The good, obedient child.'

'Do you want to stay out late? Something like that?'

She gave him a glance of withering scorn. 'Honestly, Alan! And you're at Oxford. I find that so depressing.'

It seemed that everything was turned on its head. Mary should have been the one to hate all this. Instead, with her new painted face she went racing with zest, while Deb trailed along somewhat dismally. George Reynolds, lugubriously saddling the Murray-Gill horse, looked at her and said, 'You look different. Prettier.'

'Thanks,' said Mary. 'Has this one got a chance?'

'He's a possible. Not like Belarus in the fourth. I'll swear he'll break down.'

Mary resolved to back Belarus and leave this one well alone.

Peter Murray-Gill was on edge. His mother was there, eyeing Mary from the safety of a box. 'She wants to meet you,' he told Mary, who looked appalled and said, 'I certainly don't want to meet her, thank you very much! I hardly know you.'

'All the same. After the horse has run. Come up and drink champagne.'

'Only if Deb comes too. She's much better at this sort of thing.'

The horse ran a dismal third, and Mary wasted time in the unsaddling enclosure, listening to Reynolds talking bankruptcy. But Lady Murray-Gill was waving a gloved hand down at them, and Deb was under siege from yet more indigent suitors, so it had to be. Glumly they were escorted to the box.

'Mary. Deborah. I've heard so much about you.'

Deborah murmured politely, but Mary said, 'I can't think how. I only met Peter last week and he was terribly drunk.'

'I was ill,' he said hurriedly. 'I explained all that. Anyway, Mother's heard lots from other people. The glamorous Cooper girls. Everyone's talking.'

'Deb's the glamorous one,' said Mary. 'I sort of bask in her reflected glory. Do you know, she's had three proposals of marriage in two weeks?'

'And not one of them sober,' said Deb, moving smoothly into the conversation. She wasn't about to let Mary be as shocking as she wished. The Murray-Gills knew people, Mary couldn't upset them without suffering for it in some way. 'Were you pleased with the way your horse ran, Lady Murray-Gill?'

'Moderately. We bred him ourselves. We may change trainers.'

'The trainer thinks he's lazy,' said Mary airily. 'And puts it down to the breeding, says the sire was just the same. He's going to try blinkers. You might get a couple of good runs before he gets used to them and goes on strike.'

'I didn't know you were such an expert, Mary?' said Lady Murray-Gill frostily.

She responded with a brilliant smile. 'I'm no expert of course. But I know something about horses.'

'There you are, Mother,' declared Peter triumphantly. 'I told you she was just right!'

'Just right for what?' demanded Mary, looking from one to the other. Deb's eyebrows rose expressively.

'If you'll excuse us?' stammered Mary, suddenly taking fright. 'I did say I'd help Mr Reynolds in the paddock.' She made a run for the door.

Peter followed her down the stairs. 'You were wonderful,' he declared. 'Mother likes a girl to have character.'

'I don't have character. I was being rude.'

They emerged from the stand into the sunlit afternoon. Peter glanced up. 'Look, she's smiling and waving. That proves it. She likes you a lot.'

'I *am* glad. You can go off for a bit if you like, Peter. There's George Reynolds.' Seeing Mary, the trainer beckoned furiously. But Peter hung to her arm. 'So you see, you've got to take me seriously,' he said. 'She'll invite you for the shooting.'

'What? To Scotland?' Mary was appalled.

'August. Do make sure you're free.'

She backed away, and he let her go. In the paddock, making sticky conversation with the owners while Reynolds sobbed under his breath, she kept looking up to see him watching her. She felt like a mouse being watched by a very large bird. What did he want from her? Why? She barely knew the boy!

That evening, Lady Murray-Gill telephoned Rosalind. It emerged that to her mind Mary might not be the beauty of the family, but she was: 'An interesting girl with the right sort of spirit. Not the type to mope when her husband's away. A girl with a good strong mind.'

'Murray-Gill women get left to defend the castle while their husbands live it up elsewhere,' declared Deborah, flopping into a chair in the garden. 'You've been chosen, Mary. There's nothing you can do.'

281

'You must admit, it's wonderfully flattering,' said Rosalind, sipping a well-earned gin and tonic. She had, after all, sustained her end of the conversation rather well, she thought. Mary's worthy but unglamorous background had been whisked over as, if not gold-plated, at least more than substantial.

Mary herself sprawled on the grass in a pair of threadbare shorts, her marks once more in evidence, her hair a tangle. 'I don't understand it,' she sighed. 'I've only met him twice.'

'And you don't like his whisky,' giggled Deb. 'Perhaps the worst Murray-Gill wives have to be dried out once a year. You're the first girl who's showed any sign of abstinence!'

Rosalind and Deborah between them became more and more silly. They sketched for Mary a vision of the ideal Murray-Gill wife, rocklike but still of leonine courage, tender only to horses and dogs, able to bear children while at the same time weaving the family coat of arms out of barbed wire. 'She eats only curried ghillie,' declared Deborah. Rosalind said, 'Not curried, dear. Too foreign. I think – stewed.' She awarded herself another drink on the strength of the invention.

'I think you're all mad,' said Mary. 'I'm going to ring Mum and tell her.'

'Say I'll telephone tomorrow,' called Rosalind as she went indoors. 'I can tell her what really happened. Not your silly tale.'

Mary fumed as she waited for the connection. It was all very well for them to laugh. She was the one who had to deal with Peter's assumptions. He was escorting her to a party on Friday, it seemed, whether she liked it or not. When a Murray-Gill's eye lighted upon a girl, she was done for.

A voice on the telephone said, 'Hello?' It was Connor.

'Con? It's me. Look, I have to talk to Mum. I was having a super time here but now I'm being menaced by this terrible man. I mean, he's not terrible, he's all right, I suppose, but I don't want to be dragged off to his Scottish castle and made to have a dozen children while he does something more interesting! Rosalind, of course, can't wait.'

'What the hell are you on about, Mary?'

'I just told you. Connor, you're so slow.'

He took an exasperated breath. 'Try me again. There's this man. What man?'

'Peter Murray-Gill. Scottish acres, millions of them. I've only met him twice, but I've already been approved by his mother, for God's sake! It's all the fault of this make-up. You see, I can paint out the marks and suddenly everyone wants to know me. Awful, isn't it?'

Connor seemed to choke on a laugh. 'Oh, Mary.'

'Oh, Mary, what?'

'Just "oh, Mary". Why are you there and not here?'

'Don't start that again,' she said in exasperation. 'Go and cuddle Aunt Dora.'

'And don't you start *that* again! I've had an offer for your horse.'

'What? You bastard!'

'You said to sell it, Mary. Besides, I haven't accepted.'

'I should think not! What about Sweet? And the mare?'

'Sweet's sold. The mare's a pig. And the chestnut's gone lame.'

'Told you so!'

'Will you listen to the girl? Does the Scottish laird know about your temper?'

'He's a sort of English Scot actually. He seems to like my temper. In the harsh conditions of the castle they need a girl with a bit of life.'

Connor laughed incredulously. 'Oh God!'

'Yes. I've taken to praying, too.'

He said nothing for a moment. She said anxiously 'Are you still there?'

'Yes. Your mother's here. She wants to talk.'

'Oh. But Con—'

'What?'

'Nothing. Nothing much.'

'What then? Not more about the castle?'

'No. I could send you some horses, I think. Racehorses. To be retrained to jump. I haven't seen them.'

'And that is nothing much?'

'I know what you're like about horses. If I sent them they wouldn't be right.'

'Am I so much of a fool, then?'

'I don't know. Perhaps.'

There was a pause, and then Laura came on. 'Mary? Darling? Why are you upsetting Con?'

'I wasn't. Mum, would you mind terribly if I got dragged off to a castle and was never seen again? Aunt Rosalind's all for it, and so's Deb.'

The explanation took some time. As the extent of Mary's conquest unfolded she could hear Laura's pleasure in her voice. 'Well, darling! Aren't you proud of yourself? I always knew that one day you'd be a hit!'

'I don't want to be a hit, Mum!'

'Surely you want to have fun? Don't take it all too seriously, Mary. You don't have to do what this boy says.'

'Yes, but he just assumes—'

'Then he's silly to assume. Darling, I'm sure if you have any problems, Rosalind is more than able to cope.'

Mary subsided. There was no more to be said. Then she

remembered something. 'Oh, Mum, an old friend of yours is coming to lunch on Sunday. We don't even know his name, isn't that odd?'

'An old friend? What does he look like?'

'Tall, blond, foreign. Rosalind thinks you probably met him when you were in London during the war.'

'I don't remember anyone.'

'He remembers you terribly well. Says he wants to pay you back for what you did for him during the war.'

'Good heavens! Well, I must have been nice. Darling, this must be costing Rosalind a fortune. Give Deb my love, won't you? Write soon.'

Mary went back out to the garden. It was almost time for dinner and there was a gathering up of chairs and books and glasses. The sun was setting behind the trees, sinking in a welter of purple and black cloud. 'The weather's breaking,' said Rosalind. 'A sunset like that at Gunthwaite and we always brought the sheep up from the river meadows and down from the tops. We used to say you never knew what that sunset meant but it always meant trouble.'

'We still say that,' said Mary, standing with a deckchair in her hands. 'If I was at Gunthwaite now I'd help with the gather.'

'And so would I,' said Deb.

'You? You never help!'

'But if I was there now, I would. You don't realise when you're there but everything at Gunthwaite matters. And nothing here does.'

She turned and went into the house, her sandals slapping against her bare feet. A gust of wind caught a window and slammed it, and Howard could be heard calling to everyone to shut the place up. The roses were disintegrating, full blooms blown to petals. There was a dull rumble of thunder, and Mary felt a thrill of nerves. Was it just the weather? She had the distinct sensation that there was indeed trouble ahead.

Chapter Twenty-eight

To Mary's chagrin, Rosalind invited Peter Murray-Gill to Sunday's lunch. Deborah, who was being inundated with telephone calls from any of half a dozen young men, was allowed to relax with Alan, although Mary suspected that it was he himself who had precluded any other invitation. To everyone's surprise, before the guest of honour arrived, David turned up. He eyed Murray-Gill with extreme disfavour.

'Oh, yes,' he said, when introduced. 'I remember you. Some damned silly prank at a party last year. Chucked a chap out of the window. He was lucky to get away with a broken leg.'

Peter retreated to Mary's side. 'Bit straitlaced your cousin?' he remarked.

'Depends on your view of broken legs, I suppose. If the victim took it in good part, I don't suppose it matters.'

Peter chuckled. 'He threatened to sue.'

'And didn't? Why? Did your mother glare at him?'

'I suppose someone did.'

Alan said to Deb, 'If Mary lands Murray-Gill, I'll be impressed. What does he see in her?'

'Dislike,' said Deb airily. 'Reminds him of his mother. At least, it isn't him Mary hates, it's more being treated like prey. She has the feeling that he'd like to lodge her in the fork of a tree between dates.'

Alan laughed. 'No wonder everyone's in love with you, Deb.'

She walked away, her hair swinging, longer now and almost to her waist. He felt a soft swelling of desire. Deborah was sensuality and beauty mixed, a combination that attracted and intimidated at one and the same time. Men needed confidence to bid for such a prize. No wonder she thought that most men were usually drunk. He thought of Piers and wondered a little. But that was only a boy/girl thing. The truth was, the men who knew Deb well were most likely to win her favour, while the others scrabbled to catch up. And, he thought, he knew Deb as well as anyone.

There was a ring at the door. Rosalind glanced around at everyone, checking. It had to be their mystery guest. She signalled to the maid to let him in, and a moment later went smiling into the hall.

'How do you do?' she began. 'I simply must tell you how grateful we are—'

She fell silent. Her heart came up into her throat and seemed to lodge there, beating wildly. Howard, at her elbow, said, 'My God! The Pole.'

'Indeed.' The visitor clicked his heels, like the Polish cavalry officer he had once been. 'Wojtyla Zwmskorski at your service. Mrs Dalton. Mr Dalton. How kind of you to invite me to lunch.'

Rosalind was gathering her wits. 'And how unkind of you not to give your name, Mr Zwmskorski. But then, I have no doubt that you know how it would be received.'

'Can you possibly mean discourteously, Rosalind? After all I did for you and your family?'

'I know only too well what you did to our family,' she snapped. 'And I don't think ten pounds is any sort of repayment. Give him his money, Howard.'

But, even as Howard looked in vain for some cash, Zwmskorski seemed to be making himself at home. He handed his hat and coat to the bemused maid and pushed easily past Rosalind into the drawing room. 'Deborah, my dear!' He went across and took her hand, lifting it easily to his lips. 'You must tell your mother we have met. Dr Zwmskorski. She and I were such good friends when her husband was away, during the war.'

'You were nothing of the sort!' said Rosalind, her jaw set. How could she extricate herself from this mess with Peter Murray-Gill around? How could she have been so stupid?

Mary was suddenly all attention. 'During the war, you say?'

'But, yes. I remember you very well. What has happened to your forceps marks? Such stains under the skin. But that other doctor was a fool.'

'I paint the marks out,' said Mary clearly. She glanced at Peter. 'Did you know that? I'm a mess without make-up.'

He looked bemused. 'Most women are, aren't they? I'm sorry, sir, I didn't catch your name.'

The Pole smiled again, dangerously. 'Zwmskorski. And you are Murray-Gill. You lost two thousand pounds in one of my clubs just a month ago.'

Peter's face flamed. Howard said, 'I don't think we need to have all our secrets aired today, Mr Zwmskorski. Rosalind, is luncheon served? Then let's get on with it, my dear.'

Mary ate little of the meal. She was watching Zwmskorski, all the while taking note of the currents running around the table. Rosalind was desperately on edge, Howard hardly less so. But the man himself seemed relaxed, flirting easily with Deborah, and rousing Alan to tight-lipped rage. But she wasn't interested in that. Was it possible that Zwmskorski had been her mother's lover? The thought appalled her. And yet – he was attractive. He and Deborah were sparring with the easy respect of two sexual conquerors. It was a game they were both used to winning.

Because lunch had been rushed the roast beef was very underdone. Mary loved it rare but her appetite was gone, and most of the men pushed at the pink slices on their plates. Peter Murray-Gill said, 'Of course, at home we always eat our own beef. We have our own Aberdeen Angus herd.'

'We use an Angus bull for our dairy heifers,' said Mary absently. 'It makes for an easier calving.'

She became uneasily aware that Peter was trying to take hold of her hand under the table. Her innocent remark had once again proved that she was wife material. A woman who understood cattle would be a no-nonsense breeder of sons. She let him take hold and then dug her nails into his skin. He yelped, and Rosalind said, 'Is anything the matter?'

'Not at all,' he said, going pink. 'I bit my tongue.'

'I was used, in the cavalry, to help with foalings,' said Zwmskorski. 'But I was at my best helping women give birth. You remember, Rosalind, how Dora suffered? She was always grateful, ever after.'

Deborah said, 'When Piers was born, you mean? How incredible! To meet you, that is. Dora always says he nearly cost her her life.'

'It's true,' said Zwmskorski, taking a large mouthful of pink meat. Mary shivered. 'You are too small to give birth easily,' went on Zwmskorski, taking Deborah's hand. 'See this palm. So narrow. So with the hips. You are a woman to give pleasure in love and to suffer pain because of it.'

Rosalind said, 'That is quite enough, thank you!' and Deborah went rather red. As if at a signal, everyone began to talk, drowning the possibility of more underbred remarks.

'You really mustn't say things like that in front of Aunt Rosalind,' Deborah murmured to the Pole.

'Why not? You are made to be loved. It should be said. Celebrated. The new Aphrodite.'

'Don't flatter me. I'm sick of being flattered.'

He grinned. 'You remind me so much of your mother. She too knew men through and through. I wish she had trusted me.'

'Didn't she?'

'Not in the least. Because of Dora, you see.'

'Dora? You mean, you and she—?'

'I was her lover. For years. You see?'

'Yes. I think so. Goodness me.'

The maid came to collect the plates. Deborah felt a shiver run through her. She had never met a man like this in all her life. He

287

attracted her, she knew that, and also that she attracted him. It was as if a small fire had been lit deep in her belly, smouldering and smouldering, ready at any moment to burst into flame. Was it the same for him? she wondered. He looked so calm and in control, coming here today deliberately to disrupt things. Why?

'Why have you come?' she asked suddenly, ignoring some remark of Alan's as if he hadn't spoken.

'Curiosity,' said Zwmskorski. 'And you.'

'Me?'

'I have rarely seen a girl I so much wanted to take to bed.'

Deborah gasped. She couldn't help it. And she turned at once to Alan and said, 'I'm sorry. What was that?'

Zwmskorski smiled to himself, and met Rosalind's eye. She looked baleful. He knew that as soon as the meal was done she would have him out of here. He smiled again.

As soon as the cheese was served and perfunctorily offered, Rosalind leaped to her feet and insisted that the younger people go into the garden to play tennis. 'No one's dressed for it, Mother,' complained David, but Rosalind told him with some sharpness to find everyone some shoes in the garden room and not to be such a bore. David muttered but did as he was told, used from childhood to his mother's habit of venting her spleen on her family when it was impossible to relieve her feelings elsewhere. Nonetheless he grumbled to Alan.

'I'll swear she's getting worse. I tell you, if she goes absolutely ga-ga I'm putting her in a home.'

'I'd like to see you try,' remarked his brother. 'I've never seen anyone get the better of her yet. I suppose Mary can give her a run for her money, though.'

'Mary? I tell you, Alan, that girl needs taking in hand.'

Alan laughed unkindly. 'Don't dream, brother mine. Murray-Gill's bound to cut you out.'

Since the same thought was disturbing David's equilibrium, the comment did not improve his temper. He advanced on Deborah with a pair of tennis shoes and an air of determined menace. 'Here you are, my girl. About time you took some exercise, if you ask me.'

'I didn't know I was quite so obviously flabby,' said Deb, wrapping her skirt around her and raising Alan's blood pressure more than a little. Zwmskorski, seeing her from the window, made to come out. But Rosalind intercepted him.

'Right. Now you can tell me why you're really here.'

He looked down at her. 'You're getting very plain,' he said. 'And you've put on too much weight. But that's Englishwomen for you. No lasting glamour.'

288

Howard, in the act of sneaking off to his study and his books, took sudden notice. 'Good God! That is the outside of enough. It's time you left, sir. I won't have my wife insulted. I was hoping you'd go quietly, but obviously you haven't that much decency. You were a blackguard in the war, mixed up in everything unsavoury. If it had been up to me I'd have had you arrested and interned, but unfortunately fair men gave you the benefit of the doubt. You've come here to cause trouble and I tell you, I won't have it.'

Zwmskorski looked down his long, aristocratic nose. 'Shut up, little man,' he said simply, and turned to Rosalind. 'That's decided then. If you had been polite I might have considered leniency. But as it is – well, a letter to the Murray-Gills is inevitable, I think.'

Rosalind swallowed visibly. 'Saying what?'

'That the elegant Mary is not the child of good family they seem to believe. How did they come to imagine she was wealthy? You, Rosalind, and your incorrigible pretensions? You always were ashamed of being a farm girl. And then, of course, there is the little matter that Mary is the daughter of a French whore. As for her father – the parentage of anyone must be in doubt when they spring from the womb of a woman who has lain down with any passing tramp!'

Rosalind was whiter than her own snowy table linen. 'They won't believe you. And you have no proof.'

'Proof? Laura harbours two played out old whores in her own home!'

For a long second he and Rosalind stared at each other. Howard said, 'I'm calling the police.'

Zwmskorski laughed cruelly, turned on his heel and left.

That evening, Rosalind called Mary to her bedroom. Howard was still downstairs, and Rosalind sat in her dressing gown, the soft light from the garden falling kindly on her face. She caught sight of herself in the mirror and wondered if she saw what she wanted to see. Or was she really the overweight old wreck Zwmskorski had conjured? Beside Mary, so wonderfully slim, she felt huge.

'Sit down, my dear,' she said. Mary sat, looking up at her aunt. The girl wore no make-up now, and her skin bore the faint sheen of cleansing cream. The pink V on her forehead and the thumbprint beneath her eye seemed welcome and familiar. It was odd, thought Rosalind, but the marks, although every bit as visible as ever, seemed not so noticeable now. But then, Mary seemed to have forgotten them. In these few weeks the knowledge that she could banish them seemed to have changed her mind set. Even when clearly seen, Mary behaved as if they were not there.

Rosalind pulled her mind back to the matter in hand. 'That man today,' she said abruptly. 'He means to cause trouble.'

289

A tremor seemed to pass through Mary's whole body. 'Did he have an affair with my mother?' she asked bluntly.

'Good God, no!' At that moment Rosalind could willingly have strangled Laura. Had she made no attempt to explain to this girl what could and could not be said? 'Your mother couldn't stand him,' she said forcefully. 'And I have to admit, in that at least she was an excellent judge of character. Your Aunt Dora wasn't so discriminating.'

'Dora?' Mary's face was a study. 'Her? Honestly, she's no better than an alleycat!'

'Mary, please!'

Rosalind went to the window, twisting and pulling at her rings. Oh, how she longed to get away from here for a while. Biarritz seemed very tempting. But if the Murray-Gill thing were to founder, as now seemed very likely, she would have to take Mary as well as Deb. The thought was sobering. Could she endure Biarritz at the mercy of Mary's honest but blistering tongue? There was nothing for it but to tell the whole, it seemed.

'Dora had a wild affair with him,' she announced. 'Because of your mother and Gabriel, no doubt, but also because Dora's like that. Desperately oversexed, I've always thought. Anyway, he was mixed up in everything shady. He said he escaped Poland just in front of the Nazis, but I've always suspected that they sprang him from gaol. You name it, he was into it. Black market. Gun running. Someone informed on him and he had to leave Bainfield on the run. He always thought it was your mother, and it might have been. But he had enemies enough. Laura hated him particularly, though. He knew about her past.'

Mary's eyes opened very wide. 'You mean – her past in France?'

Rosalind nodded. 'I don't know the details but he threatened for years to let the cat out of the bag. He never did, probably because it didn't suit him – he hasn't anything you could call a finer feeling. Anyway, now he's looking for revenge. He's going to tell the Murray-Gills all about it.'

'Oh.' Mary looked down and chewed her lip. 'He's going to tell them that my mother was a prostitute?'

'Yes. And – and I seem to have misled people rather about Gunthwaite. I've made too much of it and he'll take the greatest pleasure in bursting that balloon. And I suppose he'll imply that you're not a Cooper.'

'As to that,' said Mary with false bravado, 'I'm not the Cooper people think I am, but I'm a Cooper still. Oh, dear. I didn't think I liked Peter very much. Is it terribly silly of me to mind?'

Tears glistened on her hands. All at once, Rosalind felt her heart go out to her. Mary was so brave, so indomitable, facing every challenge with nothing but pride as her shield. True enough, the girl lifted her head and tried to smile. 'He can't prove anything.'

'But there's Sophie. And Marie.'

'It still says nothing at all about my mother. Our mother. This is as bad for Deb as it is for me.'

'But Deb – Deb—'

'She's so pretty no one will mind, but all I have is my reputation? Well, you could be right. And it doesn't matter, because I wouldn't have liked to be Lady Murray-Gill at all really. I'm ashamed of myself for caring. I mean, it was all too much. I don't know if I even liked him. But – oh, Aunt Rosalind! I can't bear for everyone to know!'

She hid her face and sobbed. Rosalind, unused to such scenes, patted her bracingly. 'No one will know. You can carry it off by your manner. I shall tell everyone who will listen that he's a crook. He must be. Gambling clubs, and expensive cars. Howard's going to talk to the Chief Constable first thing on Monday.'

'I hate not being honest! Having to cover up the truth!'

Rosalind sighed. 'I imagine your mother's felt like that for years.'

But nothing happened for some time. The Murray-Gills invited Mary and Deb to a dance held by a Murray-Gill cousin. They attended without demur, although in ordinary circumstances Mary would probably have refused. Suddenly the prize of the Scottish estate seemed worth winning. She had thought it tawdry before. Now she didn't know whether to despise herself.

She telephoned home again, the morning after. She was tired and a little hungover, her feet aching from too much dancing, including some wild Scottish reels. Peter had been sweet to her, fetching this and that and not insisting on talking all the time. He had kissed her on the terrace. She found herself thinking, Do I love him? Shall I mind?

Now her mother was talking of the hay crop, heavy and sweet for the first time in years. 'We haven't had a drop of rain, darling. Michael's so brown you wouldn't recognise him. And Piers and Connor too. I don't know what's happened here, the house used to be such a female sort of place, and now it's full of these great big men. It's all so different.'

'Is it?' She felt her heart ache for the sameness of things. 'Has Connor sold Diablo?'

'Darling, of course not! You know he won't sell your horse.'

'I told him to. I didn't mean it. But he might have believed me.'

Laura laughed. 'I don't think Connor believes half the things you tell him. Actually, I don't think he's going to stay.'

Mary launched into a barrage of questions. Was it the horses? Was

291

it the place? Had his family in Ireland requested his return? But her mother was vague. She didn't think it was that. He and Michael had made money and could make more, but if Mary had stagnated at Gunthwaite so had Connor too. 'It isn't the place for a young man on his own,' said Laura. 'There's no adventure.'

Mary replaced the receiver thoughtfully. Vaguely, at the back of her mind, she had thought of going home. When the Murray-Gill thing fell apart, and failing a job, it might be that she had no choice. But she had meant to go home to Connor and a business, not to a world with nothing for her to do. The cloud of depression that she had warded off for days now threatened to envelop her. It was like standing on a mountain top in the mist, she thought. Cold, clammy and frightening, because one dared not take a step for fear of a fall.

It wasn't true that disaster and opportunity came hand in hand, she decided. All was either glory or despair. If you failed one exam you never came top in another. If you broke your ankle and had to sit waiting for a visitor you would at once hear that they had died. In fact, life was utterly depressing.

She was sitting at the window, watching the day cloud over, when Deb came to find her. 'That racehorse man's on the 'phone. You said you wanted to look at some horses.'

'Oh.' Mary blinked. 'I suppose I did.'

'I thought you'd be pleased. It's what you wanted, isn't it?'

'I thought it was. But Mum says Connor's leaving. The horses were for him.'

Deb chivvied her to the telephone just the same and Mary arranged to visit the stables at the weekend. Did it matter that Connor was to go? She could send the horses to Michael, if need be. Or they might be duds, and she wouldn't want them at all. At any rate, going to see George Reynolds was certain to be better than moping around here.

She wrote a nice thank you note about the party and persuaded Uncle Howard to lend her the car. She had expected Deborah to come too, but to her surprise, Deb said, 'Not more horses, please, Mary. I'll go up to town and shop.'

'On a Saturday? It's bound to be mayhem.'

Deborah grinned, her lovely face suddenly like a mischievous fairy's. 'After Gunthwaite, I like a bit of mayhem once in a while.'

So Mary drove alone. The dry spell had ended, and from time to time showers fell, lapsing once or twice into rain so heavy she was forced to pull to the side of the road. The noise of the rain drowned out everything, a curtain of water hiding all but faint glimmers of colour; the red of a pillar box, the green of a heavy-leafed tree. Mary felt cut off from everything. She had felt like this when she was in London before, rootless, cut adrift from her past with no future on which she could rely. She thought of Sandra. She hadn't seen her

292

since that first dance. But Sandra was one of those people who frightened her, not for what they might do but for what they were. The Sandras of this world hadn't found a path to follow. They drifted in misery, without hope or expectation. Yet they weren't so very different from her.

The rain was easing now. She started the car again, and drove through inches of water to the stable yard. A lad directed her to the kitchen door and she found George Reynolds inside, chewing on a cigarette and worrying about the racing being off.

'But it's been so dry,' said Mary. 'This is bound to help.'

'Haven't a horse can run on the soft,' he said dismally.

His wife, a pretty woman with an understandably grim smile, gave Mary a cup of coffee. 'George said you'd come to look at some of our failures.'

'We've got enough of those,' he said, and Mary laughed.

'They might not be total failures. Some of them could jump.'

'We haven't the time,' moaned George.

'They're just eating their heads off,' added his wife.

'What a good thing I've come to help you out,' said Mary bracingly.

Suddenly she wished that Connor was here. She could almost see him trying to keep a straight face while these two talked themselves out of a decent price. A thought occurred to her; if she sent some horses home he'd have to stay. A barn full of untouched horseflesh would be too much to resist.

She followed George out to the stables. The sun was brilliant on puddles and rivulets, and steam rose in a cloud from the muckheap behind the barn, enveloping everything in a mist that could have been romantic, if you forgot its origins. A little cat stalked along the top of a stable door, and the horse within blew at it and ruffled its fur. Yard led to yard, everywhere lined with boxes. Lads shuffled out of the way as they passed, but George said nothing to anyone. He was lost in his own worst imaginings.

At last they came to a row of boxes facing on to a muddy field. Here the paint was worn and the roofs sagging, but the horses looked well and happy. A big grey watched their arrival with a mildly interested eye. Mary said, 'He's one, is he?'

'Yes. Clumsy brute. Means well, but never did a thing. Tried him every which way, too.'

Mary peered into the box. The horse had feet like dinner plates on spindly racehorse legs. 'Never went wrong,' said George, anticipating her comment. 'Looks as if he will, though, I grant you that.'

'I'll risk it,' said Mary. 'At a price. How's that chestnut bred? Is it half a Shetland pony?'

George pulled out the diminutive horse. Mary felt her heart skip with delight. The little gelding was neat, precise and pretty, the perfect lady's horse. Remembering herself, she sighed. 'I can't think why you ever put him into training, George.'

'Had to. One of my best owners bred him. But they laughed in the paddock. Couldn't blame them. Like putting a whippet in with greyhounds.'

Mary sighed again and chewed her lip. Tearing herself away from the little horse she moved on down the boxes. There was a wild colt she considered but decided she didn't like, and a roan she did, although he looked a mess. Everything else was too dopey, too ugly or just wrong. She leaned on a gate, looked George in the eye and offered a straight price for all three. 'Take it or leave it, George. I'll take them as they stand. No guarantees.'

He glared at her under his beetling brows. 'There's never a straight price for a horse. It's always robbery.'

'These aren't easy horses though,' said Mary. 'You know there are things wrong with them you haven't said. I'm buying your problems, George. Think on.'

It was a Yorkshire-ism from the market. He chuckled and so did she. 'Add two hundred for the colt and they're yours.'

'Oh.' Mary glanced again at the wild thing, weaving and kicking at one and the same time. 'He must be horrible, then.'

'It's less than meat money.'

'People always say that.'

'He's bred like a king.'

She considered. The horse was doing no good here. At Gunthwaite they could turn him out for the winter, and see if he was sweeter in the spring. As a stallion he might be worth something, after all.

She spun on her heel. 'Done.'

They went back into the house for lunch. George was almost cheerful, which alarmed Mary more than a little. He must have sold her a real dog, she decided, and stared glumly into her wine.

Deborah was feeling adventurous. She sauntered along Bond Street, looking into the jewellers' shops, wishing that she was rich. But for the horrors of the Scottish castle she might have found the prosperous Murray-Gills of interest herself.

It was starting to rain, a fine drizzle that soon developed into a torrential downpour. She retreated into Asprey's, one of a number of refugees from the storm. The doorman courteously ushered them into the cutlery department, where they could gather out of anyone's way. Deborah found herself staring at a canteen of Dubarry, wondering if one day she might eat with such things herself. Yes, a husband would have to be rich, she decided, and began a mental inventory of everyone she knew.

The rich ones were unattractive, it seemed. Only poor young men had good teeth and broad shoulders. Although sexual attraction wasn't all about youth and good looks. A shiver ran through her. The Pole ... A gentleman at her side, also driven here out of the rain, said, 'Are you cold? I'm sure they'd bring you a cup of coffee, shall I ask?'

Deb thanked him but shook her head. She doubted the Pole would be as considerate. He looked cruel and self-interested, but that was part of his charm. For her, the world was full of easy men who would do anything to win her. She thought that Zwmskorski would do very little, but that little would count.

Soon the rain began to ease. Deborah moved into rings, driven by the attentions of her unknown admirer. He hovered, anxious to follow. Would he buy her diamonds? she wondered, looking at a magnificent stone set amidst sapphires, delicately fringed with gold. Perhaps love made diamonds unimportant. All the same, she wanted love and diamonds both.

The sun was coming out. She glanced at her watch and saw that she was going to be late. Slipping out past the doorman, long hair swinging, neat and delectable, everyone seemed to sigh. 'What a lovely young girl,' someone said. 'She should be on the stage.'

Deborah hurried along, feeling excitement build. Would he be there? He might not wait. Men always waited, she said to herself. But would he? Aunt Rosalind hated him, that much she knew, but that was to be expected. Anyone as exciting as he must be disapproved of. He ran gambling clubs and wasn't the least respectable. What respectable man would have passed her such a note so calmly? Suppose she'd shown it to her aunt?

She stopped and took stock of the street, spotting a discreet restaurant sign painted in black and gold. She crossed the road, wondering if he was watching, refusing to hurry. But when she entered, he hadn't been looking at all. He was seated at the bar, smoking Russian cigarettes, drinking vodka.

'Ah! Deborah.' He got up and kissed her quickly on both cheeks. 'Another vodka, Hans.'

'I don't drink vodka,' she said, sliding on to a bar stool. 'I'll have champagne.'

His lined, sardonic face turned towards her. 'Are you always so impertinent?'

She looked surprised. 'I'm sorry. Can't you afford champagne?'

'You spoiled little—' he took a breath. 'Hans, a bottle of Krug, if you please.'

Deborah giggled.

Oddly, he barely spoke to her. He drank some champagne, and then left it to Deb and reverted to vodka, wreathed in cigarette smoke the while. People came up and spoke to him, respectful, nervous people. That was why he had come here, she thought. He was impressing her with evidence of his power. In the middle of a conversation she interrupted and said, 'Are we going to eat? I can't stay all afternoon.'

Again he fixed her with those cold blue eyes. She stared back, refusing to be intimidated. Her own daring left her a little breathless. How far could she go? But he merely waved to the head waiter and said, 'We'll go to our table now.'

She hadn't ordered. Nonetheless food appeared before them: a salad of some kind, convoluted and delicious, and then shredded duckling on a bed of wild cherries, wrapped in a rich cream sauce. 'Polish food,' Zwmskorski explained. 'Polish food as it used to be, before the war. Nowadays it's nothing of course. Cabbage and beetroot and goat.'

'It's wonderful,' said Deb honestly. 'Now I forgive you for being so rude.'

'That was not I.'

She challenged him with her stare. 'Please. I'm not a child. Don't treat me as one.'

His attention had seemed to be everywhere but her. Now, suddenly, she could feel him watching her. Thinking of her. Wanting her. She looked at her own hand encircling her wine glass. Dainty fingers, tipped with pink varnish, so clean, so perfect. She imagined that hand touching him – a few drops of champagne spilled on to the cloth.

'You are nervous,' he said.

'No. I thought of something that disturbed me.'

'I think only of you.'

'A minute ago you thought of anything else but.'

'Because I desire you. Before was not the time. Was it desire that made you shake?'

'Yes. But not for you.'

'Who then?'

'Someone.'

'Forget him. I will make you long for no one but me.'

He leaned across the table, put his hand behind her head and pulled her to him. Their lips met, his tongue invaded her, experienced, knowing, sending shards of glass slicing down every nerve. She pulled away, and at once he let her go. 'People are looking,' she said nervously. She felt as if he had stripped her naked in public. Her whole body was on fire.

'We'll go,' he said. 'I have a place near here.'

He stood up, and in a daze she stood up with him. What was she doing? Where did he mean them to go? He held her arm above the elbow, as if to preclude an escape. Suddenly she felt trapped. The

296

game was rushing to its conclusion, and she had only just put her pieces on the board. The waiter was hailing a taxi, and she found it wasn't in her to make a scene. Not in here, not in front of everyone who had seen that kiss. On the pavement, the taxi at the kerb, she pulled back. 'No.'

He behaved as if he hadn't heard. He pushed her before him into the car, giving the driver a brief address. But the moment he followed her in, sitting, oddly, on the tip-up seat facing her, she said, 'I think you should take me to the station. I have to go home.'

His hand met hers. Before she could pull away he pressed her palm into his groin. Her eyes flew to his, wide with shock. He said nothing. Involuntarily, knowledgeably, she closed her fingers briefly on his massive erection. He gave a grunt, and let her go.

'You are a virgin still?' he said in a low voice.

She nodded.

'A boy won't please you. You've let them fumble you, of course. You like it. But you can't go too far in case it gets known. But with me – there's no risk. No one will ever know.'

There was an ache between her legs. Her breasts burned and throbbed. He was right, she couldn't do this with anyone else, she was doomed to years of boyish fumblings in a car. The taxi was drawing up outside a large white building, its door flanked with the bells of many flats. Zwmskorski threw a note at the driver and got out. This time, Deborah followed of her own free will.

He didn't touch her in the lift. He seemed irritable and impatient. He got out on the third floor, the hall of which was opulently carpeted, and opened a large mahogany door. They entered a flat luscious with riches; dark velvet curtains hung at the windows, and tapestries glowed on the walls. Deb looked about her, surprised. He said, 'Come into the bedroom. As you said, you haven't all afternoon.'

When she saw the double bed her stomach lurched. Not looking at her, Zwmskorski was taking off his jacket and tie, and throwing off his shirt. He had a muscled, wiry body, the chest covered in pale blond hair. She stood quite still, watching him. Quite unselfconscious, he threw off his trousers and underpants. His erection, a little diminished, stuck out from him like a growth.

'Oh God.' Deb covered her mouth with her hand. He turned and looked at her, and she saw he didn't care what she thought. Suddenly she was afraid. He could do anything he liked to her. And she had come here of her own free will.

She was wearing a long straight skirt, down past her knees, with a tight white top tucked into it. He crossed the room to her and pulled her top free, pushing it above her breasts. Today she had worn her prettiest bra, a film of lace in which her breasts hung suspended. He

297

closed his hand on it and ripped it away. She let out a small scream, and at once his hand closed on her breast, stopping just short of pain. 'Don't make a noise,' he whispered.

She whispered back. 'Don't ruin my clothes. They'll know at home.'

'Perhaps a wild animal mauled you.'

He left her for a moment and went to a table by the bed. She heard him fiddling with something, and thought vaguely that he was taking care not to make her pregnant. But he turned back without anything. Instead, he switched on a bright, overhead light.

'No,' she said involuntarily.

'But I want to see you, my love.'

He bent his head and took her nipple in his mouth, teasing it with his tongue. She groaned, and closed her fingers in his hair, feeling the desire begin again, wanting more and yet wanting none of it, eager and yet afraid. His hands pushed her skirt to her waist, holding her thighs, his penis brushing against the skin above her stockings. A blind worm, she thought distractedly, looking for a home in the dark, hiding from the light. She began to shudder, and the man lifted his head. 'What a slut you are,' he said dispassionately. 'Kneel on the bed.'

She was beyond resistance. She did as she was told, feeling his hand come up between her legs and rip away her best silk panties. She would go home half naked, she thought in some part of her mind. But her body precluded thinking. She was responding to an age-old call, and could not resist.

He lay on the bed, his head by her knees. She was bewildered. What did he mean to do? An odd, mechanical clicking sounded at intervals. She found herself wondering vaguely what it was.

'Come here.' He pulled her over his face. Her mind froze into immobility. She slumped forward, her hands on either side of him, suddenly realising, suddenly experiencing something she had never imagined. His tongue stroked her, sending messages to her womb. She could feel an explosion building. It was frightening yet irresistible, obscene but somehow right. All at once her body spun out of control. She fell sideways away from him, heart pounding, breath coming in pants. Was that the reason for this? Was that its purpose? Again the mechanical clicking. She moved away from him, repelled by his slack, wet mouth.

'My God,' he said. 'You're a whore. Just like your priggish, stupid mother.'

Catching her breath and finding her voice, Deb croaked, 'Did you do this with my mother?'

'Her? You must be joking. She wouldn't stoop to such as me. When in Paris she'd taken money for it from anyone who could pay!

You knew that, did you? Your mother was a whore. And so, it seems, are you.'

He reared up on the bed, ready to come at her, ready to finish all this. His face was suffused with lustful loathing. He would do to Deborah what he had never managed with her mother, and have his cruel revenge. But his timing was at fault. He had satisfied her and she was herself again. Suddenly everything looked different. He was just an ageing man on a huge green bed, and she a half-dressed young fool. He had brought her here to harm her, because he hated her mother and hated her. She had to get out!

He was so sure of himself. He reached out at full stretch to catch hold of her arm. Deb evaded him by a hairsbreadth, falling off the bed, grabbing at her shoes. She rolled to the open door, seeing her bag and seizing it, scrambling to her feet. There was the front door. She scrabbled at the handle. In his haste he hadn't turned the lock.

'Come back here, you bitch!' he was roaring. 'Come back or I'll see you dead, you little slut!'

She fell into the hall, slamming the door behind her. He had no clothes on, but he might not care. There was no one out here, no one at all. A deathly quiet hung over the place. She found herself gibbering with fright.

The lift was out of the question. She ran for the stairs, shielded by a heavy fire door. For a second it wouldn't give. But then she was through, half falling down the first flight, hearing him come after her. She dared not look back and ran on, pulling her top down one-handed, her mind dividing itself in two. What would she look like in the street? What if he caught her? Both thoughts ran on, side by side. She must escape to people, and be safe.

A glass door led on to the street. Bare feet were padding on the stairs behind her. She put both hands to the bar that held the door shut, throwing her weight behind them. The bar gave quite easily and she fell on to the pavement, picking herself up and running.

'What the devil . . . ?' A man walking his dog stood staring. She looked back, taking a second to struggle into her shoes, seeing the naked figure of Zwmskorski standing in the doorway. Defiance surged.

'So there!' she yelled at him. 'So there!'

Then she turned again and ran.

Chapter Twenty-nine

Deborah sat on the train and stared resolutely at her reflection in the window. It was amazing how normal you could look under the most extreme circumstances, she reflected. There she was, mauled and abused, naked but for her skirt and top, and no one knew. And her bodily ills were the least of it. Inside she was shaking with shame and fright. No one in the world had ever behaved so badly, she thought. If anyone ever found out then she would die.

She took a taxi from the station, although she had said she would telephone to be collected. Somehow she couldn't stand waiting around, wondering if people were looking at her, wondering if by some ghastly chance Zwmskorski had come looking for her and was there. All her instincts were to run towards safety as fast as she could go. But where was safety to be found? Zwmskorski knew where she lived. He knew her family. He could find her whenever he chose.

She entered the house quietly. No one was around. She ran quickly upstairs, looking out from the landing window and seeing that Rosalind and Alan were in the garden. In a way she was relieved, she could bathe and change without difficulty, and yet she would have liked them to be nearer at hand. Her lingering impression was that the Pole would leap out at her. That it was impossible made the thought no less real. If only Mary would come back!

She bathed in water as hot as she could bear. The thought of Zwmskorski's hands, his mouth, turned her skin to flame even before the heat of the bath. The worst of it, she thought in agony, was that she had enjoyed it so! All the things he had said. She turned everything over, hating herself to the core of her soul.

She didn't stay in the bath long. The noise of the water obscured the sound of whoever might be approaching. She went into the bedroom and dressed in a skirt she hated and a blouse two sizes too big. She didn't want to look pretty tonight. She didn't want to look pretty ever again. Just as she was brushing her hair, ready to fold it up into a tight pleat, Mary came in.

'Hi,' she said happily. 'I've bought four horses.'

'Have you?' Deb didn't turn from the mirror.

'Well, take some notice, won't you? They're a really mixed bag – one's a lunatic, but there's always one, and there's the prettiest little gelding, a doll-sized horse, and one with these feet . . . Deb? Deb, are you listening?'

'Not really,' she said, again in that odd sort of voice.

Mary put down her bag and crossed the room towards her. She looked at Deb's tight, unhappy face and sat on the bed. 'What's happened?'

Deb tried to take a deep breath. She managed only a gulp. 'It was that man. The Pole. I went to see him. To his flat. And, Mary – oh, Mary, it was horrible!'

She burst into shuddering sobs. Mary put out her arms and drew her sister down. Her own heart was hammering wildly. 'Did he rape you?' she asked in a voice so ordinary she might have been asking if he'd offered her a drink.

Deb shook her head and tried to sit up. The first wild admission over, she wanted to tell it, all of it, and be done. 'He almost didn't have to,' she said calmly. 'I went there to sleep with him. He – he did things. And I let him, Mary. I wanted what he did. And then – he called me names. And Mum. He said I was a whore, just like her. And I came to my senses and ran.'

Relief made Mary light-headed. After a moment she said, 'We need a drink. Let's go downstairs and steal some of Howard's horrible wine.'

Deb tried to laugh. 'If we're going to steal something, make it something decent. But I'd rather have a gin.'

They crept into the sitting room and poured two gin and tonics each, taking the brimming glasses back with them. After the first, Deb began to relax. Suddenly she was telling every horrible, shaming detail. At the end, she said matter-of-factly 'So you see, I've been disgusting. It's been coming for a while, I suppose, but in the end I just went mad.'

Mary sat quietly. Then she sighed. 'I thought he was going to ruin me,' she said. 'I didn't realise he had it in for both of us. He was probably going to make you pregnant. But he got as carried away as you, and it all got out of hand.'

Deb said, 'He said he'd take care of me. I thought—' When Mary said nothing, she went on, 'How did he mean to ruin you?'

'He was going to spill the beans to the Murray-Gills about Mum. It's true, you see. She was a prostitute. In France, when she was young. I mean, with Sophie and Marie – well, we might have guessed.'

Deborah went very quiet. Mary passed her another gin, and began her second. 'So it's in the genes,' said Deb at last. 'A depraved appetite.'

'I don't think there's anything depraved about it,' said Mary staunchly.

301

'Perhaps it hasn't come out in you.'

'For God's sake, Deb! Mum never wanted to be a prostitute! You've no idea what it's like trying to survive on your own. If I hadn't known – if I hadn't been lucky – it could have been me!'

Deborah rose and went to the window. Rosalind and Alan were preparing to come in, gathering up glasses and newspapers, folding deckchairs. It hadn't rained here. They had spent all day in peaceful relaxation. She had the desperate feeling that she too should have been here, been spared today. She didn't want to know what she knew now. In one moment, in one day, she had lost so much. Her self-respect, her optimism, her ordered, simple life.

Mary, sensing it all, said, 'Don't let it spoil things, Deb. Really, nothing's changed. He didn't hurt you. Everything's the same as this morning. You, me, Mum. I know how it feels to find out, but honestly, everything's the same.' But even as she said it, she knew that for Deborah, as for her, nothing was.

Days passed. Nothing happened, nothing was said. Neither Mary nor Deb found that time improved things. Each day meant slowly gathering tension, a tightening screw that must in the end reach breaking point. At night the scene played and replayed in Deborah's head. She began to wonder about things: the light, the mechanical clicking. She sat up suddenly in bed. He had gone to the side table, she didn't know for what. Suppose – suppose he had set up a camera?

She went ice cold. Her teeth began to chatter. Her instinct was to fall out of bed and tell Mary, but when she looked across at her sleeping sister she remained still. How could you admit to such stupidity? She couldn't face Mary, let alone the world. If there were pictures – and how she prayed she was wrong – she would die rather than have anyone know.

Deborah became more and more withdrawn. She developed recurrent headaches, excusing herself from this or that party. Rosalind began taking her to the eye hospital. 'There's no point suffering dear, just because you don't want to wear glasses. I'm sure you'd look ravishing in them. You always do.' But Deborah, wan and tired, always promised to be better in the morning. She seldom was.

As for Mary, she was sucked more and more into the world of the Murray-Gills. On Wednesday Peter telephoned to ask if she could join a houseparty at the weekend. 'I know it's short notice Mary, but someone's dropped out. It's Mother's idea. You'll get some riding in, but not much more. Still, it could be fun.'

She couldn't decide. Waiting like this, expecting it to end, she was taking it further than she had intended. 'I can't really leave Deb,' she prevaricated, but straight away Peter invited her too. For once

Rosalind would not take no for an answer, and Mary agreed. Deborah needed a change of scene. They would both be happy to come.

Connor stood in the yard, staring in disbelief at the horses filing one after another out of the wagon. There had been no message, no telegram, nothing. Just four deadbeat horses, driven north by a racing stable's travelling lad, off to Birmingham to see his parents. Connor said to him again, 'You're sure they're for here? From this Reynolds chap?'

The man nodded. But then, unbending a little, he said, 'Young lady bought them. Great friends they are, her and the boss. Thick as thieves.'

'Indeed?' Connor fixed him with a dark stare.

'Never seen the boss so cheerful,' added the lad. He'd taken to Mary, with her bluntness and her lack of airs and graces, and was more than happy to boost her credit at home. Connor scowled still more.

He perfunctorily offered a cup of tea, making it plain that he had better things to do than entertain. The lad declined, he had to drive a fair way back south before dark, and might not make Birmingham at all. As he drove away, leaving his four charges staring wistfully after him, Connor let out a resounding curse. 'That sodding girl!'

Laura, coming out to see what was causing the commotion, was taken aback. 'Did Mary send these?' She gestured to the four weary nags. 'Who can say?' he snarled. 'Not a word has she vouchsafed about one of them. And what do we have? A thing which looks as if it's wearing boots; a rocking horse, give or take an inch; something which might be OK if it wasn't such a dishwater colour; and this.' He put out a hand to the black and it snatched at him, teeth meeting with a click. 'A wrong-headed stallion.'

'Oh dear,' said Laura. 'And you were leaving on Friday.'

'I imagine it's her little joke.' He walked around the four, assessing them as best he could. Their heads followed him. It had been a very long drive and they were wondering about food and bed. They had the ill-founded optimism of all well cared for horses, expecting the best wherever they found themselves. Much as Connor raged at Mary, he couldn't disappoint the creatures. He stomped past them into the barn to prepare some boxes. The stallion tried to catch him with a kick.

Laura went on through the yard and up into the meadow. Michael was baling hay with Piers, the last of the crop and hard won. Rain had soaked it twice and they had laboriously dried it each time. She leaned on the gate for a moment, watching them. Piers drove the little tractor she had bought in the war, ancient now and many times

303

repaired. He was bare-headed in the sun, his hair golden and thick. He had filled out this summer, reminding her more than ever of Gabriel when he was young. But he had none of Gabriel's youthful insouciance. It was in Piers' nature to expect the worst, he was always surprised by good fortune.

He saw her, pulled up the turner and came to the gate. He switched off and jumped down, his shirt pulled open, smelling of hay and sweat. She thought how attractive he was. 'Has something happened?' he demanded.

'Nothing awful,' she said easily. 'Mary's sent four horses and Connor's in a rage. They're quite out of the blue.'

'Oh.' He hesitated. 'Any post?'

'Circulars and bills. Nothing more.'

Deborah hadn't written in two weeks. As the days passed Piers was becoming more and more downcast. Sorry as she felt for him, Laura wasn't displeased. He was a difficult boy at the best of times. Since the letters dried up he had taken to driving into Bainfield after work, turning up the following morning, bleary and sick.

Michael drove across, the baler clanking angrily. He climbed stiffly down from the tractor cab, saying to Piers, 'The knotter's gone again. Do what you can. I'll go back to the house for an hour.'

In contrast to the boy he looked grey with dust and weariness. Laura took his arm, waiting until they were out of earshot to say, 'Is it your head?'

He grimaced. 'I'll have some tea and five minutes on the bed.'

But when he came to the yard and saw Connor leading the first of the horses to their new quarters, the weariness fell quite away. He strode across, his face crinkling with laughter. 'Is this Mary's doing? That girl! Where does she get it from?'

'She got these from the reject pile of a racing stable,' said Connor thinly. 'I should have known she'd try something like this. Her sort of horses, every one of them.'

Michael nodded to the little gelding. 'He's small, I'll give you that. But the mare went well. She'll do for a girl.'

'There isn't a girl here to ride him,' snapped Connor. 'That could be it, I suppose. She's hoping I'll beg her to come back and show me how it's done.'

Laura bridled. 'I don't imagine Mary does things solely to upset you, Connor. She'll have got a good deal. She always could spot a bargain.'

'And I can't, I suppose?' It was his turn to rise.

'You say yourself you like to buy good horses. It takes Mary to see promise where you least expect it.'

Connor was silent. Laura knew she had offended him, and so did Michael; he was looking at her with a shading of reproach. But she would not retract it! Since the girls had gone to London Laura had felt them to be supplanted by male energy, male strength, male single-mindedness. She was standing up for her daughters' subtlety, acknowledging too how great a gap their absence made in her own life.

She turned aside and went quickly into the house. Michael wouldn't come in now. Tired as he was, he would stay in the stables with Connor, talking horses, joining with him in his tacit accusation of Mary. But then, to her surprise, a moment later Michael followed her in.

'She's a cunning one,' he said, sinking into a chair and leaning his head back. 'She's landed Connor in a fix. He can't leave now.'

'I don't suppose she thought of that at all,' said Laura primly. 'She saw some good horses and that was that. And I wish you'd stop letting Connor talk her down. He's too full of himself, that boy.' She plonked a mug of tea in front of him.

Michael said, 'Connor's too full of himself and Piers is too wild. But the girls are very near perfect.'

Laura blushed. 'I don't say that.'

'Do you not? I must have misheard. Perhaps it's just that since those two went away, you've forgotten a few things.'

'The things I've forgotten aren't the ones you have,' said Laura. 'You still wish we'd had a boy. Don't you?'

He lifted his head to meet her eye. 'It's the only thing I wish,' he admitted, his voice suddenly soft. 'But not instead of our girls, Laura. If I'm honest I'd have welcomed a dozen more – boys, girls, whatever. For Gunthwaite. And for us.'

She swallowed. 'I just want the two we have.'

'We can't hold on to them, love. You've said that yourself.'

'And I can't help wanting to.'

For a moment she looked bereft. Michael reached out a hand to her, drawing her to him to stand close by his chair. He encircled her waist with his brawny farmer's arm, trying to give her some of his own calm confidence. She had known who she was when the girls were young, as a mother and a wife. She was a wife still, but motherhood no longer filled her days. Her life had lost its purpose, and with it had gone her calm. He had offered her amusements – hunting, joining the Beachams' party set – but that wasn't Laura. She had no wish to pass her days in trivia. But whatever she did wish for, whatever it was that would fill the hollow he sensed deep within, he simply did not know.

He pressed his lips against the soft skin of her neck. She looked at him, and without a word went to the stairs. He sighed. She never refused him, was always sexually obedient. He followed her up, and stood watching her undress. She could still excite him, still rouse him to boyish urgency. If only he didn't feel he was imposing himself on

305

her! She lay down and he moved at once to cover her, quick, deliberate, confining himself to those actions which he simply could not resist. Sometimes, moved to passion, he closed his hands on her breasts, and her face contorted, just enough. Was it pleasure or pain? Did she hate this, as he suspected? He could never tell. He felt himself begin to pulsate, delicious, heady release. Beneath him, his wife's closed eyes still hid from him.

That night Connor tried to telephone Mary. At last when the phone had rung for ten minutes or so in an apparently empty house, Howard answered, somewhat testily, only to say that Rosalind and the girls were out. 'Can you tell me where they've gone, sir?' asked Connor. 'It's important I speak to Mary.'

'Mary's at a dance of some sort, that's all I know. No doubt this Murray-Gill character's taken her, he's running after her pretty hard. As for Deborah, I assume she's gone too. But there's no saying. To tell you the truth, young man, we have telephone calls all day and all night for Deborah.'

'Can I telephone when they get back?'

'Most certainly not! I have no wish to be wakened at three in the morning, or thereabouts. Call again tomorrow, not before twelve. Good evening to you.'

Connor stormed back into the kitchen. Laura was alone sewing, and looked up enquiringly. He snapped, 'Out on the tiles. She's doing pretty well for a girl who hates parties. To tell the truth, I begin to wonder if I know Mary at all. She's not the girl she pretends to be, that's for sure.'

'I hope she's gained some confidence,' said Laura, in what she hoped were mild tones.

He spread the newspaper in front of his face, rustling the pages furiously. 'Confidence? Is that what you call it? If that girl got any more confident she'd be in real trouble!'

Laura looked at him in confusion. He was clearly very angry about something. Suddenly the paper fell and he met her eyes. 'If you only knew,' he said pityingly.

'Knew what?'

'You ought to have her home. She needs some proper control.'

'Mary? I assure you, she's really very sensible!'

'And that's all that counts is it? This man, that man, but as long as she's sensible!'

Laura put her hand to her face. 'You can't be serious?'

'Of course I am. She told me herself.'

'And you believed her? Connor, have some sense. Mary might want you to think her sophisticated but she certainly isn't. Or at least, wasn't. Heaven knows what she's doing right now.'

306

His face grew very black. He pushed himself up and stormed to the door, only to stop and stand quite still. Then he turned. 'That's what the horses are for. To keep me here. Stop me getting down there and finding out what's really going on.'

'What?'

'She's a conniving little bitch!'

'Don't call my daughter a bitch, Connor! I won't have it!'

'And what will you have? She doesn't know what she's doing. She thinks she can behave like a man and it won't matter. If she goes on like this she'll have nothing of a reputation and nothing of a future. I tell you, it's time she was stopped!'

He was out in the yard, striding across the cobbles in the dark. In the barn she heard him blundering for the light switch, falling over something and cursing. She stood in the doorway, quite bemused, until Michael came downstairs and asked why she was freezing the house.

She closed the door and said slowly, 'Connor seems to think Mary's leading a life of vice. Men. You know.'

'Good God!'

'And of course she isn't. I think he's gone mad, Michael. I know he's been lonely here. Sitting in, night after night. He's been brooding I suppose.'

Michael said, 'He didn't like Mary half so well when she was here, you know. This is a fine time to play the neglected lover.'

'Is that what he's doing, do you think?' She sat down heavily by the fire. 'I don't understand all this. I was never a girl like Mary and Deb. My life was so much more serious.'

She looked up at her husband, those great pale eyes full of the pain of remembering. He moved, as always, to take that pain away. 'Shall we have a warm drink?' he said encouragingly. 'To help you get some sleep. The girls are fine, love. And I'll speak to Connor.'

He watched her as she moved about the kitchen. He used to love to look at her, taking strength from her slim, lithe form. But these days he felt a heaviness about her, in her heart if not her body. Yet they had been so lucky together. They had given each other so much happiness. Why should it be now that it all had to wither away?

Mary was packing for the weekend and Rosalind was sitting on the bed. Mary said, 'I shouldn't be going, of course. The further things go, the worse it's going to be when everything comes out.'

Rosalind said bracingly, 'It might not come out. Zwmskorski might have meant none of it.'

Mary made a face. 'I think it's more likely he's going to pop up at the altar and stop the wedding.'

'You don't really think Peter Murray-Gill's going to—'

'No! No, of course not. I was just saying.'

But Rosalind was alight with pleasure. 'If he did, Mary! You couldn't accept, of course, you haven't known him long enough. But he could visit your father; make his intentions known. And then, in August, in the heather—'

'Oh, Rosalind!' They giggled at each other. Rosalind thought how odd it was that after such unpromising beginnings she had come to like Mary so much.

Deborah came in. She was wearing a dress that should have had a belt, but today preferred it to hang in baggy folds. Rosalind looked askance at her. 'Why on earth are you looking such a wreck, my dear?'

'To stop men leering at me,' said Deborah flatly. 'I've had enough of it.'

Rosalind said nothing. She had her suspicions, and was intelligent enough not to investigate further. Deborah had been badly frightened, and this weekend was just the thing to reassure her once again. Laura had neglected her daughters in one very important respect: she hadn't taught them about difficult men. No doubt Deborah had become involved in a wrestling match that had got a little out of hand, and innocent that she was, had taken fright.

She pulled out Deborah's case and began to select dresses from the wardrobe. 'You won't want to ride particularly, will you, dear? Don't look so anxious! I understand from Lady Murray-Gill that there are only two young men besides Peter, and both of them are charming. One's something to do with a dukedom, so you're quite beneath his touch, and the other's something in tea.'

When she had gone Mary said sardonically, 'You realise you're being trailed under a future duke's nose?'

Deb threw herself on the bed. 'I don't care. I don't want to meet anybody.'

'You don't have to let anyone do anything you don't want.'

'But suppose I do want? What then? I can't trust myself, Mary. I see that now.'

Mary went and knelt down beside her, taking her sister's hand. 'Well, you can trust me, can't you? I promise I won't let you out of my sight. Or at least, if it's unavoidable, I'll make sure you're firmly nailed to the hem of some dowager. Then you can't be dragged off to the conservatory and made to do things against your better nature.'

'I haven't got a better nature,' said Deborah gloomily. 'I'm just a mass of desires.'

'So's everybody,' declared Mary. 'You have more opportunity to find out about them, that's all. Everyone wants to get you in a compromising position, so obviously it's harder.'

As if to reinforce this point of view, Alan knocked at the door. 'Coming for a walk, Deb?' he asked, poking his head into the room. 'We could go for a drink at the Nelson.'

'It's going to rain,' she said, turning her back on him.

'We'll take an umbrella. Please come, Deb. You're going to be away all weekend and I won't see you at all.'

'Just as well,' said Mary, getting up to shut the door on him. 'You have to realise, Alan, Deb isn't interested.'

When his shocked face had been excluded, Deb said, 'That was mean.'

'I don't care. You've got to start being firm with them. You didn't like having him trail after you, did you?'

'No. Yes. I don't want him glaring at me, that's all.'

'Be nice to him at dinner. Give him hope.'

'Like you do to David?'

Mary snorted. 'Him! If you saw his other girlfriends you'd know why he hangs after me. I should feel sorry for him, I suppose. But I'm not sorry enough to put up with him. He's a damned nuisance.'

True to form, David took the opportunity of driving them down to Camborough Place the next morning to deliver a lecture on Mary's conduct during the weekend. The girls were to chaperone each other at all times. Mary was not to show anyone up by her superior riding skills. She was not to show any preference at all for Peter Murray-Gill: 'Because he's only amusing himself with you, Mary. At the end of the day you don't want people to know he got bored.'

'Really!' Deborah took up the cudgels in Mary's defence. 'How do you know he doesn't adore her? He looks as if he does. He positively beams when he sees her come into a room.'

'Don't be foolish, Deborah,' said David loftily. 'You're far too young to know anything about it.'

'Thanks a lot! I'll look for my dummy,' retorted his unrepentant cousin, and leaned between the front seats to turn on the radio and drown out further talk.

Camborough Place was a large mansion set in rolling parkland complete with lake, fountains and deep drifts of celandine under the trees. They were all impressed and in consequence David managed to park in an obvious show of bad temper, showering gravel everywhere. Nonetheless Mary said goodbye quite nicely. 'If you can't pick us up on Monday, say so,' she said ingenuously. 'I'm sure Peter can give us a lift...'

'Failing any other chauffeur, I shall be here at ten,' said David. 'And do remember my advice, Mary. I was there the last time you fell flat on your face.'

He was infuriating! Mary and Deb went into the house, followed by a footman and their luggage. They were greeted by the housekeeper, and conducted to their rooms. Maids would be sent to unpack for them, while their hostess, and the rest of the houseparty, would be encountered when they came down for luncheon. It was to be eaten in the yellow dining room, to which a footman would be waiting to escort them in just over half an hour. Following her up the wide stairs, the girls exchanged panicked glances. This was frightful! They should never have come!

But in her room, looking out through long windows across the lake, Mary began to revive. The maid was quick and unobtrusive, and Mary thanked God she had let Rosalind pack. She checked in the mirror that her make-up was good, wondering not for the first time if she ought to ask Kristian about the tell-tale smudge under her eyebrow. But it seemed greedy to want everything, she decided, and then looked again. Some people lived perfect lives. Why not her?

She changed into a cream linen suit, beautiful but liable to crease. She fluffed her hair back from her face. Did she look elegant? She fancied so. She thought of Peter and felt the warmth of a familiar friend. They got on very well.

When she was quite ready she went next door to Deb. She was sitting on the bed in her slip, looking hopelessly out at the view. Mary went to the wardrobe and said, 'Why not the blue? That's nice and demure.'

'Is it? I'm not sure that I can tell.'

Mary dressed her and brushed her hair, almost frog-marching her into the corridor when the footman knocked. They went downstairs together, side by side on the sweeping stair, and in the hall below them Peter and his mother stood to wait for them. Lady Murray-Gill came forward with a smile. 'What a picture you two make!'

Mary smiled in return. What fun all this was! Even if nothing came of this, even if she never experienced anything like this again, she would remember this weekend for the rest of her life.

'All right then, David! Where is she?'

Connor marched into Rosalind's drawing room and confronted his friend. David, sprawling on the sofa thinking about having a whisky, sat up with a start. 'Who? Mary? What's she done now?'

'Nothing to concern anyone but me. I wish to speak to her. Now.'

Rosalind, hurrying in, said, 'Connor, please! Mary's away for the weekend, a guest of the Murray-Gills. But you're welcome to stay until Monday. Sit down, do.'

'I've no wish to sit down, Mrs Dalton. And thank you for your kind invitation, but I have to see Mary. Her behaviour's quite unacceptable.'

'Couldn't agree more,' said David. 'I told Mother the girl was playing fast and loose.'

'I knew it!' said Connor, slapping a fist into his palm. 'Laura tried to tell me I was imagining things, of course. Well, I suppose a mother ought to retain some illusions. The full extent of it would break her heart.'

Rosalind rang the bell for the drinks trolley. She felt in need of immediate refreshment. 'What do you imagine Mary is doing, Connor?'

'Being loose,' he declared, looking her straight in the eye. 'This weekend will be a cover for it. She told me herself she was up to all the tricks. And this racehorse trainer. He's another one of her pick-ups, I don't doubt.'

'George Reynolds?' Rosalind was aghast.

'And this other one – Murray-Gill. And I don't know who else.'

The maid pushed the trolley into the room, whispering to Rosalind that dinner would be served in fifteen minutes, and did she want an extra place? Rosalind nodded distractedly, and pushed a whisky and soda at her unexpected guest. He turned his burning gaze upon her. 'And she had the nerve to accuse me!'

Rosalind sat uneasily in her chair. 'Can you tell me how you know all this?'

Connor nodded. 'She sent me some racehorses. The driver of the wagon let a few things slip. And Mary herself. Well, I knew she was no angel, but now she's full of her tales. It must be her face, makes her want to prove something. It's really tragic.'

'The man who did her make-up!' said David suddenly. 'I had a strange feeling about him at the time. Didn't believe it, though.'

'I know it's hard,' said Connor. 'A girl like that. But there's no use deceiving yourself.'

Rosalind put down her cup. She thought of all the times she had assumed that Mary was with Deborah, or in a group. She might have been with someone. On her own. She thought of her blithe assumption that George Reynolds and she merely had horses in common. Had she not wished her well on a day with him in the country? Suddenly she felt herself to be foolishly blind. If Mary was as Connor said, her aunt had given her freedom without restraint. 'You don't imagine she'll show herself up on this weekend?' she asked plaintively. 'Lady Murray-Gill is there. Surely she'll keep everything respectable?'

'She'll go off riding with him,' declared Connor. 'She knows how well she looks on a horse. I'd better get out there tonight.'

Rosalind glanced at the clock. 'You wouldn't be there before eleven. You'll have to go in the morning.'

'The morning! My God!'

'My good fellow, if Mary's really behaving as you say, I don't suppose one night's going to make any difference! Besides, you can't crash a houseparty at eleven o'clock at night. Whatever you think might be going on. It just wouldn't do.'

'God forbid that anyone should be embarrassed,' declared Connor, leaping up and striding about the room. 'The girl's lost all sense of decency, but why should that concern us? Embarrassment's the thing.'

Rosalind's mind whirled. She thought of Zwmskorski and the threat that hung over them still. Mary had been so sensible about it. Suppose that she was in fact tormented? Might she not be behaving as Connor supposed? Expecting to be ruined, she might think she had nothing to lose. What should Rosalind do?

Howard came in, in slippers and sports jacket, looking surprised at the unexpected guest. Alan trailed lackadaisically after him.

'Connor's staying the night, dear,' explained Rosalind. 'He's going to see Mary at Camborough Place in the morning. He's got something important to discuss.'

'In the middle of a houseparty?' said Alan, eating peanuts without bothering to offer them round.

'It can't wait,' said Connor grimly. In his mind's eye, whenever he forgot his anger, he saw Mary's face. He felt as if he could reach out and gently trace the pink outlines of her marks, like borders on a map. He thought of this Murray-Gill character, and the trainer, blank faces that he could not know. She was a mixed-up kid, that was all. He'd known that from the first. Why then had he let her go?

312

Chapter Thirty

A light wind was blowing across the park. Mary sat easily astride a thoroughbred mare, feeling her dance and sidle beneath her. There was really nothing like a blood horse, she thought to herself. Connor was right. If you wanted the ultimate in spirit and responsiveness, to feel as if the wind itself was harnessed to your hand, then nothing would do but pure thoroughbred blood. Although of course, she reasoned, watching Peter struggle with an over-oated hunter, the same applied if you wanted nerves and stupidity and unsoundness.

She put her mare into a half-pass and came up beside Peter. 'He's above himself. Will a gallop help?'

He looked at her, half in appeal, half in shame. 'Don't know. Might make him boil over.'

'We can swap, if you like. The mare should carry you. And I'm quite good with the nervy ones.'

'It's all right. You couldn't possibly . . .'

But at that moment, sensing his inattention, his mount half-reared and dropped a shoulder. Peter crashed off on to springy turf. 'Damn!'

Mary slid off her mare and helped him up. 'I'll take yours,' she said firmly. 'Really. I like idiot horses.'

'Everyone will know I couldn't manage him!'

'They thought neither of us could. They want us to have a horrible time, didn't you see the grooms laugh?'

'Yes. Are you sure you'll be OK?'

'Positive.'

Mary let him leg her into the saddle. She felt protective towards him, as if he was a favoured child. As expected, the horse was very light, she kept her hands like feathers and sat absolutely still. The slightest breath of movement brought a response. She wondered who in the stables thought of him as their very own, and kept everyone else off. If she and Connor hired a groom they must avoid possessive ones.

Peter was looking much more contented on the mare. Mary showed off a little, setting her horse into a collected canter, circling and changing leg. It was wonderful to elicit response with so little work! If Connor rode this hunter, she found herself thinking, he'd make the horse sit up and beg.

313

They set off after the others. The party was riding sedately through the park, a little trot here, a short canter there. That was never Mary's style. When she saw them at the end of a ride and her own horse started to pull, she shouted to Peter, 'Let's go!' and unleashed a rocket. They fizzed past the willows, hurtled through the oaks and took the curve of the lake with Mary's knee touching the rushes. A drumming of hooves told her that Peter was keeping more or less in touch. She was aware of startled faces ahead of her, and a general shifting of position. They thought she couldn't stop. She sat up and back, taking in rein and squeezing the horse up into her hands. He came back to her like a dream, as she had known he would. What a horse!

'Hello, everyone.' She took off her hat and grinned at them, happy, alive.

Someone said, 'What on earth's happened to your face?'

The smile froze. Mary put her hat back on and said quickly, 'I don't know. I suppose I'm too hot. This horse is hardly blowing, let's get on, shall we?' She should have known the make-up wouldn't withstand a hectic ride. She'd been too slapdash, she ought not to have put it on for something like this. But she couldn't bear to have people look at her in surprise and distaste. What would Peter do when he saw her? She didn't want to know.

She sent her horse forward in a high-stepping trot, leaving the others behind. Her inner turmoil made her hold him so tight between leg and hand that his stride began to bounce, he was floating like a dressage star. 'My word,' said the heir to the dukedom, 'she's an absolutely brilliant rider!'

Lady Murray-Gill, torn between admiration and chagrin at her son's poor performance, said, 'But what is the matter with her face?'

Mary kept her horse moving. She didn't care if she got lost, didn't care what happened so long as she didn't have to confront them all before she found a mirror. There was something so humiliating about being seen to have covered something up. It let people know she was ashamed of her marks, when all her life she had struggled to make it seem as if she didn't care. Of course she cared! Who wouldn't? But to be seen to do so was intolerable.

She pulled the horse to a walk and took up her leathers a couple of holes. She was going to jump her way home across the post and rail fences, none of the others would follow. At that moment she saw a Land Rover heading out from the stables across the fields. It seemed to be coming towards her. At once she set off, taking an oblique line, one eye on the Land Rover, the other on her goal, and nothing for the fences in between.

But she and the horse were of the same mind. They had faith in each other. Soon they were winging their way home, meeting each obstacle on an even stride, leaving it clean and clear. Despite herself Mary was exhilarated, she couldn't care about her face with a good horse in the summer air and the grass like a well-sprung bed. She sent the gelding dancing across a paddock, flying the far fence, looking at once for the next to jump. Suddenly she realised she had lost concentration. The Land Rover in the next field was pulling across her path. She would have to turn and retreat.

She pulled the horse up, and spun him round on his hocks. But then a familiar voice raked the air, like Irish butter mixed with coals of fire. 'Mary! Mary, you ride away from me again and so help me I'll skin you!'

She turned to stare back at him. Connor was vaulting the fence, putting mud on his good flannel trousers. She thought of her face and set her legs to the horse, but she was too urgent and he spun round in a bewildered circle. By the time she'd collected herself and him, Connor was there. He grabbed her reins and hung on.

'Don't you dare try and ride me down. You hellion!'

She didn't want to look at him. He would see what a fool she'd been, trying to hide what could never be hidden. But there was nothing else to be done. She gazed down at him, standing panting, his hair on end, eyes blazing with unspecified rage. 'What do you think you're doing?' she enquired icily.

'Stopping you making a complete fool of yourself,' he declared. 'My God, but you should be ashamed.'

'I was only riding the horse home,' she said awkwardly. 'Is it the horse that worries you? Or the ground? I haven't cut it up much.'

'I don't give a damn about the horse! Why is it always horses? It's time you came away from here and behaved yourself. I know what you've been doing.'

'Do you?' She didn't know what he meant.

'There's no point denying it. If that's the sort of girl you are. But in years to come you'll thank me for stopping you. When you've got over all this. When the urges aren't so strong.'

'What urges?' She fastened on to the one solid fact in this mish-mash of talk.

'Don't try and pull the wool, Mary Cooper! Tell me, was it worth it? In the cold light of day, wouldn't you rather have gone to bed alone?'

Her breath deserted her. She could feel a laugh bubbling deep inside, somewhere beneath her outrage. He found it so easy to believe the worst of her! It was what he expected! She struggled for a voice.

'You mean – instead of with Peter?'

'Yes! And then there's the man sold you the horses. If you wanted it that much, Mary – if it couldn't be denied – you could have come to me.'

She turned her head fully towards him, colour flooding into her skin. Her eyes were dark with unexpressed rage and her hands closed fiercely on the reins. 'That would have been an act of charity on your part!' she hissed. 'Going from one bitch on heat to another, with barely a pause in between. But you can get back to Dora with a clear conscience. I hate to disappoint you, Connor, but if I was dying of lust you'd be the last man I'd want. And, for your information, though it's no concern of yours, I have never slept with anyone. But I'll make sure I do before the day's out! The girl you think I am is having a whale of a time, it seems to me. I think I'll join her!'

She pulled the horse round, shaking Connor's hand from the reins with a well-aimed kick from her boot.

She galloped back to the stableyard without pause. As she arrived the grooms erupted from the tack room, coffee cups and cigarettes in evidence. 'One of you can cool this horse down,' snarled Mary. 'And I'll thank you not to give him to just anyone in future. You'll have him sent to the knacker as unmanageable.'

She left the horse standing wearily, head down, reins hanging in loops. She heard his groom rush up to him, chirruping in distress. It was the stupid little fat one, then. She must ride well. Mary pushed open the door of the stable cloakroom and confronted the mirror.

Sweat had lifted away most of her make-up. The mark beneath her eye was clearly visible, while her forehead V showed as a rising pink tide beneath the skin. Impatience had been her undoing, as in so many things.

She ran across the drive to the house. God forbid that anyone should see her until she reached the sanctuary of her room. But Deb was in the hall, resisting the attentions of the teaplanter. The moment she saw Mary she beamed, only for the smile to freeze on her face.

'I must dash,' said Mary, heading determinedly for the stairs. 'Connor's here. Can you field him, Deb?'

'Connor? Yes. But why? Mary?' She stared up at Mary's rapidly disappearing feet.

Once in her room, the door locked and the bath running, she felt calmer. She sat at her dressing table and creamed away the last of the make-up. Then she stared at herself, seeing the marks anew, wondering that such a slight discoloration could blight her so. Did Connor think her marks were behind everything? He probably imagined she offered her virtue as the only thing she had. He didn't know she could be pretty, when she chose. The trouble was, she knew her prettiness to be more than ordinarily superficial, when her marks, superficial themselves, were so much more. Bearing them all these years had caused damage that make-up could never erase.

316

She bathed, getting rid of sweat and horsehair, turning herself into a society girl once again. She stared at her long legs in the water, wondering if the bush of hair at their fork was repellently long and black. She knelt in the bath, trying to see herself in the mirror above the basin, taking in a section of herself from breast to crotch. Her breasts were so small still. She remained so very thin. Didn't Connor see that someone like Murray-Gill liked her because she was so unattractive? People like him married horsey, practical, ordinary girls. She was a useful everyday commodity.

She thought of Peter looking at her like this. He wouldn't despise her. But Connor would compare her to Dora, luscious, golden Dora, with her full breasts and insatiable desires. Didn't he realise she wasn't like Dora, inside or out? Or did he think all women were Doras in disguise?

She applied her make-up with stiff, angry fingers. No doubt he'd been sleeping with Dora again. Bound to have been. All the time she was here, safely out of the way, he did as he liked and then excused himself by imagining that she was doing much the same. She sat, drumming her fingers, waiting for a coat of make-up to dry. While she waited she began to mascara her lashes. On the next coat she painted her nails. At the last, lacquered, immaculate, she slipped into a dress of dark blue silk.

A knock came on the door. Deb's voice said, 'Mary? Mary, you really must come.'

'Nearly ready. Is Connor making a scene?'

'He had a go at me. I told him where to get off. But it isn't that. Mary, there's something in the paper. About us.'

The world seemed to stop for a moment. Mary felt very calm. She took a breath. 'Zwmskorski, of course. Well, it had to come. Don't worry, Deb. I'm coming down.'

She descended the stairs as if fifty people stood below, looking up at her. But there was only Deborah, flanked by the heir to the dukedom and his teaplanting rival. She was looking impatient, wanting rid of them, wanting to talk. The teaplanter said, 'This is all quite dreadful, of course. I am so sorry.'

Mary smiled a little, and swept gracefully past into the drawing room. Connor was standing glowering by the window, an untouched glass of whisky in his hand. Everyone else was reading the newspapers.

Lady Murray-Gill looked up, her jaw set. 'Miss Cooper,' she said in cool tones. 'There's been something of an upset.'

'Really?' Mary raised her eyebrows in mild interest. 'It's not that dreadful man Zwmskorski again, is it? I'm starting to think he's deranged.'

She took the paper from Lady Murray-Gill's fingers, much as she

317

would some distasteful rag. There was an enormous picture of Deb looking beautiful, and a much smaller one of herself, looking bored. They must have been taken at that first ball, she thought. Deborah had that look of wide-eyed delight that had lately turned to restlessness. The headline read SHAME OF SOCIETY GIRLS in large black letters.

Mary and Deborah Cooper, two of the season's brightest and most glamorous sirens, must today face the world knowing their secret is out. Despite their best efforts at concealment, it has been revealed that their mother, far from being the respected chatelaine of a Yorkshire estate, is in fact an ex-prostitute. One of London's most prominent club owners, Mr Wojtyla Zwmskorski, approached this newspaper with the shocking revelation that Mrs Laura Cooper, married for more than twenty years to Michael, of Gunthwaite Hall in Yorkshire, spent her youth in Paris, selling herself to the highest bidder in the notorious Rue de Claret. What's more, two old friends from those days are today resident in a cottage on the Gunthwaite Hall estate.

When questioned, a local said yesterday, 'We often wondered about them. Couple of right old tarts we've always thought them, but Mrs Cooper, well, we thought she was just being kind. And they add a bit of colour to the place. There've been stories, of course. Bound to be. But no one ever took them serious.'

The question now is, how seriously will these revelations be taken by Sir Robert and Lady Murray-Gill, whose son Peter is known to be keeping company with the vivacious Mary Cooper? Heir to a title that harks back to Norman times, Peter Murray-Gill cannot afford to besmirch the family escutcheon.

Beneath the article were three blurred photographs; one of Laura, looking alarmed, the others of Sophie and Marie, looking like elderly Frenchwomen and nothing more.

Mary looked up. Everyone was staring at her. But only Connor met her eye, his mouth twisting ruefully. What a day to come storming in, intent on saving the rags of her virtue! She giggled. It was all such a farce.

Lady Murray-Gill said, 'I'm glad you find it amusing. Perhaps you'd be kind enough to tell us exactly what has given rise to this vulgar article?'

'No,' said Mary. 'Actually, I wouldn't.'

Deborah let out a gasp. 'Mary! Mary, of course you must explain.'

'There's no of course about it,' retorted her sister. 'If people think it matters what my mother may or may not have done years ago,

318

according to some gangster club owner who ought to be in gaol, then I'm sorry for them. I'm me. What you see is what you get. Except Peter, I should tell you, I have some marks on my face, forceps marks, I cover them with make-up.'

'Oh,' he said feebly. Then, tellingly, he glanced at his mother. Mary felt her face stiffen. Whatever he thought about her, he would do as his mother said.

'What about these women?' said Lady Murray-Gill. 'Does your mother really harbour ex-prostitutes?'

'They live in one of our cottages, certainly,' declared Mary. 'As to what they used to do, I've really no idea. They were evacuated to us during the war. Fleeing Nazi intolerance, I believe. They seemed to think that the British weren't like that. A misconception, as we now can see. When I was little Marie used to tell me she set up the Resistance single-handed, but nowadays I'm a little more sceptical. They probably kept guns under the bed.'

'Oh, Mary, you disappoint me.' Connor moved around a sofa towards her. 'I believed all that! Are you saying they didn't marshal teams of butchers and bakers and teach them to blow up bridges?'

She chuckled. 'Connor, you know Marie can't so much as wind a watch. And Sophie can't be trusted with the stove.'

'There you are then.' He grinned down at her. 'Another illusion shattered.' He lifted his glass and drank to her.

The teaplanter moved to take Deb's unresponsive hand. 'So you see, Deborah! A storm in a tea-cup, no more.'

But Lady Murray-Gill said thinly, 'Miss Cooper is certainly very plausible. I wonder if she can also explain who this gentleman is? You certainly seem to be on very intimate terms with him.'

Connor beetled his brows. 'Intimate? What do you mean, intimate? If anyone's being intimate it's that frog-faced son of yours, who ought to know better. He's the one can't keep his hands to himself!'

Mary's blush ran from her toes to her scalp. Thankfully, only her neck turned red. 'How dare you all discuss my personal life?' she blazed. 'Whatever I may or may not have done, none of you has the right to question me about it in public!'

Peter said, 'Really Mother—' in anguished tones, and Connor looked at him with scorn. 'Is he the best you can do, Mary?'

Lady Murray-Gill rose to her feet. 'All things considered,' she said, 'I think it might be best if these young ladies returned home. In my experience these things never blow over quite as one would wish. It is a sad fact of life that rumours never die. No doubt your mother would like you with her at this difficult time, Mary.'

It was a public and pointed snub. Lady Murray-Gill didn't care whether or not what was said was true. The rumour itself was what mattered. She was not prepared to spend years reading allusions to it in the gossip columns at any mention of the Murray-Gill name. Mary wasn't prize enough for such a price to be paid. She was expendable.

Mary felt the tears welling, whatever she did. She pushed past them all to run outside and to everyone's surprise Peter put down his glass and followed her.

She was on the terrace, leaning against a gargoyle. He said awkwardly, 'I'm terribly sorry about all that, you know. I shan't mind if you cry.'

'My make-up will run,' said Mary tightly. 'And then you'd see what I really look like. Do you really care if my mother was a prostitute?'

He said, truthfully, 'I don't know. What's she like?'

'More of a lady than your mother will ever be! And that's the truth, Peter. If you met her you'd like her. Everyone does.'

'Including your Irish friend, no doubt?'

She took a breath, the urge to cry for a week receding into a dull ache. It was all right, provided she didn't think about it. Everyone looking. Everyone talking. Everyone knowing that Lady Murray-Gill had thrown her out. 'Connor's no one,' she said shortly.

'He's obviously in love with you.'

Her eyes met his in shock. 'Connor? He couldn't care less about me. He only pretends to be worried about my morals because his own are despicable, and I've told him so. Honestly, Peter. You must see that I'm not the sort of girl people fall for. Not me.'

He sighed, heavily. 'I think I've fallen for you. All the same.'

'Nonsense! You just thought I'd suit. The castle and all that.'

'There's a million girls would suit that. But they wouldn't suit me. Look, Mary, I won't say it would be easy, with my mother against you. But I'd be on your side. If you'd like – we could still get married.'

She turned to face him, looking up at him in sudden concern. She hadn't taken him seriously. She hadn't taken any of this seriously. It had been an interlude, occupying her mind and her time while she decided what she would really do in life. But this could be her life. If she chose.

His expression was anxious, like a gundog bringing a present from the garden that might or might not be well received. He was a kind, predictable man, she thought. Marrying her would be his cue to settle down to the kind of life his father lived. But she would be condemned to be a consort, living anonymously, her only claim to fame the disfavour of his mother, and her murky past. No doubt there'd be a portrait of her. In years to come, guides would pause briefly and say, 'Lady Mary Murray-Gill is of little interest. Her mother-in-law hated her, we understand.' Nothing else. Nothing she could achieve would make her notable in the Murray-Gill hall of fame. She thought, If I loved him I wouldn't care.

She looked up into his worried face. 'I'm sorry, Peter. I can't.'

'Is it Mother? I hope it's not me.'

'We couldn't be happy. Not if she feels the way she does. You don't want to lead a miserable life, Peter. I like you far too much to inflict it on you.'

'But if we tried – if you wanted to try—'

She took a deep breath. 'But I don't think I do. There. That's being honest. I couldn't wake every day and know we had to stand up to her. She and my grandmother would make a good pair, you know. She hated my mother just as your mother hates me. And it never worked out. I don't want that, and neither would you.'

'But, Mary—'

She put a hand over his mouth. There wasn't any point in saying more. From the house his mother called, 'Peter! It's time Miss Cooper was on her way. Everything's packed.'

'You see?' She smiled at him, elfin, courageous, her blue eyes full of light. Suddenly it was all too much. He turned away and hid his face.

Crammed into the Land Rover with Connor at the wheel, Deborah leaned over from the back seat and said, 'All right, then. How did he get out of it?'

Connor said, 'Give you three guesses. The family name.'

'He did offer it to me,' said Mary, studying her fingernails.

'What?' Connor swerved violently and Deborah yelped.

'Stop it, Con! You mean he proposed?'

Mary nodded. 'I said no. I couldn't bear to be at the mercy of his mother all my life. He was terribly sweet, actually. I like him much more than I did.' She sighed. 'I'm really going to miss him.'

No one said anything for a moment. Then Connor forced a crack of laughter. 'I suppose you know we don't believe you?'

Mary said distantly, 'I don't care whether you do or not. You may not have noticed, Connor, but I'm not very pleased with you right now. You've been a complete pain.'

'*I've* been a pain?' The car swerved again and Deborah moaned. He went on forcefully 'I haven't been gallivanting all over London! In fact, I managed to spend months here without ever once getting my name in the papers on a charge of dropping litter, let alone a major scandal. But don't let me worry you, Mary. The truth, in your mind, has always been a movable feast.'

'Like decent behaviour to yours,' she said sweetly. 'Or is that something you only expect from other people?'

'I wish you'd both shut up,' said Deborah quietly. 'I don't know why you have to squabble all the time. I don't even know why you're here, Con.'

'A little matter of four useless horses,' he retorted.

321

'Useless? The trouble with you, Connor, is you don't know a good horse unless it's got a ten thousand price tag. You have no judgment of your own at all.'

'If it's judgment we're talking,' flamed Connor, 'there's no judgment in buying something with carthorse feet on racehorse legs.'

'That horse will never go wrong! I'll stake my life on it.'

'If you don't shut up and let him drive, we'll all stake our lives on it!' shrieked Deborah. 'Will you both, for God's sake, shut up!'

They subsided, muttering. Connor turned his mind to driving and contented himself with cornering expertly at speed.

The mood, when Rosalind saw them, became leaden. The telephone rang constantly, friends, reporters, until Howard took it off the hook.

'Your mother might not have seen it,' said Rosalind anxiously. 'It won't be in the *Yorkshire Post*.'

'She's bound to find out sooner or later,' said Mary. 'But I won't ring. She mustn't think that it matters.'

Rosalind moaned. 'If only she knew! I never could stand the Murray-Gill woman. Anyone would think she was the queen.'

'It doesn't matter!' said Mary stoically. 'Most of the papers hint that Zwmskorski's a rat. I don't suppose anyone really important will take a blind bit of notice.'

But she was speaking out of bravado. She wondered if they ought to run home. Far better that than to be systematically excluded, although to run would look like an admission of guilt. And they had nothing to be guilty about! She tossed her head defiantly at an imagined world, only to see that Connor stood in the doorway, watching her.

'What are you doing?'

'Nothing much.' She pushed her fingers through her hair, feeling embarrassed, feeling trapped.

He came into the room, closing the door behind him. She struggled with her breathing. 'Your face looks great,' he remarked.

'As good as Dora's? Or is that too much to ask?'

'A great deal too much. I tell you that's finished but still you won't believe me. But then, you're such a liar yourself.'

'I am not!'

'You are so. I don't know what to believe about you any more.'

She went to the window and looked out into the gathering night. 'Why believe anything? I am what you see.'

'But for an expensive haircut and some very sophisticated paint. For once, just tell me the truth, Mary.'

'What about?'

'You very well know. But you'll make me say it, I suppose. Are you a virgin?'

322

She spun round to face him. 'You have no right to ask me that.'

'Granted. All the same.'

'Why should it matter? Either way?'

'Because – because I don't like to think of men having you.'

'But you expect me to like Dora having you?'

'It isn't the same!'

'You don't want it to be, you mean. Because that would sadly cramp your style.'

He stood looking at her, his hair falling into his eyes. He was too thin, she thought, bony shoulders, the muscles unshielded by comforting flesh. She thought of his black chest hair, and caught her breath. She thought of Dora's long, painted nails tangling in it. She hated him.

'I wish Dora had never happened,' he said thickly.

'Huh!'

'Can't you at least acknowledge my apology? I made a mistake! I'm sorry.'

'It doesn't matter to me.'

'But you matter to me. You matter more than anything. Are you pleased now? Two men in one day kneeling to you.'

Her mouth was dry. What was he saying to her? She didn't know what to think. 'You didn't believe me. About Peter.'

'Mary, Mary!' He came towards her, hands outstretched. 'How can I know when you're lying and when you're not? You turn me round in circles, you tie me up in knots. And I'm so lonely without you.'

But she put up her hands to fend him off, retreating behind a chair. She knew Connor too well. Most competitive of men, he was staking a claim he might not mean to hold. He was only waiting for her acquiescence to laugh at her. And then she would lie down and die.

'I don't care for you,' she said abruptly. 'So you can stop this. Leave me alone.'

'You don't mean that,' he said.

'You're so conceited, Con! I wasn't waiting for this, you know. I suppose you thought you were doing me a favour?'

'Why do you always have to fight me?'

She blazed at him: 'Because if I didn't, you'd use me as a doormat, Connor, and don't you dare deny it! You know it's true!'

He said nothing. He leaned on the mantel and looked at her. She felt a shiver run down her spine, wondering what he saw, what he was thinking. If only she was beautiful! When men looked at Deborah they could feast their eyes, there was no need to excuse thin legs, a flat chest, arms like twigs. When they rubbed Deb's cheek there was no danger that the paint would come off. Why wasn't Deb happy, she found herself thinking? How could it be that such beauty wasn't enough?

323

She said awkwardly, 'Zwmskorski. This might not be all he means to do.'

'What else is there?'

It was awkward. Difficult. A confidence. She said, 'He seemed very nice at first. And he's quite old and seems sophisticated. The sort of man – well, a young girl could fall for him. These things happen after all. Something happened – I haven't said this to Deb. But there might have been a camera. I keep thinking it's the sort of thing he'd do. Do you see?'

His face turned a dark, angry red. 'I see all right,' he said shortly. 'I see what a fool I've been. God, Mary!'

'What?' She looked at him bemusedly. 'What have you to be angry about?'

'I tell you I love you and you confess something like that!'

'Do you love me?'

He came towards her, caught her by the shoulders and then pushed her away. 'No! I refuse ever to love someone so undeserving!'

'But it wasn't me. It was Deb.'

After a moment, he took a long breath through his nose. He said, 'I need a drink.'

He had a whisky, and she a strong gin. She sat in the armchair, and he on the sofa, staring fixedly at the wall. Mary tried, haltingly, to explain about Deb. 'All these men, you see,' she managed. 'She finds it very hard.'

'So she goes to bed with a Polish crook?'

'No. Not quite. But – things happened. If any of it came out she'd die of shame.'

He thought for a moment. 'We need to know what's going on. We can't just sit here and let him do whatever he means to do. Where does he live?'

Mary shrugged. 'No idea. Deb went to his flat, but she couldn't find it again. We know his clubs of course. But I couldn't go there.'

'I could. Get changed, girl. I'll drive you up to town.'

Chapter Thirty-one

Mary was very tired. She wished vaguely that they had stayed at home, letting events take their course, instead of venturing out into a chill evening breeze with no real purpose in view. She wound up the window and hunched down a little in her seat. The lights of Leicester Square winked and glittered, and she shivered even though she was warm. She half expected to see her old self walking along the pavement, a tall, thin girl in chambermaid's shoes, her bag full of leftover food, if she was lucky. She touched Connor's sleeve.

'Stop here. There's a girl I know. Works the station.'

He looked at her sardonically. 'The way people do.'

He wouldn't drop her off, and insisted on finding a parking space. Mary was impatient, too late and Sandra wouldn't be there. She moved off to the back streets after ten.

Parked at last, they walked quickly back to the station. Connor's presence felt comforting, insurance against yesterday, living proof that those days were gone. But it all seemed horribly familiar. She found herself looking nervously at the men walking past. Stevie was somewhere about. Zwmskorski. Despite herself, she was afraid.

The usual knot of girls stood about amidst the pillars and the timetables, smoking, talking, some of them almost respectable, some like caricatures of women, all high heels and nipped in waists and bulging blouses. Sandra was slumped against a pillar, the roots of her hair showing black against blonde dye. When she saw Mary she looked at her at first without recognition. Then she said, 'Hello, love! What are you doing here? He's not put you on the game, has he?'

'Him?' Mary glanced at Connor. He was looking inscrutable, which usually meant he disapproved. She said, 'Actually he does like pushing women around. But we wanted to talk. Fancy a coffee?'

Sandra glanced round. 'OK,' she conceded. 'Ten minutes, that's all. It's a slow night. And I don't get the hotel trade like I did. Now the escort work should have worked out nicely, no standing about ruining your feet, but I couldn't take to it. You'd be a winner, Mary love. Nice and posh.'

They bore her off to a coffee bar, still talking, and bought her coffee and cake. She sat facing the window, watching nervously in case Stevie came by. 'How's it going with him?' asked Mary.

325

Sandra shrugged. 'Up and down. He did three months a while back. Peaceful, it was. But I missed him.'

'You must be mad,' said Mary honestly, and Sandra laughed. 'He's not so bad! You bring out his nasty side. Too posh. He can be nice, can Stevie.'

Mary did not reply. Connor, who had so far taken a back seat, said, 'We've come to ask you about someone, Sandra. A Polish club owner.'

'Oh. Him.' She made a face. 'Keep clear of him. None of the girls will work his clubs no more. Sooner or later he calls you up to his rooms and you end up in hospital. He's that sort.'

'Do you know where he lives?' asked Mary.

'Now why would you want to know that?' Sandra looked wary. 'You want that sort of thing and you're talking money.'

'Sandra!' Mary was shocked, but the girl was unrepentant.

'I don't have no young man taking care of me,' she said with feeling. 'I got Stevie taking everything I earn! And no nice hotel work nowadays. You want that address, you pay for it.'

Sighing, Mary looked at Connor. He reached for his wallet. Sandra said, 'There! Isn't that nice. Lives on Fulham Broadway, he does. Very smart flat. Sends the girls down the fire escape when he's done with them. One or two ain't never been seen again.'

They walked back to the car in silence. Mary felt worse than ever. The hour was late, she'd been up since dawn, and the day had brimmed with events. She felt the need to assimilate some of them, and distance herself in sleep. But Connor was wide awake and determined.

'He won't be at his flat now,' reasoned Mary. 'He has clubs to run. And even if he was there, I don't want to see him.'

'All the same. I want to see what he's like.'

But before she could reply she shrank back in her seat. Stevie was walking down the pavement towards them. Mary let out a little, strangled shriek.

He stopped by the car, looking down at her. 'Drive off,' said Mary in a whisper. 'It's Stevie. Please, Con!'

Instead, he got out of the car. 'Good evening to you,' he said easily.

'She was never so polite,' said Stevie. He was fingering something in his pocket. 'Been talking to Sandra, I hear.'

Connor leaned on the car roof, apparently relaxed. 'Sandra's a nice sort of girl,' he remarked. 'But Mary's always needed discipline. She can get very out of hand.'

'Can't they all?' said Stevie, and laughed.

After a moment he said, 'And I'm not the only one she's crossed. You should be careful, you should. Now the Pole's after her.'

'But no one remembers yesterday's stories.'

'He's got more up his sleeve than that!' retorted the man. 'Pictures, they say. Word is, he means to take the whole family to the cleaners.'

'What sort of pictures?'

Stevie grinned. 'Now, how would I know that? You'll just have to wait until they turn up in the papers. Won't you, me old china?'

Suddenly his hand came out of his pocket. He jabbed something at the window, up against the glass beside Mary's face. It was a knife. She fell back, gasping, and Stevie chuckled. 'Discipline. That's what they need. Women need to be kept in order.'

He sauntered off down the street, dapper, sure of himself. Mary had never hated anyone as much as him. He was such an unsophisticated villain, without apology, without pretence. Stevie was a distillation of all that was worst in people: the cowardice, the self-interest, the ignorance and lack of love. Even the Pole, for all his scheming, wasn't so utterly without good qualities. Hadn't he delivered babies, and done it well? If Stevie had ever committed an act of kindness, Mary was sure it had been by mistake.

Connor started the car and said, 'Nasty little chap, that.'

'Yes.' She shivered and slid down in her seat. 'We're not going to the flat, are we? I don't feel very brave.'

'Imagine how Deborah will feel if those pictures hit the newsstands.'

Mary was silent for a moment. She felt cold and her head was aching. If the pictures were really obscene, Zwmskorski might not publish them at all. He had merely to send them to a few selected addresses – one of them Gunthwaite Hall – and Deborah would be ruined. Every time she showed her face in public someone, somewhere would turn and murmur, 'Did you see those photographs? Unbelievable.'

She wondered what Connor meant to do. Ransack the place? Appeal to Zwmskorski's better nature? Nothing else occurred. He drove off, saying nothing, and she wished with all her heart that she was a child again, in the orchard at home, with life an uneaten apple. She had been happy, and hadn't known it. Now it seemed impossible that she could ever be again.

They parked on the pavement outside the flats, seeing how characterless the place was. People resided here, living their lives in some other, more vibrant place. Or perhaps the people here remained encapsulated in their sterile homes, taking little from the world and returning nothing. As they approached the door of the flat, Mary knew instinctively that no one here would respond to a scream. Whatever Zwmskorski wanted to do he could.

She tugged at Connor's sleeve. 'He won't be in. Let's go.'

But Connor knocked firmly, and after a moment the door opened on the chain. 'Yes?' Mary flinched at the foreign intonation.

'Mr Zwmskorski? I've brought Mary Cooper to see you.'

327

At once the door swung wide.

He was wearing a red silk dressing gown. It suited him, lifting the pallor of his cheeks and restoring colour to his hair. He had the cold, severe good looks of a foreign aristocrat, thought Mary. One of the crueller Tsars. Here was a man who wouldn't hesitate to bury peasants alive.

'Would you like my fingerprints too?' he asked bleakly, responding to her stare.

'I should think the police have those already,' she retorted, and then wished she had held her tongue. There was no need to alienate the man still further.

He held her gaze until she dropped her eyes. 'No looks, and intelligence you don't use,' he remarked. 'So unlike your lovely sister.'

Connor, ignored, went to the hall table and turned over some papers.

The impertinence ruffled the Pole, he said sharply, 'I'll thank you to leave that alone. Come into the drawing room, if you must.'

It was a large, half-panelled room with windows overlooking the park. A huge painting of a cavalry horse dominated one wall, the rider with blood dripping from a wound, the horse wild-eyed and foaming. It was lurid yet arresting. Mary said, 'That's amazing.'

'You think so?' Zwmskorski glanced at her oddly. 'You surprise me. The English are so suburban about art. Watercolours and landscapes.'

Connor said, 'You've a taste for blood, I see.'

Zwmskorski laughed. 'And now who is being melodramatic?'

'It comes from reading so many newspapers,' said Con. 'But you'll be glad to know that Mary had no intention of marrying Murray-Gill – article or none. So that was a pretty damp squib.'

The Pole inclined his head. 'But something brought you here. I wonder what?'

Connor turned on his heel and surveyed the room. Polished tables stood about, and on them rested sculptures, horses, busts; arresting, burgeoning shapes. The floor was strewn with silk rugs and on the wall above the picture rested two crossed swords, their hilts gilded and engraved. 'Well,' he said, letting his admiration show, 'you have no need for blackmail at all events.'

'Blackmail? An interesting choice of words. I see you are aware that I possess – some interesting snaps.'

'Can we see them?' demanded Mary. 'It's only fair.'

'I don't keep them here. Naturally.'

Mary dropped her eyes and turned away. He said, in a harsh, uncompromising voice, 'Who told you about the pictures?'

Mary said nothing. But Connor said, 'Stevie. A pimp.'

'Dear me. The company you keep. Wait one moment.' He went to the telephone, dialled, and then spoke briefly to someone.

'What will happen to him?' asked Mary fearfully.

Zwmskorski said, 'I've really no idea. Such things are best left to others. Do sit down, or do you mean to stand all evening?'

Mary sat edgily in a chair. Connor, more relaxed, leaned back on the sofa. Zwmskorski went to a cupboard and poured three glasses of vodka. Mary drank cautiously. The spirit was strong enough to make her gasp. Zwmskorski said conversationally, 'Your sister is a slut, of course. She needed no persuasion to come here. Your mother was just the same, prancing about in Paris before the war, wearing a pert little hat. Then back to the brothel to let fat old men use her body. She was sold as a virgin every night for a month, I believe. She had the tightest—'

'Shut up!' Connor got to his feet and advanced on him. 'You'll not infect us with your filth. I know Mrs Cooper, and she was never what you say. Whatever she did, she had to do. I'm sure of that.'

'Dear me.' Zwmskorski struck a camp attitude, his hand against his cheek. 'Your boyfriend's in love with your mother, child. Or perhaps she obliges him in – certain ways.'

In a bored voice Mary said, 'He has Aunt Dora to see to that. But then, you'd know all about her. And I daresay she could tell some tales about you, couldn't she? We might ask her to.'

'My dear girl.' He was contemptuous. 'Pictures of Deborah today against tales from a very long time ago? There's no comparison. Besides, I like to see what people will do when threatened. Especially people who once threatened me.'

Connor got to his feet. 'Mary. Time to leave.'

'But we haven't—'

'He's not going to do a deal. Take my word for it. He's going to torment us for as long as it suits him. And then some.'

'At last!' said Zwmskorski. 'Someone who appreciates that life is about power. Deborah – such a sweet girl, and so very, very stupid. She can have her fun. But let her remember that sooner or later everything will come out. That's my promise.'

Connor frogmarched Mary out to the lift. She tried to talk all the way down but he would have none of it. At last, in the street, she burst out, 'You didn't try to persuade him! And now we have to tell Deb about the pictures and tell her there's nothing we can do!'

'We need not tell her,' said Connor.

'And then what? Wait until she's engaged to some earl and watch the whole thing fall apart? That's what he means, Con. He's waiting to do maximum damage.'

He unlocked the car and pushed her inside. Mary was shivering again, with anger and fright. 'We must tell your mother,' he said. 'She knows him better than us. So does Dora. They may come up with something.'

'We can't tell Mum,' said Mary heavily. 'Deb would be so ashamed.'

'Dora, then. Anyway. I think you and Deb ought to lie low for a bit. And there's four horses to see to.'

'Your job,' said Mary.

'I was going to leave.'

'And will you? Now?'

He said nothing. A light rain began to fall. Lulled by the tyres on the road, soothed by every yard between her and the city, Mary fell quietly asleep.

Harvest was in full swing. The giant combine, on contract from another farm, clattered and rumbled through the yard and out to the barley. Michael stood in the arch of the barn, feeling his stomach knot with nerves. They should have been here last week. The crop was steely days ago, heaven knows what had been lost since then. At least when the horses ruled he had sent them in as and when he pleased, without waiting on a neighbour's pleasure. He hated to admit how much he wanted to go into the kitchen and tell Laura of a good yield; how much he would hate to report that it was light.

Mary came sauntering out of the kitchen door. She was wearing shorts and a loose white blouse, her hair tied up on her head in a frivolous knot. It showed off her marks quite clearly, but for some reason she didn't seem to care. It was as if, knowing she could hide them, she no longer felt the need.

'Doesn't the air smell good?' She put an arm around his neck to give him a brief hug.

'Diesel and bad temper.'

'Your nerves are showing. Don't worry, Dad! There's hardly any gone down. Now, last year you had a right to complain. Whole fields were laid.'

He put his hands in his pockets and sighed. 'Aye. And that gave me an excuse for poor yields. This year – do they laugh at me, Mary? In the village? The poor old fool who still won't put anything but muck on his land?'

'I'm a London girl,' said Mary expansively, spreading the legs of her shorts in a mock curtsey. 'No one knows anything about farming in London. No, I tell a lie. Peter Murray-Gill was an expert on deer. And he'd approve of the way you farm. But then, they're horribly rich.'

'Sounds a good fellow,' said Michael awkwardly. 'Pity nothing came of it.'

They had given a censored version of events at Camborough Place.

330

The scurrilous newspaper article was no doubt circulating in Bainfield and beyond, but no trace of it had filtered through to Gunthwaite. Mary wouldn't have been surprised to discover that old Mrs Tims at the Post Office had removed the paper from sale, as she had when a local man had been convicted of rape in Nottingham. 'His family don't need the upset,' she had declared. 'That's more important than a bit of news. Rubbish they writes, all of them.' And that had been that.

Mary wandered to the gate and stood looking across the fields. How had she survived without this wonderful, cleansing air? Connor was bringing two horses in, but the combine was clattering wildly and he had been forced to retreat into a gateway. She watched him hanging on to the pair, pulled this way and that. His voice came faintly to them: 'Whoa! Steady, my boys. Steady.'

She felt her usual unspecified irritation. What was it about him? Just to see him, bare-headed and competent, annoyed her.

Michael said, 'So. Will you be home long? We expected a card from Biarritz.'

'We were homesick, Dad. For the farm. And everyone.'

'We're always here for you, lass. You know that. But we'd have been here after Biarritz. What are you not telling me?'

She felt her blush rising. 'Nothing. Really. Nothing.'

'Well, your mother's glad to have you home at any rate. Tell me when you're ready, Mary. Nothing will change.'

But he spoke from ignorance, she thought. If he knew about the newspaper, if he knew about Deb, if he looked into that part of his daughter's life that should always be private, hidden from her parents, before anyone, there would be no going back. Laura would be wrecked. Deborah would be walled off from them by shame. The wall was there now, if Michael but knew. Mary could see it in Deb's awkward, silent stance. She kept imagining that they knew.

Deborah walked quickly through the fields. Below she could hear the combine, crashing through the day with all its mechanised lack of care. She walked to be away from it, out of earshot of anything manmade. She wanted to be free of the idiocy of communal living, with its strictures, its restraints, its littleness. What was society but a group of silly people, banded together by sillier rules and sillier prejudice? She was well out of it, she thought grimly. She hadn't liked it at all.

But what did she like? She felt miserable and restless. Even as the din of the combine receded, to be replaced by the trilling of the skylark high in the blue, she felt at odds with the world. There was nothing for her here. The world she had hoped for had failed her too. It was all very well to be admired and talked about, to be approached by this man and that, trying to be special to you, trying to be noticed. But in the end, what was it for? Not for her, the real Deb, product of this place. She felt like a cardboard cutout of a woman, without substance of any kind, and she knew that if she had been just that no one would have cared. She would still have been beautiful; men would have imagined owning her and delighted in the thought. No one would have cared that she was nothing.

She sat on a tussock of grass and hunched over her knees. She felt so tense and miserable. Alan had telephoned the night before, ostensibly to see if they had arrived safely, in reality to press his suit. Something he had said lingered with her: 'Nobody knows you as I do, Deb. You want to remember that. When it comes down to basics, none of the others ever looks beyond your face.' But Alan knew no more of her than the others did. He liked to think that he had noticed her in childhood, but it wasn't true.

She had never before thought that she wished to be Mary. But she did, she did! Mary was Mary, liked or loathed, everyone who met her fell into one or other camp. But Deborah was always bland; the pretty, good girl. That was what she had been for years, only for it all to fall apart. If only they knew!

Someone was coming across the turf towards her. She stared at the figure, dark against the sun. Wide shoulders, thick with a young man's muscle, a narrow waist arrowing down into long, long legs. She felt a lurch of attraction before she recognised him, and hated herself anew. It was Piers.

He sat down beside her, saying nothing. She had forgotten how calm he was with silence. She was always uncomfortable, longing to fill up the space with chatter. But chatter was the last thing on her mind. She couldn't pretend.

At last Piers said, 'I've missed you terribly. Did you miss me?'

She lifted her shoulders in a shrug. 'I don't know. It was all so different. So many people.'

'Alan, I suppose.'

'Him. Lots of others. I felt like a prize cow at a big show.'

'Were you miserable?'

She glanced at him. He was looking down across the valley, not at her at all. 'Yes, actually. Sometimes I was.'

'Good. You deserved to be.'

'Thanks very much!'

His blue eyes turned to her. She realised that his calm disguised raw anger. A muscle was flickering at the corner of his eye and she suddenly thought, He might kill me. Out here, far from anyone, he could do anything. Her heart came up into her throat.

'I didn't owe you a thing,' she said tremulously. 'Just because a few things happened – kids' things – it didn't mean I'd stay.'

'You can't ever be honest, can you, Deb? You said you loved me. You said you wanted me with you forever. And now you're saying it was all schoolgirl rubbish.'

'Yes! No. We were both so lonely, Piers. You know we were. All the trouble with Mary and your mother. When you asked if I'd missed you – I'm not even sure I know you very well. I know there were letters, hundreds of letters, but that isn't the same. Sometimes I don't understand about you. Like now.'

'What about now?'

'I keep thinking you're going to lean over and strangle me.'

He sat so very still. She couldn't breathe, felt all the terror of Zwmskorski rise up again, now, with weeks of imagination to enhance it, more vivid and more real than at the time. She folded in on herself, hiding her face against her knees, letting out a low, strangled moan. Piers said, 'What's the matter? What is it?'

She found she was crying, great gasping sobs. 'I'm so afraid,' she murmured, and then in a scream of release, 'I'm so afraid!'

'Of me? Honestly, Deb, you're going loopy. You know I won't hurt you!'

'Won't you? You're so angry. Everyone's angry. It's all my fault.'

He was bewildered. He had come here today, hurt and sore, wanting to have it out with her, once and for all. If she was tired of him then he wanted to know. He couldn't go on in limbo, waiting and hoping for something she did not mean to give. But she seemed to think he meant to murder her. Why?

He put an arm tentatively round her shoulders. She wailed, like an animal in pain, so he put his other arm around her and held her like a child. 'I love you,' he said simply. 'Don't worry, Deb. I love you, and whatever's happened I'm not going to mind.'

'You will! You'll hate me. Everyone will.'

'If you tell me then you'll know. You can't not tell me now.'

'I'm so ashamed! Oh, Piers, I didn't care, you see, I didn't want to care. It was all so hard. I just wanted – it was all so – I didn't mean to let him touch me!'

His head was against hers, he was holding her, rocking her. He realised he didn't care what she had to tell. Whatever she had done, to have her here, needing him, confiding in him, filled him with strength. He could take anything she had to say.

'So,' he said. 'You had sex with someone?'

'No! No. Not that far.'

'Then what? What we used to do?'

She clung to him, her face against his shoulder. He could barely hear what she whispered. 'I let him – touch me. With his mouth. And then I ran away. And – and I think now – that he took pictures. Oh, Piers, Piers, if people see what I did I shall die!'

333

He held her very close. Her tears were soaking through his shirt and he could feel her breasts soft against his chest. He should have been angry, he realised. She should have felt for him the exclusive passion that he felt for her. She did not. She had not. And yet, he was the one she had told.

He said, 'Why did you do it? Were you in love with him?'

She was calming and pushed a little away from him, dragging wet strands of hair from her face. 'I hardly knew him,' she confessed. 'But he knew me. He used to live round here during the war, he's got some grudge against us. He's physically very attractive. He – he excited me. I thought I could do it with him, and no one would ever know.'

'Not even me.'

'No. Not even you.'

A gentle breeze was stirring the hairs on his arms. A shudder ran through him. Deborah the child was a child no more. He remembered how easily he had led her on in the wood. She had done what he wanted because she wanted it too. The untrammelled, unawakened virgin, because of him and in spite of him, had become a beautiful woman with deep sexual needs, the expression of which seemed so unacceptable that she had given herself to a stranger.

Suddenly he pushed his hand between her legs. She fell back on the grass, looking up at him with wide eyes. 'You let him,' said Piers, rubbing his palm against the lace of her underwear, 'and he cared nothing for you.'

'Do as you like,' said Deb bitterly, closing her eyes and turning her face to the soil. 'If you want me you can have me. I'm that sort of girl, anyone will do. So the first one might just as well be you.'

'You don't mean that.' He took his hand away and she gave a little moan.

'Don't I?' She sat up and looked at him. 'I'm so miserable, Piers. I keep thinking about what he did. I go over it again and again. And I want it again. I hate myself for wanting it but I do.'

She stared up at him, hardly caring what he thought of her. Perhaps some of it was his fault, anyway. He had lit the tiny flame that was now a fire that threatened to consume her. His kisses, his fumblings, his pleas for her to touch, to stroke, to hold, had all conspired to bring her to this. Besides, nothing mattered any more. She was degraded and lost.

She stood up and began to unfasten her blouse. She slipped it off and let it fall to the ground, closing her eyes and lifting her face to the sun. She lifted her arms to push them through her tear-soaked hair, and he thought he had never seen such a goddess. She was wanton and irresistible.

334

'We'd better go up to the rocks,' he said shortly. 'No one ever goes there.'

'I don't care. Really I don't.' She spun round, arms held high, utterly abandoned.

He realised she was almost hysterical. He put his arms around her waist and pulled her to him and she became still. He could hear her uneven breathing. She said, 'Don't worry, Piers. I'm sure this is right.'

He led her to a fold of dry earth between two rocks. They were hidden from everywhere but the empty sky, bright with sunshine. She took off her clothes, quickly, urgently, feeling no trace of the fever that had sent her to Zwmskorski. Piers took off his shirt, and held her to him. Her breasts were cradled against his chest, but her sex was chafed by his denims. She pushed herself hard into him, relishing the pain.

'Stop it,' he said. 'There's no need to hate yourself. God, you don't know what I've done lately.'

'I hope you've had women,' she said shortly. 'Then you'll know what to do with me.'

'I know. Believe me, I know.'

He pushed her to the earth, pulling his jeans open. The size of him made her tremble. He nudged at her body, probing, cautious, and for the first time she was afraid. Why was she doing this? What was it for? He grunted and she spread her legs wide, pushing off the ground, tensing against him, his face an inch from hers. He whispered, 'It's all right. Really.'

And for the first time in her life a man pushed aside her defences and entered her.

He asked if it hurt her. She shook her head. She couldn't speak, she never wanted to speak again. He began to move in her, and the sensation took her by surprise. She held on to his shoulders, uttering little groans, suddenly aware that her body was made for this. He and she fitted together like two halves of a whole. She had spent years waiting for someone to fill her up. Why had she waited so long?

Feeling was radiating from deep within. Some part of her, some sore and damaged part, was bathed in the warmth and rightness of it all. What the Pole had done was a travesty of this. Each gave to the other, and was complete.

When her climax came she was past caring. Just to be joined to this man was satisfaction enough. She felt him throbbing inside her, and for the first time, wondered what they had done. But at that moment nothing more mattered.

He rolled away from her, gasping. She said slowly, 'I didn't realise. I didn't know.'

'Neither did I.'

335

'But I thought—'

'I'd never done it before. I wouldn't, with anyone but you. That's the difference, you see, Deb. I love you.'

She knelt up on the dry earth, spreading her arms, delighting in the warmth of the sun on bare breasts, bare arms, her bloody crotch. 'I might love you,' she declared. 'I can't tell. It felt so right, didn't it? The two of us?'

'Yes.'

They dressed slowly. He put an arm around her; she knew he could easily want her again. But she wanted to keep this time special and of itself. She wanted to lie in bed and think of every moment. Then she would be ready again.

They walked down the hill and stopped at the top of Stony Slide.

'Will you tell anyone?' he asked.

She shook her head. 'It's too special.'

'Next time I'll use something.'

'Will you? I hadn't thought. I don't think I could ever have a baby. But if I did I wouldn't mind.'

'Oh, Deb.' He looked at her and laughed. She realised she had hardly seen him laugh in months. 'You're such an idiot sometimes.'

'I don't feel an idiot now,' she confessed. 'It's better, isn't it? Being together like this.'

He turned away, admitting gruffly that it was.

Deborah went into the house. Her mother was in the kitchen, making bread, and heard her run upstairs. She went into the hall. 'Deborah? Are you all right?'

'Yes, Mum. Fine.' She appeared on the upstairs landing, bright-eyed, a little flushed, a different girl from the tense and miserable figure of this morning. 'Shall we go into Bainfield this afternoon?' she asked brightly. 'It might be fun.'

Her mother agreed, wondering privately what had happened. She had never thought that Deborah would cause her great anxiety. Mary was the child who bore the burdens in this household. But it seemed that not even Deborah's beauty had insulated her from life. Although she was smiling now, wasn't she? She had come home. Against all her instincts, Laura struggled for an optimistic frame of mind.

Chapter Thirty-two

Gabriel got stiffly out of the car. He was feeling old today, the result of a hangover. He had spent the best part of yesterday in Leeds, negotiating the purchase of a derelict factory that was certain to be a prime site for a shopping centre, and the deal completed, he'd come home to celebrate. Needless to say, with Dora bored and snide, and the constraints of a house that wasn't really his, there had been precious little celebration.

He sighed, and breathed deep of the clean, morning air. Time was he'd spent his days making more than money. There were planes flying today that wouldn't have got off the ground but for his technical input. But this was easier – if much less satisfying. Nothing won without pain ever counted for anything, he thought.

Mary came out of the barn, leading a neat little horse. When she saw him she stopped, her expression hardening. 'What do you want?'

'Nothing that's any business of yours.'

'I doubt that very much.'

At that moment Connor came out also, leading a much larger horse with feet like dinner plates. 'Good morning, sir,' he said politely and Mary turned on him.

'You talk like a stable lad, damn it! He of all people doesn't need to be called sir. I won't have it.'

'Shut up, Mary,' said Connor dispassionately. 'It's his money we live by, I'll have you remember. Would you like to see these two go, Mr Cooper?'

'He'll see them when we're good and ready and not before,' declared Mary.

'We are good and ready,' said Connor. 'I hope you'll excuse her, sir. She's in a temper this morning. She can't take being bested.'

'In what?' asked Gabriel, wishing he could clear the fog from his brain. These two needle wits were exhausting.

'In a race of two horses, the faster one is usually victorious,' said Mary sweetly. 'He was on the faster, that's all.'

'Of course, if I'd ridden the other it would also have been the best,' went on Connor. 'She has the innate ability to make a good horse relax to the point of idleness.'

Mary glared at him, ready to fight on, only to see that he was

337

laughing at her. He ran rings round her, did Connor. 'I hate you to death!' she declared, and swung up on to her little horse.

'Is Michael about?' called Gabriel, as she prepared to clatter from the yard.

'At market,' she shouted back. 'But you never have mastered the telephone, have you? Or was it Mum you wanted to see all the time?'

'Have some manners, Mary Cooper,' barked Connor, mounting and riding in her wake. He put his legs to his horse and it bucketed three canter strides, neatly cutting Mary off at the gate. Not to be outdone, the moment they were through, she sent her little horse nipping past him, and trotted briskly down the track.

As the sound of their hooves faded Gabriel went into the kitchen. Laura was sitting at the table, reading yesterday's paper. She looked up and said, 'There's tea in the pot. Pour yourself some.'

He did as he was told. The room was peaceful but untidy, covered in everyone's bits and pieces. After a while Laura put down the paper. 'Was it Michael you wanted to see?'

'Not really. I was feeling lonely. I clinched a big deal yesterday and no one cares.'

'Poor you.'

He grinned. 'I thought so. I want to be congratulated. I'm almost a tycoon.'

'Well done!' said Laura, clapping her hands in mock delight. 'Will I like you when you've become one altogether?'

'I don't know. Do you like me now?'

She considered, putting her head on one side in one of her few remaining French gestures. 'If you weren't here I'd miss you,' she conceded. 'Will that do?'

'Oh, yes.'

They grinned at one another. Laura thought how strange it was that after everything, they should have managed to come to this. They were easy together; but that ease was spiced with wariness, because each knew that a passing breeze could fan the embers of the old romance. There was something a little delicious in the knowledge, she thought, and at once cringed inwardly. How could Michael trust her? There was nothing in her to trust.

Gabriel said, 'Why have the girls come home? Do you know?'

'What?' Laura gathered her wits. 'I really don't know. I thought it was because Mary had a run-in with some young man, but she doesn't mention him. And Deb's been very odd. And I had a peculiar 'phone call from Rosalind, too. I'm not sure she wants the girls back.'

Gabriel snorted. 'I could have told her she'd never cope with Mary! That girl is a complete rogue.'

Laura chuckled. 'Not such a rogue as she was, I don't think. Oh, Gabriel, don't you think she's looking lovely? When she does herself up, I'm not surprised Connor's besotted.'

'Him? Good God. I thought they fought all the time.'

'They do. It's all part of it. Surely you can see?'

He felt angry suddenly. How was it possible that other men could gain Mary's affection when he earned only her venomous dislike? He never had any real success with women. Mary would do anything rather than please him. Dora would do nothing that caused her any personal inconvenience. And Laura had never for one moment thought more of him than Michael. Even after all these years, all the little victories, he could never overcome that.

He got briskly to his feet, although his head was throbbing and his mouth tasted foul. 'I'm taking you out to lunch,' he said determinedly. 'I insist.'

'And I won't let you,' said Laura.

'But you must! Run upstairs and change your shoes or something. Michael won't mind. I'd take him too if he was here. Please, Laura. Rosalind asked me to talk to you.'

It was a lure, designed to catch a prize salmon. Laura resisted, but of course she wanted to go. He tempted her with a restaurant on the Harrogate road, with a French chef and good wines. 'Just the sort of place where we can talk.'

'But what did Rosalind say exactly? You never said she'd rung?'

'I was going to tell you over lunch.'

At last she went upstairs and changed. Gabriel scrawled a note and left it on the kitchen table: 'Mike – came to take you and Laura out to lunch, and failing you, couldn't disappoint your good lady. Expect us back mid-afternoon.'

As they were leaving Piers drove the tractor into the yard. He looked brown and happy, light years away from the sulky youth he had been when first he started here. When he saw his father his face changed. He came across and said, 'Going off somewhere?'

'Lunch, that's all. I've left a note for Mike. How are you, Piers?'

'Pretty well. I need to talk to you, as it happens.'

'Oh?' Gabriel had never known anyone with worse timing. 'When we get back, perhaps. Or another day. You can always 'phone.'

'I work until seven and by then you're usually drunk.'

'Don't exaggerate, Piers! Good God, when I think of your benders my occasional whisky seems positively respectable. I said, I'll talk to you another time.'

He got in the car, moving quickly as if afraid that Laura would escape if left too long. Piers stood looking after them. The air was heavy with coming rain, the beeches sighed and rustled as the wind blew up. He had to get a hundred bales of hay under cover before the storm, with only one man to help. He looked at the house and thought of Deborah, wishing they could find an hour, even half, to be together. But the house remained closed and silent. Did she love him? If she did, wouldn't she sense that he was there? It seemed impossible that she could exist and not know that he stood yards away, thinking of her, yearning for just a smile.

Mary and Connor were clattering back into the yard, their horses sweating. Try as he would he couldn't see riding as work. They frittered their days in play with never a thought for anything but themselves. Suddenly angry, he called out to them: 'There's a field of hay to get in before the rain. You can give me a hand.'

'Can we now?' Mary was pert and difficult. But then, she always was.

Connor, possibly to spite her, said, 'You'll have to move sharp. I'm with you.'

'What about you, Mary?'

'Oh, if he can toss bales then so can I. And Deb.'

'We don't need Deb!'

But Mary had slipped from her horse to run to the house and shout: 'Deb! Deb, Piers has got in a mess with the hay. Come down, will you?'

She took her time, but was ready by the time the horses were put away. She smiled lazily at Piers and he felt his skin prickle. Oh, if she didn't mean to love him, she should never have given herself. He might have recovered before, but now? Now he was infected through and through, there was no part of him that did not burn and ache for her.

Out in the field, tossing leaden bales on to a sledge, he stayed close to Deb. She had her hair tied up with a scarf, just as she had when she fell from the horse. She knew he was watching her. It was in every swing of her hips, every turn of her head. When their eyes met he was on fire!

Mary, taking a rest after a dozen bales, murmured to Connor, 'Have you seen those two?'

He tossed a bale up and said laconically, 'If you mean they're working harder than you, then yes, I have seen. You're a slacker, Mary Cooper.'

'And you're a tyrant. I don't mean that. There's something going on.'

'But you knew that already. He's always fancied her.'

'It's different now.'

But Connor didn't understand. He didn't know Deb as did her sister. He couldn't see how depressed she had been, and the sudden lifting of the cloud. He hadn't been in London, when it all went wrong.

Mary felt a sudden shiver of nerves. Suppose Zwmskorski did his worst? A wave of dizziness came over her. She stopped in the act of heaving at a bale, and stood bent over it, panting. Connor said, 'You're a slacker if ever I saw one. There's no strength to you, it comes from having no flesh on your bones. Go and drive the tractor.'

'I'm all right.'

'Do as you're told, girl!'

She went, edging the tractor beside them at walking pace. She knew she must speak to someone about Zwmskorski. Deb might be carefree today, but for how long? Mary looked behind to see that the sledge was full and everyone climbing aboard for a ride back to the yard. She set off at speed, the tractor roaring. There was no time to be lost.

The rain held off until two. Laura and Gabriel were finishing a caramel, and thinking about coffee. There was the murmur of civilised talk and the gentle clatter of spoons on good china, mingled now with the soft spatter of raindrops against the window pane. Laura closed her eyes for a moment. This should be wonderful. Why should it be that she could never feel properly happy?

Gabriel said, 'This is marvellous, isn't it?'

'Yes,' she said obediently. He reached for her hand across the table and she let him take it. Would it be better if Michael was here? She doubted it. The longer she lived and the more people she gathered about her, the more she felt alone.

She roused herself to speech. 'What did Rosalind say? You were going to tell me.'

'Was I? Oh. Well, this boyfriend of Mary's was pretty keen, I gather. Rosalind thinks he proposed, but that's probably Mary making things up.'

'I'm sure it wasn't! Good heavens.' Laura took back her hand and sat up. Hadn't she always known that Mary could be a success? Girls didn't all have to be pretty and docile to be loved.

She noticed Gabriel looking at her with his old, speculative stare. She felt nervous suddenly. Nothing stayed comfortable when Gabriel was around. 'I've had an idea,' he said. 'It's really why I wanted to talk.'

'Oh, yes?'

'Well, I've made quite a bit of money, as you know. And Dora and I never did mean to stay at Fairlands. Things drifted on, you know how it is. But the time's come to find somewhere for ourselves.'

'The parents won't conveniently die, you mean?' said Laura with some asperity.

'There is something in that. They seem very hale and hearty. And

Dora's been fighting with her mother rather a lot lately. Bored, you see. Needs a new challenge. I thought – well, it seemed obvious, since Gunthwaite's eventually coming to me.'

In a voice of ice, Laura said, 'What seemed obvious?'

'To move to Gunthwaite.'

She did not speak for some minutes. Then, 'Where do you expect me and Michael to go?'

'You don't have to make it sound as if I was evicting you! After all, you know the old place needs a heap of cash spending on it. Nothing's been done since you put in electricity, and that was on a shoestring. I'd pay you out, of course, and you could find something really nice in the village. All mod cons. You know how Michael's headaches are troubling him. He's finding the farm uphill work. And Piers is on top of things now. He and I could work together, so to speak. And if Mary and her Irishman wanted to keep going with the horses then they could. I'd even put up with Sophie and Marie. So you see, it would be best all round. I'd get the farm when I could really make a difference, spend some real money, make the place just right!'

'How very kind.'

'Not kind, Laura. Fair. And Michael could take things easy for the first time in his life.'

She looked at him and felt the strongest emotion she had known in years. Hatred. It seemed so simple to him, so sensible, so easy. He needed a new house, Dora wanted an amusement, and between them they saw Gunthwaite as the prize. Never mind that it was her sanctuary, Michael's life. Never mind that her children would be dispossessed years before their time. It suited him and therefore it must suit them. It was all quite straightforward.

'No wonder you didn't want Michael to come,' she said bitterly. 'He might have made a scene.'

'Mike? Why should he?'

'If you don't know that I can't explain. What's happened to you, Gabriel? I used to think that you were really a good, kind man. Perhaps you are. The trouble is, you're so wrapped up in yourself and your concerns that you can't show it. Your selfishness always wins through.'

'Be reasonable, Laura! Think a little. Something that suits all of us can't be my selfishness!'

'You're so sure the world should be viewed from your own limited perspective that you can't see anything else! I blame your mother. She spent years behaving as if the universe had been created solely for your amusement.'

'You always hated her.'

'I never liked her, that's true. How could I? She thought you were the new Messiah.'

'I should have known you'd never agree that anything I did was worth anything.'

She was silent. Her hands were shaking. She wanted to escape from here and get back to her home, shutting the door on Gabriel and the outside world. He had never brought her anything but trouble, from the very first moment her door opened in the Rue de Claret and he was there.

They left the restaurant without another word spoken between them. In the car, Gabriel tried to take her hand but she turned her light eyes on him with a glare. He recoiled, thinking how far from his vision of today was the reality. He had intended to win her over. He had intended to kiss her in the car. He had thought that she would magically dispel his ills and his depression and make him happy.

As they neared Gunthwaite he looked at her rigid profile and said, 'Will you at least think about it? Talk it over with Michael? Sensibly.'

'There's nothing sensible that can be said. Michael won't ever leave Gunthwaite.'

'He doesn't think he can, that's all. You know yourself he needs a rest. It's obvious the place needs updating. The world's changed, Laura. Not even Gunthwaite can stand still.'

When he had gone she didn't immediately go into the house. She walked into the fields, still wet from the storm, one or two broken hay bales all that remained to tell of this morning's labour. A hare started up from the hedge and raced across the field, stopping halfway to sit up and look back at her. She knew that hare. Whenever she walked in this field he started. If modern ways came to Gunthwaite there'd be chemicals and ploughings and fields put down to high-yielding barley that would leave the soil drained and lifeless. Michael said that a few years of that would take twice as long to put right. But Michael farmed for fifty years hence, not just tomorrow.

She went to sit under the hawthorn tree, its dense canopy keeping the earth dry and bare. Was Gabriel right? They weren't making enough, that was true. Michael's ways took people and time, to garner a meagre harvest. They bred and sold good cows too, but that wasn't done every day. What's more, Michael was happiest with the horses nowadays. Would it be best to take Gabriel's money, find somewhere new, not in the village, not that, but nearby? A few small fields, a line of stabling, and Mike could relax and take pleasure in things.

She couldn't see it somehow. She knew that Michael and she woke every morning with a sense that they belonged. Looking out across these fields and hills soothed and satisfied.

Suddenly her mind switched back to London. The flat. The gas. The longing for nothing more to come. She couldn't have felt like that

343

here. Cows calved, sheep lambed, birds nested, and even in the hardest winter something bloomed. In the midst of such a testament to life, untimely death seemed a vulgarity; a rejection of the natural cycle in which they all lived. She knew, more than anyone, that Gunthwaite could stifle you with loneliness, starve you of variety, crush you with work. But a bargain was always made. What was taken was paid for, in fullest and satisfying measure.

Laura rose to her feet, feeling the creaking in her hips that reminded her that she was no longer young. Nonetheless, old age was yet to be confronted. Her hair was still lustrous, her skin still soft. She wasn't ready to hand over Gunthwaite, all meek and mild, and let Gabriel do as he wished. So many lives depended on things going on as they had always done, not the least of them the hare's. She wouldn't let Michael give in.

As soon as the hay was safely under cover Mary rolled her sleeves down her arms where the hay had scratched them and said to Connor, 'Well then. Are you coming?'

'Where?'

'You don't have to if you don't want. I'll perfectly understand.'

'Don't be cryptic.' He leaned against the wall by her head. He smelled strongly of sweat and horses and hay, with rivulets of moisture marking the dust on his face. Mary felt herself shiver and said briskly, 'I'm going to see Dora, as you very well know. But it's all right. I know you'd rather not bother.'

He said nothing for a moment. Mary busied herself tidying bridles into neat lengths to hang with military precision on the walls. It was blatantly unnecessary. She wondered what he had said to Dora when they parted. She wondered if he went to see her still. You could never really tell about someone. Not even Deb.

He said, 'All right. I'll come.'

'You don't have to. I said.'

'Don't blame me if the whole thing degenerates into one of Dora's fits. But you're right. We should go with Gabriel out of the way.'

He went to wash, emerging minutes later in a smart blue suit and tie. Mary, in jodhpurs and shirt, felt criticised, and at once went to change into a skirt. She looked speculatively at her face. She never wore make-up when working horses nowadays, it took too long, and besides, she couldn't always rely on Kristian to send replacement bottles. He sent them eventually, with cryptic notes, tempting her to go and see him. She grinned ruefully. She had very much better continue to write, Kristian was way out of her depth. But, despite the dwindling level of supplies, if she'd thought earlier she'd have put some on. It would have been so nice to parade before Dora with an apparently flawless complexion.

344

She brushed her hair to fluff it up, and outlined her eyes in black. That was better. For too long she had allowed her face to intimidate her, when it was worth making the effort to beat the marks into second place. She put on a slash of dark red lipstick, and wiped it off again. There. The bee-stung look was all the rage, so people said.

As she was going, Deborah came to the door and said, 'Will you be long?'

'Quite a while,' replied Mary. She looked askance at Piers, lurking – why? – in the kitchen. 'What are you going to do? Mum won't be back until mid-afternoon.'

'I might do some baking,' promised Deb. 'Piers can help me. There's not much he can get on with in the rain.'

'No.' Mary left doubtfully. She felt sure she knew exactly what Piers and Deborah had planned for the afternoon. She wondered if she should go back and have a hissed conversation with her sister, and then thought, what would she say? Deborah already knew more about sex than she did. She had aeons more experience of men. And Deborah, more than anyone, must surely know the problems that arose when things got out of hand. As an elder sister Mary knew she had often been found wanting, but in this instance, surely the sisterly thing was not to interfere?

But she was quiet as Connor drove away. After half a mile of total silence he said, 'Have I done something I don't know about?'

'What?' She gathered her wits. 'No. It's Deb. And Piers. They're in the house. All alone.'

'Shock, horror, shame!'

'Well. It might be. I know you think people should be absolutely liberal about sex, but that's just you. People like Deb shouldn't.'

He said nothing. Then, negotiating a bend, 'What about people like you?'

She coloured, and was the old Mary again, scarlet and unhappy. 'You know that was all silly. It's mean of you to mention it.'

'I wasn't. I mean, that wasn't what I meant. What I should have said is – what about you and me?'

She sat frozen in her seat for a long second. Then, 'You swine,' she muttered. 'I suppose your thoughts turn to such things when we're off to visit your one-time mistress. I'm no replacement for Dora, I'll have you know.'

'Mary, I—'

'Don't try and excuse yourself! If you think I'm going to fall into bed with you just because you've been halfway decent lately then you've got a very long think coming.'

'I didn't suggest bed!'

'Then what did you suggest?'

He ran his hand through his hair. 'Nothing! Ever. God help me if

345

I'm ever so foolish as to think about physical contact with you. It would be like an embrace from a man-eating tiger.'

'I'm glad you realise it,' said Mary, turning her profile towards him and studying the road. They said nothing more until they arrived at Fairlands.

Dora was in the drawing room, leafing through a copy of *Vogue*. She was dressed in a pair of immaculately tailored slacks and a wrapover blouse in bronze silk that failed entirely to restrain her breasts. As Mary and Con entered and she rose to greet them, they were greeted with a view of her magnificent cleavage, bounded by two luscious hills. Mary felt her self-esteem wither like a pricked balloon. Her own breasts were mere goosepimples beside those.

Dora stretched out her hands to Con. 'How lovely of you to come! So sweet of you to visit an old woman like me.'

'Indeed,' said Connor dryly.

Mary, astounded by his lack of gallantry, mumbled, 'Old? You? Good heavens,' when she would much rather have extended a cool and distant handshake.

'You children sit right by me and tell me why you're here,' said Dora, drawing Connor down on a two-seater sofa. Mary, excluded, perched uncomfortably on a gilded chair. It was some time since she had been to Fairlands and the changes surprised her. All the old furniture seemed to have vanished, and in its place stood elegant, airy pieces covered in green damask and gold. The old, faded paper was gone from the walls and in its place was a riot of birds and flowers, against which real flowers in towering arrangements stood like extravagant statues. There were pictures in light white frames, and others in surrounds of cherrywood and elm. The room wasn't comfortable any more perhaps, but in its place was genuine grace.

'Did you do all this?' demanded Mary, in her usual straightforward way.

'Why, yes, dear. Don't you like it?' Dora patted Connor's knee in a gesture of maternal reassurance.

'It's fantastic,' admitted Mary. 'I didn't know you had it in you, Aunt Dora.'

'We all have hidden talents,' replied her aunt. 'I don't think anyone here has any idea of the sort of person I really am.'

'I think they do,' said Mary, and could have bitten her tongue out. 'I mean – I think they realise you're really very accomplished.'

'Yes.' Dora gave her a jaundiced stare.

Connor turned in his confined seat, trying to distance his body from Dora by resigning himself to nudging knees. Dora crossed hers provocatively, and leaned forward a little, again giving him a clear view of her breasts. He cleared his throat. 'We met an old friend of yours in London, Dora. A Polish gentleman.'

346

Dora sat up as if she had been stuck with a cattle prod. 'What? Who? Not – not Wodgy?'

'A Mr Zwmskorski,' supplied Mary. 'Dr Zwmskorski. I don't know him well enough for nicknames. But he tried to get to know Deb. If you know what I mean.'

Dora got up restlessly, and went to a cigarette box on a table, hastily lighting up and puffing. 'Know what you mean? I should say I do. She ought to keep clear of him. The most dangerous man I ever knew, and that's saying something. Oh, Wodgy. What times we had.' She looked into the air, as if those times could still be seen, a film repeating in her head.

'He remembers too,' said Mary. 'He didn't know you'd come back to this country.'

'No. I haven't been in touch since – well, since the war. How does he look?'

'Handsome,' supplied Connor. 'Cold.'

'He was hot when he wanted to be,' said Dora. 'Redhot. But I could cope with him. Well, I learned to. It was either that or—'

'He's violent to women,' said Mary stiffly. 'A girl I met says he's known for it.'

'Depends on how you handle him.' Dora allowed herself a small, pleased smile. 'He didn't hurt me. Not really. He knew that he'd suffer if he did. Life – wouldn't be so pleasant. You know, I'd have thought he'd grown out of that by now. Most men mellow, don't they? I mean, look at Gabriel. All his urges drowned in whisky. And Wodgy used to drink.'

'He takes photographs now,' said Connor. 'Photographs of Deb.'

Dora looked at him in puzzlement. Then, her brow darkening, she exploded. 'The silly cow! The stupid little cow! Getting involved with a man like that and letting him take photographs.'

'She didn't let him,' said Mary grimly. 'He took them just the same.'

'My God,' whispered Dora. 'My God.' And then, recovering, 'What does he mean to do?'

Mary shrugged. 'Ruin Deb's life, I suppose. Show Mum and Dad. And the papers, and anyone she's fond of. As a way of getting back at us, you see. At Mum.'

'Yes. He and Laura never could stand each other. I suppose she came over Miss Morality. Well, that was Laura for you. One moment anybody's, the next touch-me-not. She was tough in those days. Not so washed out. She was even admirable, in a way.'

'Were you?' asked Connor softly. 'Then.'

Dora looked at him. She grinned. 'Oh, Connor. How you'd like to despise me now. Don't worry, my dear. I never bear grudges.' She looked into his eyes. He held her gaze and she began to smile, her mouth curving in a taunting, seductive line.

The colour flooded Mary's skin and she stood up, saying abruptly, 'So we need to know, Aunt Dora. Can we get back at this man? You might know something we could use. To make him give up.'

Dora turned to her. She seemed to sneer. 'Really, dear, you have such a simplistic view of things,' she purred. 'What could I possibly know that would still have relevance after all these years? Zwmskorski was into everything: black market, gun running, drugs. He never got caught. Once or twice he had to make himself scarce, but he always came back. You know, believe it or not, I once had Gabriel arrange to have him threatened with the police. He never found out, thank God. And he was the reason I went abroad. I knew if I stayed here he'd never leave me alone. If I'd known anything don't you think I'd have used it then?'

She walked across the room with tight strides, stopping to grind out her cigarette into an ashtray. Mary and Connor exchanged glances. Connor said, 'He must have thought a great deal of you.'

She laughed mirthlessly. 'More than anyone else, perhaps. That isn't saying much. Not with Wodgy. But you can never tell, can you, about people? I mean, look at Laura. Mrs Butter-wouldn't-melt, and I'll bet her past would make your hair stand on end.'

She turned to Mary suddenly, extending a long finger, complete with scarlet, varnished nail. 'I'll tell you this, Mary Cooper. Your mother would be a great deal happier if she could come to terms with what she used to be. Don't think I haven't read the papers, and sooner or later so will she. There've been rumours for years, and there she sits, terrified that one day someone will turn up and there'll be nothing she can say. But I ask you, who cares? Michael? Why doesn't she tell him and have done with it? Why doesn't she stand up one day, look in the mirror and see herself for what she is, warts and all? We all have that to do. We all have to know ourselves.'

Connor said, 'What if you can't like what you know?'

'Oh, my poor boy.' Dora clicked across in her heels, and put an arm around his shoulder. 'You adore yourself, we all know that. We all do, at your age. It's later the cracks appear. But it's all about honesty. We have to be honest with ourselves, if no one else. Not like Laura. She lies to herself all the time.'

'Yes,' said Mary tightly. 'She can't relax. She's always keeping things hidden, locked away. It takes all her strength.'

'Exactly!'

Dora went to a cupboard, and poured herself a gin. 'Anything for you two? No, I thought not. Sorry I can't help you though. Tell you what – why don't you give me Wodgy's address? At least I could talk to him. Don't you think?'

348

'Would you?' Mary's face lit up.

But Connor said, 'Are you sure, Dora? He hasn't mellowed, that's for sure.'

'Thank God,' said Dora. 'I should hate to think that in the end everyone ends up house-trained. That would mean it could even happen to me.' She took a mouthful of gin and winked at him, jiggling those magnificent breasts. He laughed.

Outside in the car, Mary said furiously, 'She's outrageous! How could you laugh? I've never been so embarrassed.'

'Don't be po-faced, Mary! She's going to try and help. Can't you be magnanimous for once in your life?'

'Not with her.'

'And why not? Are you jealous then?'

'No!'

She turned her head to stare resolutely out of the window. But, beyond the drive, he pulled over into a wood. 'Is something the matter with the car?' asked Mary frostily.

'No. Yes. I can't drive it. I want to kiss you.'

'You want to kiss her, you mean! But failing her, with her bosom the size of a rubber dinghy, you'll make do with me.'

'You don't want to drive me back into her arms, do you?'

'I won't take you into mine to stop you!'

'Keep your arms by your sides, then. It's a kiss I want.'

He leaned across. Mary turned her face away, like a child refusing food. She could feel him nuzzling her neck. 'Oh, Mary,' he whispered. 'You smell so good.'

'You smell of horse,' she said unkindly.

'You like horses. And I washed. Mary, Mary, your skin's like silk.'

'If it's silk you want, consult a dressmaker,' she snapped. But her resolve was weakening. His mouth felt so moist. His teeth were nibbling at tiny pinches of skin. She could feel her nipples prickling, tensing, her very mouth was watering! She swallowed noisily, and was embarrassed. She turned to say, 'I'm sorry,' but in that instant of inattention his mouth was on hers.

She was stunned by him. In an instant she realised how much her body had longed for this. Try as she might, every sense in her responded to his tongue, his teeth, the simple warmth of human touch. Peter Murray-Gill had never kissed like this, she thought. No one in the world had ever done so. To touch another's tongue with your own was a gesture more intimate and more exciting than she could have known.

She broke away, gasping for breath. 'You're not supposed to stop breathing,' said Connor.

'Shut up, will you? I didn't want to be kissed.'

'No one was kissed. We were both kissing.'

349

'I know. I don't want it. Next thing you'll be talking about sex again and telling me it's all OK. And then you'll be back to Ireland and I'll be left. And I'll have to live with being a fool.'

'It isn't foolish to want to make someone happy.'

'Should I want that for you? Why don't you want it for me? I don't want this, Connor. Truly. My mother was a prostitute, for God's sake, doing it for money and nothing else. But when I make love with a man it has to be love, real love, not just anything. We have to want the same things. To be together, to be important to each other, not just today but for always.'

'The wedding ring,' said Connor in a singsong voice.

'Not the ring exactly,' replied Mary. 'Just the commitment.'

'Oh. The lifetime thing. Just that.'

He turned back to the wheel again, taking hold of it aggressively. Dora had excited him right enough, but only on top of weeks of Mary. Only a kiss and he was on fire for her. Except Mary, being Mary, would never simply give in. He felt like a knight challenged to greater and greater things. Mary knew all about torture, he thought. But he looked at her face, brow creased, rumpling the mark on her forehead into an ugly scar. He felt his heart ache for her, knew he wouldn't care half so much if she was perfect. It was her flaws he desired, within and without. But was she worth the price she set upon herself? Was he prepared to pay it? He simply didn't know.

Chapter Thirty-three

Michael returned from market weary. He had stood in a chill wind for hours, watching fat cattle through the ring, waiting for his own select crop. They had made a fair price, but he knew that if he hadn't stood by them the auctioneer would have let them go for less. To him, it felt symptomatic of the times. Everyone wanted an easy life, abundant profit for little effort. Extorting an extra five pounds a head from tightfisted butchers was considered very hard work, and only the farmer's uncompromising stance in the ring, standing amidst the shining rumps of his prize beasts shaking his head and refusing to budge, made a quick sale impossible.

People had talked about him in the market café. He had heard a man say, a man he thought not much of, but all the same: 'Cooper's a good sort but he doesn't move with the times. Thinks the old ways are best, doesn't hold with science. He'll go under, mark my words.'

He had come home thinking grimly of the harvest. Was he old-fashioned to believe, still, that the thin soils of his hilly fields could not take rough treatment? On all sides men urged him to spray this, plough that, plant the other. Men further down the valley had this year taken a hay crop weeks before his, mowing fields of lush green grass, weedless, flowerless, perfect. His own crop, so much lighter, smelling of meadow thyme and cocksfoot, would have given him great satisfaction years ago. He had coaxed it from difficult land, after all. Was he, in honesty, so wrong?

Laura put a cup of tea on the table for him, with a large piece of cake. 'Deb made this,' she said. 'I was out. Gabriel took me to lunch. We left a note, but you didn't get back.'

'I was well down the list. It took forever. I've heard of a man with a good tup that might suit us, though. Our sort. Good, big animal with some flesh on him.'

'I thought our sheep were thought to be too big already. The fashion's for smaller joints now.'

'The fashion! Since when had fashion anything to do with farming?'

Mary, coming in and hearing this, exchanged glances with her mother. Michael so rarely showed temper. Mary sat down opposite him and said, 'Bad price then, Dad? They were beautiful beasts.'

Michael sipped his tea. In a changing world at least a good cup of tea remained the same. 'I got the price they deserved. But I had to stand over the man to get it. He'd have knocked them down ten minutes earlier, and been glad to get on.'

'Was it Jenkins' son?' asked Laura. 'He's a slimy boy. Just like his father.'

But Mary, shrewd in the ways of the market, said, 'I suppose everyone said you were being difficult. They always moan about Gunthwaite. Just because we produce top quality and it makes them all feel bad.'

Michael said nothing. He sipped again at his tea and nibbled his piece of cake. He thought how good it was to have Mary home again, with her staunch and loyal heart. He looked at Laura, and could see she was thinking the same. They smiled at one another.

Later, after supper, with Mary gone to the stables to groom horses and Connor trailing bad-temperedly behind, Deborah said, 'Can I have the car tomorrow? Piers is going to teach me to drive.'

'You wouldn't learn when I offered,' reminded her father. 'What's different?'

'Piers is more fun,' said Deborah.

Laura looked up from some mending. 'You know what we think about Piers, dear. He's a nice boy, I grant you. But he is a bit – well – wayward.'

'That's just his family. With parents like his anyone would be unstable. I'm sorry, Dad, but how did you ever get a brother like that?'

She got up and flounced off to her room. Laura sighed. 'Didn't I say, Michael? But you would employ the boy. If only she'd met somebody in London.'

'Deb hasn't decided on Piers,' he said peaceably. 'The more fuss you make the worse she'll be.'

'Are you sure Piers hasn't decided on Deb?' challenged his wife. 'That's the real trouble. If she goes on like this she might find herself in so deep she can't get out. And what then? You know what the boy's like when he's upset. He's the sort – well, he's the type to take a gun to them both.'

Michael got up and went over to her. He put a firm hand on her shoulder. Laura shook her head, fighting tears, fighting the sensation that her insides were jelly, shaking and dissolving into nothing. 'What is it? What is it really?' he asked.

She rested her head against his arm. What would she do but for Michael? There would be nothing solid in the whole world.

'It's Gabriel. He wants the farm. He's offering to buy us out and improve everything, let Dora turn my house into some magazine version of a country home! And I know we're very shabby. I know I should rip out the plywood cupboards and put in real oak, and have

352

proper heating and something more than a bare bulb in the hall. And she'll do it beautifully. But I can't bear to think of going and leaving everything!'

Michael patted her shoulder in a steady, careful rhythm. 'No doubt he'd like a double herringbone milking parlour too. And for that he'd need a new building. One of those block and asbestos jobs. And tractors in a new shed, and a silage clamp. The old barn would be nothing but a museum piece.'

'He'll do it in the end,' said Laura miserably. 'That's the trouble. Now he's prepared to let Mary stay on with her horses, and Sophie and Marie keep the cottage. If we make him wait, what then?'

'He'd be just the same,' said Michael. 'You could always twist Gabriel around your little finger.'

'I think he's changed. He doesn't listen to me any more. He thinks I've gone to pieces. I suppose he's right.'

Michael was quiet. If the truth was obvious and there was nothing to say, he never felt the need to fill the silence with empty words. Of course she had gone to pieces. She was like a piece of broken china, mended enough to be serviceable but always obviously flawed. She felt again the gnawing of anxiety, that nameless, baseless feeling that scarred her days. What was it that frightened her? It might even be fear itself. But every day and every hour she forced it down, contained it, denied that it was there.

Michael yawned capaciously. 'Time we stopped this and went to bed,' he said, and Laura got up and began settling the house for the night.

Later, in bed, he turned to her. She lay still, as always, merely spreading her legs for him. He was silent, quick, as if what he did was an affront to her and must be soon finished. When he rolled aside she lay listening to his breathing, hearing it subside into the gentle rhythms of sleep. She felt desperate suddenly. Tears ran from the corners of her eyes on to her pillow. If only Gabriel lay beside her, she thought. Then at least she would have found some release. She let her mind dwell on the thought. Gabriel's kiss, Gabriel's hands on her breasts, his presence within her. Her eyes opened wide against the dark. She longed for it! The touch of a man she knew to be nothing beside her husband!

She got out of bed and went out to the landing. A window looked on to the yard and tonight there was a moon. She sat in the wide embrasure, cold in her nightgown, the moisture between her legs drying unpleasantly. There was a light on in the flat above the barn. Piers was awake still. She felt angry with him for intruding on her nighttime solitude and turned instead to look across the fields, to where the owls were hunting the shadowed hedges. If she had continued to look for a moment longer she would have seen two figures silhouetted against the lighted window. A man and a woman, both naked. The woman linked her hands behind his hand, leaned to let her heavy hair fall down her back, and gave her young breasts up to him.

Two days later, Gabriel came again to the house. He found Michael in the sheep pen, trimming feet. To his chagrin Piers was there too, cutting out the worst ones and handing them on. 'I suppose Laura told you my plan?' began Gabriel hopefully. 'I thought we could talk about it in private.'

Michael took the ewe that Piers presented, saying irritably, 'She was missed last time. Must have been. What are you thinking of, boy?'

'She was missed when we gathered the moor,' said Piers equably. 'She'd have stayed out this time but her feet were sore. She's a devil.'

Gabriel wondered why he hadn't flared at Michael as he did at his father. He and Piers were always at loggerheads. But Michael's criticism was untypical, caused by his brother's presence. Michael was always irritated by the thought that Gunthwaite wasn't his to leave as he wished.

The job was messy, but Michael did it neatly. Piers daubed on the treatment, a stinking, gluey mix that seemed to work. 'You know there's a new spray for that?' said Gabriel helpfully. 'I saw it at an exhibition.'

'If I wanted to treat this ewe every day I might consider it,' said Michael. 'It doesn't do for this land. Not with sheep on the moor.'

'You should bring them indoors in winter,' went on Gabriel. 'Build a new shed and have done with tramping the hills in the snow.'

Michael pushed the ewe through the race into the next pen. 'If we must talk, we must,' he said shortly, and led the way to the barn.

'I know Laura's told you my plan,' Gabriel began. 'And I know initially she wasn't keen, but if you think a little, Mike—'

'I've thought a lot. The answer's no.'

Gabriel said nothing. Michael's tone was enough. He stood looking at his big, workworn brother, shabby overalls over a patched sweater, hands covered in nicks and splashes of tar. Laura felt sorry for him, he reasoned. She must. But he had to see reason.

'You're not up to it any more, Mike,' he said kindly. 'You look exhausted. And you know Laura isn't herself these days. All things considered, I think you might take what I say seriously.'

'Do you now?'

'Yes. This farm is more or less a shambles. You've got good stock, I grant you, but you could run twice the number. I've been looking at the figures for a modern farm and—'

'A modern farm. You want to bring Gunthwaite bang up to date?'

'Of course. You owe it to the land, Mike. After all, it's my inheritance.'

'Only because we never had a boy!'

'Agreed. Nonetheless, it passes to me. I have every right to suggest a scheme that would stop this land becoming wasted and derelict.'

Michael felt the anger ignite within him. Even as he felt it rise up, he was amazed at himself. What a thing to get angry about! Land!

'Are you saying this farm has gone backwards under my care? Are you? Has the bracken taken over, the walls gone down? Don't my stock still command the highest prices at market? If you, the rich playboy, think you can take this thin soil and put heart in it from a bag and expect miracles, then you know nothing! We have machines that can do what horses never could, but no one stops to ask if it should be done. And I say it should not!'

But Gabriel persisted. 'Mike, even Laura farms more progressively than you. She pushed yields skyhigh in the war.'

'By ploughing grassland! We needed corn then but we don't now. There are farms in the East Riding can produce bushels more than me, on good rich land. Let them. Gunthwaite's always going to lose that race. But good, hardy stock, no one beats us there.'

'And you'll end your days in poverty, brother mine.'

Gabriel kicked out at a pile of junk in a corner. Ropes, chains, an oil can. The detritus of a working farm. 'You can't afford the men to run this place. You can't pay them. You realise what's going to happen, don't you? You'll get older, poorer, the farm will go down and down. Rotten timbers you can't replace, tractors you can't repair. No use coming to me for cash. Oh, no. You had your chance.'

'Chance? Is that what you call it? To live in some tidy box, looking out on other boxes, instead of with this?' Michael spread his arms wide, taking in the high arches of the barn, the lime-splashed beams where the swallows nested, the gentle stirrings of the horses in their straw. 'You'll not imprison me like that. Not while I have breath.'

He set off back to the sheep, fulminating, his stride fast and furious. Mary was riding the stallion back home and slithered to halt as her father marched past.

'You could at least think of Laura!' yelled Gabriel. 'Does this make her happy? You can deceive yourself about everything Michael, but not that!'

Mary, her mount startled and plunging beneath her, hung on and for once agreed.

Dora sat before her dressing table, looking at herself. She wondered if she had changed more than she knew. When Zwmskorski last saw her she was slender, svelte, her blonde hair entirely due to nature's beneficence. She wasn't so slender now. What's more there were lines on her face nothing could disguise, and her hair had become a careful blend of silver-gilt. But men, both young and old, still found her toothsome. Even Gabriel, who might reasonably be expected to have tired of his marital duties by now, still, when sober, liked to see what she had to offer.

She sighed. He was so rarely sober at night. If she wanted sex she had to inveigle him into the bedroom well before evening. So she satisfied herself with what she could get, a couple of people at the golf club, who each thought her exclusively theirs, and anyone at a party who caught her eye. None of them was a patch on Zwmskorski.

He had written her a vicious letter at the end. Her mother had forwarded it unopened, but it should have been burned. He had called down every curse imaginable on her head, wishing her a life of misery. Had she been miserable? Not very. If she was honest with herself, a life of settled monogamy wasn't really her thing.

She picked up a lipbrush and began briskly to outline her lips in dark red. She filled the centres with deep coral, more flattering than pink or apricot, she thought. And it teamed with her suit, a youthful trousers and jacket combination over a tight white top. Before she put on the jacket she admired herself in profile. Her breasts had certainly gained over the years. Good underwear and good posture ensured that she could never be labelled matronly because of it. What could she be called? Voluptuous? Yes.

She looked around the room. She didn't want to arrive in London and find she had left behind some vital part of her toilette. Her equilibrium would be tenuous enough without that. She picked up her case, mentally rehearsing various clothing combinations. Evening dress – gilt sandals. Cocktail frock – cream high heels, small leather bag. Damn it, wasn't she past this? If she did leave anything all she had to do was pop into Bond Street and indulge herself. She wasn't the well-bred but obscure little girl she had once been, after all. She was a wealthy, experienced woman.

Her mood of determined optimism lasted as far as her London hotel. But when the door closed behind the porter she felt fear begin again. She went at once to the fridge and poured herself a large gin, deciding to make this the only one. All the same, she soon drank another. There. That was better. Now she could think.

She opened the telephone book and ran her fingers down the entries. To her surprise he was there, she hadn't expected that. The only Zwmskorski, but not the only Pole. She wondered if he had a woman in his life. Certain to. It might even be another Pole, some glamorous aristocrat like himself, well versed in cruelty and excess. The gin in the fridge was gone so she rang down for a full-sized bottle. There was nothing to do while she waited for it. She sat down, cursed herself for a coward and dialled.

The telephone rang four times. She counted. When it was answered and he said, still with that distinctive intonation, 'Hello? Zwmskorski?' for a moment she couldn't speak. 'Hello?' he said again, irritable, just as she remembered.

'Wodgy,' she breathed.

'What? What did you say?'

'I said Wodgy.'

There was a long silence. Then he said clearly, 'I have been expecting you. For years. Where are you, I will pick you up.'

She told him her hotel, which was stupid. Hadn't she learned anything over the years? He'd taught her well enough.

She was in the lobby when he called, still in her trousers. She didn't want to dress up for the evening and look eager. She saw him the moment he stepped out of his chauffeur-driven car. Tall, she had forgotten how tall, but his thin, muscular limbs had always added to his height. His hair had faded. Not his eyes. When he saw her and looked without smiling, she felt her guts turn to water.

'Did you miss me?' she asked boldly.

He didn't reply. He said, 'You must come to my club, The Vermilion. I always go there in the early-evening. We have some serious gamblers call then.'

'Don't you dare disrupt your routine just for me,' said Dora in mock humility.

'I won't. You disrupted my life enough, Dora.'

'Me? Liar. You haven't changed.'

'You have. Now you want to know me.'

He took her arm and led her to his car. It was a Rolls-Royce with soft leather seats and a smoked glass partition from front to back. Once inside, he pulled open a cocktail cabinet and poured vodka in tiny silver cups. Dora took hers and said, 'What shall we drink to? Old times? Or new ones?'

'Old enemies,' said Zwmskorski, and she laughed.

'Still the same old Wodgy. You were never my enemy. You tried to own me, that's all. I didn't like that. You wreck the things you own.'

He looked at her thoughtfully. 'That's very true. Are you going to surprise me, Dora? Have you grown up?'

'I was always grown up with you,' she said, and laughed again. 'Don't you remember?'

He downed his vodka in one, turned and tried to put his hand on her breast. She caught his wrist and held him off. 'Careful. You'll spill my drink. We don't have to rush at things, do we? Not nowadays. It isn't as if we expect to get hit by a bomb at any moment, after all.'

'Unless the Irish turn difficult again.'

'Wodgy, if the Irish try and blow us up, I promise I'll think of it as

357

wartime and act accordingly. God, all that screwing we used to do! If I'd known I was going to live this long I might have been more careful.'

'What about? Doing it with a filthy foreigner?'

'Don't be a fool, Wodgy. I don't need your hurt pride. I'm here now, after all these years, and that will just have to do. If I'd stayed, you'd have tired of me by now. You know that. I knew it then. I backed a distance horse instead of a sprinter with doubtful temperament.'

She leaned her head back and drained her little cup. Zwmskorski seized upon her moment of inattention to put his hand inside her jacket and hold her breast. She stayed very still and he chuckled.

'You see,' he said calmly. 'I play by no rules but my own.'

Dora lowered the cup and turned very slowly to look at him. 'You want to have fun, don't you? I know what you like. And if you don't behave you won't get it.'

It was a tactic she had learned from him. The blackmail of pleasure. He held her gaze, smiled and removed his hand. 'Oh, Dora. Perhaps I have missed you after all.'

The Vermilion was large and rather flashy. It catered for gamblers – not of the highest class who had their own exclusive dens to which Zwmskorski could never gain entrance. He would hold influence though. One day. He looked around at The Vermilion's collection of Chinese businessmen and middle-aged clerks from suburbia risking their savings and longed to abandon them for aristocrats. He would delight in watching old England lose its shirt. He remembered Dora's mother and her pained, strained face, concealing none of her dislike. She deserved his revenge.

Dora took hold of his wrist in both hands. 'Don't look so angry. You've done OK for yourself. This place is booming.'

'Yes.' He looked across at the Blackjack table. The girl was dealing somewhat absently. She was one he slept with now and then, one of the conceited, ambitious kids who thought they were special. All the girls thought his bed was a shortcut to ease and prosperity. However many came and went, they always thought that for them it would be different. Sometimes it was. More different than they could believe.

He signalled to his manager. 'Take Audrey off that table. She's playing badly. Giving a bad impression.'

'Yes, Mr Zwmskorski.'

As the girl was pushed aside she turned and stared at him. Then her eyes moved to Dora, on a stool at the bar, her long legs in their coral silk trousers nonchalantly crossed. Dora raised her glass in a mocking salute and the girl's sallow face flamed.

'You're still a bitch,' said Zwmskorski, taking the seat beside her.

'And you're still a womaniser. Do you lay all the kids in here? You could always get anyone you liked.'

'Except Laura.'

Dora threw back her head and laughed. 'Her? Did you honestly try her? She's more or less frigid, you know. Always was probably, even with Gabriel. God, Wodgy, if you saw her now you'd be amazed. She tried to kill herself once. As it is she drags herself around looking more than half dead. I haven't the least idea why.'

'It's the whoring,' he remarked. 'Come back to haunt her, now she's respectable. She was never cut out for it. Unlike you.'

She leaned back, letting her jacket fall open. She could feel her nipples standing out like twin bellpushes. 'Do you think I'd be in demand, Wodgy? Do you think I'd have anything to offer?'

He stared at her, his eyes harder than pebbles on a winter beach. She felt the snake of her desire start to uncoil itself, its forked tongue flickering over her loins. God, but she wanted him! The more frightened she was the better it felt. And in all these years, she'd learned a thing or two about pleasing a man.

The manager was hovering. 'Mr Zwmskorski – we're being asked to accept a note of hand.'

'Whose?' The cold eyes raked the room.

'Mr Nesbitt. You remember, his wife asked—'

'Oh, yes. We've gone as far as we can with him. Throw him out.'

'Yes, sir.'

Dora put a hand on Zwmskorski's expensive black sleeve. 'Are you being charitable, Wodgy? It's not like you.'

'The man's ruined. His notes are worthless. Now, let's go upstairs.'

She looked back at her drink. There was half a glass still remaining. 'Not yet, Wodgy. Later.'

'Damn you Dora, I—'

She stood up, felt between his legs as he sat on the stool. She pressed her thigh against his genitals, feeling his hardness. 'Don't be impatient,' she murmured, putting her hands on his knees. 'You've had your women too easy. You must learn to wait.'

'And why should I learn?' He took hold of her wrist, tightening his grip until her bones cracked. She let out a gasp and then laughed. 'Same old Wodgy. You still like to hear a woman scream.'

'You never screamed.'

'Didn't I? I wonder why not.'

They were both aroused, both eager. Although she had meant to torment him half the night, suddenly she couldn't bear to wait. She tried to think what to do, remembered Deborah and said, 'My hotel. I want it to be there.'

'No. Here, or my flat.'

'Don't think I trust you! The hotel or nowhere.'

He glared at her, and she pulled away, downing her drink. He said harshly, 'All right. If you want. Don't let this be a trap!'

'God, but you've grown paranoid! Come on, Wodgy! I'm sick of this place. Nothing but foreigners and miserable old men.'

In the car she realised she was close to being drunk. She opened the window and breathed deep of the night air. This was no time to lose her wits. Zwmskorski drank two quick vodkas, but seemed none the worse for them. She thought of Gabriel, snoring and incapable. The Pole was a man all right. Gabriel's manhood was senseless most of the time.

The foyer of the hotel seemed far too brightly lit. They crossed it without speaking, ascending in the lift with other people. When at last they were alone in Dora's room she suddenly felt sober and wide awake. The excitement had gone. The fever had ebbed away.

'I knew we should not have come here,' snapped Zwmskorski, searching the fridge for vodka. 'This stupid, cheap hotel.'

'It's a very expensive hotel,' said Dora, switching on table lamps, wishing that the heating didn't hiss.

'He turned out rich then? Your husband.'

'Yes. Very. In fact, there's not much to choose between you. Except that he's drunk all the time. Why aren't you?'

'Drink helps me. Makes me angry. I'm angry now.'

'So I see.'

She bent to move a table between two chairs. Zwmskorski reached out without warning and hit her hard across the bottom. She gasped and half fell, striking her breast against the table edge. She remained crouched, clutching her bosom. 'Bastard,' she whispered.

'You know that already. And still you came back.' He moved to kick her between the legs. Suddenly she rolled away, striking out at random, catching him on the knee. He fell across her. She felt his wrist before her face and, without thinking, sank her teeth to the bone. He gave a short, stifled cry. Gagging on blood, she lay beneath him, wondering if he would kill her. She could feel him moving against her. The violence had excited him again. What's more, it had excited her.

She crawled away from him, stripping off her top and bra. He too began to undress, the blood from his wrist covering everything in fine droplets. Dora's breast bore the sharp line of the table edge in an aching bruise. He came to her and began licking it, now and then nibbling at her, suddenly taking her breast in his teeth and biting to draw blood. She retaliated, clawing her long nails down his naked back.

She stripped off her trousers and pants and threw herself naked on to the bed. He undressed watching her, and she saw that his erection was hard and thick. She rose up to meet him, encircling him with her thighs, forcing him to come into her. He grunted and pushed her back on to the bed. She brought up her knee, hitting him on the ribs, and he pulled back his hand to slap her.

'Don't,' she said warningly. 'That will show.'

'Do you think I care?'

'You will, if you mark me.' She gazed up at him with cold, hard menace. Suddenly, he felt triumph, exhilaration. He'd never met anyone more able to match him than Dora. He'd never met anyone who could fight back with his very own weapons. They were both sexual bullies, forcing others to do as they wished. Together they were capable of so much more than mere satisfaction. With Dora, he could explore fear, pleasure and pain. It was a delicious thought.

'Dora, Dora, I worship you,' he cried.

She looked up at him, the veins in her neck as taut as in her girlhood. 'Worship away, Wodgy,' she instructed.

Over the next few days, Dora and the Pole were seldom apart. It was soon apparent that he had become what events from his youth had promised, a major racketeer. Half the clubs in which he had no interest paid protection money to him, and the other half lived uneasily in his shadow. Drug dealing on his premises occurred only when he had been paid his cut, and girls on his gambling tables moved freely from club to escort agency as required, or found themselves bleeding in the street.

'Did you keep up with the gun running?' asked Dora, idly leafing through a magazine one sunny morning, surrounded by the aftermath of a busy clubland night. A waiter was sweeping away broken glass and clearing out washroom flowerpots full of the tinfoil remains of heroin smoking.

'I never had the capital to get really involved,' said Zwmskorski, running his eye down the accounts.

She thought how unlike himself he looked, half-moon glasses on the end of his long nose, checking suppliers' invoices at random. He might almost be respectable.

'I'm surprised you never married,' she said. 'I can see you in the stockbroker belt, with a wife you cheat on and children you bully. And a dog, perhaps. A miserable dog, that knows what you're like.'

He said nothing. But all at once Dora realised. 'You did it, didn't you?' she said incredulously. 'There is a wife! Who is she? Wodgy, you've got to tell!'

'She's stupid,' he said shortly. 'And my children are stupid because of her. All I asked was a little privacy. They had everything.'

'And she found out about the girls! Well, what did you expect? This isn't pre-war Poland, Wodgy! Women don't expect their husbands to get through a girl a night.'

He slammed the accounts book shut. 'Come,' he said. 'I will show you.'

It was a two-hour drive, presumably less on the train. A green and leafy suburb, woodland and grassy track interspersed with solid brick houses. They stopped at a large, respectable dwelling, its porch supported on white-painted pillars, the windows criss-crossed with leading. Dora put up her hand to hide a giggle. 'How very – suburban.'

'She liked it,' said Zwmskorski. 'She said it would make her happy. I thought, for a year or so. But now I'm not allowed to be here.'

'Why? I suppose she got the law on you. Well, if you will do these things.'

She turned her attention back to the house. A door opened and a child came out. A little boy. The man beside her tensed, his hand clenching on the seat. Another child appeared, a girl, some years older. 'Just like her mother,' he hissed.

'Her mother must be pretty.'

'I hate pretty women.'

Dora felt her breath hard in her throat. 'Is that why you did as you did to Deborah? Or was that Laura's fault?'

He turned and stared at her in silence. She forced herself to stare back. She felt a frisson of excitement, a sense of tempting fate. He might kill her, she thought. With a man like him, you never knew what he might do.

'Is this why you came to see me?'

'It's how I knew where you were. Deb's not a bad girl. Impossibly young, of course, and too pretty for her own good. She could marry anyone.'

'Not if I have a hand in it.'

Dora chuckled. 'What a brute you are! You can't really hate her that much.'

For answer, he rapped on the partition and the chauffeur drove off. There was a lake a mile or so on, and they stopped to walk. Dora was wearing unsuitable shoes, and teetered after Zwmskorski as he strode along, his black coat flapping. Suddenly he turned on her. 'You have no idea. None of you. How it is to be treated like – like a piece of unpleasant garbage. That is how it is to be foreign in this country. To be different.'

'To be a crook, you mean,' said Dora. 'That's what made people hate you.'

'You believe that? You are a fool.'

He stood gazing out over the water. Some ducks were squabbling, flapping and pecking wildly. Dora said, 'If you want to believe a sob story, it doesn't bother me. But Laura didn't do you much harm, believe me.'

He looked at her. 'She did you enough. She stole your husband.'

'I don't think he was mine in the first place, to be absolutely frank. And now – now I'm glad I had the sense to pick up something much more to my taste when I had the chance.'

She reached up to trace the long, cruel lines from his nose to his mouth. His face was so lean, so uncompromising, she thought. Everything firm and functional, no spare flesh anywhere. He had no compassion, she thought. If there was gentleness in him it was buried very deep. It made him – invulnerable. 'Let's go in the bushes,' she murmured.

'You are only here to save Deborah. Admit it!'

'I'm here because I want to be. It's up to you to decide about Deborah. I can't make you do anything at all.'

He took her in the bushes, a wild, brutal coupling against a tree. Dora closed her eyes and thought of Gabriel. Did he know what she was doing? Did he care? But then the base pleasure of the act engulfed her, flooding like a tide of white-hot metal, burning thought away.

Chapter Thirty-four

Deborah wandered disconsolate from the hall. Laura glanced up from her sewing. 'One of your London friends?' she asked.

Deb shook her head. 'Not this time. Graham Beacham. Wants me to go over for dinner.'

'That should be nice.'

Deb flung herself down on the sofa. 'I said no.'

Laura sighed, and tried to rouse herself to spirited persuasion. 'Now that was silly. You like Graham Beacham. And you never go out! Deb, it's time you started doing something with your life and not simply hanging about here.'

'You want me married off,' said Deb bleakly. 'I didn't manage to hook anyone in London so you're hoping for someone round here.'

'Or a job,' said Laura, hearing her voice beginning to plead. 'You can't do nothing, Deb! If – if you can't find anything else then it's got to be a job.'

Deb cupped her chin in her hands and stared into the flames of the fire. The evenings were chill at this time of year. A crackling log or two revived the spirits as well as warming the room. But her spirits felt precarious at the best of times. Only a little while ago she had been the lucky child, the blessed one. Her future had seemed very clear; marriage, children, a settled and prosperous home. But all that had gone, and she was back at Gunthwaite, with nothing to hope for. If it wasn't for Piers, she didn't know what she would do.

'I suppose – well, I could go back to London, couldn't I? Next year?'

'I don't know why you left in the first place,' said her mother in bewilderment. 'Honestly, Deb, I thought you were having fun. Rosalind said that you were. Did something happen? Did you have a fright?'

Deborah shook her head. 'Mary and I got tired of it, that's all. We wanted to come home. Well, you know what Mary's like.'

'I'm not sure that I do any more.'

Laura looked down at her work. She was darning a tablecloth, one that Sophie and Marie had made when first they came to Gunthwaite. The embroidery was exquisite, but they had used too fine a linen and the years had taken their toll. Little holes had appeared, and Laura could spend hours carefully filling them in with tiny running stitches, creating a web of threads. She liked to do it. There was something soothing in mindless activity. It spared her the need to think.

Mary and Connor were out looking at a horse and Michael was in the barn, seeing to a cow that was taking its time calving. Deborah got up abruptly and said, 'I'll go and see how Dad's getting on.'

'Deb—' Her mother turned and looked at her.

Deborah sighed. It was no use her mother wanting things for her, planning things for her. She'd made a mess of everything, brought disaster to the door, and these conversations only made things worse. She couldn't tell her mother what she'd done! If she and Dad ever found out, Deb thought she'd rather be dead. And there were simply no plans she could make. She couldn't get on with her life, wondering if one day it was all going to fall apart. There was only Piers, she thought, and felt her depression lighten. Only with him could she feel hopeful and happy.

When she went outside the evening struck cold. She shivered and hurried into the barn. Michael was sitting patiently by a cow as the animal stood, head lowered, huffing and puffing, occasionally lifting her nose to moo. 'Poor old girl,' said Deb sympathetically. 'Shall I get Piers for you, Dad? You might have to pull.'

'I'll give her another half hour. Go and tell him if you like.'

She ran up to the loft, calling softly, 'Piers? Piers, it's me. Dad's going to need some help with a calving.'

He opened the door and stood grinning at her. She felt herself blushing. It was like this every time they met now, remembering what they had done before. Sometimes, if he came to breakfast in the house, she couldn't meet his eye at all. It was so hard to behave normally when they had shared so much.

She went in and sat in the one easy chair. 'Mum's going on again. Graham Beacham invited me to dinner and I said no.'

Piers bent and kissed her hair. 'Beacham needs his teeth down his throat. Smug little prick.'

'Piers!'

'Sorry. But he is, Deb. Loved by all who know him.'

'Except me. Because I love you.'

He stood in front of her, suddenly serious. 'Do you mean that? I thought you loved me before but you went away. The truth is, Deb, you love me when there's no one better.'

'I do not! Piers, that isn't true.'

She got up to put her arms around him, but his expression made her turn away. Was it true? She'd liked nearly all the men in London, had not once thought of Piers. It was only when she came back hurt and bewildered that she turned to him. Her own weakness challenged her. 'Perhaps I can't love,' she admitted. 'Not really. I might be that sort of girl.'

With that sudden swing of which Piers was so alarmingly capable, he burst out 'That's not you, Deb! I don't know why I said that. We love each other perfectly. We always have.'

He came to hug her and she let him. In a moment they would start to kiss and then everything would be simple. But in that second Deborah felt very calm and clear. Piers needed her so. He had no one to love him but her. And although at this moment he filled the gaping void that used to hold her future, would he always? She felt afraid suddenly. Where did you turn when familiar sanctuary was no more? She put her face to his and began feverishly to kiss.

Connor whistled tunelessly between his teeth. Mary said, 'Do shut up,' but he took no notice. The evening had been wasted. The horse had turned out to be knock-kneed and spavined, and possibly half-witted as well. Mary had recommended that the owners find some sentimental lady rider who would prefer doctoring this dim equine to riding him. There were enough of them about.

'Why are you always so bloody rude?' asked Connor.

'Don't swear. I was not.'

'You were so.' He buzzed around a corner, because he knew it made her nervous and he wanted to see her cringe. Satisfyingly he saw her reach out and clutch the dash. He said, 'I take it Dora's not back?'

'I thought you'd be the first to know if she was.'

'Don't be tedious, Mary!'

'Well, stop trying to scare me. I haven't heard anything. Look, why don't we stop for a drink?'

Obligingly he pulled over at a pub. Once small and characterful, it had been ruthlessly modernised, turning the place into one vast room full of carpet and fruit machines. Stopping at the door Mary said, 'This is horrible. Let's not stay.'

'Snob. You're no better than you should be, you know.'

'I never know what that means. Anyway, you're no horny-handed son of toil, either. Your family's quite something in Ireland, isn't it?'

'How do you know that?' He looked at her incredulously and she laughed.

'I didn't. I guessed. And I'm right.'

In one of her infuriating contradictions she danced to the bar and ordered drinks. Connor followed, irritated, not wanting to stay in this unpleasant pub at all. Seated at a plastic table in the large and threatening space, Mary said, 'So, what are you really?'

He sipped at the thin beer. 'Third son of a very successful racehorse trainer. He wanted me in the business, but the others are in it too and

I won't dance to their tune. We had a bust-up. I said I'd make my own way, and that I mean to do.'

'Don't you ever mean to go home?'

He lifted an eyebrow at her. 'It was what I was planning to do when some hussy foisted her racing breakdowns on me. She's a witch, this woman. Heartless. Cruel. Makes a man do and say the things he never thought he would.'

'What things are they?'

'Did I tell you too that she's no memory? What's said to her is forgotten in a flash.'

He was looking at her hard. She felt a blush beginning, and put up a hand to see if she was wearing make-up. Nowadays whether she was or not she felt more or less the same. But at least, wearing make-up she could blush.

'You don't have to bother with that stuff on my account,' said Connor, noting the gesture.

'I wear it for me, not you,' snapped Mary. 'Why would you care what I look like?'

'Like I said. No memory at all.'

'If you're talking about – before – we were squabbling, weren't we? You never meant what you said.'

'I always mean what I say.'

Her head came up. 'No you don't! Connor, you liar! In one breath you say I'm the worst woman in the world and in the next—'

Suddenly he reached out and took hold of her wrist. She squirmed in his grasp, but he held on. His dark eyes were fixed on hers and she tried to look away, but then it was worse. She found herself looking back at him, facing him, for the first time in weeks. He stared into her face, her poor, imperfect face, and she wished more than anything that she could be different, just for him. 'Has my make-up smudged?' she asked, hating herself for such a silly, mundane comment.

But all he said was, 'It has a bit. Why do you talk of such things when you know what I want to say?'

'I don't know. At least—'

'I want to tell you I love you.'

'Why?'

'Why do I want to say it?'

'No! Why do you? If you do?'

'And me such a liar! I don't know. It happened. I love you. Even though you're such a bitch.'

She sat up, flicked into anger. 'I am not! You don't love me at all really. Do you?'

He reached out and took her other hand. Again she tried and failed to look away, there was nowhere but his eyes in this huge, cold room full of strangers. He said, 'I do. I love you. I always will.'

367

She began to cry. But he held her hands still and she couldn't wipe the tears. 'You love the man in London,' said Connor sadly. 'I knew that must be it.'

'I do not love him! And you know it. You just want me to say things.'

'And why won't you? Why must it always be me?'

She looked at him in agony. She wasn't used to being defenceless. She had spent her life hiding behind words, too proud and too angry to let anyone see behind her rickety defences. But he wanted her to drop her guard, to come out and face him in honesty and truth. Once she'd said it he wouldn't love her any more. And she would be fatally struck.

'This isn't the place,' she said, trying to break free.

'It's the place we are. Say it, Mary!'

'I can't! You know I can't!'

'I know nothing of the sort. Do you love me, Mary Cooper?'

'You know it. You don't have to ask.'

'But I'm asking. If you love me you'll say.'

'Will I? Should I?' She stared at him miserably. She knew everyone was looking. Why wouldn't he let her go, why wouldn't he take it for granted? But she wouldn't want him to be the sort of man who settled for less than his due. She bent her head and whispered, 'I love you.'

'What?' He pulled her closer, putting his face inches from hers. She lifted her head, glared at him and yelled, 'I love you, Connor, you bastard!'

There was silence in the pub. Connor started to laugh and after a moment so did she. As the people in the pub started to clap they got up and fled.

They were still laughing when they drove into Gunthwaite's yard. There was a light in the barn, and they knew it was the calving. Mary moved to open her door to get out and help, but Connor caught her arm.

'Not yet.'

'All right. I'll stay a minute.'

He bent his head to kiss her. She opened her lips beneath his, held in wonderment by pleasure. Kisses were entrancing when you kissed out of love, she thought. Connor felt dearer to her than her own self, more precious than any jewel, to think of him ill or unhappy made her want to weep. 'I didn't know it was going to be like this,' she murmured.

He whispered, 'I did. I've known from the first. But you were always a difficult girl.'

'So you don't love me, then?'

'I think I must. To put up with you.'

He kissed her again, and she put her arms around him and felt him against her, exciting, alien, and yet so much loved. What would she feel tomorrow? Happiness? Joy? Perhaps only sweet contentment.

A long moo from the barn roused them. They dragged themselves apart and climbed from the car, coming together again to touch and kiss and hold hands. 'Don't let them see,' whispered Mary. 'I should be embarrassed.'

'We'll not let them see yet, then.'

They dropped hands as they entered the barn, and at once yearned to touch each other. Piers was fixing calving ropes to the protruding feet of what looked to be a very large calf. Michael turned, saw their faces and looked away.

'Right then,' he said, suddenly very cheerful. 'Right. We can get on now there's enough of us.'

They began to pull, working with the cow and not against her. After a while Deb appeared and sat on a bale to watch. 'You could help, you know,' said Mary caustically, but Deb said, 'You've more than enough. The poor beast's being pulled backwards as it is.'

'Go to her head then, Deb,' said Michael.

But they seemed to be getting nowhere. They started to glance at Michael to see if he was going to give up, but he showed no sign. He went and spoke soothingly to the cow. 'Come along, girl. You make the effort and we'll join you. Just once more.' The cow seemed to sigh and strain, and at that moment the calf began to come.

'Pull!' yelled Connor, he and Mary on one rope, Michael and Piers on the other.

'Poor girl! Poor love!' said Deb, as the cow's chain cracked with the strain. The calf began to slither out, its head swollen and misshapen from the protracted birth. But its tongue was moving in its mouth. It was alive.

Mary grinned at Connor. It was an omen, a sign of good luck. But then there came a sound. A strangled sob. Marie was standing in the huge arch of the barn. She was wearing her lace peignoir, more draggled and stained than ever. Her face, without make-up, was ghost white, while her eyes were red-rimmed and painful. She was holding a cup.

'Marie? What is it?' Mary went to her, seeing that she was holding a tisane, the inevitable tisane.

The old woman's mouth moved but nothing came out. She waved the cup as if that would explain. But all at once Mary knew what she wanted to say. 'That was for Sophie, wasn't it?' she asked. 'Sophie's dead.'

Laura sat by the bed, feeling the chill of the little house enter her bones. She shouldn't have let them stay here each winter. The Hall

369

was altogether warmer, they should have been there. But they had never complained. Not once, in all the years she had known them, had they complained to her that what she gave them wasn't enough.

Of course some people would say she had given more than was their due. People who didn't know. People who didn't understand that you couldn't give too much when all you had was because Sophie had noticed you, taken you, helped you to live. She put her hand towards the bed, intending to touch Sophie's aged and wrinkled fingers. But she held back. Throughout her life she had had to fight against revulsion where Sophie was concerned; dirt, drink, neglect, they all conspired to make her adult self forget that this was the adored grand lady who had saved her.

Determinedly, she reached out and took hold of the dead fingers. She loved Sophie. She had always loved her, even when she was sick and had lice and the smell of her made you gag. Loving was always like that, thought Laura. It was never easy, it was always a fight. Even loving Michael had always meant pretending, living a life to which she could never be entitled, because she was never of sufficient worth. Was it like that for everyone? Or was it all part of the plot? To keep the beggar child, the bastard, in her place?

They hadn't managed, she thought, tightening her hold. And that was Sophie's doing. She alone had found room in her generous, erratic heart for someone else's child. She had loved simply because she didn't know how not to, because by some miracle nothing in her life had ever extinguished her warmth. Other people might see nothing to admire in this worn-out old whore. But for whatever reasons, and whether she willed it or not, Sophie had been good.

Marie came into the room. She stood at the foot of the bed, looking down at the bloated face, the cheeks slackened in death. 'I never liked her, you know,' she remarked. 'Not in Paris. A very irritating woman, one of the stupid ones.'

'I know,' said Laura.

'We all thought she shouldn't have charge of you. That was why we bothered, you know. Not because of you, so much. Because we thought she wasn't good enough. Too stupid, too silly to care. We didn't see beyond. In these last years, only – and she irritated still. Sometimes I liked her. Sometimes I even admired her. But I bit her head off just the same.'

'I loved you both,' said Laura diplomatically.

'No you didn't! It was Sophie all the time. And why not? She was the only one prepared to take a risk for you. The rest of us – well, we did what cost us nothing. Nothing much. And that was all. I've imposed on you all these years. Don't think I don't know. I rode here on Sophie's back and never tried to get off.'

Laura felt the weight of her responsibilities crushing her. Marie needed comfort she had no strength to give. She knew the words, knew they should be said, but the strength to utter them seemed beyond her. With a last mighty effort she gave tongue. 'You've been – welcome. Very welcome. Done so much.'

'Have I?' The gargoyle face cracked in a smile. 'It's kind of you to say. I like to think I haven't been totally worthless all my life.'

The room grew colder still. Laura sat on, keeping watch, with no clear idea why. It seemed right, though. As if Sophie's soul might still be here, and needed to know that it was loved. Only then could it leave, slipping through the opened window to some new dimension. Was Sophie happy? She deserved happiness. And surely there was fairness after death.

Someone was coming up the stairs. It was Michael. He came into the room, smelling of cows and birth, and stood at the foot of the bed looking down at the dead woman. 'I always liked her,' he said quietly. 'But we never really spoke. It was the language, I suppose. But we never tried.'

'She didn't want to try,' said Laura. 'She was a little scared of you, I think.'

He came to put his hand on his wife's shoulder. She was rigid with tension, and chilled through and through. He began urging her to come home, but she sat quite still, not answering, not resisting, simply remaining where she was. At length, seeing he could not shift her, he went back to the house. Then Mary came, climbing the narrow stairs in the cottage, standing by the bed.

'Oh, Mum,' she said sadly. 'I didn't think she was so old. Now we'll never know.'

Laura turned her head stiffly to look at her. 'Know what?'

'About you, of course! Sophie knew more than anyone. And we never asked.'

'There was nothing to ask. Why should anyone want to?'

Mary looked at her mother. She seemed almost as pale as the corpse. Only a day ago all this would have been too frightening to bear, Sophie dead, her mother once again shivering in distress. But today, and only today, Mary had taken her first true step away from her mother. And for the first time, she could see her as she was. Suddenly, safe in her new-found happiness, she knew she had to speak.

'We have to know who you are,' said Mary quietly. 'We don't know anything. And it wouldn't matter if you were happy. But you're not.'

'I can't ever be happy,' whispered her mother.

'I know that's not true. You used to be. You could be. But not if you go on like this.'

Laura looked away. She let go of Sophie's fingers and buried her face in her hands.

They buried her in Gunthwaite churchyard three days later. To everyone's surprise, Dora was there. She arrived at the graveside moments before the coffin, not as elegant as usual, somehow lacking her usual self-assurance. She almost looked embarrassed, thought Mary. Perhaps almost – happy. The emotion was inappropriate, she frowned on it in herself as much as in Dora. It seemed obscene next to the misery of Laura and Marie. They stood and watched the coffin sink into the earth, and their tears fell with it, a rain of sorrow.

'We brought nothing into this world and it is certain we can carry nothing out,' intoned the vicar. But Sophie had possessed nothing in between. She had been indigent from first to last.

'The Lord gave and the Lord taketh away.' What had he ever given Sophie? A warm heart that led her into trouble and distress.

Laura turned from the graveside, her face contorted, pushing past Michael as if he wasn't there. Going blindly through the small group they parted for her, not sure what to do. But Dora, on the edge, caught her arm. Laura stopped, gazing at her in wild-eyed distress.

'I can't – I can't—' she panted.

'Then don't,' said Dora. 'Come along, do.'

Holding Laura firmly by the arm, she escorted her out of the churchyard and away.

The service droned on. Mary felt tortured by things she didn't wish to see: the ugly vicar, Marie in her grief, the coffin. There was Michael, of course, but behind him stood Gabriel, looking bored and restless. He was probably thinking of his next drink. She turned to rest her eyes on the church, lovely even on this chill autumn day, its ageless beauty settling her thoughts. Connor's hand took hers. She thought, Everyone will know. But of course, that didn't matter. Nothing mattered but that Sophie was gone, as they all must go, leaving behind success or failure, each the same.

She couldn't think of it for herself. Death seemed an impossibility, even now. But she thought of her mother and felt cold. What if Laura had died in London, what if she died now? Everything would be ended miserably and there would never be another chance to make it right.

The service ground to its inevitable conclusion. Marie, gaunt and suddenly tearless, took up earth and tossed it into the grave, handful after handful. Her little frenzy exhausted her and she stood panting. Michael gently took her arm and led her away.

Deborah and Piers were sneaking off into the fields, climbing over the low stone wall. Mary snorted and said, 'Typical! They won't do their duty at the funeral tea.'

'They might turn up,' said Connor enigmatically. 'Later.'

'Later than what?' She stared at him, not understanding. Sometimes he could be very obscure.

He said nothing. On the way back to the car, struggling against the urge to indecent haste, she suddenly said, 'We can't leave it any longer, you know. Mum's in such a state.'

'Leave what?'

Mary sighed and linked her fingers in front of her. 'Sorting her out. Someone's got to, Con!'

'Mary Cooper, psychiatrist,' he said with heavy irony. 'Life's little sadnesses alleviated on request.'

'Hers isn't a little sadness!' She turned to him, her hair blowing across her face, her eyes glowing with cold and agitation. He thought how lovely she looked; how much he loved her. He hardly heard what she had to say.

'This isn't really about Sophie at all. My mother isn't a whole person, Con. She's in two parts. The person she was and the person she's become. But the girl she used to be won't die, however hard she tries to kill her. She's tried everything, Gabriel and all. For a while it was all right, she had the girl under control, but the minute she drops her guard there she is again, whispering. Reminding. Mum's haunted, Connor. Haunted by herself.'

'You talk such rubbish, child!' He shivered, and told himself it was the cold autumn wind.

'You know it's nothing of the kind. You see, Con, we've got to find the girl she used to be. Find out who she was, where she came from, what really happened. Mum doesn't know. She's shut everything up so tight she can't remember a thing. We've got to rediscover her. And let her be whole again.'

He said nothing. Mary waited and waited, but he walked to the car and started the engine without speaking once. Did he really think her a fool? Didn't he see that she was right? His crooked, Irish profile gave nothing away.

Back at the house Laura was piling sandwiches erratically on to plates. Mary went to help her, and saw that Dora was leaning on the dresser, smoking an idle cigarette. 'Your mother's not up to all this, Mary,' she declared. 'You ought to get that sister of yours to use her energy productively. Instead of reproductively. If you understand me.'

Mary shot her a furious glance. No doubt she knew everything about Deborah now. She had visited Zwmskorski merely to satisfy a vulgar curiosity, she'd do nothing to help. Mary pushed a plate of fruit cake at her aunt and said crisply, 'Pass this round, would you, Dora? I really don't know what Deborah's doing, and neither do you.'

'I think I can guess,' said Dora, and blew a cloud of smoke over the cake. Mary shoved the plate willy-nilly into her hands and bustled off.

The gathering flourished, as such things do when death is neither untimely nor unexpected. People said, 'She was a game old girl, I'll say that for her. No idea where she came from. Gave the word colourful a whole new meaning!' And they laughed, because they dared not say what they really thought. That the old woman was a burned out whore, and they couldn't believe that they were here. Who went to a whore's funeral, after all? The mind boggled.

Mary drank two quick glasses of sherry. The room buzzed a little less threateningly. Suddenly she saw her mother, sitting outside on the terrace. She was alone, without a coat, wearing only a thin blue dress. Even from here Mary could see that she shivered. She made to rush out to her, but Connor, appearing soundlessly beside her, caught her arm. They stood together, watching, as Laura leaned back to the wall of the house, hitting her head sharply against the stone. For a second her face cleared. She looked momentarily relaxed. Then she leaned forward again, pushed back again, and struck herself once more. It was a gesture she was constantly repeating.

Connor turned and met Mary's wide, anguished eyes. 'Go and fetch her, will you? I don't know if we can put her together. But you must be right. In the name of God, we have to try.'

Chapter Thirty-five

The ferry was heaving and bucking on a gale-whipped sea. Beyond the heavy glass of the windows white horses charged upon them, like ranks of unending cavalry. A trawler, some distance off, was tossing in and out of view. Mary and Connor sat side by side and stared at it.

After a while Connor got up, went hastily to the washroom and returned, looking like a ghost. A waiter, smugly efficient, cleared full ashtrays and dirty glasses. As the smell of stale cigarettes hit, Mary lurched to her feet and paid her own visit. When she returned she and Connor leaned against each other, like weary drunks.

'Oh God,' he said. 'There's another hour at least.'

'I should have listened to you,' said Mary. 'I've never been on a boat before.'

'We could have waited a week, though. At this time of year.'

'If I'd known it was going to be like this, I'd have waited forever!'

But a deck door was being unlocked. With one accord they staggered to their feet and launched themselves into the wind and spray. At once they began to feel better. 'If it wasn't so cold,' said Mary, her teeth chattering.

'Rather this than the collywobbles.' Connor pulled her close in the lee of a lifeboat. He wrapped his arms around her, revelling in the sensation of her body against his, thighs, belly, breasts. 'God, but you excite me,' he whispered.

'Don't.' She was blushing, pulling half-heartedly away. There were people near.

He let her go, and she wouldn't look at him. They'd discussed nothing of this. They had come away together with no clear understanding of what each of them meant by it. Would they book two rooms tonight? What did Connor expect? Mary felt shy and at a loss.

She said hurriedly, 'Did Marie tell you anything useful? You didn't say.'

'Just that Sophie brought your mother back from a village near Arras. She thought it had a name like Chouilly. Or something like that.'

'Oh.' Mary studied her glove. 'What was Sophie doing there in the first place?'

'No idea. And what was your mother doing there? She always says her mother was English.'

'She might have made that up,' said Mary. 'I always thought she wanted to be English. At least, she thought Michael wanted it. She's got the oddest ideas about Dad.'

The boat gave a more than usually sickening roll and plunge. Mary fell against Connor, and he held her, breathing hard. She was aware of him as never before, hard, urgent. She was suddenly more than a little frightened. Everything was changing, nothing was familiar. Despite her good French, the French waiters and crew seemed foreign and slightly threatening. And now Connor was different too. She looked up at him, her eyes full of fear. But all he said was 'Your make-up's run. You shouldn't wear it. It hides you too much.'

'Sometimes I like to hide.' She shuddered and pulled away from him.

'Not from me, Mary. Never from me.'

Was that a plea or another threat? She went to the rail and stood looking into the murk. The French coast seemed very close, but the storm had blown them off course and they could be anywhere. Little, red-roofed houses crouched near the water's edge, and beyond, on roads of grey silk, lorries and vans chugged by. It wasn't English. It wasn't home. She wished she had never come this far, she didn't know why she had.

But passengers were starting to collect their things. While they had been on deck an announcement had been made. They went back into the hot, smelly cabin and stood, suitcases in hand. 'It's about time we had an adventure,' said Connor, and grinned at her. She tried to grin back.

They caught a train near the port, to Paris. A trim guard paraded along the carriage, his ludicrous hat perched between his eyes. 'Mesdames, Messieurs,' he intoned, punching tickets.

'How long to Paris?' asked Mary in French hesitantly.

'Half an hour, Mam'selle.' He went his way, leaving them looking at each other.

'We'll get a hotel straight off,' said Connor. 'You look exhausted.'

'Yes.' She studied her gloves again. They hadn't talked about this, except that, when Michael asked if they would have separate rooms, she had looked outraged and said, 'Of course!' What had she meant? What had Connor thought she meant? Oh, if only now she could be at home in her own small room at Gunthwaite.

The station was noisy and crowded. They pushed through the people, heading for the street, engulfed in a Babel of language. Mary's ear wasn't used to so much French, she felt overwhelmed. Everyone seemed very crisp and purposeful. There were men in lemon waistcoats and girls in short raincoats belted tight. Chic women with heavy lipstick pushed past as if she wasn't there. Connor, carrying the cases, said cheerfully, 'Great, isn't it? Wow!'

She felt as she had that time in London. Small. Frightened. But, spurred by Connor's enthusiasm, she smiled and agreed. They found a Tourist Information office, and were given a list of possible hotels. They took a taxi, and stopped outside a tall, thin house with green shutters. 'Wait here,' said Connor, and ran in to make enquiries. He came back, grinning, and paid off the taxi. 'The place is great. Like a new pin, and flowers everywhere. From our room you can see the Eiffel Tower.'

She followed him up the stairs, past smiling Madame and ingratiating chambermaid. He had taken one room with a very large, very high double bed.

When the door was closed and they were alone she went to sit very quietly on the edge of the bed. Connor was at the window, remarking on the lace curtains, the quaint rug, the old-fashioned chamber pot. 'But there's a bathroom down the landing, thank God. Everything's enormous, you'll never dare to have a bath.'

His conversation dwindled at last. He stood silent by the window, looking at her obliquely, rubbing his thumb against his forefinger in a nervous tic. He drew in his breath. 'Come on, Mary,' he said at last. 'This is our adventure! It was your idea.'

'The double bed wasn't.'

'So it's that, is it? You can't turn prudish on me now! Not after everything.'

'What's everything? Did you only come because of the double bed? Not for me or my mother at all?'

'No!'

But his own vehemence betrayed him. He ran his hands through his hair and came to sit beside her, saying urgently, 'You can't pretend you don't want this too! We're in love, aren't we? We've been happier these last weeks than ever before. And there's nothing to be frightened of. I mean, if you're worried – I've taken care of all that.'

'Ready for anything,' said Mary bitterly. 'But I'm not ready to be taken for granted.'

'There's no need to be a bloody fool! Mary, we're in the modern world now. Look at Deborah and Piers.'

She swung round to look at him. 'What about them?'

'Don't play the innocent, Mary! You must know they're at it day and night.'

'At what?'

'Oh, Mary, come on!'

Her cheeks suddenly flamed. She could feel the heat consuming her, making even her eyes burn. 'She couldn't! Deb wouldn't be so silly.'

377

'What's silly about it? They're in love, just like us.'

'No, they're not. Piers might be. Deb's just – oh Deb, Deb!'

She got up and paced the room, her fists clenched. If only she'd realised before she left! Did her mother know? She was certain she did not. But Dora did. She'd bank on it. All the half-understood hints that Dora had tossed her way now became glassy clear. She wouldn't stir herself on Deb's behalf now. Why should she? Piers had stood ready for Deb's fall, and had found it worth the wait. Deb would never get free.

She swung round on Con. 'I don't want it. Not now.'

Reaching out to soothe her, he said, 'You're just tired, that's all. Have a rest, we'll have some tea—'

'Madame said no drinks in the rooms. But even so. I don't want it like this. Because we're here, because no one will know, because everyone does. It isn't right, Connor! It isn't – isn't—' She flailed for a word that would suit. He supplied it. 'Romantic,' he said, with heavy irony. 'You want the ring and the flowers and the pink mists. When it comes down to it, Mary, when you leave aside all your youthful protestations, you're just too bloody conventional!'

Mary said nothing. She went to sit on the bed again, a tentative perching. Oh, but she was tired. After a while, as Connor still stood, large and gloomy, she rested her head on the pillow. And after a little while longer she took off her shoes and lay down altogether. Dozing, she was vaguely aware that he had come to lie beside her.

Later that night she awoke. There was a glow from a street lamp, reminding her again of London. Connor was sprawled on the bed, still dressed. She slipped off her skirt and blouse, and wriggled quickly under the covers. She felt better now. She thought how mean she had been not to make everything clear before. But she hadn't been clear about it herself until the room and the bed confronted her. It was just – she didn't want to be a Dora in Con's life. She knew she wasn't, knew she couldn't be, but like this – it had the smell of that other relationship. She wasn't a Dora, nor even a Deb. She couldn't be casual about making love. If Connor hadn't realised how important this was to her then he didn't know her at all.

She tried to sleep again. The bed was warm and comfortable, smelling of starch and dried rosemary. It reminded her of the pot pourri at Fairlands, prepared each year by Mrs Fitzalan-Howard and set in little bowls here and there. Gabriel had toyed with some when she talked to him last week. She hadn't wanted to go. It was Connor who insisted. She could see Gabriel now, thinner, more gaunt, the whites of his eyes flecked with yellow and his hands playing restlessly with the petals of the summer past. 'I should come with you,' he'd said at last, suddenly staring at her. 'I knew her in Paris. I was seventeen, she was – what? Thirteen? Fourteen? Madame said thirteen, but then she would. Wanted me to think I'd done it with a child, you see. God. We were both children.'

'You – you slept with her, you mean?' Mary had felt her throat almost close on the words.

But Gabriel only nodded. 'Yes. Look, I don't need your disapproval! I was seventeen, I didn't know. I went to a Paris brothel when I should have been going round the Louvre, and there she was. This girl. Naturally I thought – but I was wrong. Well, they all have to start somewhere, I suppose. And then, years later, I met her again. In London. I hadn't forgotten one moment. I was still bearing a grudge.'

'You? What about *her*?' Mary's outrage burned in her eyes, Gabriel's own eyes, staring back at him.

'If it hadn't been me it would have been someone else!' he snarled. 'And believe me, I was humiliated. The women in those houses are different. I was robbed, insulted and thrown half-dressed on to the street. I warn you, Mary, you don't know the first thing about places like that. Madame was a creature from hell. Bonacieux her name was. The biggest, fattest, hardest old harridan that ever ran a house in the Rue de Claret.'

Mary lay and thought of Gabriel. Gabriel and her mother, aged thirteen – fourteen? A child, lying with a stranger, because there was nothing else. And here she was, a grown woman, choosing to love or not, on a whim, a fancy. It wasn't fair, she thought bitterly. It was as if her mother's good fortune had been taken at birth and locked away. Was it Mary's now? Did she have the key? She lay in the gloom, trying to will herself to refuse her mother's rightful, misplaced blessing. She needed it so much more than her daughter. If only it could descend upon her now.

She stirred restlessly and Connor woke. 'Get undressed and come under the covers,' whispered Mary.

'What for? A change of heart?'

'No. Not yet. Just to be – close.'

But he wouldn't hold her. He held her hand instead, and she thought, I love him, truly I do. If he had reached for her then he would have found no resistance. But he only said, 'Were you thinking about your mother?'

'Yes. In a brothel at thirteen.'

'Don't expect it still to be there.'

'I don't. But if it is, and I go in – what if they won't let me out?'

'You'll end up in the harem of a sultan, no less. Don't worry, the moment they find out what you're really like they'll have you out of there faster than you can blink.'

'Beast.'

'Harpy. Go to sleep.'

At Gunthwaite, Laura lay wakeful. For weeks past she had barely done more than catnap. Her thoughts wandered from place to place, year to year. Sometimes she could almost believe herself back in that flat with Sophie, watching the drunks through the crack in the door. Then there was the farm and Jean – Jean! She sat up, gasping and panting.

Michael reached out sleepily and pulled her down again. 'Don't,' he murmured. 'Laura, don't.'

'No.'

He was reaching beneath her nightgown, beginning the usual, cursory coupling. She lay rigid beneath him. Waiting. Refusing to feel. Sometimes, when she was least in control, when her mind was flying apart like a cracked plate, the sensations would come, like it or not. The tingling, burning, building excitement that was not and must never be part of Michael's wife. He would hate her for that, hate her and know her at last! The whore. The used, insatiable streetgirl who knew everything because she'd done everything. And she had. She had. Beyond counting. Never knowing their names. Feeling them within her – just like this.

She turned her face to the pillow, opening her mouth in a soundless scream.

Mary looked up at a tall, imposing house. There were green velvet curtains at the upstairs windows and neat windowboxes, empty now but no doubt bright with geraniums in summer. The brass knocker was polished, the steps swept, and the expected brass plate advertising a doctor or a dentist or even an embassy for a minor state was nowhere to be seen.

'Perhaps it's a private house now,' said Mary doubtfully.

'I should say it's a bit big.' Connor stood back and stared again at the windows. A face looked down at him. A pretty, blonde girl gave him a meaningful grin.

Without another word he ran up the steps to knock. But even before his hand fell, the door opened before him. 'Monsieur,' intoned a voice. A doorman stood respectfully aside, waiting for him to enter a large mirrored hallway, dominated by a crystal chandelier and a wide staircase.

Connor glanced back towards Mary. She was standing wide-eyed at the bottom of the steps, as if expecting him at any moment to disappear and never be seen again. 'Come on!' he called robustly. 'This is certainly the place.'

As Mary ascended the steps under the surprised gaze of the doorman, Connor dazzled him with a smile. 'Madame Bonacieux,' he declared. '*Tout de suite.*'

The words were electric. The moment Mary was in the hall the door was shut and a torrent of French erupted. Mary replied tentatively, in nervous half sentences. Connor put his hand on her arm. 'Tell him we have to see her. Tell him we'll pay.'

Mary shot him a surprised glance. They had money, but not much. And in Paris, a cup of coffee cost pounds.

But, obediently, she said, 'We'll pay. We have to see Madame. My mother used to be one of her girls.'

There was a silence. The doorman was grizzled enough to have seen very many girls. He looked from Mary to Connor assessingly, before saying in English, 'I will speak to Madame. I will ask if she will see you.' He walked away, giving no hint that they should follow. Standing by themselves in the hall, they looked around. The blonde girl was watching from the landing. She was wearing a silk robe, hanging open to show a black bra, black stockings and nothing else. When Connor looked up she leaned on the banister, giving a friendly smile.

'My God,' said Mary with feeling. 'What next?'

'Madame Bonacieux, I hope,' murmured Connor. 'How can you deny me, girl? Deny me and then bring me to this?'

'It just wasn't right,' said Mary in confusion. 'You can't think that I – I mean, you wouldn't want me to—' She jerked her head in the direction of the landing.

'Believe me, I didn't know *anyone* did that,' said Connor. 'Travel certainly broadens something. But I'm not sure it's my mental capacities, somehow.'

The girl on the landing was beginning to do stretch and bend exercises. Mary could feel hysterical giggles beginning, and was more than thankful to see the grizzled doorman return. She took a step back, expecting to be thrown out, hoping that's what he would do. But he gave his disdainful sniff and said, 'Come. Madame will see you. Don't stay long.'

They followed him through a door and down a corridor. He opened another door and stood aside. Lying on a bed, dressed entirely in purple silk, was the biggest, fattest, ugliest old woman they had ever imagined they might see.

She gazed out at them unsmiling, from button eyes sunk within folds of flesh. 'Don't tell me,' she said contemptuously. 'I might have known. Lori's girl.'

They perched uncomfortably on small gilt chairs. A bell was rung, and in a moment a maid brought a silver tray, bearing three exquisite glasses. Connor took one and blinked at the weight. The twisted dark red stem swirled out into a heavy bowl of pinkish glass, colouring the liquid within. He sipped but didn't recognise the taste. For a wild moment he thought the woman might be drugging them, only to find that she was watching him, his thought anticipated.

'It is only cassis,' she said in heavily accented English. 'Did Lori tell you I was dangerous?'

'She's never said anything about you,' said Mary, out of courtesy speaking French. 'She never says anything about her past.'

The old woman grinned and lapsed into French also. 'Not many of my girls do. And not many are as lucky as your mother, child. But it wasn't luck. Brains, she had. Could have been the mistress of a king, could Lori, and I'd taught her all the tricks. A man never left her bed unsatisfied. Can you say that, girl? Can you? Don't you let this black-haired boy have it easy. Ask your mother. You want them begging to get between your legs.'

Mary was scarlet with embarrassment. She found she could hardly breathe. She said, gasping, 'We wanted some help, Madame. My mother's been unhappy lately. Very unhappy.'

Madame shrugged her massive shoulders. 'So? Whores always are. They hate doing it and hate giving it up. And she always thought too much. A man had her when she was a child, on some stinking farm way out in the country. She never quite got over it.'

'Do you know which farm, Madame?' asked Mary, suddenly eager. 'Do you know where she came from? If you know anything about her, anything at all, please tell.'

But all at once Madame's eyes were like pebbles. 'And why should I tell you anything?' she asked softly. 'What's past is past. She had a rough life, rougher than most by all accounts, but there isn't a girl here who didn't. Best forgotten, lives like that. Your mother's still alive, isn't she? Why should she want to remember?'

Suddenly Mary found courage. 'She doesn't,' she said softly. 'The trouble is, she can't forget. It's haunting her. I thought, if she knew everything, knew the truth—'

'Rubbish!' Madame sat up and waved her hands at them. 'She doesn't need truth! Tell her to drink more, and take a new lover. A woman doesn't need the past. Not a woman like her. I tell you, she was the best trained girl I ever had. Politicians, scientists, everyone wanted her. And she wasn't a beauty, no more than you are, girl, but she had that look about her – wasn't a man didn't think he'd make her love him. Except the one who beat her, of course, but there's always one of those. She'd have got over it. A girl like her who hasn't a family, hasn't any love, she needs the men. Feels like love to her too, you see? Wonderful workers, girls like that.'

Mary sighed and got to her feet. Madame said sharply, 'Angry now, are you? Because I won't do as you say? You owe me twenty francs.'

382

'You didn't tell us anything,' snapped Mary. 'Besides, you've made enough from my mother by the sound of it.'

'Nasty, aren't you? Tell you what, get rid of the boyfriend and come round tonight. I'll teach you how to hump him. For free!'

Mary grabbed Connor's hand and dragged him from the room. They stood for a moment beyond the closed door, listening to Madame chuckling to herself. 'She said – she said she'd teach me!' whispered Mary, wide-eyed. 'She meant it too.'

'Did she tell you anything?'

'She never meant to. The old bitch!'

Connor said nothing. They went together to the front door, and the doorman stood up. Connor said, 'You go on, Mary. I won't be long.'

'What?' She opened her eyes wide. The blonde girl was gone from the stairs, but from a distant room there came the sound of knowing laughter. 'Go on, Mary! Wait down the street.'

She went outside. The afternoon was mild, as if winter had decided not to bite that year. It seemed strange to be out in the normal world. In that house everything was about sex, there was nothing that did not concern it. She thought of the blonde, her pubic hair darkest gold. A beautiful woman, more beautiful than Mary would ever be. Of course Connor must want her!

She sat on a wall, chewing at her lip. Suddenly the door of the house opened and Connor came walking quickly down the street. She got up, staring at him, trying to read his thoughts in his face. 'What's the matter?' he asked, staring at her. 'Did you think I'd not come out?'

'I thought – I thought you might want – that girl.'

'Her? Bit of a Dora type, if you ask me. Not really my style.'

'What did you stay for then?'

He grinned at her, obviously pleased with himself. Then he took her hand and swung her along the street, saying, 'Wouldn't you like to know? What will you give me when I tell you?'

'Tell me what? Was it the doorman? Did he know?'

'The name of the village? Yes.'

He tempted her with the wait, rounding the corner before he said, 'It's a place called Chaillot. Madame sent Sophie there one year to recover from – well, an operation.'

'An abortion, you mean.'

'I suppose so. It wasn't the usual place. Sophie had a lover at the time, Madame gave her the address as a favour. He only remembers because Sophie left the inn and didn't pay, and she was tracked here months later. The police came, I think, it was a bit garbled. His English is very hit and miss. In the end Madame agreed to settle up if Sophie paid her off in instalments, and the doorman trekked out to the village with the cash. In the middle of nowhere, he says.'

383

Mary let go his hand and began to gnaw the edge of her thumb. She felt more nervous than excited. She hadn't told Connor anything Madame had said. Might her mother still long for this life? She looked covertly at the men passing by, tall, short, fat, thin. A prostitute must lie with them all. And she wouldn't lie with a man for love.

They checked out of the hotel within the hour, but even so it was almost four before they were on a train. They wouldn't reach Arras much before eight, so the guard said. They were to change at Amiens. Lunch had been no more than a snack, grabbed from a café near the station; they had seen nothing of Paris. Mary wasn't sure that she minded. The Rue de Claret had shocked her more than she'd expected. Paris seemed tainted now. The loveliness of the skyline beyond the river seemed nothing but a sham.

Connor put down the map and looked across at her. 'Are you all right?' he asked softly.

'Yes. Why shouldn't I be?' She managed a bright, false smile.

'I thought you wanted to do this. But if you're going to be upset—'

'I'm not. Really.'

The other people in the carriage glanced at them. Perhaps they understood. Mary wished she did. What was she going to say to her mother about Madame Bonacieux? Old, cynical and corrupt, she created victims and then saved them. Mary wasn't at all surprised at what had happened to her mother in that house. Perhaps the greatest surprise was that her mother had survived it.

She dozed until Amiens, and then sat sour-mouthed on the station waiting for a train. Connor went to a kiosk and brought back strong coffee laced with spirits. Every sip bolstered Mary's flagging energies. She looked up at Connor, marvelling at his continuing enthusiasm. He was a natural traveller, she realised. Not for him the timid thoughts of home. Secure and self-contained, as perhaps only a man can be, he was revelling even in this chilly wait.

He looked down at her and she saw his face change. What was he thinking? She looked away, wondering if this morning had changed his mind. He might see her as plain and ordinary, a bad bargain after all, when a few francs would buy him a blonde and a free tomorrow. But Connor, looking down into her pale face, had thought his heart would break for loving her. She seemed so young and so frail. The flame of her spirit seemed to gutter when harsh winds blew, but the clear, bright fire never diminished. He thought her the bravest girl he had ever known. He might have spoken. But then she looked away.

When the train at last came in it was old and wheezing. A man two seats away reeked of garlic, and the air was thick with cigarette smoke. They were both very hungry, and as the train stuttered along, stopping at every halt and junction, even Connor began to look grim. The guard proved to have been guessing about times, and it was almost nine before they came to Arras. Mary stood on the windy platform, overwhelmed by her day, little knowing that her mother had felt much the same, so many years before.

The station emptied quickly. Soon they were looking out at a deserted street, the wind blowing leaves and rubbish. A man with a very small dog was striding along the pavement, the dog's legs a blur of movement at his heels. Without a word of discussion, Connor and Mary followed him, soon finding themselves in a maze of little streets. Charming shops selling bric-à-brac and paintings were dotted here and there amidst neat houses, and there was a restaurant, brilliantly lit.

'We should find somewhere to stay first,' said Mary doubtfully. 'It's so late.'

'If we don't eat we'll not have the strength to find somewhere to stay,' said Connor. 'Look! Everyone's drinking gallons of red wine. We'll have a gallon each.'

They sat at a table and drank, gnawing on bread the while. The room was warm, the setting indisputably strange. The morning's disturbing talk seemed years past; here it was just Mary and Connor, feeling their way. They ordered the cheapest menu, soup and some sort of stew, and it was hot and filling and good. Mary plucked up her courage and asked the patron if he could recommend somewhere for them to stay, and he shouted across the room to a small, square man with a moustache, whose wife let rooms in the summer. He eyed them thoughtfully. One room or two? One, said Mary, and the man said he'd go and telephone his wife.

She turned back to face Connor, her face hot. She could see he'd understood. 'Let's look at it as an economy measure,' said Con, with his white-toothed, wolfish grin. She didn't know what to say to him. She didn't know what to think. This was a dance of measured and difficult steps.

The room was very small and very clean, above the kitchen in a tall thin townhouse. The bathroom was shared with the family, and they would breakfast with them as well, Monsieur and Madame, Madame's ancient mother and three neat children. Mary undressed while Connor did likewise in the bathroom, and then they sat, in their nightclothes, side by side in the hard bed. They could faintly hear the old lady mumbling to herself in another room, and, nearer at hand, Monsieur and Madame arguing. Immediately behind the bed, sounding as if it might almost be in the same room, one of the children coughed. They rocked with silent laughter. They dared do nothing that might make a noise.

Mary slid beneath the covers, and Connor slid down to join her.

They kissed, in absolute silence. His hands touched her breasts, lightly brushing the nipples, and she let out a gasp. Her own hands pressed against his chest, her thighs against his, her breath warm on his neck. He groaned, very softly. And let her go and turned his back.

In the morning they walked to the town and bought a map, sitting in a café poring over the fine print. It was raining, a steadily thickening drizzle through which cars and lorries swished continuously, spattering the café windows with mud. But Mary and Connor were in good spirits this morning. They were learning to be comfortable together. Little by little the intimacies of life were becoming known to them, the compromises, the tactful agreements. He knew she hated to be watched while she did her make-up. She knew he liked to write his diary in peace. Mary's thoughts kept darting to a future in which they would live together always, arranging their lives around each other's habits, fitting neatly together like parts of a fine machine. The thought pleased her. She wondered how it was that they used to squabble so.

'I can't see it anywhere,' said Connor grumpily. 'I was a fool. I should have asked the man for directions, I just assumed we'd find it on a map.'

'We could ask,' said Mary hopefully. But they questioned the waitress, and then the owner, and no one knew of Chaillot. They were advised to try at the library, but they got lost looking for it. Eventually they slumped, weary-footed, near a taxi rank.

'We could ask a taxi-driver,' suggested Mary, without conviction.

'OK.' Connor got up to try his painstaking French. As the days passed he was starting to be more confident in his usage, although his ear was still confounded by the relentless speed of the natives. Mary, brought up on Sophie's lightning delivery, was quite at home.

She stood beneath an awning, watching a group of men gather around Connor, all of them short, all of them gesticulating. He rose up above them like a different sort of tree, the Celt amidst Gauls. Familiarity with his face, his hair, the slight crookedness of his nose, made him seem more handsome to her than perhaps he really was. He made a gesture she recognised, pointing down with one finger and describing a circle. For some silly reason it made her heart contract.

Then he came back to her. She was caught up with her thoughts and barely heard what he said. 'Believe it or not, they know Chaillot. At least, it might be my French, but it's twenty or so miles from here. Not all that small either. It's called Remy-Chaillot on the map.'

'It might not be the same place.'

'No idea. But someone's brother's got a car-hire business. He's going to bring us his cheapest model. God knows what.'

They ate lunch with the taxi drivers in a small, smelly café. The tables were plastic-topped, the wine thin and vinegary, served without asking as you sat down. The meal for the day was cassoulet, great lumps of meat and vegetables with unappetising pieces of what looked like bacon fat floating like icebergs in the murk. Connor chewed manfully through them and said they were delicious, but Mary was a coward and hid them under her fork. The wine took the edge off the discomforts of the place; the draughts, the smell, the dampness of their coats. A small grey 2CV drew up at the door and the driver came in. It was the brother. This was their car.

Connor haggled with determination, refusing all blandishments in the form of cognac and cigarettes. Mary's skill with the language seemed more of a handicap than an asset in negotiation, Connor thrived on the thunderous '*Non!*' accompanied by firmly crossed arms. Her more tentative assertion that a car with no rear seats and a hole in the floor could not possibly be expensive was greeted with profound silence. She felt as if she had said something terribly rude.

Suddenly there were handshakes all round. The cigarettes were offered again, and the cognac came out, compulsory glasses. The car, complete with rattles, bangs and disconcerting groaning on corners, was theirs.

They set off at once. Somehow the little car gave them a feeling of security, as if they were snails with their house on their backs. The weather invited early-evening gloom, and they were woozy from drink. But the taxi drivers had all leaped into their cabs and roared off regardless, so that must be the French way. They struggled with the roadsigns and the coming dark, battling their way through the incipient Arras rush-hour, trying to find the St Quentin road. Three miles outside town they had their first puncture, and found there was no jack. When at last, at eight in the evening, they limped into a village, they took the only room going at the café, ate pickled fish, and lay next to one another listening to the television in the bar.

'Still no romance,' said Connor ruefully. 'I can't be trying hard enough.'

Mary said, 'I didn't know you were trying at all.'

He took her hand beneath the clammy covers. 'Well, I am, sweetheart. Don't think I'm not. But life's against me.'

She giggled. She thought how nightmarish this would seem on her own. Yet with Connor each day was a present, unwrapped bit by bit, new and exciting even when opened and you could see what it was. She didn't mind the café or the car or the rain, or even the pickled fish. With Connor, anywhere, she was happy.

Chapter Thirty-six

Dora flung down her hairbrush and turned irritably from her dressing table. She was wearing only bra and pants, showing her to advantage as a full-bodied, sensual woman. She liked the way she looked just now. She liked to see the bruises on her nipples glowing darkly through the lace of her bra. They reminded her.

Gabriel was lying on the bed, not yet dressed, staring at her in the mirror. Dora flared at him, 'Will you stop looking at me like that? I didn't come home to be stared at first thing in the morning by a drunk.'

'What did you come home for then?'

'I can't imagine.'

She went to the wardrobe and rifled vigorously through the clothes. Her hands touched a red silk dress – she paused, caught by a thought. Wodgy had said she looked ravishing in this. Wearing her red dress, she had danced and gambled until she could tell from his eyes that he wanted her and wouldn't wait. They had gone upstairs and everything was ready: champagne, silk sheets – the leather thongs he liked.

It always began quite calmly, of course. It was only later that the fights began. She never dared let him tie her up completely, whatever he promised, whatever he said. After all, when she had him trussed, arms and legs spread, fighting to get away, even she felt the urge to torture. It was the look of panic, the intake of breath – the power. If ever he had her in that position he'd never confine himself to little, cruel excesses, she thought, closing her hand again on the red dress. He'd destroy her.

The thought was almost orgasmic. She shuddered, and Gabriel said, 'Good, was he?'

She turned. 'Yes,' she said shortly. 'Very good. But then, he doesn't let drink turn him into a gelding.'

'Bitch.'

He lay there, watching her. God, but she had wonderful breasts! He thought of another man with her, on her, in her. Did she tell him about her useless, newly impotent husband? He'd never be impotent with Laura, he thought. If he'd had Laura he'd never have turned out like this. Suddenly he was aroused, suddenly he

388

wanted to show his bitch of a wife that he was still something of a man!

He flung off the bed and grabbed Dora's arms. She turned on him like a tigress, striking out. He'd forgotten she was so strong. Somehow he got her to the bed, got on top of her, his knee between hers. Her face snarled up at him, excited, alive. He realised she was enjoying this. 'Do it,' she hissed. 'Go on, do it if you're man enough.'

He dragged at her underclothes, discovering hot, wet hair. He'd forgotten how intoxicating his own wife could be! He fumbled at himself, reaching for what she needed, discovering – softness. Even now, suffused with aggressive desire, he was barely semi-erect. Not now, he thought desperately. Let me not fail now!

Dora reached down and felt him. 'Oh God,' she said contemptuously. 'I might have known.' She rolled out from underneath and went without speaking to her wardrobe once again.

Gabriel said, 'I'll be OK in a minute. You've got to give me some time.'

'I don't have to give you a damn' thing,' snapped Dora. She found a clean pair of pants and eased herself into them. 'Even Piers can do better than you nowadays. He's got Deborah flat on her back a dozen times a day, and loving every minute of it. You were never like that. Even when we married I was the one who had to make all the moves. God! Why didn't I see what I could have been doing? I must have spent years waiting for you to get it up.'

'That isn't how it was and you know it. And you can stop spreading stories about Piers. He'll never get near Deborah Cooper. She's much too pretty.'

Dora stopped in the act of putting on a pair of slacks. 'For your information, Piers is screwing Deborah every blessed night. I agree, he's done well for himself. And she could certainly do better. But I suppose that when a girl's had to run from London in case some pornographic photographs of herself turn up, then she wants any masculine comfort that's available.'

'What?' Gabriel stared at her in amazement and Dora looked back, wide-eyed. 'Didn't I tell you? Somebody took some photographs of Deborah in a very compromising position. That poor girl is living in dread that one day Laura will come down to breakfast and find herself looking at her daughter's arse in a totally new way. No wonder she lets Piers shag her. There's not much else she can do.'

She shrugged herself into a sweater, picked up a brush and swept her hair vigorously back from her face. Gabriel looked stunned and she was glad of it. She was sick of him lying there, sick of him looking at her, sick of him being no use to her, ever, drunk or sober. It was time he realised what was really going on in the world. He was even being defeated by his son.

When she had gone Gabriel, still lying on the bed, listened for long minutes to the sound of his own grating breaths. Then he rolled towards the cupboard. Taking out a whisky bottle, he took a long, desperate pull.

Gabriel sat slumped by the gate. He had intended to walk through, but sudden wooziness had overtaken him. He leaned against the gatepost, looking up at the sky, wondering how it was that he could feel sober in his mind while his legs betrayed him.

How much had he had that day? A bottle? More? It was barely four o'clock. He felt ashamed of himself suddenly. Suppose someone came and saw him? Michael, for instance. Laura. But Michael would be worse. When you'd spent a lifetime being the golden boy, being admired as better than your brother, to be looked down on as a drunk by that selfsame brother was more than a man could bear. But the face that came and looked down at him belonged to neither Michael nor Laura. It was Piers.

He said nothing for a long, thoughtful moment. Gabriel glowered up at him, trying to think of something pertinent to say. Finally he muttered, 'If you can't help me up you can sod off.'

Piers said, 'I've got a load of muck to bring through here. I'm trying to decide whether to move you or bring it through regardless.'

'Is that supposed to be amusing? Your parochial idea of a joke?'

He saw his son's eyes narrow. 'Actually it was the truth.'

Piers flung the gate open, grabbed his father by the armpits and hauled him bodily to the side. Gabriel's legs felt like pieces of string, attached to him but not part of him. He wondered why he wasn't more embarrassed. Too drunk, probably. 'You'll be like this one day,' he said, as his son deposited him on a grassy knoll.

Piers cast him a look of loathing. 'I'd die first. As it happens, Dad, I've given up the drink. Deborah made me see that there wasn't a lot of point in following my parents' well-worn tracks to the bar. It hasn't made either of you happy.'

'The drink doesn't make people miserable,' said Gabriel. 'It's what they do to make it better when they are. But you wouldn't understand that. Not you. Too busy mooning after a girl who'll come to her senses and leave you flat. Don't flatter yourself, Piers, my boy. One of these days you'll wake up to find her in bed with someone who's worth something, not just a glorified farm labourer.'

Piers said nothing. He got back in his tractor and drove on, leaving the gate swinging. Perhaps the sheep would get out. He didn't care. Better an hour spent chasing them with the dogs than five more minutes listening to his father spit venom. Was he right? Was the day

390

fast approaching when Piers would wake in a bed that bore no trace of Deborah's warm body? The thought was like a stone within him. He had nothing without Deborah.

She came to him every night now, leaving just after five, to creep back into the house. It had become routine, almost casual. Sometimes now, when he reached for her, she would yawn and say, 'Be quick, won't you? I'm terribly tired.'

He stopped the tractor and sat, looking down across Gunthwaite's broad, green acres. Good hearted land, stripped and ready for winter. The hoggetts were at a lowland farm this year, to return to the hill in spring. It was to make room for the horses. Those useless toys. Piers clenched his fist and struck the wheel of the tractor a heavy, meaningful blow. When Gunthwaite was his entirely he would keep nothing but the old shire mares, and that for Michael's sake. The others would be gone and the land returned to its true duty, that of raising sheep and crops and good cattle.

He wondered at his own vehemence. It wasn't something he liked to think deeply about. But it centred, he realised, on his need to claim Gunthwaite entirely, completely, casting off all others. Connor for instance. Too tall, too easy, too charming for anyone's good, and Michael's undoubted friend. It enraged Piers to see how comfortable Michael was with him. How without reservation. If Connor were to ask for Mary's hand there was no doubt that Michael would be delighted. But if Piers asked for Deb? Another story.

The trouble was, he was still considered the wayward young boy, in need of guidance and restraint. He was too the son of parents of whom no one could easily approve. He was rich enough, that was true – unless his father was disposed to disinherit him – but in the eyes of Michael and Laura that was hardly a consideration. He had never known two people less impressed by material wealth. To them, true wealth was in the life you led, in the people who loved you, in the place you could call your home. He wanted Gunthwaite to be his home. He was destined to own it.

When he returned the gate was closed and Gabriel gone. He drove back to the farm, scanning the ditches now and then to see if his father might be drowning in one. He let his mind dwell on the pleasure of discovering his father's lifeless body. What a delight!

But in the yard, as he unhitched the trailer, he saw Gabriel's bleached blond head, framed in the kitchen window. Piers felt a shaft of hatred, piercing him like a white-hot lance. As it abated, he felt shaken and stunned. He hadn't known he hated his father quite so much.

In the kitchen, Michael was making his brother a cup of tea. 'It's awfully good of you, Mike,' Gabriel was saying, drawling his words, as so often when he was drunk. 'Laura not about?'

'She's having a rest. One of her bad days. You know.'

'Time you gave up this place, Mike. It's too much for her, haven't I told you often enough? Get out of here, man, while you've still got a life to live.'

'Like you, you mean?'

'Don't start that. My God, as if I haven't got enough excuse. With Dora.'

He leaned forward over the kitchen table. 'She's got a new man. In London. Doesn't care if I know or not. God! One of these days I'll show her what I know. One of these days she's going to go too far. The time's not far off when I'm going to hit her so hard she'll be grinning on the other side of her face. If she's got a face at all.'

'Stop it, Gabe.' Michael put the tea in front of him. 'You don't make it better by dwelling on it.'

'Forgetting it doesn't do much, I can promise you! She's making a bloody fool of me. Christ! Look at us! Why should I expect you to be sorry because my wife's a nymphomaniac? Yours is half-crazed most of the time.'

Michael stood apart from his brother, facing the wall. He felt a great revulsion suddenly. Gabriel had promised so much in his youth, an intelligent, handsome, gifted boy. Yet because of some flaw, some undiscovered weakness, everything had turned rotten. Whatever he might have been, he had become drink-sodden, coarse and crude. He might not have deserved Dora once. Now, they deserved each other.

He made a conscious effort to be kind. 'Have you thought about divorce? Dora might be more than willing right now.'

'Divorce? Her?' Gabriel's laugh turned into a bronchial cough. 'She'd take me for as much as she could get. The law's an ass where divorce is concerned. She'd throw up all my old peccadilloes and no one would see that this is nothing like that. To be honest, I wouldn't mind if she upped and left. I'm sick of trying to suit her. This is the place I should be, and no bloody Dora. Gunthwaite. You, me and Laura, the way it used to be.'

Michael was suddenly stunned by his own rage. That Gabriel should imagine he could come here, live here, be part of this life! It was unthinkable, and yet Gabriel went on thinking it. After everything that had happened. He burst out, 'For God's sake, Gabriel, can't you ever understand about this place? We do not intend to let you have it until the day I'm carried out of that door in a box. Laura and I aren't sharing it. Neither are we giving it up. And if we had a son, then you and yours wouldn't ever set foot over this threshold! This is mine, Gabriel. Mine! Until the day I die!'

Gabriel looked at him bad-temperedly. He hated Michael interrupting his thoughts. 'You were never man enough to have a son,' he said dispassionately. And grinned to himself, the slack-mouthed grimace of the long-time drunk. 'At least I managed that. He may be good for nothing but screwing your daughter, but then, that's his mother in him.'

'What on earth do you mean?' Michael stared at him. He'd been about to telephone to Fairlands for Gabriel to be taken home. 'What are you saying about Deborah?'

Gabriel propped his head on his hand. 'Dora spotted it first. She would, of course. Darling Deborah's turned out a tart, it seems. Didn't you think it odd the way she ran home? Dora knows the whole thing. Dirty photographs in London. Dear little Deb let someone stick his camera up her skirt. So now she lets Piers stick something else. Don't look so shocked, Mike. I told you it was time you got out of Gunthwaite and into the real world. Your daughter certainly did.'

Michael reached out, picked up his brother by his collar, and flung him like a rag into the yard.

The little town of Remy-Chaillot might have been justifiably called a village a few years before, were it not for the large and imposing church that dominated its centre. Built with a round tower (the spire was a later, badly executed addition in need of restoration), the nave was wide enough to take two farm carts side by side and the Lady chapel, glowing with stained glass, contained two noteworthy statues. The people of Chaillot, as the region was colloquially called, had been prosperous in centuries past. In this last period, no sooner had they recovered from one tumultuous war than another assailed them. They had become resigned to struggle, although in recent years resignation had palled. Many of the younger inhabitants had left for Amiens, or Paris.

Connor and Mary drove down the wide main street, past the haberdasher's, with its fearsome pink displays of underwear, past the shoeshop with its farm boots and dated court shoes. The butcher's was far enough behind the times still to display a dead horse's head on a hook beside that of a sheep and a pig. Mary swallowed convulsively. It was, she knew, a British affectation to find horsemeat loathsome, but all the same . . .

Connor said, 'There's a hotel over there. Bit grand, would you say?'

Mary peered over the rusting bonnet. The Hôtel du Maréchal was an imposing structure, although most of the shutters were pulled to. They decided to find somewhere less intimidating, but twenty minutes later, as darkness fell and one or another passer-by directed them firmly to the Hôtel du Maréchal, they bowed to pressure.

The hotel was cold, dark, fusty and unwelcoming. They were taken to a chilly room containing a huge mahogany four-poster, surrounded by curtains of heavy green cloth, smelling of dust. When Mary folded back the bedclothes the sheets were icy to the touch. Madame fixed her with an equally chilly stare and said that a warming pan was available, but it was extra.

'We'll pay the extra,' said Mary.

They were beginning to dislike Chaillot. Since it was raining they committed themselves to the hotel restaurant, and sat in a silent room, separated from the few other diners by acres of white-clothed tables. The food was dull and came from a kitchen so far removed that everything was cold. They whispered about other, better meals and other, better hotels. Madame toured the room, twitching cloths and asking grimly if everything was to their satisfaction. 'Tell her the soup was colder than ice cream,' instructed Connor, but Mary lacked the nerve and muttered: '*Merci*. Everything was fine.'

They retreated back upstairs. The warming pan, a huge brass thing full of coals, was in residence in the bed. When Connor ill-advisedly tried to move it, he tipped it on the way to the door and showered the carpet with burning embers. Black holes appeared instantly. The pan was flung down as they scrabbled to stop a conflagration.

'Grab it! Quick! Not that, this!' A jug of water put out any blaze. But there was the carpet, blackened and soaked. Very quietly, while Connor cracked his muscles holding the bed an inch from the floor, Mary rolled up the carpet. Turning it carefully to ensure that the burned part was under the bed this time, they laid it down again. The room was covered in a fine layer of dust and the condition of the bed had reverted to icy. What's more the warming pan was cold.

They lay together shivering. Mary put her arms around Connor's neck. 'You can't be serious,' he said.

'No, I'm not. Not after today. But I will be serious. Soon.'

'How soon?' He breathed the scent of her, the perfume of her hair, her skin, her lips.

She pressed kisses to his face, delighting in him, delighting in this time of grace. 'Very soon,' she whispered.

Virginity was no prize if held too long. It was a gift, to be freely given, out of love and respect. This time was the remnant of her girlhood, when she stood on the threshold of a truly adult life. When she gave herself to Connor she would give up her past. Her life would be his life too, they would build a life together, on the wide green plains of their maturity. And there they would linger, perhaps for many years, until the time came to walk down again, down the slopes and rugged gorges, to the valley of their quiet old age. The thought made her peaceful and happy. She felt that everything was all planned out.

Connor rolled away, restless with desire. Mary said anxiously, 'We don't have to wait. Not if you don't want—'

'Not here,' said Connor shortly. 'Even I wouldn't want it to be somewhere this miserable. God, but this place is a nightmare.'

Mary curled against his back. They slept fitfully, only achieving warmth in the morning, when a gong startled them awake and a rap on the door demanded that they attend for breakfast.

But the day was something of an improvement. A stiff breeze was drying the streets, while the sun peeped in and out of scudding clouds, brightening the church and the windblown flowerbeds. Neat children with satchels were running down the street, late for school. Connor turned to Mary and said expectantly, 'Right. What's the plan?'

She pretended not to have heard him. After a moment he said in exasperation, 'You must have something to go on! What did Marie say?'

'Only that Sophie had come back from the country with this child. And I didn't dare ask my mother. Not as she was.'

'No.' They stood looking at the retreating schoolchildren. An old lady came into view, hobbling with a stick, her shopping bag clutched beneath her shapeless bosom. 'We'll have to ask people, that's all,' went on Connor. 'You can start with her.'

The old lady was nervous at first. She pretended deafness, and then, when curiosity got the better of her, a failing mind. She looked coquettishly at Connor. 'So long ago, you say! I was almost a child myself!'

'My mother was very young,' said Mary. 'Hair the same colour as mine. And her mother was English, so she says.'

'English?' The old lady's nose twitched. 'The only English girl I recall was the one out at the Girand place. Miserable creature, she was. Died young. Now, she had a child . . . Was she the one who saw the vision in the church? Yes, indeed she was. Some people believed it, but if you ask me it was that Madame Girand. She was a hag, if you like!'

'Vision?' Mary blinked.

'Certainly. Go and ask the priest if you don't believe me. And don't go near that farm. The old man's dangerous!'

She went on her way, hurrying now, stopping at the corner to wave her hand to them. They waved back, elated. 'Did you get all that?' demanded Mary. 'The farm and the vision? Let's go and see the priest.'

But Connor caught her arm. 'It might not be right, Mary. Don't get carried away.'

'I'll be carried away if I want to, thank you very much! Take some photographs, will you, Con? We can show Mum and everything. We've discovered her!'

He looked down into her flushed face, the marks clear as beacons. She was so sure that finding out all this would help her mother become well. He wanted to believe it, for Mary's sake as much as Laura's. Mary wanted to fling wide the windows of her mother's mind, letting in light and air and understanding. But there were shadows in Laura's mind that no sunshine could dispel. Memories.

The church was empty but for a cleaning woman. She directed them to the priest's house, where a young man in a soutane was hurrying to his car. Mary hovered between him and his garden gate, while he tried to dodge round her, obviously inured to the demands of his flock. 'It's about the vision,' said Mary eagerly. 'My mother's vision. In your church.'

The priest gave her a cool smile. 'No vision, Mam'selle. The old Father believed in it, but it was never supported.'

'But if my mother was the one who saw it—'

'I know nothing of this at all, Mam'selle. I only came here two years ago. And I must be excused—'

Mary caught his arm, refusing to be brushed aside. 'You don't understand!' she burst out, only to find him staring at her with cold dislike.

'Indeed?'

'It's just – if the girl was my mother – we know nothing of her. We're trying to find out who she was—'

'I'm sorry. There's nothing I can do.' He stepped neatly round her, got into his smart Peugeot and drove away.

Mary stood looking after him. 'And he's a man of God!' she said furiously. 'I've a mind to stay here all day and make him miserable as hell when he comes back.'

But Connor had eased past her. A tiny little woman was polishing the knocker on the door, smiling at them brightly now and then. She was grey-haired under a neat red scarf, and her eyes were wreathed in wrinkles. '*Bonjour*, Madame,' said Connor in his halting French. 'Is the old priest perhaps still about?'

'He most certainly is,' she declared. 'And he tells me to have patience. In forty years the young one might have learned enough to be human. I tell him I can't wait that long.'

'No,' agreed Mary. 'Can we see him?'

The old woman squinted up at the sun, making an estimate of the time. 'He'll be in his garden just now. The house with the green door, just along there. The new young man hates him being so near, of course, now he's retired. But we got used to him, over the years. There might not be enough years to get used to what we've got now.'

They almost ran along the street. In this sheltered spot the breeze did little more than gust now and then, stirring the leaves to a gentle rustling. An old man – a very old man – was poking at a flowerbed with a hoe. Arriving at his gate, Mary stood awkwardly, not knowing what to say. He turned and squinted at her against the sun.

'Hello,' she said nervously. 'I've come to ask you about my mother. She lived on a farm here long ago. I think she saw a vision. She had hair the same colour as me, and her mother was English I think, and—'

'Little Lori.' The old man's face split into a wonderful smile. 'Little Lori's daughter. By the Good God! I've often thought about her. Come in.'

Together, cautiously, Connor and Mary opened the gate and stepped into the old man's garden.

Deborah was wringing out clothes. They had once possessed an old-fashioned mangle, but the years had taken their toll and it worked no more. Nowadays Laura washed in the old copper and wrung out by hand, hanging everything up in the wash house on bad days and in the orchard on good. She said there was no need to buy anything modern, now there was so much nylon and no babies any more. Perhaps she enjoyed this drudgery, thought Deborah sourly. She looked down at her own reddened hands and felt oppressed.

She was sick of this life, she thought. Every day was made up of hard labour. And while she acknowledged that she had to do something, she couldn't see why it had to be something so primitive as wringing washing by hand. A washing machine wasn't an out of the way expense, either, it was simply that Laura never wanted change. The effort of a trip to Bainfield, choosing a machine, fitting, everything, was beyond her.

Deborah leaned against the copper. It was still warm. In a few weeks there would be few enough warm places around Gunthwaite, when the winter winds began howling about, seeking every crevice and crack. She thought with sudden longing of Aunt Rosalind's house, with its central heating and deep pile carpets, warm bathrooms and immaculate lawns. That life could have suited her – would have suited her – and she had wilfully thrown it away.

She felt the sudden dive into depression that she had learned to dread. It was like a blight in her mind, changing everything, making everything grey. She didn't mind boredom, or irritation, or even misery. It was this cloud that she dreaded, taking away hope, mocking the future, blotting out the sun.

She turned her mind deliberately to Piers. Wasn't he something to feel good about? She was so comfortable with him. It was the ease of long familiarity, the knowledge that with this person she could always be at peace. But did she want to be at peace? At her age, peace was a double-edged sword. She should be adventuring, discovering, achieving something in the world, not – not mouldering peacefully here!

Deborah slumped on to the slatted wooden stool. She felt

exhausted, but it was only depression. She ought not to let life defeat her so, she thought. There was more to life than Aunt Rosalind's world. Zwmskorski wasn't everywhere. It might even be that if she went to him, talked to him perhaps, he might be persuaded to give up the photographs. And if he wouldn't, then at least she would know where she stood.

Suddenly she was excited. She would tell Piers and her father that she was going to stay with a schoolfriend for a few days. Her mother would accept anything without question just now, but the others needed a convincing lie. She'd wear her cream wool coat, that she never wore here because life didn't permit cream wool to survive untrammelled, even on a sheep, but it set off her hair wonderfully. She'd wear high heels again, and make-up, and feel she was doing something at last!

She swept into the house singing happily. To her surprise her father was standing by the table, as if he had been there for hours. 'Has something happened? Is it Mum?'

'She's all right. Deborah – I heard something today. Something about you.'

'Oh, yes?' She took half a step backwards. Her mind raced through the possibilities. She felt sick suddenly, as if someone had opened a box and shown her a decomposing body.

'Are you – physically involved – with Piers?'

She swallowed. He was looking at her so hard, as if his eyes would bore into her soul. She couldn't bear him to think – to know—

'Someone's being telling you lies,' she whispered. 'You know I wouldn't do anything to disgrace you, Daddy.'

'And – in London. Nothing happened, did it? Nothing that would cause you such embarrassment that you had to come home?'

He knew, she thought desperately. Oh God, he knew! Had the photographs arrived at last? How could he know?

'What do you mean?' she asked, her voice croaking in her throat.

'My brother told me that there were some photographs. Unpleasant photographs. Can you say to me honestly that it isn't so?'

She took in her breath, trying to frame the lie. At that moment it seemed more important that he should believe her innocent than anything in the world. He wouldn't despise her, she knew that. But he'd be so dreadfully disappointed.

'I've never seen any photographs,' she said clearly. 'What has Uncle Gabriel heard, I wonder? Was he drunk again? Or perhaps it was Dora telling him things. I don't know what goes on in that woman's mind. I think she's unbalanced.'

Michael came round the table, put out his arms and embraced her. 'Thank God,' he said with feeling. 'I couldn't bear to think that you'd

398

gone too far with Piers. I know how much he cares for you, Deb, but –
well, you know what he can be like. There's violence in him.
Everything he thinks or feels or does is so intense. And you could
take your pick of any young man you chose.'

'Could I, Dad?' She gazed up at him, so beautiful, so pure, so
apparently guileless. He thought how lucky he was to have such a
daughter. 'Yes, darling. You could.'

She went on her visit buoyed up by her father's relief. Piers was less
easy to placate, but she told him she had to shop, she had nothing to
wear. He pulled her back on the bed, mouthing the naked underside
of her breast. 'I like you best like this,' he whispered. 'Don't you like
it too?'

'Yes,' she agreed, opening her legs. His hand began to touch and
excite her. She thought, there wasn't any need to talk when you could
do this. Through this one act she and Piers could communicate as
much as they wished. He never seemed to tire of wanting her.
Perhaps it wasn't the sex, she thought, letting her hands drift across
the golden haze on his chest, down to his belly, down, down – he
gasped as she touched him and said, 'Oh Deb! Deb!' It was the act of
possession, she thought with sudden acuteness. He needed to possess
her. In this act of love he was reassured that for this time at least, she
was utterly his.

When she arrived in London she went at once to an hotel Aunt
Rosalind sometimes used, a small, family-run place that served real
butter at breakfast and gave all its guests a key. She felt strangely
furtive. When she walked the streets she expected at any moment to
see someone she knew, and expected too that they would look, show
surprise, and cut her dead. She knew it wouldn't happen, of course.
Ever since she'd returned to Yorkshire there had been invitation
after invitation, trying to tempt her south. The newspaper piece had
been discounted as meaningless gossip, an excuse for the Murray-
Gills to disengage from a family much less rich than they had
supposed, and no one had taken it up. But the burden of guilt
distorted everything. If only she had never gone with Zwmskorski! If
only she'd had some sense!

She left her case in her room, not even bothering to unpack, and
went to the mirror to look at herself. The coat wasn't quite as good as
she remembered it. But then, she didn't look quite as pretty as she
used to think she did. Was she fading so soon? Or was it guilt again?
She felt an upsurge of panic that her looks, taken for granted for so
long, should be deserting her. Today of all days she needed beauty.

She put on a slash of lipstick, picked up her bag and rushed out. She
felt flustered and unsettled, but she couldn't help that. The sooner

she saw Zwmskorski the better, she thought fervently. Then at least she'd know where she stood.

But the block of flats surprised her. Unsure of where he lived she had found the address in the telephone book, and in her imagination had remembered the place as huge and fearsome. To see again just an ordinary, blank-faced building took her by surprise. She went up in the lift, counting floors, remembering last time, hating herself. How could she have done all that? How could she have been such a fool?

Outside his door she felt like crying and waited a moment until the feeling went away. She knocked, and knocked again, harder, in case she might not be heard. There were voices. Someone was coming to the door, calling to someone else. The door opened and Zwmskorski stood there. He grinned when he saw her, and she thought, What am I doing here? I must be mad. But then he turned and called out, 'Dora! You won't believe this. Deborah is here.'

Chapter Thirty-seven

The old man toyed with his spectacles. His eyes were misty with age, and from time to time he peered at Mary, as if trying to see her through a fog. 'I wouldn't have known you,' he said at last. 'It's so long ago, of course. She wasn't pretty. Just so pathetic; dirty, hungry, frightened. She never spoke, you see. But, when I got the old woman to bring her to the nativity, then she did. She called Our Lady her mother. And people say to me today, and they said then, it's nothing of a vision, and perhaps it isn't. But Our Lady had blessed her. I knew it then. And I expected every day some miracle to take her away from that farm.'

'Was Sophie a miracle, then?' asked Mary. 'The woman who came?'

'Well, she must have been,' said the priest. 'I saw her as such. The child was suffering and needed to be saved. I don't think she'd have lived another year with Madame as she was. Although Madame herself died not three years on. Left the farm to that ruffian son of hers. The other son came back too, Luc, he was called, but they've never got on. Don't go to the farm, I beg of you. Jean's not to be trifled with.'

'Why not?'

The old priest reached out and took her hand. 'My child, it isn't given to everyone to have your innocence. He was always a cruel man. Stupid. Brutish. I've thought so many times of what your mother had to suffer. I should have done more. Ask her to forgive me, please. I did so little.'

Mary didn't know what to say. She glanced at Connor, only to find that he was looking at the priest and not at her. He said suddenly, in his halting French, 'Father, will you give us your blessing?' He moved to kneel before the old man. Embarrassed, without his Irish acceptance of such things, Mary knelt too. The priest laid his hands on their heads and blessed them. She felt tearful all of a sudden.

'Bless my mother, too,' she said softly. 'She needs it so much.'

The old man's misty eyes looked sorrowfully down at her. 'I shall hold her in my prayers and intercede for her in heaven,' he said. 'Let her know the love of the Good God, Jesus Christ and his Blessed Mother. No pain can stand against it.'

Outside, in the bright air, Mary felt self-conscious. She said to Connor, 'All that mumbo-jumbo.'

'Don't mock,' he said. 'Your mother needs something, that's for certain. Forgiveness, blessing, call it what you will.'

'We'll go to the farm, of course,' said Mary. 'What shall we say? We don't want to enrage this man Jean.'

'Let's play it by ear.'

He looked down at her, and grinned. She caught his hand, and they ran laughing back to their car.

Dora was wearing harem trousers in red silk, with a white cross-over top. She looked hard and lascivious, Deborah thought. She shivered. Was this a vision of her own unappetising future?

Deb sat on a chair, legs crossed decorously. Zwmskorski came and began stroking her hair. She said nothing, although she wanted to ask him to stop. The stroking continued. She was aware of each and every strand of hair moving gently against her head. There was something erotic in the sensation; she could feel an unspecified desire. Despite herself, she shifted uncomfortably in her chair. 'You see, Dora?' said Zwmskorski conversationally. 'She is really one of us.'

Deborah twisted from the chair and stood up. 'I'm nothing like either of you,' she said fiercely, her cheeks burning, her fists clenched. Then she remembered her errand. 'At least – I didn't think I was. I suppose you mean – sexual things.'

'He does indeed,' said Dora, spreading herself languidly on a sofa. 'You're lucky, my dear. The pleasures of the flesh aren't given to everyone to enjoy. Far too many people lead such miserable, inhibited lives. You will too. If you stick with Piers.'

Deborah's chin came up. 'You must hate him terribly,' she said and Dora fixed her with a hard stare. 'I don't hate him at all, as it happens,' she said in clipped, hard tones. 'I'm really quite fond of him. So fond that I'd rather he didn't end up shackled to a girl who won't stay. Because you're not the type to be a farm wife, Deborah. And believe me, I should know. I tried to be a business wife and that was a complete waste of time. I assure you, my dear, you'll do well to abandon all that moral brainwashing and do what your instincts command.'

'Or what my instincts command,' added Zwmskorski, moving towards her. He put his hands on her waist and drew her to him, pressing his thighs into hers. She could feel his erection, hard against her belly.

Dora said irritably, 'Stop it, Wodgy! You can have your showgirls while I'm not here. Deborah didn't come for that.'

Zwmskorski let her go and moved to the fireplace. He found a cigarette box on the marble overmantel and lit up. 'First it was your

402

sister, then it was Dora, and now it is you,' he remarked. 'You want the photographs?'

'Yes.'

'What will you give me for them? I don't need money.'

'I don't have any money. I suppose you want – bed.'

'Is that what you're offering? Shut up, Dora!' He turned on her with violence. She fell back, her face suddenly stiff, looking from Deborah to her lover, eyes wide.

Deborah could feel temptation pulling at her. One part of her mind screamed, 'No! No!' while a voice kept whispering, 'Why not?' If she slept with this man he might give her the photographs. If so, she would have won. And if not – she shuddered. He was the most sensually aware man she had ever met. He could take her to places she had never known might exist. He was like a lion amongst tame cats, stripping her to the bone with one casual slash of his claws. She knew why Dora was here. It was the lure of the sexual king.

She turned away and said, 'I don't think so, somehow.'

He came behind her and put his hands on her hips. 'You liked it before. Look, I'll show you the photographs. Let you see.'

Dora said, 'You told me they weren't here! God, but I hate you! One of these days I'll make you pay.'

She went to the bar and poured herself a drink. When Zwmskorski came back with the photographs, although apparently not paying attention, Dora lunged suddenly and grabbed the envelope. Then she retreated behind the sofa, pulling the pictures out, one eye on the Pole.

'Let's see what's really here,' she said teasingly. 'Oh God! Oh my God!' She threw them in a shower towards the girl. Deborah grabbed one and stared at it, then another, and another. Then she picked up the last and stood silent.

Zwmskorski chuckled. 'Of course, I shall keep the negatives,' he murmured.

'Of course.' She stood looking down at pictures of a woman – any woman. She was exposed from the waist down, kneeling on a bed. No face could be seen, and it was only clear that she was naked. But on the last picture – her hand trembled. Her face was half-hidden by her hair, but to anyone who knew her it was still recognisably her. She knelt on the bed, her skirts above her waist, while a man's unmistakable hand fondled her. There was almost a strange beauty about the picture. An artistic pose of a woman being seduced.

She thought of Michael seeing this. Dora said shrilly, 'You know it won't be the end, don't you? And you don't care. You silly child, you can't handle him! You haven't got a hope!'

But Zwmskorski stood at her shoulder, touching her, murmuring,

403

'You're so beautiful. Dora's jealous, don't listen to her. You want some excitement, don't you? Some pleasure? I've been cruel, but not any more. You need to be loved.'

At the same time as Dora stood, outraged, watching them, he slipped his hand in the crease of Deborah's bottom and caressed her. Arousal was clouding her judgment, she thought, staring at herself in the photograph, her half-hidden rapt expression. She felt heavy with need, dizzy with desire. Suddenly Dora crossed the room, swung back her hand and struck her niece hard across the face.

The farm looked almost deserted. At this distance it was little more than a tumbledown wreck, a jumble of old buildings crouched against the land. But a dog barked incessantly at them and a wisp of smoke curled from a dilapidated chimney. The poplars guarding the drive were gap-toothed, and pools of water lay in the fields. A few miserable cows gazed at them through a hedge, their eyes darkly sunken. Mary felt the beginnings of outrage against whoever had caused this. She was enough Michael's daughter to loathe bad husbandry.

Con said, 'They'll know we're here. We might as well go up.'

'He might have a gun. Everyone warned us.'

'People are always like that in the country. A couple of old hermits, that's all they are.'

She was uneasy though. The place was so far from town. The fields rolled away on all sides, flat and uninteresting, and less than a mile back they had passed a heap of dead crows, tossed anyhow against the hedge. She had hesitated about taking a photograph. Was that the sort of thing her mother needed to remember?

Connor put the little car into gear and they motored up the potholed drive. The dog was in a frenzy now, twisting wildly on the end of an insecure chain. There was barely room to pass it en route to the door, but they inched past, evading the foam-flecked jaws. It was probably rabid, thought Mary. But it looked too ill-fed for anything except bad temper.

No one answered their knock. After a while Con began walking round the house, peering in at the windows. Mary went to the barn, to a stinking shed where it seemed the cows were milked. Next to it she found three or four huge vats of wine, or spirits or whatever. They were open to the skies, the top crusted with inches of dust and dead flies. As she reached in a tentative finger to see if the crust was solid, a voice said in rough French, 'What the shit do you want?'

She turned. A man stood there, square, muscled, not very tall. His hair was long, and although he looked old, it was only streaked with white. Mary said, 'Are you Jean? Or Luc?'

He stood looking at her. She could feel herself colouring and longed for the make-up that disguised her. He would think her ugly, her mother a dead loss.

'I'm Luc,' he said gruffly. 'If it was Jean had found you, he'd have shot you for sure.'

'So they said. In town. Why?'

The man shrugged. 'He's like that. Why are you here?'

'My mother used to live here. As a child. She was called Lori then. When your mother was alive.'

His head came up. He looked at her for long seconds, and then turned away, shaking his grizzled locks. 'Lori's girl. Little Lori. I thought it all ended, at last. Oh my God.'

'What was ended? Why was she here? We've come from England to discover it all. Please tell us.'

'Who else is here?' he barked at her, and for the first time she was truly afraid. Had he meant to murder her? Was he in fact Jean?

'My friend,' she said cautiously. 'A man of honour and under-standing.'

'You don't say?' He spat glutinously into the dirt.

He took her back to the house. They found Connor trying to befriend the enraged dog, but Luc merely kicked at it and it slunk into its kennel. They went into a kitchen, strewn on every surface with plates and tins and disorder. The place smelled worse than the farmyard. Seeing that Luc cared nothing, Mary prowled about opening doors, finding the stairs, the front room, a store room smelling of rotten meat. Everywhere except the kitchen held the cold of long disuse. Above the range was a picture of a stern old woman.

'Madame?' enquired Mary, and the man nodded. 'She took her in. Your mother's mother. Someone had to.'

He sloshed wine from an open unmarked bottle, into three stained glasses. Then he watched to see if they drank. When he saw them both do so he grinned and drank his own, then took up the bottle and filled all the glasses again. 'I didn't care for the kid,' he said slowly. 'But I wouldn't have minded. Not if I'd given her one of my own. But that never happened. And then it couldn't be, I wasn't spending my life raising a brat that wasn't mine. I'd have gone on, though. But for her.' He raised a horny thumb in the direction of his mother's picture. 'She wouldn't let her be. Worked her to death. Killed her in the fields. She was never strong.'

'Where did she come from?' asked Mary softly. 'Was she English? My mother always said so.'

He drank from his glass and nodded. 'She was English all right. Came from England to find her brother. He was wounded in the Great War, and gassed so they say. I believe she found him, but he died soon after. She should have gone home, but she got mixed up with someone. Got her in the family way. Next thing, she's here, giving birth in that room above the store. God knows who the father was.' He drank again, and turned his eyes sorrowfully to them both. 'She was sweet, you see. Defenceless. The way she'd been brought up, she didn't know about men. I wanted her from the first, but Jean wouldn't have that. I only ever got his leavings. And I would have married her. Yes, married her! A woman like that.'

Mary sat very still. The old man scrubbed at his eyes, leaving a clean mark in the all-pervading dirt. 'But who was she?' she asked softly. 'Didn't anyone ever know?'

'My mother never wanted to know. She had an unpaid servant. And what did it matter? The girl couldn't go home, not with the brat. If we'd married, perhaps then she could have written. Not otherwise.'

'No.'

Connor said haltingly, 'So there were no papers, then? Nothing?'

The man looked at him, clearly surprised that he could speak French even a little. 'You didn't ask about papers,' he said. 'My mother hid them all.'

'Perhaps – if we saw them?' Mary's heart was beating so fast she thought she might faint.

'If Jean was here you wouldn't.'

'Jean isn't here.'

'No, thank God.'

He got up and shuffled out of the room and up the stairs. Mary cast a look at Connor, who got up and gestured that they should follow. They crept up the narrow, bare wooden treads, turning off at the first landing into the main bedroom of the house. It was surprisingly empty. A large low bed stood to one side, a chest at its foot, and a huge clothes press loomed beside the window. Mouse droppings rolled like tiny marbles underfoot.

Luc knelt beside the chest and opened the lid. It was piled high with papers: old advertisements, old certificates, official letters. He dug down, messily disturbing things and tearing pages. Mary gritted her teeth, longing to push him aside and look herself. At last he brought out an old tin box. 'There's stuff in here,' he said laconically.

Mary tried not to snatch it from his grasp. She forced herself to show some staged reluctance, taking it diffidently. The picture on the box was of Napoleon reviewing his troops. 'Let's take this downstairs, shall we?' she said with assumed insouciance.

They followed one another down the dark stairs. The box was burning Mary's fingers, as if it was on fire. There'll be nothing in it, she told herself. Luc's careless handling will have ripped up the letters that really matter. We'll know nothing but that my grandmother was a silly slut who'd sleep with anyone, and I can't tell my mother that!

Connor said, 'We really ought to look at this quite carefully. Is there a table we can use?'

'A table?' Luc looked bemusedly round at the piled up mess on tables, chairs, dressers, mantelshelves. 'There isn't one here.'

He sat down again in his fireside chair, sipping his wine, smacking his lips like a baby. Mary wondered if he might be simple. He had a certain childlike manner. 'You can take all that,' he said then, as if to support her view. 'No one looks at that any more. Not since Mother died.'

'Was your mother a terrible woman?' Mary asked straight out.

Luc smacked his lips again. 'She was after the war,' he said thoughtfully. 'We were trying to get things built up again. She was a strong woman, you see, and the girl wasn't strong. She couldn't fight! With the kid I suppose it was hard, but all the same – and my mother could cook! Oh, how she could cook. Her stuffing with truffles was the talk of the neighbourhood. Mwah!' He put his fingers to his lips and kissed them ecstatically. Mary and Connor laughed.

They got to their feet, preparing to sidle out, murmuring about coming again. But then there were footsteps outside the door. Luc made a sound between a whine and a moan, and got up to hide behind his chair. The door was flung wide and they all stood staring. A big, white-haired, furious old man stood there. He was brandishing a gun.

'So,' he said softly. 'Visitors.'

'I see you've been hunting, Monsieur Jean,' said Mary, her voice piping with terror.

'You see right. What do they want, Brother?'

'They were asking about Lori. This is Lori's child.'

'What?'

Jean's eyes fixed on Mary, a horrible staring gaze. He looked mad, she thought. Really crazy.

'We were just going,' she whispered, and Connor said, in English, 'Let's get out. Any way we can.'

Mary whispered, 'There isn't another door.'

'I knew she'd come back,' Jean was muttering. 'One day, I knew she'd come. It was those eyes. Horrible, white eyes, staring at me. I knew she'd come. This one hasn't got the eyes, but she's come just the same. I'll see to her. I've had enough.'

He was fumbling in his pocket for shotgun cartridges. Mary clutched the tin to her breast, unable to think or move, but then Connor grabbed her arm and dragged her forward. He elbowed Jean aside, forcing Mary through the door, kicking a wild foot at the dog as he passed. Suddenly energised, she ran for the car and scrambled in, listening in agony to the leisurely whirring of the starter. At last the engine caught! Connor flung the car into gear and set it on its rocking, swaying departure.

The gun went off behind them. Shotgun pellets fizzed against the rear of the car and they began to lurch from side to side. 'Puncture,' said Connor succinctly. 'But I'm damned if I'll stop.'

'He's mad,' whispered Mary, her lips stiff with fright. 'Really, thoroughly mad.'

Connor wrenched the wheel sideways and hauled the little car forcibly out of a rut. 'Tell me. What good will knowing this do your mother?'

Mary said nothing. She was clutching the tin still, holding it close to her heart. If there was nothing inside she would die, she thought. There had to be something. She couldn't go home without discovering something. She thought of the cold, unpleasant room at the Hôtel du Maréchal, and thought too of Jean storming in with his gun in the middle of the night. It didn't bear thinking of. As so often sharing her thoughts, Connor said shortly, 'We'll check out right away, get the wheel changed and be off. I don't care where we stay tonight.'

'We could sleep in the car,' said Mary. 'I wouldn't mind.'

'Wouldn't you?' He reached out and took her hand, as it held tight to the tin box. Suddenly, and to her surprise, she found that she was crying.

Deborah fell back against a chair, the other woman's heavy body bearing down on her. Dora was furious, her fingers hooked like claws. Deb felt a nail rake down her cheek and struck out, catching her aunt on the breast. Dora grunted, using her weight to crush the younger girl and subdue her.

The terror that Deb had so far suppressed suddenly bubbled to the surface. Dora was angry enough to gouge out an eye, to claw a furrow in Deborah's smooth and lovely cheek. The girl kicked without direction, putting up her hands to defend herself. Dora's face was within inches of her own, a mask of rage and hatred. Dimly, as if from a long way away, she could hear Zwmskorski laughing. He wanted this, thought Deborah suddenly. Two women fighting gave him a particular thrill.

Dora's fingers were biting into her arms. Deb wrenched one wrist free, and gripped the older woman's perfectly coiffed hair. She pulled Dora's head back, and her aunt let out a yelp of pain. 'Get her off me!' yelled Deborah to Zwmskorski. 'You can see she's gone mad!'

For a minute the Pole did nothing. But Dora was fighting like a tigress, her hands reaching for Deborah's vulnerable face. The girl wriggled away, still clutching the hair, containing but not subduing her opponent. But then, Zwmskorski gripped Dora's wrists and pulled her to her feet. Deb let go. Her lip was bleeding and she could taste her own blood, while her fingers still held a clump of her aunt's blonde hair.

'Hold still, Dora,' Zwmskorski was saying as the woman still struggled. 'Do you want me to hit you or tie you up?'

'How dare you torment me like this? I'll not be treated like one of your nothing girls. I won't let you humiliate me! I won't let her! She's nothing but a stupid child!'

He held her and laughed. It was a mistake. The bones of her face seemed suddenly very sharp and clear. She bent her head, like a darting snake, and sank her teeth into his hand, touching bone. He howled, flung her away, and then struck her. There was a crack like breaking wood, and Dora fell unconscious to the floor.

'Oh my God,' said Deborah very quietly. 'You've killed her.'

He was bending over the woman, the fingers of his unbitten hand against her neck. 'She's out, that's all,' he said shortly. 'I should know better with Dora. I always underestimate her.'

'You suit each other,' said Deb.

'*We* suit each other too,' he said, getting to his feet. 'And I'm really a lot fonder of you than I expected to be. Dora's right. You'll never stay on a farm.'

'That doesn't mean I want to get involved with you,' she retorted. But her voice quavered, as if she didn't entirely mean what she said. He came and stood over her, very tall, very commanding. All at once she remembered why everything had happened; this man bemused her. His arrogance and his magnetism stultified her wits.

'You don't have to mind about Dora,' he was saying. 'I'll deal with her. You could have a flat somewhere. Buy some new clothes. Have some fun.'

'Be your mistress, you mean?' whispered Deb.

'If you like. But I'm divorced, you know. I might like to have a beautiful new wife.'

He was very close now, holding the ends of her hair and brushing them against her lips. She tried to think of Piers, of her mother, of anything except this incredible man. His lips were on hers, gentle at first, but then bruising. She opened her mouth beneath his, felt his tongue like raw muscle within her. But some part of her still retained sanity. She turned her head aside and fought for breath.

'What will you do with the photographs?'

He mouthed her neck. 'Keep them, of course. If you come to me then they're worthless. If you don't I shall send them to your mother. So you see. You have everything to gain and everything to lose.'

'You wouldn't give up Dora.'

'She's married. She'd come to terms.'

'And we'd be fighting over you. I knew you liked that.'

'Of course you knew. You, Deborah, are a deeply sensual woman. It must be your mother in you. One of the few women I've wanted and never had.'

409

Suddenly Deb thought of Mary. Even as Zwmskorski reached into her blouse and held her naked breast, sending darts of feeling to pierce her soul, she thought of her sister observing all this. The blood, the violence, the raw, undisciplined emotion. Mary would be appalled! she thought. She'd have Deb out of here before she could blink.

'I've got to go to the bathroom,' she said urgently. 'I'm sorry.'

He stared irritably down at her. She slipped away, before he could think, into a cool white room. She rested her head against the tiles above the basin, and then looked up into the mirror. Her lips were swollen. Her eyes were heavy with desire. She thought again of Mary, held the thought of her firm and clear and decided. She washed her face and passed water, feeling herself hot and swollen. Her breasts ached as if filled with molten lead, and she unfastened her blouse to look at herself. Small drops of milky fluid were leaking from her nipples. She met her own eyes in the mirror. What was it? What did it mean?

Zwmskorski, outside the door, said, 'Deborah? Are you all right? Your aunt is coming round.'

'I'm all right,' she said, fastening her blouse. She flushed the lavatory and rinsed her hands once again, pressing them against her flushed cheeks. Then she unlocked and opened the door.

In the sitting room Dora was sprawled on the sofa, muttering curses against the Pole. 'I'll make you pay for this, Wodgy. That's what you forget about me. You don't beat me up and get away with it.'

He said to Deborah 'Ignore her. I'll get a doctor and have her sent home.'

'Don't bother.' Deb reached for her cream wool coat and stood holding it. 'You want us both, I suppose. Two women you can play with, tormenting Dora and blackmailing me. But I've been stupid enough as far as you're concerned. I think I'll show that picture to my mother myself.'

She took up the photograph and slipped it inside her coat. Zwmskorski chuckled. 'She'll throw you out. She won't want a daughter like you.'

Deborah shuddered and closed her eyes for a second. 'I don't know what she'll say. We'll just have to see.'

He went with her to the front door. He was complacent, she realised, sure that sooner or later she'd be back. 'Such beauty,' he murmured, running his finger down the curve of her cheek. 'You'll never waste it all on that boy.'

She looked up at him. If he had the capacity to love she knew he would never love her. If he loved Dora it was a macabre and twisted thing. He damaged the people he touched, she thought. Like all evil people he had the ability to make others discover the evil in themselves.

'Goodbye,' she said politely, as if she'd been invited to tea.

'Au revoir,' said Zwmskorski, and waited in the hallway until she was safely in the lift.

Deborah returned home that night. She sat on the train, wrapped in a cloak of thought. The stations crawled by, one after another, a slow progression northwards. She thought of what she might do when she reached home. It would be late, perhaps three in the morning. She could go to Piers, and have him love her in place of the love she had refused. It ought to be enough, she thought, that sort of love.

But she rather thought she would go to her own bed, in the white-painted room high under Gunthwaite's ancient roof. She would be alone there and think of what had happened, drawing strength from a childhood happy and secure. She wished she had never grown up, she thought dismally. She wanted again to be the golden child, beautiful, loved and serene. She had made such a mess of everything.

At Leeds she had trouble persuading a taxi driver to take her so far, and then he made the journey anxious by telling her how lovely she was and asking if she wanted to stop. She ached to be rid of him, ached to be home. When at last she saw Gunthwaite's bulk against the night sky, she wanted to curl up on the ground, in her good cream coat, and give thanks for her return.

Instead she paid the driver and went to the big oak front door which they never locked because it took a knack to open it, and only the family knew how. The house smelled of polish and last summer's lavender. She stood in the hall and took it in, feeling her heart swell with misery and guilt.

'Deborah?' Her mother stood on the stair. She was wearing her old cotton nightgown, enveloping her to neck, wrist and ankle. Her hair was a black cascade down her back and her pale eyes glowed with an eerie light. She said, 'I knew you'd lied to me. I take it something's the matter?'

Deb tried to shake her head. She wanted to deny everything, rub out everything, but the words wouldn't come. Instead she ran to her mother, wordless, sobbing, to the shelter of those loved and welcoming arms.

Chapter Thirty-eight

The room was small and very plain. There was a stone pitcher in the corner and a chipped china basin on a shelf, but the bed was high and covered with a fine patchwork quilt. There were books too, four in all, French tracts on hunting and the chase. Connor glanced at one, apparently interested, but Mary knew he was shamming. Neither of them could think of anything but the tin box.

'I keep thinking he's going to burst through the door,' she said at last.

'Not him. I doubt he leaves the farm. He stank, did you notice? Worse than a billygoat.'

'I noticed.'

She set the box carefully in the middle of the bed. They both stared at it for long seconds. 'Shall we eat dinner first?' asked Mary.

But Connor exploded. 'For God's sake! How much longer do we have to suffer? Open it girl, and see what's what.'

She sat on the bed and slid her nails beneath the box's rusted rim. The lid wouldn't lift, she had to wrestle with it, and eventually Connor used her steel nail file and forced it back. Inside was a pile of envelopes and folded paper, and on top a photograph. Mary looked at it dubiously. A man and a woman stood smiling awkwardly at the camera. The woman was dark, her hair in a heavy bun at the nape of her neck, and she wore an ankle-length dress with a draped bodice. It made her appear shapeless and lumpen. In contrast the man was dapper, in an un-British uniform. Connor, who knew more about such things than Mary, took the photograph to the window. 'French, I think,' he said. 'Some sort of officer.'

All at once Mary was breathless with excitement. Her heart was rattling against her ribs. The box was as she had hoped! Everything was going to be known and revealed. Why, the very first thing had shown her two people who were certainly her grandparents. She looked again at the photograph and tried not to wish that they had been taller, or much better-looking. They might have been stunning in their day. After all, standards changed. But, looking at the girl's happy but lopsided smile, she doubted it.

She and Connor began to sort through the letters. Most were in one hand, but here and there was one in neat copperplate, or the rounded, childish writing once much favoured by provincial schools. Mary looked at the simple writing first.

My dear Avril,
Much saddened by your news. Auntie Beth and Uncle Gerald came over and spoke this afternoon, and agree that your brother is best off where he is, in the arms of his Maker. As for you, it is time you came home. You have adventured long enough, and your mother would be shocked if she was still alive. Needless to say, your father says nothing on the subject, and you know my views there.

Donald Fulshaw's been asking after you. He's a good boy, if not as dashing as some. You could do worse, and like as not will if you persist in this gallivanting. We expect you home, Avril.

Yours truly,
Auntie Elsie

So, Avril's mother was dead. Mary turned quickly to the copperplate hand:

Dearest Avril
Stricken by your news. That fool Elsie came tattling it, in advance of your letter. I tried not to weep in front of her, but I was a little the worse for wear and tears overcame me. I make no excuses; if James had come home there was nothing for him, the debts are crippling. I am going to sell Home Farm, and the house if I can. There's nothing left for me now.

As for you, Avril, get yourself married to someone worth something, not some jumped up tradesman with ideas above himself. You're still a lady, after all. Despite everything I remain still, I hope, a gentleman.

Yours affectionately,
Father

Mary leafed quickly through the copperplate letters again. All predated the one she had read. There was much about money, crop failures, a hunter gone lame, a gambling debt. There was a great deal of grumbling about Elsie and the rest, yeoman stock appalled by the high-handed extravagance of this relative by marriage. All Elsie's letters returned again and again to the same theme – Avril was to give up France, come home and marry.

Mary and Connor passed the letters between them, reading one after another. In the middle of it, someone rapped on the door and a child's voice called out that Mother had cooked dinner and was waiting and had been five minutes or more. Mary and Connor leaped up, leaving the letters in a heap on the bed.

Dinner was rich and delicious. They began with cheese bread-crumbed and fried, served with an end of summer salad of beans and olives. It was followed by a casserole of partridge, the gravy thick enough to cut, eaten with bread and mustard sauce. As her hunger faded and the need to placate Madame passed, Mary said, 'She was a misfit in England, wasn't she? Avril. Between classes. Her father had married beneath him.'

'If you can call it that,' said Connor reasonably. 'The man was a waster. Estate mortgaged to the hilt and he admits himself he drank. Her mother's family couldn't stick him at all.'

'But they wanted poor Avril to marry Donald Fulshaw, and you can tell he was ugly and stupid.'

'Just because Elsie liked him! Avril would have done better with him than the French officer. Let that be a lesson to you, girl! Take honest worth above dash.'

Mary held his eyes while she crunched her teeth into some bread. 'That rules you out then,' she said with her mouth full.

'Does it now? To be sure, I thought taking risks ran in the family.'

'Would I be taking a risk?' She looked away, trying to keep her voice light, letting instead a note of anxiety creep into it.

Connor took her wrist and held it. 'I'm not a drunkard. And I don't yet smell. Neither do I chase all visitors with a gun. And who can tell but that Donald Fulshaw did all those things in the end? Avril might have known her own business best.'

Madame returned with the casserole, and saw him holding Mary's hand. She beamed and muttered something to her husband. They thought them newlyweds, thought Mary. They imagined the long hours upstairs were spent making love. She felt as embarrassed as if that might be the case, and allowed Madame to press some more meat upon her, although she was more than full. Beyond that there was a compôte of bottled raspberries, with a home-made wafer each, and then a glass of Monsieur's schnapps to help it down. Connor looked at her and said, 'They want to celebrate with us. And so they should. It's finished.'

'We don't know anything yet,' said Mary.

'But we're going to know. And that's almost better.'

She thought then how much she loved him. He was more hopeful than she, more optimistic. He had a faith in life that she had yet to acquire. Somehow her mother's insecurities had filtered through over the years, helped by her marked skin and the contrast with Deb's unusual beauty. She didn't believe in happiness as Connor did. She was frightened to reach out and take it.

414

Upstairs again, in the room, they sat either side of the bed. Now the bulk of the unread letters was in the unknown hand. Mary looked at one – the date merely read 'Wednesday'. 'There's no way of telling what happened when,' she complained. 'We'll have to read them in any order.'

'Do we have to do it now?'

She didn't look at him. She knew what she would see. Tonight he would insist that she face him, and decide. They had come so far together, had done so much. They could be no closer unless she willed it. She wanted to say so much, to ask him if he loved her, if he had ever felt this for someone else. But she dared not let him see her insecurities. They had nothing to do with Connor after all, just her own lack of esteem, rising up once again to torment her. In the end, knowing herself, there was nothing he might want that she would refuse.

She began to fold the letters up once again. But a passage caught her eye, written in bold black ink. 'I long for you,' it said. 'I long for your body through all the nights of filth and noise and terror. Only you can protect me, giving so much of your strength that I am strong again. I come to you as a bee to a flower, feeding deep within you that I might survive.'

This unknown woman had loved unwisely, she thought, moving all the while to slip off her shoes, her jacket, begin to unfasten her blouse. She too had thought that love would always be enough. She looked up at Connor and said jerkily, 'What will happen afterwards? Will it all go wrong?'

He came and held her, in her stockinged feet suddenly short against him. 'Whisht, no,' he murmured. 'They couldn't be happy. The times were wrong. This is our good fortune, to have love and the times all on our side. Nothing can ever go wrong.'

So she let him undress her, easing straps from her shoulders, freeing her sad little breasts. Her hands fluttered across them. Surely he must want a more womanly woman? But he kissed her and nuzzled her. 'I don't know how I've borne it all,' he murmured. 'From the very first I couldn't wait to touch you. All that slimness and strength. All this vulnerable blue skin. I could worship your skin!'

Tiny rivulets of feeling coursed through her, coming together into a rush of heat. She wanted something – anything – more of him, more of this!

He was stopping to see to things. She wished he hadn't, wished he wouldn't, wanted not to think about anything. Thought had no place here, in this quiet room, this warm bed, this temple of feeling. He was pressing against her, rubber clad. She thought she would rather be ten times pregnant than have this disgusting mundanity intrude. She thought of her mother, no more than a child; her sister, more child

415

than she. This was a woman's lot, it seemed, to want love and instead to suffer brutishness. He pressed harder and she took in her breath. All at once he was within.

She looked into his face in surprise. 'All right?' he whispered. She could only nod. There was right in all of this. She knew now why the goose submitted to the gander, why the sow stood firm beneath the boar. There was communion here, a stretching back to the beginnings of life. She had needed this man, as much as he needed her. She wanted what he had to give.

He began to move in her, and she heard her own breathing quicken. What was happening to her? The slow burn of her feelings was become a forest fire, racing through her body. If he stopped she would die, if he didn't stop he would surely kill her! She dug her nails into his back and whimpered, the sound growing and growing until she let out one sharp, triumphant cry.

They could hardly bear to part. He lay with her, joined to her by a film of sweat, unable to think of anything but love. Life seemed to stretch out before him, and he knew himself powerful enough to do as he liked with it. What greater power was there than to love and be loved? He'd loved her forever, and now she was his. Death and betrayal were for others to suffer, not them. Not ever.

Laura brought up two mugs of cocoa. Deborah was white as the walls of her room, her hair still glowing but her eyes quite lacking in colour. Waking at the sound of the car, Laura had known who it would be. She had known from the first that Deb was lying to her. Had known for weeks that somewhere behind her daughter's lovely face there lurked something far from sweet. But misery insulated you, prevented you from feeling as you should feel, seeing clearly what was plain to a mother's knowing eye. Deborah was miserably unhappy.

She sat on the bed and waited. At last, Deb whispered, 'I'm sorry. I just can't say.'

'It can't be so terrible,' said Laura. 'Have you hurt someone? Is it a crime?'

'No! No.' Deb's hands closed on the sheet. Laura thought she had rarely seen anyone so keyed up. Her daughter was like a bough on a laden apple tree, bent to the ground, only needing a second's more pressure to break altogether. She let the silence build, let the seconds pass. Suddenly Deborah reached for something from under the bed and thrust it into her mother's hands. Laura was looking at the photograph.

She said nothing at first. Then she looked at her daughter and gave a little smile. 'Who is the man? Someone horrible, I imagine, to take photographs.'

'He's – someone you used to know. Someone Aunt Dora knows. A Pole.'

'Zwmskorski? Oh. I see.'

Laura put the photograph face up on the bed. Deborah burst out, 'What will happen when Dad sees? He'll make sure Dad sees. He'll send him one in the post, perhaps, or have something published in a paper.'

'Papers don't publish pictures like that,' said Laura reasonably.

'But he'll do something! He won't rest until everyone sees what I'm like! I thought I'd buy him off, I was going to sleep with him and see then – but Dora was there. I didn't know what to do. He makes me feel so – so—'

'Yes,' said Laura. 'That sort of man always does.'

She looked calmly into her daughter's lovely face, so much lovelier than her own. Even so, it was almost like seeing herself. There was the same guilt and shame, the same terror that the world would see you for what you really were and be revolted. And yet, looking now at Deborah, she felt only compassion. A young girl had fallen foul of an evil man. He had taken her strong, natural desires and used them against her, to damage her and satisfy him. And she, in her innocence, thought that no one would ever understand.

Laura looked into her daughter's eyes. She knew, because she knew so much, what Deborah might or might not have done. Every shameful, exploitative act, every gratification of her own and another's instincts, was more clearly seen by her mother than Deb could possibly know. And Deb had to know. She had to understand that one slip such as this was no absolute fall from grace. In comparison with her mother's life, she had done nothing!

'By the time I was your age,' Laura began quietly, 'I had worked as a prostitute for years. I'd done everything. Things you can't even imagine. I'd been beaten up and even got pregnant, although naturally I got rid of it. I didn't want the child of some man I didn't know. Some brute. But really I was lucky. I hadn't got a disease, I hadn't gone mad, I wasn't scarred – on the outside, anyway. I got out and came here. I married your father and had two lovely girls.'

She took a breath. How hard this was, how difficult to say. She had spent years not saying these words. She went on. 'I should have been happy. But all my life I've been ashamed and frightened because of what I did. So ashamed – you can't know!' For a moment she closed her eyes tight, like a child hiding from the dark. 'Now, I could say to myself it wasn't my fault, I hadn't any choice, that I was a victim and no more. But that wouldn't be true. What I did was a choice, as what you did was a choice too. That's what life is, darling. Choices. And sometimes you make a terrible mistake. Mine was in the money and the power and the excitement. Not making the effort to find another

417

way. But I was so young! I'm not sure if I had it to do again I could have done any different.'

'I was old enough,' whispered Deb. 'I knew what I was doing.'

'Did you? I imagine you thought you were going to enjoy sex with an attractive man. Zwmskorski was always that, you know. You didn't mean to ruin your life for ever.'

Deb took a shuddering breath. 'Mary would never have done it. When I went to see him today I kept thinking what Mary would do. She'd never have let him touch her!'

Laura chuckled. 'She'd have hit him with the poker, we both know that. But Mary's different, darling! We're all different. Mary's naturally the sort only to love and want one man, and she'll love and want him always. As for me – I shall never stop loving your father, loving him with every fibre of my soul, but I've wanted others.'

Deborah whispered, 'I'm the same as you, then. It must be the eyes.'

'You're not the same as me! I've been stupid in my marriage, I know that. I've – I've denied your father the chance really to know me. You can't know how hard I've worked to be the sort of woman I thought he wanted, and here I am, the sort of woman no one could ever want. Neurotic. Miserable. And why? Because I can't admit the mistakes I made. I can't forgive myself for them. Deborah, please don't do the same.'

Her daughter was pleating the sheet. Slow tears began to dribble down her cheeks on to the working hands. 'I think I'm pregnant,' she whispered.

Laura felt all her calm erupt into cold, consuming panic. Not her daughter! Not now! But not a muscle moved except in her jaw, clenching her teeth tight together, preventing her crying out. After a moment, she said, 'Is Zwmskorski the father?'

Deb shook her head. 'I never actually did it with him in the end. I came back here and did it with Piers instead.'

'Oh.' In that one syllable Laura expressed everything she had ever felt about Piers. Hadn't she told Michael she didn't want him? Hadn't he and Gabriel insisted? She had known that no young girl could resist such devotion, that in the end, battered by life, she might fall into his waiting arms. And now it had happened. She wanted to run to her bedroom and beat Michael over the head with her bare fists!

Instead, she said mildly, 'What do you want to do?'

Deb hunched a shoulder. 'I don't know. I'm not even sure. Except I am. There's a baby inside me. I know.'

So had Laura known, all those years ago in the Rue de Claret, waking each morning and praying that she might be wrong. Was this a punishment, to see her own daughter repeating her own mistakes? She felt terrible despair. 'If you want,' she said jerkily, 'we could get rid of it. But I tell you, it half killed me. After, I thought I'd never have a child.'

Deb made a face. 'I don't want to do that. I don't really want to do anything. I want it – not to be there.'

'But it is.'

Their eyes met. Suddenly Laura couldn't bear it. She reached out and hugged her daughter, holding her close, letting her weep tears of pain and shame and renewal. If I could have wept like this, she thought, would it have made me happy? She didn't know.

The coffee smelled delicious that day. Mary munched her croissant with relish, although normally she thought them greasy and not very nice. Today, though, even the chipped paint on the windows of the little inn seemed charming and rustic.

Connor spread thin French jam and dribbled it on his shirt. 'Damn! Now you'll have to wash it.'

'Wash it yourself, clumsy,' retorted Mary and he chuckled. 'The wonders of love.'

They gazed adoringly at each other. Just to sit here and look was a pleasure in itself. They knew they would never tire of it, and would spend years of their lives together studying each separate inch of skin or hair or soft, secret place. Connor said, 'Well, there's no point messing about now, is there? We'll get married and start having babies.'

'Shall we? We can't. We've nowhere to live.'

'Do you care for that, my gypsy queen?'

'Actually – not in the least.'

They grinned at each other, and drank more coffee, which later gave them indigestion. They didn't care. The day was cool but windless, and they drove the little hire car to a muddy pond where they could sit and look at the ducks and finish the letters. Mary picked up one which seemed more worn than the rest:

My darling
I adore you! I worship you! I can never thank you enough. What you gave me last night was a treasure I thought never to receive in this world. I write now at the station, and all I can think is how much I love you. Your exquisite body excites me still, your kisses are sweet on my tongue. I die until I am with you again.
Your beloved,
Nicolas

She looked again at the photograph. Nicolas. Perhaps he was good-looking – or at least, might have appeared so to a girl being told to marry Donald Fulshaw. She leafed through the rest of the letters.

419

Connor said, 'They get shorter. Either he was getting bored or there was something going on.'

'He was killed. I'm sure of it,' declared Mary. 'They were going to marry but he was killed and she was left pregnant and alone.'

'Er – no.' Connor was looking at a letter in a very different hand. Sloping lines, very straight and angular, as if the letter had been written and then copied in this precise way. 'This is in French. I think it's from his wife.'

Mary took it, wide-eyed. Haltingly, stumbling over the exact meaning, she began to translate:

Dear Miss Halston,
I am writing on behalf of my husband Nicolas. You had with him a relationship – that is, you used to have a relationship – oh, I can't get that quite right – when he was based at Amiens. He has now returned home to me, his lawful wife, and his two young sons, and to his profession as a notary. I trust that being the sort of woman that you are – I think she might mean prostitute, I'm not sure – you will stop – cease – all communications forthwith.
                    Severine Lussiez

They stared at each other. 'Did he know she was pregnant?' asked Connor. 'Does anything say?'

They rifled through the box, looking at each of the letters. If Avril had told him, he had never referred to the fact. Had she written to him at his home? If so, there could be no greater callousness than to let his wife make this cold reply.

'I don't think she ever told him,' said Mary slowly. 'I think her pride stopped her. If he wouldn't come to her because he loved her, then she didn't want him just because she had a child.'

'I wonder if she still thought that a year later?' said Connor bitterly. 'With Madame working her to death and Jean terrorising the child.'

'She slept with Jean,' said Mary quietly. 'She had to. To survive.'

The box was empty. They had read it all. But right at the bottom, as big as the tin itself, was a child's book, in English. *Peter Rabbit*.

'Oh,' said Mary, looking at it. 'My mother's favourite. How odd.'

To her surprise, Connor snatched it from her, thrust it back into the box and jammed on the lid. 'I've had enough of this,' he flared. 'The poor, stupid, silly girl! She couldn't cope with France or the French – Nicolas, Madame, Jean. She was too soft, too much a lady, without Elsie's primness or her father's selfishness. She couldn't cope! I want to despise her. Look at the trouble she caused! She never learned to toughen up.'

'She died. She didn't have time to learn.'

'But she could have gone home! Back to Elsie. Lied about a marriage, taken the child.'

'Everyone would have known, whatever she said.'

'And who would care? Her pride was the death of her. She was too proud to admit a mistake, reach out and ask for help. And she didn't pay the price. Her daughter did.'

Mary said nothing for a long time. On the pond before them a heron began fishing, imagining the battered grey car to be part of the natural scene. At length she turned to Connor and said, 'My mother's got something, hasn't she? I think you're half in love with her yourself.'

'Would you mind if I was?'

She almost smiled. 'Not really. She'll never love anyone as she loves Michael. And as long as you're whole in love with me.'

He looked at her fiercely. 'I wouldn't ever leave you like that. I want you to understand. I will never do that to you.'

'I know.' Mary took his hand, tracing the veins with a long, slim finger. 'Her tragedy is that she didn't know. And if she'd been the type to know then she'd have coped anyway. So none of it was really her fault. It happened, that's all.'

'Will your mother understand that?'

Mary looked out at the waters of the pond, ruffling now in a slight breeze. The willows were almost bare, trailing their branches like dank hair amidst the rushes. Like a chorus of women, mourning the foolishness that led them to trust the untrustworthy and give their love to those who did not deserve it. Would her mother understand? Mary simply didn't know.

Chapter Thirty-nine

Michael was out with the shires in Long Acre. He was taking the chain harrow over the grass, raking through the seed bed and letting in air. He said he used the horses because they damaged the land less than a tractor, but in truth he liked the work. The harrow was light, it barely needed a pair, and he could stride up and down the field behind two beautiful glossy rumps, turning them with a singsong command, stopping them with one long, easy: 'Whoooooa.' The work soothed him. It reminded him of times past and gave him faith in times to come.

As he turned by the old holly bush, where thrushes nested each and every spring, he saw Laura coming across the field towards him, her long wool skirt blowing about her legs. He was surprised. She didn't often leave the house nowadays, seeming more and more to need the security of Gunthwaite's walls. Seeing her leaning against the wind, her hair clasped tight in one hand, he was taken back suddenly to her very first days here. She had looked like this then. Full of colour, and energy, and life.

'Whoooooa,' he called to the horses as she approached. 'Whoooaaa. Stand up there, Bonny. Easy, Blossom. Easy now.' They stood obediently still, well up in their collars, heads lowered. He looped the reins around the harrow; he prided himself that his horses would stand where commanded for as long as he chose. Although, as Mary said, he never chose for long. Michael had never abused a horse's patience in his life.

Laura came panting up to him. She was flushed and tangled by the wind. He let himself look at her for a moment. 'My,' he said at last. 'You look so well.'

'Do I? I shouldn't. Michael, we've got to talk. It's Deborah.'

He said nothing, merely going to the horses, turning them and sending them back to the hedge. There he unhitched the harrow, and looped up the traces, so that the horses could stand tied and idle for a while. At last, task completed, he came and drew Laura into the shelter of the holly. The ground was dry there, in the lee of the weather. She sank down and clasped her arms around her knees. She looked up at her husband.

'It's men,' she said simply. 'Piers here and someone else in

422

London. She's so upset and ashamed, she thinks you won't want to know her any more if you find out what she's done. And I know she's been silly – and I know how you feel about these things – Michael, you won't be angry when you know?'

He sat at her side. 'I don't know why you should be worried that I might be,' he said reasonably. 'Was I angry with Mary and all her silliness? I didn't think myself an angry sort of man.'

Laura reached out and touched his cheek. 'No. Of course you're not. But sex is different, isn't it? Men want their wives and daughters to be pure.'

He looked at her. She tried to hold his gaze, but all at once she blushed and turned away. 'I'm sorry, Michael,' she said hurriedly. 'I shouldn't bother you with these things. You needn't know what's happened, I'll deal with it myself, if you'll just not – not notice anything. Not be different with her.' She tried to scramble up, but he caught her arm.

'Stop it, Laura. Why won't you tell me? Why are you afraid?'

She was shivering uncontrollably, although she was well wrapped up. It was as if she was ill, racked by fever. 'I thought I could tell you – I can't, that's all. You'll hate her and me and everything. It's my fault, you see. I never told her things. I knew what the world was like, but I didn't tell her because I didn't want her to know. And now this. That evil man, Zwmskorski, trying to wreck us, wreck her! I always hated him and he knew it. He's waited years to get his revenge.'

'Laura.' He held her on the ground, firm hands stained with earth, gripping her tight. 'Laura, there's nothing you can't speak to me about. Nothing at all. Believe me, there's nothing you can tell me that will ever change the way I feel about you or Deborah or Mary.'

'It will! I know it will.'

'Tell me, then. Let's see.'

'But then there's no going back!'

'We can never go back. We must always move on, changing and growing. That's for all of us, Laura. Me as well as you and Deborah. Don't try and shut me out.'

She took a long, anguished breath. 'Deborah – Deborah went to Zwmskorski's flat to make love. She let him touch her, and he took photographs. She realised what was happening and ran away, but then he began blackmailing her and that's why she came home. She was so upset – so in need of comfort – that she began sleeping with Piers. And now she's pregnant. Oh God, Michael, what are we going to do?'

His dark eyes continued to look at her. She waited, in agony, for his response. At last he said, 'You were right about Piers. He should never have come here.'

423

Laura relaxed within his grasp. 'But it's my fault, you must realise that. I've been so wrapped up in myself, I didn't see what was happening to her. Or rather, I didn't choose to see. And now this!'

'Poor Deb,' said Michael softly. 'Our poor, lovely girl. This is the worst of children. Watching them hurt themselves like this.'

'Because of me!' insisted Laura.

'No! Laura, I'll not have you indulging yourself like this! Deborah's mistakes are her own, and no one else's. She's more than our daughter now. She's a woman, responsible for herself. What she's done is her own responsibility, not ours. We'll give her help, of course. We'll give her anything she wants. But Deb's life is her own now.'

Laura sat back, quite deflated. 'I thought you might at least insist that Piers marry her?' she said mildly.

'If she wants to marry him, then no doubt she will. But she could rear the child at Gunthwaite if she wished.'

Laura made a face. 'And what would people say?'

He snorted. 'They've said enough about us over the years! Haven't you heard them at market? That's the Coopers of Gunthwaite. The ones who house the French whores. When we were all younger half the village believed I had a harem, a different woman every night.'

Laura had never felt so surprised. She looked at her husband, seeing the greying hair, the wide shoulders, the crease in his forehead that deepened when his headaches began. He seemed much the same. But for him to say that he must surely be different. She had never expected to hear Michael speak so in all her life. She said 'But I thought – I never thought you knew.'

He chuckled. 'I was never so stupid as all that, love.'

'I think I've been the stupid one. Do you know – do you know about me too?'

He looked deep into her eyes, those strange, glassy eyes that sometimes seemed blue and sometimes grey and sometimes no colour at all. 'I know everything I need to know,' he said softly. 'I know that I love you. That I loved you from the first, the very first, when you were so nervous and so sure we'd turn you out. I know that nothing anyone said then, or that anyone says now, will ever stop me loving you. I know that your life before was very hurtful and I know that it hurts you still. You used to be happiest not remembering and I only ever wanted to make you happy. But if that isn't enough any more – if you want to tell me, if it will do you good – then I'll listen. And I'll love you just the same.'

She licked her lips. She felt frightened, as if she stood on a precipice and the wind was blowing so hard she might fall off. But things weren't always as they seemed. Perhaps she wouldn't fall at all,

424

perhaps she could spread her arms and find them wings, and take to the air and fly. She tried to think of all the things she might say. Nothing came to mind.

She tried to summon up one thing, one single thing that she simply must let out. But somehow, knowing that whatever she said wouldn't change him, suddenly knowing that that was true – she had nothing she really wanted to say. Except perhaps – she swallowed and licked her lips again. 'I have nightmares,' she whispered. 'It's Jean, you see, at the farm, when I was very small. He used to come upstairs at night. Into my room. My bed. Into – me. On a windy night, when the stairs creak – I think it's him! Coming back! And I can't think, I can't breathe, I'm so terribly, terribly scared!' Rushing up from nowhere the tears came. A child's tears, wept now because she could not weep them then. She rubbed her fists into her eyes as a child might. A very young, very miserable child.

Michael's face contorted suddenly. He reached out and embraced her, hugging her close. 'My poor girl! My poor darling. Why don't you ever wake me? Oh, I could weep for you and that poor little girl.'

Laura was sobbing less violently now. 'She *was* a poor little girl, wasn't she? Her mother was dead. She was cold and hungry and she hadn't any clothes. And that brute of a man!'

'It happens. There are such people. The world isn't kind enough yet.'

He was holding her, rocking her, soothing her. She thought, I'm his child as much as his lover. And all these years, I've refused to see his strength. I thought my secrets would destroy him, and they've only destroyed me.

'I hate myself,' she whispered. 'I've never been worthy of you.'

'Rubbish!' He put her away and held her a foot from him. 'I was never loved until you. I learned to love because of you. Can't you see, Laura, can't you see that I'm nothing without you? Just a shell. A cowardly shell. I've let you go on in your misery because I didn't dare try and make you better in case it went wrong. In case I lost you and had to be alone. Can't you see? The one thing I could never bear is being alone.'

'But I've betrayed you in so many things.'

'But do you love me? That's all I've ever asked.'

She broke free from his grasp and struck at him, her fists on his shoulders. 'Love you? Do I love you? After all these years, how dare you ask that? I've given you the last vestige of my soul!'

He was laughing, catching her fists, subduing her so easily. Her heart was melting inside her, dissolving into glory. She had suffered too much for one life, had believed herself cursed. But to balance that misfortune she had been given a gift that few can claim. A true companion.

They walked back to the house together behind the horses, the rest of the field left unharrowed. Laura was conscious of something she hadn't felt in many a long day; peace was spreading through her, dissolving all the knots and tensions that had made her so thoroughly unhappy. She thought of Deborah and felt ashamed. 'I shouldn't feel like this,' she said to Michael. 'Deb will see.'

'That we're happy? I hope she does see that. It might give her hope.'

But Deborah wasn't there when they returned to the house.

Deborah sat by the railway, high on the embankment, looking down at the tracks. She didn't need to make any sort of decision yet. The choice had to be made when the trains came, the local one ten past every hour, and the express every two hours or so. The express was probably the one to choose. To be struck by a train travelling so fast must mean instant oblivion, whilst the local puffer might take long, horrible seconds.

But she hadn't definitely decided. She tried to marshal her thoughts into logical trains themselves, first the engine, then the tender, then the carriages one after another. But she couldn't think like that today. Instead there was a jumble in her head, a great confusion of tangles, like knitting wool left to a kitten. She thought, No more knitting. No more kittens. Everything gone.

She should never have told her mother. Now her father would know, and he'd want to kill Piers, but then he'd see the photograph and know that she was to blame. He'd never love her after that. He couldn't. She was his lovely, innocent daughter, innocent no more.

The baby was innocent. At least, that's what was always said about babies, unless you were Catholic, in which case you thought them brimming with sin. She didn't know many babies, so it was hard to judge. A man like Zwmskorski had probably brought some sins with him. So perhaps had she. But it didn't feel like that somehow. It seemed more that all had been going well in her life until she was ambushed – almost kidnapped – by desire. She hadn't been ready for that. She hadn't known what to do with it. If she had it all to do again, she knew she'd do it better.

But what would she have done differently? It was all very well to sit now, on this cold embankment, waiting for a train, and say she'd have exercised restraint. Well she knew that she wasn't the restraining type. Men saw her as an icon, a symbol of loveliness and purity, to be owned, to be corrupted, to be desired. None of them knew her. Not even Piers. For a man to know her properly he would probably have to be blind.

The local train was coming. She crouched on the bank, gripping tight to the grass, thinking that if she was going to do it this would be

426

her very last sensation in life. But she wouldn't do it this time. She hadn't finished thinking.

The train chugged past, the faces in the windows looking out at her, a procession of eyes. What would they think? That a madwoman was there, crouched on the embankment, tearing at the grass? Perhaps she was mad. Perhaps that was the cause of everything. She had a definite and strange insanity.

Madwomen shouldn't ever be mothers. This child within her might end up mad too. Was it a boy or a girl? She put her hand on her belly, but no whisper of certainty came. It was there, though. She was sure of that. A life was growing in her, despite her reluctance, despite the stupidity of choosing her to shelter it. She was nothing but a face, a lovely face masking a corrupt soul. Would anyone care if she died? Really care? Her parents didn't know her. No one did. Except Piers.

She felt uncertain suddenly. A minute ago she had decided she was a stranger to him, and now she felt that he alone understood. How could she decide whether to live or die, when her thoughts kept shifting like this? She needed certainty, not these contradictory thoughts. Did anyone ever know anyone all through? Did Piers know as much as it was possible to know about her? After all, she knew more than was comfortable about him. The wind was growing colder, a sparrow fluttered by. She'd rather think of the sparrow than of Piers. What would he do when she was gone?

She tried to imagine the life he would lead. He'd have to leave Gunthwaite, of course. Her father would never let him stay. And there'd be talk, they'd know she was pregnant from the inquest. Although of course, her body might be battered to bloody crumbs. That would be best. If it wasn't though – was the baby conscious yet? Would it know that it was dying? Piers would know she had killed their child. What then?

The express was coming. She crouched again, ready, tense, imagining the act, preparing for it. She couldn't be held responsible for what happened next. Even Piers would come to see that she couldn't have gone on. She didn't want to be the sort of girl who gave birth to bastard babies, nor even the sort that had to be married off because of her immoral ways. She wouldn't be that girl. The express would see to that.

Last thoughts flashed through her brain, like photographs in an album. Mary; her parents; Zwmskorski; Piers asleep, Piers dead drunk, Piers smiling. He'd take this worse than anyone. But the train was coming, and she'd decided. She didn't want to be in this situation, and this was the best way out. Neat. Final. She would step off the stage and let other, better actors finish the play. She could hear her own breathing, and hear too the express coming closer. She must wait until it reached the green signal, and then start to fall. There'd be no

427

time for it to brake, and she'd be fully on the line for at least a second before it struck. She'd have time to think of something, some last, important thing. What?

'Deborah!' Someone was calling. She turned her head away, refusing to hear. No one she knew would come to this place. It was her mind, playing tricks in her last minutes of life.

'Deborah!'

She looked up. Gabriel was climbing through the fence and slithering down the bank towards her. She felt bewildered. What was he doing? Why was he here? As he came level she tried to get up and slide down towards the track, but he reached out and grabbed her wrist. 'No you don't, my girl,' he declared. 'Not this time.'

The express was coming. Deb looked down the line and saw the long snake of carriages rocking towards them. She started to struggle, twisting and turning against her uncle's iron hand. He shouldn't have been able to hold her. He was a drunk, wasn't he? He was past it. But he held her all the same, his eyes fixed on hers, his face white and grim. The express came level and rattled past, carriage after carriage. The noise was intense, until suddenly, abruptly, it was gone. Without a word spoken, Gabriel hauled her to the top of the bank. His car was there. He opened the door and pushed her roughly inside.

He came to sit behind the wheel, reaching at once for a hip flask. He offered it to her first. 'I suggest you have some. It's not often someone tries to commit suicide.'

'I didn't try,' said Deb grimly. 'You wouldn't let me.'

'Indeed I did not.' He took a pull from the flask himself. 'I saw you from the train, of course. I'd been to town. Grabbed the car at the station and drove like a bat out of hell. Will you tell me why?'

'If I'd done it you'd have known.'

'Why? It's not Piers, is it? I told him he wasn't the man for you.'

She shook her head, miserably. 'It's not that. I don't want to tell you.'

'Well, you'll have to tell somebody. I'm taking you straight home and telling your parents the whole story.'

'No!'

She turned burning eyes on him. Gabriel felt his stomach lurch. God, but she was beautiful. Her skin was pale as marble, the veins at her temples standing out like dark blue threads. As she leaned towards him her bosom seemed to swell invitingly, as if she wanted it touched. He blinked and shook his head. It was coming to something when he couldn't help lusting after his own niece.

Suddenly Deborah began to cry. Tears welled from her lovely eyes and fell in rivers. It gave her a welcome normality and Gabriel fished for his handkerchief with the sense that at least this was within his experience. No longer the goddess, her sorrow had rendered her

428

human again. 'I'm pregnant,' she sobbed. 'Piers didn't take enough care and now I'm pregnant, and my mother's telling Dad right now and he's going to hate me!'

'And that's all?' Gabriel looked at her incredulously.

'It's enough, isn't it? I'm a slut. I'll go with anyone.'

'I thought you said Piers was the father?'

'He is! I meant – I'm the sort of girl who might go with anyone.'

'Well, looking as you do, I expect you get more offers than most. That's something you've got to realise. Life's never without temptation.'

She felt another wave of despair begin to build and knew that in a moment it would crash on her helpless head. She fumbled for the door handle but Gabriel leaned across and stopped her. 'It isn't so bad, you know,' he said. 'I married Dora because I got her in the family way. I admit, we're not suited and never were, but even if we hadn't married she'd have been OK. Better, possibly. It's no fun being married to someone who's in love with someone else.'

'Were you in love with someone else?'

He nodded. 'Always have been. You must have realised. Your mother.'

Deborah said nothing. It seemed to her entirely likely that Gabriel would love Laura instead of his wayward wife. He went on, 'I think Piers is the same about you. Terrible shame, really. He'd be much happier loving someone a bit more his style. He's such a loser, you see. Would rather spend his days driving tractors and forking muck than using an ounce of brain. Why not have an op and get rid of the thing? What happens to Piers is his own problem after all. If you haven't told him, the chances are he'll never know.'

'I don't know that I want to do that,' she said quietly.

'Why not? Better than killing yourself over it.'

'It's not really the pregnancy, you see – it's me. I hate myself.'

'For getting pregnant? You've got far too nice a conscience, my girl. A bit of sexual misjudgment's inevitable at your age. I dare say you've made a few mistakes. Got yourself in a few situations you'd rather not remember. That's growing up, Deborah. Being human. It's life.'

He pulled at the flask once again. Deborah thought how much she disliked him. He might love Laura, but he loved neither himself, nor Piers, nor any other living thing. Why couldn't he care about Piers for once? she found herself thinking. He couldn't look elsewhere for a father who would serve him better. This father was all he had.

Gabriel looked at her blearily. He seemed to pick up her thoughts, in the uncanny way he had always had, disconcerting people over the years.

'When you think about it, though, you're all Piers has got,' he

429

muttered. 'And bloody lucky to have you. Why not have the kid? Then if you go off you can leave him something. Some part of you. To keep him company.'

'You're mad,' said Deborah bleakly. 'Children aren't things to be left here and there.'

'Aren't they? We always managed. Better that than giving up your life to some ungrateful brat.' He leaned back in his seat. He was very drunk now. She knew that if she wished she could slip from the car and fling herself on the railway line and he wouldn't do a thing to stop her. But the urge had gone now. She was thinking instead that it was time she went home. Her parents would be looking for her. And she had to speak to Piers.

Gabriel was starting to snore. She said, 'You come over here and I'll drive.'

'What? I'm OK. Take you home. God, but you're gorgeous. Laura's eyes. Ought to be me giving you a bit, instead of that son of mine.'

Deborah took him by the arm and wrenched him from the seat. 'Never in a million years,' she declared, and climbed behind the wheel.

Piers was getting ready for milking. In these high hills the cattle came in early and now they stood in the yard, looking mournfully out at him. He felt mournful too. It was the old, empty feeling when the tighter he held to things the more they slipped away. Deborah was growing cold towards him. She'd gone away in a rush, come back in a rush, and wanted nothing from him at all.

He pushed open the yard gate and let the first six cows into the parlour. They bustled in, all gloom gone, thinking about their suppers. He wished he was a cow, or at least a beast of some kind, satisfied so easily, cared for so well. He wished someone would care enough to take pains over him. Once there had been his grandmother, the rock of his childhood, but in the time that he was gone she had built another life for herself. He had come back older, tougher, and she hadn't seemed to know him any more. So he had reached out and taken hold of what he wanted, gripping tight, refusing to let it go. But you couldn't hold on to happiness like that. He had opened his hands to find his fragile bird quite dead.

He began washing udders, finding the work physically painful, as if his heart had really turned to stone. Deb was leaving him. He knew that now. There was something about him which meant he could never be properly loved. He felt a great rage within him, a huge explosion of fire. It was all his parents' fault! Whether they had caused him to be like this, or merely reacted to the essential awfulness that was him, they might at least have tried a little. If he'd had some

430

love, or at least the approximation of it, he might have learned to be lovable. But every time he asked Deb to come to him, stay with him, tell him where she was going, hearing the note of desperation in his voice, he hated himself and knew she must too. Sometimes he watched Connor, so easy, so light, and tried to copy the way he was. He had done the same with his father when first he went to live with him. The trouble was, you couldn't wear a personality like a cloak. It blew open at the first breeze and everyone saw that you were naked. And everyone laughed.

He moved to the next cow. She shuffled uncomfortably and he saw that she had gashed her udder. He went for the iodine stick, washing and anointing her with infinite care. Laura, coming into the barn and seeing him, was amazed at his tenderness. She had never realised that Piers could be so gentle.

'Hello,' she said. 'I wondered if you knew where Deb's got to?'

He glanced up at her and shook his head. Something about his face disturbed her. He looked very white and tense.

'She was in quite a state when she came back last night,' Laura went on. 'I wondered if you knew why?'

'No.'

The uncompromising statement took her aback. She sat down on an upturned crate, emphasising that she wasn't going to be fobbed off quite so easily, and said with some asperity, 'I'm glad to find you so interested, Piers. Since I gather that you and Deborah have been having a relationship that could well be described as intimate – in fact, I think very intimate might be appropriate – I think you might show a little more concern.'

He dropped the iodine into his bucket. Laura felt a surge of satisfaction. That had wiped the indifference off his face. But then, unexpectedly, she saw that his head was bent. He was crouched by the udder of a big, old cow and he was crying.

'Oh,' said Laura doubtfully. 'Oh dear. Piers, please don't upset yourself. I thought perhaps – I thought perhaps after everything, you really didn't care.'

He got to his feet, startling the cow into a sideways shuffle. Laura thought how young he looked, the misery taking away all his assumed adult composure. He always managed this, she thought despairingly. He infuriated and then undermined you. Just as you had decided never to forgive him again, he demanded compassionate forgiveness.

'She'll never love me the way I love her,' he burst out. 'Nothing I do will ever make it right.'

Laura sighed. 'I don't think you can know that,' she said quietly.

'If I don't, then who does? She's shutting me out. Not talking to me. Going away. Even in bed she's not the way she was! The truth is, she wants rid of me and can't find the words. And even if she could

431

she doesn't know what she'd do afterwards with me hanging around the place, getting on her nerves. If she had her way she'd wake up one morning and find me vanished into thin air. Then she could do as she liked and never think about me ever again.'

'I don't think that's the truth as she sees it,' said Laura.

'God damn it, it is!'

He picked up the bucket and slammed it against the wall. The contents exploded everywhere, deluging Laura, the cows, Piers himself. One of the younger cows, thoroughly panicked, broke her halter and tried to get out. Laura, on her feet now, stood in the passage and blocked the way, saying, 'Whisht, whisht,' gently, to calm and distract the beast.

Piers said, 'Don't look so shocked. It's only what you expected of me, after all! I can't be trusted.'

Laura took hold of the cow's halter and led her back to the stall. 'I don't know that. It was something I was going to find out.'

'You hate me! You always have, you've always hated me and Deb. I don't know why you just can't admit it.'

She looked at him over the cow's nervous back. 'I want my daughters to be happy. You might be right for Deb, I don't know. She thinks you are.'

'Don't make me laugh!'

Suddenly Laura was angry. She left the cow and came out into the passage, by the speed of her approach backing Piers against the wall. She glared at him, furious, crusading on her daughter's behalf.

'Nobody's laughing, Piers,' she said in a soft, menacing voice. 'In fact, I'm very far from being in the least amused. Shall I tell you what's the matter with Deb? Are you sure you want to know? Or are you so wrapped up in your own feelings and self pity that you can't spare the time?'

'What do you mean?'

'Deborah's pregnant! You've made her pregnant! And all you can do is weep into a bucket and terrify the cows!'

She turned away, and for something to do began to attach a cluster to the first cow. She hadn't often done it of late and she was clumsy. After a moment Piers came and took over. He seemed bemused.

They worked together in silence for some minutes. Then, as the milk began to flow and the cows to develop the required state of peaceful rumination, he said, 'Why hasn't she told me?'

Laura sighed. 'I don't know. Because she might have an abortion. Because she might not. Because she thinks you'll take it for granted that you'll marry. That's what you want, isn't it?'

He nodded. 'It's bound to be what's best.'

'Who for? You? The baby? Deborah?'

'You don't know her. She's better settled.'

432

Laura moved to the first cow again and removed the cluster. Was it right to believe that of Deb? She had always seemed so tranquil next to highstrung, wilful Mary. When the fires of youth had died down a little, would she in fact find contentment in a settled, quiet life?

The door opened and Michael came in. He said to Piers, 'You should be done with this by now.'

'I know. Sorry. We were talking.'

'Yes. There'll be a lot of talking over the next days. Come along, Laura. He'd best get on.'

Out in the yard she said, 'I thought you weren't going to be angry?'

'I know. I never meant to be. It's easier to have him to blame. And she still isn't home.'

It was getting dark. The starlings were roosting in the trees by the gate, a chattering mass of wings. It was a sign of winter. Laura felt fear stirring in her, the gnawing, crawling anxiety of the mother whose child is lost. Where was Deb? What was happening to her?

Lights appeared on the road. Michael rubbed his eyes and peered through the gloom. 'Whose car?'

'Gabriel's, I think. It won't be Deb.'

But as it turned into the gate and they saw that it was indeed Deb, she felt a flood of joyful relief. What price a baby, what price shame, if Deborah was safe? Laura knew she would pay any price for that.

Gabriel had climbed out of the car and was staggering towards them, leaving Deb closing windows and switching off lights and engine. He said, 'You'll never guess what! Going to throw herself under a train, and all because of that idiot son of mine. You'd think he'd have a bit more sense. Know everything they do, nowadays. Not like us.'

'Deb.' She hung back in the shadows and Michael went to her. 'Come here, my Deb.'

He enfolded her in his arms, smelling of wool and horses and grass. It was the scent of home, of safety, and it was more than she could bear. 'I'm so sorry, Dad,' she burst out, shaking with sobs.

'No need. No need. We'll help you through.'

'I wanted you to be proud of me.'

'And so we are. We don't stop being proud because things have gone a little wrong, you know.'

He led her into the house and sat talking quietly to her. Gabriel followed, expansive, erratic, demanding that Laura find them all something to drink. She put the kettle on the range and made him coffee. He sank into a chair, and suddenly the drunkenness fell away. He looked up at Laura and said, 'Takes you back, doesn't it? Everything happening again. Me and Dora.'

'That wasn't at all the same.'

'Suppose not.'

433

He looked across at Deborah, sitting crying quietly into her father's shoulder. He said, 'It could have been you and me, Laura. It was my fault. I had the chance and I didn't take it. I was such a fool.'

'We've both been fools,' said Laura. She sat at the table opposite him and met his eye. 'I thought I couldn't be honest with Michael. At the start, probably I couldn't. But I never saw that things had changed. We've lived together so long and yet I never really looked at Michael and saw what he was. All the things I was hiding – we've built a life together! How can ancient history harm that?'

Gabriel suddenly closed his eyes. Laura looked at him, puzzled. But then he whispered, 'I always thought – in the end – you'd come to me. I've been waiting, you know.'

'Waiting? Really?'

He nodded. 'I knew you'd have to come in the end!'

She took in her breath in surprise. She had never once considered leaving Michael. Didn't Gabriel see himself, see the drunken, overblown figure he'd become? Or perhaps he saw himself too clearly. Perhaps the drink was a necessary veil.

She said, 'What would you have done if I had? I mean, what then?'

He shrugged. 'I don't know. A house somewhere. Spend some money, have some fun. You've hardly travelled, you know. You could have a life so much easier than this. You still could.'

'I never wanted an easy life, Gabriel.'

'Didn't you? I wonder why not.'

She turned the question in her head. She had worked all her days, at one thing or another. The worst thing about her depression had been that it sapped her strength, oppressing her with tasks undone as well as misery. But she had the sense that work mattered, that she was not on this earth to do nothing and watch the birds. She liked to feel that all her labour and all her struggle would ultimately mean that the world was a better place.

It was foolishness of course. There was work for as long as anyone wanted to do it, and more besides. It wasn't your deeds that mattered in life. Even the greatest achievement was no more than a speck in a timeless waste. It seemed to her then that what mattered was the person you became. What was required was that a journey should be made. She had made her journey. If she travelled not an inch further she would have come quite far enough. After years of imprisonment she had at last set her spirit free.

Piers rapped on the back door and came in. Deb glanced up and looked away, but he stood his ground, saying fiercely, 'Deb. Your mother told me. We've got to talk.'

She turned to her father, as if trying to become a child again. But he put her away and said, 'Go on, Deborah. You've got to decide.'

She got up. Piers stretched out his hand to her. She shivered, as if about to make an enormous decision. He had the tense, desperate look of someone expecting the worst. Suddenly, her heart ached for him, she knew she could never hurt him as he must be hurt, if she did anything but go with him now. Hadn't he been there when she needed him? Wouldn't he always? And if she must leave her father's love and protection then surely she must look for it elsewhere. She crossed the floor to Piers, her steps light across the flags, and took his hand. He drew her close and held her.

A spasm crossed Gabriel's face. He said jerkily, 'You'll see it's for the best, Deborah. Besides, it'll keep Gunthwaite in the family. I know how sensitive Michael is about that.'

'Shut up, Gabe,' said Michael laconically. 'Give me a minute and I'll drive you home.'

Gabriel said, 'I am so sick of calling that place home.'

'Then move,' said Piers. 'Get out of here and make a life. You can't batten on to Deb and me. I'll not give you the time of day.'

'Oh, for Christ's sake!' Gabriel lurched to his feet and came across to his son. 'Didn't anyone teach you any manners? Don't you know I could buy and sell this place ten times over? If you want a sniff of that money, if you want a penny of it, you'd better learn to be decently polite!'

'I don't need anything from you.' Piers' voice was shaking with hatred. 'You've never given me anything I needed in all my life. Michael's given me more than you. A hundred times more!'

'He has, has he? How wonderful! What a wonderful brother I have! One of the most boring, conservative, unimaginative blockheads the world has seen, but a saint. A positive saint.'

Michael said, 'I'll take you home,' and moved to take his arm. But Gabriel fought free and lurched to the door.

'I'll take myself home! Believe me, I'd rather die in a ditch than suffer your kindness. How I must amuse you all! I warn you, if I ever get my hands on Gunthwaite you'll laugh on the other side of your face.'

Cold air whistled into the room as he left. Laura moved to close the door. It seemed very quiet and still. Piers said to Michael, 'I'm sorry it happened like this. But you know I love Deb. I promise I'll make her happy.'

Michael spoke softly to them, and Laura thought, Happiness can't be promised. It's a blessing, bestowed when you least expect it, a sudden ambush in the midst of your daily toil. Perhaps it would come to Deborah. She prayed that it might. Her lovely daughter surely deserved a little.

There was the sound of an engine in the yard. She assumed it was Gabriel and took no notice. She went back to her husband by the fire.

435

Chapter Forty

Connor and Mary drew up in the yard. Gabriel sat in his car directly in front of them, staring out with unblinking eyes. 'Good God,' said Mary. 'Is he dead, do you think?'

'Drunk, of course. Will you drive him back or shall I?'

Mary reached out and touched his cheek. 'I will. Then I don't have to face them straight away. I feel so shy.'

'But you know they'll be thrilled for us.' He took her hand and held it, pressing the ring they had bought in Amiens, an old gold rope studded with amethysts the colour of Mary's eyes.

'All the same. You tell them. Then when I get there we can talk about the letters and everything. It's too much all at once.'

She scrambled out of the car and he let her go. He had no wish to spoil this evening with a trail to Fairlands in the company of a bad-tempered drunk. If Mary preferred it to her family's rejoicings then that was her privilege. He'd pave the way for her indoors.

She pulled open Gabriel's door without ceremony. 'Move over,' she commanded. 'Come on, I'll drive you home.'

He seemed to waken out of a trance. 'Oh God. You.'

'Yes, me. Have you emptied that flask? Your liver must be pickled. I'm surprised Dad let you drive home.'

'Michael's halo was somewhat lacking in polish this evening.'

Mary chuckled. 'Like that, is it? Believe me, that's one emotion I do understand.'

She manoeuvred the car expertly out of the yard. After a moment Gabriel said, 'Let's not go straight back. Dora's not there and her parents will be in bed. I'll be alone.'

'But you don't want me for company.'

'Don't I? Mary, you'd be surprised.'

He sank his face into his hands. She drew the car to a standstill at the side of the road and said gently, 'It's all right, you know. You can tell me what it is.'

'I don't need to be comforted by my high-handed, self-opinionated, bastard daughter!'

'Yes, you do,' said Mary, quite unmoved by the insults. 'I mean, if I don't, who else will? Dora's off you, Piers hates you, you hate Michael and Mum's not interested.'

'But she ought to be! She damn well bloody ought to be! I've waited years!'

'And it's all been a waste of time.'

He looked at her. She was so blindingly, cruelly honest. He felt himself smile. 'Do you think it really is all her fault? I might have wasted my life anyway. I was never brave enough or clever enough. Not really.'

'Brave enough and clever enough for what?' demanded his daughter. 'You've made a stack of money. And I've no doubt you could have been happy, if you'd stopped mooning after Mum. You could be happy still. Stop drinking and find yourself some innocent young thing and you could have a whole new family in five minutes. Rich men can always do things like that.'

'I don't want a whole new family! I want the family I should have had!'

Mary snorted and started the car. 'In that case, you deserve everything you haven't got.'

As they neared Fairlands he said, 'You're heartless, of course. Always have been.'

'I probably get it from you.'

'I doubt it! It's probably Laura. You'd have to be heartless to survive her life.'

'People aren't heartless because they don't give in to you, you know.'

'Don't give me your homespun philosophy!'

'Then spare me your horrible self-pity. I should tell you, I'm sick of your drinking. I don't think I've ever known you when you weren't drunk. It's a shame. I might like you sober.'

He gave a guffaw of laughter. 'Is that supposed to reform me?'

'Not likely! You won't stop. But it's a shame, for all that. We might have something in common.'

They passed the Fairlands gates and crunched on new gravel Gabriel had paid for. 'I remember when you wrecked all this on the old man's hunter.'

'Yes. I never did ride him in a point to point. And now I won't.'

'Why not?'

'I'm getting married and having babies. Then, when I get back to it, the Bombardier won't be around. It's the way of things. Opportunities don't wait.'

'More homespun philosophy?'

'Home truths, Father.'

She drew the car to a halt in front of the house. 'I'll drive this back. You can send someone over for it tomorrow.'

'Do you want me to thank you?'

She grinned. 'No. Definitely not. It would be so out of character.'

437

He hesitated. Then he said, 'Thank you. Thank you very much indeed.'

'What for?'

'For being the only person in the world I think might understand me. When you go back – tell Piers I wish him every happiness. I can't say it. He'd spit in my face. And I might not mean it then. But I want to mean it. Go home, Mary, then you'll understand.'

She sat still, reluctant to leave. He looked so strange, so different. As if he'd suddenly woken up from a long and troubled sleep. He alarmed her, and intrigued her at the same time. But home meant Connor and her mother, and all the poignancy of their news. She couldn't stay with this odd old man.

He stood watching as she turned the car and began to drive away. He thought how strange it was that at the moment in his life when he most needed someone, that someone should be Mary. He'd lost his nerve for a second, that was all. He'd found himself teetering on the edge of despair. He wasn't far away now. How could he be? You didn't progress far in half an hour. But he knew he had begun a journey, taken the steps he should have taken years ago. He didn't know where he was going just yet. But he could see signposts to guide him, labelled pride, dignity and self-respect. He was so very sick of despising himself!

The moon was rising above Gunthwaite woods. He looked up at the hills and saw the faint light that was Gunthwaite itself. They would all be there now. Michael had gathered his family about him. And the moon would swing in the sky overhead, and the struggles and triumphs would pass away and leave the moon unchanging as ever. There was something comforting in that. Gabriel turned and went into the house.

The shires were fastened to the cart once again, their tails bound up with ropes of corn, their manes entwined with flowers. They had paraded like this when Laura and Michael married, just before the war. But Laura had only borrowed them. Mary was a Gunthwaite bride in her own right, and was entitled to every privilege.

Deborah, heavily pregnant, took a seat in the car and tried not to mind. They had done their best for her, rushing out the invitations, choosing an expensive dress. But Mary's wedding was the product of months of planning. The horses were in summer condition, whereas for her they were thick with winter hair. The dress had cost less than Deb's, but it had been made by a local seamstress, and fitted like a skin of pure white silk. Even Mary's hair had necessitated a visit to London, whereas Deb's had been looped on top of her head by Mrs Fitzalan-Howard, who was good at such things, and was lending a pearl tiara besides.

438

It was all stupidity, of course. Deborah knew that she had looked magnificent on the day. The people from the village, come to stand outside the church, had broken into spontaneous applause. 'He's done well for himself,' she heard them mutter. 'That girl's a marvel.' But now, looking at Mary, whose flawless complexion was due to make-up, whose perfect dress had taken hours of fitting and a discreetly padded bra, Deborah felt the pangs of pointless regret.

Piers climbed in beside her. 'All right?' he asked anxiously.

'Yes. Fine.' She smiled at him. He always needed to be reassured, she thought despondently. He could never let her alone with her mood, to suffer or enjoy it, as she chose. He had to check that she was happy, probe if she was sad, enquire if neither state was immediately apparent.

'The horses look wonderful,' she said determinedly.

'Yes. You're not upset, are you? I mean, ours was a winter wedding. There wasn't any choice.'

'I know that!' She turned her shoulder to him. How could she forget, when she was as big as a house? She heard him sigh and knew that she was being difficult and cruel. Everyone was trying to humour her nowadays.

The car filled out with various Cooper relatives, and Graham, the tractor man, got in to drive. At the church one or other of Deborah's acquaintances caught her arm and stopped her. 'My, you're looking big! You didn't waste any time, did you?'

'Not an instant,' replied Deb with a brilliant smile. 'We're rather embarrassed about it, actually. It looks so bad.'

'Don't you care what people think! Spoil anything, some people. Pretty as a picture still, I see. Just you take care.'

She went to take her seat in the church. Piers reached for her hand but she evaded him. People were turning in their seats to glance at her, and she could tell they thought she looked good. She was feeling a little better. She might not be the most beautiful young girl to be seen, but she was still the loveliest mother to be.

She felt ashamed of herself suddenly. She had never thought herself so vain. This was Mary's day, and they must all feel happy for her. Besides, she herself had a loving husband, a baby to come and a life of peace and plenty.

High heels were clacking authoritatively on the flags. Deborah turned her head and saw Dora coming in. She felt cold. For a moment she expected to see Zwmskorski. But of course, that wasn't going to happen. He wouldn't dare show his face here. Instead Gabriel appeared, slimmer and paler than only a few months ago. He caught her eye and gave her a wink. She tried to smile but it wobbled.

Sliding into the row behind her, he leaned forward and murmured, 'Chin up. These ghastly rites improve the moment you get out of church. Just think, in a year's time she'll be every bit as big as you and looking a lot less glamorous.'

Deborah whispered, 'Is it mean of me to feel fed up?'

'Probably. Who cares? Mary's one of the lucky ones in life. She knows what she wants and she's getting it.'

Piers was reaching for her hand again. This time she let him take it. Dora, sitting next to Gabriel, but with feet of space between them, hissed through her teeth. Let her hiss, thought Deborah. She had turned her back on Dora's sort of life. She and Piers were living quietly, contentedly in their cottage. One day, perhaps a day not so distant, Michael and Laura would take the cottage and she and Piers would have the house. Mary and Connor were going on honeymoon to Ireland, but would come back to live in Piers' old flat above the barn. They were supposed to be running their horse business, but Deb suspected and Piers hoped that they'd live in Ireland in the end. Connor was being enticed back home, to the racing stables. It would be best if they were gone, thought Deborah. She was the future mistress of Gunthwaite, and Mary wouldn't understand.

The organ wheezed into the wedding march. Laura, just arrived and summery in lavender silk, hurried to her place. Everyone stood, craning their heads for a glimpse of the bride. Connor, immaculate in dark broadcloth, had somehow managed to turn up one side of his collar. As Mary came towards him, so tall, so lovely, he gave a broad grin of pleasure and stretched out his hand. She took it, leaning across at the same time and putting his collar straight. A chuckle ran round the church. Deborah prayed, Let her be happy. Let me be happy too. Make the thing I did be the right thing for Piers and me and the baby. Don't let me hate my life!

Laura, glancing back at Deborah's lovely face, had no inkling of any unease. There wasn't room for it today. She felt light with happiness, watching Mary on Michael's proud arm, seeing Connor so sure, Mary so confident. Deborah and Piers set the seal on everything, she decided. Piers had settled so well since he and Deb married. Everything had turned out for the best.

'Dearly Beloved,' began the vicar, evoking thoughts of weddings over seventy years or more. Gabriel stamped restlessly in his seat, and wished he could have a drink at the reception.

All the guests reached Gunthwaite Hall before the bridal pair, clopping slowly along the road behind the horses. They lined the drive to welcome them, cheering and clapping and making the horses shy. Connor had to stand up and take the reins from the old carter or they'd have ended up run away with. Michael, a whisky already under his belt, came rushing up, red-faced, saying, 'What did I say, Con? Too many oats. You'll never make a horseman.'

440

'He's not used to carthorses, Dad,' said Mary, hitching up her skirts and climbing nimbly down. 'And you're not used to whisky.'

'If I can't get drunk today, when can I? My, but you do look well. Mrs O'Malley!'

But Mary was swept away into the throng, and the horses danced and the carter cursed and Michael had to put them away in his best suit because he doubted that anyone else would manage. When he came back into the house Laura had to take his jacket and brush it with lavender water, to get rid of the smell of horse.

The day rolled on, full of food and wine and good humour. One of Connor's brothers made a speech as best man that had everyone rocking with laughter. Michael, giving his own good wishes, was caught on the edge of tears, Again and again Gabriel looked at the wine and wrestled with himself. Finally, as the speeches at last closed, he got up from the table and went to the bathroom, splashing cold water on his face and wishing he could go straight home. But it wouldn't do. He owed Mary his presence here at least. Giving way at last to the urgent rappings of others on the door, he considered going back into the party. He would, but not just yet. He'd walk around outside for a while.

Others had had the same idea. People were sitting on the garden wall or in the stables, talking to the horses. Some were in the pasture, admiring Michael's crop of orchids. Looking for solitude, Gabriel headed for the orchard. The gate was stiff and heavy. Few would enter here.

He looked around in curiosity. He hadn't been here himself in many a long year. The trees were heavy with leaf, sheltering tiny apples, plums and cherries. Underfoot the grass was springy, as befitted a sheep-grazed pasture. He leaned against a gnarled old apple tree, the trunk crooked and bent. It was quiet out here. The air drifted softly through the canopy above him. He might have been six years old again.

A voice said, 'Hello.'

He gasped and looked up. Mary was sitting in the tree. Her wedding dress was bunched in a heap around her.

'My God,' he said. 'Your mother will be furious if you ruin that dress.'

'I'm being careful. I just couldn't bear them all any more. Did you sit here when you were small?'

'Yes. Me and Mike and Rosalind. We all did.'

'I wouldn't let Deb. I used to yell at her. I was terribly mean.'

He said nothing. A bird fluttered up into the branches, saw Mary and flashed away. 'There's a nest here,' she said. 'I'd better come down.'

'I'll catch you.' He spread out his arms and she let go, descending in

441

a flurry of silk and twigs and leaves. He held her for longer than was necessary, saying, 'Well then.'

'What?' She looked up at him calmly.

'I'm going away,' he said. 'Dora's going to live in London. We won't divorce, there's no point. I'm going to Brazil. There's money to be made out there. I've bought an engineering factory.'

'You should get divorced,' said Mary. 'Then you can find someone new.'

'I don't want anyone new, thanks. The old's enough for me.'

She said nothing. If she lost Connor, she thought, would she ever want someone else? It seemed impossible. She let her fingers brush Gabriel's cheek, a gesture of friendship and understanding. He caught her hand and touched it with his lips. 'I'm happy for you,' he said. 'Try and be kind to Deb.'

'I don't think I'm unkind to her. Why?'

He shrugged. 'I don't know. She's doing what she should. I'm not sure if it's what she wants.'

'You don't need to hate Piers so,' said Mary.

'I don't hate him! He irritates me though. It's the way he is.'

They were silent. The party could be heard, distant laughter, voices raised in song. Connor's voice called, 'Mary! Mary?' She knew she would have to go.

Gabriel said, 'Have a dozen babies. But call one of them after me.'

'What? You've done nothing to deserve that!'

'I know. All the same.'

She grinned at him. He thought, One day I'll come back and there will be my grandchild Gabriel. He longed already for that return, wished he could sleep away the years between. Connor was calling again and Mary moved away, not bothering to open the gate but hitching up her skirt and climbing over with a flash of white-stockinged legs. Gabriel moved to follow her and the bird at once fluttered back to its nest. When next he was here, would he find Gabriel sitting in this tree? Or would it be Piers' child, who would never carry his name, pushing the others out? He wanted to know, he thought, he wanted to see what was to be. He hadn't the patience any more to wait out the years.

Someone was playing the fiddle. It was a jig, come out of Ireland, reminding these Yorkshire folk of other worlds and other rhythms. Gabriel felt a sudden lift of enthusiasm, a sudden surge of curiosity.

There was more to the world than the littleness of things here. When next he returned he would have tales to tell, and they would sit at the old kitchen table in the lamplight and be amazed. He too climbed over the orchard gate, his legs only a little stiff, his ankles jarring on the ground. Not so old, then. Young enough for adventure.

442